Praise for Robert Galbraith

'A master storyteller'
Daily Telegraph

'Unputdownable ... Irresistible'
Sunday Times

'Will keep you up all night'
Observer

'One of the most unique and compelling detectives
I've come across in years'
Mark Billingham

'A thoroughly enjoyable classic'
Peter James, *Sunday Express*

Praise for *Lethal White*

'A blistering piece of crime writing'
Sunday Times

'Confirms [Galbraith's] exceptional ability as a storyteller'
Daily Mail

'Highly inventive storytelling'
Guardian

'Outrageously entertaining'
Financial Times

'Come for the twists and turns and stay for the
beautifully drawn central relationship'
Independent

Also by Robert Galbraith

The Cuckoo's Calling
The Silkworm
Career of Evil
Lethal White

ROBERT GALBRAITH

TROUBLED BLOOD

A *STRIKE* NOVEL

SPHERE

First published in Great Britain in 2020 by Sphere

1 3 5 7 9 10 8 6 4 2

A CIP catalogue record for this book
is available from the British Library.

Hardback ISBN 978-0-7515-7993-2
Trade paperback ISBN 978-0-7515-7994-9

Typeset in Bembo by M Rules
Printed and bound in Great Britain by Clays Ltd, Elcograf S.p.A.

Papers used by Sphere are from well-managed forests
and other responsible sources.

MIX
Paper from
responsible sources
FSC FSC® C104740
www.fsc.org

Sphere
An imprint of
Little, Brown Book Group
Carmelite House
50 Victoria Embankment
London EC4Y 0DZ

An Hachette UK Company
www.hachette.co.uk

www.littlebrown.co.uk

To Barbara Murray,
social worker, WEA worker, teacher,
wife, mother, grandmother,
demon bridge player
and
world's best mother-in-law

There they her sought, and euery where inquired,
Where they might tydings get of her estate;
Yet found they none. But by what haplesse fate,
Or hard misfortune she was thence conuayd,
And stolne away from her beloued mate,
Were long to tell . . .

Edmund Spenser
The Faerie Queene

For, if it were not so, there would be something disappearing
into nothing, which is mathematically absurd.

Aleister Crowley
The Book of Thoth

PART ONE

Then came the iolly Sommer . . .

Edmund Spenser
The Faerie Queene

1

'You're a Cornishman, born and bred,' said Dave Polworth irritably. '"Strike" isn't even your proper name. By rights, you're a Nancarrow. You're not going to sit here and say you'd call yourself English?'

The Victory Inn was so crowded on this warm August evening that drinkers had spilled outside onto the broad stone steps which led down to the bay. Polworth and Strike were sitting at a table in the corner, having a few pints to celebrate Polworth's thirty-ninth birthday. Cornish nationalism had been under discussion for twenty minutes, and to Strike it felt much longer.

'Would I call myself English?' he mused aloud. 'No, I'd probably say British.'

'Fuck off,' said Polworth, his quick temper rising. 'You wouldn't. You're just trying to wind me up.'

The two friends were physical opposites. Polworth was short and spare as a jockey, weathered and prematurely lined, his sunburned scalp visible through his thinning hair. His T-shirt was crumpled, as though he had pulled it off the floor or out of a washing basket, and his jeans were ripped. On his left forearm was tattooed the black and white cross of St Piran; on his right hand was a deep scar, souvenir of a close encounter with a shark.

His friend Strike resembled an out-of-condition boxer, which

3

in fact he was; a large man, well over six feet tall, with a slightly crooked nose, his dense dark hair curly. He bore no tattoos and, in spite of the perpetual shadow of the heavy beard, carried about him that well-pressed and fundamentally clean-cut air that suggested ex-police or ex-military.

'You were born here,' Polworth persisted. 'So you're Cornish.'

'Trouble is, by that standard, you're a Brummie.'

'Fuck off!' yelped Polworth again, genuinely stung. 'I've been here since I was two months old and my mum's a Trevelyan. It's identity – what you feel here,' and Polworth thumped his chest over his heart. 'My mum's family goes back centuries in Cornwall—'

'Yeah, well, blood and soil's never been my—'

'Did you hear about the last survey they done?' said Polworth, talking over Strike. '"What's your ethnic origin?" they asked, and half – *half* – ticked "Cornish" instead of "English". Massive increase.'

'Great,' said Strike. 'What next? Boxes for Dumnones and Romans?'

'Keep using that patronising fucking tone,' said Polworth, 'and see where it gets you. You've been in London too fucking long, boy . . . There's nothing wrong with being proud of where you came from. Nothing wrong with communities wanting some power back from Westminster. The Scots are gonna lead the way, next year. You watch. When they get independence, that'll be the trigger. Celtic peoples right across the country are going to make their move.

'Want another one?' he added, gesturing towards Strike's empty pint glass.

Strike had come out to the pub craving a respite from tension and worry, not to be harangued about Cornish politics. Polworth's allegiance to Mebyon Kernow, the nationalist party he'd joined at sixteen, appeared to have gained a greater hold over him in the year or so since they had last seen each other. Dave usually made Strike laugh like almost nobody else, but he brooked no jokes upon Cornish independence, a subject that for Strike had all the appeal of soft furnishings or train-spotting. For a second Strike considered saying that he needed to get back to his aunt's house, but the prospect of that was almost more depressing than his old friend's invective against supermarkets that resisted putting the cross of St Piran on goods of Cornish origin.

'Great, thanks,' he said, passing his empty glass to Dave, who headed up to the bar, nodding left and right to his many acquaintances.

Left alone at the table, Strike's eyes roamed absently over the pub he'd always considered his local. It had changed over the years, but was still recognisably the place in which he and his Cornish mates had met in their late teens. He had an odd double impression of being exactly where he belonged, and where he'd never belonged, of intense familiarity and of separateness.

As his gaze moved aimlessly from timber floor to nautical prints, Strike found himself looking directly into the large, anxious eyes of a woman standing at the bar with a friend. She had a long, pale face and her dark, shoulder-length hair was streaked with grey. He didn't recognise her, but he'd been aware for the past hour that certain locals were craning their necks to look at him, or else trying to catch his eye. Looking away, Strike took out his mobile and pretended to be texting.

Acquaintances had a ready excuse for conversation, if he showed the slightest sign of encouraging them, because everyone in St Mawes seemed to know that his aunt Joan had received a diagnosis of advanced ovarian cancer ten days previously, and that he, his half-sister, Lucy, and Lucy's three sons had hastened at once to Joan and Ted's house to offer what support they could. For a week now he'd been fielding enquiries, accepting sympathy and politely declining offers of help every time he ventured out of the house. He was tired of finding fresh ways of saying 'Yes, it looks terminal and yes, it's shit for all of us.'

Polworth pushed his way back to the table, carrying two fresh pints.

'There you go, Diddy,' he said, resuming his bar stool.

The old nickname hadn't been bestowed, as most people assumed, in ironic reference to Strike's size, but derived from 'didicoy', the Cornish word for gypsy. The sound of it softened Strike, reminding him why his friendship with Polworth was the most enduring of his life.

Thirty-five years previously, Strike had entered St Mawes Primary

5

School a term late, unusually large for his age and with an accent that was glaringly different from the local burr. Although he'd been born in Cornwall, his mother had spirited him away as soon as she'd recovered from the birth, fleeing into the night, baby in her arms, back to the London life she loved, flitting from flat to squat to party. Four years after Strike's birth, she'd returned to St Mawes with her son and with her newborn, Lucy, only to take off again in the early hours of the morning, leaving Strike and his half-sister behind.

Precisely what Leda had said in the note she left on the kitchen table, Strike had never known. Doubtless she'd been having a spell of difficulty with a landlord or a boyfriend, or perhaps there was a music festival she particularly wanted to attend: it became difficult to live exactly as she pleased with two children in tow. Whatever the reason for her lengthening absence, Leda's sister-in-law, Joan, who was as conventional and orderly as Leda was flighty and chaotic, had bought Strike a uniform and enrolled him in the local school.

The other four-and-a-half-year-olds had gawped when he was introduced to the class. A few of them giggled when the teacher said his first name, Cormoran. He was worried by this school business, because he was sure that his mum had said she was going to 'home school' him. He'd tried to tell Uncle Ted that he didn't think his mum would want him to go, but Ted, normally so understanding, had said firmly that he had to, so there he was, alone among strangers with funny accents. Strike, who'd never been a great crier, had sat down at the old roll-top desk with a lump like an apple in his throat.

Why Dave Polworth, pocket don of the class, had decided to befriend the new boy had never been satisfactorily explained, even to Strike. It couldn't have been out of fear of Strike's size, because Dave's two best friends were hefty fishermen's sons, and Dave was in any case notorious as a fighter whose viciousness was inversely proportional to his height. By the end of that first day Polworth had become both friend and champion, making it his business to impress upon their classmates all the reasons that Strike was worthy of their respect: he was a Cornishman born, a nephew to Ted Nancarrow of the local lifeguard, he didn't know where his mum was and it wasn't his fault if he spoke funny.

Ill as Strike's aunt was, much as she had enjoyed having her nephew to stay for a whole week and even though he'd be leaving the following morning, Joan had virtually pushed him out of the house to celebrate 'Little Dave's' birthday that evening. She placed immense value on old ties and delighted in the fact that Strike and Dave Polworth were still mates, all these years later. Joan counted the fact of their friendship as proof that she'd been right to send him to school over his feckless mother's wishes and proof that Cornwall was Strike's true home, no matter how widely he might have wandered since, and even though he was currently London-based.

Polworth took a long pull on his fourth pint and said, with a sharp glance over his shoulder at the dark woman and her blonde friend, who were still watching Strike,

'Effing emmets.'

'And where would your garden be,' asked Strike, 'without tourists?'

'Be ansom,' said Polworth promptly. 'We get a ton of local visitors, plenty of repeat business.'

Polworth had recently resigned from a managerial position in an engineering firm in Bristol to work as head gardener in a large public garden a short distance along the coast. A qualified diver, an accomplished surfer, a competitor in Ironman competitions, Polworth had been relentlessly physical and restless since childhood, and time and office work hadn't tamed him.

'No regrets, then?' Strike asked.

'Fuck, no,' said Polworth fervently. 'Needed to get my hands dirty again. Need to get back outside. Forty next year. Now or never.'

Polworth had applied for the new job without telling his wife what he was doing. Having been offered the position, he'd quit his job and gone home to announce the fait accompli to his family.

'Penny come round, has she?' Strike asked.

'Still tells me once a week she wants a divorce,' Polworth answered indifferently. 'But it was better to present her with the fact, than argue the toss for five years. It's all worked out great. Kids love the new school, Penny's company let her transfer to the office in the Big

City', by which Polworth meant Truro, not London. 'She's happy. Just doesn't want to admit it.'

Strike privately doubted the truth of this statement. A disregard for inconvenient facts tended to march hand in hand with Polworth's love of risk and romantic causes. However, Strike had problems enough of his own without worrying about Polworth's, so he raised his fresh pint and said, hoping to keep Polworth's mind off politics:

'Well, many happy returns, mate.'

'Cheers,' said Polworth, toasting him back. 'What d'you reckon to Arsenal's chances, then? Gonna qualify?'

Strike shrugged, because he feared that discussing the likelihood of his London football club securing a place in the Champions League would lead back to a lack of Cornish loyalties.

'How's your love life?' Polworth asked, trying a different tack.

'Non-existent,' said Strike.

Polworth grinned.

'Joanie reckons you're gonna end up with your business partner. That Robin girl.'

'Is that right?' said Strike.

'Told me all about it when I was round there, weekend before last. While I was fixing their Sky Box.'

'They didn't tell me you'd done that,' said Strike, again tipping his pint towards Polworth. 'That was good of you, mate, cheers.'

If he'd hoped to deflect his friend, he was unsuccessful.

'Both of 'em. Her and Ted,' said Polworth, 'both of 'em reckon it's Robin.'

And when Strike said nothing, Polworth pressed him, 'Nothing going on, then?'

'No,' said Strike.

'How come?' asked Polworth, frowning again. As with Cornish independence, Strike was refusing to embrace an obvious and desirable objective. 'She's a looker. Seen her in the paper. Maybe not on a par with Milady Berserko,' Polworth acknowledged. It was the nickname he had long ago bestowed on Strike's ex-fiancée. 'But on the other hand, she's not a fucking nutcase, is she, Diddy?'

Strike laughed.

'Lucy likes her,' said Polworth. 'Says you'd be perfect together.'

'When were you talking to Lucy about my love life?' asked Strike, with a touch less complaisance.

'Month or so ago,' said Polworth. 'She brought her boys down for the weekend and we had them all over for a barbecue.'

Strike drank and said nothing.

'You get on great, she says,' said Polworth, watching him.

'Yeah, we do,' said Strike.

Polworth waited, eyebrows raised and looking expectant.

'It'd fuck everything up,' said Strike. 'I'm not risking the agency.'

'Right,' said Polworth. 'Tempted, though?'

There was a short pause. Strike carefully kept his gaze averted from the dark woman and her companion, who he was sure were discussing him.

'There might've been moments,' he admitted, 'when it crossed my mind. But she's going through a nasty divorce, we spend half our lives together as it is and I like having her as a business partner.'

Given their longstanding friendship, the fact that they'd already clashed over politics and that it was Polworth's birthday, he was trying not to let any hint of resentment at this line of questioning show. Every married person he knew seemed desperate to chivvy others into matrimony, no matter how poor an advertisement they themselves were for the institution. The Polworths, for instance, seemed to exist in a permanent state of mutual animosity. Strike had more often heard Penny refer to her husband as 'that twat' than by his name, and many was the night when Polworth had regaled his friends in happy detail of the ways in which he'd managed to pursue his own ambitions and interests at the expense of, or over the protests of, his wife. Both seemed happiest and most relaxed in the company of their own sex, and on those rare occasions when Strike had enjoyed hospitality at their home, the gatherings always seemed to follow a pattern of natural segregation, the women congregating in one area of the home, the men in another.

'And what happens when Robin wants kids?' asked Polworth.

'Don't think she's does,' said Strike. 'She likes the job.'

'They all say that,' said Polworth dismissively. 'What age is she now?'

'Ten years younger than us.'

'She'll want kids,' said Polworth confidently. 'They all do. And it happens quicker for women. They're up against the clock.'

'Well, she won't be getting kids with me. I don't want them. Anyway, the older I get, the less I think I'm the marrying kind.'

'Thought that myself, mate,' said Polworth. 'But then I realised I'd got it all wrong. Told you how it happened, didn't I? How I ended up proposing to Penny?'

'Don't think so,' said Strike.

'I never told you about the whole Tolstoy thing?' asked Polworth, surprised at this omission.

Strike, who'd been about to drink, lowered his glass in amazement. Since primary school, Polworth, who had a razor-sharp intelligence but despised any form of learning he couldn't put to immediate, practical use, had shunned all printed material except technical manuals. Misinterpreting Strike's expression, Polworth said,

'Tolstoy. He's a writer.'

'Yeah,' said Strike. 'Thanks. How does Tolstoy—?'

'Telling you, aren't I? I'd split up with Penny the second time. She'd been banging on about getting engaged, and I wasn't feeling it. So I'm in this bar, telling my mate Chris about how I'm sick of her telling me she wants a ring – you remember Chris? Big guy with a lisp. You met him at Rozwyn's christening.

'Anyway, there's this pissed older guy at the bar on his own, bit of a ponce in his corduroy jacket, wavy hair, and he's pissing me off, to be honest, because I can tell he's listening, and I ask him what the fuck he's looking at and he looks me straight in the eye,' said Polworth, 'and he says: "You can only carry a weight and use your hands, if you strap the weight to your back. Marry, and you get the use of your hands back. Don't marry, and you'll never have your hands free for anything else. Look at Mazankov, at Krupov. They've ruined their careers for the sake of women."

'I thought Mazankov and Krupov were mates of his. Asked him

what the fuck he was telling me for. Then he says he's quoting this writer, Tolstoy.

'And we got talking and I tell you this, Diddy, it was a life-changing moment. The light bulb went on,' said Polworth, pointing at the air over his balding head. 'He made me see it clearly. The male predicament, mate. There I am, trying to get my hole on a Thursday night, heading home alone again, poorer, bored shitless; I thought of the money I've spent chasing gash, and the hassle, and whether I want to be watching porn alone at forty, and I thought, this is the whole point. What marriage is for. Am I going to do better than Penny? Am I enjoying talking shit to women in bars? Penny and me get on all right. I could do a hell of a lot worse. She's not bad-looking. I'd have my hole already at home, waiting for me, wouldn't I?'

'Pity she can't hear this,' said Strike. 'She'd fall in love with you all over again.'

'I shook that poncey bloke's hand,' said Polworth, ignoring Strike's sarcasm. 'Made him write me down the name of the book and all. Went straight out that bar, got a taxi to Penny's flat, banged on the door, woke her up. She was fucking livid. Thought I'd come round because I was pissed, couldn't get anything better and wanted a shag. I said, "No, you dozy cow, I'm here because I wanna marry you."'

'And I'll tell you the name of the book,' said Polworth. '*Anna Karenina*.' He drained his pint. 'It's shit.'

Strike laughed.

Polworth belched loudly, then checked his watch. He was a man who knew a good exit line and had no more time for prolonged leave-taking than for Russian literature.

'Gonna get going, Diddy,' he said, getting to his feet. 'If I'm back before half eleven, I'm on for a birthday blowie – which is the whole point I'm making, mate. Whole point.'

Grinning, Strike accepted Polworth's handshake. Polworth told Strike to convey his love to Joan and to call him next time he was down, then squeezed his way out of the pub, and disappeared from view.

2

Heart, that is inly hurt, is greatly eas'd
With hope of thing, that may allay his Smart . . .

Edmund Spenser
The Faerie Queene

Still grinning at Polworth's story, Strike now realised that the dark woman at the bar was showing signs of wanting to approach him. Her spectacled blonde companion appeared to be advising against it. Strike finished his pint, gathered up his wallet, checked his cigarettes were still in his pocket and, with the assistance of the wall beside him, stood up, making sure his balance was everything it should be before trying to walk. His prosthetic leg was occasionally uncooperative after four pints. Having assured himself that he could balance perfectly well, he set off towards the exit, giving unsmiling nods to those few locals whom he could not ignore without causing offence, and reached the warm darkness outside without being importuned.

The wide, uneven stone steps that led down towards the bay were still crowded with drinkers and smokers. Strike wove his way between them, pulling out his cigarettes as he went.

It was a balmy August night and tourists were still strolling around the picturesque seafront. Strike was facing a fifteen-minute walk, part of it up a steep slope, back to his aunt and uncle's house. On a whim he turned right, crossed the street and headed for the high stone wall separating the car park and ferry point from the sea. Leaning against it, he lit a cigarette and stared out over the smoke grey and silver ocean, becoming just one more tourist in the darkness, free to smoke quietly without having to answer questions about cancer, deliberately postponing the moment when he'd have to return to the uncomfortable sofa that had been his bed for the past six nights.

On arrival, Strike had been told that he, the childless single man and ex-soldier, wouldn't mind sleeping in the sitting room 'because *you'll* sleep anywhere'. She'd been determined to shut down the possibility, mooted by Strike on the phone, that he might check into a bed and breakfast rather than stretch the house to capacity. Strike's visits were rare, especially in conjunction with his sister and nephews, and Joan wanted to enjoy his presence to the full, wanted to feel that she was, once again, the provider and nurturer, currently weakened by her first round of chemotherapy though she might be.

So the tall and heavy Strike, who'd have been far happier on a camp bed, had lain down uncomplainingly every night on the slippery, unyielding mass of satin-covered horsehair, to be woken each morning by his young nephews, who routinely forgot that they had been asked to wait until eight o'clock before barging into the sitting room. At least Jack had the decency to whisper apologies every time he realised that he'd woken his uncle. The eldest, Luke, clattered and shouted his way down the narrow stairs every morning and merely sniggered as he dashed past Strike on his way to the kitchen.

Luke had broken Strike's brand-new headphones, which the detective had felt obliged to pretend didn't matter in the slightest. His eldest nephew had also thought it amusing to run off into the garden with Strike's prosthetic leg one morning, and to stand waving it at his uncle through the window. When Luke finally brought it back, Strike, whose bladder had been very full and who was incapable of hopping up the steep stairs to the only toilet, had delivered Luke a quiet telling-off that had left the boy unusually subdued for most of the morning.

Meanwhile, Joan told Strike every morning, 'you slept well', without a hint of enquiry. Joan had a lifelong habit of subtly pressurising the family into telling her what she wanted to hear. In the days when Strike was sleeping in his office and facing imminent insolvency (facts that he had admittedly not shared with his aunt and uncle), Joan had told him happily 'you're doing awfully well' over the phone, and it had felt, as it always did, unnecessarily combative to challenge her optimistic declaration. After his lower leg had been blown off in Iraq, a tearful Joan had stood at his hospital bed as he tried to focus through a fog of morphine, and told him 'You feel comfortable, though. You aren't in pain.' He loved his aunt, who'd raised him for significant chunks of his childhood, but extended periods in her company made him feel stifled and suffocated. Her insistence on the smooth passing of counterfeit social coin from hand to hand, while uncomfortable truths were ignored and denied, wore him out.

Something gleamed in the water – sleek silver and a pair of soot-black eyes: a seal was turning lazily just below Strike. He watched its revolutions in the water, wondering whether it could see him and, for reasons he couldn't have explained, his thoughts slid towards his partner in the detective agency.

He was well aware that he hadn't told Polworth the whole truth about his relationship with Robin Ellacott, which, after all, was nobody else's business. The truth was that his feelings contained nuances and complications that he preferred not to examine. For instance, he had a tendency, when alone, bored or low-spirited, to want to hear her voice.

He checked his watch. She was having a day off, but there was an outside chance she'd still be awake and he had a decent pretext for texting: Saul Morris, their newest subcontractor, was owed his month's expenses, and Strike had left no instructions for sorting this out. If he texted about Morris, there was a good chance that Robin would call him back to find out how Joan was.

'Excuse me?' a woman said nervously, from behind him.

Strike knew without turning that it was the dark woman from the pub. She had a Home Counties accent and her tone contained that precise mixture of apology and excitement that he usually encountered in those who wanted to talk about his detective triumphs.

'Yes?' he said, turning to face the speaker.

Her blonde friend had come with her: or perhaps, thought Strike, they were more than friends. An indefinable sense of closeness seemed to bind the two women, whom he judged to be around forty. They wore jeans and shirts and the blonde in particular had the slightly weather-beaten leanness that suggests weekends spent hill walking or cycling. She was what some would call a 'handsome' woman, by which they meant that she was bare faced. High-cheekboned, bespectacled, her hair pulled back into a ponytail, she also looked stern.

The dark woman was slighter in build. Her large grey eyes shone palely in her long face. She had an air of intensity, even of fanaticism, about her in the half-light, like a medieval martyr.

'Are you ... are you Cormoran Strike?' she asked.

'Yes,' he said, his tone uninviting.

'Oh,' she breathed, with an agitated little hand gesture. 'This is – this is so strange. I know you probably don't want to be – I'm sorry to bother you, I know you're off duty,' she gave a nervous laugh, 'but – my name's Anna, by the way – I wondered,' she took a deep breath, 'whether I could come – whether I could come and talk to you about my mother.'

Strike said nothing.

'She disappeared,' Anna went on. 'Margot Bamborough's her name. She was a GP. She finished work one evening, walked out of her practice and nobody's seen her since.'

'Have you contacted the police?' asked Strike.

Anna gave an odd little laugh.

'Oh yes – I mean, they knew – they investigated. But they never found anything. She disappeared,' said Anna, 'in 1974.'

The dark water lapped the stone and Strike thought he could hear the seal clearing its damp nostrils. Three drunk youths went weaving past, on their way to the ferry point. Strike wondered whether they knew the last ferry had been and gone at six.

'I just,' said the woman in a rush, 'you see – last week – I went to see a medium.'

Fuck, thought Strike.

He'd occasionally bumped up against the purveyors of paranormal insights during his detective career and felt nothing but contempt for them: leeches, or so he saw them, of money from the pockets of the deluded and the desperate.

A motorboat came chugging across the water, its engine grinding the night's stillness to pieces. Apparently this was the lift the three drunk boys were waiting for. They now began laughing and elbowing each other at the prospect of imminent seasickness.

'The medium told me I'd get a "leading",' Anna pressed on. 'She told me, "You're going to find out what happened to your mother. You'll get a leading and you must follow it. The way will become clear very soon." So when I saw you just now in the pub – *Cormoran Strike*, in the Victory – it just seemed such an incredible coincidence and I thought – I had to speak to you.'

A soft breeze ruffled Anna's dark, silver-streaked hair. The blonde said crisply,

'Come on, Anna, we should get going.'

She put an arm around the other's shoulders. Strike saw a wedding ring shining there.

'We're sorry to have bothered you,' she told Strike.

With gentle pressure, the blonde attempted to turn Anna away. The latter sniffed and muttered,

'Sorry. I . . . probably had too much wine.'

'Hang on.'

Strike often resented his own incurable urge to know, his inability to leave an itch unscratched, especially when he was as tired and aggravated as he was tonight. But 1974 was the year of his own birth. Margot Bamborough had been missing as long as he'd been alive. He couldn't help it: he wanted to know more.

'Are you on holiday here?'

'Yes.' It was the blonde who had spoken. 'Well, we've got a second home in Falmouth. Our permanent base is in London.'

'I'm heading back there tomorrow,' said Strike (*What the fuck are you doing?* asked a voice in his head), 'but I could probably swing by and see you tomorrow morning in Falmouth, if you're free.'

'Really?' gasped Anna. He hadn't seen her eyes fill with tears, but he knew they must have done, because she now wiped them. 'Oh, that'd be *great*. Thank you. *Thank you!* I'll give you the address.'

The blonde showed no enthusiasm at the prospect of seeing Strike again. However, when Anna started fumbling through her handbag, she said, 'It's all right, I've got a card', pulled a wallet out of her back pocket, and handed Strike a business card bearing the name 'Dr Kim Sullivan, BPS Registered Psychologist', with an address in Falmouth printed below it.

'Great,' said Strike, inserting it into his own wallet. 'Well, I'll see you both tomorrow morning, then.'

'I've actually got a work conference call in the morning,' said Kim. 'I'll be free by twelve. Will that be too late for you?'

The implication was clear: you're not speaking to Anna without me present.

'No, that'll be fine,' said Strike. 'I'll see you at twelve, then.'

'Thank you so much!' said Anna.

Kim reached for Anna's hand and the two women walked away. Strike watched them pass under a street light before turning back towards the sea. The motorboat carrying the young drinkers had now chugged away again. It already looked tiny, dwarfed by the wide bay, the roar of its engine gradually deadened into a distant buzz.

Forgetting momentarily about texting Robin, Strike lit a second cigarette, took out his mobile and Googled Margot Bamborough.

Two different photographs appeared. The first was a grainy head-and-shoulders shot of an attractive, even-featured face with wide-set eyes, her wavy, dark blonde hair centre-parted. She was wearing a long-lapelled blouse over what appeared to be a knitted tank top.

The second picture showed the same woman looking younger and wearing the famous black corset of a Playboy Bunny, accessorised with black ears, black stockings and white tail. She was holding a tray of what looked like cigarettes, and smiling at the camera. Another young woman, identically dressed, stood beaming behind her, slightly bucktoothed and curvier than her willowy friend.

Strike scrolled down until he read a famous name in conjunction with Margot's.

... young doctor and mother, Margaret **'Margot' Bamborough**, whose disappearance on 11 October 1974 shared certain features with Creed's abductions of Vera Kenny and Gail Wrightman.

17

Bamborough, who worked at the St John's Medical Practice in Clerkenwell, had arranged to meet a female friend in the local Three Kings pub at six o'clock. She never arrived.

Several witnesses saw a small white van driving at speed in the area around the time that **Bamborough** would have been heading for her rendezvous.

DI Bill Talbot, who led the investigation into **Bamborough**'s disappearance, was convinced from an early stage that the young doctor had fallen victim to the serial killer known to be at large in the south east area. However, no trace of **Bamborough** was discovered in the basement flat where Dennis Creed imprisoned, tortured and killed seven other women.

Creed's trademark of beheading the corpses of his victims . . .

3

But now of Britomart it here doth neede,
The hard aduentures and strange haps to tell

Edmund Spenser
The Faerie Queene

Had her day gone as planned, Robin Ellacott would have been tucked up in bed in her rented flat in Earl's Court at this moment, fresh from a long bath, her laundry done, reading a new novel. Instead, she was sitting in her ancient Land Rover, chilly from sheer exhaustion despite the mild night, still wearing the clothes she'd put on at four-thirty that morning, as she watched the lit window of a Pizza Express in Torquay. Her face in the wing mirror was pale, her blue eyes bloodshot, and the strawberry blonde hair currently hidden under a black beanie hat needed a wash.

From time to time, Robin dipped her hand into a bag of almonds sitting on the passenger seat beside her. It was only too easy to fall into a diet of fast food and chocolate when you were running surveillance, to snack more often than needed out of sheer boredom. Robin was trying to eat healthily in spite of her unsociable hours, but the almonds had long since ceased to be appetising, and she craved nothing more than a bit of the pizza she could see an overweight couple enjoying in the restaurant window. She could almost taste it, even though the air around her was tangy with sea salt and underlain by the perpetual fug of old Wellington boots and wet dog that imbued the Land Rover's ancient fabric seats.

The object of her surveillance, whom she and Strike had

nicknamed 'Tufty' for his badly fitting toupee, was currently out of view. He'd disappeared into the pizzeria an hour and a half previously with three companions, one of whom, a teenager with his arm in a cast, was visible if Robin craned her head sideways into the space above the front passenger seat. This she did every five minutes or so, to check on the progress of the foursome's meal. The last time she had looked, ice cream was being delivered to the table. It couldn't, surely, be much longer.

Robin was fighting a feeling of depression which she knew was at least partly down to utter exhaustion, to the stiffness all over her body from many hours in the driving seat, and to the loss of her long-awaited day off. With Strike unavoidably absent from the agency for an entire week, she'd now worked a twenty-day stretch without breaks. Their best subcontractor, Sam Barclay, had been supposed to take over the Tufty job today in Scotland, but Tufty hadn't flown to Glasgow as expected. Instead, he'd taken a surprise detour to Torquay, leaving Robin with no choice but to follow him.

There were other reasons for her low spirits, of course, one of which she acknowledged to herself; the other, she felt angry with herself for dwelling on.

The first, admissible, reason was her ongoing divorce, which was becoming more contentious by the week. Following Robin's discovery of her estranged husband's affair, they'd had one last cold and bitter meeting, coincidentally in a Pizza Express near Matthew's place of work, where they'd agreed to seek a no-fault divorce following a two-year separation. Robin was too honest not to admit that she, too, bore responsibility for the failure of their relationship. Matthew might have been unfaithful, but she knew that she'd never fully committed to the marriage, that she'd prioritised her job over Matthew on almost every occasion and that, by the end, she had been waiting for a reason to leave. The affair had been a shock, but a release, too.

However, during the twelve months that had elapsed since her pizza with Matthew, Robin had come to realise that far from seeking a 'no-fault' resolution, her ex-husband saw the end of the marriage as entirely Robin's responsibility and was determined to make her pay, both emotionally and financially, for her offence. The joint bank account, which held the proceeds of the sale of their old house, had been frozen while the lawyers wrangled over how much Robin could reasonably expect when she had been earning so much less than Matthew, and had – it had been strongly hinted in the last letter – married him purely with a view to obtaining a pecuniary advantage she could never have achieved alone.

Every letter from Matthew's lawyer caused Robin additional stress, rage and misery. She hadn't needed her own lawyer to point out that Matthew appeared to be trying to force her to spend money she didn't have on legal wrangling, to run down the clock and her resources until she walked away with as close to nothing as he could manage.

'I've never known a childless divorce be so contentious,' her lawyer had told her, words that brought no comfort.

Matthew continued to occupy almost as much space in Robin's head as when they'd been married. She thought she could read his thoughts across the miles and silence that separated them in their widely divergent new lives. He'd always been a bad loser. He had to emerge from this embarrassingly short marriage the winner, by walking away with all the money, and stigmatising Robin as the sole reason for its failure.

All of this was ample reason for her present mood, of course, but then there was the other reason, the one that was inadmissible, that Robin was annoyed with herself for fretting about.

It had happened the previous day, at the office. Saul Morris, the agency's newest subcontractor, was owed his month's expenses, so, after seeing Tufty safely back into the marital home in Windsor, Robin had driven back to Denmark Street to pay Saul.

Morris had been working for the agency for six weeks. He was an ex-police officer, an undeniably handsome man, with black hair and bright blue eyes, though something about him set Robin's teeth on edge. He had a habit of softening his voice when he spoke to her; arch asides and over-personal comments peppered their most mundane interactions, and no double entendre went unmarked if Morris was in the room. Robin rued the day when he'd found out that both of them were currently going through divorces, because he seemed to think this gave him fertile new ground for assumed intimacy.

She'd hoped to get back from Windsor before Pat Chauncey, the agency's new office manager, left, but it was ten past six by the time Robin climbed the stairs and found Morris waiting for her outside the locked door.

'Sorry,' Robin said, 'traffic was awful.'

She'd paid Morris back in cash from the new safe, then told him briskly she needed to get home, but he clung on like gum stuck in her hair, telling her all about his ex-wife's latest late-night texts. Robin tried to unite politeness and coolness until the phone rang on her old desk. She'd ordinarily have let it go to voicemail, but so keen was she to curtail Morris's conversation that she said,

'I've got to get this, sorry. Have a nice evening,' and picked up the receiver.

'Strike Detective Agency, Robin speaking.'

'Hi, Robin,' said a slightly husky female voice. 'Is the boss there?'

Given that Robin had only spoken to Charlotte Campbell once, three years previously, it was perhaps surprising that she'd known instantly who was on the line. Robin had analysed these few words of Charlotte's to a perhaps ludicrous degree since. Robin had detected an undertone of laughter, as though Charlotte found Robin amusing. The easy use of Robin's first name and the description of Strike as 'the boss' had also come in for their share of rumination.

'No, I'm afraid not,' Robin had said, reaching for a pen while her heart beat a little faster. 'Can I take a message?'

'Could you ask him to call Charlotte Campbell? I've got something he wants. He knows my number.'

'Will do,' said Robin.

'Thanks very much,' Charlotte had said, still sounding amused. 'Bye, then.'

Robin had dutifully written down 'Charlotte Campbell called, has something for you' and placed the message on Strike's desk.

Charlotte was Strike's ex-fiancée. Their engagement had been terminated three years previously, on the very day that Robin had come to work at the agency as a temp. Though Strike was far from communicative on the subject, Robin knew that they'd been together for sixteen years ('on and off', as Strike tended to emphasise, because the relationship had faltered many times before its final termination), that Charlotte had become engaged to her present husband just two weeks after Strike had left her and that Charlotte was now the mother of twins.

But this wasn't all Robin knew, because after leaving her husband, Robin had spent five weeks living in the spare room of Nick and Ilsa Herbert, who were two of Strike's best friends. Robin and Ilsa had struck up their own friendship during that time, and still met regularly for drinks and coffees. Ilsa made very little secret of the fact that she hoped and believed that Strike and Robin would one day, and preferably soon, realise that they were 'made for each other'. Although Robin regularly asked Ilsa to desist from her broad hints, asserting that she and Strike were perfectly happy with a friendship and working relationship, Ilsa remained cheerfully unconvinced.

Robin was very fond of Ilsa, but her pleas for her new friend to forget any idea of matchmaking between herself and Strike were genuine. She was mortified by the thought that Strike might think she herself was complicit in Ilsa's regular attempts to engineer foursomes that increasingly had the appearance of double dates. Strike had declined the last two proposed outings of this type and, while the agency's current workload certainly made any kind of social life difficult, Robin had the uncomfortable feeling that he was well aware of Ilsa's ulterior motive. Looking back on her own brief married life, Robin was sure she'd never been guilty of treating single people as she now found herself treated by Ilsa: with a cheerful lack of concern for their sensibilities, and sometimes ham-fisted attempts to manage their love lives.

One of the ways in which Ilsa attempted to draw Robin out on the subject of Strike was to tell her all about Charlotte, and here, Robin felt guilty, because she rarely shut the Charlotte conversations down, even though she never left one of them without feeling as though she had just gorged on junk food: uncomfortable, and wishing she could resist the craving for more.

She knew, for instance, about the many me-or-the-army ultimatums, two of the suicide attempts ('The one on Arran wasn't a proper one,' said Ilsa scathingly. 'Pure manipulation') and about the ten days' enforced stay in the psychiatric clinic. She'd heard stories that Ilsa gave titles like cheap thrillers: the Night of the Bread Knife, the Incident of the Black Lace Dress and the Blood-Stained Note. She knew that in Ilsa's opinion, Charlotte was bad, not mad, and that the worst rows Ilsa and her husband Nick had ever had were on the subject of Charlotte, 'and she'd have bloody loved knowing that, too,' Ilsa had added.

And now Charlotte was phoning the office, asking Strike to call her back, and Robin, sitting outside the Pizza Express, hungry and exhausted, was pondering the phone call yet again, much as a tongue probes a mouth ulcer. If she was phoning the office, Charlotte clearly wasn't aware that Strike was in Cornwall with his terminally ill aunt, which didn't suggest regular contact between them. On the other hand, Charlotte's slightly amused tone had seemed to hint at an alliance between herself and Strike.

Robin's mobile, which was lying on the passenger seat beside the bag of almonds, buzzed. Glad of any distraction, she picked it up and saw a text message from Strike.

Are you awake?

Robin texted back:

No

As she'd expected, the mobile rang immediately.

'Well, you shouldn't be,' said Strike, without preamble. 'You must be knackered. What's it been, three weeks straight on Tufty?'

'I'm still on him.'

'What?' said Strike, sounding displeased. 'You're in Glasgow? Where's Barclay?'

24

'In Glasgow. He was ready in position, but Tufty didn't get on the plane. He drove down to Torquay instead. He's having pizza right now. I'm outside the restaurant.'

'The hell's he doing in Torquay, when the mistress is in Scotland?'

'Visiting his original family,' said Robin, wishing she could see Strike's face as she delivered the next bit of news. 'He's a bigamist.'

Her announcement was greeted with total silence.

'I was outside the house in Windsor at six,' said Robin, 'expecting to follow him to Stansted, see him safely onto the plane and let Barclay know he was on the way, but he didn't go to the airport. He rushed out of the house looking panicky, drove to a lock-up, took his case inside and came out with an entirely different set of luggage and minus his toupee. Then he drove all the way down here.

'Our client in Windsor's about to find out she's not legally married,' said Robin. 'Tufty's had this wife in Torquay for twenty years. I've been talking to the neighbours. I pretended I was doing a survey. One of the women along the street was at the original wedding. Tufty travels a lot for business, she said, but he's a lovely man. Devoted to his sons.

'There are two boys,' Robin continued, because Strike's stunned silence continued unabated, 'students, both in their late teens and both the absolute spit of him. One of them came off his motorbike yesterday – I got all this out of the neighbour – he's got his arm in a cast and looks quite bruised and cut up. Tufty must've got news of the accident, so he came haring down here instead of going to Scotland.

'Tufty goes by the name of Edward Campion down here, not John – turns out John's his middle name, I've been searching the online records. He and the first wife and sons live in a really nice villa, view of the sea, massive garden.'

'Bloody hell,' said Strike. 'So our pregnant friend in Glasgow—'

'—is the least of Mrs-Campion-in-Windsor's worries,' said Robin. 'He's leading a triple life. Two wives and a mistress.'

'And he looks like a balding baboon. There's hope for all of us. Did you say he's having dinner right now?'

'Pizza with the wife and kids. I'm parked outside. I didn't manage to get pictures of him with the sons earlier, and I want to, because they're a total giveaway. Mini-Tuftys, just like the two in Windsor. Where d'you think he's been pretending to have been?'

'Oil rig?' suggested Strike. 'Abroad? Middle East? Maybe that's why he's so keen on keeping his tan topped up.'

Robin sighed.

'The client's going to be shattered.'

'So's the mistress in Scotland,' said Strike. 'That baby's due any minute.'

'His taste's amazingly consistent,' said Robin. 'If you lined them up side by side, the Torquay wife, the Windsor wife and the mistress in Glasgow, they'd look like the same woman at twenty-year intervals.'

'Where are you planning to sleep?'

'Travelodge or a B&B,' said Robin, yawning again, 'if I can find anything vacant at the height of the holiday season. I'd drive straight back to London overnight, but I'm exhausted. I've been awake since four, and that's on top of a ten-hour day yesterday.'

'No driving and no sleeping in the car,' said Strike. 'Get a room.'

'How's Joan?' asked Robin. 'We can handle the workload if you want to stay in Cornwall a bit longer.'

'She won't sit still while we're all there. Ted agrees she needs some quiet. I'll come back down in a couple of weeks.'

'So, were you calling for an update on Tufty?'

'Actually, I was calling about something that just happened. I've just left the pub . . .'

In a few succinct sentences, Strike described the encounter with Margot Bamborough's daughter.

'I've just looked her up,' he said. 'Margot Bamborough, twenty-nine-year-old doctor, married, one-year-old daughter. Walked out of her GP practice in Clerkenwell at the end of a day's work, said she was going to have a quick drink with a female friend before heading home. The pub was only five minutes' walk away. The friend waited, but Margot never arrived and was never seen again.'

There was a pause. Robin, whose eyes were still fixed on the window of the pizza restaurant, said,

'And her daughter thinks you're going to find out what happened, nearly four decades later?'

'She seemed to be putting a lot of store on the coincidence of spotting me in the boozer right after the medium told her she'd get a "leading".'

'Hmm,' said Robin. 'And what do *you* think the chances are of finding out what happened after this length of time?'

'Slim to non-existent,' admitted Strike. 'On the other hand, the truth's out there. People don't just vaporise.'

Robin could hear a familiar note in his voice that indicated rumination on questions and possibilities.

'So you're meeting the daughter again tomorrow?'

'Can't hurt, can it?' said Strike.

Robin didn't answer.

'I know what you're thinking,' he said, with a trace of defensiveness. 'Emotionally overwrought client – medium – situation ripe for exploitation.'

'I'm not suggesting *you'd* exploit it—'

'Might as well hear her out, then, mightn't I? Unlike a lot of people, I wouldn't take her money for nothing. And once I'd exhausted all avenues—'

'I know you,' said Robin. 'The less you found out, the more interested you'd get.'

'Think I'd have her wife to deal with unless I got results within a reasonable period. They're a gay couple,' he elaborated. 'The wife's a psychol—'

'Cormoran, I'll call you back,' said Robin, and without waiting for his answer, she cut the call and dropped the mobile back onto the passenger seat.

Tufty had just ambled out of the restaurant, followed by his wife and sons. Smiling and talking, they turned their steps towards their car, which lay five behind where Robin sat in the Land Rover. Raising her camera, she took a burst of pictures as the family drew nearer.

By the time they passed the Land Rover, the camera was lying in her lap and Robin's head was bowed over her phone, pretending to be texting. In the rear-view mirror she watched as the Tufty family got into their Range Rover and departed for the villa beside the sea.

Yawning yet again, Robin picked up her phone and called Strike back.

'Get everything you wanted?' he asked.

'Yeah,' said Robin, checking the photographs one-handedly with the phone to her ear, 'I've got a couple of clear ones of him and the boys. God, he's got strong genes. All four kids have got his exact features.'

She put the camera back into her bag.

'You realise I'm only a couple of hours away from St Mawes?'

'Nearer three,' said Strike.

'If you like—'

'You don't want to drive all the way down here, then back to London. You've just told me you're knackered.'

But Robin could tell that he liked the idea. He'd travelled down to Cornwall by train, taxi and ferry, because since he had lost a leg, long drives were neither easy nor particularly pleasurable.

'I'd like to meet this Anna. Then I could drive you back.'

'Well, if you're sure, that'd be great,' said Strike, now sounding cheerful. 'If we take her on, we should work the case together. There'd be a massive amount to sift through, cold case like this, and it sounds like you've wrapped up Tufty tonight.'

'Yep,' sighed Robin. 'It's all over except for the ruining of half a dozen lives.'

'*You* didn't ruin anyone's life,' said Strike bracingly. 'He did that. What's better: all three women find out now, or when he dies, with all the effing mess that'll cause?'

'I know,' said Robin, yawning again. 'So, do you want me to come to the house in St M—'

His 'no' was swift and firm.

'They – Anna and her partner – they're in Falmouth. I'll meet you there. It's a shorter drive for you.'

'OK,' said Robin. 'What time?'

'Could you manage half eleven?'

'Easily,' said Robin.

'I'll text you a place to meet. Now go and get some sleep.'

As she turned the key in the ignition, Robin became conscious that her spirits had lifted considerably. As though a censorious jury were watching, among them Ilsa, Matthew and Charlotte Campbell, she consciously repressed her smile as she reversed out of the parking space.

4

Begotten by two fathers of one mother,
Though of contrarie natures each to other . . .

Edmund Spenser
The Faerie Queene

Strike woke shortly before five the following morning. Light was already streaming through Joan's thin curtains. Every night the horsehair sofa punished a different part of his body, and today he felt as though he had been punched in a kidney. He reached for his phone, noted the time, decided that he was too sore to fall back asleep, and raised himself to a sitting position.

After a minute spent stretching and scratching his armpits while his eyes acclimatised to the odd shapes rising on all sides in the gloom of Joan and Ted's sitting room, he Googled Margot Bamborough for a second time and, after a cursory examination of the picture of the smiling, wavy-haired doctor with widely spaced eyes, he scrolled through the results until he found a mention of her on a website devoted to serial killers. Here he found a long article punctuated with pictures of Dennis Creed at various ages, from pretty, curly-haired blond toddler all the way through to the police mugshot of a slender man with a weak, sensual mouth and large, square glasses.

Strike then turned to an online bookstore, where he found an account of the serial killer's life, published in 1985 and titled *The Demon of Paradise Park*. It had been written by a well-respected investigative journalist, now dead. Creed's nondescript face appeared in colour on the cover, superimposed over ghostly black and white images of the seven women he was known to have tortured and killed. Margot Bamborough's face wasn't among them. Strike ordered the second-hand book, which cost £1, to be delivered to the office.

He returned his phone to its charging lead, put on his prosthetic leg, picked up his cigarettes and lighter, navigated around a rickety nest of tables with a vase of dried flowers on it and, being careful not to nudge any of the ornamental plates off the wall, passed through the doorway and down three steep steps into the kitchen. The lino, which had been there since his childhood, was icy cold on his remaining foot.

After making himself a mug of tea, he let himself out of the back door, still clad in nothing but boxers and a T-shirt, there to enjoy the cool of early morning, leaning up against the wall of the house, breathing in salt-laden air between puffs on his cigarette, and thinking about vanished mothers. Many times over the past ten days had his thoughts turned to Leda, a woman as different to Joan as the moon to the sun.

'Have you tried smoking yet, Cormy?' she'd once asked vaguely, out of a haze of blue smoke of her own creation. 'It isn't good for you, but God, I love it.'

People sometimes asked why social services never got involved with Leda Strike's family. The answer was that Leda had never stayed still long enough to present a stable target. Often her children remained in a school for mere weeks before a new enthusiasm seized her, and off they went, to a new city, a new squat, crashing on her friends' floors or, occasionally, renting. The only people who knew what was going on, and who might have contacted social services, were Ted and Joan, the one fixed point in the children's lives, but whether because Ted feared damaging the relationship between himself and his wayward sister, or because Joan worried that the children might not forgive her, they'd never done so.

One of the most vivid memories of Strike's childhood was also one of the rare occasions he could remember crying, when Leda had made an unannounced return, six weeks into Strike's first term at St Mawes Primary School. Amazed and angry that such definitive steps as enrolling him in school had been taken in her absence, she'd ushered him and his sister directly onto the ferry, promising them all manner of treats up in London. Strike had bawled, trying to explain to her that he and Dave Polworth had been going to explore smugglers' caves at the weekend, caves that might well have had no existence except in Dave's imagination, but which were no less real to Strike for that.

'You'll see the caves,' Leda had promised, plying him with sweets once they were on the train to London. 'You'll see what's-his-name soon, I promise.'

'Dave,' Strike had sobbed, 'he's called D-Dave.'

Don't think about it, Strike told himself, and he lit a second cigarette from the tip of his first.

'Stick, you'll catch your death, out there in boxers!'

He looked around. His sister was standing in the doorway, wrapped in a woollen dressing gown and wearing sheepskin slippers. They were physically so unalike that people struggled to believe that they were related, let alone half-siblings. Lucy was small, blonde and pink-faced, and greatly resembled her father, a musician not quite as famous as Strike's, but far more interested in maintaining contact with his offspring.

'Morning,' he said, but she'd already disappeared, returning with his trousers, sweatshirt, shoes and socks.

'Luce, it's not cold—'

'You'll get pneumonia. Put them on!'

Like Joan, Lucy had total confidence in her own judgement of her nearest and dearest's best interests. With slightly better grace than he might have mustered had he not been about to return to London, Strike took his trousers and put them on, balancing awkwardly and risking a fall onto the gravel path. By the time he'd added a shoe and sock to his real foot, Lucy had made him a fresh mug of tea along with her own.

'I couldn't sleep, either,' she told him, handing over the mug as she sat down on the stone bench. It was the first time they'd been entirely alone all week. Lucy had been glued to Joan's side, insisting on doing all the cooking and cleaning while Joan, who found it inconceivable that she should sit down while the house was full of guests, hovered and fussed. On the rare moments that Joan wasn't present, one or more of Lucy's sons had generally been there, in Jack's case wanting to talk to Strike, the other two generally badgering Lucy for something.

'It's awful, isn't it?' said Lucy, staring out over the lawn and Ted's carefully tended flower-beds.

'Yeah,' sighed Strike. 'But fingers crossed. The chemo—'

'But it won't cure her. It'll just prolong – pro—'

Lucy shook her head and dabbed at her eyes with a crumpled piece of toilet roll she pulled out of her dressing-gown pocket.

'I've rung her twice a week for nigh on twenty years, Stick. This place is a second home for our boys. She's the only mother I've ever known.'

Strike knew he oughtn't to rise to the bait. Nevertheless, he said, 'Other than our actual mother, you mean.'

'Leda wasn't my mother,' said Lucy coldly. Strike had never heard her say it in so many words, though it had often been implied. 'I haven't considered her my mother since I was fourteen years old. Younger, actually. *Joan's* my mother.'

And when Strike made no response, she said,

'You chose Leda. I know you love Joan, but we have entirely different relationships with her.'

'Didn't realise it was a competition,' Strike said, reaching for another cigarette.

'I'm only telling you how I feel!'

And telling me how I feel.

Several barbed comments about the infrequency of Strike's visits had already dropped from his sister's lips during their week of enforced proximity. He'd bitten back all irritable retorts. His primary aim was to leave the house without rowing with anyone.

'I always hated it when Leda came to take us away,' said Lucy now, 'but you were glad to go.'

He noted the Joan-esque statement of fact, the lack of enquiry.

'I wasn't always glad to go,' Strike contradicted her, thinking of the ferry, Dave Polworth and the smugglers' caves, but Lucy seemed to feel that he was trying to rob her of something.

'I'm just saying, you lost *your* mother years ago. Now I'm – I might be – losing mine.'

She mopped her eyes again with the damp toilet roll.

Lower back throbbing, eyes stinging with tiredness, Strike stood smoking in silence. He knew that Lucy would have liked to excise Leda for ever from her memory, and sometimes, remembering a few of the things Leda had put them through, he sympathised. This morning, though, the wraith of Leda seemed to drift on his cigarette smoke around him. He could hear her saying to Lucy, 'Go on and have a good cry, darling, it always helps', and 'Give your old mum a fag, Cormy'. He couldn't hate her.

'I can't *believe* you went out with Dave Polworth last night,' said Lucy suddenly. 'Your last night here!'

'Joan virtually shoved me out of the house,' said Strike, nettled. 'She loves Dave. Anyway, I'll be back in a couple of weeks.'

'Will you?' said Lucy, her eyelashes now beaded with tears. 'Or will you be in the middle of some case and just forget?'

Strike blew smoke out into the constantly lightening air, which had that flat blue tinge that precedes sunrise. Far to the right, hazily visible over the rooftops of the houses on the slope that was Hillhead, the division between sky and water was becoming clearer on the horizon.

'No,' he said, 'I won't forget.'

'Because you're good in a crisis,' said Lucy, 'I don't deny that, but it's keeping a commitment going that you seem to have a problem with. Joan'll need support for months and months, not just when—'

'I know that, Luce,' said Strike, his temper rising in spite of himself. 'I understand illness and recuperation, believe it or—'

'Yeah, well,' said Lucy, 'you were great when Jack was in hospital, but when everything's fine you simply don't bother.'

'I took Jack out two weeks ago, what're you—?'

'You couldn't even make the effort to come to Luke's birthday party! He'd told all his friends you were going to be there—'

'Well, he shouldn't have done, because I told you *explicitly* over the phone—'

'You said you'd try—'

'No, *you* said I'd try,' Strike contradicted her, temper rising now, in spite of his best intentions. '*You* said "You'll make it if you can, though." Well, I couldn't make it, I told you so in advance and it's not my fault you told Luke differently—'

'I appreciate you taking Jack out every now and then,' said Lucy, talking over him, 'but has it never occurred to you that it would be nice if the other two could come, too? Adam *cried* when Jack came home from the War Rooms! And then you come down here,' said Lucy, who seemed determined to get everything off her chest now she'd started, 'and you only bring a present for Jack. What about Luke and Adam?'

'Ted called with the news about Joan and I set straight off. I'd been saving those badges for Jack, so I brought them with me.'

'Well, how do you think that makes Luke and Adam feel? Obviously they think you don't like them as much as Jack!'

'I don't,' said Strike, finally losing his temper. 'Adam's a whiny little prick and Luke's a complete arsehole.'

He crushed out his cigarette on the wall, flicked the stub into the hedge and headed back inside, leaving Lucy gasping for air like a beached fish.

Back in the dark sitting room, Strike blundered straight into the table nest: the vase of dried flowers toppled heavily onto the patterned carpet and before he knew what he was doing he'd crushed the fragile stems and papery heads to dust beneath his false foot. He was still tidying up the fragments as best he could when Lucy strode silently past him towards the door to the stairs, emanating maternal outrage. Strike set the now empty vase back on the table and, waiting until he heard Lucy's bedroom door close, headed upstairs for the bathroom, fuming.

Afraid to use the shower in case he woke Ted and Joan, he peed, pulled the flush and only then remembered how noisy the old toilet was. Washing as best he could in tepid water while the cistern refilled with a noise like a cement mixer, Strike thought that if anyone slept through that, they'd have to be drugged.

Sure enough, on opening the bathroom door, he came face to face with Joan. The top of his aunt's head barely came up to Strike's chest. He looked down on her thinning grey hair, into once forget-me-not blue eyes now bleached with age. Her frogged and quilted red dressing gown had the ceremonial dignity of a kabuki robe.

'Morning,' Strike said, trying to sound cheerful and achieving only a fake bonhomie. 'Didn't wake you, did I?'

'No, no, I've been awake for a while. How was Dave?' she asked.

'Great,' said Strike heartily. 'Loving his new job.'

'And Penny and the girls?'

'Yeah, they're really happy to be back in Cornwall.'

'Oh good,' said Joan. 'Dave's mum thought Penny might not want to leave Bristol.'

'No, it's all worked out great.'

The bedroom door behind Joan opened. Luke was standing there in his pyjamas, rubbing his eyes ostentatiously.

'You woke me up,' he told Strike and Joan.

'Oh, sorry, love,' said Joan.

'Can I have Coco Pops?'

'Of course you can,' said Joan fondly.

Luke bounded downstairs, stamping on the stairs to make as much noise as possible. He was gone barely a minute before he came bounding back towards them, glee etched over his freckled face.

'Granny, Uncle Cormoran's broken your flowers.'

You little shit.

'Yeah, sorry. The dried ones,' Strike told Joan. 'I knocked them over. The vase is fine—'

'Oh, they couldn't matter less,' said Joan, moving at once to the stairs. 'I'll fetch the carpet sweeper.'

'No,' said Strike at once, 'I've already—'

'There are still bits all over the carpet,' Luke said. 'I trod on them.'

I'll tread on you in a minute, arsehole.

Strike and Luke followed Joan back to the sitting room, where Strike insisted on taking the carpet sweeper from Joan, a flimsy, archaic device she'd had since the seventies. As he plied it, Luke stood in the kitchen doorway watching him, smirking while shovelling Coco Pops into his mouth. By the time Strike had cleaned the carpet to Joan's satisfaction, Jack and Adam had joined the early morning jamboree, along with a stony-faced Lucy, now fully dressed.

'Can we go to the beach today, Mum?'

'Can we swim?'

'Can I go out in the boat with Uncle Ted?'

'Sit down,' Strike told Joan. 'I'll bring you a cup of tea.'

But Lucy had already done it. She handed Joan the mug, threw Strike a filthy look, then turned back to the kitchen, answering her sons' questions as she went.

'What's going on?' asked Ted, shuffling into the room in pyjamas, confused by this break-of-dawn activity.

He'd once been nearly as tall as Strike, who greatly resembled him. His dense, curly hair was now snow white, his deep brown face more cracked than lined, but Ted was still a strong man, though he stooped a little. However, Joan's diagnosis seemed to have dealt him a physical blow. He seemed literally shaken, a little disorientated and unsteady.

'Just getting my stuff together, Ted,' said Strike, who suddenly had an overpowering desire to leave. 'I'm going to have to get the first ferry to make the early train.'

'Ah,' said Ted. 'All the way back up to London, are you?'

'Yep,' said Strike, chucking his charging lead and deodorant back into the kit bag where the rest of his belongings were already neatly stowed. 'But I'll be back in a couple of weeks. You'll keep me posted, right?'

'You can't leave without breakfast!' said Joan anxiously. 'I'll make you a sandwich—'

'It's too early for me to eat,' lied Strike. 'I've had a cup of tea and I'll get something on the train. Tell her,' he said to Ted, because Joan wasn't listening, but scurrying for the kitchen.

'Joanie!' Ted called. 'He doesn't want anything!'

Strike grabbed his jacket off the back of a chair and hoisted the kit bag out to the hall.

'You should go back to bed,' he told Joan, as she hurried to bid him goodbye. 'I really didn't want to wake you. Rest, all right? Let someone else run the town for a few weeks.'

'I wish you'd stop smoking,' she said sadly.

Strike managed a humorous eye roll, then hugged her. She clung to him the way she had done whenever Leda was waiting impatiently to take him away, and Strike squeezed her back, feeling again the pain of divided loyalties, of being both battleground and prize, of having to give names to what was uncategorisable and unknowable.

'Bye, Ted,' he said, hugging his uncle. 'I'll ring you when I'm home and we'll fix up a time for the next visit.'

'I could've driven you,' said Uncle Ted feebly. 'Sure you don't want me to drive you?'

'I like the ferry,' lied Strike. In fact, the uneven steps leading down to the boat were almost impossible for him to navigate without assistance from the ferryman, but because he knew it would give them pleasure, he said, 'Reminds me of you two taking us shopping in Falmouth when we were kids.'

Lucy was watching him, apparently unconcerned, through the door from the sitting room. Luke and Adam hadn't wanted to leave their Coco Pops, but Jack came wriggling breathlessly into the tiny hall to say,

'Thanks for my badges, Uncle Corm.'

'It was a pleasure,' said Strike, and he ruffled the boy's hair. 'Bye, Luce,' he called. 'See you soon, Jack,' he added.

5

He little answer'd, but in manly heart
His mightie indignation did forbeare,
Which was not yet so secret, but some part
Thereof did in his frouning face appeare . . .

Edmund Spenser
The Faerie Queene

The bedroom in the bed and breakfast where Robin spent the night barely had room for a single bed, a chest of drawers and a rickety sink plumbed into the corner. The walls were covered in a mauve floral wallpaper that Robin thought must surely have been considered tasteless even in the seventies, the sheets felt damp and the window was imperfectly covered by a tangled Venetian blind.

In the harsh glare of a single light bulb unsoftened by its shade of open wickerwork, Robin's reflection looked exhausted and ill-kempt, with purple shadows beneath her eyes. Her backpack contained only those items she always carried on surveillance jobs – a beanie hat, should she need to conceal her distinctive red-blonde hair, sunglasses, a change of top, a credit card and ID in a couple of different names. The fresh T-shirt she'd just pulled out of her backpack was heavily creased and her hair in urgent need of a wash; the sink was soapless and she'd omitted to pack toothbrush or toothpaste, unaware that she was going to be spending the night away from home.

Robin was back on the road by eight. In Newton Abbot she stopped at a chemist and a Sainsbury's, where she purchased, in addition to basic toiletries and dry shampoo, a small, cheap bottle of

4711 cologne. She cleaned her teeth and made herself as presentable as possible in the supermarket bathroom. While brushing her hair, she received a text from Strike:

I'll be in the Palacio Lounge café in The Moor, middle of Falmouth. Anyone will tell you where The Moor is.

The further west Robin drove, the lusher and greener the landscape became. Yorkshire-born, she'd found it extraordinary to see palm trees actually flourishing on English soil, back in Torquay. These twisting, verdant lanes, the luxuriance of the vegetation, the almost sub-tropical greenness was a surprise to a person raised among bare, rolling moors and hillside. Then there were the glints to her left of a quicksilver sea, as wide and gleaming as plate glass, and the tang of the salt now mixed with the citrus of her hastily purchased cologne. In spite of her tiredness she found her spirits buoyed by the glorious morning, and the idea of Strike waiting at journey's end.

She arrived in Falmouth at eleven o'clock, and drove in search of a parking space through streets packed with tourists and past shop doorways accreted in plastic toys and pubs covered in flags and multi-coloured window boxes. Once she'd parked in The Moor itself – a wide open market square in the heart of the town – she saw that beneath the gaudy summertime trappings, Falmouth boasted some grand old nineteenth-century buildings, one of which housed the Palacio Lounge café and restaurant.

The high ceilings and classical proportions of what looked like an old courthouse had been decorated in a self-consciously whimsical style, which included garish orange floral wallpaper, hundreds of kitschy paintings in pastel frames, and a stuffed fox dressed as a magistrate. The clientele, which was dominated by students and families, sat on mismatched wooden chairs, their chatter echoing through the cavernous space. After a few seconds Robin spotted Strike, large and surly-looking at the back of the room, seeming far from happy beside a pair of families whose many young children, most of whom were wearing tie-dyed clothing, were racing around between tables.

Robin thought she saw the idea of standing to greet her cross

Strike's mind as she wound her way through the tables towards him, but if she was right, he decided against. She knew how he looked when his leg was hurting him, the lines around his mouth deeper than usual, as though he had been clenching his jaw. If Robin had looked tired in the dusty bed and breakfast mirror three hours previously, Strike looked utterly drained, his unshaven jaw appearing dirty, the shadows under his eyes dark blue.

'Morning,' he said, struggling to make himself heard over the merry shrieking of the hippy children. 'Get parked OK?'

'Just round the corner,' she said, sitting down.

'I chose this place because I thought it would be easy to find,' he said.

A small boy knocked into their table, causing Strike's coffee to slop over onto his plate, which was littered with croissant flakes, and ran off again. 'What d'you want?'

'Coffee would be great,' said Robin loudly, over the cries of the children beside them. 'How're things in St Mawes?'

'Same,' said Strike.

'I'm sorry,' said Robin.

'Why? It's not your fault,' grunted Strike.

This was hardly the greeting Robin had expected after a two-and-a-half drive to pick him up. Possibly her annoyance showed, because Strike added,

'Thanks for doing this. Appreciate it. *Oh, don't pretend you can't see me, dipshit*,' he added crossly, as a young waiter walked away without spotting his raised hand.

'I'll go to the counter,' said Robin. 'I need the loo anyway.'

By the time she'd peed and managed to order a coffee from a harassed waiter, a tension headache had begun to pound on the left-hand side of her head. On her return to the table she found Strike looking like thunder, because the children at the next tables were now shrieking louder than ever as they raced around their oblivious parents, who simply shouted over the din. The idea of giving Strike Charlotte's telephone message right now passed through Robin's mind, only to be dismissed.

In fact, the main reason for Strike's foul mood was that the end of his amputated leg was agony. He'd fallen (*like a total tit*, as he told himself) while getting onto the Falmouth ferry. This feat required a precarious descent down worn stone steps without a handhold, then a step down into the boat with only the boatman's hand for assistance. At sixteen stone, Strike was hard to stabilise when he slipped, and slip he had, with the result that he was now in a lot of pain.

Robin took paracetamol out of her bag.

'Headache,' she said, catching Strike's eye.

'I'm not bloody surprised,' he said loudly, looking at the parents shouting at each other over the raucous yells of their offspring, but they didn't hear him. The idea of asking Robin for painkillers crossed Strike's mind, but this might engender enquiries and fussing, and he'd had quite enough of those in the past week, so he continued to suffer in silence.

'Where's the client?' she asked, after downing her pills with coffee.

'About five minutes' drive away. Place called Wodehouse Terrace.'

At this point, the smallest of the children racing around nearby tripped and smacked her face on the wooden floor. The child's shrieks and wails of pain pounded against Robin's eardrums.

'Oh, Daffy!' said one of the tie-dyed mothers shrilly, '*what* have you done?'

The child's mouth was bloody. Her mother crouched beside their table, loudly castigating and soothing, while the girl's siblings and friends watched avidly. The ferry-goers this morning had worn similar expressions when Strike had hit the deck.

'He's got a false leg,' the ferryman had shouted, partly, Strike suspected, in case anyone thought the fall was due to his negligence. The announcement had in no way lessened Strike's mortification or the interest of his fellow travellers.

'Shall we get going?' Robin asked, already on her feet.

'Definitely,' said Strike, wincing as he stood and picked up his holdall. 'Bloody kids,' he muttered, limping after Robin towards the sunlight.

6

Faire Lady, hart of flint would rew
The vndeserued woes and sorrowes, which ye shew.

Edmund Spenser
The Faerie Queene

Wodehouse Terrace lay on a hill, with a wide view of the bay below. Many of the houses had had loft conversions, but Anna and Kim's, as they saw from the street, had been more extensively modified than any other, with what looked like a square glass box where once there had been roof.

'What does Anna do?' asked Robin, as they climbed the steps towards the deep blue front door.

'No idea,' said Strike, 'but her wife's a psychologist. I got the impression she isn't keen on the idea of an investigation.'

He pressed the doorbell. They heard footsteps on what sounded like bare wood, and the door was opened by Dr Sullivan, tall, blonde and barefoot in jeans and a shirt, the sun glinting off her spectacles. She looked from Strike to Robin, apparently surprised.

'My partner, Robin Ellacott,' Strike explained.

'Oh,' said Kim, looking displeased. 'You do realise – this is only supposed to be an exploratory meeting.'

'Robin happened to be just up the coast on another case, so—'

'I'm more than happy to wait in the car,' said Robin politely, 'if Anna would rather speak to Cormoran alone.'

'Well – we'll see how Anna feels.'

43

Standing back to admit them, Kim added, 'Straight upstairs, in the sitting room.'

The house had clearly been remodelled throughout and to a high standard. Everywhere was bleached wood and glass. The bedroom, as Robin saw through an open door, had been relocated to the ground floor, along with what looked like a study. Upstairs, in the glass box they'd seen from the street, was an open-plan area combining kitchen, dining and sitting room, with a dazzling view of the sea.

Anna was standing beside a gleaming, expensive coffee machine, wearing a baggy blue cotton jumpsuit and white canvas shoes, which to Robin looked stylish and to Strike, frumpy. Her hair was tied back, revealing the delicacy of her bone structure.

'Oh, hello,' she said, starting at the sight of them. 'I didn't hear the door over the coffee machine.'

'Annie,' said Kim, following Strike and Robin into the room, 'this is Robin Ellacott, er – Cameron's partner. She's happy to go if you'd rather just talk to—'

'Cormoran,' Anna corrected Kim. 'Do people get that wrong a lot?' she asked Strike.

'More often than not,' he said, but with a smile. 'But it's a bloody stupid name.'

Anna laughed.

'I don't mind you staying,' she told Robin, advancing and offering a handshake. 'I think I read about you, too,' she added, and Robin pretended that she didn't notice Anna glancing down at the long scar on her forearm.

'Please, sit down,' said Kim, gesturing Strike and Robin to an inbuilt seating area around a low Perspex table.

'Coffee?' suggested Anna, and both of them accepted.

A ragdoll cat came prowling into the room, stepping delicately through the puddles of sunlight on the floor, its clear blue eyes like Joan's across the bay. After subjecting both Strike and Robin to dispassionate scrutiny, it leapt lightly onto the sofa and into Strike's lap.

'Ironically,' said Kim, as she carried a tray laden with cups and biscuits to the table, 'Cagney absolutely *loves* men.'

Strike and Robin laughed politely. Anna brought over the coffee pot, and the two women sat down side by side, facing Strike and Robin, their faces in the full glare of the sun until Anna reached for a remote control, which automatically lowered cream-coloured sun blinds.

'Wonderful place,' said Robin, looking around.

'Thanks,' said Kim. '*Her* work,' she said, patting Anna's knee. 'She's an architect.'

Anna cleared her throat.

'I want to apologise,' she said, looking steadily at Strike with her unusual silver-grey eyes, 'for the way I behaved last night. I'd had a few glasses of wine. You probably thought I was a crank.'

'If I'd thought that,' said Strike, stroking the loudly purring cat, 'I wouldn't be here.'

'But mentioning the medium probably gave you entirely the wrong . . . because, believe me, Kim's already told me what a fool I was to go and see her.'

'I don't think you're a fool, Annie,' Kim said quietly. 'I think you're vulnerable. There's a difference.'

'May I ask what the medium said?' asked Strike.

'Does it matter?' asked Kim, looking at Strike with what Robin thought was mistrust.

'Not in an investigative sense,' said Strike, 'but as he — she? — is the reason Anna approached me—'

'It was a woman,' said Anna, 'and she didn't really tell me anything useful . . . not that I . . . '

With a nervous laugh, she shook her head and started again.

'I know it was a stupid thing to do. I — I've been through a difficult time recently — I left my firm and I'm about to turn forty and . . . well, Kim was away on a course and I — well, I suppose I wanted—'

She waved her hands dismissively, took a deep breath and said,

'She's quite an ordinary-looking woman who lives in Chiswick. Her house was full of angels — made of pottery and glass, I mean, and there was a big one painted on velvet over the fireplace.

'Kim,' Anna pressed on, and Robin glanced at the psychologist, whose expression was impassive, 'Kim thinks she – the medium – knew who my mother was – that she Googled me before I arrived. I'd given her my real name. When I got there, I simply said that my mother died a long time ago – although of course,' said Anna, with another nervous wave of her thin hands, 'there's no proof that my mother's dead – that's half the – but anyway, I told the medium she'd died, and that nobody had ever been clear with me about how it happened.

'So the woman went into a – well, I suppose you'd call it a trance,' Anna said, looking embarrassed, 'and she told me that people thought they were protecting me for my own good, but that it was time I knew the truth and that I would soon have a "leading" that would take me to it. And she said "your mother's very proud of you" and "she's always watching over you", and things like that, I suppose they're boilerplate – and then, at the end, "she lies in a holy place".

'"Lies in a holy place"?' repeated Strike.

'Yes. I suppose she thought that would be comforting, but I'm not a churchgoer. The sanctity or otherwise of my mother's final resting place – if she's buried – I mean, it's hardly my primary concern.'

'D'you mind if I take notes?' Strike asked.

He pulled out a notebook and pen, which Cagney the cat appeared to think were for her personal amusement. She attempted to bat the pen around as Strike wrote the date.

'Come here, you silly animal,' said Kim, getting up to lift the cat clear and put her back on the warm wooden floor.

'To begin at the beginning,' said Strike. 'You must've been very young when your mother went missing?'

'Just over a year old,' said Anna, 'so I can't remember her at all. There were no photographs of her in the house while I was growing up. I didn't know what had happened for a long time. Of course, there was no internet back then – anyway, my mother kept her own surname after marriage. I grew up as Anna Phipps, which is my father's name. If anybody had said "Margot Bamborough" to me before I was eleven, I wouldn't have known she had any connection to me.

'I thought Cynthia was my mum. She was my childminder when I was little,' she explained. 'She's a third cousin of my father's and quite a bit younger than him, but she's a Phipps, too, so I assumed we were a standard nuclear family. I mean – why wouldn't I?

'I do remember, once I'd started school, questioning why I was calling Cyn "Cyn" instead of "Mum". But then Dad and Cyn decided to get married, and they told me I could call her "Mum" now if I wanted to, and I thought, oh, I see, I had to use her name before, because they weren't married. You fill in the gaps when you're a child, don't you? With your own weird logic.

'I was seven or eight when a girl at school said to me, "That's not your real mum. Your real mum disappeared." It sounded mad. I didn't ask Dad or Cyn about it. I just locked it away, but I think, on some deep level, I sensed I'd just been handed the answer to some of the strange things I'd noticed and never been given answers to.

'I was eleven when I found out properly. By then, I'd heard other things from other kids at school. "Your real mum ran away" was one of them. Then one day, this really *poisonous* boy said to me, "Your mum was killed by a man who cut off her head."'

'I went home and I told my father what that boy had said. I wanted him to laugh, to say it was ridiculous, what a horrible little boy . . . but he turned white.

'That same evening he and Cynthia called me downstairs out of my bedroom, sat me down in the sitting room and told me the truth.

'And everything I thought I knew crumbled away,' said Anna quietly. 'Who thinks something like this has happened in their own family? I adored Cyn. I got on better with her than with my father, to tell you the truth. And then I found out that she wasn't my mum at all, and they'd both lied – lied in fact, lied by omission.

'They told me my mother walked out of her GP's practice one night and vanished. The last person to see her alive was the receptionist. She said she was off to the pub, which was five minutes up the road. Her best friend was waiting there. When my mother didn't turn up, the friend, Oonagh Kennedy, who'd waited an hour, thought she must have forgotten. She called my parents' house. My mother wasn't there. My father called the practice, but it was closed. It got dark. My mother didn't come home. My father called the police.

'They investigated for months and months. Nothing. No clues, no sightings – at least, that's what my father and Cyn said, but I've since read things that contradict that.

'I asked Dad and Cyn where my mother's parents were. They said they were dead. That turned out to be true. My grandfather died of a heart attack a couple of years after my mother disappeared and my grandmother died of a stroke a year later. My mother was an only child, so there were no other relatives I could meet or talk to about her.

'I asked for photographs. My father said he'd got rid of them all, but Cyn dug some out for me, a couple of weeks after I found out. She asked me not to tell my father she'd done it; to hide them. I did: I had a pyjama case shaped like a rabbit and I kept my mother's photographs in there for years.'

'Did your father and stepmother explain to you what *might* have happened to your mother?' Strike asked.

'Dennis Creed, you mean?' said Anna. 'Yes, but they didn't tell me details. They said there was a chance she'd been killed by a – by a bad man. They had to tell me that much, because of what the boy at school had said.

'It was an appalling idea, thinking she might have been killed by Creed – I found out his name soon enough, kids at school were happy to fill me in. I started having nightmares about her, head-less. Sometimes she came into my bedroom at night. Sometimes I dreamed I found her head in my toy chest.

'I got really angry with my father and Cyn,' said Anna, twisting her fingers together. 'Angry that they'd never told me, obviously, but I also started wondering what else they were hiding, whether they were involved in my mother disappearing, whether they'd wanted her out of the way, so they could marry. I went a bit off the rails, started playing truant . . . one weekend I took off and was brought home by the police. My father was livid. Of course, I look back, and after what had happened to my mother . . . obviously, me going missing, even for a few hours . . .

'I gave them hell, to tell you the truth,' said Anna shamefacedly. 'But all credit to Cyn, she stuck by me. She never gave up. She and Dad had had kids together by then – I've got a younger brother and sister – and there was family therapy and holidays with bonding activities, all led by Cyn, because my father certainly didn't want to do it. The subject of my mother just makes him angry and aggrieved. I remember him yelling at me, didn't I realise how terrible it was for *him* to have it all dragged up again, how did I think *he* felt . . .

'When I was fifteen I tried to find my mother's friend, Oonagh, the one she was supposed to be meeting the night she disappeared. They were Bunny Girls together,' said Anna, with a little smile, 'but I didn't know that at the time. I tracked Oonagh down in Wolverhampton, and she was quite emotional to hear from me. We had a couple of lovely phone calls. She told me things I really wanted to know, about my mother's sense of humour, the perfume she wore – Rive Gauche, I went out and blew my birthday money on a bottle next day – how she was addicted to chocolate and was an obsessive Joni Mitchell fan. My mother came more alive to me when I was talking to Oonagh than through the photographs, or anything Dad or Cyn had told me.

'But my father found out I'd spoken to Oonagh and he was furious. He made me give him Oonagh's number and called her and accused her of encouraging me to defy him, told her I was troubled, in therapy and what I didn't need was people "stirring". He told me not to wear the Rive Gauche, either. He said he couldn't stand the smell of it.

'So I never did meet Oonagh, and when I tried to reconnect with her in my twenties, I couldn't find her. She might have passed away, for all I know.'

'I got into university, left home and started reading everything I could about Dennis Creed. The nightmares came back, but it didn't get me any closer to finding out what really happened.

'Apparently the man in charge of the investigation into my

mother's disappearance, a detective inspector called Bill Talbot, always thought Creed took her. Talbot will be dead by now; he was coming up for retirement anyway.

'Then, a few years out of uni, I had the bright idea of starting a website,' said Anna. 'My girlfriend at the time was tech-savvy. She helped me set it up. I was very naive,' she sighed. 'I said who I was and begged for information about my mother.

'You can probably imagine what happened. All kinds of theories: psychics telling me where to dig, people telling me my father had obviously done it, others telling me I wasn't really Margot's daughter, that I was after money and publicity, and some really malicious messages as well, saying my mother had probably run off with a lover and worse. A couple of journalists got in touch, too. One of them ran an awful piece in the *Daily Express* about our family: they contacted my father and that was just about the final nail in the coffin for our relationship.

'It's never really recovered,' said Anna bleakly. 'When I told him I'm gay, he seemed to think I was only doing it to spite him. And Cyn's gone over to his side a bit, these last few years. She always says, "I've got a loyalty to your dad, too, Anna." So,' said Anna, 'that's where we are.'

There was a brief silence.

'Dreadful for you,' said Robin.

'It is,' agreed Kim, placing her hand on Anna's knee again, 'and I'm wholly sympathetic to Anna's desire for resolution, of course I am. But is it realistic,' she said, looking from Robin to Strike, 'and I mean this with no offence to you two, to think that you'll achieve what the police haven't, after all this time?'

'Realistic?' said Strike. 'No.'

Robin noticed Anna's downward look and the sudden rush of tears into her large eyes. She felt desperately sorry for the older woman, but at the same time she respected Strike's honesty, and it seemed to have impressed the sceptical Kim, too.

'Here's the truth,' Strike said, tactfully looking at his notes until Anna had finished drying her eyes with the back of her hand. 'I think we'd have a reasonable chance of getting hold of the old police file, because we've got decent contacts at the Met. We can sift right through the evidence again, revisit witnesses as far as that's possible, basically make sure every stone's been turned over twice.

'But it's odds on that after all this time, we wouldn't find any more than the police did, and we'd be facing two major obstacles.

'Firstly, zero forensic evidence. From what I understand, literally no trace of your mother was ever found, is that right? No items of clothing, bus pass – nothing.'

'True,' mumbled Anna.

'Secondly, as you've just pointed out, a lot of the people connected with her or who witnessed anything that night are likely to have died.'

'I know,' said Anna, and a tear trickled, sparkling, down her nose onto the Perspex table. Kim reached out and put an arm around her shoulders. 'Maybe it's turning forty,' said Anna, with a sob, 'but I can't stand the idea that I'll go to my grave never knowing what happened.'

'I understand that,' said Strike, 'but I don't want to promise what I'm unlikely to be able to deliver.'

'Have there,' asked Robin, 'been any new leads or developments over the years?'

Kim answered. She seemed a little shaken by Anna's naked distress, and kept her arm around her shoulders.

'Not as far as we know, do we, Annie? But any information of that kind would probably have gone to Roy – Anna's father. And he might not have told us.'

'He acts as though none of it ever happened; it's how he copes,' said Anna, wiping her tears away. 'He pretends my mother never existed – except for the inconvenient fact that if she hadn't, I wouldn't be here.

'Believe it or not,' she said, 'it's the possibility that she just went away of her own accord and never came back, never wanted to see how I was doing, or let us know where she was, that really haunts me. That's the thing I can't bear to contemplate. My grandmother on my father's side, who I never loved – she was one of the meanest women I've ever met – took it upon herself to tell me that it had always been her private belief that my mother had simply run away. That she didn't like being a wife and a mother. That hurt me more than I can tell you, the thought that my mother would let everyone go through the horror of wondering what had happened to her, and never check that her daughter was all right . . .

'Even if Dennis Creed killed her,' said Anna, 'it would be terrible – awful – but it would be over. I could mourn rather than live with the possibility that she's out there somewhere, living under a different name, not caring what happened to us all.'

There was a brief silence, in which both Strike and Robin drank coffee, Anna sniffed, and Kim left the sofa area to tear off kitchen roll, which she handed to her wife.

A second ragdoll cat entered the room. She subjected the four humans to a supercilious glare before lying down and stretching in a patch of sunlight.

'That's Lacey,' said Kim, while Anna mopped her face. 'She doesn't really like anyone, even us.'

Strike and Robin laughed politely again.

'How would this work?' asked Kim abruptly. 'How d'you charge?'

'By the hour,' said Strike. 'You'd get an itemised monthly bill. I can email you our rates,' he offered, 'but I'd imagine you two will want to talk this over properly before coming to a decision.'

'Yes, definitely,' said Kim, but as she gave Strike her email address she looked with concern again at Anna, who was sitting with head bowed, still pressing kitchen roll to her eyes at regular intervals.

Strike's stump protested at being asked to support his weight again so soon after sitting down, but there seemed little more to discuss, especially as Anna had regressed into a tearful silence. Slightly regretting the untouched plate of biscuits, the detective shook Anna's cool hand.

'Thanks, anyway,' she said, and he had the feeling that he had disappointed her, that she'd hoped he would make her a promise of the truth, that he would swear upon his honour to do what everyone else had failed to do.

Kim showed them out of the house.

'We'll call you later,' she said. 'This afternoon. Will that be all right?'

'Great, we'll wait to hear from you,' said Strike.

Robin glanced back as she and Strike headed down the sunlit garden steps towards the street, and caught Kim giving them a strange look, as though she'd found something in the pair of visitors that she hadn't expected. Catching Robin's eye, she smiled reflexively, and closed the blue door behind them.

7

Long they thus traueiled in friendly wise,
Through countreyes waste, and eke well edifyde . . .

Edmund Spenser
The Faerie Queene

As they headed out of Falmouth, Strike's mood turned to cheerfulness, which Robin attributed mainly to the interest of a possible
new case. She'd never yet known an intriguing problem to fail to
engage his attention, no matter what might be happening in his
private life.

She was partially right: Strike's interest had certainly been piqued
by Anna's story, but he was mainly cheered by the prospect of keeping
weight off his prosthesis for a few hours, and by the knowledge that
every passing minute put further distance between himself and his
sister. Opening the car window, allowing the familiar sea air to rush
bracingly inside the old car, he lit a cigarette and, blowing smoke
away from Robin, asked,

'Seen much of Morris while I've been away?'

'Saw him yesterday,' said Robin. 'Paid him for his month's
expenses.'

'Ah, great, cheers,' said Strike, 'I meant to remind you that needed
doing. What d'you think of him? Barclay says he's good at the job,
except he talks too much in the car.'

'Yeah,' said Robin noncommittally, 'he does like to talk.'

'Hutchins thinks he's a bit smarmy,' said Strike, subtly probing.

He'd noticed the special tone Morris reserved for Robin. Hutchins had also reported that Morris had asked him what Robin's relationship status was.

'Mm,' said Robin, 'well, I haven't really had enough contact with him to form an opinion.'

Given Strike's current stress levels and the amount of work the agency was struggling to cover, she'd decided not to criticise his most recent hire. They needed an extra man. At least Morris was good at the job.

'Pat likes him,' she added, partly out of mischief, and was amused to see, out of the corner of her eye, Strike turn to look at her, scowling.

'That's no bloody recommendation.'

'Unkind,' said Robin.

'You realise in a week's time it's going to be harder to sack her? Her probation period's nearly up.'

'I don't want to sack her,' said Robin. 'I think she's great.'

'Well, then, on your head be it if she causes trouble down the line.'

'It won't be on my head,' said Robin. 'You're not pinning Pat on me. Hiring her was a joint decision. You were the one who was sick of temps— '

'And you were the one who said "it might not be a bad idea to get a more traditional manager in" and "we shouldn't discount her because of her age"—'

'—I know what I said, and I stand by the age thing. We *do* need someone who understands a spreadsheet, who's organised, but you were the one who—'

'—I didn't want you accusing me of ageism.'

'—*you were the one who offered her the job,*' Robin finished firmly.

'Dunno what I was bloody thinking,' muttered Strike, flicking ash out of the window.

Patricia Chauncey was fifty-six and looked sixty-five. A thin woman with a deeply lined, monkeyish face and implausibly jet-black hair, she vaped continually in the office, but was to be seen drawing deeply on a Superking the moment her feet touched the pavement at the end of the day's work. Pat's voice was so deep and rasping that she was often mistaken for Strike on the phone. She sat at what once had been Robin's desk in the outer office and had taken over the bulk of the agency's phone-answering and administrative duties now that Robin had moved to full-time detection.

Strike and Pat's relationship had been combative from the start, which puzzled Robin, who liked them both. Robin was used to Strike's intermittent bouts of moodiness, and prone to give him the benefit of the doubt, especially when she suspected he was in pain, but Pat had no compunction about snapping 'Would a "thanks" kill you?' if Strike showed insufficient gratitude when she passed him his phone messages. She evidently felt none of the reverence some of their temps had displayed towards the now famous detective, one of whom had been sacked on the spot when Strike realised she was surreptitiously filming him on her mobile from the outer office. Indeed, the office manager's demeanour suggested that she lived in daily expectation of finding out things to Strike's discredit, and she'd displayed a certain satisfaction on hearing that the dent in one of the filing cabinets was due to the fact that he'd once punched it.

On the other hand, the filing was up to date, the accounts were in order, all receipts were neatly docketed, the phone was answered promptly, messages were passed on accurately, they never ran out of teabags or milk, and Pat had never once arrived late, no matter the weather and irrespective of Tube delays.

It was true, too, that Pat liked Morris, who was the recipient of most of her rare smiles. Morris was always careful to pay Pat his full tribute of blue-eyed charm before turning his attention to Robin. Pat was already alert to the possibility of romance between her younger colleagues.

'He's lovely-looking,' she'd told Robin just the previous week, after Morris had phoned in his location so that the temporarily unreachable Barclay could be told where to take over surveillance on their biggest case. 'You've got to give him that.'

'I haven't got to give him anything,' Robin had said, a little crossly.

It was bad enough having Ilsa badger her about Strike in her leisure time without Pat starting on Morris during her working hours.

'Quite right,' Pat had responded, unfazed. 'Make him earn it.'

'Anyway,' said Strike, finishing his cigarette and crushing the stub out in the tin Robin kept for that purpose in the glove compartment, 'you've wrapped up Tufty. Bloody good going.'

'Thanks,' Robin said. 'But there's going to be press. Bigamy's always news.'

'Yeah,' said Strike. 'Well, it's going to be worse for him than us, but it's worth trying to keep our name out of it if we can. I'll have a word with Mrs-Campion-in-Windsor. So that leaves us,' he counted the names on his thick fingers, 'with Two-Times, Twinkletoes, Postcard and Shifty.'

It had become the agency's habit to assign nicknames to their targets and clients, mainly to avoid letting real names slip in public or in emails. Two-Times was a previous client of the agency, who'd recently resurfaced after trying other private detectives and finding them unsatisfactory. Strike and Robin had previously investigated two of his girlfriends. At a superficial glance, he seemed most unlucky in love, a man whose partners, initially attracted by his fat bank balance, seemed incapable of fidelity. Over time, Strike and Robin had come to believe that he derived obscure emotional or sexual satisfaction from being cheated on, and that they were being paid to provide evidence that, far from upsetting him, gave him pleasure. Once confronted with photographic evidence of her per-fidy, the girlfriend of the moment would be confronted, dismissed and another found, and the whole pattern repeated. This time round, he was dating a glamour model who thus far, to Two-Times' poorly concealed disappointment, seemed to be faithful.

Twinkletoes, whose unimaginative nickname had been chosen by Morris, was a twenty-four-year-old dancer who was currently having an affair with a thirty-nine-year-old double-divorcee, notable mainly for her history of drug abuse and her enormous trust fund. The socialite's father was employing the agency to discover anything they could about Twinkletoes' background or behaviour, which could be used to prise his daughter away from him.

Postcard was, so far, an entirely unknown quantity. A middle-aged and, in Robin's opinion, fairly unattractive television weather forecaster had come to the agency after the police had said there was nothing they could do about the postcards that had begun to arrive at his place of work and, most worryingly, hand delivered to his house in the small hours. The cards made no threats; indeed, they were often no more than banal comments on the weatherman's choice of tie, yet they gave evidence of knowing far more about the man's movements and private life than a stranger should have. The use of postcards was also a peculiar choice, when persecution was so much easier, these days, online. The agency's subcontractor, Andy Hutchins, had now spent two solid weeks' worth of nights parked outside the weatherman's house, but Postcard hadn't yet shown themselves.

Last, and most lucrative, was the interesting case of Shifty, a young investment banker whose rapid rise through his company had generated a predictable amount of resentment among overlooked colleagues, which had exploded into full-blown suspicion when he'd been promoted to the second-in-command job ahead of three undeniably better qualified candidates. Exactly what leverage Shifty had on the CEO (known to the agency as Shifty's Boss or SB) was now a matter of interest not only to Shifty's subordinates, but to a couple of suspicious board members, who'd met Strike in a dark bar in the City to lay out their concerns. Strike's current strategy was to try to find out more about Shifty through his personal assistant, and to this end Morris had been given the job of chatting her up after hours, revealing neither his real name nor his occupation, but trying to gauge how deep her loyalty to Shifty ran.

'D'you need to be back in London by any particular time?' Strike asked, after a brief silence.

'No,' said Robin, 'why?'

'Would you mind,' said Strike, 'if we stop for food? I didn't have breakfast.'

Despite remembering that he had, in fact, had a plate full of croissant crumbs in front of him when she arrived at the Palacio Lounge, Robin agreed. Strike seemed to read her mind.

'You can't count a croissant. Mostly air.'

Robin laughed.

By the time they reached Subway at Cornwall Services, the

atmosphere between the two of them had become almost light-hearted, notwithstanding their tiredness. Once Robin, mindful of her resolution to eat more healthily, had started on her salad and Strike had taken a few satisfying mouthfuls of his steak and cheese sandwich, he emailed Kim Sullivan their form letter about billing clients, then said,

'I had a row with Lucy this morning.'

Robin surmised that it must have been a bad one, for Strike to mention it.

'Five o'clock, in the garden, while I was having a quiet smoke.'

'Bit early for conflict,' said Robin, picking unenthusiastically through lettuce leaves.

'Well, it turns out we're competing in the Who Loves Joan Best Handicap Stakes. Didn't even know I'd been entered.'

He ate in silence for a minute, then went on,

'It ended with me telling her I thought Adam's a whiny prick and Luke's an arsehole.'

Robin, who'd been sipping her water, inhaled, and was seized by a paroxysm of coughs. Diners at nearby tables glanced round as Robin spluttered and gasped. Grabbing a paper napkin from the table to mop her chin and her streaming eyes, she wheezed,

'What – on *earth* – did you say that for?'

'Because Adam's a whiny prick and Luke's an arsehole.'

Still trying to cough water out of her windpipe, Robin laughed, eyes streaming, but shook her head.

'Bloody hell, Cormoran,' she said, when at last she could talk properly.

'You haven't just had a solid week of them. Luke broke my new headphones, then ran off with my leg, the little shit. Then Lucy accuses me of favouring Jack. Of course I favour him – he's the only decent one.'

'Yes, but telling their *mother*—'

'Yeah, I know,' said Strike heavily. 'I'll ring and apologise.' There was a brief pause. 'But for fuck's sake,' he growled, 'why do I have to take all three of them out together? Neither of the others give a toss about the military. "Adam cried when you came back from the

War Rooms", my arse. The little bastard didn't like that I'd bought Jack stuff, that's all. If Lucy had her way, I'd be taking them on group outings every weekend, and they'd *take turns* to choose; it'll be the zoo and effing go-karting, and everything that was good about me seeing Jack'll be ruined. I *like* Jack,' said Strike, with what appeared to be surprise. 'We're interested in the same stuff. What's with this mania for treating them all the same? Useful life lesson, I'd have thought, realising you aren't owed. You don't get stuff automatically because of who you're related to.

'But fine, she wants me to buy the other two presents,' and he framed a square in mid-air with his hands. '"Try Not Being a Little Shit". I'll get that made up as a plaque for Luke's bedroom wall.'

They bought a bag of snacks, then resumed their drive. As they turned out onto the road again, Strike expressed his guilt that he couldn't share the driving, because the old Land Rover was too much of a challenge with his false leg.

'It doesn't matter,' said Robin. 'I don't mind. What's funny?' she added, seeing Strike smirking at something he had found in their bag of food.

'English strawberries,' he said.

'And that's comical, why?'

He explained about Dave Polworth's fury that goods of Cornish origin weren't labelled as such, and his commensurate glee that more and more locals were putting their Cornish identity above English on forms.

'Social identity theory's very interesting,' said Robin. 'That and self-categorisation theory. I studied them at uni. There are implications for businesses as well as society, you know . . . '

She talked happily for a couple of minutes before realising, on glancing sideways, that Strike had fallen fast asleep. Choosing not to take offence, because he looked grey with tiredness, Robin fell silent, and other than the occasional grunting snore, there was no more communication to be had from Strike until, on the outskirts of Swindon, he suddenly jerked awake again.

'Shit,' he said, wiping his mouth with the back of his hand, 'sorry. How long was I asleep?'

'About three hours,' said Robin.

'Shit,' he said again, 'sorry,' and immediately reached for a ciga-rette. 'I've been kipping on the world's most uncomfortable sofa and the kids have woken me up at the crack of fucking dawn every day. Want anything from the food bag?'

'Yes,' said Robin, throwing the diet to the winds. She was in urgent need of a pick-me-up. 'Chocolate. English or Cornish, I don't mind.'

'Sorry,' Strike said for a third time. 'You were telling me about a social theory or something.'

Robin grinned.

'You fell asleep around the time I was telling you my fascinating application of social identity theory to detective practice.'

'Which is?' he said, trying to make up in politeness now what he had lost earlier.

Robin, who knew perfectly well that this was why he had asked the question, said,

'In essence, we tend to sort each other and ourselves into group-ings, and that usually leads to an overestimation of similarities between members of a group, and an underestimation of the simi-larities between insiders and outsiders.'

'So you're saying all Cornishmen aren't rugged salt-of-the-earthers and all Englishmen aren't pompous arseholes?'

Strike unwrapped a Yorkie and put it into her hand.

'Sounds unlikely, but I'll run it past Polworth next time we meet.'

Ignoring the strawberries, which had been Robin's purchase, Strike opened a can of Coke and drank it while smoking and watch-ing the sky turn bloody as they drew nearer to London.

'Dennis Creed's still alive, you know,' said Strike, watching trees blur out of the window. 'I was reading about him online this morning.'

'Where is he?' asked Robin.

'Broadmoor,' said Strike. 'He went to Wakefield initially, then Belmarsh, and was transferred to Broadmoor in '95.'

'What was the psychiatric diagnosis?'

'Controversial. Psychiatrists disagreed about whether or not he was sane at his trial. Very high IQ. In the end the jury decided he was capable of knowing what he was doing was wrong, hence prison, not hospital. But he must've developed symptoms since that to justify medical treatment.

'On a very small amount of reading,' Strike went on, 'I can see why the lead investigator thought Margot Bamborough might have been one of Creed's victims. Allegedly, there was a small van seen speeding dangerously in the area, around the time she should have been walking towards the Three Kings. Creed used a van,' Strike elucidated, in response to Robin's questioning look, 'in some of the other known abductions.'

The lamps along the motorway had been lit before Robin, having finished her Yorkie, quoted:

'"She lies in a holy place".'

Still smoking, Strike snorted.

'Typical medium bollocks.'

'You think?'

'Yes, I bloody think,' said Strike. 'Very convenient, the way people can only speak in crossword clues from the afterlife. Come off it.'

'All right, calm down. I was only thinking out loud.'

'You could spin almost anywhere as "a holy place" if you wanted. Clerkenwell, where she disappeared – that whole area's got some kind of religious connection. Monks or something. Know where Dennis Creed was living in 1974?'

'Go on.'

'Paradise Park, Islington,' said Strike.

'Oh,' said Robin. 'So you think the medium *did* know who Anna's mother was?'

'If I was in the medium game, I'd sure as hell Google clients' names before they showed up. But it could've been a fancy touch designed to sound comforting, like Anna said. Hints at a decent burial. However bad her end was, it's purified by where her remains are. Creed admitted to scattering bone fragments in Paradise Park, by the way. Stamped them into the flower-beds.'

Although the car was still stuffy, Robin felt a small, involuntary shudder run through her.

'Fucking ghouls,' said Strike.

'Who?'

'Mediums, psychics, all those shysters ... preying on people.'

'You don't think some of them believe in what they're doing? Think they really are getting messages from the beyond?'

'I think there are a lot of nutters in the world, and the less we reward them for their nuttery, the better for all of us.'

The mobile rang in Strike's pocket. He pulled it out.

'Cormoran Strike.'

'Yes, hello – it's Anna Phipps. I've got Kim here, too.'

Strike turned the mobile to speakerphone.

'Hope you can hear us all right,' he said, over the rumble and rattle of the Land Rover. 'We're still in the car.'

'Yes, it is noisy,' said Anna.

'I'll pull over,' said Robin, and she did so, turning smoothly onto the hard shoulder.

'Oh, that's better,' said Anna, as Robin turned off the engine. 'Well, Kim and I have talked it over, and we've decided: we *would* like to hire you.'

Robin felt a jolt of excitement.

'Great,' said Strike. 'We're very keen to help, if we can.'

'But,' said Kim, 'we feel that, for psychological and – well, candidly, financial – reasons we'd like to set a term on the investigation, because if the police haven't solved this case in nigh on forty years – I mean, you could be looking for the next forty and find nothing.'

'That's true,' said Strike. 'So—'

'We think a year,' said Anna, sounding nervous. 'What do you – does that seem reasonable?'

'It's what I would have suggested,' said Strike. 'To be honest, I don't think we've got much chance in anything under twelve months.'

'Is there anything more you need from me to get started?' Anna asked, sounding both nervous and excited.

'I'm sure something will occur to me,' said Strike, taking out his notebook to check a name, 'but it would be good to speak to your father and Cynthia.'

63

The other end of the line became completely silent. Strike and Robin looked at each other.

'I don't think there's any chance of that,' said Anna. 'I'm sorry, but if my father knew I was doing this, I doubt he'd ever forgive me.'

'And what about Cynthia?'

'The thing is,' came Kim's voice, 'Anna's father's been unwell recently. Cynthia is the more reasonable of the two on this subject, but she won't want anything to upset Roy just now.'

'Well, no problem,' said Strike, raising his eyebrows at Robin. 'Our first priority's got to be getting hold of the police file. In the meantime, I'll email you one of our standard contracts. Print it out, sign it and send it back, we'll get going.'

'Thank you,' said Anna and, with a slight delay, Kim said, 'OK, then.'

They hung up.

'Well, well,' said Strike. 'Our first cold case. This is going to be interesting.'

'And we've got a year,' said Robin, pulling back out onto the motorway.

'They'll extend that if we look as though we're onto something,' said Strike.

'Good luck with that,' said Robin sardonically. 'Kim's prepared to give us a year so she can tell Anna they've tried everything. I'll bet you a fiver right now we don't get any extensions.'

'I'll take that bet,' said Strike. 'If there's a hint of a lead, Anna's going to want to see it through to the end.'

The remainder of the journey was spent discussing the agency's four current investigations, a conversation that took them all the way to the top of Denmark Street, where Strike got out.

'Cormoran,' said Robin, as he lifted the holdall out of the back of the Land Rover, 'there's a message on your desk from Charlotte Campbell. She called the day before yesterday and asked you to ring her back. She said she's got something you want.'

There was a brief moment where Strike simply looked at Robin, his expression unreadable.

'Right. Thanks. Well, I'll see you tomorrow. No, I won't,' he instantly contradicted himself, 'you've got time off. Enjoy.'

And with a slam of the rear door he limped off towards the office, head down, carrying his holdall over his shoulder, leaving an exhausted Robin no wiser as to whether he did or didn't want whatever it was that Charlotte Campbell had.

PART TWO

Then came the Autumne all in yellow clad . . .

Edmund Spenser
The Faerie Queene

8

Full dreadfull thinges out of that balefull booke
He red . . .

Edmund Spenser
The Faerie Queene

When Strike and Robin broke the news of her husband's bigamy, the white-faced woman they now called the Second Mrs Tufty had sat in silence for a couple of minutes. Her small but charming house in central Windsor was quiet that Tuesday morning, her son and daughter at primary school, and she'd cleaned before they arrived: there was a smell of Pledge in the air and Hoover marks on the carpet. Upon the highly polished coffee table lay ten photographs of Tufty in Torquay, minus his toupee, laughing as he walked out of the pizza restaurant with the teenage boys who so strongly resembled the young children he'd fathered in Windsor, his arm around a smiling woman who might have been their client's older sister.

Robin, who could remember exactly how she'd felt when Sarah Shadlock's diamond earring had fallen out of her own marital bed, could only guess at the scale of pain, humiliation and shame behind the taut face. Strike was speaking conventional words of sympathy, but Robin would have bet her entire bank account that Mrs Tufty hadn't heard a word – and knew she'd been right when Mrs Tufty suddenly stood up, shaking so badly that Strike also struggled to his feet, mid-sentence, in case she needed catching. However, she walked jerkily past him out of the room. Shortly afterwards, they heard the front door open and spotted their client through the net curtain, approaching a red Audi Q3 parked in front of the house with a golf club in her hand.

'Oh shit,' said Robin.

By the time they reached her, the Second Mrs Tufty had smashed the windscreen and put several deep dents in the roof of the car. Gawping neighbours had appeared at windows and a pair of Pomeranians were yapping frenziedly behind glass in the house opposite. When Strike grabbed the four iron out of her hand, Mrs Tufty swore at him, tried to wrestle it back, then burst into a storm of tears.

Robin put her arm around their client and steered her firmly back into the house, Strike bringing up the rear, holding the golf club. In the kitchen, Robin instructed Strike to make strong coffee and find brandy. On Robin's advice, Mrs Tufty called her brother and begged him to come, quickly, but when she'd hung up and begun scrolling to find Tufty's number, Robin jerked the mobile out of her well-manicured hand.

'Give it back!' said Mrs Tufty, wild-eyed and ready to fight. 'The bastard . . . the bastard . . . I want to talk to him . . . give it back!'

'Bad idea,' said Strike, putting coffee and brandy in front of her. 'He's already proven he's adept at hiding money and assets from you. You need a shit-hot lawyer.'

They remained with the client until her brother, a suited HR executive, arrived. He was annoyed that he'd been asked to leave work early, and so slow at grasping what he was being told that Strike became almost irate and Robin felt it necessary to intervene to stop a row.

'Fuck's sake,' muttered Strike, as they drove back towards London. '*He was already married to someone else when he married your sister.* How hard is that to grasp?'

'Very hard,' said Robin, an edge to her voice. 'People don't expect to find themselves in these kinds of situations.'

'D'you think they heard me when I asked them not to tell the press we were involved?'

'No,' said Robin.

She was right. A fortnight after they'd visited Windsor, they woke to find several tabloids carrying front-page exposés of Tufty and his three women, a picture of Strike in all the inside pages and his name in one of the headlines. He was news in his own right now, and the juxtaposition of famous detective and squat, balding, wealthy man who'd managed to run two families and a mistress was irresistible.

Strike had only ever given evidence at noteworthy court cases while sporting the full beard that grew conveniently fast when he needed it, and the picture the press used most often was an old one that showed him in uniform. Nevertheless, it was an ongoing battle to remain as inconspicuous as his chosen profession demanded, and being badgered for comment at his offices was an inconvenience he could do without. The storm of publicity was prolonged when both Mrs Tuftys formed an offensive alliance against their estranged husband. Showing an unforeseen taste for publicity, they not only granted a women's magazine a joint interview, but appeared on several daytime television programmes together to discuss their long deception, their shock, their newfound friendship, their intention to make Tufty rue the day he'd met either of them and to issue a thinly veiled warning to the pregnant mistress in Glasgow (who, astonishingly, seemed disposed to stand by Tufty) that she had another think coming if she imagined he'd have two farthings to rub together once his wives had finished with him.

September proceeded, cool and unsettled. Strike called Lucy to say sorry for being rude about her sons, but she remained cold even after the apology, doubtless because he'd merely expressed regret for voicing his opinion out loud, and hadn't retracted it. Strike was relieved to discover that her boys had weekend sporting fixtures now that school had started again, which meant he didn't have to sleep on the sofa on the next visit to St Mawes, and could devote himself to Ted and Joan without the distraction of Lucy's tense, accusatory presence.

Though as desperate to cook for him as ever, his aunt was already enfeebled by the chemotherapy. It was painful to watch her dragging herself around the kitchen, but she wouldn't sit down, even when Ted implored her to do so. On Saturday night, his uncle broke down after Joan had gone to bed, and sobbed into Strike's shoulder. Ted had once seemed an unperturbable, invulnerable bastion of strength to his nephew, and Strike, who could normally sleep under almost any conditions, lay awake past two in the morning, staring into the darkness that was deeper by far than a London night, wondering whether he should stay longer, and despising himself for deciding that it was right that he should return to London.

In truth, the agency was so busy that he felt guilty about the burden it was placing on Robin and his subcontractors by taking a long weekend in Cornwall. In addition to the five open cases still on the agency's books, he and Robin were juggling increased management demands made by the expanded workforce, and negotiating a year's extension on the office lease with the developer who'd bought their building. They were also trying, though so far without luck, to persuade one of the agency's police contacts to find and hand over the forty-year-old file on Margot Bamborough's disappearance. Morris was ex-Met, as was Andy Hutchins, their most longstanding subcontractor, a quiet, saturnine man whose MS was thankfully in remission, and both had tried to call in favours from former colleagues as well, but so far, responses to the agency's requests had ranged from 'mice have probably had it' to 'fuck off, Strike, I'm busy'.

One rainy afternoon, while tailing Shifty through the City, trying not to limp too obviously and inwardly cursing the second pavement seller of cheap umbrellas who'd got in his way, Strike's mobile rang. Expecting to be given another problem to sort out, he was caught off guard when the caller said,

'Hi, Strike. George Layborn here. Heard you're looking at the Bamborough case again?'

Strike had only met DI Layborn once before, and while it had been in the context of a case where Strike and Robin had given material assistance to the Met, he hadn't considered their association close enough to ask Layborn for help on getting the Bamborough file.

'Hi, George. Yeah, you heard right,' said Strike, watching Shifty turn into a wine bar.

'Well, I could meet you tomorrow evening, if you fancy it. Feathers, six o'clock?' said Layborn.

So Strike asked Barclay to swap jobs, and headed to the pub near Scotland Yard the following evening, where he found Layborn already at the bar, waiting for him. A paunchy, grey-haired, middle-aged man, Layborn bought both of them pints of London Pride, and they removed themselves to a corner table.

'My old man worked the Bamborough case, under Bill Talbot,' Layborn told Strike. 'He told me all about it. What've you got so far?'

'Nothing. I've been looking back at old press reports, and I'm trying to trace people who worked at the practice she disappeared from. Not much else I can do until I see the police file, but nobody's been able to help with that so far.'

Layborn, who had demonstrated a fondness for colourfully obscene turns of phrase on their only previous encounter, seemed oddly subdued tonight.

'It was a fucking mess, the Bamborough investigation,' he said quietly. 'Anyone told you about Talbot yet?'

'Go on.'

'He went off his rocker,' said Layborn. 'Proper mental breakdown. He'd been going funny before he took on the case, but you know, it was the seventies – looking after the workforce's mental health was for poofs. He'd been a good officer in his day, mind you. A couple of junior officers noticed he was acting odd, but when they raised it, they were told to eff off.

'He'd been heading up the Bamborough case six months before his wife called an ambulance in the middle of the night and got him sectioned. He got his pension, but it was too late for the case. He died a good ten years ago, but I heard he never got over fucking up the investigation. Once he recovered he was mortified about how he'd behaved.'

'How was that?'

'Putting too much stock in his own intuitions, didn't take evidence properly, had no interest in talking to witnesses if they didn't fit his theory—'

'Which was that Creed abducted her, right?'

'Exactly,' said Layborn. 'Although Creed was still called the Essex Butcher back then, because he dumped the first couple of bodies in Epping Forest and Chigwell.' Layborn took a long pull on his pint. 'They found most of Jackie Aylett in an industrial bin. He's an animal, that one. Animal.'

'Who took over the case after Talbot?'

'Bloke called Lawson, Ken Lawson,' said Layborn, 'but he'd lost six months, the trail had gone cold and he'd inherited a right balls-up. Added to which, she was unlucky in her timing, Margot Bamborough,' Layborn continued. 'You know what happened a month after she vanished?'

'What?'

'Lord Lucan disappeared,' said Layborn. 'You try and keep a missing GP on the front pages after a peer of the realm's nanny gets bludgeoned to death and he goes on the run. They'd already used the Bunny Girl pictures – did you know Bamborough was a Bunny Girl?'

'Yeah,' said Strike.

'Helped fund her medical degree,' said Layborn, 'but according to my old man, the family didn't like that being dragged up. Put their backs right up, even though those pictures definitely got the case a bit more coverage. Way of the world,' he said, 'isn't it?'

'What did your dad think happened to her?' asked Strike.

'Well, to be honest,' sighed Layborn, 'he thought Talbot was probably right: Creed had taken her. There were no signs she meant to disappear – passport was still in the house, no case packed, no clothes missing, stable job, no money worries, young child.'

'Hard to drag a fit, healthy twenty-nine-year-old woman off a busy street without someone noticing,' said Strike.

'True,' said Layborn. 'Creed usually picked them off when they were drunk. Having said that, it was a dark evening and rainy. He'd pulled that trick before. And he was good at lulling women's suspicions and getting their sympathy. A couple of them walked into his flat of their own accord.'

'There was a van like Creed's seen speeding in the area, wasn't there?'

'Yeah,' said Layborn, 'and from what Dad told me it was never checked out properly. Talbot didn't want to hear that it might have been someone trying to get home for their tea, see. Routine work just wasn't done. For instance, I heard there was an old boyfriend of Bamborough's hanging around. I'm not saying the boyfriend killed

74

her, but Dad told me Talbot spent half the interview trying to find out where this boyfriend had been on the night Helen Wardrop got attacked.'

'Who?'

'Prostitute. Creed tried to abduct her in '73. He had his failures, you know. Peggy Hiskett, she got away from him and gave the police a description in '71, but that didn't help them much. She said he was dark and stocky, because he was wearing a wig at the time and all padded out in a woman's coat. They caught him in the end because of Melody Bower. Nightclub singer, looked like Diana Ross. Creed got chatting to her at a bus stop, offered her a lift, then tried to drag her into the van when she said no. She escaped, gave the police a proper description and told them he'd said his house was off Paradise Park. He got careless towards the end. Arrogance did for him.'

'You know a lot about this, George.'

'Yeah, well, Dad was one of the first into Creed's basement after they arrested him. He wouldn't ever talk about what he saw in there, and he'd seen gangland killings, you name it … Creed's never admitted to Bamborough, but that doesn't mean he didn't do it. That cunt will keep people guessing till he's dead. Evil fucking bastard. He's played with the families of his known victims for years. Likes hinting he did more women, without giving any details. Some journalist interviewed him in the early eighties, but that was the last time they let anyone talk to him. The Ministry of Justice clamped down. Creed uses publicity as a chance to torment the families. It's the only power he's got left.'

Layborn drained the last of his pint and checked his watch.

'I'll do what I can for you with the file. My old man would've wanted me to help. It never sat right with him, what happened with that case.'

The wind was picking up by the time Strike returned to his attic flat. His rain-speckled windows rattled in their loose frames as he sorted carefully through the receipts in his wallet for those he needed to submit to the accountant.

At nine o'clock, after eating dinner cooked on his single-ringed hob, he lay down on his bed and picked up the second-hand

biography of Dennis Creed, *The Demon of Paradise Park,* which he'd
ordered a month ago and which had so far lain unopened on his
bedside table. Having undone the button on his trousers to better
accommodate the large amount of spaghetti he'd just consumed, he
emitted a loud and satisfying belch, lit a cigarette, laid back against
his pillows and opened the book to the beginning, where a timeline
laid out the bare bones of Creed's long career of rape and murder.

1937	Born in Greenwell Terrace, Mile End.
1954	April: began National Service.
	November: raped schoolgirl **Vicky Hornchurch**, 15.
	Sentenced to 2 years, Feltham Borstal.
1955–61	Worked in a variety of short-lived manual and office jobs. Frequented prostitutes.
1961	July: raped and tortured shop assistant **Sheila Gaskins**, 22.
	Sentenced to 5 years HMP Pentonville.
1968	April: abducted, raped, tortured and murdered schoolgirl **Geraldine Christie**, 16.
1969	September: abducted, raped, tortured and murdered secretary and mother of one **Jackie Aylett**, 29.
	Killer dubbed 'The Essex Butcher' by press.
1970	January: moved to Vi Hooper's basement in Liverpool Road, near Paradise Park.
	Gained job as dry-cleaning delivery man.
	February: abducted dinner lady and mother of three **Vera Kenny**, 31. Kept in basement for three weeks. Raped, tortured and murdered.
	November: abducted estate agent **Noreen Sturrock**, 28. Kept in basement for four weeks. Raped, tortured and murdered.
1971	August: failed to abduct pharmacist **Peggy Hiskett**, 34.
1972	September: abducted unemployed **Gail Wrightman**, 30. Kept imprisoned in basement. Raped and tortured.

1973   January: murdered Wrightman.
        December: failed to abduct prostitute and mother of
        one **Helen Wardrop**, 32.
1974   September: abducted hairdresser **Susan Meyer**, 27.
        Kept imprisoned in basement. Raped and tortured.
1975   February: abducted PhD student **Andrea Hooton**,
        23. Hooton and Meyer were held concurrently in
        basement for 4 weeks.
        March: murdered Susan.
        April: murdered Andrea.
1976   January 25th: attempted to abduct nightclub singer
        Melody Bower, 26.
        January 31st: landlady Vi Hooper recognises Creed
        from description and photofit.
        February 2nd: Creed arrested.

Strike turned over the page and skim-read the introduction, which featured the only interview ever granted by Creed's mother, Agnes Waite.

... She began by telling me that the date given on Creed's birth certificate was false.

'It says he was born December 20th, doesn't it?' she asked me. 'That's not right. It was the night of November 19th. He lied about it when he registered the birth, because we were outside the time you were supposed to do it.'

'"He" was Agnes's stepfather, William Awdry, a man notorious in the local area for his violent temper ...

'He took the baby out of my arms as soon as I'd had it and said he was going to kill it. Drown it in the outside toilet. I begged him not to. I pleaded with him to let the baby live. I hadn't known till then whether I wanted it to live or die, but once you've seen them, held them ... and he was strong, Dennis, he wanted to live, you could tell.

'It went on for weeks, the threats, Awdry threatening to kill him. But by then the neighbours had heard the baby crying and probably heard what [Awdry] was threatening, as well. He knew

77

there was no hiding it; he'd waited too long. So he registered the birth, but lied about the date, so nobody would ask why he'd done it so late. There wasn't nobody to say it had happened earlier, not anybody who'd count. They never got me a midwife or a nurse or anything . . .'

Creed often wrote me fuller answers than we'd had time for during face-to-face interviews. Months later he sent me the following, concerning his own suspicions about his paternity:

'I saw my supposed step-grandfather looking at me out of the mirror. The resemblance grew stronger as I got older. I had his eyes, the same shaped ears, his sallow complexion, his long neck. He was a bigger man than I was, a more masculine-looking man, and I think part of his great dislike of me came from the fact that he hated to see his own features in a weak and girlish form. He despised vulnerability . . .'

'Yeah, of course Dennis was his,' Agnes told me. 'He [Awdry] started on me when I was thirteen. I was never allowed out, never had a boyfriend. When my mother realised I was expecting, Awdry told her I'd been sneaking out to meet someone. What else was he going to say? And Mum believed him. Or she pretended to.'

Agnes fled her stepfather's overcrowded house shortly before Dennis's second birthday, when she was sixteen-and-a-half.

'I wanted to take Dennis with me, but I left in the middle of the night and I couldn't afford to make noise. I had nowhere to go, no job, no money. Just a boyfriend who said he'd look after me. So I went.'

She was to see her firstborn only twice more. When she found out William Awdry was serving nine months in jail for assault, she returned to her mother's house in hopes of snatching Dennis away.

'I was going to tell Bert [her first husband] he was my nephew, because Bert didn't know anything about that whole mess. But Dennis didn't remember me, I don't think. He wouldn't let go of my mum, wouldn't talk to me, and my mum told me it was too late now and I shouldn't have left him if I wanted him so bad. So I went away without him.'

The last time Agnes saw her son in the flesh was when she made a trip to his primary school and called him over to the fence to speak to her. Though he was barely five, Creed claimed in our second interview to remember this final meeting.

'She was a thin, plain little woman, dressed like a tart,' he told me. 'She didn't look like the other boys' mothers. You could tell she wasn't a respectable person. I didn't want the other children to see me talking to her. She said she was my mother and I told her it wasn't true, but I knew it was, really. I ran away from her.'

'He didn't want nothing to do with me,' said Agnes. 'I gave up after that. I wasn't going to go to the house if Awdry was there. Dennis was in school, at least. He looked clean . . .

'I used to wonder about him, how he was and that,' Agnes said. 'Obviously, you do. Kids come out of you. Men don't understand what that is. Yeah, I used to wonder, but I moved north with Bert when he got the job with the GPO and I never went back to London, not even when my mum died, because Awdry had put it about that if I turned up he'd kick off.'

When I told Agnes I'd met Dennis a mere week before visiting her in Romford, she had only one point of curiosity.

'They say he's very clever, is he?'

I told her that he was, undoubtedly, very clever. It was the one point on which all his psychiatrists agreed. Warders told me he read extensively, especially books of psychology.

'I don't know where he got that from. Not me . . .

'I read it all in the papers. I saw him on the news, heard everything he did. Terrible, just terrible. What would make a person do that?

'After the trial was over, I thought back to him, all naked and bloody on the lino where I'd had him, with my stepfather standing over us, threatening to drown him, and I swear to you now,' said Agnes Waite, 'I wish I'd let it happen.'

Strike stubbed out his cigarette and reached for the can of Tennent's sitting beside the ashtray. A light rain pattered against his windows as he flicked a little further on in the book, pausing midway through chapter two.

... grandmother, Ena, was unwilling or unable to protect the youngest member of the household from her husband's increasingly sadistic punishments.

Awdry took a particular satisfaction in humiliating Dennis for his persistent bedwetting. His step-grandfather would pour a bucket of water over his bed, then force the boy to sleep in it. Creed recalled several occasions on which he was forced to walk to the corner shop without trousers, but still wearing sodden pyjama bottoms, to buy Awdry cigarettes.

'One took refuge in fantasy,' Creed wrote to me later. 'Inside my head I was entirely free and happy. But there were, even then, props in the material world that I enjoyed incorporating into my secret life. Items that attained a totemic power in my fantasies.'

By the age of twelve, Dennis had discovered the pleasures of voyeurism.

'It excited me,' he wrote, after our third interview, 'to watch a woman who didn't know she was being observed. I'd do it to my sisters, but I'd creep up to lit windows as well. If I got lucky, I'd see women or girls undressing, adjusting themselves or even a glimpse of nudity. I was aroused not only by the obviously sensual aspects, but by the sense of power. I felt I stole something of their essence from them, taking that which they thought private and hidden.'

He soon progressed to stealing women's underwear from neighbours' washing lines and even from his grandmother, Ena. These he enjoying wearing in secret, and masturbating in ...

Yawning, Strike flicked on, coming to rest on a passage in chapter four.

... a quiet member of the mailroom staff at Fleetwood Electric, who astonished his colleagues when, on a works night out, he donned the coat of a female co-worker to imitate singer Kay Starr.

'There was little Dennis, belting out "Wheel of Fortune" in Jenny's coat,' an anonymous workmate told the press after Creed's arrest. 'It made some of the older men uncomfortable. A couple of them thought he was, you know, queer, after. But the younger ones, we all cheered him like anything. He came out of his shell a bit after that.'

But Creed's secret fantasy life didn't centre on a life of amateur theatrics or pub singing. Unbeknownst to anyone watching the tipsy sixteen-year-old onstage, his elaborate fantasies were becoming ever more sadistic . . .

Colleagues at Fleetwood Electric were appalled when 'little Dennis' was arrested for the rape and torture of Sheila Gaskins, 22, a shop assistant whom he'd followed off a late night bus. Gaskins, who survived the attack only because Creed was scared away by a nightwatchman who heard sounds down an alleyway, was able to provide evidence against him.

Convicted, he served five years in HMP Pentonville. This was the last time Creed would give way to sudden impulse.

Strike paused to light himself a fresh cigarette, then flicked ten chapters on through the book, until a familiar name caught his eye.

. . . Dr Margot Bamborough, a Clerkenwell GP, on October 11th 1974.

DI Bill Talbot, who headed the investigation, immediately noted suspicious similarities between the disappearance of the young GP and those of Vera Kenny and Gail Wrightman.

Both Kenny and Wrightman had been abducted on rainy nights, when the presence of umbrellas and rainwashed windscreens provided handy impediments to would-be witnesses. There was a heavy downpour on the evening Margot Bamborough disappeared.

A small van with what were suspected to be fake number plates had been seen in both Kenny's and Wrightman's vicinities shortly before they vanished. Three separate witnesses came forward to say that a small white van of similar appearance had been seen speeding away from the vicinity of Margot Bamborough's practice that night.

Still more suggestive was the eyewitness account of a driver who saw two women in the street, one of whom seemed to be infirm or faint, the other supporting her. Talbot at once made the connection both with the drunk Vera Kenny, who'd been seen getting into a van with what appeared to be another woman, and the testimony of Peggy Hiskett, who'd reported the man dressed as a woman at a lonely bus stop, who'd tried to persuade her to drink a bottle of beer with him, becoming aggressive before, fortunately, she managed to attract the attention of a passing car.

Convinced that Bamborough had fallen victim to the serial killer now dubbed the Essex Butcher, Talbot—

Strike's mobile rang. Trying not to lose his page, Strike groped for it and answered it without looking at the caller's identity.

'Strike.'

'Hello, Bluey,' said a woman, softly.

Strike set the book on the bed, pages down. There was a pause, in which he could hear Charlotte breathing.

'What d'you want?'

'To talk to you,' she said.

'What about?'

'I don't know,' she half-laughed. 'You choose.'

Strike knew this mood. She was halfway into a bottle of wine or had perhaps enjoyed a couple of whiskies. There was a moment of drunkenness – not even of drunkenness, of alcohol-induced soften- ing – where a Charlotte emerged who was endearing, even amusing, but not yet combative or maudlin. He'd asked himself once, towards the end of their engagement, when his own innate honesty was forc- ing him to face facts and ask hard questions, how realistic or healthy it was to wish for a wife forever very slightly drunk.

'You didn't call me back,' said Charlotte. 'I left a message with your Robin. Didn't she give it to you?'

'Yeah, she gave it to me.'

'But you didn't call.'

'What d'you want, Charlotte?'

The sane part of his brain was telling him to end the call, but still he held the phone to his ear, listening, waiting. She'd been like a drug to him for a long time: a drug, or a disease.

'Interesting,' said Charlotte dreamily. 'I thought she might have decided not to pass on the message.'

He said nothing.

'Are the two of you together yet? She's quite good-looking. And always there. On tap. So conven—'

'Why are you calling?'

'I've told you, I wanted to talk to you . . . d'you know what day it is today? The twins' first birthday. The entire *famille Ross* has turned up to fawn over them. This is the first moment I've had to myself all day.'

He knew, of course, that she'd had twins. There'd been an announcement in *The Times*, because she'd married into an aristocratic family that routinely announced births, marriages and deaths in its columns, although Strike had not, in fact, read the news there. It was Ilsa who'd passed the information on, and Strike had immediately remembered the words Charlotte had said to him, over a restaurant table she had tricked him into sharing with her, more than a year previously.

All that's kept me going through this pregnancy is the thought that once I've had them, I can leave.

But the babies had been born prematurely and Charlotte had not left them.

Kids come out of you. Men don't understand what that is.

There'd been two previous tipsy phone calls to Strike like this one in the past year, both made late at night. He'd ended the first one mere seconds in, because Robin was trying to reach him. Charlotte had hung up abruptly a few minutes into the second.

'Nobody thought they'd live, did you know that?' Charlotte said now. 'It's,' she whispered, '*a miracle.*'

'If it's your kids' birthday, I should let you go,' said Strike. 'Goodnight, Char—'

'Don't go,' she said, suddenly urgent. 'Don't go, please don't.'

Hang up, said the voice in his head. He didn't.

'They're asleep, fast asleep. They don't know it's their birthday, the whole thing's a joke. Commemorating the anniversary of that fucking nightmare. It was hideous, they cut me open—'

'I've got to go,' he said. 'I'm busy.'

'*Please*,' she almost wailed. 'Bluey, I'm so unhappy, you don't know, I'm so fucking miserable——'

'You're a married mother of two,' he said brutally, 'and I'm not an agony aunt. There are anonymous services you can call if you need them. Goodnight, Charlotte.'

He cut the call.

The rain was coming down harder. It drummed on his dark windows. Dennis Creed's face was now the wrong way up on the cast-aside book. His light-lashed eyes seemed reversed in the upside-down face. The effect was unsettling, as though the eyes were alive in the photograph.

Strike opened the book again and continued to read.

9

Faire Sir, of friendship let me now you pray,
That as I late aduentured for your sake,
The hurts whereof me now from battell stay,
Ye will me now with like good turne repay.

Edmund Spenser
The Faerie Queene

George Layborn still hadn't managed to lay hands on the Bamborough file when Robin's birthday arrived.

For the first time in her life, she woke on the morning of October the ninth, remembered what day it was and experienced no twinge of excitement, but a lowering sensation. She was twenty-nine years old today, and twenty-nine had an odd ring to it. The number seemed to signify not a landmark, but a staging post: 'Next stop: THIRTY'. Lying alone for a few moments in her double bed in her rented bedroom, she remembered what her favourite cousin, Katie, had said during Robin's last trip home, while Robin had been helping Katie's two-year-old son make Play-Doh monsters to ride in his Tonka truck.

'It's like you're travelling in a different direction to the rest of us.'

Then, seeing something in Robin's face that made her regret her words, Katie had hastily added,

'I don't mean it in a bad way! You seem really happy. Free, I mean! Honestly,' Katie had said, with hollow insincerity, 'I really envy you sometimes.'

Robin hadn't known a second's regret for the termination of a

85

marriage that, in its final phase, had made her deeply unhappy. She could still conjure up the mood, mercifully not experienced since, in which all colour seemed drained from her surroundings – and they had been pretty surroundings, too: she knew that the sea captain's house in Deptford where she and Matthew had finally parted had been a most attractive place, yet it was strange how few details she could remember about it now. All she could recall with any clarity was the deadened mood she'd suffered within those walls, the perpetual feelings of guilt and dread, and the dawning horror which accompanied the realisation that she had shackled herself to somebody whom she didn't like, and with whom she had next to nothing in common.

Nevertheless, Katie's blithe description of Robin's current life as 'happy' and 'free' wasn't entirely accurate. For several years now, Robin had watched Strike prioritise his working life over everything else – in fact, Joan's diagnosis had been the first occasion she'd known him to reallocate his jobs, and make something other than detection his top concern – and these days Robin, too, felt herself becoming taken over by the job, which she found satisfying to the point that it became almost all-consuming. Finally living what she'd wanted ever since she first walked through the glass door of Strike's office, she now understood the potential for loneliness that came with a single, driving passion.

Having sole possession of her bed had been a great pleasure at first: nobody sulking with their back to her, nobody complaining that she wasn't pulling her weight financially, or droning on about his promotion prospects; nobody demanding sex that had become a chore rather than a pleasure. Nevertheless, while she missed Matthew not at all, she could envisage a time (if she was honest, was perhaps already living it) when the lack of physical contact, of affection and even of sex – which for Robin was a more complicated prospect than for many women – would become, not a boon, but a serious absence in her life.

And then what? Would she become like Strike, with a succession of lovers relegated firmly to second place, after the job? No sooner had she thought this than she found herself wondering, as she'd done almost daily since, whether her partner had called Charlotte Campbell back. Impatient with herself, she threw back the covers and, ignoring the packages lying on top of her chest of drawers, went to take a shower.

Her new home in Finborough Road occupied the top two floors of a terraced house. The bedrooms and bathroom were on the third floor, the public rooms on the fourth. A small terraced area lay off the sitting room, where the owner's elderly rough-coated dachshund, Wolfgang, liked to lie outside on sunny days.

Robin, who was under no illusions about property available in London for single women on an average wage, especially one with legal bills to pay, considered herself immensely fortunate to be living in a clean, well-maintained and tastefully decorated flat, with a double room to herself and a flatmate she liked. Her live-in landlord was a forty-two-year-old actor called Max Priestwood, who couldn't afford to run the place without a tenant. Max, who was gay, was what Robin's mother would have called ruggedly handsome: tall and broad-shouldered, with a full head of thick, dark blond hair and a perpetually weary look about his grey eyes. He was also an old friend of Ilsa's, who'd been at university with his younger brother.

In spite of Ilsa's assurances that 'Max is absolutely lovely', Robin had spent the first few months of her tenancy wondering whether she'd made a huge mistake in moving in with him, because he seemed sunk in what seemed perpetual gloom. Robin tried her very best to be a good flatmate: she was naturally tidy, she never played music loudly or cooked anything very smelly; she made a fuss of Wolfgang and remembered to feed him if Max was out; she was punctilious when it came to replacing washing-up liquid and toilet roll; and she made a point of being polite and cheery whenever they came into contact, yet Max rarely if ever smiled, and when she first arrived, he'd seemed to find it an immense effort to talk to her. Feeling paranoid, Robin had wondered at first whether Ilsa had strong-armed Max into accepting her as a tenant.

Conversation had become slightly easier between them over the months of her tenancy, yet Max was never loquacious. Sometimes Robin was grateful for this monosyllabic tendency, because when she came in after working a twelve-hour stretch of surveillance, stiff and tired, her mind fizzing with work concerns, the last thing she wanted was small talk. At other times, when she might have preferred to go upstairs to the open-plan living area, she kept to her room rather than feel she was intruding upon Max's private space.

She suspected the main reason for Max's perennially low mood was his state of persistent unemployment. Since the West End play in which he had had a small part had ended four months ago, he hadn't managed to get another job. She'd learned quickly not to ask him whether he had any auditions lined up. Sometimes, even saying 'How was your day?' sounded unnecessarily judgemental. She knew he'd previously shared his flat with a long-term boyfriend, who by coincidence was also called Matthew. Robin knew nothing about Max's break-up except that his Matthew had signed over his half of the flat to Max voluntarily, which to Robin seemed remarkably generous compared with the behaviour of her own ex-husband.

Having showered, Robin pulled on a dressing gown and returned to her bedroom to open the packages that had arrived in the post over the past few days, and which she'd saved for this morning. She suspected her mother had bought the aromatherapy bath oils that were ostensibly from her brother Martin, that her veterinarian sister-in-law (who was currently pregnant with Robin's first niece or nephew) had chosen the homespun sweater, which was very much Jenny's own style, and that her brother Jonathan had a new girlfriend, who'd probably chosen the dangly earrings. Feeling slightly more depressed than she had before she'd opened the presents, Robin dressed herself all in black, which could take her through a day of paperwork at the office, a catch-up meeting with the weatherman whom Postcard was persecuting, all the way to birthday drinks that evening with Ilsa and Vanessa, her policewoman friend. Ilsa had suggested inviting Strike, and Robin had said that she would prefer it to be girls only, because she was trying to avoid any further occasions on which Ilsa might try and matchmake.

On the point of leaving her room, Robin's eye fell on a copy of *The Demon of Paradise Park* which she, like Strike, had bought online.

Her copy was slightly more battered than his and had taken longer to arrive. She hadn't yet read much of it, partly because she was generally too tired of an evening to do anything other than fall into bed, but partly because what she had read had already caused a slight recurrence of the psychological symptoms she had carried with her ever since her forearm had been sliced open one dark night. Today, however, she stuffed it into her bag to read on the Tube.

A text from her mother arrived while Robin was walking to the station, wishing her a happy birthday and telling her to check her email account. This she did, and saw that her parents had sent her a one-hundred-and-fifty-pound voucher for Selfridges. This was a most welcome gift, because Robin had virtually no disposable income left, once her legal bills, rent and other living expenses had been paid, to spend on anything that might be considered self-indulgent.

Feeling slightly more cheerful as she settled into a corner of the train, Robin took *The Demon of Paradise Park* from her bag and opened it to the page she had last reached.

The coincidence of the first line caused her an odd inward tremor.

Chapter 5

Little though he realised it, Dennis Creed was released from prison on his true 29th birthday, 19th November, 1966. His grandmother, Ena, had died while he was in Brixton and there was no question of him returning to live with his step-grandfather. He had no close friends to call on, and anyone who might have been well disposed to him prior to his second rape conviction was, unsurprisingly, in no rush to meet or help him. Creed spent his first night as a free man in a hostel near King's Cross.

After a week sleeping in hostels or on park benches, Creed managed to find himself a single room in a boarding house. For the next four years, Creed would move between a series of rundown rooms and short-term, cash-in-hand jobs, interspersed with periods of rough living. He admitted to me later that he frequented prostitutes a good deal at this time, but in 1968 he killed his first victim.

Schoolgirl Geraldine Christie was walking home—

Robin skipped the next page and a half. She had no particular desire to read the particulars of the harm Creed had visited upon Geraldine Christie.

> ... until finally, in 1970, Creed secured himself a permanent home in the basement rooms of the boarding house run by Violet Cooper, a fifty-year-old ex-theatre dresser who, like his grandmother, was an incipient alcoholic. This now demolished house would, in time, become infamous as Creed's 'torture chamber'. A tall, narrow building of grubby brick, it lay in Liverpool Road, close to Paradise Park.
>
> Creed presented Cooper with forged references, which she didn't bother to follow up, and claimed he'd recently been dismissed from a bar job, but that a friend had promised him employment in a nearby restaurant. Asked by defending counsel at his trial why she'd been happy to rent a room to an unemployed man of no fixed abode, Cooper replied that she was 'tender-hearted' and that Creed seemed 'a sweet boy, bit lost and lonely'.
>
> Her decision to rent, first a room, then the entire basement, to Dennis Creed, would cost Violet Cooper dearly. In spite of her insistence during the trial that she had no idea what was happening in the basement of her boarding house, suspicion and opprobrium have been attached to the name Violet Cooper ever since. She has now adopted a new identity, which I agreed not to disclose.
>
> 'I thought he was a pansy,' Cooper says today. 'I'd seen a bit of it in the theatre. I felt sorry for him, that's the truth.'
>
> A plump woman whose face has been ravaged by both time and drink, she admits that she and Creed quickly struck up a close friendship. At times during our conversation she seemed to forget that young 'Den' who spent many evenings with her upstairs in her private sitting room, both of them tipsy and singing along to her collection of records, was the serial killer who dwelled in her basement.
>
> 'I wrote to him, you know,' she says. 'After he was convicted. I said, "If you ever felt anything for me, if any of it was real, tell me whether you did any of them other women. You've got nothing

to lose now, Den," I says, "and you could put people's minds at rest."'

But the letter Creed wrote back admitted nothing.

'Sick, he is. I realised it, then. He'd just copied out the lyrics from an old Rosemary Clooney song we used to sing together, "Come On-A My House". You know the one ... "*Come on-a my house, my house, I'm-a gonna give you candy ...*" I knew then he hated me as much as he hated all them other women. Taunting me, he was.'

However, back in 1970, when Creed first moved into her basement, he'd been keen to ingratiate himself with his landlady, who admits he swiftly became a combination of son and confidant. Violet persuaded her friend Beryl Gould, who owned a dry-cleaner's, to give young Den a job as a delivery man, and this gave him access to the small van that would soon become notorious in the press ...

Twenty minutes after boarding the train, Robin got out at Leicester Square. As she emerged into daylight, her mobile phone vibrated in her pocket. She pulled it out and saw a text from Strike. Drawing aside from the crowd emerging from the station, she opened it.

News: I've found Dr Dinesh Gupta, GP who worked with Margot at the Clerkenwell Practice in 1974. He's 80-odd but sounds completely compos mentis and is happy to meet me this afternoon at his house in Amersham. Currently watching Twinkletoes having breakfast in Soho. I'll get Barclay to take over from me at lunchtime and go straight to Gupta's. Any chance you could put off your meeting with Weatherman and come along?

Robin's heart sank. She'd already had to change the time of the weatherman's catch-up meeting once and felt it unfair to do so a second time, especially at such short notice. However, she'd have liked to meet Dr Dinesh Gupta.

I can't mess him around again, she typed back. **Let me know how it goes.**

Right you are, replied Strike.

Robin watched her mobile screen for a few more seconds. Strike had forgotten her birthday last year, realising his omission a week late and buying her flowers. Given that he'd seemed to feel guilty about the oversight, she'd imagined that he might make a note of the date and perhaps set an alert on his mobile this year. However, no 'Happy birthday, by the way!' appeared, so she put her mobile back in her pocket and, unsmiling, walked on towards the office.

10

'You are thinking,' said the small, spectacled, elderly doctor, who was dwarfed by both his suit and his upright armchair, 'that I look like Gandhi.'

Strike, who'd been thinking exactly that, was surprised into a laugh.

The eighty-one-year-old doctor appeared to have shrunk inside his suit; the collar and cuffs of his shirt gaped and his ankles were skinny in their black silk socks. Tufts of white hair appeared both in and over his ears, and he wore horn-rimmed spectacles. The strongest features in his genial brown face were the aquiline nose and dark eyes, which alone appeared to have escaped the ageing process, and were as bright and knowing as a wren's.

No speck of dust marred the highly polished coffee table between them, in what bore the appearance of a seldom-used, special occasion room. The deep gold of wallpaper, sofa and chairs glowed, pristine, in the autumn sunshine diffused by the net curtains. Four gilt-framed photographs hung in pairs on the wall on either side of the fringed drapes. Each picture showed a different dark-haired young woman, all wearing mortarboards and gowns, and holding degree certificates.

Mrs Gupta, a tiny, slightly deaf, grey-haired woman, had already

93

told Strike what degrees each of her daughters had taken — two medicine, one modern languages and one computing — and how well each was doing in her chosen career. She'd also shown him pictures of the six grandchildren she and her husband had been blessed with so far. Only the youngest girl remained childless, 'but she will have them,' said Mrs Gupta, with a Joan-ish certainty. 'She'll never be happy without.'

Having provided Strike and her husband with tea served in china cups, and a plate of fig rolls, Mrs Gupta retreated to the kitchen, where *Escape to the Country* was playing with the sound turned up high.

'As it happens, my father met Gandhi as a young man when Gandhi visited London in 1931,' said Dr Gupta, selecting a fig roll. 'He, too, had studied law in London, you see, but a while after Gandhi. But ours was a wealthier family. Unlike Gandhi, my father could afford to bring his wife to England with him. My parents decided to remain in the UK after Daddy qualified as a barrister.

'So my immediate family missed partition. Very fortunate for us. My grandparents and two of my aunts were killed as they attempted to leave East Bengal. Massacred,' said Dr Gupta, 'and both my aunts were raped before being killed.'

'I'm sorry,' said Strike, who, not having anticipated the turn the conversation had taken, had frozen in the act of opening his notebook and now sat feeling slightly foolish, his pen poised.

'My father,' said Dr Gupta, nodding gently as he munched his fig roll, 'carried the guilt with him to his grave. He thought he should have been there to protect them all, or to have died alongside them.

'Now, *Margot* didn't like hearing the truth about partition,' said Dr Gupta. 'We all wanted independence, naturally, but the transition was handled very badly, very badly indeed. Nearly three million went missing. Rapes. Mutilation. Families torn asunder. Dreadful mistakes made. Appalling acts committed.

'Margot and I had an argument about it. A friendly argument, of course,' he added, smiling. 'But Margot romanticised uprisings of people in distant lands. She didn't judge brown rapists and torturers by the same standards she would have applied to white men who drowned children for being the wrong religion. She believed, I think, like Suhrawardy, that "bloodshed and disorder are not necessarily evil in themselves, if resorted to for a noble cause".'

Dr Gupta swallowed his biscuit and added,

'It was Suhrawardy, of course, who incited the Great Calcutta Killings. Four thousand dead in a single day.'

Strike allowed a respectful pause to fill the room, broken only by the distant sound of *Escape to the Country*. When no further mention of bloodshed and terror was forthcoming, he took the opening that had been offered to him.

'Did you like Margot?'

'Oh yes,' said Dinesh Gupta, still smiling. 'Although I found some of her beliefs and her attitudes shocking. I was born into a traditional, though Westernised, family. Before Margot and I went into practice together, I had never been in daily proximity to a self-proclaimed *liberated* lady. My friends at medical school, and the partners in my previous practice, had all been men.'

'A feminist, was she?'

'Oh, very much so,' said Gupta, smiling. 'She would tease me about what she thought were my regressive attitudes. She was a great improver of people, Margot — whether they wished to be improved or not,' said Gupta, with a little laugh. 'She volunteered at the WEA, too. The Workers' Educational Association, you know? She'd come from a poor family, and she was a great proponent of adult education, especially for women.

'She would certainly have approved of my girls,' said Dinesh Gupta, turning in his armchair to point at the four graduation photographs behind him. 'Jheel still laments that we had no son, but I have no complaints. No complaints,' he repeated, turning back to face Strike.

'I understand from the General Medical Council records,' said Strike, 'that there was a third GP at the St John's practice, a Dr Joseph Brenner. Is that right?'

'Dr Brenner, yes, quite right,' said Gupta. 'I doubt he's still alive, poor fellow. He'd be over a hundred now. He'd worked alone in the area for many years before he came in with us at the new practice. He brought with him Dorothy Oakden, who'd done his typing

95

for twenty-odd years. She became our practice secretary. An older lady – or so she seemed to me at the time,' said Gupta, with another small chuckle. 'I don't suppose she was more than fifty. Married late and widowed not long afterwards. I have no idea what became of her.'

'Who else worked at the practice?'

'Well, let's see . . . there was Janice Beattie, the district nurse, who was the best nurse I ever worked with. An Eastender by birth. Like Margot, she understood the privations of poverty from personal experience. Clerkenwell at that time was by no means as smart as it's become since. I still receive Christmas cards from Janice.'

'I don't suppose you have her address?' asked Strike.

'It's possible,' said Dr Gupta. 'I'll ask Jheel.'

He made to get up.

'Later, after we've talked, will be fine,' said Strike, afraid to break the chain of reminiscence. 'Please, go on. Who else worked at St John's?'

'Let's see, let's see,' said Dr Gupta again, sinking slowly back into his chair. 'We had two receptionists, young women, but I'm afraid I've lost touch with both of them . . . now, what were their names . . . ?'

'Would that be Gloria Conti and Irene Bull?' asked Strike, who'd found both names in old press reports. A blurry photograph of both young women had shown a slight, dark girl and what he thought was probably a peroxide blonde, both of them looking distressed to be photographed as they entered the practice. The accompanying article in the *Daily Express* quoted 'Irene Bull, receptionist, aged 25', as saying *'It's terrible. We don't know anything. We're still hoping she'll come back. Maybe she's lost her memory or something.'* Gloria was mentioned in every press report he'd read, because she'd been the last known person to see Margot alive. *'She just said "Night, Gloria, see you tomorrow." She seemed normal, well, a bit tired, it was the end of the day and we'd had an emergency patient who'd kept her longer than she expected. She was a bit late to meet her friend. She put up her umbrella in the doorway and left.'*

'Gloria and Irene,' said Dr Gupta, nodding. 'Yes, that's right. They were both young, so they should still be with us, but I'm afraid I haven't the faintest idea where they are now.'

'Is that everyone?' asked Strike.

'Yes, I think so. No, wait,' said Gupta, holding up a hand. 'There was the cleaner. A West Indian lady. What was her name, now?'

He screwed up his face.

'I'm afraid I can't remember.'

The existence of a practice cleaner was new information to Strike. His own office had always been cleaned by him or by Robin, although lately, Pat had pitched in. He wrote down 'Cleaner, West Indian'.

'How old was she, can you remember?'

'I really couldn't tell you,' said Gupta. He added delicately, 'Black ladies – they are much harder to *age*, aren't they? They look younger for longer. But I think she had several children, so not *very* young. Mid-thirties?' he suggested hopefully.

'So, three doctors, a secretary, two receptionists, a practice nurse and a cleaner?' Strike summarised.

'That's right. We had,' said Dr Gupta, 'all the ingredients of a successful business – but it was an unhappy practice, I'm afraid. Unhappy from the start.'

'Really?' said Strike, interested. 'Why was that?'

'Personal chemistry,' said Gupta promptly. 'The older I've grown, the more I've realised that the team is everything. Qualifications and experience are important, but if the team doesn't *gel* . . .' He interlocked his bony fingers, '. . . forget it! You'll never achieve what you should. And so it was at St John's.

'Which was a pity, a very great pity, because we had potential. The practice was popular with ladies, who usually prefer consulting members of their own sex. Margot and Janice were both well liked.

'But there were internal divisions from the beginning. Dr Brenner joined us for the conveniences of a newer practice building, but he never acted as though he was part of the team. In fact, over time he became openly hostile to some of us.'

'Specifically, who was he hostile to?' asked Strike, guessing the answer.

'I'm afraid,' said Dr Gupta, sadly, 'he didn't like Margot. To be quite frank, I don't think Joseph Brenner liked *ladies*. He was rude to the girls on reception, as well. Of course, they were easier to bully than Margot. I think he respected Janice – she was very efficient, you know, and less combative than Margot – and he was always polite to Dorothy, who was fiercely loyal to him. But he took against Margot from the start.'

'Why was that, do you think?'

'Oh,' said Dr Gupta, raising his hands and letting them fall in a gesture of hopelessness, 'the truth is that Margot – now, I liked her, you understand, our discussions were always good-humoured – but she was a *Marmite* sort of person. Dr Brenner was no feminist. He thought a woman's place was at home with her children, and Margot leaving a baby at home and coming back out to work full time, he disapproved of that. Team meetings were very uncomfortable. He'd wait for Margot to start talking and then talk over her, very loudly.

'He was something of a bully, Brenner. He thought our reception-ists were no better than they should be. Complained about their skirt lengths, their hairstyles.

'But actually, although he was *especially* rude to ladies, it's my opinion that he didn't really like *people*.'

'Odd,' said Strike. 'For a doctor.'

'Oh,' said Gupta, with a chuckle, 'that's by no means as unusual as you might think, Mr Strike. We doctors are like everybody else. It is a popular myth that all of us must love humanity in the round. The *irony* is that our biggest liability as a practice was Brenner himself. He was an addict!'

'Really?'

'Barbiturates,' said Gupta. 'Barbiturates, yes. A doctor couldn't get away with it these days, but he over-ordered them in massive quantities. Kept them in a locked cupboard in his consulting room. He was a very difficult man. Emotionally shut down. Unmarried. And this secret addiction.'

'Did you talk to him about it?' asked Strike.

'No,' said Gupta sadly. 'I put off doing so. I wanted to be sure of my ground before I broached the subject. From quiet enquiries I made, I suspected that he was still using his old practice address in addition to ours, doubling his order and using multiple pharmacies. It was going to be tricky to prove what he was up to.

'I might never have realised if Janice hadn't come to me and said she'd happened to walk in on him when his cupboard was open, and seen the quantities he'd amassed. She then admitted that she'd found him slumped at his desk in a groggy state one evening after the last patient had left. I don't think it ever affected his judgement, though. Not *really*. I'd noticed that at the end of the day he might have been a little glazed, and so on, but he was nearing retirement. I assumed he was tired.'

'Did Margot know about this addiction?' asked Strike.

'No,' said Gupta, 'I didn't tell her, although I should have done. She was my partner and the person I ought to have confided in, so we could decide what to do.

'But I was afraid she'd storm straight into Dr Brenner's consulting room and confront him. Margot wasn't a woman to back away from doing what she thought was right, and I did sometimes wish that she would exercise a little more *tact*. The fallout from a confrontation with Brenner was likely to be severe. Delicacy was required – after all, we had no absolute proof – but then Margot went missing, and Dr Brenner's barbiturate habit became the least of our worries.'

'Did you and Brenner continue working together after Margot disappeared?' asked Strike.

'For a few months, yes, but he retired not long afterwards. I continued to work at St John's for a short while, then got a job at another practice. I was glad to go. The St John's practice was full of bad associations.'

'How would you describe Margot's relationships with the other people at work?' Strike asked.

'Well, let's see,' said Gupta, taking a second fig roll. 'Dorothy the secretary never liked her, but I think that was out of loyalty to Dr Brenner. As I say, Dorothy was a widow. She was one of those *fierce* women who attach themselves to an employer they can defend and champion. Whenever Margot or I displeased or challenged Joseph in any way, our letters and reports were sure to go straight to the bottom of the typing pile. It was a joke between us. No computers in those days, Mr Strike. Nothing like nowadays – Aisha,' he said, indicating the top right-hand picture on the wall behind him, 'she types everything herself, a computer in her consulting room, everything computerised, which is much more efficient, but we were at the mercy of the typist for all our letters and reports.

'No, Dorothy didn't like Margot. Civil, but cold. Although,' said Gupta, who had evidently just remembered something, 'Dorothy *did* come to the barbecue, which was a surprise. Margot held a barbecue at her house one Sunday, the summer before she disappeared,' he explained. 'She knew that we weren't pulling together as a team, so she invited us all around to her house. The barbecue was supposed to . . .' and, wordlessly this time, he again illustrated the point by interlacing his fingers. 'I remember being surprised that Dorothy attended, because Brenner had declined. Dorothy brought her son, who was thirteen or fourteen, I think. She must have given birth late, especially for the seventies. A boisterous boy. I remember Margot's husband telling him off for smashing a valuable bowl.'

A fleeting memory of his nephew Luke carelessly treading on Strike's new headphones in St Mawes crossed the detective's mind.

'Margot and her husband had a very nice house out in Ham. The husband was a doctor too, a haematologist. Big garden. Jheel and I took our girls, but as Brenner didn't go, and Dorothy was offended by Margot's husband telling off her son, Margot's objective wasn't achieved, I'm afraid. The divisions remained entrenched.'

'Did everyone else attend?'

'Yes, I think so. No – wait. I don't think the cleaning lady – *Wilma!*' said Dr Gupta, looking delighted. 'Her name was Wilma! I had no idea I still knew it . . . but her surname . . . I'm not even sure I knew it back then . . . No, Wilma didn't come. But everyone else, yes.

'Janice brought her own little boy – he was younger than Dorothy's and far better behaved, as I remember. My girls spent the afternoon playing badminton with the little Beattie boy.'

'Was Janice married?'

'Divorced. Her husband left her for another woman. She got on with it, raised her son alone. Women like Janice always do get on with it. Admirable. Her life wasn't easy when I knew her, but I believe she married again, later, and I was glad when I heard about it.'

'Did Janice and Margot get along?'

'Oh yes. They had the gift of being able to disagree without taking personal offence.'

'Did they disagree often?'

'No, no,' said Gupta, 'but decisions must be made in a working environment. We were – or tried to be – a democratic business . . .

'No, Margot and Janice were able to have rational disagreements without taking offence. I think they liked and respected each other. Janice was hit hard by Margot's disappearance. She told me the day I left the practice that a week hadn't passed since it happened that she hadn't dreamed about Margot.

'But none of us were ever quite the same afterwards,' said Dr Gupta quietly. 'One does not expect a friend to vanish into thin air without leaving a single trace behind them. There is something – uncanny about it.'

'There is,' agreed Strike. 'How did Margot get along with the two receptionists?'

'Well, now, Irene, the older of the two,' sighed Gupta, 'could be a handful. I remember her being – not rude, but a little cheeky – to Margot, at times. At the practice Christmas party – Margot organised that, as well, still trying to force us all to get along, you know – Irene had rather a lot to drink. I remember a slight *contretemps*, but I really couldn't tell you what it was all about. I doubt it was anything serious. They seemed as amicable as ever the next time I saw them. Irene was quite hysterical after Margot disappeared.'

There was a short pause.

'*Some* of that may have been theatrics,' Gupta admitted, 'but the underlying distress was genuine, I'm sure.

'Gloria – poor little Gloria – *she* was devastated. Margot was more than an employer to Gloria, you know. She was something of an older sister figure, a mentor. It was Margot who wanted to hire her, even though Gloria had almost no relevant experience. And I must admit,' said Gupta judiciously, 'she turned out to be a good appointment. Hard worker. Learned fast. You only had to correct her once. I believe she was from an impoverished background. I know Dorothy looked down on Gloria. She could be quite unkind.'

'And what about Wilma, the cleaner?' asked Strike, reaching the bottom of his list. 'How did she get on with Margot?'

'I'd be lying if I said I could remember,' said Gupta. 'She was a quiet woman, Wilma. I never heard that they had any kind of problem.'

After a slight pause, he added,

'I hope I'm not inventing things, but I *seem* to remember that Wilma's husband was something of a bad lot. I *think* Margot told me that Wilma ought to divorce him. I don't know whether she said that directly to Wilma's face – though she probably did, knowing Margot ... as a matter of fact,' he continued, 'I heard, after I left the practice, that Wilma had been fired. There was an allegation of drinking at work. She always had a Thermos with her. But I may be misremembering that, so please don't set too much store by it. As I say, I'd already left.'

The door to the sitting room opened.

'More tea?' enquired Mrs Gupta, and she removed the tray and the now-cooling teapot, telling Strike, who had risen to help her, to sit back down and not to be silly. When she'd left, Strike said,

'Could I take you back to the day Margot disappeared, Dr Gupta?'

Appearing to brace himself slightly, the little doctor said,

'Of course. But I must warn you: what I mostly remember about that day now is the account of it I gave the police at the time. Do you see? My actual memories are hazy. Mostly, I remember what I told the investigating officer.'

Strike thought this an unusually self-aware comment for a witness. Experienced in taking statements, he knew how wedded people became to the first account they gave, and that valuable information, discarded during that first edit, was often lost for ever beneath the formalised version that now stood in for actual memory.

'That's all right,' he told Gupta. 'Whatever you can remember.'

'Well, it was an entirely ordinary day,' said Gupta. 'The *only* thing that was *slightly* different was that one of the girls on reception had a dental appointment and left at half past two – Irene, that was.'

'We doctors were working as usual in our respective consulting rooms. Until half past two, both girls were on reception, and after Irene left, Gloria was there alone. Dorothy was at her desk until five, which was her regular departure time. Janice was at the practice until lunchtime, but off making house calls in the afternoon, which was quite routine. I saw Margot a couple of times in the back, where we had, not exactly a kitchen, but a sort of nook where we had a kettle and a fridge. She was pleased about Wilson.'

'About who?'

'Harold Wilson,' said Gupta, smiling. 'There'd been a general election the day before. Labour got back in with a majority. He'd been leading a minority government since February, you see.'

'Ah,' said Strike. 'Right.'

'I left at half past five,' said Gupta. 'I said goodbye to Margot, whose door was open. Brenner's door was closed. I assumed he was with a patient.

'Obviously, I can't speak with authority about what happened after I left,' said Gupta, 'but I can tell you what the others told me.'

'If you wouldn't mind,' said Strike. 'I'm particularly interested in the emergency patient who kept Margot late.'

'Ah,' said Gupta, now placing his fingertips together and nodding, 'you know about the mysterious dark lady. Everything I know about *her* came from little Gloria.

'We operated on a first-come, first-served basis at St John's. Registered patients came along and waited their turn, unless it was an emergency, of course. But this lady walked in off the street. She wasn't registered with the practice, but she had severe abdominal pain. Gloria told her to wait, then went to see whether Joseph Brenner would see her, because he was free, whereas Margot was still with her last registered patient of the day.

'Brenner made heavy weather of the request. While Gloria and Brenner were talking, Margot came out of her consulting room, seeing off her last patients, a mother and child, and offered to see the emergency herself as she was going from the practice to the pub with a friend, which was just up the road. Brenner, according to Gloria, said "good of you" or something like that – which was friendly, for Brenner – and he put on his coat and hat and left.

'Gloria went back into the waiting room to tell the lady Margot would see her. The lady went into the consulting room and stayed there longer than Gloria expected. Fully twenty-five, thirty minutes, which took the time to a quarter past six, and Margot was supposed to be meeting her friend at six.

'At last the patient came out of the consulting room and left. Margot came out shortly afterwards in her coat. She told Gloria that she was late for the pub, and asked Gloria to lock up. She walked out into the rain . . . and was never seen again.'

The door of the sitting room opened and Mrs Gupta reappeared with fresh tea. Again, Strike stood to help her, and was again shooed back into his chair. When she'd left, Strike asked,

'Why did you call the last patient "mysterious"? Because she was unregistered, or—?'

'Oh, you didn't know about that business?' said Gupta. 'No, no. Because there was much discussion afterwards as to whether or not she was actually a lady.'

Smiling at Strike's look of surprise, he said,

'Brenner started it. He'd walked out past her and told the investigating officer that he'd thought, on the brief impression he had of her, that she was a man and was surprised afterwards to hear that she was female. Gloria said she was a thickset young lady, dark – gypsy-ish, was her word – not a very *politically correct* term, but that's what Gloria said. Nobody else saw her, of course, so we couldn't judge.

'An appeal was put out for her, but nobody came forward, and in the absence of any information to the contrary, the investigating officer put a great deal of pressure on Gloria to say that she thought the patient was really a man in disguise, or at least, that she could have been mistaken in thinking she was a lady. But Gloria insisted that she knew a lady when she saw one.'

'This officer being Bill Talbot?' asked Strike.

'Precisely,' said Gupta, reaching for his tea.

'D'you think he wanted to believe the patient was a man dressed as a woman because—'

'Because Dennis Creed sometimes cross-dressed? Yes,' said Gupta. 'Although we called him the Essex Butcher back then. We didn't know his real name until 1976. And the only physical description of the Butcher at the time said he was dark and squat – I suppose I see why Talbot was suspicious but . . .'

'Strange for the Essex Butcher to walk into a doctor's surgery in drag and wait his turn?'

'Well . . . quite,' said Dr Gupta.

There was a brief silence while Gupta sipped tea and Strike flicked back through his notes, checking that he had asked everything he wanted to know. It was Gupta who spoke first.

'Have you met Roy? Margot's husband?'

'No,' said Strike. 'I've been hired by her daughter. How well did you know him?'

'Only very slightly,' said Gupta.

He put the teacup down on the saucer. If ever Strike had seen a man with more to say, that man was Dinesh Gupta.

'What was your impression of him?' asked Strike, surreptitiously clicking the nib back out of his pen.

'Spoiled,' said Gupta. 'Very spoiled. A handsome man, who'd been made a prince by his mother. We Indian boys know something about that, Mr Strike. I met Roy's mother at the barbecue I mentioned. She singled me out for conversation. A snob, I should say. She didn't consider receptionists or secretaries worth her time. I had the strong impression that she thought her son had married beneath him. Again, this opinion is not unknown among Indian mothers. He's a haemo-philiac, isn't he?' asked Gupta.

'Not that I've heard,' said Strike, surprised.

'Yes, yes,' said Gupta 'I think so, I think he is. He was a haema-tologist by profession, and his mother told me that he had chosen the specialty because of his own condition. You see? The clever, fragile little boy and the proud, overprotective mother.

'But then the little prince chose for a wife somebody utterly unlike his mother. Margot wasn't the kind of woman to leave her patients, or her adult learners, to rush home and cook Roy's dinner for him. Let him get his own, would have been her attitude . . . or the little cousin could have cooked, of course,' Gupta went on, with something of the delicacy he had brought to the mention of 'black ladies'. 'The young woman they paid to look after the baby.'

'Was Cynthia at the barbecue?'

'That was her name, was it? Yes, she was. I didn't talk to her. She was carrying Margot's daughter around, while Margot mingled.'

'Roy was interviewed by the police, I believe,' said Strike, who in fact took this for granted rather than knowing it for certain.

'Oh yes,' said Gupta. 'Now, *that* was a curious thing. Inspector Talbot told me at the start of my own police interview that Roy had been completely ruled out of their enquiries – which I've always thought was an odd thing to tell me. Don't you find it so? This was barely a week after Margot's disappearance. I suppose it was only just dawning on us all that there really was no mistake, no innocent explanation. We'd all had our hopeful little theories in the first couple of days. She'd maybe felt stressed, unable to cope, and gone off alone somewhere. Or perhaps there'd been an accident, and she was lying unconscious and unidentified in a hospital. But as the days went by, and the hospitals had been checked, and her photograph had been in all the papers and still there was no news, everything started to look more sinister.

'I found it most peculiar that Inspector Talbot informed me, unasked, that Roy wasn't under suspicion, that he had a complete alibi. Talbot struck all of us as peculiar, actually. Intense. His questions jumped around a lot.

'I *think* he was trying to reassure me,' said Gupta, taking a third fig roll and examining it thoughtfully as he continued. 'He wanted me to know that my brother doctor was in the clear, that I had nothing to fear, that he knew no doctor could have done anything so terrible as to abduct a woman, or – by then, we were all starting to fear it – to kill her . . .

'But Talbot thought it was Creed, of course, from the very start – and he was probably right,' sighed Gupta, sadly.

'What makes you think so?' asked Strike. He thought Gupta might mention the speeding van or the rainy night, but the answer was, he thought, a shrewd one.

'It's very difficult to dispose of a body as completely and cleanly as Margot's seems to have been hidden. Doctors know how death smells and we understand the legalities and procedures surrounding a dead human. The ignorant might imagine it is nothing more than disposing of a table of equivalent weight, but it is a very different thing, and a very difficult one. And even in the seventies, before DNA testing, the police did pretty well with fingerprints, blood groups and so forth.

'How has she remained hidden for so long? Somebody did the job very cleverly and if we know anything about Creed, it's that he's very clever, isn't that so? It was living ladies who betrayed him in the end, not dead. He knew how to render his corpses mute.'

Gupta popped the end of the fig roll in his mouth, sighed, brushed his hands fastidiously clean of crumbs, then pointed at Strike's legs and said,

'Which one is it?'

Strike didn't resent the blunt question, from a doctor.

'This one,' he said, shifting his right leg.

'You walk very naturally,' said Gupta, 'for a big man. I might not have known, if I hadn't read about you in the press. The prosthetics were not nearly as good in the old days. Wonderful, what you can buy now. Hydraulics reproducing natural joint action! Marvellous.'

'The NHS can't afford those fancy prosthetics,' said Strike, slipping his notebook back into his pocket. 'Mine's pretty basic. If it's not too much trouble,' he continued, 'could I ask you for the practice nurse's current address?'

'Yes, yes, of course,' said Gupta. He succeeded in rising from his armchair on the third attempt.

It took the Guptas half an hour to find, in an old address book, the last address they had for Janice Beattie.

'I can't swear it's current,' said Gupta, handing the slip of paper to Strike in the hall.

'It'll give me a head start on finding her, especially if she's got a different married name now,' said Strike. 'You've been very helpful,

Dr Gupta. I really appreciate you taking the time to talk to me.'

'Of course,' said Dr Gupta, considering Strike with his shrewd, bright brown eyes, 'it would be a miracle if you found her, after all this time. But I'm glad somebody's looking again. Yes, I'm very glad somebody's looking.'

11

It fortuned forth faring on his way,
He saw from far, or seemed for to see
Some troublous vprore or contentious fray

Edmund Spenser
The Faerie Queene

Strike walked back towards Amersham station, past the box hedges and twin garages of the professional middle classes, thinking about Margot Bamborough. She'd emerged from the old doctor's reminiscences as a vivid and forceful personality and, irrationally, this had been a surprise. In vanishing, Margot Bamborough had assumed in Strike's mind the insubstantiality of a wraith, as though it had always been predestined that she would one day disperse into the rainy dusk, never to return.

He remembered the seven women depicted on the front cover of *The Demon of Paradise Park*. They lived on in ghostly black and white, sporting the hairstyles that had become gradually more unfashionable with every day they'd been absent from their families and their lives, but each of those negative images represented a human whose heart had once beaten, whose ambitions and opinions, triumphs and disappointments had been as real as Margot Bamborough's, before they ran into the man who was paid the compliment of full colour in the cover photograph of the dreadful story of their deaths. Strike still hadn't finished the book, but knew that Creed had been responsible for the deaths of a diverse array of victims, including a schoolgirl, an estate agent and a pharmacist. That had been part of the terror of

109

the Essex Butcher, according to the contemporary press: he wasn't confining his attacks to prostitutes who, it was implied, were a killer's natural prey. In fact, the only working girl who was known to have been attacked by him had survived.

Helen Wardrop, the woman in question, had told her story in a television documentary about Creed, which Strike had watched on YouTube a few nights previously while eating a Chinese takeaway. The programme had been salacious and melodramatic, with many poorly acted reconstructions and music lifted from a seventies horror movie. At the time of filming, Helen Wardrop had been a slack-faced, slow-spoken woman with dyed red hair and badly applied fake eyelashes, whose glazed affect and monotone suggested either tranquillisers or neurological damage. Creed had struck the drunk and screaming Helen what might have been a fatal blow to the head with a hammer in the course of trying to force her into the back of his van. She turned her head obligingly for the interviewer, to show the viewers a still-depressed area of skull. The interviewer told her she must feel very lucky to have survived. There was a tiny hesitation before she agreed with him.

Strike had turned off the documentary at that point, frustrated by the banality of the questioning. He, too, had once been in the wrong place at the wrong time, and bore the lifelong consequences, so he perfectly understood Helen Wardrop's hesitation. In the immediate aftermath of the explosion that had taken Strike's foot and shin, not to mention the lower half of Sergeant Gary Topley's body and a chunk of Richard Anstis's face, Strike had felt a variety of emotions which included guilt, gratitude, confusion, fear, rage, resentment and loneliness, but he couldn't remember feeling lucky. 'Lucky' would have been the bomb not detonating. 'Lucky' would have meant still having both his legs. 'Lucky' was what people who couldn't bear to contemplate horrors needed to hear maimed and terrorised survivors call themselves. He recalled his aunt's tearful assertion that he wasn't in pain as he lay in his hospital bed, groggy with morphine, her words standing in stark contrast to the first Polworth had spoken to him, when he visited Strike in Selly Oak Hospital.

'Bit of a fucker, this, Diddy.'

'It is, a bit,' Strike had said, his amputated leg stretched in front of him, nerve endings insisting that the calf and foot were still there.

Strike arrived at Amersham station to discover he'd just missed a train back to London. He therefore sat down on a bench outside in the feeble autumn sunshine of late afternoon, took out his cigarettes, lit one, then examined his phone. Two texts and a missed call had come in while he'd been interviewing Gupta, his mobile on mute.

The texts were from his half-brother Al and his friend Ilsa, and could therefore wait, whereas the missed call was from George Layborn, whom he immediately phoned back.

'That you, Strike?'

'Yeah. You just phoned me.'

'I did. I've got it for you. Copy of the Bamborough file.'

'You're kidding!' said Strike, exhaling on a rush of exhilaration. 'George, that's phenomenal, I owe you big time for this.'

'Buy me a pint and mention me to the press if you ever find out who did it. "Valuable assistance." "Couldn't have done it without him." We can decide the wording after. Might remind this lot I deserve promotion. Listen,' added Layborn, more seriously, 'it's a mess. The file. Real mess.'

'In what way?'

'Old. Bits missing, from what I've seen, though they might just be in the wrong order – I haven't had time to go systematically through the whole thing, there's four boxes' worth here – but Talbot's record-keeping was all over the place and Lawson coming in and trying to make sense of it hasn't really helped. Anyway, for what it's worth, it's yours. I'll be over your way tomorrow and drop it in at the office, shall I?'

'Can't tell you how much I appreciate this, George.'

'My old man would've been dead happy to know someone was going to take another look,' said Layborn. 'He'd've loved to see Creed nailed for another one.'

Layborn rang off and Strike immediately lit a cigarette and called Robin to give her the good news, but his call went straight to voicemail. Then he remembered that she was in a meeting with the persecuted weatherman, so he turned his attention to the text from Al.

Hey bruv, it began, chummily.

Al was the only sibling on his father's side with whom Strike maintained any kind of ongoing relationship, spasmodic and one-sided thought it was, Al making all the running. Strike had a total of six Rokeby half-siblings, three of whom he'd never even met, a situation which he felt no need to remedy, finding the stresses of his known relatives quite sufficient to be going on with.

As you know, the Deadbeats are celebrating 50 years together next year—

Strike hadn't known this. He'd met his father, Jonny Rokeby, who was lead singer of the Deadbeats, exactly twice in his life and most of the information he had about his rock-star father had come either from his mother Leda, the woman with whom he had carelessly fathered a child in the semi-public corner of a party in New York, or from the press.

As you know, the Deadbeats are celebrating 50 years together next year and (super confidential) they're going to drop a surprise new album on 24th May. We (families) are throwing them a big London bash that night at Spencer House to celebrate the launch. Bruv, it would mean the world to all of us, especially Dad, if you came. Gaby's had the idea of getting a picture taken of all the kids together, to give him as a present on the night. First ever. Getting it framed, as a surprise. Everyone's in. We just need you. Think about it, bruv.

Strike read this text through twice, then closed it without replying and opened Ilsa's, which was far shorter.

It's Robin's birthday, you total dickhead.

12

With flattering wordes he sweetly wooed her,
And offered faire guiftes, t'allure her sight,
But she both offers and the offerer
Despysde, and all the fawning of the flatterer.

Edmund Spenser
The Faerie Queene

The television weatherman brought his wife to the catch-up meeting with Robin. Once ensconced in the agency's inner office, the couple proved hard to shift. The wife had arrived with a new theory to present to Robin, triggered by the most recent anonymous postcard to arrive by post at the television studio. It was the fifth card to feature a painting, and the third to have been bought at the National Portrait Gallery shop, and this had caused the weatherman's thoughts to turn to an ex-girlfriend, who'd been to art school. He didn't know where the woman was now, but surely it was worth looking for her?

Robin thought it was highly unlikely that an ex-girlfriend would choose anonymous postcards to reconnect with a lost love, given the existence of social media and, indeed, the publicly available contact details for the weatherman, but she agreed diplomatically that this was worth looking into, and took down as many details of this long-vanished love interest as the weatherman could remember. Robin then ran through all the measures the agency was so far taking to trace the sender of the cards, and reassured husband and wife that they were continuing to watch the house at night, in the hopes that Postcard would show themselves.

113

The weatherman was a small man with reddish-brown hair, dark eyes and a possibly deceptive air of apology. His wife, a thin woman several inches taller than her husband, seemed frightened by the late-night hand deliveries, and slightly annoyed by her husband's half-laughing assertions that you didn't expect this sort of thing when you were a weatherman, because, after all, he was hardly the *film star* type, and who knew what this woman was capable of?

'Or man,' his wife reminded him. 'We don't *know* it's a woman, do we?'

'No, that's true,' said her husband, the smile fading slowly from his face.

When at last the couple had left, walking out past Pat, who was stoically typing away at her desk, Robin returned to the inner office and re-examined the most recent postcard. The painting on the front featured the portrait of a nineteenth-century man in a high cravat. *James Duffield Harding*. Robin had never heard of him. She flipped the card over. The printed message read:

HE ALWAYS REMINDS ME OF YOU.

She turned the card over again. The mousy man in side-whiskers *did* resemble the weatherman.

A yawn caught her by surprise. She'd spent most of the day clearing paperwork, authorising payment of bills and tweaking the rota for the coming fortnight to accommodate Morris's request for Saturday afternoon off, so that he could go and watch his three-year-old daughter perform in a ballet show. Checking her watch, Robin saw that it was already five o'clock. Fighting the low mood that had been held at bay by hard work, she tidied away the Postcard file, and switched her mobile ringer back on. Within seconds, it had rung: Strike.

'Hello,' said Robin, trying not to sound peeved, because as the hours had rolled by it had become clear to her that Strike had indeed forgotten her birthday yet again.

'Happy birthday,' he said, over the sound of what Robin could tell was a train.

'Thanks.'

'I've got something for you, but I won't be back for an hour, I've only just got on the train back from Amersham.'

Have you hell got something, thought Robin. *You forgot. You're just going to grab flowers on the way back to the office.*

Robin was sure Ilsa must have tipped Strike off, because Ilsa had called her just before the client had arrived, to tell Robin that she might be unavoidably late for drinks. She'd also asked, with unconvincing casualness, what Strike had bought her, and Robin had answered truthfully, 'Nothing'.

'That's nice, thanks,' Robin said now, 'but I'm just leaving. Going out for a drink tonight.'

'Oh,' said Strike. 'Right. Sorry – couldn't be helped, you know, with coming out here to meet Gupta.'

'No,' said Robin, 'well, you can leave them here in the office—'

'Yeah,' said Strike, and Robin noted that he didn't dispute the word 'them'. It was definitely going to be flowers.

'Anyway,' said Strike, 'big news. George Layborn's got hold of a copy of the Bamborough file.'

'Oh, that's great!' said Robin, enthusiastic in spite of herself.

'Yeah, isn't it? He's going to bring it over tomorrow morning.'

'How was Gupta?' asked Robin, sitting down on her side of the partners' desk which had replaced Strike's old single one.

'Interesting, especially about Margot herself,' said Strike, who became muffled as, Robin guessed, the train went through a tunnel. Robin pressed the mobile closer to her ear and said,

'In what way?'

'Dunno,' said Strike distantly. 'From the old photo, I wouldn't have guessed an ardent feminist. She sounds much more of a personality than I'd imagined, which is stupid, really – why shouldn't she have a personality, and a strong one?'

But Robin knew, somehow, what he meant. The hazy picture of Margot Bamborough, frozen in blurry time with her seventies middle parting, her wide, rounded lapels, her knitted tank top, seemed to belong to a long-gone, two-dimensional world of faded colour.

'Tell you the rest tomorrow,' said Strike, because their connection

115

was breaking up. 'Reception's not great here. I can hardly hear you.'

'OK, fine,' said Robin loudly. 'Speak tomorrow.'

She opened the door into the outer office again. Pat was just turning off Robin's old PC, electronic cigarette sticking out of her mouth.

'Was that Strike?' she asked, crow-like, with her jet-black hair and her croak, the fake cigarette waggling.

'Yep,' said Robin, reaching for her coat and bag. 'He's on his way back from Amersham. Lock up as usual though, Pat, he can let himself in if he needs to.'

'Has he remembered your birthday yet?' asked Pat, who seemed to have taken sadistic satisfaction in news of Strike's forgetfulness that morning.

'Yes,' said Robin, and out of loyalty to Strike she added, 'he's got a present for me. I'll get it tomorrow.'

Pat had bought Robin a new purse. 'That old one was coming apart at the seams,' she said, when Robin unwrapped it. Robin, touched in spite of the fact that she might not have chosen bright red, had expressed warm thanks and at once transferred her money and cards across into the new one.

'Good thing about having one in a nice bright colour, you can always find it in your bag,' Pat had said complacently. 'What's that Scottish nutter got you?'

Barclay had left a small wrapped package with Pat to give to Robin that morning.

'Cards,' said Robin, smiling as she unwrapped the package. 'Sam was telling me all about these, look, when we were out on surveillance the other night. Cards showing Al-Qaeda's most wanted. They gave packs out to the American troops during the Iraq War.'

'What's he given you those for?' said Pat. 'What are you supposed to do with them?'

'Well, because I was interested, when he told me,' said Robin, amused by Pat's disdain. 'I can play poker with them. They've got all the right numbers and everything, look.'

'Bridge,' Pat had said. 'That's a proper game. I like a nice game of bridge.'

As both women pulled on their coats, Pat asked,

'Going anywhere nice tonight?'

'For a drink with a couple of friends,' said Robin. 'But I've got a Selfridges voucher burning a hole in my pocket. Think I might treat myself first.'

'Lovely,' croaked Pat. 'What d'you fancy?'

Before Robin could answer, the glass door behind her opened and Saul Morris entered, handsome, smiling and a little breathless, his black hair sleek, his blue eyes bright. With some misgiving, she saw the wrapped present and card clutched in his hand.

'Happy birthday!' he said. 'Hoped I'd catch you.'

And before Robin could prevent it, he'd bent down and kissed her on the cheek; no air kiss, this, but proper contact of lips and skin. She took half a step backwards.

'Got you a little something,' he said, apparently sensing nothing amiss, but holding out to her the gift and card. 'It's nothing really. And how's Moneypenny?' he said, turning to Pat, who had already removed her electronic cigarette to smile at him, displaying teeth the colour of old ivory.

'*Moneypenny*,' repeated Pat, beaming. 'Get on with you.'

Robin tore the paper from her gift. Inside was a box of Fortnum & Mason salted caramel truffles.

'Oh, *very* nice,' said Pat approvingly.

Chocolates, it seemed, were a far more appropriate gift for a young woman than a pack of cards with Al-Qaeda members on them.

'Remembered you like a bit of salted caramel,' said Morris, looking proud of himself.

Robin knew exactly where he'd got this idea, and it didn't make her any more appreciative.

A month previously, at the first meeting of the entire expanded agency, Robin had opened a tin of fancy biscuits that had arrived in a hamper sent by a grateful client. Strike had enquired why everything these days was salted caramel flavour, and Robin had replied that it didn't seem to be stopping him eating them by the handful. She'd expressed no personal fondness for the flavour, but Morris had evidently paid both too little and too much attention, treasuring up his lazy assumption for use at some later date.

'Thanks very much,' she said, with a bare minimum of warmth. 'I'm afraid I've got to dash.'

And before Pat could point out that Selfridges would still be there in a half an hour, Robin had slid past Morris and started down the metal stairs, his card still unopened in her hand.

Exactly why Morris grated on her so much, Robin was still pondering as she moved slowly around Selfridges' great perfume hall half an hour later. She'd decided to buy herself some new perfume, because she'd been wearing the same scent for five years. Matthew had liked it, and never wanted her to change, but her last bottle was down to the dregs, and she had a sudden urge to douse herself in something that Matthew wouldn't recognise, and possibly wouldn't even like. The cheap little bottle of 4711 cologne she'd bought on the way to Falmouth was nowhere near distinctive enough for a new signature scent, and so she wandered through a vast maze of smoked mirrors and gilded lights, between islands of seductive bottles and illuminated pictures of celebrities, each little domain presided over by black-clad sirens offering squirts and testing strips.

Was it pompous of her, she wondered, to think that Morris the subcontractor ought not to assume the right to kiss an agency partner? Would she mind if the generally reserved Hutchins kissed her on the cheek? No, she decided, she wouldn't mind at all, because she'd now known Andy over a year, and in any case, Hutchins would do the polite thing and make the greeting a matter of brief proximity of two faces, not a pressing of lips into her face.

And what about Barclay? He'd never kissed her, though he had recently called her 'ya numpty' when, on surveillance, she had accidentally spilled hot coffee all over him in her excitement at seeing their target, a civil servant, leaving a known brothel at two o'clock in the morning. But she hadn't minded Barclay calling her a numpty in the slightest. She'd *been* a numpty.

Turning a corner, Robin found herself facing the Yves Saint Laurent counter, and with a sudden sharpening of interest, her eyes focused on a blue, black and silver cylinder bearing the name Rive Gauche. Robin had never knowingly smelled Margot Bamborough's favourite perfume before.

'It's a classic,' said the bored-looking salesgirl, watching Robin spraying Rive Gauche onto a fresh testing strip and inhaling.

Robin tended to rate perfumes according to how well they reproduced a familiar flower or foodstuff, but this wasn't a smell from nature. There was a ghostly rose there, but also something strangely metallic. Robin, who was used to fragrances made friendly with fruit and candy, set down the strip with a smile and a shake of her head and walked on.

So that was how Margot Bamborough had smelled, she thought. It was a far more sophisticated scent than the one Matthew had loved on Robin, which was a natural-smelling concoction of figs, fresh, milky and green.

Robin turned a corner and saw, standing on a counter directly ahead of her, a faceted glass bottle full of pink liquid: Flowerbomb, Sarah Shadlock's signature scent. Robin had seen it in Sarah and Tom's bathroom whenever she and Matthew had gone over for dinner. Since leaving Matthew, Robin had had ample time to realise that the occasions on which he had changed the sheets mid-week, because he'd 'spilled tea' or 'thought I'd do it today, save you doing it tomorrow' must have been as much to wash away that loud, sweet scent, as any other, more obviously incriminating traces that might have leaked from careful condoms.

'It's a modern classic,' said the hopeful salesgirl, who'd noticed Robin looking at the glass hand grenade. With a perfunctory smile, Robin shook her head and turned away. Now her reflection in the smoked glass looked simply sad, as she picked up bottles and smelled strips in a joyless hunt for something to improve this lousy birthday. She suddenly wished that she were heading home, and not out for drinks.

'What are you looking for?' said a sharp-cheekboned black girl, whom Robin passed shortly afterwards.

Five minutes later, after a brief, professional interchange, Robin was heading back towards Oxford Street with a rectangular black bottle in her bag. The salesgirl had been highly persuasive.

' . . . and if you want something *totally* different,' she'd said, picking up a fifth bottle, spraying a little onto a strip and wafting it around, 'try Fracas.'

She'd handed the strip to Robin, whose nostrils were now burning from the rich and varied assault of the past half hour.

'Sexy but grown-up, you know? It's a real classic.'

And in that moment, Robin, breathing in heady, luscious, oily tuberose, had been seduced by the idea of becoming, in her thirtieth year, a sophisticated woman utterly different from the kind of fool who was too stupid to realise that what her husband told her he loved, and what he liked taking into his bed, bore about as much resemblance as a fig to a hand grenade.

13

Thence forward by that painfull way they pas,
Forth to an hill, that was both steepe and hy;
On top whereof a sacred chappell was,
And eke a little hermitage thereby.

Edmund Spenser
The Faerie Queene

In retrospect, Strike regretted the first gift he'd ever given Robin Ellacott. He'd bought the expensive green dress in a fit of quixotic extravagance, feeling safe in giving her something so personal only because she was engaged to another man and he was never going to see her again, or so he'd thought. She'd modelled it for Strike in the course of persuading a saleswoman into indiscretions, and that girl's evidence, which Robin had so skilfully extracted, had helped solve the case that had made Strike's name and saved his agency from bankruptcy. Buoyed by a tide of euphoria and gratitude, he'd returned to the shop and made the purchase as a grand farewell gesture. Nothing else had seemed to encapsulate what he wanted to tell her, which was 'look what we achieved together', 'I couldn't have done it without you' and (if he was being totally honest with himself) 'you look gorgeous in this, and I'd like you to know I thought so when I saw you in it'.

But things hadn't panned out quite as Strike had expected, because within an hour of giving her the green dress he'd hired her as a full-time assistant. Doubtless the dress accounted for at least some of the profound mistrust Matthew, her fiancé, had henceforth felt towards the detective. Worse still, from Strike's point of view, it had set the bar uncomfortably high for future gifts. Whether consciously or not, he'd lowered expectations considerably since, either by forgetting to buy Robin birthday and Christmas gifts, or by making them as generic as was possible.

He purchased stargazer lilies at the first florist he could find when he got off the train from Amersham, and bore them into the office for Robin to find next day. He'd chosen them for their size and powerful fragrance. He felt he ought to spend more money than he had on the previous year's belated bunch, and these looked impressive, as though he hadn't skimped. Roses carried an unwelcome connotation of Valentine's Day, and nearly everything else in the florist's stock – admittedly depleted at half past five in the afternoon – looked a little bedraggled or underwhelming. The lilies were large and yet reassuringly impersonal, sculptural in quality and heavy with fragrance, and there was safety in their very boldness. They came from a clinical hothouse; there was no romantic whisper of quiet woods or secret garden about them: they were flowers of which he could say robustly 'nice smell', with no further justification for his choice.

Strike wasn't to know that Robin's primary association with stargazer lilies, now and for evermore, would be with Sarah Shadlock, who'd once brought an almost identical bouquet to Robin and Matthew's housewarming party. When she walked into the office the day after her birthday and saw the flowers standing there on the partners' desk, stuck in a vase full of water but still in their cellophane, with a large magenta bow on them and a small card that read 'Happy birthday from Cormoran' (no kiss, he never put kisses), she was affected exactly the same way she'd been by the hand-grenade-shaped bottle in Selfridges. She didn't want these flowers; they were a double irritant in reminding her of Strike's forgetfulness and Matthew's infidelity, and if she had to look at or smell them, she resolved, it wouldn't be in her own home.

So she'd left the lilies at the office, where they stubbornly refused to die, Pat conscientiously refilling their water every morning and taking such good care of them that they lived for nearly two weeks. Even Strike was sick of them by the end: he kept getting wafts of something that reminded him of his ex-girlfriend Lorelei's perfume, an unpleasant association.

By the time the waxy pink and white petals began to shrivel and fall, the thirty-ninth anniversary of Margot Bamborough's disappearance had passed unmarked and probably unnoticed by anyone except, perhaps, her family, Strike and Robin, who both registered the fateful date. Copies of the police records had been brought to the office as promised by George Layborn, and now lay in four cardboard boxes under the partners' desk, which was the only place the agency had room for them. Strike, who was currently the least encumbered by the agency's other cases, because he was holding himself in readiness to go back down to Cornwall should the need arise, set himself to work systematically through these files. Once he'd digested their contents, he intended to visit Clerkenwell with Robin, and retrace the route between the old St John's practice where Margot had last been seen alive, and the pub where her friend had waited for her in vain.

So, on the last day of October, Robin left the office at one o'clock and hurried, beneath a threatening sky and with her umbrella ready in her hand, onto the Tube. She was quietly excited by the prospect of this afternoon, the first she and Strike would spend working the Bamborough case together.

It was already drizzling slightly when Robin caught sight of Strike, standing smoking as he surveyed the frontage of a building halfway down St John's Lane. He turned at the sound of her heels on the wet pavement.

'Am I late?' she called, as she approached.

'No,' said Strike, 'I was early.'

She joined him, still holding her umbrella, and looked up at the tall, multi-storey building of brown brick, with large, metal-framed windows. It appeared to house offices, but there was no indication of what kind of businesses were operating inside.

'It was right here,' said Strike, pointing at the door numbered 29. 'The old St John's Medical Practice. They've remodelled the front of the building, obviously. There used to be a back entrance,' he said. 'We'll go round and have a shufti in a minute.'

Robin turned to look up and down St John's Lane, which was a long, narrow one-way street, bordered on either side by tall, multi-windowed buildings.

'Very overlooked,' commented Robin.

'Yep,' said Strike. 'So, let's begin with what Margot was wearing when she disappeared.'

'I already know,' said Robin. 'Brown corduroy skirt, red shirt, knitted tank top, beige Burberry raincoat, silver necklace and ear-rings, gold wedding ring. Carrying a leather shoulder bag and a black umbrella.'

'You should take up detection,' said Strike, mildly impressed. 'Ready for the police records?'

'Go on.'

'At a quarter to six on the eleventh of October 1974 only three people are known to have been inside this building: Margot, who was dressed exactly as you describe, but hadn't yet put on her rain-coat; Gloria Conti, who was the younger of the two receptionists; and an emergency patient with abdominal pain, who'd walked in off the street. The patient, according to the hasty note Gloria took, was called "Theo question mark". In spite of the male name, and Dr Joseph Brenner's assertion that he thought the patient looked like a man, and Talbot trying hard to persuade her that Theo was a man dressed as a woman, Gloria never wavered in her assertion that "Theo" was a woman.

'All the other employees had left before a quarter to six, except Wilma the cleaner, who hadn't been there at all that day, because she didn't work Fridays. More of Wilma later.

'Janice, the nurse, was here until midday, then making house visits the rest of the afternoon and didn't return. Irene, the receptionist, left at half past two for a dental appointment and didn't come back. According to their statements, each of which were corroborated by some other witness, the secretary, Dorothy, left at ten past five, Dr Gupta at half past and Dr Brenner at a quarter to six. Police were happy with the alibis all three gave for the rest of the evening: Dorothy went home to her son and spent the evening watching TV with him. Dr Gupta attended a large family dinner to celebrate his mother's birthday and Dr Brenner was with the spinster sister he shared his house with. Both Brenners were seen through the sitting-room window later that evening, by a dog walker.

'The last registered patients, a mother and child, were Margot's, and they left the practice shortly before Brenner did. The patients testified that Margot was fine when they saw her.

'From that point on, Gloria is the only witness. According to Gloria, Theo went into Margot's consulting room and stayed there longer than expected. At a quarter past six, Theo left, never to be seen at the practice again. A police appeal was subsequently put out for her, but nobody came forward.

'Margot left no notes about Theo. The assumption is that she intended to write up the consultation the following day, because her friend had now been waiting for her in the pub for a quarter of an hour and she didn't want to make herself even later.

'Shortly after Theo left, Margot came hurrying out of her consulting room, put on her raincoat, told Gloria to lock up with the emergency key, walked out into the rain, put up her umbrella, turned right and disappeared from Gloria's sight.'

Strike turned and pointed up the road towards a yellow stone arch of ancient appearance, which lay directly ahead of them.

'Which means she was heading in that direction, towards the Three Kings.'

For a moment, both of them looked towards the old arch that spanned the road, as though some shadow of Margot might materialise. Then Strike ground out his cigarette underfoot and said,

'Follow me.'

He walked the length of number 28, then paused to point up a dark passageway the width of a door, called Passing Alley.

'Good hiding place,' said Robin, pausing to look up and down the dark, vaulted corridor through the buildings.

'Certainly is,' said Strike. 'If somebody wanted to lie in wait for her, this is tailor made. Catch her by surprise, drag her up here – but after that, it'd get problematic.'

They walked along the short passage and emerged into a sunken garden area of concrete and shrubs that lay between two parallel streets.

'The police searched this whole garden area with sniffer dogs. Nothing. And if an assailant dragged her onwards, through there,' Strike pointed to the road that ran parallel to St John's Lane, 'onto St John Street, it would've been well-nigh impossible to go unde-tected. The street's far busier than St John's Lane. And that's assuming a fit, tall twenty-nine-year-old wouldn't have shouted and fought back.'

He turned to look at the back entrance.

'The district nurse sometimes went in the back, rather than going through the waiting room. She had a little room to the rear of the building where she kept her own stuff and sometimes saw patients. Wilma the cleaner sometimes went out the back door as well. Otherwise it was usually locked.'

'Are we interested in people being able to enter or leave the build-ing through a second door?' asked Robin.

'Not especially, but I want to get a feel for the layout. It's been nearly forty years: we've got to go back over everything.'

They walked back through Passing Alley to the front of the building.

'We've got one advantage over Bill Talbot,' said Strike. 'We know the Essex Butcher turned out to be slim and blond, not a swarthy thickset person of gypsy-ish appearance. Theo, whoever she was, wasn't Creed. Which doesn't necessarily make her irrelevant, of course.

'One last thing, then we're done with the practice itself,' said Strike, looking up at number 29. 'Irene, the blonde receptionist, told the police that Margot received two threatening, anonymous notes shortly before she disappeared. They're not in the police file, so we've only got Irene's statement to go on. She claims she opened one, and that she saw another on Margot's desk when bringing her tea. She says the one she read mentioned hellfire.'

'You'd think it was the secretary's job to open mail,' commented Robin. 'Not a receptionist's.'

'Good point,' said Strike, pulling out his notebook and scrib-bling, 'we'll check that ... It seems relevant to add here that Talbot thought Irene was an unreliable witness: inaccurate and prone to exaggeration. Incidentally, Gupta said Irene and Margot had what he called a "contretemps" at a Christmas party. He didn't think it was a particularly big deal, but he'd remembered it.'

'And is Talbot—?'

'Dead? Yes,' said Strike. 'So's Lawson, who took over from him. Talbot's got a son, though, and I'm thinking of getting in touch with him. Lawson never had kids.'

'Go on, about the anonymous notes.'

'Well, Gloria, the other receptionist, said Irene showed her one of the notes, but couldn't remember what was in it. Janice, the nurse, confirmed that Irene had told her about them at the time, but said she hadn't personally seen them. Margot didn't tell Gupta about them – I called him to check.

'Anyway,' said Strike, giving the street one last sweeping look through the drizzle, 'assuming nobody abducted Margot right outside the practice, or that she didn't get in a car yards from the door, she headed towards the Three Kings, which takes us this way.'

'D'you want to come under this umbrella?' Robin asked.

'No,' said Strike. His densely curling hair looked the same wet or dry: he had very little vanity.

They continued up the street and passed through St John's Gate, the ancient stone arch decorated with many small heraldic shields, emerging onto Clerkenwell Road, a bustling two-way street, which they crossed, arriving beside an old-fashioned scarlet phone box which stood at the mouth of Albemarle Way.

'Is that the phone box where the two women were seen struggling?' asked Robin.

Strike did a double take.

'You've read the case notes,' he said, almost accusingly.

'I had a quick look,' Robin admitted, 'while I was printing out Two-Times' bill last night. I didn't read everything; didn't have time. Just looked at a few bits and pieces.'

'Well, that *isn't* the phone box,' said Strike. 'The important phone box – or boxes – come later. We'll get to them in due course. Now follow me.'

Instead of proceeding into a paved pedestrian area that Robin, from her own scant research, knew Margot must have crossed if she had been heading for the Three Kings, Strike turned left, up Clerkenwell Road.

'Why are we going this way?' asked Robin, jogging to keep up.

'Because,' said Strike, stopping again and pointing up at a top window on the building opposite, which looked like an old brick warehouse, 'some time after six o'clock on the evening in question, a fourteen-year-old schoolgirl called Amanda White swore she saw Margot at the top window, second from the right, banging her fists against the glass.'

'I haven't seen *that* mentioned online!' said Robin.

'For the good reason that the police concluded there was nothing in it.

'Talbot, as is clear from his notes, disregarded White because her story couldn't be fitted into his theory that Creed had abducted Margot. But Lawson went back to Amanda when he took over, and actually walked with her along this stretch of road.

'Amanda's account had a few things going for it. For one thing, she told the police unprompted that this had happened the evening after the general election, which she remembered because she had an argument with a Tory schoolfriend. The pair of them had been kept back after school for a detention. They'd then gone for a coffee together, over which the schoolfriend went into a huff when Mandy said it was good that Wilson had won, and refused to walk home with her.

'Amanda said she was still angry about her friend getting stroppy when she looked up and saw a woman pounding on the glass with her fists. The description she gave was a good one, although by this time, a full description of Margot's appearance and clothing had been in the press.

'Lawson contacted the business owner who worked on the top floor. It was a paper design company run by a husband and wife. They produced small runs of pamphlets, posters and invitations, that kind of stuff. No connection to Margot. Neither of them were registered with the St John's practice, because they lived out of the area. The wife said she sometimes had to thump the window frame to make it close. However, the wife in no way resembled Margot, being short, tubby and ginger-haired.'

'And someone would've noticed Margot on her way up to the third floor, surely?' said Robin, looking from the top window to the front door. She moved back from the kerb: cars were splashing through the puddles in the gutter. 'She'd have climbed the stairs or used the lift, and maybe rung the doorbell to get in.'

'You'd think so,' agreed Strike. 'Lawson concluded that Amanda had made an innocent mistake and thought the printer's wife was Margot.'

They returned to the point where they had deviated from what Robin thought of as 'Margot's route'. Strike paused again, pointing up the gloomy side road called Albemarle Way.

'Now, disregard the phone box, but note that Albemarle Way is the first side street since Passing Alley I think she could plausibly have entered – voluntarily or not – without necessarily being seen by fifty-odd people. Quieter, as you can see – but not *that* quiet,' admitted Strike, looking towards the end of Albemarle Way, where traffic was passing at a steady rate. Albemarle Way was narrower than St John's Lane, but similar in being bordered by tall buildings in unbroken lines, which kept it permanently in shadow. 'Still a risk for an abductor,' said Strike, 'but if Dennis Creed was lurking somewhere in his van, waiting for a lone woman – any woman – to walk past in the rain, this is the place I can see it happening.'

It was at this moment, as a cold breeze whistled up Albemarle Way, that Strike caught a whiff of what he had thought were the dying stargazer lilies, but now realised was coming from Robin herself. The perfume wasn't exactly the same as the one that Lorelei had worn; his ex's had been strangely boozy, with overtones of rum (and he'd liked it when the scent had been an accompaniment to easy affection and imaginative sex; only later had he come to associate it with passive-aggression, character assassination and pleas for a love he could not feel). Nevertheless, this scent strongly resembled Lorelei's; he found it cloying and sickly.

Of course, many would say it was rich for him to have opinions about how women smelled, given that his signature odour was that

129

of an old ashtray, overlain with a splash of Pour Un Homme on special occasions. Nevertheless, having spent much of his childhood in conditions of squalor, Strike found cleanliness a necessary trait in anyone he could find attractive. He'd liked Robin's previous scent, which he'd missed when she wasn't in the office.

'This way,' he said, and they proceeded through the rain into an irregular pedestrianised square. A few seconds later, Strike suddenly became aware that he'd left Robin behind, and walked back several paces to join her in front of St John Priory Church, a pleasingly symmetrical building of red brick, with long windows and two white stone pillars flanking the entrance.

'Thinking about her lying in a holy place?' he asked, lighting up again while the rain beat down on him. Exhaling, he held the cigarette cupped in his hand, to prevent its extinguishment.

'No,' said Robin, a little defensively, but then, 'yes, all right, maybe a bit. Look at this ...'

Strike followed her through the open gates into a small garden of remembrance, open to the public and full (as Robin read off a small sign on the inner wall) of medicinal herbs, including many used in medieval times, in the Order of St John's hospitals. A white figure of Christ hung on the back wall, surrounded with the emblems of the four evangelists: the bull, the lion, the eagle and the angel. Fronds and leaves undulated gently beneath the rain. As Robin's eyes swept the small, walled garden, Strike, who'd followed her, said,

'I think we can agree that if somebody buried her in here, a cleric would have noticed disturbed earth.'

'I know,' said Robin. 'I'm just looking.'

As they returned to the street, she added,

'There are Maltese crosses everywhere, look. They were on that archway we just passed through, too.'

'It's the cross of the Knights Hospitaller. Knights of St John. Hence the street names and the emblem of St John ambulance; they've got their headquarters back in St John's Lane. If that medium Googled the area Margot went missing, she can't have missed Clerkenwell's associations with the Order of St John. I'll bet you that's where she got the idea for that little bit of "holy place" padding. But bear it in mind, because the cross is going to come up again once we reach the pub.'

'You know,' said Robin, turning to look back at the Priory, 'Peter Tobin, that Scottish serial killer – he attached himself to churches. He joined a religious sect at one point, under an assumed name. Then he got a job as a handyman at a church in Glasgow, where he buried that poor girl beneath the floorboards.'

'Churches are good cover for killers,' said Strike. 'Sex offenders, too.'

'Priests and doctors,' said Robin thoughtfully. 'It's hardwired in most of us to trust them, don't you think?'

'After the Catholic Church's many scandals? After Harold Shipman?'

'Yes, I think so,' said Robin. 'Don't you think we tend to invest some categories of people with unearned goodness? I suppose we've all got a need to trust people who seem to have power over life and death.'

'Think you're onto something there,' said Strike, as they entered a short pedestrian lane called Jerusalem Passage. 'I told Gupta it was odd that Joseph Brenner didn't like people. I thought that might be a basic job requirement for a doctor. He soon put me right.'

'Let's stop here a moment,' Strike said, doing so. 'If Margot got this far – I'm assuming she'd've taken this route, because it's the shortest and most logical way to the Three Kings – this is the first time she'd have passed residences rather than offices or public buildings.'

Robin looked at the buildings around them. Sure enough, there were a couple of doors whose multiple buzzers indicated flats above.

'Is there a chance,' said Strike, 'however remote, that someone living along this lane could have persuaded or forced her inside?'

Robin looked up and down the street, the rain pattering onto her umbrella.

'Well,' she said slowly, 'obviously it *could* have happened, but it seems unlikely. Did someone wake up that day and decide they wanted to abduct a woman, reach outside and grab one?'

'Have I taught you nothing?'

'OK, fine: *means before motive*. But there are problems with the means, too. This is really overlooked as well. Does nobody see or hear her being abducted? Doesn't she scream or fight? And I assume the abductor lives alone, unless their housemates are also in on the kidnapping?'

'All valid points,' admitted Strike. 'Plus, the police went door to door here. Everyone was questioned, though the flats weren't searched.

'But let's think this through . . . She's a doctor. What if someone shoots out of a house and begs her to come inside to look at an injured person – a sick relative – and once inside, they don't let her go? That'd be a good ploy for getting her inside, pretending there was a medical emergency.'

'OK, but that presupposes they knew she was a doctor.'

'The abductor could've been a patient.'

'But how did they know she'd be passing their house at that particular time? Had she alerted the whole neighbourhood that she was about to go to the pub?'

'Maybe it was a random thing, they saw her passing, they knew she was a doctor, they ran out and grabbed her. Or – I dunno, let's say there really was a sick or dying person inside, or someone's had an accident – perhaps there's an argument – she disagrees with the treatment or refuses to help – the fight becomes physical – she's accidentally killed.'

There was a short silence, while they moved aside for a group of chattering French students. When these had passed, Strike said,

'It's a stretch, I grant you.'

'We can find out how many of these buildings are occupied by the same people they were thirty-nine years ago,' said Robin, 'but we've still got the problem of how they've kept her body hidden for nearly four decades. You wouldn't dare move, would you?'

'That's a problem, all right,' admitted Strike. 'As Gupta said, it's not like disposing of a table of equivalent weight. Blood, decomposition, infestation . . . plenty have tried keeping bodies on the premises. Crippen. Christie. Fred and Rose West. It's generally considered a mistake.'

'Creed managed it for a while,' said Robin. 'Boiling down severed hands in the basement. Burying heads apart from bodies. It wasn't the corpses that got him caught.'

'Are you reading *The Demon of Paradise Park*?' asked Strike sharply.

'Yes,' said Robin.

'D'you want that stuff in your head?'

'If it helps us with the case,' said Robin.

'Hmm. Just thinking of my health and safety responsibilities.'

Robin said nothing. Strike gave the houses a last, sweeping look, then invited Robin to walk on, saying,

'You're right, I can't see it. Freezers get opened, gas men visit and notice a smell, neighbours notice blocked drains. But in the interests of thoroughness, we should check who was living here at the time.'

They now emerged onto the busiest road they had yet seen. Aylesbury Street was a wide road, lined with more office blocks and flats.

'So,' said Strike, pausing again on the pavement, 'if Margot's still walking to the pub, she would've crossed here and turned left, into Clerkenwell Green. But we're pausing to note that it was *there*,' Strike pointed some fifty yards to the right, 'that a small white van nearly knocked down two women as it sped away from Clerkenwell Green that evening. The incident was witnessed by four or five onlookers. Nobody got the registration number— '

'But Creed was putting fake licence plates on the delivery van he was using,' said Robin, 'so that might not help anyway.'

'Correct. The van seen by witnesses on the eleventh of October 1974 had a design on the side. The onlookers didn't all agree what it was, but two of them thought a large flower.'

'And we also know,' said Robin, 'that Creed was using removable paint on the van to disguise its appearance.'

'Correct again. So, on the surface, this looks like our first proper hint that Creed might've been in the area. Talbot, of course, wanted to believe that, so he was uninterested in the opinion of one of the witnesses that the van actually belonged to a local florist. However, a junior officer, presumably one of those who'd realised that his lead investigator was going quietly off his onion, went and questioned the florist, a man called Albert Shimmings, who absolutely denied driving a speeding van in this area that night. He claimed he'd been giving his young son a lift in it, miles away.'

'Which doesn't necessarily mean it *wasn't* Shimmings,' said Robin. 'He might have been worried about being done for dangerous driving. No CCTV cameras . . . nothing to prove it one way or the other.'

'My thoughts exactly. If Shimmings is still alive, I think we should check his story. He might've decided it's worth telling the truth now a speeding charge can't stick. In the meantime,' said Strike, 'the matter of the van remains unresolved and we have to admit that one possible explanation is that Creed was driving it.'

'But where did he abduct Margot, if it *was* Creed in the van?' asked Robin. 'It can't've been back in Albemarle Way, because this isn't how he'd have left the area.'

'True. If he'd grabbed her in Albemarle Way, he'd've joined Aylesbury Street much further down and he definitely wouldn't have come via Clerkenwell Green – which leads us neatly to the Two Struggling Women by the Phoneboxes.'

They proceeded through the drizzle into Clerkenwell Green, a wide rectangular square which boasted trees, a pub and a café. Two telephone boxes stood in the middle, near parked cars and a bike stand.

'Here,' said Strike, coming to a halt between the phone boxes, 'is where Talbot's craziness really starts messing with the case. A woman called Ruby Elliot, who was unfamiliar with the area, but trying to find her daughter and son-in-law's new house in Hayward's Place, was driving around in circles in the rain, lost.

'She passed these phone boxes and noticed two women struggling together, one of whom seemed, in her word, "tottery". She has no particularly distinct memory of them – remember, it's pouring with rain and she's anxiously trying to spot street signs and house numbers, because she's lost. All she can tell the police is that one of them was wearing a headscarf and the other a raincoat.

'The day after this detail appeared in the paper, a middle-aged woman of sound character came forward to say that the pair of women Ruby Elliot had seen had almost certainly been her and her aged mother. She told Talbot she'd been walking the old dear across Clerkenwell Green that night, taking her home after a little walk. The mother, who was infirm and senile, was wearing a rainhat, and she herself was wearing a raincoat similar to Margot's. They didn't have umbrellas, so she was trying to hurry her mother along. The old lady didn't take kindly to being rushed and there was a slight alter- cation here, right by the phone boxes. I've got a picture of the two of them, incidentally: the press got hold of it – "sighting debunked".

'But Talbot wasn't having it. He flat-out refused to accept that the two women hadn't been Margot and a man dressed like a woman. The way he sees it: Margot and Creed meet here by the phone boxes, Creed wrestles her into his van, which presumably was parked *there –*' Strike pointed to the short line of parked cars nearby, 'then Creed takes off at speed, with her screaming and banging on the sides of the van, exiting down Aylesbury Street.'

'But,' said Robin, 'Talbot thought *Theo* was Creed. Why would Creed come to Margot's surgery dressed as a woman, then walk out, leaving her unharmed, walk to Clerkenwell Green and grab her here, in the middle of the most public, overlooked place we've seen?'

'There's no point trying to make sense of it, because there isn't any. When Lawson took over the case, he went back to Fiona Fleury, which was the respectable middle-aged woman's name, questioned her again and came away completely satisfied that she and her mother had been the women Ruby Elliot saw. Again, the general election was useful, because Fiona Fleury remembered being tired and not particularly patient with her difficult mother, because she'd sat up late the night before, watching election coverage. Lawson concluded – and I'm inclined to agree with him – that the matter of the two struggling women had been resolved.'

The drizzle had thickened: raindrops were pounding on Robin's umbrella and rendering the hems of her trousers sodden. They now turned up Clerkenwell Close, a curving street that rose towards a large and impressive church with a high, pointed steeple, set on higher ground.

'Margot can't have got this far,' said Robin.

'You say that,' said Strike, and to her surprise he paused again, look- ing ahead at the church, 'but we now reach one last alleged sighting.

'A church handyman – yeah, I know,' he added, in response to Robin's startled look, 'called Willy Lomax claims he saw a woman in a Burberry raincoat walking up the steps to St James-on-the-Green that evening, around the time Margot should've been arriving at the pub. He saw her from behind. These were the days, of course, when churches weren't locked up all the time.

'Talbot, of course, disregarded Lomax's evidence, because if Margot was alive and walking into churches, she couldn't have been speeding away in the Essex Butcher's van. Lawson couldn't make much of Lomax's evidence. The bloke stuck fast to his story: he'd seen a woman matching Margot's description go inside but, being a man of limited curiosity, didn't follow her, didn't ask her what she was up to and didn't watch to see whether she ever came out of the church again.

'And now,' said Strike, 'we've earned a pint.'

14

In which there written was with cyphres old . . .

Edmund Spenser
The Faerie Queene

On the opposite side of the road from the church hung the sign of the Three Kings. The pub's curved, tiled exterior wall mirrored the bend in the road.

As she followed Strike inside, Robin had the strange sensation of walking back in time. Most of the walls were papered in pages from old music papers dating back to the seventies: a jumble of reviews, adverts for old stereo systems and pictures of pop and rock stars. Hallowe'en decorations hung over the bar, Bowie and Bob Marley looking down from framed prints, and Bob Dylan and Jimi Hendrix looked back at them from the opposite wall. As Robin sat down at a free table for two and Strike headed to the bar, she spotted a newspaper picture of Jonny Rokeby in tight leather trousers in the collage around the mirror. The pub looked as though it hadn't changed in many years; it might even have had these same frosted windows, these mismatched wooden tables, bare floorboards, round glass wall lamps and candles in bottles back when Margot's friend sat waiting for her in 1974.

For the first time, looking around this quirky, characterful pub, Robin found herself wondering exactly what Margot Bamborough had been like. It was odd how professional people's jobs defined them in the imagination. 'Doctor' felt, in many ways, like a complete identity. Waiting for her companion to buy the drinks, her eyes drifting from the skulls hanging from the bar to the pictures of dead rock stars, Robin was struck by the odd idea of a reverse nativity. The three Magi had journeyed towards a birth; Margot had set out for the Three Kings and, Robin feared, met death along the way.

Strike set Robin's wine in front of her, took a satisfying mouthful of Sussex Best, sat down and then reached inside his overcoat and pulled out a roll of papers. Robin noticed photocopied newspaper reports among the typed and handwritten pages.

'You've been to the British Library.'

'I was there all day yesterday.'

He took the top photocopy and showed it to Robin. It showed a small clipping from the *Daily Mail*, featuring a picture of Fiona Fleury and her aged mother beneath the caption: *Essex Butcher Sighting 'Was Really Us'*. Neither woman would have been easy to mistake for Margot Bamborough: Fiona was a tall, broad woman with a cheery face and no waist; her mother was shrivelled with age and stooped.

'This is the first inkling that the press were losing confidence in Bill Talbot,' said Strike. 'A few weeks after this appeared, they were baying for his blood, which probably didn't help his mental health . . . Anyway,' he said, his large, hairy-backed hand lying flat on the rest of the photocopied paper. 'Let's go back to the one, incontrovertible fact we've got, which is that Margot Bamborough was still alive and inside the practice at a quarter to six that night.'

'At a quarter *past* six, you mean,' said Robin.

'No, I don't,' said Strike. 'The sequence of departures goes: ten past five, Dorothy. Half past five, Dinesh Gupta, who catches sight of Margot inside her consulting room before he leaves, and walks out past Gloria and Theo.

'Gloria goes to ask Brenner if he'll see Theo. He refuses. Margot comes out of her consulting room and her last scheduled patients, a mother and child, come out at the same time and leave, also walking out past Theo in the waiting room. Margot tells Gloria she's happy to see Theo. Brenner says "good of you" and leaves, at a quarter to six.

'From then on, we've only got Gloria's uncorroborated word for anything that happened. She's the only person claiming Theo and Margot left the surgery alive.'

Robin paused in the act of taking a sip of wine.

'Come on. You aren't suggesting they never left? That Margot's still there, buried under the floorboards?'

'No, because sniffer dogs went all over the building, as well as the garden behind it,' said Strike. 'But how's this for a theory? The reason Gloria was so insistent that Theo was a woman, not a man, was because he was her accomplice in the murder or abduction of Margot.'

'Wouldn't it have been more sensible to write down a girl's name instead of "Theo" if she wanted to hide a man's identity? And why would she ask Dr Brenner if he could see Theo, if she and Theo were planning to kill Margot?'

'Both good points,' admitted Strike, 'but maybe she knew perfectly well Brenner would refuse, because he was a cantankerous old bastard, and was trying to make the thing look natural to Margot. Humour me for a moment.

'Inert bodies are heavy, hard to move and difficult to hide. A living, fighting woman is even harder. I've seen press photographs of Gloria and she was what my aunt would call a "slip of a girl", whereas Margot was a tall woman. I doubt Gloria could have killed Margot without help, and she definitely couldn't have lifted her.'

'Didn't Dr Gupta say Margot and Gloria were close?'

'*Means before motive.* The closeness could've been a front,' said Strike. 'Maybe Gloria didn't like being "improved" after all, and only acted the grateful pupil to allay Margot's suspicions.

'Be that as it may, the last time there are multiple witnesses to Margot's whereabouts was half an hour before she supposedly left the building. After that, we've only got Gloria's word for what happened.'

'OK, objection sustained,' said Robin.

'So,' said Strike, as he took his hand off the pile of paper, 'having granted me that, forget for a moment any alleged sightings of her at windows or walking into churches. Forget the speeding van. It's entirely possible that *none* of that had anything to do with Margot.

'Go back to the one thing we know for certain: Margot Bamborough was still alive at a quarter to six.

'So now we turn to three men the police considered plausible suspects at the time and ask ourselves where they were at a quarter to six on the eleventh of October 1974.'

'There you go,' he said, passing Robin a photocopy of a tabloid news story dated 24 October 1974. 'That's Roy Phipps, otherwise known as Margot's husband and Anna's dad.'

The photograph showed a handsome man of around thirty, who strongly resembled his daughter. Robin thought that if she had been looking to cast a poet in a cheesy movie, she'd have put Roy Phipps's headshot to the top of the pile. This was where Anna had got her long, pale face, her high forehead and her large, beautiful eyes. Phipps had worn his dark hair down to his long-lapelled collar in 1974, and he stared up out of this old newsprint harrowed, facing the camera, looking up from the card in his hand. The caption read: *Dr Roy Phipps, appealing to the public for help.*

'Don't bother reading it,' said Strike, already placing a second news story over the first. 'There's nothing in there you don't already know, but *this* one will give you a few titbits you don't.'

Robin bent obediently over the second news story, of which Strike had photocopied only half.

her husband, Dr Roy Phipps, who suffers from von Willebrand Disease, was ill at home and confined to bed at the marital home in Ham on the 11th October.

'Following several inaccurate and irresponsible press reports, we would like to state clearly that we are satisfied that Dr Roy Phipps had nothing to do with his wife's disappearance,' DI Bill Talbot, the detective in charge of the investigation, told newsmen. 'His own doctors have confirmed that walking and driving would both have been beyond Dr Phipps on the day in question and both Dr Phipps' nanny and his cleaner have given sworn statements confirming that Dr Phipps did not leave the house on the day of his wife's disappearance.'

'What's von Willebrand Disease?' asked Robin.

'A bleeding disorder. I looked it up. You don't clot properly. Gupta remembered that wrong; he thought Roy was a haemophiliac.

'There are three kinds of von Willebrand Disease,' said Strike. 'Type One just means you'd take a bit longer than normal to clot, but it shouldn't leave you bedbound, or unable to drive. I'm assuming Roy Phipps is Type Three, which can be as serious as haemophilia, and could lay him up for a while. But we'll need to check that.

'Anyway,' said Strike, turning over the next page. 'This is Talbot's record of his interview with Roy Phipps.'

'Oh God,' said Robin quietly.

The page was covered in small, slanting writing, but the most distinctive feature of the record were the stars Talbot had drawn all over it.

'See there?' said Strike, running a forefinger down a list of dates that were just discernible amid the scrawls. 'Those are the dates of the Essex Butcher abductions and attempted abductions.

'Talbot loses interest halfway down the list, look. On the twenty-sixth of August 1971, which is when Creed tried to abduct Peggy Hiskett, Roy was able to prove that he and Margot were on holiday in France.

'So that was that, as far as Talbot was concerned. If Roy hadn't tried to abduct Peggy Hiskett, he wasn't the Essex Butcher, and if he wasn't the Essex Butcher, he couldn't have had anything to do with Margot's disappearance.

'But there's a funny thing at the bottom of Talbot's list of dates. All refer to Creed's activities except that last one. He's circled December twenty-seventh, with no year. No idea why he was interested in December twenty-seventh.'

'Or, presumably, why he went Vincent van Gogh all over his report?'

'The stars? Yeah, they're a feature on all Talbot's notes. Very strange. Now,' said Strike, 'let's see how a statement *should* be taken.'

He turned the page and there was a neatly typewritten, double-spaced statement, four pages long, which DI Lawson had taken from Roy Phipps, and which had been duly signed on the final page by the haematologist.

'You needn't read the whole thing now,' said Strike. 'Bottom line is, he stuck to it that he'd been laid up in bed all day, as the cleaner and his nanny would testify.

'But now we go to Wilma Bayliss, the Phippses' cleaner. She also happened to be the St John's practice's cleaner. The rest of the practice didn't know at the time that she'd been doing some private work for Margot and Roy. Gupta told me that he thought Margot might've been encouraging Wilma to leave her husband, and giving her a bit of extra work might've been part of that scheme.'

'Why did she want Wilma to leave her husband?'

'I'm glad you asked that,' said Strike, and he turned over another piece of paper to show a tiny photocopied news clipping, which was dated in Strike's spiky and hard-to-read handwriting: 6 November 1972.

Rapist Jailed

Jules Bayliss, 36, of Leather Lane, Clerkenwell was today sentenced at the Inner London Crown Court to 5 years' jail for 2 counts of rape. Bayliss, who previously served two years in Brixton for aggravated assault, pleaded Not Guilty.

'Ah,' said Robin. 'I see.'

She took another slug of wine.

'Funnily enough,' she added, though she didn't sound amused, 'Creed got five years for his second rape as well. After they let him out, he started killing women as well as raping them.'

'Yeah,' said Strike. 'I know.'

For the second time, he considered questioning the advisability of Robin reading *The Demon of Paradise Park*, but decided against.

'I haven't yet managed to find out what became of Jules Bayliss,' he said, 'and the police notes regarding him are incomplete, so I can't be sure whether he was still in the nick when Margot was abducted.

'What's relevant to us is that Wilma told a different story to Lawson to the one she told Talbot — although Wilma claimed she had, in fact, told Talbot, and that he didn't record it, which is possible, because, as you can see, his note-taking left a lot to be desired.

'Anyway, one of the things she told Lawson was that she'd sponged blood off the spare-room carpet the day Margot disappeared. The other was that she'd seen Roy walking through the garden on the day he was supposedly laid up in bed. She also admitted to Lawson that she hadn't actually seen Roy in bed, but she'd heard him talking from the master bedroom that day.'

'Those are . . . pretty major changes of story.'

'Well, as I say, Wilma's position was that she wasn't changing her story, Talbot simply hadn't recorded it properly. But Lawson seems to have given Wilma a very hard time about it, and he re-interviewed Roy on the strength of what she'd said, too. However, Roy still had Cynthia the nanny as his alibi, who was prepared to swear to the fact that he'd been laid up all day, because she was bringing him regular cups of tea in the master bedroom.'

'I know,' he said, in response to Robin's raised eyebrows. 'Lawson seems to have had the same kind of dirty mind as us. He questioned Phipps on the precise nature of his relationship with Cynthia, which led to an angry outburst from Phipps, who said she was twelve years younger than he was and a cousin to boot.'

It flitted across both Strike's and Robin's minds at this point that there were ten years separating them in age. Both suppressed this unbidden and irrelevant thought.

'According to Roy, the age difference and the blood relationship ought to have constituted a total prohibition on the relationship in the minds of all decent people. But as we know, he managed to overcome those qualms seven years later.

'Lawson also interrogated Roy about the fact that Margot had met an old flame for a drink three weeks before she died. In his rush to exonerate Roy, Talbot hadn't paid too much attention to the account of Oonagh Kennedy—'

'The friend Margot was supposed to be meeting in here?' said Robin.

'Exactly. Oonagh told both Talbot and Lawson that when Roy found out Margot had been for a drink with this old boyfriend, he'd been furious, and that he and Margot weren't talking to each other when she disappeared.

'According to Lawson's notes, Roy didn't like any of this being brought up—'

'Hardly surprising—'

'—and got quite aggressive. However, after speaking to Roy's doctors, Lawson was satisfied that Roy had indeed had a serious episode of bleeding after a fall in a hospital car park, and would have found it well nigh impossible to drive to Clerkenwell that evening, let alone kill or kidnap his wife.'

'He could have hired someone,' suggested Robin.

'They checked his bank accounts and couldn't find any suspicious payments, but that obviously doesn't mean he didn't find a way. He's a haematologist; he won't be lacking in brains.'

Strike took a further swig of beer.

'So that's the husband,' he said, flipping over the four pages of Roy's statement. 'Now for the old flame.'

'God above,' said Robin, looking down at another press photograph.

The man's thick, wavy hair reached well past his shoulders. He stood, unsmiling, with his hands on his narrow hips beside a painting of what appeared to be two writhing lovers. His shirt was open almost to his navel and his jeans were skin tight at the crotch and extremely wide at the ankle.

'I thought you'd enjoy that,' said Strike, grinning at Robin's reaction. 'He's Paul Satchwell, an artist – though not a very highbrow one, by the sounds of it. When the press got onto him, he was designing a mural for a nightclub. He's Margot's ex.'

'She's just gone *right* down in my estimation,' muttered Robin.

'Don't judge her too harshly. She met him when she was a Bunny Girl, so she was only nineteen or twenty. He was six years older than her and probably seemed like the height of sophistication.'

'In *that* shirt?'

'That's a publicity photo for his art show,' said Strike. 'It says so below. Possibly he didn't show as much chest hair in day-to-day life. The press got quite excited at the thought an ex-lover might be involved, and let's face it, a bloke who looked like that was a gift to the tabloids.'

Strike turned to another example of Talbot's chaotic note-taking, which like the first was covered in five-pointed stars and had the same list of dates, with scribbled annotations beside them.

'As you can see, Talbot didn't start with anything as mundane as "Where were you at a quarter to six on the night Margot disappeared?" He goes straight into the Essex Butcher dates, and when Satchwell told him he was celebrating a friend's thirtieth birthday on September the eleventh, which was when Susan Meyer was abducted, Talbot basically stopped asking him questions. But once again, we've got a date unconnected with Creed heavily circled at the bottom, with a gigantic cross beside it. April the sixteenth this time.'

'Where was Satchwell living when Margot disappeared?'

'Camden,' said Strike, turning the page to reveal, again, a conventional typewritten statement. 'There you go, look, it's in his statement to Lawson. Not all that far from Clerkenwell.

'To Lawson, Satchwell explained that after a gap of eight years, he and Margot met by chance in the street and decided to go for a catch-up drink. He was quite open with Lawson about this, presumably because he knew Oonagh or Roy would already have told them about it. He even told Lawson he'd have been keen to resume an affair with Margot, which seems a bit *too* helpful, although it was probably meant to prove he had nothing to hide. He said he and Margot had a volatile relationship for a couple of years when she was much younger, and that Margot finally ended it for good when she met Roy.

'Satchwell's alibi checked out. He told Lawson he was alone in his studio, which was also in Camden, for most of the afternoon on the day Margot disappeared, but took a phone call there round about five. Landlines – far harder to monkey about with than mobiles when you're trying to set up an alibi. Satchwell ate in a local café, where he was known, at half past six, and witnesses agreed they'd seen him. He then went home to change before meeting some friends in a bar around eight. The people he claimed to have been with confirmed it all and Lawson was satisfied that Satchwell was in the clear.

'Which brings us to the third, and, I'd have to say, most promising suspect – always excepting Dennis Creed. This,' said Strike, moving Satchwell's statement from the top of a now greatly diminished pile of paper, 'is Steve Douthwaite.'

If Roy Phipps would have been a lazy casting director's idea of a sensitive poet, and Paul Satchwell the very image of a seventies rock star, Steve Douthwaite would have been hired without hesitation to play the cheeky chap, the wisecracking upstart, the working-class Jack the Lad. He had dark, beady eyes, an infectious grin and a spiky mullet that reminded Robin of the young men featured on an old Bay City Rollers LP which Robin's mother, to her children's hilarity, still cherished. Douthwaite was holding a pint in one hand, and his other arm was slung around the shoulder of a man whose face had been cropped from the picture, but whose suit, like Douthwaite's, looked cheap, creased and shiny. Douthwaite had loosened his kipper tie and undone his top shirt button to reveal a neck chain.

'Ladykiller' Salesman Sought Over Missing Doctor

Police are anxious to trace the whereabouts of double-glazing salesman Steve Douthwaite, who has vanished following routine questioning over the disappearance of Dr Margot Bamborough, 29.

Douthwaite, 28, left no forwarding address after quitting his job and his flat in Percival Street, Clerkenwell.

A former patient of the missing doctor's, Douthwaite raised suspicion at the medical practice because of his frequent visits to see the pretty blonde doctor. Friends of the salesman describe him as 'smooth talking' and do not believe Douthwaite suffered any serious health issues. Douthwaite is believed to have sent Dr Bamborough gifts.

Douthwaite, who was raised in foster care, has had no contact with friends since February 7th. Police are believed to have searched Douthwaite's home since he vacated it.

Tragic Affair

'He caused a lot of trouble round here, a lot of bad feeling,' said a co-worker at Diamond Double Glazing, who asked not to be named. 'Real Jack the Lad. He had an affair with another guy's wife. She ended up taking an overdose, left her kids without a mum. Nobody was sorry when Douthwaite took off, to be honest. We were happy to see the back of him. Too interested in booze and girls and not much cop at the job.'

Doctor Would Be 'A Challenge'

Asked what he thought Douthwaite's relationship with the missing doctor had been, his co-worker said,

'Chasing girls is all Steve cares about. He'd think a doctor was a challenge, knowing him.'

Police are eager to speak to Douthwaite again and appeal to any members of the public who might know his whereabouts.

When Robin had finished reading, Strike, who'd just finished his first pint, said,

'Want another drink?'

'I'll get these,' said Robin.

She went to the bar, where she waited beneath the hanging skulls and fake cobwebs. The barman had painted his face like Frankenstein's monster. Robin ordered drinks absent-mindedly, thinking about the Douthwaite article.

When she'd returned to Strike with a fresh pint, a wine and two packets of crisps, she said,

'You know, that article isn't fair.'

'Go on.'

'People don't necessarily tell their co-workers about their medical problems. Maybe Douthwaite *did* seem fine to his mates when they were all down the pub. That doesn't mean he didn't have anything wrong with him. He might have been mentally ill.'

'Not for the first time,' said Strike, 'you're bang on the money.'

He searched the small number of photocopied papers remaining in his pile and extracted another handwritten document, far neater than Talbot's and devoid of doodles and random dates. Somehow Robin knew, before Strike had said a word, that this fluid, rounded handwriting belonged to Margot Bamborough.

'Copies of Douthwaite's medical records,' said Strike. 'The police got hold of them. "Headaches, upset stomach, weight loss, palpitations, nausea, nightmares, trouble sleeping",' Strike read out. 'Margot's conclusion, on visit four – see there? – is "personal and employment-related difficulties, under severe strain, exhibiting signs of anxiety".'

'Well, his married girlfriend had killed herself,' said Robin. 'That'd knock anyone except a psychopath for six, wouldn't it?'

Charlotte slid like a shadow across Strike's mind.

'Yeah, you'd think. Also, look there. He'd been the victim of an assault shortly before his first visit to Margot. "Contusions, cracked rib." I smell angry, bereaved and betrayed husband.'

'But the paper makes it sound as though he was stalking Margot.'

'Well,' said Strike, tapping the photocopy of Douthwaite's medical notes, 'there are a hell of a lot of visits here. He saw her three times in one week. He's anxious, guilty, feeling unpopular, probably didn't expect his bit of fun to end in the woman's death. And there's a good-looking doctor offering no judgement, but kindness and support. I don't think it's beyond the realms of possibility to think he might have developed feelings for her.

'And look at this,' Strike went on, turning over the medical records to show Robin more typed statements. 'These are from Dorothy and Gloria, who both said Douthwaite came out of her room the last time he saw Margot, looking – well, this is Dorothy,' he said, and he read aloud, '"*I observed Mr Douthwaite leaving Dr Bamborough's surgery and noticed that he looked as though he had had a shock. I thought he also looked angry and distressed. As he walked out, he tripped over the toy truck of a boy in the waiting room and swore loudly. He seemed distracted and unaware of his surroundings.*" And Gloria,' said Strike, turning over the page, 'says: "*I remember Mr Douthwaite leaving because he swore at a little boy. He looked as though he had just been given bad news. I thought he seemed scared and angry.*"

'Now, Margot's notes of her last consultation with Douthwaite don't mention anything but the same old stress-related symptoms,' Strike went on, turning back to the medical records, 'so she definitely hadn't just diagnosed him with anything life-threatening. Lawson speculated that she might've felt he was getting over-attached, and told him he had to stop taking up valuable time that could be given to other patients, which Douthwaite didn't like hearing. Maybe he'd convinced himself his feelings were reciprocated. All the evidence suggests he was in a fragile mental state at the time.

'Anyway, four days after Douthwaite's last appointment, Margot vanishes. Tipped off by the surgery that there was a patient who seemed a bit over-fond of her, Talbot called him in for questioning. Here we go.'

Once again, Strike extracted a star-strewn scrawl from amid the typewritten pages.

'As usual, Talbot starts the interrogation by running through the list of Creed dates. Trouble is, Douthwaite doesn't seem to remember what he was doing on any of them.'

'If he was already ill with stress—' began Robin.

'Well, exactly,' said Strike. 'Being interrogated by a police officer who thinks you might be the Essex Butcher wouldn't help your anxiety, would it?

'And look at this, Talbot adds a random date again: twenty-first February. But he also does something else. Can you make anything of that?'

Robin took the page from Strike and examined the last three lines of writing.

'Pitman shorthand,' said Robin.

'Can you read it?'

'No. I know a bit of Teeline; I never learned Pitman. Pat can do it, though.'

'You're saying she might be useful for once?'

'Oh sod off, Strike,' said Robin, crossly. 'You want to go back to temps, fine, but I like getting accurate messages and knowing the filing's up to date.'

She took a photograph on her phone and texted it to Pat, along with a request to translate it. Strike, meanwhile, was reflecting that Robin had never before called him 'Strike' when annoyed. Perversely, it had sounded more intimate than the use of his first name. He'd quite enjoyed it.

'Sorry for impugning Pat,' he said.

'I just told you to sod off,' said Robin, failing to suppress a smile. 'What did Lawson make of Douthwaite?'

'Well, unsurprisingly, when he tried to interview him and found out he'd left his flat and job, leaving no forwarding address, he got quite interested in him. Hence the tip-off to the papers. They were trying to flush him out.'

'And did it work?' asked Robin, now eating crisps.

'It did. Douthwaite turned up at a police station in Waltham Forest the day after the "Ladykiller" article appeared, probably terrified he'd soon have Fleet Street and Scotland Yard on his doorstep. He told them he was unemployed and living in a bedsit. Local police called Lawson, who went straight over there to interview him.

'There's a full account here,' said Strike, pushing some of the last pages of the roll he had brought with him towards Robin. 'All written by Lawson: "appears scared" – "evasive" – "nervous" – "sweating" – and the alibi's not good. Douthwaite says that on the afternoon of Margot's disappearance he was out looking for a new flat.'

'He claims he was already looking for a new place when she disappeared?'

'Coincidence, eh? Except that upon closer questioning he couldn't say which flats he'd seen and couldn't come up with the name of anyone who'd remember seeing him. In the end he said his flat-hunting had involved sitting in a local café and circling ads in the paper. Trouble was, nobody in the café remembered him being there.

'He said he'd moved to Waltham Forest because he had bad associations with Clerkenwell after being interviewed by Talbot and made to feel as though he was under suspicion, and that, in any case, things hadn't been good for him at work since his affair with the co-worker's suicidal wife.'

'Well, that's credible enough,' said Robin.

'Lawson interviewed him twice more, but got nothing else out of him. Douthwaite came lawyered up to interview three. At that point, Lawson backed off. After all, they had nothing on Douthwaite, even if he was the fishiest person they interviewed. And it was – just – credible that the reason nobody had noticed him in the café was because it was a busy place.'

A group of drinkers in Hallowe'en costumes now entered the pub, giggling and clearly already full of alcohol. Robin noticed Strike casting an automatic eye over a young blonde in a rubber nurse's uniform.

'So,' she said, 'is that everything?'

'Almost,' said Strike, 'but I'm tempted not to show you this.'

'Why not?'

'Because I think it's going to feed your obsession with holy places.'

'I'm not—'

'OK, but before you look at it, just remember that nutters are always attracted by murders and missing person cases, all right?'

'Fine,' said Robin. 'Show me.'

Strike flipped over the piece of paper. It was a photocopy of the crudest kind of anonymous note, featuring letters cut out of magazines.

If YOU WaNt TO kNOw WhEre MɑrgOt BaamBorOu gh IS bURied DiG hERe

'Another St John's Cross,' said Robin.

'Yep. That arrived at Scotland Yard in 1985, addressed to Lawson, who'd already retired. Nothing else in the envelope.'

Robin sighed and leaned back in her chair.

'Nutter, obviously,' said Strike, now tapping his photocopied articles and statements back into a pile and rolling them up again. 'If you really knew where a body was buried, you'd include a bloody map.'

It was nearly six o'clock now, close to the hour at which a doctor had once left her practice and had never been seen again. The frosted pub windows were inky blue. Up at the bar, the blonde in the rubber uniform was giggling at something a man dressed as the Joker had told her.

'You know,' said Robin, glancing down at the papers sitting beside Strike's pint, 'she was late . . . it was pouring with rain . . .'

'Go on,' said Strike, wondering whether she was about to say exactly what he'd been thinking.

'Her friend was waiting in here, alone. Margot's late. She would've wanted to get here as quickly as possible. The simplest, most plausible explanation I can think of is that somebody offered her a lift. A car pulled up—'

'Or a van,' said Strike. Robin had, indeed, reached the same conclusion he had. 'Someone she knew—'

'Or someone who seemed safe. An elderly man—'

'Or what she thinks is a woman.'

'Exactly,' said Robin.

She turned a sad face to Strike.

'That's it. She either knew the driver, or the stranger seemed safe.'

'And who'd remember that?' said Strike. 'She was wearing a nondescript raincoat, carrying an umbrella. A vehicle pulls up. She bends down to the window, then gets in. No fight. No conflict. The car drives away.'

'And only the driver would know what happened next,' said Robin.

Her mobile rang: it was Pat Chauncey.

'She always does that,' said Strike. 'Text her, and she doesn't text back, she calls—'

'Does it matter?' said Robin, exasperated, and answered.

'Hi, Pat. Sorry to bother you out of hours. Did you get my text?'

'Yeah,' croaked Pat. 'Where did you find that?'

'It's in some old police notes. Can you translate it?'

'Yeah,' said Pat, 'but it doesn't make much sense.'

'Hang on, Pat, I want Cormoran to hear this,' said Robin, and she changed to speakerphone.

'Ready?' came Pat's rasping voice.

'Yes,' said Robin. Strike pulled out a pen and flipped over his roll of paper so that he could write on the blank side.

'It says: *"And that is the last of them, comma, the twelfth, comma, and the circle will be closed upon finding the tenth, comma"* – and then there's a word I can't read, I don't think it's proper Pitman – and after that another word, which phonetically says Ba – fom – et, full stop. Then a new sentence, *"Transcribe in the true book."*'

'Baphomet,' repeated Strike.

'Yeah,' said Pat.

'That's a name,' said Strike. 'Baphomet is an occult deity.'

'OK, well, that's what it says,' said Pat, matter-of-factly.

Robin thanked her and rang off.

'*"And that is the last of them, the twelfth, and the circle will be closed upon finding the tenth – unknown word – Baphomet. Transcribe in the true book,"*' Strike read back.

'How d'you know about Baphomet?' asked Robin.

'Whittaker was interested in all that shit.'

'Oh,' said Robin.

Whittaker was the last of Strike's mother's lovers, the man Strike believed had administered the overdose that had killed her.

'He had a copy of *The Satanic Bible*,' said Strike. 'It had a picture of Baphomet's head in a penta – shit,' he said, rifling back through the loose pages to find one of those on which Talbot had doodled many five-pointed stars. He frowned at it for a moment, then looked up at Robin.

'I don't think these are stars. They're pentagrams.'

PART THREE

. . . Winter, clothëd all in frieze . . .

Edmund Spenser
The Faerie Queene

15

Wherein old dints of deepe woundes did remaine . . .
                                        Edmund Spenser
                                        The Faerie Queene

In the second week of November, Joan's chemotherapy caused her white blood cell count to plummet dangerously, and she was admitted to hospital. Strike left Robin in charge of the agency, Lucy left her three sons in the care of her husband, and both hurried back to Cornwall.

Strike's fresh absence coincided with the monthly team meeting, which for the first time Robin led alone, the youngest and arguably least experienced investigator at the agency, and the only woman.

Robin wasn't sure whether she had imagined it, but she thought Hutchins and Morris, the two ex-policemen, put up slightly more disagreement about the next month's rota, and about the line they ought to take on Shifty, than they would have done had Strike been there. It was Robin's opinion that Shifty's PA, who'd now been extensively wined and dined at the agency's expense without revealing anything about the hold her boss might have over his CEO, ought to be abandoned as a possible source. She'd decided that Morris ought to see her one last time to wrap things up, allaying any suspicion about what he'd been after, after which Robin thought it time to try and infiltrate Shifty's social circle with a view to getting information direct from the man they were investigating. Barclay was the only subcontractor who agreed with Robin, and backed her up when she insisted that Morris was to leave Shifty's PA well alone. Of course, as Robin was well aware, she and Barclay had once gone digging for a body together, and such things create a bond.

The memory of the team meeting was still bothering her as she sat with her legs up on the sofa in the flat in Finborough Road later, now in pyjamas and a dressing gown, working on her laptop. Wolfgang the dachshund was curled at her bare feet, keeping them warm.

Max was out. He'd suddenly announced the previous week-end that he feared he was in danger of passing from 'introvert' to 'recluse', and had accepted an invitation to go to dinner with some actor friends, even though, in his bitter words on parting, 'They'll all be pitying me, but I suppose they'll enjoy that'. Robin had taken Wolfgang for a quick walk around the block at eleven, but otherwise had spent her evening on the Bamborough case, for which she'd had no time while Strike had been in St Mawes, because the other four cases on the agency's books were absorbing all working hours.

Robin hadn't been out since her birthday drinks with Ilsa and Vanessa, which hadn't been as enjoyable as she'd hoped. The conversation had revolved entirely around relationships, because Vanessa had arrived with a brand-new engagement ring on her finger. Since then, Robin had used pressure of work during Strike's absence to avoid nights out with either of her friends. Her cousin Katie's words, *it's like you're travelling in a different direction to the rest of us*, were hard to forget, but the truth was that Robin didn't want to stand in a bar while Ilsa and Vanessa encouraged her to respond to the advances of some overfamiliar, Morris-like man with a line in easy patter and bad jokes.

She and Strike had now divided between them the people they wished to trace and re-interview in the Bamborough case. Unfortunately, Robin now knew that at least four of her allocated people had passed beyond the reach of questioning.

After careful cross-referencing of old records, Robin had managed to identify the Willy Lomax who'd been the long-serving handyman of St James's Church, Clerkenwell. He'd died in 1989 and Robin had so far been unable to find a single confirmed relative.

Albert Shimmings, the florist and possible driver of the speeding van seen on the night of Margot's disappearance, had also passed away, but Robin had emailed two men she believed to be his sons. She sincerely hoped she'd correctly identified them, otherwise an insurance agent and a driving instructor were both about to get truly mystifying messages. Neither had yet responded to her request to talk to them.

Wilma Bayliss, the ex-practice cleaner, had died in 2003. A mother of two sons and three daughters, she'd divorced Jules Bayliss in 1975. By the time she died, Wilma hadn't been a cleaner, but a social worker, and she'd raised a high-achieving family, including an architect, a paramedic, a teacher, another social worker and a Labour councillor. One of the sons now lived in Germany, but Robin nevertheless included him in the emails and Facebook messages she sent out to all five siblings. There'd been no response so far.

Dorothy Oakden, the practice secretary, had been ninety-one when she died in a North London nursing home. Robin hadn't yet managed to trace Carl, her only child.

Meanwhile, Margot's ex-boyfriend, Paul Satchwell, and the receptionist, Gloria Conti, were proving strangely and similarly elusive. At first Robin had been relieved when she'd failed to find a death certificate for either of them, but after combing telephone directories, census records, county court judgments, marriage and divorce certificates, press archives, social media and lists of company staff, she'd come up with nothing. The only possible explanations Robin could think of were changes of name (in Gloria's case, possibly by marriage) and emigration.

As for Mandy White, the schoolgirl who'd claimed to have seen Margot at a rainy window, there were so many Amanda Whites of approximately the right age to be found online that Robin was starting to despair of ever finding the right one. Robin found this line of inquiry particularly frustrating, firstly because there was a good chance that White was no longer Mandy's surname, and secondly because, like the police before her, Robin thought it highly unlikely that Mandy had actually seen Margot at the window that night.

Having examined and discounted the Facebook accounts of another six Amanda Whites, Robin yawned, stretched and decided she was owed a break. Setting her laptop down on a side table, she swung her legs carefully off the sofa so as not to disturb Wolfgang, and crossed the open-plan area that combined kitchen, dining and living rooms, to make herself one of the low-calorie hot chocolates she was trying to convince herself was a treat, because she was still, in the middle of this long, sedentary stretch of surveillance, trying to keep an eye on her waistline.

As she stirred the unappetising powder into boiling water, a whiff of tuberose mingled with the scent of synthetic caramel. In spite of her bath, Fracas still lingered in her hair and on her pyjamas. This perfume, she'd finally decided, had been a costly mistake. Living in a dense cloud of tuberose made her feel not only perpetually on the verge of a headache, but also as though she were wearing fur and pearls in broad daylight.

Robin's mobile, which was lying on the sofa beside Wolfgang, rang as she picked up her laptop again. Startled from his sleep, the disgruntled dog rose on arthritic legs. Robin lifted him to safety before picking up her phone and seeing, to her disappointment, that it wasn't Strike, but Morris.

'Hi, Saul.'

Ever since the birthday kiss, Robin had tried to keep her manner on the colder side of professional when dealing with Morris.

'Hey, Robs. You said to call if I had anything, even if it was late.'

'Yes, of course.' *I never said you could call me 'Robs', though.* 'What's happened?' asked Robin, looking around for a pen.

'I got Gemma drunk tonight. Shifty's PA, you know. Under the influence, she told me she thinks Shifty's got something on his boss.'

Well, that's hardly news, thought Robin, abandoning the fruitless search for a writing implement.

'What makes her think so?'

'Apparently he's said stuff to her like, "Oh, he'll always take *my* calls, don't worry", and "I know where all the bodies are buried".'

An image of a cross of St John slid across Robin's mind and was dismissed.

'As a joke,' Morris added. 'He passed it off like he was joking, but it made Gemma think.'

'But she doesn't know any details?'

'No, but listen, seriously, give me a bit more time and I reckon I'll be able to persuade her to wear a wire for us. Not to blow my own horn here – can't reach, for one thing – no, seriously,' he said, although Robin hadn't laughed, 'I've got her properly softened up. Just give me a bit more time—'

'Look, I'm sorry, Saul, but we went over this at the meeting,' Robin reminded Morris, suppressing a yawn, which made her eyes water. 'The client doesn't want us to tell any of the employees we're investigating this, so we can't tell her who you are. Pressuring her to investigate her own boss is asking her to risk her job. It also risks blowing the whole case if she decides to tell him what's going on.'

'But again, not to toot—'

'Saul, it's one thing her confiding in you when she's drunk,' said Robin (why wasn't he listening? They'd been through this endlessly at the team meeting). 'It's another asking a girl with no investigative training to work for us.'

'She's all over me, Robin,' said Morris earnestly. 'It'd be crazy not to use her.'

Robin suddenly wondered whether Morris had slept with the girl. Strike had been quite clear that that wasn't to happen. She sank back down on the sofa. Her copy of *The Demon of Paradise Park* was warm, she noticed, from the dachshund lying on it. The displaced Wolfgang was now gazing at Robin from under the dining table, with the sad, reproachful eyes of an old man.

'Saul, I really think it's time for Hutchins to take over, to see what he can do with Shifty himself,' said Robin.

'OK, but before we make that decision, let me ring Strike and—'

'You're not ringing Strike,' said Robin, her temper rising. 'His aunt's – he's got enough on his plate in Cornwall.'

'You're so sweet,' said Morris, with a little laugh, 'but I promise you, Strike would want a say in this—'

'He left me in charge,' said Robin, anger rising now, 'and I'm telling you, you've taken it as far as you can with that girl. She doesn't know anything useful and trying to push her further could backfire badly on this agency. I'm asking you to give it up now, please. You can take over on Postcard tomorrow night, and I'll tell Andy to get to work on Shifty.'

There was a pause.

'I've upset you, haven't I?' said Morris.

'No, you haven't upset me,' said Robin. After all, 'upset' wasn't quite the same as 'enrage'.

'I didn't want to—'

'You haven't, Saul, I'm only reminding you what we agreed at the meeting.'

'OK,' he said. 'All right. Hey – listen. Did you hear about the boss who told his secretary the company was in trouble?'

'No,' said Robin, through clenched teeth.

'He said, "I'm going to have to lay you or Jack off." She said, "Well, you'll have to jack off, because I've got a headache."'

'Ha ha,' said Robin. 'Night, Saul.'

Why did I say 'ha ha'? she asked herself furiously, as she set down her mobile. *Why didn't I just say, 'Stop telling me crap jokes?' Or say nothing! And why did I say sorry when I was asking him to do what we all agreed at the meeting? Why am I cossetting him?*

She thought of all those times she'd pretended with Matthew. Faking orgasms had been nothing compared to pretending to find him funny and interesting through all those twice-told tales of rugby club jokes, through every anecdote designed to show him as the cleverest or the funniest man in the room. *Why do we do it?* she asked herself, picking up *The Demon of Paradise Park* without considering what she was doing. *Why do we work so hard to keep the peace, to keep them happy?*

Because, suggested the seven ghostly black and white faces behind Dennis Creed's, *they can turn nasty, Robin. You know just how nasty they can turn, with your scar up your arm and your memory of that gorilla mask.*

But she knew that wasn't why she'd humoured Morris, not really. She didn't expect him to become abusive or violent if she refused to laugh at his stupid jokes. No, this was something else. The only girl in a family of boys, Robin had been raised, she knew, to keep everyone happy, in spite of the fact that her own mother had been quite the women's libber. Nobody had meant to do it, but she'd realised during the therapy she'd undertaken after the attack that had left her forearm forever scarred, that her family role had been that of 'easy child', the non-complainer, the conciliator. She'd been born just a year before Martin, who had been the Ellacotts' 'problem child': the most scattered and impetuous, the least academic and conscientious, the son who still lived at home at twenty-eight and the brother with whom she had least in common. (Though Martin had punched Matthew on the nose on her wedding day, and the last time she'd been home she'd found herself hugging him when he offered, on hearing how difficult Matthew was being about the divorce, to do it again.)

Wintry specks of rain were dotting the window behind the dining table. Wolfgang was fast asleep again. Robin couldn't face perusing the social media accounts of another fifty Amanda Whites tonight. As she picked up *The Demon of Paradise Park*, she hesitated. She'd made a rule for herself (because it had been a long, hard journey to reach the place where she was now, and she didn't want to lose her current good state of mental health) not to read this book after dark, or right before bed. After all, the information it contained could be found summarised online: there was no need to hear in his own words what Creed had done to each of the women he'd tortured and killed.

Nevertheless, she picked up her hot chocolate, opened the book to the page she had marked with a Tesco receipt, and began to read at the point she'd left off three days previously.

> Convinced that Bamborough had fallen victim to the serial killer now dubbed the Essex Butcher, Talbot made enemies among his colleagues with what they felt was his obsessive focus on one theory.
>
> 'They called it early retirement,' said a colleague, 'but it was basically dismissal. They said he wasn't interested in anything other than the Butcher, but here we are, 9 years on, and no-one's ever found a better explanation, have they?'
>
> Margot Bamborough's family failed to positively identify any of the unclaimed jewellery and underwear found in Creed's basement flat when he was arrested in 1976, although Bamborough's husband, Dr Roy Phipps, thought a tarnished silver locket which

had been crushed, possibly by blunt force, might have resembled one that the doctor was believed to have been wearing when she disappeared.

However, a recently published account of Bamborough's life, *Whatever Happened to Margot Bamborough?* [4] written by the son of a close friend of the doctor, contains revelations about the doctor's private life which suggest a new line of enquiry – and a possible connection with Creed. Shortly before her disappearance, Margot Bamborough booked herself into the Bride Street Nursing Home in Islington, a private facility which in 1974 provided discreet abortions.

16

Behold the man, and tell me Britomart,
If ay more goodly creature thou didst see;
How like a Gyaunt in each manly part
Beares he himselfe with portly maiestee . . .

Edmund Spenser
The Faerie Queene

Four days later, at a quarter past five in the morning, the 'Night Riviera' sleeper train pulled into Paddington station. Strike, who'd slept poorly, had spent long stretches of the night watching the ghostly grey blur of the so-called English Riviera slide past his compartment window. Having slept on top of the covers with his prosthesis still attached, he turned down the proffered breakfast on its plastic tray, and was among the first passengers to disembark into the station, kit bag over his shoulder.

There was a nip of frost in the early morning air and Strike's breath rose in a cloud before him as he walked down the platform, Brunel's steel arches curving above him like the ribs of a blue whale's skeleton, cold dark sky visible through the glass ceiling. Unshaven and slightly uncomfortable on the stump that had missed its usual nightly application of soothing cream, Strike headed for a bench, sat down, lit a much-needed cigarette, pulled out his mobile and phoned Robin.

He knew she'd be awake, because she'd just spent the night parked in Strike's BMW outside the house of the weatherman, watching for Postcard. They'd communicated mostly by text while he'd been in Cornwall, while he divided his time between the hospital in Truro

165

and the house in St Mawes, taking it in turns with Lucy to sit with Joan, whose hair had now fallen out and whose immune system appeared to have collapsed under the weight of the chemotherapy, and to minister to Ted, who was barely eating. Before returning to London, Strike had cooked a large batch of curry, which he left in the freezer, alongside shepherd's pies made by Lucy. When he raised his cigarette to his mouth he could still smell a trace of cumin on his fingers, and if he concentrated, he could conjure up the deadly smell of hospital disinfectant underlain with a trace of urine, instead of cold iron, diesel and the distant waftings of coffee from a nearby Starbucks.

'Hi,' said Robin, and at the sound of her voice Strike felt, as he had known he would, a slight easing of the knot of tension in his stomach. 'What's happened?'

'Nothing,' he said, slightly surprised, before he recollected that it was half past five in the morning. 'Oh – yeah, sorry, this isn't an emergency call, I've just got off the sleeper. Wondered whether you fancied getting breakfast before you head home to bed.'

'Oh, that'd be wonderful,' said Robin, with such genuine pleasure that Strike felt a little less tired, 'because I've got Bamborough news.'

'Great,' said Strike, 'so've I. Be good to have a catch-up.'

'How's Joan?'

'Not great. They let her go home yesterday. They've assigned her a Macmillan nurse. Ted's really low. Lucy's still down there.'

'You could've stayed,' said Robin. 'We can cope.'

'It's fine,' he said, screwing his eyes up against his own smoke. A shaft of wintry sunlight burst through a break in the clouds and illuminated the fag butts on the tiled floor. 'I've told them I'll go back for Christmas. Where d'you want to meet?'

'Well, I was planning to go to the National Portrait Gallery before I went home, so—'

'You were what?' said Strike.

'Planning to go to the National Portrait Gallery. I'll explain when I see you. Would you mind if we meet somewhere near there?'

'I can get anywhere,' said Strike, 'I'm right by the Tube. I'll head that way and whoever finds a café first can text the other.'

Forty-five minutes later, Robin entered Notes café, which lay on St Martin's Lane and was already crowded, though it was so early in the morning. Wooden tables, some of them as large as the one in her parents' kitchen in Yorkshire, were crammed with young people with laptops and businessmen grabbing breakfast before work. As she queued at the long counter, she tried to ignore the various pastries and cakes spread out beneath it: she'd taken sandwiches with her to her overnight surveillance of the weatherman's house, and those, she told herself sternly, ought to suffice.

Having ordered a cappuccino, she headed for the back of the café, where Strike sat reading *The Times* beneath an iron chandelier that resembled a large spider. She seemed to have forgotten over the previous six days how large he was. Hunched over the newspaper, he reminded her of a black bear, stubble thick on his face, tucking into a bacon and egg ciabatta roll, and Robin felt a wave of liking simply for the way he looked. Or perhaps, she thought, she was merely reacting against clean-jawed, slim and conventionally handsome men who, like tuberose perfumes, seemed attractive until prolonged exposure made you crave escape.

'Hi,' she said, sliding into the seat opposite him.

Strike looked up, and in that moment, her long shining hair and her aura of good health acted upon him like an antidote to the fug of clinical decay in which he had spent the past five days.

'You don't look knackered enough to have been up all night.'

'I'll take that as a compliment and not as an accusation,' said Robin, eyebrows raised. 'I *was* up all night and Postcard still hasn't shown herself – or himself – but another card came yesterday, addressed to the television studio. It said Postcard loved the way he smiled at the end of Tuesday's weather report.'

Strike grunted.

Robin said, 'D'you want to go first on Bamborough, or shall I?'

'You first,' said Strike, still chewing, 'I'm starving.'

'OK,' said Robin. 'Well, I've got good news and bad. The bad news is nearly everyone I've been trying to trace is dead, and the rest might as well be.'

She filled Strike in on the deceased status of Willy Lomax, Albert

Shimmings, Wilma Bayliss and Dorothy Oakden, and on the steps she'd taken, so far, to contact their relatives.

'Nobody's got back in touch except one of Shimmings' sons, who seems worried that we're journalists trying to pin Margot's disappearance on his father. I've written a reassuring email back. Hope it works.'

Strike, who had paused in his steady demolition of the roll to drink half a mug of tea, said,

'I've been having similar problems. That "two women struggling by the phone boxes" sighting is going to be nigh on impossible to check. Ruby Elliot, who saw them, and the Fleury mother and daughter, who almost certainly *were* them, are all dead as well. But they've both got living descendants, so I've fired off a few messages. Only one response so far, from a Fleury grandson who doesn't know what the hell I'm talking about. And Dr Brenner doesn't seem to have a single living relative that I can see. Never married, no kids, and a dead sister who didn't marry, either.'

'D'you know how many women there are out there called Amanda White?' sighed Robin.

'I can imagine,' said Strike, taking another large bite of roll. 'That's why I gave her to you.'

'You—?'

'I'm kidding,' he said, smirking at her expression. 'What about Paul Satchwell and Gloria Conti?'

'Well, if they're dead, they didn't die in the UK. But here's something really weird: I can't find a single mention of either of them after '75.'

'Coincidence,' said Strike, raising his eyebrows. 'Douthwaite, he of the stress headaches and the dead mistress, has disappeared as well. He's either abroad, or he's changed his identity. Can't find any address for him after '76, and no death certificate, either. Mind you, if I were in his shoes, I might've changed my name, as well. His press reviews weren't good, were they? Crap at his job, sleeping with a colleague's wife, sending flowers to a woman who then disappears—'

'We don't know it was flowers,' said Robin, into her coffee cup. *Other kinds of presents are available, Strike.*

'Chocolates, then. Same applies. Harder to see why Satchwell and Conti took themselves off the radar, though,' said Strike, running his hand over his unshaven chin. 'The press interest in them died away fairly fast. And you'd have found Conti online if it was a simple case of a married name. There can't be as many "Gloria Contis" as there are Amanda Whites.'

'I've been wondering whether she went to live in Italy,' said Robin. 'Her dad's first name was Ricardo. She could've had relatives there. I've sent off a few Facebook enquiries to some Contis, but the only people who've responded so far don't know a Gloria. I'm pretending I'm doing genealogical research, because I'm worried she might not respond if I mention Margot straight off.'

'Think you're probably right,' said Strike, adding more sugar to his tea. 'Yeah, Italy's a good idea. She was young, might've fancied a change of scene. Satchwell disappearing's odd, though. That photo didn't suggest a shy man. You'd think he'd have popped up some-where by now, advertising his paintings.'

'I've checked art exhibitions, auctions, galleries. It really is as though he dematerialised.'

'Well, I've made *some* progress,' said Strike, swallowing the last mouthful of his roll and pulling out his notebook. 'You can get a surprising amount of work done, sitting around in a hospital. I've found four living witnesses, and one of them's already agreed to talk: Gregory Talbot, son of Bill who went off his rocker and drew pen-tagrams all over the case file. I explained who I am and who hired me, and Gregory's quite amenable to a chat. I'm going over there on Saturday, if you want to come.'

'I can't,' said Robin, disappointed. 'Morris and Andy have both got family stuff on. Barclay and I have got to cover the weekend.'

'Ah,' said Strike, 'shame. Well, I've also found two of the women who worked with Margot at the practice,' said Strike, turning a page in his notebook. 'The nurse, Janice, is still going by her first married name, which helped. The address Gupta gave me was an old one, but I traced her from there. She's now in Nightingale Grove—'

'Very appropriate,' said Robin.

'—in Hither Green. And Irene Bull's now Mrs Irene Hickson,

widow of a man who ran a successful building contractor's. She's living in Circus Street, Greenwich.'

'Have you phoned them?'

'I decided to write first,' said Strike. 'Older women, both living alone – I've set out who we are and who's hired us, so they've got time to check us out, make sure we're kosher, maybe check with Anna.'

'Good thinking,' said Robin.

'And I'm going to do the same with Oonagh Kennedy, the woman waiting for Margot in the pub that night, once I'm sure I've got the right one. Anna said she was in Wolverhampton, but the woman I've found is in Alnwick. She's the right age, but she's a retired *vicar.*'

Robin grinned at Strike's expression, which was a mixture of suspicion and distaste.

'What's wrong with vicars?'

'Nothing,' he said, adding a moment later, 'much. Depends on the vicar. But Oonagh was a Bunny Girl back in the sixties. She was standing beside Margot in one of the pictures the press used, named in one of the captions. Don't you think the transition from Bunny Girl to vicar is fairly unlikely?'

'Interesting life trajectory,' Robin admitted, 'but you're speaking to a temporary secretary who became a full-time detective. And speaking of Oonagh,' she added, drawing her copy of *The Demon of Paradise Park* out of her handbag and opening it. 'I wanted to show you something. There,' she said, holding it out to him. 'Read the bit I've marked with pencil.'

'I've already read the whole book,' said Strike. 'Which bit—?'

'Please,' Robin insisted, 'just read where I've marked.'

Strike wiped his hand on a paper napkin, took the book from Robin and read the paragraphs next to which she had made a thick pencil line.

Shortly before her disappearance, Margot Bamborough booked herself into the Bride Street Nursing Home in Islington, a private facility which in 1974 provided discreet abortions.

The Bride Street Nursing Home closed its doors in 1978 and no records exist to show whether Bamborough had the procedure.

However, the possibility that she allowed a friend to use her name is mooted by the author of *Whatever Happened to Margot Bamborough?*, who notes that the Irish woman and fellow Bunny Girl Bamborough was supposedly meeting in the pub that night might have had good reason for maintaining the pub story, even after Bamborough's death.

Bride Street Nursing Home lay a mere eight minutes' walk from Dennis Creed's basement flat on Liverpool Road. The possibility remains, therefore, that Margot Bamborough never intended to go to the pub that night, that she told the lie to protect herself, or another woman, and that she may have been abducted, not from a street in Clerkenwell, but a short distance from Creed's house near Paradise Park.

'What the—?' began Strike, looking thunderstruck. 'My copy hasn't got this bit. You've got an extra three paragraphs!'

'I *thought* you hadn't read it,' said Robin, sounding satisfied. 'Yours can't be a first edition. Mine is. Look here,' she said, flicking to a place at the back of the book, while Strike still held it. 'See there, the endnote? "*Whatever Happened to Margot Bamborough?* by C. B. Oakden, published 1985." Except it wasn't published,' said Robin. 'It was pulped. The author of this,' she said, tapping *The Demon of Paradise Park*, 'must've got hold of an advance copy. I've been digging,' Robin went on. 'All this happened pre-internet, obviously, but I found a couple of mentions of it online, in legal articles about suing for libel to stop publication.

'Basically, Roy Phipps and Oonagh Kennedy brought a joint action against C. B. Oakden and won. Oakden's book was pulped and there was a hasty reprint of *The Demon of Paradise Park*, without the offending passage.'

'C. B. Oakden?' repeated Strike. 'Is he—?'

'Dorothy-the-practice-secretary's son. Exactly. Full name: Carl Brice Oakden. The last address I've got for him was in Walthamstow, but he's moved and I haven't managed to track him down yet.'

Strike re-read the paragraphs relating to the abortion clinic, then said,

'Well, if Phipps and Kennedy succeeded in suing to stop publication, they must have convinced a judge that this was partly or completely false.'

'Horrible thing to lie about, isn't it?' said Robin. 'Bad enough if he was saying Margot had the abortion, but hinting that Oonagh had it, and was covering up where Margot was that night—'

'I'm surprised he got it past lawyers,' said Strike.

'Oakden's publisher was a small press,' said Robin. 'I looked them up, too. They went out of business not long after he had his book pulped. Maybe they didn't bother with lawyers.'

'More fool them,' said Strike, 'but unless they had some kind of death wish, this can't have been *entirely* invented. He must've had something to base it on. And *this* bloke,' he held up *The Demon of Paradise Park*, 'was a proper investigative journalist. He wouldn't have theorised without seeing some proof.'

'Can we check with him, or is he—?'

'Dead,' said Strike, who sat for a moment, thinking, then went on: 'The appointment must've been made in Margot's name. The question is whether she had the procedure, or whether somebody used her name without her knowing.' Strike re-read the first few lines of the passage. 'And the date of the appointment isn't given, either. "Shortly before her disappearance" ... weasel words. If the appointment had been made for the day she disappeared, the author would say so. That'd be a major revelation and it'd have been investigated by the police. "Shortly before her disappearance" is open to wide interpretation.'

'Coincidence, though, isn't it?' said Robin. 'Her making an appointment so close to Creed's house?'

'Yeah,' said Strike, but after a moment's consideration he said, 'I don't know. Is it? How many abortion clinics were there in London in 1974?'

Handing the book back to Robin, he continued,

'This might explain why Roy Phipps was jumpy about his daughter talking to Oonagh Kennedy. He didn't want her telling his teenage daughter her mother might've aborted her sibling.'

'I thought of that, too,' said Robin. 'It'd be an awful thing to hear.

172

Especially when she's lived most of her life wondering whether her mother ran out on her.'

'We should try and get hold of a copy *Whatever Happened to Margot Bamborough?*' said Strike. 'There might still be copies in existence if they got as far as printing them. He could've given some away. Review copies and the like.'

'I'm already on it,' said Robin. 'I've emailed a few different second-hand book places.'

This wasn't the first time she had found herself doing something for the agency that made her feel grubby.

'Carl Oakden was only fourteen when Margot disappeared,' she continued. 'Writing a book about her, milking the connection, claiming Margot and his mother were close friends—'

'Yeah, he sounds a common-or-garden shit,' Strike agreed. 'When did he leave his address in Walthamstow?'

'Five years ago.'

'Had a look on social media?'

'Yes. Can't find him.'

Strike's mobile vibrated in his pocket. Robin thought she saw a flicker of panic in his face as he fumbled to find it, and knew that he was thinking of Joan.

'Everything all right?' she asked, watching his expression darken as he looked down at his mobile screen.

Strike had just seen:

Bruv, can we please talk this over face to face? The launch and the new album are a big deal for Dad. All we're asking—

'Yeah, fine,' he said, stuffing the phone back in his pocket, the rest of the message unread. 'So, you wanted to go to—?'

For a moment, he couldn't remember the unlikely place Robin had told him she wanted to visit, and which was the reason they were currently sitting in this particular café.

'The National Portrait Gallery,' she said. 'Three of Postcard's postcards were bought in their gift shop.'

'Three of – sorry, what?'

He was distracted by what he'd just read. He'd been quite clear with his half-brother that he had no wish either to attend the party celebrating his father's new album, or to feature in the photograph with his half-siblings which was to be their congratulatory gift to him.

'Postcard's postcards – the person who's persecuting our weatherman,' she reminded him, before mumbling, 'it doesn't matter, it was just an idea I had.'

'Which was?'

'Well, the last-but-one picture Postcard sent was of a portrait they said "always reminded" them of our weatherman. So I thought . . . maybe they see that painting a lot. Maybe they work at the gallery. Maybe they secretly want him to know that, to come looking for them?'

Even as she said it, she thought the theory sounded far-fetched, but the truth was that they had absolutely no leads on Postcard. He or she had failed to turn up at the weatherman's house since they'd been watching it. Three postcards bought in a single place might mean something, or perhaps nothing at all. What else did they have?

Strike grunted. Unsure whether this indicated a lack of enthusiasm for her theory about Postcard, Robin returned her copy of *The Demon of Paradise Park* to her handbag and said,

'Heading for the office after this?'

'Yeah. I told Barclay I'll take over watching Twinkletoes at two.' Strike yawned. 'Might try and get a couple of hours' kip first.'

He pushed himself into a standing position.

'I'll call you and let you know how I get on with Gregory Talbot. And thanks for holding the fort while I was away. Really appreciate it.'

'No problem,' said Robin.

Strike hoisted his kit bag onto his shoulder and limped out of the café. With a slight feeling of anti-climax, Robin watched him pause outside the window to light a cigarette, then walk out of sight. Checking her watch, Robin saw that there was still an hour and a half before the National Portrait Gallery opened.

There were doubtless more pleasurable ways of whiling away that time than in wondering whether the text that Strike had just received had come from Charlotte Campbell, but that was the distraction that occurred to Robin, and it occupied her for a surprising proportion of the time she had left to kill.

17

But thou . . . whom frowning froward fate
Hath made sad witnesse of thy fathers fall . . .

Edmund Spenser
The Faerie Queene

Jonny Rokeby, who'd been almost entirely absent from his eldest son's life, had nevertheless been a constant, intangible presence, especially during Strike's childhood. Parents' friends had owned his father's albums, had Rokeby's poster on their bedroom walls as teenagers and regaled Strike with their fond memories of Deadbeats' concerts. A mother at the school gate had once begged the seven-year-old Strike to take a letter from her to his father. His mother had burned it later, at the squat where they were then staying.

Until he joined the army, where, by his choice, nobody knew either his father's name or his profession, Strike regularly found himself contemplated like a specimen in a jar, bothered by questions that under normal conditions would be considered personal and intrusive, and dealing with unspoken assumptions that had their roots in envy and spite.

Rokeby had demanded Leda take a paternity test before he'd accept that Strike was his son. When the test came back positive, a financial settlement had been reached which ought to have ensured that his young son would never again have to sleep on a dirty mattress in a room shared with near-strangers. However, a combination of his mother's profligacy and her regular disputes with Rokeby's representatives had merely ensured that Strike's life became a series of confusing bouts of affluence that usually ended in abrupt descents back into chaos and squalor. Leda was prone to giving her children wildly extravagant treats, which they enjoyed while wearing too-small shoes, and to taking off on trips to the Continent or to America to see her favourite bands in concert, leaving her children with Ted and Joan while she rode around in chauffeured cars and stayed in the best hotels.

He could still remember lying in the spare room in Cornwall, Lucy asleep in the twin bed beside him, listening to his mother and Joan arguing downstairs, because the children had arrived back at their aunt and uncle's in the middle of winter, without coats. Strike had twice been enrolled in private schools, but Leda had both times pulled him out again before he'd completed more than a couple of terms, because she'd decided that her son was being taught the wrong values. Every month, Rokeby's money melted away on handouts to friends and boyfriends, and in reckless ventures – Strike remembered a jewellery business, an arts magazine and a vegetarian restaurant, all of which failed, not to mention the commune in Norfolk that had been the worst experience of his young life.

Finally, Rokeby's lawyers (to whom the rock star had delegated all matters concerning the well-being of his son) tied up the paternity payments in such a way that Leda could no longer fritter the money away. The only difference this made to the teenage Strike's day-to-day life had been that the treats had stopped, because Leda wasn't prepared to have her spending scrutinised in the manner demanded by the new arrangement. From that point onwards, the paternity payments had sat accumulating quietly in an account, and the family had survived on the smaller financial contributions made by Lucy's father.

Strike had only met his father twice and had unhappy memories of both encounters. For his part, Rokeby had never asked why Strike's money remained unspent. A tax exile of long standing, he had a band to front, several homes to maintain, two exes and a current wife to keep happy, five legitimate and two illegitimate children. Strike, whose conception had been an accident, whose positive paternity test had broken up Rokeby's second marriage and whose whereabouts were usually uncertain, came low on his list of priorities.

Strike's uncle had provided the model of manhood to which Strike had aspired through his mother's many changes of lover, and a childhood spent in the long shadow cast by his biological father. Leda had always blamed Ted, the ex-military policeman, for Strike's unnatural interest in the army and investigation. Speaking from the middle of a blue haze of cannabis smoke, she would earnestly attempt to dissuade her son from a career in the army, lecturing him on Britain's shameful military history, on the inextricable links between imperialism and capitalism, and trying, without success, to persuade him to learn the guitar or, at the very least, to let his hair grow.

Yet with all the disadvantages and pain they had brought, Strike knew that the peculiar circumstances of his birth and upbringing had given him a head start as an investigator. He'd learned early how to colour himself according to his environment. From the moment he learned that penalties attached to not sounding like everyone else, his accent had switched between London and Cornwall. Before the loss of a leg had hampered his full range of physical movement, he'd been able, in spite of his distinctive size, to move and talk in ways that made him appear smaller than he really was. He'd also learned the value of concealing personal information, and of editing the stories you told about yourself, to avoid becoming entangled in other people's notions of who you must be. Most importantly of all, Strike had developed a sensitive radar for the changes in behaviour that marked the sudden realisation that he was a famous man's son. He'd been wise to the ways of manipulators, flatterers, liars, chancers and hypocrites ever since he was a child.

These dubious gifts were the best his father had given him, for, apart from child support, there'd never been a birthday card or a Christmas present. It had taken his leg being blown off in Afghanistan for Rokeby to send Strike a handwritten note. Strike had asked Charlotte, who had been sitting next to his hospital bed when he received it, to put it in the bin.

Since Strike had become of interest to the newspapers in his own right, Rokeby had made further tentative attempts to reconnect with his estranged son, going so far as to suggest in recent interviews that they were on good terms. Several of Strike's friends had sent him links to a recent online interview with Rokeby in which he'd spoken of his pride in Strike. The detective had deleted the messages without a response.

Strike was grudgingly fond of Al, the half-brother whom Rokeby had recently used as an emissary. Al's dogged pursuit of a relationship with Strike had been maintained in spite of his older brother's initial resistance. Al appeared to admire in Strike those qualities of self-reliance and independence that the latter had had no choice but to develop. Nevertheless, Al was showing an antagonising bull-headedness in continuing to push Strike into celebrating an anniversary which meant nothing to Strike, except in serving as yet another reminder of how much more important Rokeby's band had always been to him than his illegitimate son. The detective resented the time he spent on Saturday morning, crafting a response to Al's latest text message on the subject. He finally chose brevity over further argument:

Haven't changed my mind, but no hard feelings or bitterness this end. Hope all goes well & let's get a beer when you're next in town.

Having taken care of this irksome bit of personal business, Strike made himself a sandwich, put on a clean shirt over his T-shirt, extracted from the Bamborough case file the page on which Bill Talbot had written his cryptic message in Pitman shorthand, and set off by car for West Wickham, where he had an appointment with Gregory Talbot, son of the late Bill.

Driving through intermittent sun and rain, and smoking as he went, Strike refocused his mind on business, mulling not only the questions he planned to ask the policeman's son, but also the various concerns related to the agency that had arisen since his return. Certain issues that needed his personal attention had been raised by Barclay the previous day. The Scot, who Strike was inclined to rate as his best investigator after Robin, had firstly expressed himself with characteristic bluntness on the subject of the West End dancer on whom they were supposed to be finding dirt.

'We're not gonnae get anythin' on him, Strike. If he's shaggin' some other bird, she must be livin' in his fuckin' wardrobe. I ken e's wi' oor lassie for her credit card, but he's too smart tae fuck up a good thing.'

'Think you're probably right,' said Strike, 'but I said we'd give the client three months, so we keep going. How're you getting on with Pat?' he added. He was hoping that somebody else found the new secretary as much of a pain in the arse as he did, but was disappointed.

'Aye, she's great. I ken she sounds like a bronchial docker, but she's very efficient. But if we're havin' an honest talk aboot new hires, here ...' Barclay said, his large blue eyes looking up at his boss from under thick brows.

'Go on,' said Strike. 'Morris not pulling his weight?'

'I wouldnae say that, exactly.'

The Glaswegian scratched the back of his prematurely grey head, then said,

'Robin not mentioned anything to ye?'

'Has there been trouble between them?' asked Strike, more sharply.

'Not tae say trouble, exactly,' said Barclay slowly, 'but he doesnae like takin' orders from her. Makes that plain behind her back.'

'Well, that'll have to change. I'll have a word.'

'An' he's got his own ideas aboot the Shifty case.'

'Is that right?' said Strike.

'He still thinks he's gonnae win over the PA. Robin told him it wus time tae let it go, time tae put Hutchins in. She's found oot—'

'That Shifty belongs to Hendon Rifle Club, yeah, she emailed me. And she wants to get Hutchins in there, to try and befriend him. Smart plan. Shifty fancies himself a bit of a macho man, from all we know about him.'

'But Morris wants tae do it his way. He said tae her face he was happy wi' the new plan, but—'

'You think he's still seeing the PA?'

'"Seein'" might be a polite way o' puttin' it,' said Barclay.

So Strike had called Morris into the office and laid it down in plain language that he was to leave Shifty's PA alone, and concentrate for the next week on Two-Times' girlfriend. Morris had raised no objections: indeed, his capitulation had been tinged with obsequious-ness. The encounter had left a slightly unpleasant aftertaste. Morris was, in nearly all respects, a desirable hire, with many good contacts in the force, but there had been something in his manner as he hur-ried to agree that denoted a slipperiness Strike couldn't like. Later that night, while Strike was following the taxi containing Twinkletoes and his girlfriend through the West End, he remembered Dr Gupta's interlaced fingers, and the old doctor's verdict that what made a suc-cessful business was the smooth functioning of a team.

Entering West Wickham, he found rows of suburban houses with bay windows, broad drives and private garages. The Avenue, where Gregory Talbot lived, was lined with solid family residences that spoke of conscientious middle-class owners who mowed their lawns and remembered bin day. The houses weren't as palatial as the detached houses on Dr Gupta's street, but were many times more spacious than Strike's attic flat over the office.

Turning into Talbot's drive, Strike parked his BMW behind a skip that blocked the front of the garage. As he switched off his engine, a pale, entirely bald man with large ears and steel-rimmed glasses opened his door looking cautiously excited. Strike knew from his online research that Gregory Talbot was a hospital administrator.

'Mr Strike?' he called, while the detective was getting carefully out of the BMW (the drive was slick with rain and the memory of tripping on the Falmouth ferry, still fresh).

'That's me,' said Strike, closing his car door and holding out his hand as Talbot came walking towards him. Talbot was shorter than Strike by a good six inches.

'Sorry about the skip,' he said. 'We're doing a loft conversion.'

As they approached the front door, a pair of twin girls Strike guessed to be around ten years old came bursting outside, almost knocking Gregory aside.

'Stay in the garden, girls,' called Gregory, though Strike thought the more pressing problem was surely that they had bare feet, and that the ground was cold and wet.

'*Thtay in the garden, girlth,*' imitated one of the twins. Gregory looked mildly over the top of his glasses at the twins.

181

'Rudeness isn't funny.'

'It bloody is,' said the first twin, to the raucous laughter of the second.

'Swear at me again, and there'll be no chocolate pudding for you tonight, Jayda,' said Gregory. 'Nor will you borrow my iPad.'

Jayda pulled a grotesque face but did not, in fact, swear again.

'We foster,' Gregory told Strike as they stepped inside. 'Our own kids have left home. Through to the right and have a seat.'

To Strike, who lived in a slightly Spartan minimalism by choice, the cluttered and very untidy room was unappealing. He wanted to accept Gregory's invitation to sit down, but there was nowhere he could do so without having to first shift a large quantity of objects, which felt rude. Oblivious to Strike's plight, Gregory glanced through the window at the twins. They were already running back indoors, shivering.

'They learn,' he said, as the front door slammed and the twins ran upstairs. Turning back to face the room, he became aware that none of the seats were currently useable.

'Oh, yeah, sorry,' he said, though with none of the embarrassment that Strike's Aunt Joan would have displayed had a casual visitor found her house in this state of disorder. 'The girls were in here this morning.'

Gregory swiftly cleared a leaking bubble-gun, two naked Barbie dolls, a child's sock, a number of small bits of brightly coloured plastic and half a satsuma off the seat of an armchair to allow Strike to sit down. He dumped the homeless objects onto a wooden coffee table that was already piled high with magazines, a jumble of remote controls, several letters and empty envelopes and further small plastic toys, including a good deal of Lego.

'Tea?' he offered. 'Coffee? My wife's taken the boys swimming.'

'Oh, there are boys, too?'

'Hence the loft conversion,' said Gregory. 'Darren's been with us nearly five years.'

While Gregory fetched hot drinks, Strike picked up the official sticker album of this year's Champions League, which he'd spotted lying on the floor beneath the coffee table. He turned the pages with a feeling of nostalgia for the days when he, too, had collected football stickers. He was idly pondering Arsenal's chances of winning the cup when a series of crashes directly overhead, which made the pendant light sway very slightly, made him look up. It sounded as though the twins were jumping on and off their bed. Setting the sticker book down, he pondered, without finding an answer, the question of what could have motivated Talbot and his wife to bring into their home children with whom they had no biological relationship. By the time Gregory reappeared with a tray, Strike's thoughts had travelled to Charlotte, who had always declared herself entirely unmaternal, and whose premature twins she'd vowed, while pregnant, to abandon to the care of her mother-in-law.

'Would you mind shifting—?' Gregory asked, eyes on the coffee table.

Strike hastened to move handfuls of objects off it, onto the sofa.

'Cheers,' said Gregory, setting down the tray. He scooped yet another mound of objects off the second armchair, dumped them, too, onto the now considerable pile on the sofa, picked up his mug, sat down and said,

'Help yourself,' indicating a slightly sticky sugar bowl and an unopened packet of biscuits.

'Thanks very much,' said Strike, spooning sugar into his tea.

'So,' said Gregory, looking mildly excited. 'You're trying to prove Creed killed Margot Bamborough.'

'Well,' said Strike, 'I'm trying to find out what happened to her and one possibility, obviously, is Creed.'

'Did you see, in the paper last weekend? One of Creed's drawings, selling for over a grand?'

'Missed that,' said Strike.

'Yeah, it was in the *Observer*. Self-portrait in pencil, done when he was in Belmarsh. Sold on a website where you can buy serial-killer art. Crazy world.'

'It is,' agreed Strike. 'Well, as I said on the phone, what I'd really like to talk to you about is your father.'

'Yes,' said Gregory, and some of his jauntiness left him. 'I, er, I don't know how much you know.'

'That he took early retirement, following a breakdown.'

'Well, yes, that's it in a nutshell,' said Gregory. 'His thyroid was at the bottom of it. Overactive and undiagnosed, for ages. He was losing weight, not sleeping ... There was a lot of pressure on him, you know. Not just from the force; the press, as well. People were very upset. Well, you know – a missing doctor – Mum put him acting a bit oddly down to stress.'

'In what way was he acting oddly?'

'Well, he took over the spare room and wouldn't let anyone in there,' said Gregory, and before Strike could ask for more details, he continued: 'After they found out about his thyroid and got him on the right drugs, he went back to normal, but it was too late for his career. He got his pension, but he felt guilty about the Bamborough case for years. He blamed himself, you know, thinking that if he hadn't been so ill, he might've got him.

'Because Margot Bamborough wasn't the last woman Creed took – I suppose you'll know all about that? He abducted Andrea Hooton after he took Bamborough. When they arrested him and went into the house and saw what was in the basement – the torture equipment and the photos he'd taken of the women – he admitted he'd kept some of them alive for months before he killed them.

'Dad was really upset when he heard that. He kept going back over it in his head, thinking if he'd caught him earlier, Bamborough and Hooton might've still been alive. He beat himself up for getting fixated—'

Gregory cut himself off.

'—distracted, you know.'

'So, even once your father had recovered, he still thought Creed had taken Margot?'

'Oh yeah, definitely,' said Gregory, looking mildly surprised that this was in question. 'They ruled out all the other possibilities, didn't they? The ex-boyfriend, that dodgy patient who had a thing for her, they all came up clean.'

Rather than answering this with his honest view, which was that Talbot's unfortunate illness had allowed valuable months to pass in which all suspects, Creed included, had had time to hide a body, cover up evidence, refine their alibis, or all three, Strike took from an inside pocket the piece of paper on which Talbot had written his Pitman message, and held it out to Gregory.

'Wanted to ask you about something. I think that's your father's handwriting?'

'Where did you get this?' asked Gregory, taking the paper cautiously.

'From the police file. It says: *"And that is the last of them, the twelfth, and the circle will be closed upon finding the tenth"* – and then there's an unknown word – *"Baphomet. Transcribe in the true book"*,' said Strike, 'and I was wondering whether that meant anything to you?'

At that moment, there came a particularly loud crash from overhead. With a hasty 'excuse me', Gregory laid the paper on top of the tea tray and hurried from the room. Strike heard him climbing the stairs, and then a telling-off. It appeared that one of the twins had overturned a chest of drawers. Soprano voices united in exculpation and counter-accusation.

Through the net curtains, Strike now saw an old Volvo pulling up outside the house. A plump middle-aged brunette in a navy raincoat got out, followed by two boys, whom he guessed to be around fourteen or fifteen. The woman went to the boot of the car and took out two sports bags and several bags of shopping from Aldi. The boys, who'd begun to slouch towards the house, had to be called back to assist her.

Gregory arrived back at the sitting-room door just as his wife entered the hall. One of the teenage boys shoved his way past Gregory to survey the stranger with the amazement appropriate to spotting an escaped zoo animal.

'Hi,' said Strike.

The boy turned in astonishment to Gregory.

'Who's he?' he asked, pointing.

The second boy appeared beside the first, eyeing Strike with precisely the same mixture of wonder and suspicion.

'This is Mr Strike,' said Gregory.

His wife now appeared between the boys, placed a hand on their shoulders and steered them bodily away, smiling at Strike as she did so.

Gregory closed the door behind him and returned to his armchair. He appeared to have momentarily forgotten what he and Strike had been talking about before he had gone upstairs, but then his eye fell upon the piece of paper scrawled all over with his father's handwriting, dotted with pentagrams and with the cryptic lines in Pitman shorthand.

'D'you know why Dad knew Pitman shorthand?' he said, with forced cheerfulness. 'My mother was learning it at secretarial college, so he learned it as well, so he could test her. He was a good husband – and a good dad, too,' he added, a little defiantly.

'Sounds it,' said Strike.

There was another pause.

'Look,' said Gregory, 'they kept the – the specifics of Dad's illness out of the press at the time. He was a good copper and it wasn't his fault he got ill. My mother's still alive. She'd be devastated if it all got out now.'

'I can appreciate—'

'Actually, I'm not sure you can,' said Gregory, flushing slightly. He seemed a polite and mild man, and it was clear that this assertive statement cost him some effort. 'The families of some of Creed's victims, afterwards – there was a lot of ill feeling towards Dad. They blamed him for not getting Creed, for screwing it all up. People wrote to the house, telling him he was a disgrace. Mum and Dad ended up moving ... From what you said on the phone, I thought you were interested in Dad's theories, not in – not in stuff like that,' he said, gesturing at the pentagram-strewn paper.

'I'm very interested in your father's theories,' said Strike. Deciding that a little duplicity was called for, or at least a little reframing of the facts, the detective added, 'Most of what your father wrote in the case file is entirely sound. He was asking all the right questions and he'd noticed—'

'The speeding van,' said Gregory quickly.

'Exactly,' said Strike.

186

'Rainy night, exactly like when Vera Kenny and Gail Wrightman were abducted.'

'Right,' said Strike, nodding.

'The two women who were struggling together,' said Gregory. 'That last patient, the woman who looked like a man. I mean, you've got to admit, you add all that together—'

'This is what I'm talking about,' said Strike. 'He might've been ill, but he still knew a clue when he saw one. All I want to know is whether the shorthand means anything I should know about.'

Some of Gregory's excitement faded from his face.

'No,' he said, 'it doesn't. That's just his illness talking.'

'You know,' said Strike slowly, 'your father wasn't the only one who saw Creed as satanic. The title of the best biography of him—'

'*The Demon of Paradise Park.*'

'Exactly. Creed and Baphomet have a lot in common,' said Strike.

In the pause that followed, they heard the twins running downstairs and loudly asking their foster mother whether she'd bought chocolate mousse.

'Look – I'd love you to prove it was Creed,' said Gregory at last. 'Prove Dad was right all along. There'd be no shame in Creed being too clever for him. He was too clever for Lawson, as well; he's been too clever for everyone. I know there wasn't any sign of Margot Bamborough in Creed's basement, but he never revealed where he'd put Andrea Hooton's clothes and jewellery, either. He was varying the way he disposed of bodies at the end. He was unlucky with Hooton, chucking her off the cliffs; unlucky the body was found so quickly.'

'All true,' said Strike.

Strike drank his tea while Gregory absent-mindedly chewed off a hangnail. A full minute passed before Strike decided that further pressure was required.

'This business about transcribing in the true book—'

He knew by Gregory's slight start that he'd hit the bullseye.

'—I wondered whether your father kept separate records from the official file – and if so,' said Strike, when Gregory didn't answer, 'whether they're still in existence.'

Gregory's wandering gaze fixed itself once more on Strike.

'Yeah, all right,' he said, 'Dad thought he was looking for something supernatural. We didn't know that until near the end, until we realised how ill he was. He was sprinkling salt outside our bedroom doors every night, to keep out Baphomet. He'd made himself what Mum thought was a home office in the spare room, but he was keeping the door locked.

'The night he was sectioned,' said Gregory, looking miserable, 'he came running out of it, ah, shouting. He woke us all up. My brother and I came out onto the landing. Dad had left the door to the spare room open, and we saw pentagrams all over the walls and lit candles. He'd taken up the carpet and made a magic circle on the floor to perform some kind of ritual, and he claimed ... well, he thought he'd conjured some kind of demonic creature ...

'Mum called 999 and an ambulance came and ... well, you know the rest.'

'Must've been very distressing for all of you,' said Strike.

'Well, yeah. It was. While Dad was in hospital, Mum cleaned out the room, took away his tarot cards and all the occult books, and painted over the pentagrams and the magic circle. It was all the more upsetting for her, because both had been committed churchgoers before Dad had his breakdown ...'

'He was clearly very ill,' said Strike, 'which wasn't his fault, but he was still a detective and he still had sound copper sense. I can see it in the official record. If there's another set of records anywhere, especially if it contains stuff that isn't in the official file, it's an important document.'

Gregory chewed his nail again, looking tense. Finally, he seemed to reach a decision:

'Ever since we spoke on the phone, I've been thinking that maybe I should give you this,' he said, standing up and heading over to an overflowing bookcase in the corner. From the top, he took a large leather-bound notebook of old-fashioned type, which had a cord wrapped around it.

'This was the only thing that didn't get thrown away,' said Gregory, looking down at the notebook, 'because Dad wouldn't let go of it when the ambulance arrived. He said he had to record what the, ah, spirit had looked like, the thing he'd conjured . . . so the notebook got taken to hospital with him. They let him draw the demon, which helped the doctors understand what had been going on in his head, because at first he didn't want to talk to them. I found all this out afterwards; they protected me and my brother from it while it was going on. After Dad got well, he kept the notebook, because he said if anything was a reminder to take his medicine, this was it. But I wanted to meet you before I made a decision.'

Resisting the urge to hold out his hand, Strike sat trying to look as sympathetic as his naturally surly features would allow. Robin was far better at conveying warmth and empathy; he'd watched her persuading recalcitrant witnesses many times since they'd gone into business together.

'You understand,' said Gregory, still clutching the notebook, and evidently determined to hammer the point home, 'he'd had a complete mental breakdown.'

'Of course,' said Strike. 'Who else have you shown that to?'

'Nobody,' said Gregory. 'It's been up in our attic for the last ten years. We had a couple of boxes of stuff from Mum and Dad's old house up there. Funny, you turning up just as the loft was being mucked out . . . maybe this is all Dad's doing? Maybe he's trying to tell me it's OK to pass this over?'

Strike made an ambiguous noise designed to convey agreement that the Talbots' decision to clear out their loft had been somehow prompted by Gregory's dead father, rather than the need to accommodate two extra children.

'Take it,' said Gregory abruptly, holding out the old notebook. Strike thought he looked relieved to see it pass into someone else's possession.

'I appreciate your trust. If I find anything in here I think you can help with, would it be all right to contact you again?'

'Yeah, of course,' said Gregory. 'You've got my email address . . . I'll give you my mobile number . . . '

Five minutes later, Strike was standing in the hall, shaking hands with Mrs Talbot as he prepared to return to his office.

'Lovely to meet you,' she said. 'I'm glad he's given you that thing. You never know, do you?'

And with the notebook in his hand, Strike agreed that you never did.

18

So the fayre Britomart hauing disclo'ste
Her clowdy care into a wrathfull stowre,
The mist of griefe dissolu'd . . .

Edmund Spenser
The Faerie Queene

Robin, who'd recently given up many weekends to cover the agency's workload, took the following Tuesday and Wednesday off at Strike's insistence. Her suggestion that she come into the office to look at the notebook Gregory Talbot had given Strike, and to go systematically through the last box of the police file, which neither of them had yet had time to examine, had been sternly vetoed by the senior partner. Strike knew there was no time left this year for Robin to take all the leave she was owed, but he was determined that she should take as much as she could.

However, if Strike imagined that Robin derived much pleasure from her days off, he was wrong. She spent Tuesday dealing with mundanities such as laundry and food shopping, and on Wednesday morning, set off for a twice-postponed appointment with her solicitor.

When she'd broken the news to her parents that she and Matthew were to divorce a little over a year after they'd married, her mother and father had wanted her to use a solicitor in Harrogate, who was an old family friend.

'I live in London. Why would I use a law firm in Yorkshire?'

Robin had chosen a lawyer in her late forties called Judith, whose dry humour, spiky grey hair and thick black-rimmed glasses had endeared her to Robin when first they met. Robin's feeling of warmth had abated somewhat over the ensuing twelve months. It was hard to maintain fondness for the person whose job it was to pass on the latest intransigent and aggressive communications from Matthew's lawyer. As the months rolled past, Robin noticed that Judith occasionally forgot or misremembered information pertinent to the divorce. Robin, who always took care to give her own clients the impression that their concerns were upper-most in her mind at all times, couldn't help wondering whether Judith would have been more meticulous if Robin had been richer.

Like Robin's parents, Judith had initially assumed that this divorce would be quick and easy, a matter of two signatures and a handshake. The couple had been married a little over a year and there were no children, not even a pet to argue over. Robin's parents had gone so far as to imagine that Matthew, whom they'd known since he was a child, must feel such shame at his infidelity that he'd want to com-pensate Robin by being generous and reasonable over the divorce. Her mother's growing fury towards her ex-son-in-law was starting to make Robin dread her phone calls home.

The offices of Stirling and Cobbs were a twenty-minute walk away from Robin's flat, on North End Road. Zipping herself into a warm coat, umbrella in hand, Robin chose to walk that morning purely for the exercise, because she'd spent so many long hours in her car of late, sitting outside the weatherman's house, waiting for Postcard. Indeed, the last time she'd walked for a whole hour had been inside the National Portrait Gallery, a trip that had been fruitless, except for one tiny incident that Robin had discounted, because Strike had taught her to mistrust the hunches so romanticised by the non-investigative public, which, he said, were more often than not born of personal biases or wishful thinking.

Tired, dispirited and knowing full well that nothing she was about to hear from Judith was likely to cheer her up, Robin was passing a bookie's when her mobile rang. Extracting it from her pocket took a little longer than usual, because she was wearing gloves, and she consequently sounded a little panicky when she finally managed to answer the unknown number.

'Yes, hello? Robin Ellacott speaking.'

'Oh, hi. This is Eden Richards.'

For a moment, Robin couldn't for the life of her think who Eden Richards was. The woman on the end of the line seemed to divine her dilemma, because she continued,

'Wilma Bayliss's daughter. You sent me and my brothers and sisters messages. You wanted to talk to us about Margot Bamborough.'

'Oh, yes, of course, thank you for calling me back!' said Robin, backing into the bookie's doorway, her finger in the ear not pressed against the phone, to block out the sound of traffic. Eden, she now remembered, was the oldest of Wilma's offspring, a Labour councillor from Lewisham.

'Yeah,' said Eden Richards, 'well, I'm afraid we don't want to talk to you. And I'm speaking for all of us here, OK?'

'I'm sorry to hear that,' said Robin, watching abstractedly as a passing Doberman Pinscher squatted and defecated on the pavement while its scowling owner waited, a plastic bag hanging from his hand. 'Can I ask why—?'

'We just don't want to,' said Eden. 'OK?'

'OK,' said Robin, 'but to be clear, all we're doing is checking statements that were made around the time Margot—'

'We can't speak for our mother,' said Eden. 'She's dead. We feel sorry for Margot's daughter, but we don't want to drag up stuff that – it's something we don't particularly want to relive, any of our family. We were young when she disappeared. It was a bad time for us. So the answer's no, OK?'

'I understand,' said Robin, 'but I wish you'd reconsider. We aren't asking you to talk about anything pers—'

'You are, though,' said Eden. 'Yeah, you are. And we don't want to, OK? You aren't police. And by the way: my youngest sister's going through chemotherapy, so leave her alone, please. She doesn't need the grief. I'm going to go now. The answer's no, OK? Don't contact any of us again, please.'

And the line went dead.

'Shit,' said Robin out loud.

The owner of the Doberman Pinscher, who was now scooping a sizeable pile of that very substance off the pavement, said,

'You and me both, love.'

Robin forced a smile, stuffed her mobile back into her pocket and walked on. Shortly afterwards, still wondering whether she could have handled the call with Eden better, Robin pushed open the glass door of Stirling and Cobbs, Solicitors.

'*Well*,' said Judith five minutes later, once Robin was sitting opposite her in the tiny office full of filing cabinets. The monosyllable was followed by silence as Judith glanced over the documents in the file in front of her, clearly reminding herself of the facts of the case while Robin sat watching. Robin would much rather have sat for another five minutes in the waiting room than witness this casual and hasty revision of what was causing her so much stress and pain.

'Umm,' said Judith, 'yes ... just checking that ... yes, we had a response to ours on the fourteenth, as I said in my email, so you'll be aware that Mr Cunliffe isn't prepared to shift his position on the joint account.'

'Yes,' said Robin.

'So, I really think it's time to go to mediation,' said Judith Cobbs.

'And as I said in my reply to your email,' said Robin, wondering whether Judith had read it, 'I can't see mediation working.'

'Which is why I wanted to speak to you face to face,' said Judith, smiling. 'We often find that when the two parties have to sit down in the same room, and answer for themselves, especially with impartial witnesses present – I'd be with you, obviously – they become far less intransigent than they are by letter.'

'You said yourself,' Robin replied (blood was thumping in her ears: the sensation of not being heard was becoming increasingly common during these interactions), 'the last time we met – you agreed that Matthew seems to be trying to force this into court. He isn't really interested in the joint account. He can outspend me ten times over. He just wants to beat me. He wants a judge to agree that I married him for his bank account. He'll think it money well spent if he can point to some ruling that says the divorce was all my fault.'

'It's easy,' said Judith, still smiling, 'to attribute the worst possible motives to ex-partners, but he's clearly an intelligent—'

'Intelligent people can be as spiteful as anyone else.'

'True,' said Judith, still with an air of humouring Robin, 'but refusing to even *try* mediation is a bad move for both of you. No judge will look kindly on anyone who refuses to at least *try* and settle matters without recourse to the courts.'

The truth, as perhaps Judith and Robin both equally knew, was that Robin dreaded having to sit face to face with Matthew and the lawyer who had authored all those cold, threatening letters.

'I've *told* him I don't want the inheritance he got from his mother,' said Robin. 'All I want back out of that joint account is the money *my* parents put into our first property.'

'Yes,' said Judith, with a hint of boredom: Robin knew that she'd said exactly this, every time they'd met each other. 'But as you're aware, *his* position—'

'Is that I contributed virtually nothing to our finances, so he ought to keep the whole lot, because he went into the marriage out of love and I'm some kind of gold-digger.'

'This is obviously upsetting you,' said Judith, no longer smiling.

'We were together ten years,' said Robin, trying, with little success, to remain calm. 'When he was a student and I was working, I paid for everything. Should I have kept the receipts?'

'We can certainly make that point in mediation—'

'That'll just infuriate him,' said Robin.

She raised a hand to her face purely for the purpose of hiding it. She felt suddenly and perilously close to tears.

'OK, fine. We can try mediation.'

'I think that's the sensible thing to do,' said Judith Cobbs, smiling again. 'So, I'll contact Brophy, Shenston and—'

'I suppose I'll get a chance to tell Matthew he's a total shit, at least,' said Robin, on a sudden wave of fury.

Judith gave a small laugh.

'Oh, I wouldn't advise *that*,' she said.

Oh, wouldn't you really? thought Robin, as she hitched on another fake smile, and got up to leave.

A blustery, damp wind was blowing when she left the solicitor's. Robin trudged back towards Finborough Road, until finally, her face numb, her hair whipping into her eyes, she turned into a small café where, in defiance of her own healthy eating rules, she bought a large latte and a chocolate brownie. She sat and stared out at the rainswept street, enjoying the comfort of cake and coffee, until her mobile rang again.

It was Strike.

'Hi,' she said, through a mouthful of brownie. 'Sorry. Eating.'

'Wish I was,' he said. 'I'm outside the bloody theatre again. I think Barclay's right: we're not going to get anything on Twinkletoes. I've got Bamborough news.'

'So've I,' said Robin, who had managed to swallow the mouthful of brownie, 'but it isn't good news. Wilma Bayliss's children don't want to talk to us.'

'The cleaner's kids? Why not?'

'Wilma wasn't a cleaner by the time she died,' Robin reminded him. 'She was a social worker.'

Even as she said it, Robin wondered why she felt the need to correct him. Perhaps it was simply that if Wilma Bayliss was to be forever referred to as a cleaner, she, Robin, might as well be forever called 'the temp'.

'All right, why don't the *social worker's* kids want to talk to us?' asked Strike.

'The one who called me – Eden, she's the eldest – said they didn't want to drag up what had been a difficult time for the family. She said it had nothing to do with Margot – but then she contradicted herself, because when I said we only wanted to talk about Margot – I can't remember her exact words, but the sense was that talking about Margot's disappearance would involve them talking about the family's personal stuff.'

'Well, their father was in jail in the early seventies and Margot was urging Wilma to leave him,' said Strike. 'It's probably that. Think it's worth calling her back? Trying a bit more persuasion?'

'I don't think she's going to change her mind.'

'And she said she was speaking for her brothers and sisters, as well?'

196

'Yes. One of them's having chemotherapy. She warned me specif-ically away from her.'

'OK, avoid her, but one of the others might be worth a shot.'

'That'll annoy Eden.'

'Probably, but we've got nothing to lose now, have we?'

'S'pose not,' said Robin. 'So what's *your* news?'

'The practice nurse and the receptionist, the one who isn't Gloria Conti—'

'Irene Bull,' said Robin.

'Irene Bull, now Hickson, exactly – they're both happy to talk to us. Turns out they've been friends since the St John's practice days. Irene will be delighted to host Janice and us at her house on Saturday afternoon. I think we should both go.'

Robin turned her mobile to speakerphone so that she could check the rota she kept on her phone. The entry for Saturday read: *Strike's birthday/TT girlfriend*.

'I'm supposed to be following Two-Times' girlfriend,' said Robin, switching back from speakerphone.

'Sod that, Morris can do it,' said Strike. 'You can drive us – if you don't mind,' he added, and Robin smiled.

'No, I don't mind,' she said.

'Well, great,' said Strike. 'Enjoy the rest of your day off.'

He rang off. Robin picked up the rest of the brownie and finished it slowly, savouring every bite. In spite of the prospect of mediation with Matthew, and doubtless because of a much-needed infusion of chocolate, she felt a good deal happier than she had ten minutes previously.

19

Strike never told anyone that his birthday was imminent and avoided announcing it on the day itself. It wasn't that he didn't appreciate people remembering: indeed, he tended to be far more touched when they did than he ever let show, but he had an innate dislike of scheduled celebration and forced jollity, and of all inane practices, having 'Happy Birthday' sung to him was one of his least favourites.

As far back as he could remember, the day of his birth had brought up unhappy memories on which he chose, usually successfully, not to dwell. His mother had sometimes forgotten to buy him anything when he was a child. His biological father had never acknowledged the date. Birthdays were inextricably linked with the knowledge, which had long since become part of him, that his existence was accidental, that his genetic inheritance had been contested in court, and that the birth itself had been 'fucking hideous, darling, if men had to do it the human race would be extinct in a year'.

To his sister, Lucy, it would have been almost cruel to let a loved one's birthday pass without a card, a gift, a phone call or, if she could manage it, a party or at the very least a meal. This was why he usually lied to Lucy, pretending to have plans so as to avoid having to go all the way out to her house in Bromley and participate in a family dinner that she'd enjoy far more than he would. Not long ago, he'd happily have celebrated with a takeaway at his friends Nick and Ilsa's, but Ilsa had suggested Robin accompany Strike, and as Strike had decided many weeks ago that Ilsa's increasingly open attempts at matchmaking could only be successfully countered by a blanket refusal to cooperate, he'd pretended that he was going to Lucy's instead. The one joyless hope Strike had for his thirty-ninth birthday was that Robin would have forgotten it, because, if she did, his own omission would be cancelled out: they'd be quits.

He descended the metal stairs to the office on Friday morning and saw, to his surprise, two packages and four envelopes sitting beside the usual pile of mail on Pat's desk. The envelopes were all of different colours. Apparently, friends and family had decided to make sure birthday greetings reached him in time for the weekend.

'Is it your birthday?' Pat asked in her deep, gravelly voice, still staring at her monitor and typing, electronic cigarette jammed between her teeth as usual.

'Tomorrow,' said Strike, picking up the cards. He recognised the handwriting on three of them, but not the fourth.

'Many happy returns,' grunted Pat, over the clacking of her keyboard. 'You should've said.'

Some spirit of mischief prompted Strike to ask,

'Why? Would you've baked me a cake?'

'No,' said Pat indifferently. 'Might've got you a card, though.'

'Lucky I didn't say, then. One fewer tree's died.'

'It wouldn't have been a *big* card,' said Pat, unsmiling, her fingers still flying over the keyboard.

Grinning slightly, Strike removed himself, his cards and packages into the inner office, and later that evening took them upstairs with him, still unopened.

He woke on the twenty-third with his mind full of his trip to Greenwich with Robin later, and only remembered the significance of the day when he saw the presents and cards on the table. The packages contained a sweater from Ted and Joan, and a sweatshirt from Lucy. Ilsa, Dave Polworth and his half-brother Al had all sent joke cards which, while not actually making him laugh, were vaguely cheering.

He slipped the fourth card out of its envelope. It had a photograph of a bloodhound on the front, and Strike considered this for a second or two, wondering why it had been chosen. He'd never owned a dog, and while he had a mild preference for dogs over cats, having worked alongside a few in the military, he wouldn't have said dog-loving was one of his salient characteristics. Flicking the card open, he saw the words:

Happy birthday Cormoran,
Best,
Jonny (Dad)

For a few moments, Strike merely looked at the words, his mind as blank as the rest of the card. The last time he'd seen his father's writing, he'd been full of morphine after his leg had been blown off. As a child, he'd occasionally caught a glimpse of his father's signature on legal documents sent to his mother. Then, he'd stared awestruck at the name, as though he were glimpsing an actual part of his father, as though the ink were blood, and solid proof that his father was a real human being, not a myth.

Quite suddenly, and with a force that shocked Strike, he found himself full of rage, rage on behalf of the small boy who would once have sold his soul to receive a birthday card from his father. He'd grown well beyond any desire to have contact with Jonny Rokeby, but he could still recall the acute pain his father's continual and implacable absence had so often caused him as a child: while the primary class was making Father's Day cards, for instance, or when strange adults questioned him about why he never saw Rokeby, or other children jeered at him, singing Deadbeats songs or telling him his mother had got pregnant with him purely to get Rokeby's money. He remembered the longing that was almost an ache, always most acute around birthdays and Christmas, for his father to send something, or phone: anything, to show that he knew Strike was alive. Strike hated the memory of these fantasies more than he hated remembering the pain caused by their eternal unfulfillment, but most of all he hated remembering the hopeful lies he'd told himself when, as a very young boy, he'd made excuses for his father, who probably didn't know that the family had moved yet again, who'd sent things to the wrong address, who wanted to know him but simply couldn't find him.

Where had Rokeby been when his son was a nobody? Where had Rokeby been every time Leda's life came off the rails, and Ted and Joan rode, again, to the rescue? Where had he been on any of the thousands of occasions when his presence might have meant something real, and genuine, rather than an attempt to look good to the papers?

Rokeby knew literally nothing about his son except that he was a detective, and *that* explained the fucking bloodhound. *Fuck you and fuck your fucking card.* Strike tore the card in half, then into quarters, and threw the pieces into the bin. But for a disinclination to trigger the fire alarm, he might have put a match to them.

Anger pulsed like a current through Strike all morning. He hated his own rage, as it showed that Rokeby still had some emotional hold on him, and by the time he set out for Earl's Court, where Robin was picking him up, he was not far off wishing that birthdays had never been invented.

Sitting in the Land Rover just outside the station entrance some forty-five minutes later, Robin watched Strike emerge onto the pavement, carrying a leather-bound notebook, and noted that he looked as grumpy as she'd ever seen him.

'Happy birthday,' she said, when he opened the passenger door. Strike immediately noticed the card and the small wrapped package lying on the dashboard.

Fuck.

'Cheers,' and climbed in beside her, looking even grumpier.

As Robin pulled out onto the road, she said,

'Is it turning thirty-nine that's upset you, or has something else happened?'

Having no desire to talk about Rokeby, Strike decided an effort was required.

'No, I'm just knackered. I was up late last night, going through the last box of the Bamborough file.'

'I wanted to do that on Tuesday, but you wouldn't let me!'

'You were owed time off,' said Strike shortly, tearing open the envelope of her card. 'You're *still* owed time off.'

'I know, but it would've been a lot more interesting than doing my ironing.'

Strike looked down at the front of Robin's card, which featured a watercolour picture of St Mawes. She must, he thought, have gone to some trouble to find it in London. 'Nice,' he said, 'thanks.'

Flipping it open, he read,

Many happy returns, love Robin x

She'd never put a kiss on any message to him before, and he liked it being there. Feeling slightly more cheerful, he unwrapped the small package that accompanied the card, and found inside a pair of replacement headphones of the kind Luke had broken while he'd been in St Mawes over the summer.

'Ah, Robin, that's – thanks. That's great. I hadn't replaced them, either.'

'I know,' said Robin, 'I noticed.'

As Strike put her card back in its envelope, he reminded himself that he really did need to get her a decent Christmas present.

'Is that Bill Talbot's secret notebook?' Robin asked, glancing sideways at the leather-bound book in Strike's lap.

'The very same. I'll show you after we've talked to Irene and Janice. Batshit crazy. Full of bizarre drawings and symbols.'

'What about the last box of police records? Anything interesting?' Robin asked.

'Yes, as it goes. A chunk of police notes from 1975 had got mixed in with a bunch of later stuff. There were a few interesting bits.

'For instance, the practice cleaner, Wilma, was sacked a couple of months after Margot disappeared, but for petty theft, not drinking, which is what Gupta told me. Small amounts of money disappearing out of people's purses and pockets. I also found out a call was made to Margot's marital home on Anna's second birthday, from a woman claiming to be Margot.'

'Oh my God, that's horrible,' said Robin. 'A prank call?'

'Police thought so. They traced it to a phone box in Marylebone. Cynthia, the childminder-turned-second-wife, answered. The woman identified herself as Margot and told Cynthia to look after her daughter.'

'Did Cynthia think it was Margot?'

'She told police she was too shocked to really take in what the caller said. She thought it sounded a bit like her, but on balance it sounded more like someone imitating her.'

'What makes people do things like that?' Robin asked, in genuine perplexity.

'They're shits,' said Strike. 'There were also a bunch of alleged sightings of Margot after the day she disappeared, in the last box. They were all disproven, but I've made a list and I'll email them to you. Mind if I smoke?'

'Carry on,' said Robin, and Strike wound down the window. 'I actually emailed *you* a tiny bit of information last night, too. *Very* tiny. Remember Albert Shimmings, the local florist—'

'—whose van people thought they saw speeding away from Clerkenwell Green? Yeah. Did he leave a note confessing to murder?'

'Unfortunately not, but I've spoken to his eldest son, who says that his dad's van *definitely* wasn't in Clerkenwell at half past six that evening. It was waiting outside his clarinet teacher's house in Camden, where his dad drove him every Friday. He says they told the police that at the time. His dad used to wait outside for him in the van and read spy novels.'

'Well, the clarinet lessons aren't in the records, but both Talbot and Lawson believed Shimmings when they spoke to him. Good to have it confirmed, though,' he added, lest Robin think he was being dismissive of her routine work. 'Well, that means there's still a possibility the van was Dennis Creed's, doesn't it?'

Strike lit up a Benson & Hedges, exhaled out of the window, and said,

'There was some interesting material on these two women we're about to meet, in that last box of notes. More stuff that came out when Lawson took over.'

'Really? I thought Irene had a dental appointment and Janice had house visits on the afternoon Margot disappeared?'

'Yeah, that's what their original statements said,' said Strike, 'and Talbot didn't check either woman's story. Took both at their word.'

'Presumably because he didn't think a woman could be the Essex Butcher?'

'Exactly.'

Strike pulled his own notebook out of his coat pocket and opened it to the pages he'd scribbled on Tuesday.

'Irene's first statement, which she gave to Talbot, said she'd had a grumbling toothache for a few days before Margot disappeared. Her friend Janice the nurse thought it might be an abscess, so Irene made an emergency appointment for three o'clock, leaving the practice at two-thirty. She and Janice were planning to go to the cinema that evening, but Irene's face was sore and swollen after having a tooth removed, so when Janice phoned her to see how the dentist's had gone, and to check whether she still wanted to go out that night, she said she'd rather stay at home.'

'No mobile phones,' mused Robin. 'Different world.'

'Exactly what I thought when I was going over this,' said Strike. 'These days Irene's mates would've expected a minute-by-minute commentary. Selfies from the dental chair.'

'Talbot gave his officers to understand that he'd personally con-tacted the dentist to check this story, but he hadn't. Wouldn't put it past him to have consulted a crystal ball.'

'Ha ha.'

'I'm not kidding. Wait till you see his notebook.'

Strike turned a page.

'Anyway, six months later, Lawson takes over the case and goes systematically back through every single witness and suspect in the file. Irene told the dentist story again, but half an hour after she left him, she panicked and asked to see him again. This time she admit-ted she'd lied.

'There'd never been any tooth pain. She hadn't visited the dentist.

She said she'd been forced to do a lot of unpaid overtime at the surgery and resented it, and felt she was owed an afternoon off, so she faked toothache, pretended to have got an emergency appointment, then left the practice and went to the West End to do some shopping.

'She told Lawson that it was only when she got home – she was still living with her parents, incidentally – that it occurred to her that if she went out to meet Janice the nurse that evening, Janice might ask to see the place where the tooth had been extracted, or at least expect to see some swelling. So when Janice rang her to check they were still going to the cinema, she lied and said she didn't feel up to it.

'Lawson gave Irene quite a hard time, judging from his notes. Didn't she understand what a serious matter it was, lying to the police, people had been arrested for less, et cetera. He also put it to her that the new story showed she had no alibi for any point of the afternoon and evening, other than around half past six in the evening, when Janice rang her at home.'

'Where did Irene live?'

'Street called Corporation Row, which as it happens lies very close to the Three Kings, although not on the route Margot would have taken from the practice.

'Anyway, at the point alibis were mentioned, Irene became hysterical. She poured out a load of stuff about Margot having a lot of enemies, without being able to say who these enemies were, although she referred Lawson back to the anonymous letters Margot received.

'The next day, Irene went back to Lawson yet again, this time accompanied by her very angry father, who did her no favours by losing his temper at Lawson for daring to upset his daughter. In the course of this third interview, Irene presented Lawson with a receipt from Oxford Street, which was marked 3.10 p.m. on the day Margot disappeared. The receipt was for cash. Lawson probably took a lot of pleasure in telling Irene and her dad that all the receipt proved was that *somebody* had gone shopping on Oxford Street that day.'

'Still – a receipt for the right day, right time—'

'Could've been her mother's. A friend's.'

'Why would they have kept it for six months?'

'Why would she?'

Robin considered the matter. She regularly kept receipts, but these were matters of expenses while doing surveillance, to be presented to the accountant.

'Yeah, maybe it is odd she still had it,' she conceded.

'But Lawson never managed to get anything further out of her. I don't think he genuinely suspected her, mind you. I get the impression he just didn't like her. He pressed her very hard on the anonymous notes she claimed to have seen, the ones mentioning hellfire. I don't think he believed in them.'

'I thought the other receptionist confirmed she'd seen one?'

'She did. Nothing to say they weren't in cahoots, though. No trace of the notes was ever found.'

'But that'd be a serious lie,' said Robin. 'With the fake dental appointment, I can see why she fibbed and why she'd have been frightened to admit it afterwards. Lying about anonymous notes in the context of a missing person, though . . . '

'Ah, but don't forget, Irene was already telling the story of the anonymous notes before Margot went missing. It's more of the same, isn't it? The two receptionists could've invented these threatening notes for the pleasure of starting a malicious rumour, then found it impossible to back away from the lie after Margot disappeared.

'Anyway,' said Strike, flicking over a couple of pages, 'so much for Irene. Now for her best buddy, the practice nurse.

'Janice's original statement was that she drove around all after-noon, making house calls. The last visit, which was to an old lady with multiple health issues, kept her longer than she expected. She left there around six and hurried straight to a call box to ring Irene at home, to see whether they were still on for the cinema that evening. Irene said she didn't feel up to it, but Janice had already got herself a babysitter, and was desperate to see the movie – James Caan, *The Gambler* – so she went anyway. Watched the movie alone, then went back to the neighbour's, picked up her son and went home.

'Talbot didn't bother to check any of this, but a zealous junior officer did, on his own initiative, and it all checked out. All the patients confirmed that Janice had been at their houses at the right times. The babysitter confirmed that Janice returned to pick up her son when expected. Janice also produced a half-torn ticket for the movie out of the bottom of her handbag. Given that this was less than a week after Margot disappeared, it doesn't seem particularly fishy, her still having it. On the other hand, a torn ticket is no more proof that she sat through the movie than the receipt is proof Irene went shopping.'

He threw his cigarette end out of the window.

'Where did Janice's last patient of the day live?' asked Robin, and Strike knew that her mind was running on distances and timings.

'Gopsall Street, which is about a ten-minute drive from the practice. It would've been *just* possible for a woman in a car to have intercepted Margot on the way to the Three Kings, assuming Margot was walking very slowly, or was delayed somewhere along the route, or left the practice later than Gloria said she did. But it would've required luck, because as we know, some of the path Margot would've taken was pedestrianised.'

'And I can't really see why you'd make arrangements with a friend to go to the cinema if you were planning to abduct someone,' said Robin.

'Nor can I,' said Strike. 'But I'm not finished. When Lawson takes over the case he finds out that Janice lied to Talbot as well.'

'You're kidding.'

'Nope. Turned out she didn't actually have a car. Six weeks before Margot disappeared, Janice's ancient Morris Minor gave up the ghost and she sold it for scrap. From that time onwards, she was making all her house calls by public transport and on foot. She hadn't wanted to tell anyone at the practice that she was carless, in case they told her she couldn't do her job. Her husband had walked out, leaving her with a kid. She was saving up to get a new car, but she knew it was going to take a while, so she pretended the Morris Minor was in the garage, or that it was easier to get the bus, if anyone asked.'

'But if that's true—'

'It is. Lawson checked it all out, questioned the scrap yard and everything.'

'—then that surely puts her completely out of the frame for an abduction.'

'I'm inclined to agree,' said Strike. 'She could've got a cab, of course, but the cabbie would've had to be in on the abduction, too. No, the interesting thing about Janice is that in spite of believing she was entirely innocent, Talbot interviewed her a total of seven times, more than any other witness or suspect.'

'*Seven times?*'

'Yep. He had a kind of excuse at first. She was a neighbour of Steve Douthwaite's, Margot's acutely stressed patient. Interviews two and three were all about Douthwaite, who Janice knew to say hello to. Douthwaite was Talbot's preferred candidate for the Essex Butcher, so you can follow his thought processes – you *would* question neighbours if you thought someone might be butchering women at home. But Janice wasn't able to tell Talbot anything about Douthwaite beyond what we already know, and Talbot still kept going back to her. After the third interview, he stopped asking her about Douthwaite and things got very strange indeed. Among other things, Talbot asked whether she'd ever been hypnotised, whether she'd be prepared to try it, asked her all about her dreams and urged her to keep a diary of them so he could read it, and also to make him a list of her most recent sexual partners.'

'He did *what?*'

'There's a copy of a letter from the Commissioner in the file,' said Strike drily, 'apologising to Janice for Talbot's behaviour. All in all, you can see why they wanted him off the force as fast as possible.'

'Did his son tell you any of that?'

Strike remembered Gregory's earnest, mild face, his assertion that Bill had been a good father and his embarrassment as the conversation turned to pentagrams.

'I doubt he knew about it. Janice doesn't seem to have made a fuss.'

'Well,' said Robin, slowly. 'She *was* a nurse. Maybe she could tell he was ill?'

She considered the matter for a few moments, then said,

'It'd be frightening, though, wouldn't it? Having the investigating officer coming back to your house every five minutes, asking you to keep a dream diary?'

'It'd put the wind up most people. I'm assuming the explanation is the obvious one – but we should ask her about it.'

Strike glanced into the back and saw, as he'd hoped, a bag of food.
'Well, it is your birthday,' said Robin, her eyes still on the road.
'Fancy a biscuit?'

'Bit early for me. You carry on.'

As he leaned back to fetch the bag, Strike noticed that Robin
smelled again of her old perfume.

20

And if that any ill she heard of any,
She would it eeke, and make much worse by telling,
And take great ioy to publish it to many,
That euery matter worse was for her melling.

Edmund Spenser
The Faerie Queene

Irene Hickson's house lay in a short, curving Georgian terrace of yellow brick, with arched windows and fanlights over each black front door. It reminded Robin of the street where she'd spent the last few months of her married life, in a rented house that had been built for a sea merchant. Here, too, were traces of London's trading past. The lettering over an arched window read *Royal Circus Tea Warehouse*.

'Mr Hickson must've made good money,' said Strike, looking up at the beautifully proportioned frontage as he and Robin crossed the street. 'This is a long way from Corporation Row.'

Robin rang the doorbell. They heard a shout of 'Don't worry, I'll get it!' and a few seconds later, a short, silver-haired woman opened the door to them. Dressed in a navy sweater, and trousers of the kind that Robin's mother would have called 'slacks', she had a round pink and white face. Blue eyes peeked out from beneath a blunt fringe that Robin suspected she might have cut herself.

'Mrs Hickson?' asked Robin.

'Janice Beattie,' said the older woman. 'You're Robin, are you? An' you're—'

The retired nurse's eyes swept down over Strike's legs in what looked like professional appraisal.

'—Corm'ran, is that 'ow you say it?' she asked, looking back up into his face.

'That's right,' said Strike. 'Very good of you to see us, Mrs Beattie.'

'Oh, no trouble at all,' she said, backing away to let them in. 'Irene'll be wiv us in a mo.'

The naturally upturned corners of the nurse's mouth and the dimples in her full cheeks gave her a cheerful look even when she wasn't smiling. She led them through a hall that Strike found oppressively over-decorated. Everything was dusky pink: the flowered wallpaper, the thick carpet, the dish of pot-pourri that sat on the telephone table. The distant sound of a flush told them exactly where Irene was.

The sitting room was decorated in olive green, and everything that could be swagged, flounced, fringed or padded had been. Family photographs in silver frames were crowded on side tables, the largest of which showed a heavily tanned forty-something blonde who was cheek to cheek over fruit-and-umbrella-laden cocktails with a florid gentlemen who Robin assumed was the late Mr Hickson. He looked quite a lot older than his wife. A large collection of porcelain figurines stood upon purpose-built mahogany shelves against the shiny olive-green wallpaper. All represented young women. Some wore crinolines, others twirled parasols, still others sniffed flowers or cradled lambs in their arms.

'She collects 'em,' said Janice, smiling as she saw where Robin was looking. 'Lovely, aren't they?'

'Oh yes,' lied Robin.

Janice didn't seem to feel she had the right to invite them to sit down without Irene present, so the three of them remained standing beside the figurines.

'Have you come far?' she asked them politely, but before they could answer, a voice that commanded attention said,

'Hello! Welcome!'

Like her sitting room, Irene Hickson presented a first impression of over-embellished, over-padded opulence. Just as blonde as she'd been at twenty-five, she was now much heavier, with an enormous

ROBERT GALBRAITH

bosom. She'd outlined her hooded eyes in black, pencilled her sparse brows into a high, Pierrot-ish arch and painted her thin lips in scarlet. In a mustard-coloured twinset, black trousers, patent heels and a large quantity of gold jewellery, which included clip-on earrings so heavy that they were stretching her already long lobes, she advanced on them in a potent cloud of amber perfume and hairspray.

'How d'you do?' she said, beaming at Strike as she offered her hand, bracelets jangling. 'Has Jan told you? What happened this morning? *So* strange, with you coming today; *so* strange, but I've lost *count* of the number of times things like that happen to me.' She paused, then said dramatically, '*My Margot shattered.* My Margot Fonteyn, on the top shelf,' she said, pointing to a gap in the china figurines. 'Fell apart into a million pieces when I ran the feather duster over her!'

She paused, waiting for astonishment.

'That *is* odd,' said Robin, because it was clear Strike wasn't going to say anything.

'*Isn't it?*' said Irene. 'Tea? Coffee? Whatever you want.'

'I'll do it, dear,' said Janice.

'Thank you, my love. Maybe make both?' said Irene. She waved Strike and Robin graciously towards armchairs. 'Please, sit down.'

The armchairs placed Strike and Robin within view of a window framed in tasselled curtains, through which they could see a garden with intricate paving and raised beds. It had an Elizabethan air, with low box hedges and a wrought iron sundial.

'Oh, the garden was all my Eddie,' said Irene, following their gaze. 'He *loved* his garden, bless his heart. *Loved* this house. It's why I'm still here, although it's too big for me now, really ... Excuse me. I haven't been well,' she added in a loud whisper, making quite a business of lowering herself onto the sofa and placing cushions carefully around herself. 'Jan's been a *saint.*'

'I'm sorry to hear that,' said Strike. 'That you've been unwell, I mean, not that your friend's a saint.'

Irene gave a delighted peal of laughter and Robin suspected that if Strike had been sitting slightly nearer, Irene might have playfully cuffed him. With an air of giving Strike privileged information, she half-mouthed:

'Irritable bowel syndrome. It flares up. The pain is sometimes – *well*. The funny thing is, I was *fine* all the time I was away – I've been staying with my eldest daughter, they're in Hampshire, that's why I didn't get your letter straight away – but the moment I got home, I called Jan, I said, you'll have to come, I'm in *that much pain* – and my GP's no use,' she added, with a little moue of disgust. '*Woman*. All my own fault, according to her! I should be cutting out everything that makes life worth living – I was telling them, Jan,' she said, as her friend backed into the room with a laden tea tray, 'that you're a *saint*.'

'Oh, carry on. Everyone likes a good review,' said Janice cheerfully. Strike was halfway out his chair to help her with the tray, on which stood both teapot and cafetière, but like Mrs Gupta she refused help, depositing it on a padded ottoman. An assortment of chocolate biscuits, some foil-wrapped, lay on a doily; the sugar bowl had tongs and the flowered fine bone china suggested 'for best'. Janice joined her friend on the sofa and poured out the hot drinks, serving Irene first.

'Help yourself to biscuits,' Irene told her visitors, and then, eyeing Strike hungrily, 'So – the famous Cameron Strike! I nearly had a *heart attack* when I saw your name at the bottom of the letter. And you're going to try and crack Creed, are you? Will he talk to you, do you think? Will they let you go and see him?'

'We're not that far along yet,' said Strike with a smile, as he took out his notebook and uncapped his pen. 'We've got a few questions, mainly background, that you two might be able—'

'Oh, *anything* we can do to help,' said Irene eagerly. '*Anything.*'

'We've read both your police statements,' said Strike, 'so unless—'

'Oh dear,' interrupted Irene, pulling a mock-fearful expression. 'You know all about me being a naughty girl, then? About the dentist and that, do you? There'll be young girls out there doing it, right now, fibbing to get a few hours off, but just my luck I picked the day Margot – sorry, I don't mean that,' Irene said, catching herself. 'I don't. This is how I get myself in trouble,' she said, with a little laugh. '*Steady, girl*, Eddie would've said, wouldn't he Jan?' she said, tapping her friend on the arm. 'Wouldn't he have said, *steady, girl?*'

'He would,' said Janice, smiling and nodding.

'I was going to say,' Strike continued, 'that unless either of you have got anything to add—'

'Oh, don't think we haven't thought about it,' interrupted Irene again. 'If we'd remembered anything else we'd have been *straight* down the police station, wouldn't we, Jan?'

'—I'd like to clarify a few points.

'Mrs Beattie,' said Strike, looking at Janice, who was absentmindedly stroking the underside of her wedding ring, which was the only piece of jewellery she wore, 'one thing that struck me when I read the police notes was how many times Inspector Talbot—'

'Oh, you and me both, Cameron,' Irene interrupted eagerly, before Janice could open her mouth. 'You and me both! I know *exactly* what you're going to ask – *why did he keep pestering Jan?* I told her at the time – didn't I, Jan? – I said, this isn't right, you should report it, but you didn't, did you? I mean, I know he was having a breakdown, blah blah blah – *you'll* know all about that,' she said, with a nod towards Strike, that simultaneously conveyed a compliment and an eagerness to fill him in should he require it, 'but ill men are still *men*, aren't they?'

'Mrs Beattie,' repeated Strike, slightly louder, 'why do *you* think Talbot kept interviewing you?'

Irene took the broad hint and allowed Janice to answer, but her self-restraint lasted only until Janice hit her stride, at which point she set up a murmured counterpoint, echoing Janice's words, adding agreement and emphasis, and giving the general impression that she feared that if she did not make a noise every few seconds, Strike might forget she was there.

'I dunno, in all honesty,' said Janice, still fiddling with her wedding ring. 'The first few times 'e saw me it was straightforward questions—'

'At first it was, yeah,' murmured Irene, nodding along.

'—about what I done that day, you know, what I could tell 'im about people coming to see Margot, because I knew a lot of the patients—'

'We got to know them all, working at the practice,' said Irene, nodding.

'—but then, it was like 'e thought I 'ad ... well, *special powers*. I know that sounds bonkers, but I don't fink—'

'Oho, well, *I* do,' said Irene, her eyes on Strike.

'—no, I honestly *don't* fink 'e was – you know –' Janice seemed embarrassed even to say it, '*keen* on me. 'E *did* ask inappropriate things, but I could tell 'e wasn't right, you know – in the 'ead. It was an 'orrible position to be in, honestly,' Janice said, switching her gaze to Robin. 'I didn't feel like I could *tell* anyone. 'E was police! I just 'ad to keep sitting there while 'e asked me about me *dreams*. And after the first few interviews that's all he wanted to talk about, me past boyfriends and stuff, nothing about Margot or the patients—'

'He was interested in *one* patient, though, wasn't—?' began Robin.

'Duckworth!' piped up Irene excitedly.

'Douthwaite,' said Strike.

'Douthwaite, yes, that's who I meant,' muttered Irene, and to cover a slight embarrassment she helped herself to a biscuit, which meant that for a few moments, at least, Janice was able to talk uninterrupted.

'Yeah, 'e did ask me about Steve,' said Janice, nodding, ''cause 'e lived in my block of flats, down Percival Street.'

'Did you know Douthwaite well?' asked Robin.

'Not really. Ackshly, I never knew 'im at all until 'e got beaten up. I come 'ome late and found a load of people on the landing with 'im. People knew I was a nurse so – there's me wiv my son Kevin under one arm and shopping in the other hand – but Steve was in a right state, so I 'ad to 'elp. 'E didn't want the police called, but 'e'd 'ad the sort of beating that can leave you wiv internal injuries. The ovver geezer 'ad used a bat. Jealous 'usband —'

'Who had *completely* the wrong end of the stick, didn't he?' interrupted Irene. 'Because Douthwaite was queer!' she said, with a shout of laughter. 'He was only *friends* with the wife, but this jealous idiot thinks—'

'Well, I don't *know* if Steve was queer—' began Janice, but there was no stopping Irene.

'—man – woman – two and two makes five! My Eddie was *exactly the same* – Jan, bear me out, what was Eddie like?' she said, tapping Janice's arm again. '*Exactly* the same, wasn't he? I remember once, I said, "Eddie, you think if I so much *look* at a man – he can be queer, he can be Welsh –" But after you told me, Jan, I thought, yeah, that Duckworth – Douth-thing – *is* a bit camp. When he came in the surgery afterwards, I could see it. Good-looking, but a bit soft.'

'But I don't know wevver 'e *was* queer, Irene, I didn't know 'im well enough to—'

'He kept coming back to see you,' Irene chided her. 'You told me he did. Kept coming back to your place for tea and sympathy and telling you all his problems.'

'It were only a couple of times,' said Janice. 'We'd chat, passing on the stairs, and one time 'e 'elped me with my shopping and come in for a cup of tea.'

'But he asked you—' prompted Irene.

'I'm getting to that, dear,' said Janice, with what Strike thought was remarkable patience. ''E was getting 'eadaches,' she told Strike and Robin, 'an' I told 'im 'e needed to go and see a doctor for 'ead-aches, I couldn't diagnose 'im. I mean, I felt a bit sorry for 'im, but I didn't want to get in the 'abit of 'olding out-of-hours clinics in me flat. I 'ad Kevin to look after.'

'So you think Douthwaite's visits to Margot were because of his health?' asked Robin. 'Not because he had a romantic interest in—?'

'He *did* send her chocolates one time,' said Irene, 'but if you ask me, it was more like she was an agony aunt.'

'Well, 'e 'ad these 'ead pains and 'e was def'nitely nervous. Depressed, maybe,' said Janice. 'Everyone 'ad blamed him for what happened to that poor girl 'oo killed 'erself, but I don't know . . . and some of me ovver neighbours told me there were young men coming in and out of his flat—'

'There you are,' said Irene triumphantly. 'Queer!'

'Might not've been that,' said Janice. 'Coulda just been 'is mates, or drugs, or stuff falling off the back of a lorry . . . One fing I do know, 'cause people talked, locally: the 'usband of that girl who killed 'erself was knockin' twelve bells out of 'er. Tragedy, really. But the papers pinned it all on Steve an' 'e ran. Well, sex sells better'n domestic violence, doesn't it? If you find Steve,' she added, 'tell 'im I said 'ello. It wasn't fair, what the papers did.'

Robin had been trained by Strike to organise her interviews and notes into the categories of people, places and things. She now asked both women,

'Were there any other patients you can ever remember giving cause for alarm at the practice, or perhaps having an unusual relationship with Marg—?'

'*Well*,' said Irene, '*remember*, Jan, there was that one with the beard down to here . . . ' She placed her hand at waist level, ' . . . remember? *What* was he called? Apton? Applethorpe? Jan, you remember. You *do* remember, Jan, he stank like a tramp and you had to go round his house once. He used to wander around near St John's. I think he lived on Clerkenwell Road. Sometimes he had his kid with him. Really *funny*-looking kid. Massive ears.'

'Oh, *them*,' said Janice, her frown disappearing. 'But they weren't Margot's—'

'Well, *he* was stopping people on the street, afterwards, telling them he'd killed Margot!' Irene told Strike excitedly. 'Yeah! He was! He stopped Dorothy! Of course, *Dorothy* wasn't going to tell the police, not Dorothy, she was all "load of stuff and nonsense", "he's a lunatic", but I said to her, "What if he actually *did* do it, Dorothy, and you haven't told anyone?" Now, Applethorpe was a proper nutcase. He had a girl locked up—'

'She weren't *locked up*, Irene,' said Janice, for the first time showing a trace of impatience. 'Social work said she were agoraphobic, but she weren't being kept there against 'er *will*—'

'She was peculiar,' said Irene stubbornly. 'You told me she was. I think someone should've taken the kid away, personally. You said the flat was filthy—'

'You can't take people's children off them because they 'aven't cleaned the 'ouse!' said Janice firmly. She turned back to Strike and Robin. 'Yeah, I visited the Applethorpes, just the once, but I don't fink they ever met Margot. See, it was diff'rent then: doctors 'ad their own lists, and the Applethorpes were registered with Brenner. 'E asked me to go round for 'im, check on the kid.'

'Do you remember the address? Street name?'

'Oh gawd,' said Janice, frowning. 'Yeah, I think it was Clerkenwell Road. I think so. See, I only visited the once. The kid 'adn't been well and Dr Brenner wanted 'im checked and 'e'd never make an 'ouse call if 'e could avoid it. Anyway, the kid was on the mend, but I spotted right off the dad was—'

'Nutcase—' said Irene, nodding along.

'—jittery, bit out of it,' said Janice. 'I went in the kitchen to wash my 'ands and there was a load of benzedrine lying in full view on the worktop. I warned both the parents, now the kid was walking, to put it away somewhere safe—'

'*Really* funny-looking kid,' interposed Irene.

'—and I went to Brenner after, an' I said, "Dr Brenner, that man's abusing benzedrine." It was proper addictive, we all knew it by then, even in '74. 'Course, Brenner thought I was being *presumptuous*, queryin' 'is prescriptions. But I was worried, so I called social work wivout telling Brenner, and they were very good. They were already keeping a close eye on the family.'

'But the mother—' said Irene.

'You can't decide for other people what makes 'em 'appy, Irene!' said Janice. 'The mum loved that kid, even if the dad was – well, 'e *was* odd, poor sod,' Janice conceded. ''E thought 'e was a kind of – I don't know what you'd call it – a guru, or a magic man. Thought 'e could put the evil eye on people. 'E told me that durin' the 'ouse call. You do meet people wiv weird ideas, nursin'. I just used to say, "Really? 'Ow interesting." There's no point challenging 'em. But Applethorpe thought he could ill-wish people – that's what we used to call it, in the old days. 'E was worried 'is little boy 'ad got German measles because he'd got cross with 'im. 'E said 'e could do that to people . . . He died 'imself, poor sod. Year after Margot vanished.'

'Did he?' said Irene, with a trace of disappointment.

'Yeah. It would've been after you left, after you married Eddie. I remember, street cleaners found him early in the morning, curled up and dead under the Walter Street bridge. 'Eart attack. Keeled over and there was nobody there to 'elp him. Wasn't that old, neither. I remember Dr Brenner being a bit twitchy about it.'

'Why was that?' asked Strike.

'Well, 'e'd prescribed the Bennies the man was abusin', 'adn't 'e?'

To Robin's surprise, a fleeting smile passed over Strike's face.

'But it weren't just Applethorpe,' Janice went on, who didn't seem to have noticed anything odd in Strike's response. 'There was—'

'Oh, *tons* of people swore blind they'd heard something, or had a hunch, blah blah blah,' said Irene, rolling her eyes, 'and there was us, you know, who were actually *involved*, it was terrible, just – excuse me,' she said, putting her hand on her stomach, 'I must just nip to the – sorry.'

Irene left the room in something of a hurry. Janice looked after her, and it was hard, given her naturally smiley face, to tell whether she was more concerned or amused.

'She'll be fine,' she told Strike and Robin quietly. 'I 'ave *told* 'er the doc's probably right tellin' 'er to lay off the spicy food, but she wanted a curry last night . . . she gets lonely. Rings me up to come over. I stayed overnight. Eddie only died last year. Nearly ninety, bless 'im. 'E *adored* Irene and the girls. She misses 'im something rotten.'

'Were you about to tell us somebody else had claimed to know what happened to Margot?' Strike prompted her gently.

'What? Oh, yeah . . . Charlie Ramage. 'E 'ad an 'ot tub and sauna business. Wealfy man, so you'd think 'e 'ad better things to do with 'is time than make up stories, but there you go, people are funny.'

'What did he say?' asked Robin.

'Well, see, motorbikes were Charlie's 'obby. 'E 'ad loads of 'em, and 'e used to go on these long rides all over the country. 'E 'ad a bad smash and 'e was at 'ome wiv two broken legs, so I was droppin' in sev'ral times a week . . . this would've been a good two years after Margot disappeared. Well, Charlie was a man 'oo liked to talk, and one day, out of a clear blue sky, 'e swears blind 'e met Margot, about a week after she went missing, in Leamington Spa. But, you know,' Janice said, shaking her head. 'I didn't take it very serious. Lovely man, but like I say, 'e liked to talk.'

'What exactly did he tell you?' asked Robin.

'Said 'e'd been on one of 'is bike trips up north, and 'e stopped outside this big church in Leamington Spa, and 'e was leaning against the wall 'avin' a cup of tea an' a sandwich, an' there was this woman walking in the graveyard on the other side of the railings, lookin' at the graves. Not like she was in mourning or anyfing, just interested. Black 'air, accordin' to Charlie. An' 'e called out to 'er, "Nice place, innit?" and she turned to look at 'im and – well, 'e swore blind it was Margot Bamborough, wiv 'er 'air dyed. 'E said 'e told 'er she looked familiar and she looked upset and hurried off.'

'And he claimed this happened a week after she disappeared?' asked Robin.

'Yeah, 'e said 'e recognised 'er because 'er picture was still all over the papers at the time. So I says, "Did you go to the police about this, Charlie?" And 'e says, "Yeah, I did," an' 'e told me 'e was friends with a policeman, quite an 'igh up bloke, an' 'e told 'is friend. But I never saw or 'eard anyfing about it after, so, you know . . .'

'Ramage told you this story in 1976?' Strike asked, making a note.

'Yeah, musta been,' said Janice, frowning in an effort to remember, as Irene walked back into the room. 'Because they'd got Creed by then. That's 'ow it came up. 'E'd been reading about the trial in the papers and then 'e says, cool as you like, "Well, I don't fink 'e done anyfing to Margot Bamborough, because I reckon I seen 'er after she disappeared."'

'Did Margot have any connection with Leamington Spa, as far as you know?' asked Robin.

'What's this?' said Irene sharply.

'Nuffing,' said Janice. 'Just a stupid story some patient told me. Margot in a graveyard wiv dyed hair. *You* know.'

'In Leamington Spa?' said Irene, looking displeased. Robin had the impression that she greatly resented having left Janice in the spotlight while she was forced back to the bathroom. 'You never told me that. Why didn't you tell me?'

'Oh . . . well, it was in '76,' said Janice, looking slightly cowed. 'You must've just 'ad Sharon. You 'ad better fings to fink about than Charlie Ramage telling porkies.'

Irene helped herself to another biscuit, frowning slightly.

'I'd like to move on to the practice itself,' said Strike. 'How did you find Margot to—'

'To work with?' said Irene, loudly, who seemed to feel it was her turn, having missed out on several minutes of Strike's attention. 'Well, speaking *personally*—'

Her pause was that of an epicure, savouring the prospect of coming pleasure.

'—to be *totally* honest, she was one of those people who think they know best about *everything*. She'd tell you how to live your life, how to do the filing, how to make a cup of tea, blah blah blah—'

'Oh, Irene, she weren't *that* bad,' muttered Janice. 'I liked—'

'Jan, *come on*,' said Irene loftily. 'She'd never got over being the clever clogs in her family and thought all the rest of us were thick as mince! Well, maybe she didn't think *you* were,' said Irene, with an eye roll, as her friend shook her head, 'but she did me. Treated me like a moron. *Patronising* isn't it. Now, I didn't dislike her!' Irene added quickly. 'Not *dislike*. But she was *picky*. Veee-ry pleased with herself. We'd *completely* forgotten we came from a two-up, two-down in Stepney, put it that way.'

'How did *you* find her?' Robin asked Janice.

'Well—' began Janice, but Irene talked over her.

'*Snobby*. Jan, *come on*. She marries herself a rich consultant – *that* was no two-up, two-down, that place out in Ham! Proper eye-opener it was, seeing what she'd married into, and then she has the gall to come into work preaching the liberated life to the rest of us: marriage isn't the be all and end all, don't stop your career, blah blah blah. And *always* finding fault.'

'What did she—?'

'How you answered the phone, how you spoke to patients, how you dressed, even – *"Irene, I don't think that top's appropriate for work."* She was a bloody Bunny Girl! The hypocrisy of her! I didn't dislike her,' Irene insisted. 'I didn't, truly, I'm just trying to give you the full – oh, and she wouldn't let us make her hot drinks, would she, Jan? Neither of the *other* two doctors ever complained we didn't know what to do with a teabag.'

'That's not why—' began Janice.

'Jan, *come on*, you *remember* how fussy—'

'Why would *you* say she didn't like people making her drinks?'

Strike asked Janice. Robin could tell that his patience was wearing thin with Irene.

'Oh, that was 'cause of when I was washing up mugs one day,' said Janice. 'I tipped the dregs out of Dr Brenner's and I found an—'

'*Atomal* pill, wasn't it?' asked Irene.

'—Amytal capsule, stuck to the bottom. I knew what it was from the col—'

'Blue,' interjected Irene, nodding, 'weren't they?'

'Blue 'Eavens, they used to call them on the street, yeah,' said Janice. 'Downers. I always made sure everyone knew I didn't 'ave nuffing like that in me nurse's bag, when I was out makin' 'ouse calls. You 'ad to be careful, in case you got mugged.'

'How did you know it was Dr Brenner's cup?' asked Strike.

''E always used the same one, wiv his old university's coat of arms on,' said Janice. 'There'd 'ave been 'ell to pay if anyone else touched it.' She hesitated, 'I don't know wevver – if you've talked to Dr Gupta—'

'We know Dr Brenner was addicted to barbiturates,' Strike said. Janice looked relieved.

'Right – well, I knew 'e must've dropped it in there, accidental, when he was taking some. Probably didn't realise, thought it 'ad rolled away on the floor. There'd have been a lot of questions asked, usually, at a doctor's surgery, finding drugs in a drink. If something gets into someone's tea by accident, that's serious.'

'How much harm would a single capsule—?' Robin began.

'Oh, no *real* harm,' said Irene knowledgeably, 'would it, Jan?'

'No, a single capsule, that's not even a full dose,' said Janice. 'You'd've felt a bit sleepy, that's all. Anyway, Margot come out the back to make the tea when I was tryin' to get the pill off the bottom of the mug with a teaspoon. We 'ad a sink and a kettle and a fridge just outside the nurse's room. She saw me trying to scrape the pill out. So it weren't *fussiness*, 'er making 'er own drinks after that. It were precautionary. I took extra care to make sure I was drinking out of me own mug, as well.'

'Did you tell Margot how you thought the pill had got in the tea?' asked Robin.

'No,' said Janice, 'because Dr Gupta 'ad asked me not to mention Brenner's problem, so I just said "must've been an accident", which was *technically* true. I expected her to call a staff meeting and hold an enquiry—'

'Ah, well, you know my theory about why she didn't do that,' said Irene.

'Irene,' said Janice, shaking her head. 'Honestly—'

'*My* theory,' said Irene, ignoring Janice, 'is Margot thought someone *else* had put the pill in Brenner's drink, and if you're asking me *who*—'

'*Irene*,' said Janice again, clearly urging restraint, but Irene was unstoppable.

'—I'll tell you – *Gloria*. That girl was as rough as hell and she came from a criminal background – no, I'm saying it, Jan, I'm sure Cameron wants to know *everything* what was going on at that practice—'

''Ow can Gloria putting something in Brenner's tea – and by the way,' Janice said to Strike and Robin, '*I* don't fink she did—'

'Well, as I was on the desk with Gloria every day, Jan,' said Irene loftily, '*I* knew what she was really like—'

'— but even if she *did* put the pill in 'is tea, Irene, 'ow could that 'ave anything to do with Margot disappearin'?'

'I don't know,' said Irene, who seemed to be getting cross, 'but they're interested in who was working there and what went on – aren't you?' she demanded of Strike, who nodded. With a '*See?*' to Janice, Irene plunged on, 'So: Gloria came from a really rough family, a Little Italy family—'

Janice tried to protest, but Irene overrode her again.

'She *did*, Jan! One of her brothers was drug dealing, that sort of thing, she told me so! That Atomal capsule might not've come from Brenner's store at all! She could've got it off one of her brothers. Gloria *hated* Brenner. He was a miserable old sod, all right, always having a go at us. She said to me once, "Imagine living with him. If I was his sister I'd poison the old bastard's food," and Margot heard her, and told her off, because there were patients in the waiting room, and it wasn't professional, saying something like that about one of the doctors.

'Anyway, when Margot never did anything about the pill in Brenner's mug, I thought, *that's because she knows who did it*. She didn't want her little pet in trouble. Gloria was her *project*, see. Gloria spent half her time in Margot's consulting room being lectured on feminism while I was left to hold the fort on reception ... she'd've let Gloria away with murder, Margot would. Total blind spot.'

'Do either of you know where Gloria is now?' asked Strike.

'No idea. She left not long after Margot disappeared,' said Irene.

'I never saw her again after she left the practice,' said Janice, who looked uncomfortable, 'but Irene, I don't fink we should be flinging accusations—'

'Do me a favour,' said Irene abruptly to her friend, a hand on her stomach, 'and fetch that medicine off the top of the fridge for me, will you? I'm still not right. And would anyone like more tea or coffee while Jan's there?'

Janice got up uncomplainingly, collected empty cups, loaded the tray and set off for the kitchen. Robin got up to open the door for her, and Janice smiled at her as she passed. While Janice's footsteps padded away down the thickly carpeted hall, Irene said, unsmiling,

'*Poor* Jan. She's had an awful life, really. Like something out of Dickens, her childhood. Eddie and I helped her out financially a few times, after Beattie left her. She calls herself "Beattie", but he never married her, you know,' said Irene. 'Awful, isn't it? And they had a kid, too. I don't think he ever really wanted to be there, and then he walked out. Larry, though – I mean, he wasn't the brightest tool in the box,' Irene laughed a little, 'but he thought the world of her. I think she thought she could do better at first – Larry worked for Eddie, you know – not on the management side, he was just a builder, but in the end, I think she realised – well, you know, not everyone's prepared to take on a kid ... '

'Could I ask you about the threatening notes to Margot you saw, Mrs Hickson?'

'Oh, yes, of course,' said Irene, pleased. 'So *you* believe me, do you? Because the police didn't.'

'There were two, you said in your statement?'

'That's right. I wouldn't've opened the first one, only Dorothy was off, and Dr Brenner told me to sort out the post. Dorothy was *never* off usually. It was because her son was having his tonsils out. Spoiled little so-and-so, he was. That was the *only* time I ever saw her upset, when she told me she was taking him into hospital the next day. Hard as nails, usually – but she was a widow, and he was all she had.'

Janice reappeared with refilled teapot and cafetière. Robin got up and took the heavy teapot and cafetière off the tray for her. Janice accepted her help with a smile and a whispered 'thanks', so that she didn't interrupt Irene.

'What did the note say?' Strike asked.

'Well, it's *ages* ago, now,' said Irene. Janice handed her a packet of indigestion tablets, which Irene took with a brief smile, but no thanks. 'But from what I remember . . .' she popped pills out of the blister pack, 'let me see, I want to get this right . . . it was *very* rude. It called Margot the c-word, I remember *that*. And said hellfire waited for women like her.'

'Was it typed? Printed?'

'Written,' said Irene. She took a couple of tablets with a sip of tea.

'What about the second one?' said Strike.

'I don't know what that said. I had to go into her consulting room to give her a message, see, and I saw it lying on her desk. Same writing, I recognised it at once. She didn't like me seeing it, I could tell. Screwed it up and threw it in the bin.'

Janice passed round fresh cups of tea and coffee. Irene helped herself to another chocolate biscuit.

'I doubt you'll know,' said Strike, 'but I wondered if you ever had any reason to suspect that Margot was pregnant before she—'

'How d'you know about that?' gasped Irene, looking thunderstruck.

'She *was*?' said Robin.

'Yes!' said Irene. 'See – Jan, don't look like that, honestly – I took a call from a nursing home, while she was out on a house call! They called the practice to confirm she'd be in next day . . .' and she mouthed the next few words, '*for an abortion!*'

'They told you what procedure she was going in for, over the phone?' asked Robin.

For a moment, Irene looked rather confused.

'They – well, no – actually, I – well, I'm not proud of it, but I called the clinic back. Just nosy. You do that kind of thing when you're young, don't you?'

Robin hoped her reciprocal smile looked sincerer than Irene's.

'When was this, Mrs Hickson, can you remember?' Strike asked.

'Not long before she disappeared. Four weeks? Something like that?'

'Before or after the anonymous notes?'

'I don't – after, I think,' said Irene. 'Or was it? I can't remember . . .'

'Did you talk to anyone else about the appointment?'

'Only Jan, and she told me off. Didn't you, Jan?'

'I know you didn't mean any 'arm,' muttered Janice, 'but patient confidentiality—'

'Margot wasn't *our* patient. It's a different thing.'

'And you didn't tell the police about this?' Strike asked her.

'No,' said Irene, 'because I – well, I shouldn't've known, should I? Anyway, how could it have anything to do with her disappearing?'

'Apart from Mrs Beattie, did you tell anyone else about it?'

'No,' said Irene defensively, 'because – I mean, I wouldn't have told anyone *else* – you kept your mouth shut, working at a doctor's surgery. I could've told all kinds of people's secrets, couldn't I? Being a receptionist, I saw files, but of course you didn't say anything, I knew how to keep secrets, it was part of the job . . .'

Expressionless, Strike wrote 'protesting too much' in his notebook.

'I've got another question, Mrs Hickson, and it might be a sensitive one,' Strike said, looking up again. 'I heard you and Margot had a disagreement at the Christmas party.'

'*Oh*,' said Irene, her face falling. '*That*. Yes, well—'

There was a slight pause.

'I was cross about what she'd done to Kevin. Jan's son. Remember, Jan?'

Janice looked confused.

'Come on, Jan, you *do*,' said Irene, tapping Janice's arm again. 'When she took him into her consulting room and blah blah blah.'

'*Oh*,' said Janice. For a moment, Robin had the distinct impression that Janice was truly cross with her friend this time. 'But—'

'You remember,' said Irene, glaring at her.

'I . . . yeah,' said Janice. 'Yeah, I *was* angry about that, all right.'

'Jan had kept him off school,' Irene told Strike. 'Hadn't you, Jan? How old was he, six? And then—'

'What exactly happened?' Strike asked Janice.

'Kev had a tummy ache,' said Janice. 'Well, schoolitis, really. My neighbour 'oo sometimes looked after 'im wasn't well—'

'Basically,' interrupted Irene, 'Jan brought Kevin to work and—'

'Could Mrs Beattie tell the story?' Strike asked.

'Oh – yes, of course!' said Irene. She put her hand back on her abdomen again and stroked it, with a long-suffering air.

'Your usual childminder was ill?' Strike prompted Janice.

'Yeah, but I was s'posed to be at work, so I took Kev wiv me to the practice and give 'im a colouring book. Then I 'ad to change a lady's dressing in the back room, so I put Kev in the waiting room. Irene and Gloria were keeping an eye on him for me. But then Margot – well, she took 'im into her consulting room and examined 'im, stripped 'im off to the waist and everything. She *knew* 'e was my son an' she *knew* why 'e was there, but she took it upon herself . . . I was angry, I can't lie,' said Janice quietly. 'We 'ad words. I said, "All you 'ad to do was wait until I'd seen the patient and I'd've come in wiv 'im while you looked at him."

'And I've got to say, when I put it to her straight, she backed down right away and apologised. No,' Janice said, because Irene had puffed herself up, 'she *did*, Irene, she apologised, said I was quite right, she shouldn't have seen him without me, but 'e'd been holding his tummy and she acted on instinct. It wasn't badly intentioned. She just, sometimes—'

'—put people's backs up, that's what I'm saying,' said Irene. 'Thought she was above everyone else, she knew best—'

'—rushed in, I was going to say. But she were a good doctor,' said Janice, with quiet firmness. 'You 'ear it all, when you're in people's 'ouses, you 'ear what the patients think of them, and Margot was well

227

liked. She took time. She was kind – she *was*, Irene, I know she got on your wick, but that's what the patients—'

'Oh, well, maybe,' said Irene, with an if-you-say-so inflection. 'But she didn't have much competition at St John's, did she?'

'Were Dr Gupta and Dr Brenner unpopular?' Strike asked.

'Dr Gupta was lovely,' said Janice. 'A very good doctor, although some patients didn't want to see a brown man, and that's the truth. But Brenner was an 'ard man to like. It was only after he died that I understood why he might've—'

Irene gave a huge gasp and then began, unexpectedly, to laugh.

'*Tell them what you collect, Janice.* Go on!' She turned to Strike and Robin. 'If this isn't the *creepiest,* most *morbid*—'

'I don't *collect* 'em,' said Janice, who had turned pink. 'They're just something I like to *save*—'

'*Obituaries!* What d'you think of that? The rest of us collect china or snow globes, blah blah blah, but Janice collects—'

'*It isn't a collection,*' repeated Janice, still pink-faced. 'All it is—' She addressed Robin with a trace of appeal. 'My mum couldn't read—'

'*Imagine,*' said Irene complacently, stroking her stomach. Janice faltered for a moment, then said,

'—yeah, so . . . Dad wasn't bothered about books, but 'e used to bring the paper 'ome, and that's 'ow I learned to read. I used to cut out the best stories. 'Uman interest, I s'pose you'd call them. I've never been that interested in fiction. I can't see the point, things somebody's made up.'

'Oh, I *love* a good novel,' breathed Irene, still rubbing her stomach.

'Anyway . . . I dunno . . . when you read an obituary, you find out 'oo people've *really* been, don't you? If it's someone I know, or I nursed, I keep 'em because, I dunno, I felt like *somebody* should. You get your life written up in the paper – it's an achievement, isn't it?'

'Not if you're Dennis Creed, it isn't,' said Irene. Looking as though she'd said something very clever she reached forwards to take another biscuit, and a deafening fart ripped through the room.

Irene turned scarlet. Robin thought for one horrible moment that Strike was going to laugh, so she said loudly to Janice,

'Did you keep Dr Brenner's obituary?'

'Oh, yeah,' said Janice, who seemed completely unperturbed by the loud noise that had just emanated from Irene. Perhaps she was used to far worse, as a nurse. 'An' it explained *a lot*.'

'In what way?' asked Robin, determinedly not looking at either Strike or Irene.

''E'd been into Bergen-Belsen, one of the first medical men in there.'

'God,' said Robin, shocked.

'I know,' said Janice. ''E never talked about it. I'd never 'ave known, if I 'adn't read it in the paper. What 'e must have seen ... mounds of bodies, dead kids ... I read a library book about it. Dreadful. Maybe that's why 'e was the way 'e was, I dunno. I felt sorry, when I read it. I 'adn't seen 'im in years by the time 'e died. Someone showed me the obituary, knowing I'd been at St John's, and I kept it as a record of him. You could forgive Brenner a lot, once you saw what 'e'd witnessed, what 'e'd been through ... but that's true of everyone, really, innit? Once you know, ev'rything's explained. It's a shame you often *don't* know until it's too late to – you all right, love?' she said to Irene.

In the wake of the fart, Robin suspected that Irene had decided the only dignified cover-up was to emphasise that she was unwell.

'D'you know, I think it's stress,' she said, her hand down the waist-band of her trousers. 'It always flares up when I'm ... sorry,' she said with dignity to Strike and Robin, 'but I'm afraid I don't think I ... '

'Of course,' said Strike, closing his notebook. 'I think we've asked everything we came for, anyway. Unless there's anything else,' he asked the two women, 'that you've remembered that seems odd, in retrospect, or out of place?'

'We've fort, 'aven't we?' Janice asked Irene. 'All these years ... we've talked about it, obviously.'

'It *must've* been Creed, mustn't it?' said Irene, with finality. 'What other explanation is there? Where else could she have gone? *Do* you think they'll let you in to see him?' she asked Strike again, with a last flicker of curiosity.

'No idea,' he said, getting to his feet. 'Thanks very much for your hospitality, anyway, and for answering our questions ... '

Janice saw them out. Irene waved wordlessly as they left the room. Robin could tell that the interview had fallen short of her expectation of enjoyment. Awkward and uncomfortable admissions had been forced from her; the picture she'd painted of her young self had not been, perhaps, everything she would have wished – and nobody, Robin thought, shaking hands with Janice at the door, would particularly enjoy farting loudly in front of strangers.

21

Well then, sayd Artegall, let it be tride.
First in one ballance set the true aside.
He did so first; and then the false he layd
In th'other scale . . .

Edmund Spenser
The Faerie Queene

'Well, I'm no doctor,' said Strike, as they crossed the road back to the Land Rover, 'but I blame the curry.'

'Don't,' said Robin, laughing against her will. She couldn't help but feel a certain vicarious embarrassment.

'You weren't sitting as near her as I was,' said Strike, as he got back into the car. 'I'm guessing lamb bhuna—'

'Seriously,' said Robin, half-laughing, half-disgusted, 'stop.'

As he drew his seatbelt back over himself, Strike said,

'I need a proper drink.'

'There's a decent pub not far from here,' said Robin. 'I looked it up. The Trafalgar Tavern.'

Looking up the pub was doubtless yet another Nice Thing that Robin had chosen to do for his birthday, and Strike wondered whether it was her intention to make him feel guilty. Probably not, he thought, but that, nevertheless, was the effect, so he passed no comment other than to ask,

'What did you think of all that?'

'Well, there were a few cross-currents, weren't there?' said Robin, steering out of the parking space. 'And I think we were told a couple of lies.'

231

'Me too,' said Strike. 'Which ones did you spot?'

'Irene and Janice's row at the Christmas party, for starters,' said Robin, turning out of Circus Street. 'I don't think it was really about Margot examining Janice's son – although I *do* think Margot examined Kevin without permission.'

'So do I,' said Strike. 'But I agree: I don't think that's what the row was about. Irene forced Janice to tell that story, because she didn't want to admit the truth. Which makes me wonder . . . Irene getting Janice to come to her house, so we can interview them both together: was that so Irene could make sure Janice didn't tell us anything she wouldn't want told? That's the trouble with friends you've had for decades, isn't it? They know too much.'

Robin, who was busy trying to remember the route to the Trafalgar she'd memorised that morning, thought at once about all those stories Ilsa had told her about Strike and Charlotte's relationship. Ilsa had told her Strike had refused an invitation to go over to their house that evening for dinner, claiming that he had a prior arrangement with his sister. Robin found it hard to believe this, given Strike's and Lucy's recent row. Perhaps she was being paranoid, but she'd also wondered whether Strike wasn't avoiding being in her company outside work hours.

'You don't suspect Irene, do you?'

'Only of being a liar, a gossip and a compulsive attention-seeker,' said Strike. 'I don't think she's bright enough to have abducted Margot Bamborough and not given herself away in forty years. On the other hand, lies are always interesting. Anything else catch your interest?'

'Yes. There was something funny about that Leamington Spa story, or rather, Irene's reaction when she heard Janice talking about it . . . I think Leamington Spa meant something to her. And it was odd that Janice *hadn't* told her what that patient said. You'd think she definitely would have done, given that they're best friends, and they both knew Margot, and they've stayed in touch all these years. Even if Janice thought that man Ramage was making it all up, why wouldn't she tell Irene?'

'Another good point,' said Strike, looking thoughtfully at the neo-classical façade of the National Maritime Museum as they drove past wide stretches of beautifully manicured emerald lawn. 'What did you think of Janice?'

'Well, when we were allowed to hear her speak, she seemed quite decent,' said Robin cautiously. 'She seemed fair-minded about Margot and Douthwaite. Why she puts up with being treated as Irene's skivvy, though ... '

'Some people need to be needed ... and there might be a sense of obligation, if Irene was telling the truth about her and her husband helping Janice out financially when she needed it.'

Strike spotted the pub Robin had chosen from a distance. Large and opulent-looking, with many balconies and awnings, not to mention window-baskets and coats of arms, it stood on the bank of the Thames. Robin parked and they proceeded past black iron bollards to the paved area where many wooden tables afforded a view over the river, in the midst of which a life-size black statue of the diminutive Lord Nelson faced the water.

'See?' said Robin, 'you can sit outside and smoke.'

'Isn't it a bit cold?' said Strike.

'This coat's padded. I'll get the—'

'No, I will,' said Strike firmly. 'What d'you want?

'Just a lime and soda, please, as I'm driving.'

As Strike walked into the pub, there was a sudden chorus of 'Happy Birthday to You'. For a split-second, seeing helium balloons in the corner, he was horror-struck, thinking that Robin had brought him here for a surprise party; but a bare heartbeat later, it registered that he didn't recognise a single face, and that the balloons formed the figure 80. A tiny woman with lavender hair was beaming at the top of a table full of family: flashes went off as she blew out the candles on a large chocolate cake. Applause and cheers followed, and a toddler blew a feathered whistle.

Strike headed towards the bar, still slightly shaken, taking himself to task for having imagined, for a moment, that Robin would have arranged a surprise party for him. Even Charlotte, with whom he'd had the longest and closest relationship of his life, had never done that. Indeed, Charlotte had never allowed anything as mundane as his birthday to interfere with her own whims and moods. On Strike's twenty-seventh, when she'd been going through one of her intermittent phases of either rampant jealousy, or rage at his refusal to give up the army (the precise causes of their many scenes and rows tended to blur in his mind), she'd thrown his wrapped gift out of a third-floor window in front of him.

But, of course, there were other memories. His thirty-third birthday, for instance. He'd just been discharged from Selly Oak hospital, and was walking for the first time on a prosthesis, and Charlotte had taken him back to her flat in Notting Hill, cooked for him, and returned from the kitchen at the end of the meal holding two cups of coffee, stark naked and more beautiful than any woman he had ever seen. He'd laughed and gasped at the same time. He hadn't had sex for nearly two years. The night that had followed would probably never be forgotten by him, nor the way she had sobbed in his arms afterwards, telling him that he was the only man for her, that she was afraid of what she felt, afraid that she was evil for not regretting his missing lower leg if it brought her back to him, if it meant that, at last, she could look after him as he had always looked after her. And close to midnight, Strike had proposed to her, and they'd made love again, and then talked through to dawn about how he was going to start his detective agency, and she'd told him she didn't want a ring, that he was to save his money for his new career, at which he would be magnificent.

Drinks and crisps purchased, Strike returned to Robin, who was sitting on an outside bench, hands in her pockets, looking glum.

'Cheer up,' said Strike, speaking to himself as much as to her.

'Sorry,' said Robin, though she didn't really know why she was apologising.

He sat down beside her, rather than opposite, so both of them faced the river. There was a small shingle beach below them, and waves lapped the cold pebbles. On the opposite bank rose the steel-coloured office blocks of Canary Wharf; to their left, the Shard. The river was the colour of lead on this cold November day. Strike tore one of the crisp packets down the middle so that both could help themselves. Wishing she'd asked for coffee instead of a cold drink, Robin took a sip of her lime and soda, ate a couple of crisps, returned her hands to her pockets, then said,

'I know this isn't the attitude, but honestly . . . I don't think we're going to find out what happened to Margot Bamborough.'

'What's brought this on?'

'I suppose Irene misremembering names . . . Janice going along with her, covering up the reason for the Christmas party row . . . it's such a long time ago. People are under no obligation to tell the truth to us now, even if they can remember it. Factor in people getting wedded to old theories, like that whole thing about Gloria and the pill in Brenner's mug, and people wanting to make themselves important, pretending to know things and . . . well, I'm starting to think we're attempting the impossible here.'

A wave of tiredness had swept over Robin while sitting in the cold, waiting for Strike, and in its wake had come hopelessness.

'Pull yourself together,' said Strike bracingly. 'We've already found out two big things the police never knew.' He pulled out his cigarettes, lit one, then said, 'Firstly: there was a big stock of barbiturates on the premises where Margot worked. Secondly: Margot Bamborough might well have had an abortion.

'Taking the barbiturates first,' he said, 'are we overlooking something very obvious, which is that there were means on the premises to put someone to sleep?'

'Margot wasn't put to sleep,' said Robin, gloomily munching crisps. 'She walked out of there.'

'Only if we assume—'

'—Gloria wasn't lying. I know,' said Robin. 'But how do she and Theo – because Theo's still got to be in on it, hasn't she? How did Gloria and Theo administer enough barbiturates to render Margot unconscious? Don't forget, if Irene's telling the truth, Margot wasn't letting anyone else make her drinks at that point. And from what Janice said about dosage, you'd need a lot of pills to make someone actually unconscious.'

'Well reasoned. So, going back to that little story about the pill in the tea—'

'Didn't you believe it?'

235

'I did,' said Strike, 'because it seems a totally pointless lie. It's not interesting enough to make an exciting anecdote, is it, a single pill? It does reopen the question of whether Margot knew about or suspected Brenner's addiction, though. She might've noticed him being odd in his manner. Downers would make him drowsy. Perhaps she'd seen he was slow on the uptake. Everything we've found out about Margot suggests that if she thought Brenner was behaving unprofessionally, or might be dangerous to patients, she'd have waded straight in and confronted him. And we've just heard a lot of interesting background on Brenner, who sounds like a traumatised, unhappy and lonely man. What if Margot threatened him with being struck off? Loss of status and prestige, to a man who has virtually nothing else in his life? People have killed for less.'

'He left the surgery before she did, that night.'

'What if he waited for her? Offered her a lift?'

'If he did, I think she'd have been suspicious,' said Robin. 'Not that he wanted to hurt her, but that he was going to shout at her, which would've been in character, from what we know of *him*. I'd rather have walked in the rain, personally. And she was a lot younger than him, and tall and fit. I can't remember now where he lived ... '

'With his unmarried sister, about twenty minutes' drive from the practice. The sister said he'd arrived home at the usual time. A dog-walking neighbour confirmed they'd seen him through the window round about eleven ... '

'But I can think of one other possibility regarding those barbiturates,' Strike went on. 'As Janice pointed out, they had street value, and by the sounds of it, Brenner had amassed a big stock of them. We've got to consider the possibility that some outsider knew there were valuable drugs on the premises, set out to nick them, and Margot got in the way.'

'Which takes us back to Margot dying on the premises, which means—'

'Gloria and Theo come back into the frame. Gloria and Theo might have planned to take the drugs themselves. And we've just heard—'

'—about the drug-dealing brother,' said Robin.

'Why the sceptical tone?'

'Irene was determined to have a go at Gloria, wasn't she?'

'She was, yeah, but the fact that Gloria had a drug-dealing brother is information worth knowing, as is the fact that there were a stack of drugs on the premises that were ripe for nicking. Brenner wouldn't have wanted to admit he had them in the first place, so probably wouldn't have reported the theft, which makes for a situation open to exploitation.'

'A criminal brother doesn't make a person criminal in themselves.'

'Agreed, but it makes me even keener to find Gloria. The term "person of interest" fits her pretty accurately . . .'

'And then there's the abortion,' said Strike. 'If Irene's telling the truth about the nursing home calling to confirm the appointment—'

'*If*,' said Robin.

'I don't think that was a lie,' said Strike. 'For the opposite reason to the pill in Brenner's cup. That lie's too big. People don't make things like that up. Anyway, she told Janice about it at the time, and their little row about patient confidentiality rings true. And C. B. Oakden must've based the story on something. I wouldn't be at all surprised if that tip-off came from Irene. She doesn't strike me as a woman who'd turn down a chance to speculate or gossip.'

Robin said nothing. She'd only once in her life had to face the possibility that she might be pregnant, and could still remember the relief that had flooded her when it became clear that she wasn't, and wouldn't have to face still more contact with strangers, and another intimate procedure, more blood, more pain.

Imagine aborting your husband's child, she thought. Could Margot really have done that, when she already had that child's sister at home? What had been going through her mind, a month before she disappeared? Perhaps she'd been quietly breaking down, like Talbot? The past few years had taught Robin how very mysterious human beings were, even to those who thought they knew them best. Infidelity and bigamy, kinks and fetishes, theft and fraud, stalking and harassment: she'd now delved into so many secret lives she'd lost count. Nor did she hold herself superior to any of the deceived and duped who came to the agency, craving truth. Hadn't she thought she knew her own husband back to front? How many hundreds of nights had they lain entwined like Siamese twins, whispering confidences and sharing laughter in the dark? She'd spent nearly half her life with Matthew, and not until a hard, bright diamond ear stud had appeared in their bed had she realised that he was living a life apart, and was not, and perhaps never had been, the man she thought she knew.

'You don't want to think she had an abortion,' said Strike, correctly deducing at least part of the reason for Robin's silence. She didn't answer, instead asking,

'You haven't heard back from her friend Oonagh, have you?'

'Didn't I tell you?' said Strike. 'Yeah, I got an email yesterday. She *is* a retired vicar, and she'd be delighted to meet us when she comes down to London to do some Christmas shopping. Date to be confirmed.'

'That's good,' said Robin. 'You know, I'd like to talk to someone who actually *liked* Margot.'

'Gupta liked her,' said Strike. 'And Janice, she's just said so.'

Robin ripped open the second bag of crisps.

'Which is what you'd expect, isn't it?' she said. 'That people would at least *pretend* they liked Margot, after what happened. But Irene didn't. Don't you find it a bit ... *excessive* ... to be holding on to that much resentment, forty years later? She really put the boot in. Wouldn't you think it was ... I don't know, more *politic* ... '

'To claim to be friends?'

'Yes ... but maybe Irene knew there were far too many witnesses to the fact that they *weren't* friends. What did you think of the anonymous notes? True or false?'

'Good question,' said Strike, scratching his chin. 'Irene really enjoyed telling us Margot had been called "the c-word", but "hell-fire" doesn't sound like the kind of thing she'd invent. I'd have expected something more in the "uppity bitch" line.'

He drew out his notebook again, and scanned the notes he'd made of the interview.

'Well, we still need to check these leads out, for what they're worth. Why don't you follow up Charlie Ramage and Leamington Spa, and I'll look into the Bennie-abusing Applethorpe?'

'You just did it again,' said Robin.

'Did what?'

'Smirked when you said "Bennies". What's so funny about benzedrine?'

'Oh—' Strike chuckled. 'I was just reminded of something my Uncle Ted told me. Did you ever watch *Crossroads*?'

'What's *Crossroads*?'

'I always forget how much younger you are,' Strike said. 'It was a daytime soap opera and it had a character in it called Benny. He was – well, these days you'd call him special needs. Simple. He wore a woolly hat. Iconic character, in his way.'

'You were thinking of him?' said Robin. It didn't seem particularly amusing.

'No, but you need to know about him to understand the next bit. I assume you know about the Falklands War.'

'I'm younger than you, Strike. I'm not pig-ignorant.'

'OK, right. So, the British troops who went over there – Ted was there, 1982 – nicknamed the locals "Bennies", after the character on *Crossroads*. Command gets wind of this, and the order comes down the line, "Stop calling these people we've just liberated Bennies". So,' said Strike, grinning, 'They started calling them "Stills".'

'"Stills"? What does "Stills" mean?'

'"Still Bennies,"' said Strike, and he let out a great roar of laughter. Robin laughed, too, but mostly at Strike's amusement. When his guffaws had subsided, both watched the river for a few seconds, drinking and, in Strike's case, smoking, until he said,

'I'm going to write to the Ministry of Justice. Apply for permission to visit Creed.'

'Seriously?'

'We've got to try. The authorities always thought Creed assaulted or killed more women than he was done for. There was jewellery in his house and bits of clothing nobody ever identified. Just because everyone thinks it's Creed—'

'—doesn't mean it isn't,' agreed Robin, who followed the tortured logic perfectly.

Strike sighed, rubbed his face, cigarette still poking out of his mouth, then said,

'Want to see exactly how crazy Talbot was?'

'Go on.'

Strike pulled the leather-bound notebook out of the inside pocket of his coat and handed it to her. Robin opened it and turned the pages in silence.

They were covered in strange drawings and diagrams. The writing was small, meticulously neat but cramped. There was much under-lining and circling of phrases and symbols. The pentagram recurred. The pages were littered with names, but none connected with the case: Crowley, Lévi, Adams and Schmidt.

'Huh,' she said quietly, stopping on a particularly heavily embel-lished page on which a goat's head with a third eye looked balefully up at her. 'Look at this . . . '

She bent closer.

'He's using astrological symbols.'

'He's what?' said Strike, frowning down at the page she was perusing.

'That's Libra,' said Robin, pointing at a symbol towards the bottom of the page. 'It's my sign, I used to have a keyring with that on it.'

'He's using bloody *star signs*?' said Strike, pulling the book back towards him, looking so disgusted that Robin started to laugh again.

Strike scanned the page. Robin was right. The circles drawn around the goat's head told him something else, too.

'He's calculated the full horoscope for the moment he thought she was abducted,' he said. 'Look at the date there. The eleventh of October 1974. Half past six in the evening . . . fuck's sake. *Astrology* . . . he was out of his tree.'

'What's your sign?' asked Robin, trying to work it out.

'No idea.'

'Oh sod off,' said Robin.

He looked at her, taken aback.

'You're being affected!' she said. 'Everyone knows their star sign. Don't pretend to be above it.'

Strike grinned reluctantly, took a large drag on his cigarette, exhaled, then said,

'Sagittarius, Scorpio rising, with the sun in the first house.'

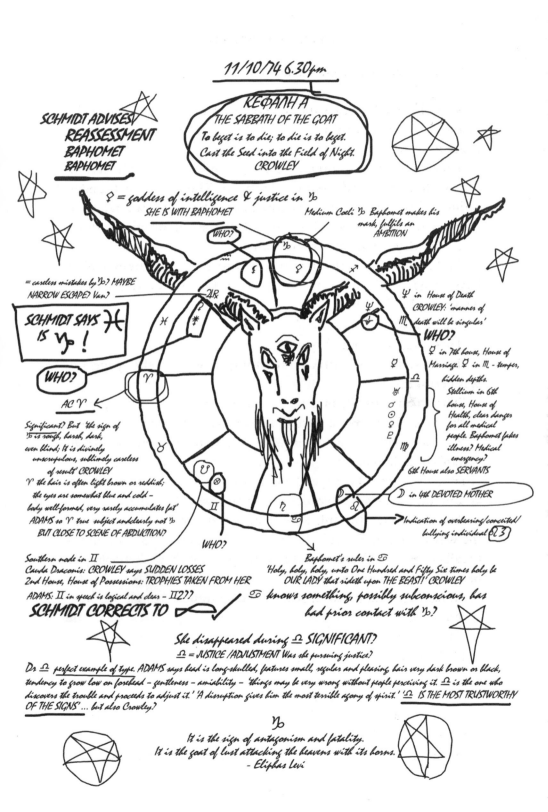

11/10/74 6.30pm

ΚΕΦΑΛΗ Α
THE SABBATH OF THE GOAT
To beget is to die; to die is to beget.
Cast the Seed into the Field of Night.
CROWLEY

SCHMIDT ADVISES REASSESSMENT
BAPHOMET
BAPHOMET

♀ = *goddess of intelligence & justice in* ♑
SHE IS WITH BAPHOMET

Medium Coeli ♑ *Baphomet makes his mark, fulfils an* AMBITION

= *careless mistakes by* ♑*? MAYBE NARROW ESCAPE? Van?*

WHO?

SCHMIDT SAYS ♓ **IS** ♑ !

WHO?

AC ♈

Significant? But 'the sign of ♑ *is rough, harsh, dark, even blind; It is divinely unscrupulous, sublimely careless of result' CROWLEY*
♈ *'the hair is often light brown or reddish; the eyes are somewhat blue and cold — body well-formed, very rarely accumulates fat' ADAMS so* ♈ *true subject and clearly not* ♑
BUT CLOSE TO SCENE OF ABDUCTION?

Ψ *in House of Death*
CROWLEY: 'manner of
♏ *death will be singular'*

WHO?

♀ *in 7th house, House of Marriage.* ♀ *in* ♏ *- temper, hidden depths.*
Stellium in 6th house, House of Health, clear danger for all medical people. Baphomet fakes illness? Medical emergency?
6th House also SERVANTS

☽ *in 4th DEVOTED MOTHER*

Indication of overbearing/conceited/bullying individual 23

WHO?

Southern node in ♊
Cauda Draconis: CROWLEY says SUDDEN LOSSES
2nd House, House of Possessions: TROPHIES TAKEN FROM HER
ADAMS: ♊ *in speech is logical and clear -* ♊*??*

SCHMIDT CORRECTS TO ♋ ✓

Baphomet's ruler in ♋
'Holy, holy, holy, unto One Hundred and Fifty Six times holy be
OUR LADY *that rideth upon* THE BEAST!' *CROWLEY*
♋ *knows something, possibly subconscious, has had prior contact with* ♑*?*

She disappeared during ♎ SIGNIFICANT?
♎ = JUSTICE /ADJUSTMENT *Was she pursuing justice?*

Dr ♎ *perfect example of type. ADAMS says head is long-skulled, features small, regular and pleasing, hair very dark brown or black, tendency to grow low on forehead – gentleness – amiability – 'things may be very wrong without people perceiving it.* ♎ *is the one who discovers the trouble and proceeds to adjust it.' 'A disruption gives him the most terrible agony of spirit.'* ♎ IS THE MOST TRUSTWORTHY OF THE SIGNS' *... but also Crowley?*

♑
It is the sign of antagonism and fatality.
It is the goat of lust attacking the heavens with its horns.
- Eliphas Levi

'You're—' Robin began to laugh. 'Did you just pull that out of your backside, or is it real?'

'Of course, it's not fucking *real*,' said Strike. '*None* of it's real, is it? But yeah. That's what my *natal horoscope* says. Stop bloody laughing. Remember who my mother was. She loved all that shit. One of her best mates did my full horoscope for her when I was born. I should have recognised that straight off,' he said, pointing at the goat drawing. 'But I haven't been through this properly yet, haven't had time.'

'So what does having the sun in the first house mean?'

'It means nothing, it's all bollocks.'

Robin could tell that he didn't want to admit that he'd remembered, which made her laugh some more. Half-annoyed, half-amused, he muttered,

'Independent. Leadership.'

'Well—'

'It's all bollocks, and we've got enough mystic crap swimming round this case without adding star signs. The medium and the holy place, Talbot and Baphomet—'

'—Irene and her broken Margot Fonteyn,' said Robin.

'Irene and her broken fucking Margot Fonteyn,' Strike muttered, rolling his eyes.

A fine shower of icy rain began to fall, speckling the table top and over Talbot's notebook, which Strike closed before the ink could run. In unspoken agreement, both got up and headed back towards the Land Rover.

The lavender-haired old lady who shared Strike's birthday was now being helped into a nearby Toyota by what looked like two daughters. All around her car stood family, smiling and talking under umbrellas. Just for a moment, as he pulled himself back inside the Land Rover, Strike wondered where he'd be if he lived to eighty, and who'd be there with him.

22

And later times thinges more vnknowne shall show.
Why then should witlesse man so much misweene
That nothing is but that which he hath seene?
What if within the Moones fayre shining spheare,
What if in euery other starre vnseene
Of other worldes he happily should heare?

Edmund Spenser
The Faerie Queene

Strike got himself a takeaway that night, to eat alone in his attic flat. As he upended the Singapore noodles onto his plate, he inwardly acknowledged the irony that, had Ilsa not been so keen to act as midwife to a romantic relationship between himself and Robin, he might now have been sitting in Nick and Ilsa's flat in Octavia Road, enjoying a laugh with two of his old friends and indeed with Robin herself, whose company had never yet palled on him, through the many long hours they had worked together.

Strike's thoughts lingered on his partner while he ate, on the kiss on the well-chosen card, on the headphones and the fact that she was now calling him Strike in moments of annoyance, or when the two of them were joking, all of them clear signs of increasing intimacy. However stressful the divorce proceedings, of which she'd shared few details, however little she might consciously be seeking romance, she was nevertheless a free agent.

Not for the first time, Strike wondered exactly how egotistical it was to suspect that Robin's feelings towards him might be warmer

than those of pure friendship. He got on with her better than he'd
ever got on with any woman. Their mutual liking had survived all
the stresses of running a business together, the personal trials each
had endured since they had met, even the major disagreement
that had once seen him sack her. She'd hurried to the hospital when
he had found himself alone with a critically ill nephew, brooking, he
had no doubt, the displeasure of the ex-husband Strike never forgot
to call 'that arsehole' inside his own head.

Nor was Strike unconscious of Robin's good looks: indeed, he'd
been fully aware of them ever since she'd taken off her coat in his
office for the first time. But her physical appeal was less of a threat to
his peace of mind than the deep, guilty liking for being, currently,
the main man in her life. Now that the possibility of something more
lay in front of him, now that her husband was gone, and she was
single, he found himself seriously wondering what would happen,
should they act upon what he was beginning to suspect was a mutual
attraction. Could the agency, for which they'd both sacrificed so
much, which for Strike represented the culmination of all his ambitions, survive the partners falling into bed together? However he
reframed this question, the answer always came back 'no', because he
was certain, for reasons that had to do with past trauma, not from any
particularly puritanical streak, that what Robin sought, ultimately,
was the security and permanence of marriage.

And he wasn't the marrying kind. No matter the inconveniences,
what he craved at the end of a working day was his private space,
clean and ordered, organised exactly as he liked it, free of emotional
storms, from guilt and recriminations, from demands to service
Hallmark's idea of romance, from a life where someone else's happiness was his responsibility. The truth was that he'd always been
responsible for some woman: for Lucy, as they grew up together in
squalor and chaos; for Leda, who lurched from lover to lover, and
whom he had sometimes had to physically protect as a teenager;
for Charlotte, whose volatility and self-destructive tendencies had
been given many different names by therapists and psychiatrists, but
whom he had loved in spite of it all. He was alone now, and at a
kind of peace. None of the affairs or one-night stands he'd had since

Charlotte had touched the essential part of him. He'd sometimes wondered since whether Charlotte had not stunted his ability to feel deeply.

Except that, almost against his will, he did care about Robin. He felt familiar stirrings of a desire to make her happy that irked him far more than the habit he'd developed of looking determinedly away when she bent over a desk. They were friends, and he hoped they'd always be friends, and he suspected the best way to guarantee that was never see each other naked.

When he'd washed up his plate, Strike opened the window to admit the cold night air, reminding himself that every woman he knew would have been complaining immediately about the draught. He then lit a cigarette, opened the laptop he'd brought upstairs and drafted a letter to the Ministry of Justice, explaining that he'd been hired by Anna Phipps, setting out his proven credentials as an investigator both within the army and outside it, and requesting permission to visit and question Dennis Creed in Broadmoor.

Once finished, he yawned, lit his umpteenth cigarette of the day and went to lie down on his bed, as usual undoing his trousers first. Picking up *The Demon of Paradise Park*, he turned to the final chapter.

> The question that haunts the officers who entered Creed's basement in 1976 and saw for themselves the combination of jail and torture chamber that he'd constructed there, is whether the 12 women he is known to have assaulted, raped and/or killed represent the total tally of his victims.
>
> In our final interview, Creed, who that morning had been deprived of privileges following an aggressive outburst against a prison officer, was at his least communicative and most cryptic.
>
> Q: People suspect there may have been more victims.
> A: Is that right?
> Q: Louise Tucker. She was sixteen, she'd run away—
> A: You journalists love putting ages on people, don't you? Why is that?

Q: Because it paints a picture. It's a detail we can all identify with. D'you know anything about Louise Tucker?

A: Yeah. She was sixteen.

Q: There was unclaimed jewellery in your basement. Unclaimed pieces of clothing.

A: ...

Q: You don't want to talk about the unclaimed jewellery?

A: ...

Q: Why don't you want to talk about those unclaimed items?

A: ...

Q: Does any part of you think, "I've got nothing to lose, now. I could put people's minds at rest. Stop families wondering"?

A: ...

Q: You don't think, it would be a kind of reparation? I could repair something of my reputation?

A: [laughs] "Reputation" ... you think I spend my days worrying about my reputation? You people really don't [indistinguishable]

Q: What about Kara Wolfson? Disappeared in '73.

A: How old was she?

Q: Twenty-six. Club hostess in Soho.

A: I don't like whores.

Q: Why's that?

A: Filthy.

Q: You frequented prostitutes.

A: When there was nothing else on offer.

Q: You tried – Helen Wardrop was a prostitute. And she got away from you. Gave a description to the police.

A: ...

Q: You tried to abduct Helen in the same area Kara was last seen.

A: ...

Q: What about Margot Bamborough?

A: ...

Q: A van resembling your van was seen speeding in the area she disappeared.

A: ...

Q: If you abducted Bamborough, she'd have been in your basement at the same time as Susan Meyer, wouldn't she?

A: ... Nice for her.

Q: Was it nice for her?

A: Someone to talk to.

Q: Are you saying you were holding both Bamborough and Meyer at the same time?

A: [smiles]

Q: What about Andrea Hooton? Was Bamborough dead when you abducted Andrea?

A: ...

Q: You threw Andrea's body off cliffs. That was a change in your m.o. Was she the first body you threw off there?

A: ...

Q: You don't want to confirm whether you abducted Margot Bamborough?

A: [smiles]

Strike put down the book and lay for a while, smoking and thinking. Then he reached for Bill Talbot's leather-bound notebook, which he'd earlier thrown onto his bed when taking off his coat.

Flicking through the densely packed pages, looking for something comprehensible, something he could connect with a solid fact or reference point, he suddenly placed a thick finger in the book to stop the pages turning, his attention caught by a sentence written mostly in English that seemed familiar.

12th (♓) found. Therefore AS EXPECTED killer is ♑

It was an effort to get up and fetch his own notebook, but this he did. Slumping back onto his bed, he found the sentence that Pat had translated for him from Pitman shorthand:

And that is the last of them, the twelfth, and the circle will be closed upon finding the tenth – unknown word – Baphomet. Transcribe in the true book.

The unknown word, Strike realised, was the same symbol that followed the word 'Killer' in Talbot's notebook.

With a feeling of both exasperation and curiosity, Strike picked up his phone and Googled 'astrological symbols'.

A few minutes later, having read a couple of astrological web pages with an expression of mild distaste, he'd successfully interpreted Talbot's sentence. It read: *'Twelfth (Pisces) found. Therefore AS EXPECTED killer is Capricorn.'*

Pisces was the twelfth sign of the zodiac, Capricorn the tenth. Capricorn was also the sign of the goat, which Talbot, in his manic state, appeared to have connected with Baphomet, the goat-headed deity.

'Fuck's sake,' muttered Strike, turning to a fresh page in his notebook and writing something.

An idea now occurred to him: those strange, unexplained dates with crosses beside them on all the male witnesses' statements. He wondered whether he could be bothered to get up and go downstairs to fetch the relevant pages from the boxes of police records. With a sigh, he decided that the answer was yes. He did up his flies, heaved himself to his feet, and fetched the office keys from their hook by the door.

Ten minutes later, Strike returned to his bedroom with both his laptop and a fresh notebook. As he settled down on top of the duvet again, he noticed that the screen of his mobile, which was lying on the duvet, was now lit up. Somebody had tried to call him while he'd been downstairs. Expecting it to be Lucy, he picked up the phone and looked at it.

He'd just missed a call from Charlotte. Strike lay the phone back down again and opened his laptop. Slowly and painstakingly, he set to work matching the unexplained dates on each male suspect's witness statements with the relevant sign of the zodiac. If his hunch that Talbot had been checking the men's star signs was correct, Steven Douthwaite was a Pisces, Paul Satchwell was an Aries and Roy Phipps, who'd been born on the twenty-seventh of December . . . was a Capricorn. Yet Talbot had cleared Roy Phipps of involvement early in the case.

12th (♓) found. Therefore AS EXPECTED killer is ♑

'Capricornus is divinely unscrupulous, sublimely careless of result... thou hast no right but to do thy will. Do that, and no other shall say nay. For pure will, unassuaged of purpose, delivered from the lust of result, is every way perfect.' – Crowley

Husband can't be true ♑, Adams says ♑ materialistic, severe, hard-bitten, thin lipped, 'eyes small and piercing'

SCHMIDT EXPLAINS → NOT ♑ BUT ♏

resourceful, sensitive, musical
"I am the secret serpent coiled about to spring; in my coiling there is joy." – CROWLEY

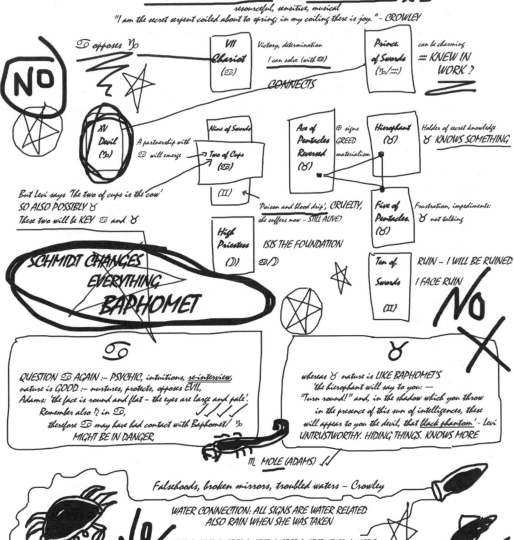

♋ opposes ♑

NO

VII Chariot (♋)   Victory, determination   I can solve (with ♊)   CONNECTS

Prince of Swords (♑/♒)   can be charming   ♒ KNEW IN WORK ?

XV Devil (♑)   A partnership with ♊ will emerge

Nine of Swords → **Two of Cups** (♊) (II)

Ace of Pentacles Reversed (♉)   ⊕ signs GREED   materialism

Hierophant (♉)   Holder of secret knowledge   ♉ KNOWS SOMETHING

But Levi says 'The two of cups is the 'cow'
SO ALSO POSSIBLY ♉
These two will be KEY ♊ and ♉

'Poison and blood drip', CRUELTY, she suffers now – STILL ALIVE?

Five of Pentacles (♉)   Frustration, impediments: ♉ not talking

High Priestess (☽))   ISIS THE FOUNDATION ♋/☽

SCHMIDT CHANGES EVERYTHING BAPHOMET

Ten of Swords (II)   RUIN – I WILL BE RUINED   I FACE RUIN   **NO**

♋

QUESTION ♋ AGAIN :– PSYCHIC, intuitions, re-interview,
nature is GOOD :– nurtures, protects, opposes EVIL,
Adams: 'the face is round and flat – the eyes are large and pale'.
Remember also ♄ in ♋,
therefore ♋ may have had contact with Baphomet/ ♑
MIGHT BE IN DANGER

♉

whereas ♉ nature is LIKE BAPHOMET'S
'the hierophant will say to you: –
"Turn round!" and, in the shadow which you throw
in the presence of this sun of intelligences, these
will appear to you the devil, that black phantom' – Levi
UNTRUSTWORTHY. HIDING THINGS. KNOWS MORE

♏ MOLE (ADAMS)

Falsehoods, broken mirrors, troubled waters – Crowley

WATER CONNECTION: ALL SIGNS ARE WATER RELATED.
ALSO RAIN WHEN SHE WAS TAKEN

NO

WATER WATER WATER WATER WATER WATER EVERYWHERE

♒ worried about how ♏ died?   SCHMIDT AGREES W ADAMS

Did ♒ challenge ♓ about ♏? Was ♋ there, did ♋ witness? ♋ is kind, instinct is to protect, INTERVIEW AGAIN.
♏ and ♒ are connected WATER WATER also ♋ and ♑ HAS A FISH'S TAIL.

The monster Cetus, Leviathan, the biblical whale
Superficial charm, evil in depths
Headstrong, enjoys spotlight
A performer, a liar

'So that makes no fucking sense,' muttered Strike to the empty room.

He put down his laptop and picked up Talbot's notebook again, reading on from the assertion that Margot's killer must be Capricorn.

'Christ almighty,' Strike muttered, trying, but not entirely succeeding, to find sense among the mass of esoteric ramblings with the aid of his astrological websites. As far as he could tell, Talbot appeared to have absolved Roy Phipps from suspicion on the grounds that he wasn't really a Capricorn, but some sign that Strike couldn't make head nor tail of, and which he suspected Talbot might have invented.

Returning to the notebook, Strike recognised the Celtic cross layout of tarot cards from his youth. Leda fancied herself a reader of tarot; many times had he seen her lay out the cards in the very formation Talbot had sketched in the middle of the page. He had never, however, seen the cards given astrological meanings before, and wondered whether this, too, had been Talbot's own invention.

His mobile buzzed again. He picked it up.

Charlotte had sent him a photograph. A naked photograph, of herself holding two coffees. The accompanying message said **6 years ago tonight. I wish it was happening again. Happy Birthday, Bluey x**

Against his will, Strike stared at the body no sentient heterosexual man could fail to desire, and at the face Venus would envy. Then he noticed the blurring along her lower stomach, where she'd airbrushed out her Caesarean scar. This took care of his burgeoning erection. Like an alcoholic pushing away brandy, he deleted the picture and returned to Talbot's notebook.

23

It is the mynd, that maketh good or ill,
That maketh wretch or happie, rich or poore:
For some, that hath abundance at his will,
Hath not enough, but wants in greatest store;
And other, that hath litle, askes no more,
But in that litle is both rich and wise.

Edmund Spenser
The Faerie Queene

Eleven days later, Robin was woken at 8 a.m. by her mobile ringing, after barely an hour's sleep. She'd spent the night on another pointless vigil outside the house of the persecuted weatherman, and had returned to her flat in Earl's Court to grab a couple of hours' sleep before hurrying out again to interview Oonagh Kennedy with Strike, in the café at Fortnum & Mason. Completely disorientated, she knocked a couple of items off the bedside table as she groped in the dark for her phone.

''Lo?'

'Robin?' said a happy shout in her ear. 'You're an aunt!'

'I'm what, sorry?' she muttered.

Wisps of her dreams still clung about her: Pat Chauncey had been asking her out to dinner, and had been deeply hurt that she didn't want to go.

'You're an aunt! Jenny's just had the baby!'

'Oh,' said Robin, and very slowly her brain computed that this was Stephen, her elder brother, on the line. 'Oh, that's wonderful . . . what—?'

'A girl!' said Stephen jubilantly. 'Annabel Marie. Eight pounds eight ounces!'

'Wow,' said Robin, 'that's – is that big? It seems—'

'I'm sending you a picture now!' said Stephen. 'Got it?'

'No – hang on,' said Robin, sitting up. Bleary-eyed, she switched to speakerphone to check her messages. The picture arrived as she was peering at the screen: a wrinkled, bald red baby swaddled in a hospital robe, fists balled up, looking furious to have been forced from a place of quiet, padded darkness into the brightness of a hospital ward.

'Just got it. Oh, Stephen, she's . . . she's beautiful.'

It was a lie, but nevertheless, tears prickled in the exhausted Robin's eyes.

'My God, Button,' she said quietly; it was Stephen's childhood nickname. 'You're a dad!'

'I know!' he said. 'Insane, isn't it? When are you coming home to see her?'

'Soon,' Robin promised. 'I'm back for Christmas. Give Jenny all my love, won't you?'

'I will, yeah. Gonna call Jon now. See you soon, Robs.'

The call was cut. Robin lay in darkness, staring at the brightly lit picture of the crumpled baby, whose puffy eyes were screwed up against a world she seemed to have decided already was not much of a place. It was quite extraordinary to think of her brother Stephen as a father, and that the family now had one more member.

Robin seemed to hear her cousin Katie's words again: *It's like you're travelling in a different direction to the rest of us.* In the old days with Matthew, before she'd started work at the agency, she'd expected to have children with him. Robin had no strong feelings *against* having children, it was simply that she knew, now, that the job she loved would be impossible if she were a mother, or at least, that it would stop being the job she loved. Motherhood, from her limited observation of those her age who were doing it, seemed to demand as much from a woman as she could possibly give. Katie had talked of the perennial tug on her heart when she wasn't with her son, and Robin had tried to imagine an emotional tether even stronger than the guilt and anger with which Matthew had tried to retain her. The problem wasn't that Robin didn't think she'd love her child. On the contrary, she thought it likely that she would love that child to the extent that this job, for which she had voluntarily sacrificed a marriage, her safety, her sleep and her financial security, would have to be sacrificed in return. And how would she feel, afterwards, about the person who'd made that sacrifice necessary?

Robin turned on the light and bent to pick up the things she had knocked off her bedside table: an empty glass, thankfully unbroken, and the thin, flimsy paperback entitled *Whatever Happened to Margot Bamborough?* by C. B. Oakden, which Robin had received in the post the previous morning, and which she'd already read.

Strike didn't yet know that she had managed to get hold of a copy of Oakden's book and Robin had been looking forward to showing him. She had a couple more fragments of Bamborough news, too, but now, perhaps because of her sheer exhaustion, the feeling of anticipation at sharing them had disappeared. Deciding that she wouldn't be able to get back to sleep, she got out of bed.

As she showered, Robin realised, to her surprise, that she was crying.

This is ridiculous. You don't even want a baby. Get a grip of yourself.

When Robin arrived upstairs, dressed, with her hair blow-dried and concealer applied to the shadows under her eyes, she found Max eating toast in the kitchen.

'Morning,' he said, looking up from a perusal of the day's news on his phone. 'You all right?'

'Fine,' said Robin, with forced brightness. 'Just found out I'm an aunt. My brother Stephen's wife gave birth this morning.'

'Oh. Congratulations,' said Max, politely interested. 'Um ... boy or girl?'

'Girl,' said Robin, turning on the coffee machine.

'I've got about eight godchildren,' said Max gloomily. 'Parents love giving the job to childless people. They think we'll put more effort in, having no kids of our own.'

'True,' said Robin, trying to maintain her cheery tone. She'd been made godmother to Katie's son. The christening had been the first time she'd been in the church in Masham since her wedding to Matthew.

She took a mug of black coffee back to her bedroom, where she opened up her laptop and decided to set down her new information on the Bamborough case in an email to Strike before they met. They might not have much time together before Oonagh Kennedy's interview, so this would expedite discussion.

Hi,

Few bits and pieces on Bamborough before I see you:

- Charles Ramage, the hot tub millionaire, is dead. I've spoken to his son, who couldn't confirm the story about the Margot sighting, but remembered Janice nursing his father after his crash and said Ramage Snr liked her and 'probably told her all his stories, he had loads of them'. Said his father never minded exaggerating if it made a story better, but was not a liar and 'had a good heart. Wouldn't have told a lie about a missing woman.' Also confirmed that his father was close friends with a 'senior police officer' (couldn't remember rank or first name) called Greene. Ramage Snr's widow is still alive and living in Spain, but she's his second wife and the son doesn't get on with her. I'm trying to get a contact number/ email address for her.

- I'm 99% sure I've found the right Amanda White, who's now called Amanda Laws. Two years ago she posted a piece on Facebook about people disappearing, which included Margot. She said in the comment that she'd been personally involved in the Margot disappearance. I've sent her a message but nothing back yet.

- I've got hold of a copy of *Whatever Happened to Margot Bamborough?* and read it (it's not long). Judging by what we know about Margot so far, it looks full of inaccuracies. I'll bring it with me this morning.

See you in a bit x

Sleep-deprived, Robin had added the kiss automatically and had sent the email before she could retract it. It was one thing to put a kiss on a birthday card, quite another to start adding them to work emails.

Shit.

She could hardly write a PS saying 'Ignore that kiss, my fingers did it without me meaning to.' That would draw attention to the thing if Strike hadn't thought anything of it.

As she closed her laptop, her mobile screen lit up: she'd received a long, excited text from her mother about baby Annabel Marie's perfection, complete with a photograph of herself cradling her new granddaughter, Robin's father beaming over his wife's shoulder. Robin texted back:

She's gorgeous!

even though the baby was quite as unprepossessing in the new photograph as she'd been in the old. Yet she wasn't really lying: the fact of Annabel's birth *was* somehow gorgeous, an everyday miracle, and Robin's mysterious shower tears had been partly in acknowledgement of the fact.

As the Tube sped her towards Piccadilly Circus, Robin took out her copy of C. B. Oakden's book, which she'd found at a second-hand bookshop in Chester, and flicked through it again. The dealer had said the book had been in his shop for several years, and had arrived in a job lot of books he'd taken off the hands of the family of an elderly local woman who'd died. Robin suspected that the dealer hadn't known of the book's murky legal status before Robin's email enquiry, but he appeared to have no particular moral qualms about selling it. As long as Robin guaranteed by phone that she wouldn't reveal where she'd got it, he was happy to part with it, for a hefty mark-up. Robin only hoped Strike would think the price justified, once he'd read it.

Robin's particular copy appeared to have escaped pulping because it had been one of the author's free copies, which must have been given to him before the court decision. An inscription on the fly-leaf read: *To Auntie May, with every good wish, CB Oakden (Carl).* To Robin, 'with every good wish' seemed an affected, grandiose message to send an aunt.

Barely a hundred pages long, the flimsy paperback had a photograph of Margot as a Bunny Girl on the cover, a picture familiar to Robin because it had appeared in so many newspaper reports of her disappearance. Half cut off in this enlarged picture was a second Bunny Girl, who Robin knew to be Oonagh Kennedy. The photograph was reproduced in its entirety in the middle of the paperback, along with other pictures which Robin thought Strike would agree were the most valuable part of the book, though only, she feared, in terms of putting faces to names rather than helping the investigation.

Robin got off the Tube at Piccadilly Circus and walked in a strong wind up Piccadilly, beneath swaying Christmas lights, wondering where she might find a baby present for Stephen and Jenny. Having passed no appropriate shops, she arrived outside Fortnum & Mason with an hour to spare before the projected meeting with Oonagh Kennedy.

Robin had often passed the famous store since she had lived in London, but never gone inside. The ornate frontage was duck-egg blue and the windows, dressed for Christmas, some of the most beautiful in the city. Robin peered through clear circles of glass surrounded by artificial snow, at heaps of jewel-like crystallised fruits, silk scarves, gilded tea canisters, and wooden nutcrackers shaped like fairy-tale princes. A gust of particularly cold, rain-flecked wind whipped at her, and, without conscious thought, Robin allowed herself to be swept inside the sumptuous seasonal fantasy, through a door flanked by a doorman in an overcoat and top hat.

The store was carpeted in scarlet. Everywhere were mountains of duck-egg blue packaging. Close at hand she saw the very truffles that Morris had bought her for her birthday. Past marzipan fruits and biscuits she walked, until she glimpsed the café at the back of the ground floor where they'd agreed to meet Oonagh. Robin turned back. She didn't want to see the retired vicar before the allotted time, because she wanted to reason herself into a more business-like frame of mind before an interview.

'Excuse me,' she asked a harried-looking woman selecting

marzipan fruits for a client, 'd'you sell anything for children in—?'

'Third floor,' said the woman, already moving away.

The small selection of children's goods available were, in Robin's view, exorbitantly priced, but as Annabel's only aunt, and only London-based relative, she felt a certain pressure to give a suitably metropolitan gift. Accordingly, she purchased a large, cuddly Paddington bear.

Robin was walking away from the till with her duck-egg carrier bag when her mobile rang. Expecting it to be Strike, she saw instead an unknown number.

'Hi, Robin here.'

'Hi, Robin. It's Tom,' said an angry voice.

Robin couldn't for the life of her think who Tom was. She mentally ran through the cases the agency was currently working on – Two-Times, Twinkletoes, Postcard, Shifty and Bamborough – trying in vain to remember a Tom, while saying with what she intended to be yes-of-course-I-know-who-you-are warmth,

'Oh, hi!'

'*Tom Turvey*,' said the man, who didn't appear fooled.

'Oh,' said Robin, her heart beginning to beat uncomfortably fast, and she drew back into an alcove where pricey scented candles stood on shelves.

Tom Turvey was Sarah Shadlock's fiancé. Robin had had no contact with him since finding out that their respective partners had been sleeping together. She'd never particularly liked him, nor had she ever found out whether he knew about the affair.

'Thanks,' said Tom. 'Thanks a *fucking bunch*, Robin!'

He was close to shouting. Robin distanced the mobile a little from her ear.

'Excuse me?' she said, but she suddenly seemed to have become all nerves and pulse.

'Didn't bother fucking telling me, eh? Just walked away and washed your hands, did you?'

'Tom—'

'She's told me *fucking* everything, and you knew a year ago and I find out today, *four weeks before my wedding*—'

'Tom, I—'

'Well, I hope you're fucking happy!' he bellowed. Robin removed the phone from her ear and held it at arm's length. He was still clearly audible as he yelled, 'I'm the only one of us who hasn't been fucking around, and I'm the one who's been *fucked over*—'

Robin cut him off. Her hands were shaking.

'*Excuse me*,' said a large woman, who was trying to see the candles on the shelves behind Robin, who mumbled an apology and walked away, until she reached a curving iron banister, beyond which was a large, circular expanse of thin air. Looking down, she saw the floors had been cut out, so that she was able to see right into the basement, where compressed people were criss-crossing the space with baskets laden with expensive hams and bottles of wine. Head spinning, hardly aware of what she was doing, Robin turned and headed blindly back towards the department exit, trying not to bump into tables piled with fragile china. Down the red carpeted stairs she walked, trying to breathe herself back to calm, trying to make sense of what she'd just heard.

'Robin.'

She walked on, and only when somebody said '*Robin*' again did she turn and realise Strike had just entered the store via a side door from Duke Street. The shoulders of his overcoat were studded with glimmering raindrops.

'Hi,' she said, dazed.

'You all right?'

For a split-second she wanted to tell him everything: after all, he knew about Matthew's affair, he knew how her marriage had ended and he'd met Tom and Sarah. However, Strike himself looked tense, his mobile gripped in his hand.

'Fine. You?'

'Not great,' he said.

The two of them moved aside to allow a group of tourists into the store. In the shadow of the wooden staircase Strike said,

'Joan's taken a turn for the worse. They've readmitted her to hospital.'

'Oh God, I'm so sorry,' said Robin. 'Listen – go to Cornwall. We'll cope. I'll interview Oonagh, I'll take care of everything—'

'No. She specifically told Ted she didn't want us all dashing down there again. But that's not like her . . . '

Strike seemed every bit as scattered and distracted as Robin felt, but now she pulled herself together. *Screw Tom, screw Matthew and Sarah.*

'Seriously, Cormoran, go. I can take care of work.'

'They're expecting me in a fortnight for Christmas. Ted says she's desperate to have us all at home. It's supposed to be just for a couple of days, the hospital thing.'

'Well, if you're sure . . . ' said Robin. She checked her watch. 'We've got ten minutes until Oonagh's supposed to be here. Want to go to the café and wait for her?'

'Yeah,' said Strike. 'Good thinking, I could use a coffee.'

'God Rest Ye Merry, Gentlemen' trilled from the speakers as they entered the realm of crystallised fruits and expensive teas, both lost in painful thought.

24

... my delight is all in ioyfulnesse,
In beds, in bowres, in banckets, and in feasts:
And ill becomes you with your lofty creasts,
To scorne the ioy, that Ioue is glad to seeke ...

Edmund Spenser
The Faerie Queene

The café was reached by a flight of stairs that placed it on a higher level than the shop floor, which it overlooked. Once he and Robin had sat down at a table for four by the window, Strike sat silently looking down into Jermyn Street, where passers-by were reduced to moving mushrooms, eclipsed by their umbrellas. He was a stone's throw from the restaurant in which he'd last seen Charlotte.

He'd received several more calls from her since the nude photograph on his birthday, plus several texts, three of which had arrived the previous evening. He'd ignored all of them, but somewhere at the back of his anxiety about Joan scuttled a familiar worry about what Charlotte's next move was going to be, because the texts were becoming increasingly overwrought. She had a couple of suicide attempts in her past, one of which had almost succeeded. Three years after he'd left her, she was still trying to make him responsible for her safety and her happiness, and Strike found it equally infuriating and saddening. When Ted had called Strike that morning with the news about Joan, the detective had been in the process of looking up the telephone number of the merchant bank where Charlotte's husband worked. If Charlotte threatened suicide, or sent any kind of final message, Strike intended to call Jago.

'Cormoran,' Robin said.

He looked round. A waiter had arrived at the table. When both had ordered coffee, and Robin some toast, each relapsed into silence. Robin was looking away from the window towards the shoppers stocking up on fancy groceries for Christmas down on the shop floor and re-running Tom Turvey's outburst in her head. The aftershocks were still hitting her. *Four weeks before my fucking wedding.* It must have been called off. Sarah had left Tom for Matthew, the man she'd wanted all along, and Robin was sure she wouldn't have left Tom unless Matthew had shown himself ready to offer her what Tom had: diamonds and a change of name. *I'm the only one of us who hasn't been fucking around.* Everyone had been unfaithful, in Tom's opinion, except poor Tom . . . so Matthew must have told his old friend that she, Robin, had been sleeping with someone else (which meant Strike, of course, of whom Matthew had been perennially jealous and suspicious from the moment Robin had gone to work for him). And even now that Tom knew about Matthew and Sarah, after his old friend's duplicity and treachery had been revealed, Tom still believed the lie about Robin and Strike. Doubtless he thought his current misery was all Robin's fault, that if she hadn't succumbed to Strike, the domino effect of infidelity would never have been started.

'You sure you're all right?'

Robin started and looked around. Strike had come out of his own reverie and was looking at her over his coffee cup.

'Fine,' she said. 'Just knackered. Did you get my email?'

'Email?' said Strike, reaching for the phone in his pocket. 'Yeah, but I haven't read it, sorry. Dealing with other—'

'Don't bother now,' said Robin hastily, inwardly cringing at the thought of that accidental kiss, even in the midst of her new troubles. 'It isn't particularly important, it'll keep. I did find this, though.'

She took the copy of *Whatever Happened to Margot Bamborough?* out of her bag and passed it over the table, but before Strike could express his surprise, she muttered,

'Give it back, give it back now,' tugged it back out of his hand and stuffed it into her bag.

A stout woman was heading towards them across the café. Two

bulging bags of Christmas fare were dangling from her hands. She had the full cheeks and large square front teeth of a cheerful-looking chipmunk, an aspect that in her youthful photos had added a certain cheeky charm to her prettiness. The hair that once had been long, dark and glossy was now chin-length and white, except at the front, where a dashing bright purple streak had been added. A large silver and amethyst cross bounced on her purple sweater.

'Oonagh?' said Robin.

'Dat's me,' she panted. She seemed nervous. 'The *queues*! Well, what do I expect, Fortnum's at Christmas? But fair play, dey *do* a lovely mustard.'

Robin smiled. Strike drew out the chair beside him.

'T'anks very much,' said Oonagh, sitting down.

Her Irish accent was attractive, and barely eroded by what Robin knew had been a longer residence in England than in the country of her birth.

Both detectives introduced themselves.

'Very nice to meet you,' Oonagh said, shaking hands before clearing her throat nervously. 'Excuse me. I was *made up* to get yer message,' she told Strike. 'Years and years I've spent, wondering why Roy never hired someone, because he's got the money to do it and the police never got anywhere. So little Anna called you in, did she? God bless that gorl, *what* she must've gone through . . . Oh, hello,' she said to the waiter, 'could I have a cappuccino and a bit of that carrot cake? T'ank you.'

When the waiter had gone, Oonagh took a deep breath and said, 'I know I'm rattlin' on. I'm nervous, that's the truth.'

'There's nothing to be—' began Strike.

'Oh, there is,' Oonagh contradicted him, looking sober. 'Whatever happened to Margot, it can't be anything good, can it? Nigh on forty years I've prayed for that girl, prayed for the truth and prayed God would look after her, alive or dead. She was the best friend I ever had and – sorry. I knew this would happen. Knew it.'

She picked up her unused cloth napkin and mopped her eyes.

'Ask me a question,' she said, half-laughing. 'Save me from meself.'

Robin glanced at Strike, who handed the interview to her with a look as he pulled out his notebook.

'Well, perhaps we can start with how you and Margot met?' Robin suggested.

'We can, o' course,' said Oonagh. 'That would've been '66. We were both auditioning to be Bunny Girls. You'll know all about that?'

Robin nodded.

'I had a decent figure then, believe it or not,' said Oonagh, smiling as she gestured down at her tubby torso, although she seemed to feel little regret for the loss of her waist.

Robin hoped Strike wasn't going to take her to task later for not organising her questions according to the usual categories of *people, places and things*, but she judged it better to make this feel more like a normal conversation, at least at first, because Oonagh was still visibly nervous.

'Did you come over from Ireland, to try and get the job?' asked Robin.

'Oh no,' said Oonagh. 'I was already in London. I kinda run away from home, truth be told. You're lookin' at a convent gorl with a mammy as strict as a prison warder. I had a week's wages from a clothes shop in Derry in my pocket, and my mammy gave me one row too many. I walked out, got on the ferry, came to London and sent a postcard home to tell 'em I was alive and not to worry. My mammy didn't speak to me for t'irty years.

'I was waitressing when I heard they were opening a Playboy Club in Mayfair. Well, the money was *crazy* good compared to what you could earn in a normal place. T'irty-five pounds a week, we started on. That's near enough six hundred a week, nowadays. There was nowhere else in London was going to pay a working-class gorl that. It was more than most of our daddies earned.'

'And you met Margot at the club?'

'I met her at the audition. Knew *she'd* get hired the moment I looked at her. She had the figure of a model: all legs, and the girl *lived* on sugar. She was t'ree years younger than me, and she lied about her age so they'd take – oh, t'ank you very much,' said Oonagh, as the waiter placed her cappuccino and carrot cake in front of her.

'Why was Margot auditioning?' Robin asked.

'Because her family had nothing – and I mean, *nothing*, now,' Oonagh said. 'Her daddy had an accident when she was four. Fell off a step-ladder, broke his back. Crippled. That's why she had no brothers and sisters. Her mammy used to clean people's houses. *My* family had more than the Bamboroughs and nobody ever got rich farming a place the size of ours. But the Bamboroughs were not-enough-to-eat poor.

'She was such a clever girl, but the family needed help. She got herself into medical school, told the university she'd have to defer for a year, then headed straight for the Playboy Club. We took to each other straight away, in the audition, because she was *so funny*.'

'Was she?' said Robin. Out of the corner of her eye, she saw Strike look up from his notebook in surprise.

'Oh, Margot Bamborough was the funniest person I ever knew in my life,' said Oonagh. 'In my *loife*, now. We used to laugh till we cried. I've never laughed like that since. Proper cockney accent and she could just make you laugh until you *dropped*.

'So we started work together, and they were *strict*, mind you,' said Oonagh, now forking cake into her mouth as she talked. 'Inspected before you walked out on the floor, uniform on properly, nails done, and then there were *rules* like you've no idea. They used to put plain-clothes detectives in the club to catch us out, make sure we weren't giving out our full names or our phone numbers.

'If you were any good at it, you could put a tidy bit of money away. Margot graduated to cigarette girl, selling them out of a little tray. She was popular with the men because she was so funny. She hardly spent a penny on herself. She split the lot between a savings account for medical school and the rest she gave her mammy. Worked every hour they'd let her. Bunny Peggy, she called herself, because she didn't want any of the punters to know her real name. I was Bunny *Una*, because nobody knew how to say "Oonagh". We got all kinds of offers – you had to say no, of course. But it was nice to be asked, right enough,' said Oonagh, and perhaps picking up on Robin's surprise, she smiled and said,

'Don't think Margot and I didn't know *exactly* what we were doin', corseted up with bunny ears on our heads. What you maybe don't realise is a woman couldn't get a mortgage in dose days without a man co-signing the forms. Same with credit cards. I squandered my money at first, but I learned better, learned from Margot. I got smart, I started saving. I ended up buying my own flat with cash. Middle-class gorls, with their mammies and daddies paying their way, they could afford to burn their bras and have hairy armpits. Margot and I, we did what we had to.

'Anyway, the Playboy Club was sophisticated. It wasn't a knocking shop. It had licences it would've lost if things got seedy. We had women guests, too. Men used to bring their wives, their dates. The worst we had was a bit of tail-pulling, but if a club member got really handsy, he lost his membership. You should've seen what I had to put up with in my job before that: hands up my skirt when I bent over a table, and worse. They looked after us at the Playboy Club. Members weren't allowed to date Bunny Girls – well, in t'eory. It happened. It happened to Margot. I was angry at her for that, I said, you're risking everything, you fool.'

'Was this Paul Satchwell?' asked Robin.

'It was indeed,' said Oonagh. 'He'd come to the club as someone's guest, he wasn't a member, so Margot t'ought it was a grey area. I was still worried she was going to lose the job.'

'You didn't like him?'

'No, I didn't like him,' said Oonagh. 'T'ought he was Robert Plant, so he did, but Margot fell for him hook, line and sinker. She didn't go out a lot, see, because she was saving. I'd been round the nightclubs in my first year in London; I'd met plenty of Satchwells. He was six years older than she was, an artist and he wore his jeans so tight you could see his cock and balls right through them.'

Strike let out an involuntary snort of laughter. Oonagh looked at him.

'Sorry,' he muttered. 'You're, ah, not like most vicars I've met.'

'I don't t'ink the Good Lord will mind me mentioning cocks and balls,' said Oonagh airily. 'He made 'em, didn't he?'

'So they started dating?' asked Robin.

'They did,' said Oonagh. '*Mad* passion, it was. You could *feel* the heat off the two of them. For Margot – see, before Satchwell, she'd always had *tunnel vision* about life, you know, eyes on the prize: become a doctor and save her family. She was cleverer than any of the boys she knew, and men don't like that much *nowadays*. She was taller than half of them, as well. She told me she'd never had a man interested in her brains before Satchwell. *Interested in her brains*, my aunt Nelly. The girl had a body like Jane Birkin. Oh, and it wasn't only *his* looks, either, she said. He'd read t'ings. He could talk about art. He could talk for the *hour* about art, right enough. I heard him. Well, *I* don't know a Monet from a poster of Margate, so I'm no judge, but it sounded a load of old bollocks to me.

'But he'd take Margot out to a gallery and educate her about art, then he'd take her home to bed. Sex makes fools of us all,' sighed Oonagh Kennedy. 'And he was her very first and it was obvious, you know,' she nodded at Robin, 'he knew what he was doing, so it was all that much more important to her. Mad in love, she was. *Mad.*

'Then, one night, just a couple o' weeks before she was supposed to be starting medical school, she turns up at my flat *howling*. She'd dropped in on Paul unexpected after work and there was another woman at the flat with him. Naked. *Modelling*, he told her. Modelling – at midnight. She turned round and ran. He went chasin' after her, but she jumped in a taxi and came to mine.

'*Heartbroken*, she was. All night, we sat up talking, me saying "You're better off without him", which was no more than the truth. I said to her, "Margot, you're about to start medical school. The place'll be *wall to wall* with handsome, clever boys training to be doctors. You won't remember Satchwell's *name* after a week or two."

'But then, near dawn, she told me a t'ing I've never told anyone before.'

Oonagh hesitated. Robin tried to look politely but warmly receptive.

'She'd let him take pictures of her. You know. *Pictures*. And she was scared, she wanted them back. I said to her, why in God's name would you let him do such a t'ing, Margot? Because it would've *killed* her mother. The pride they had in her, their only daughter, their brilliant gorl. If those photos turned up anywhere, a magazine or I don't know what, they'd have never lived it down, boastin' up and down their street about their Margot, the genius.

'So I said, I'll come with you and we'll get them back. So we went round there early and banged on his door. The bastard – excuse me, now,' she said. 'You'll rightly say, that's not a Christian attitude, but wait till you hear. Satchwell said to Margot, "I'll speak to you, but not your nanny." Your *nanny*.

'Well, now. I spent ten years working with domestic abuse survivors in Wolverhampton and it's one of the *hallmarks* of an abuser, if their victim isn't compliant, it's because she's under someone *else's* control. Her *nanny*.

'Before I know what's going on, she's inside and I'm stuck on the other side of a closed door. He'd pulled her in and slammed it in my face. I could hear them shouting at each other. Margot was giving as good as she got, God bless her.

'And then, and this is what I *really* wanted to tell you,' said Oonagh, 'and I want to get it right. I told that Inspector Talbot and he didn't listen to a word I was saying, and I told the one who took over, what was his name—?'

'Lawson?' asked Robin.

'Lawson,' said Oonagh, nodding. 'I told both of 'em: I could hear Margot and Paul screaming at each other through the door, Margot telling him to give her the pictures and the negatives – different world, you see. Negatives, you had to get, if you didn't want more copies made. But he refused. He said they were *his copyright*, the dirty bastard – so then I heard Margot say, and this is the important bit, "If you show those pictures to anyone, if they ever turn up in print, I'll go straight to the police and I'll tell them all about your little *pillow* dream—"'

'"Pillow dream"?' repeated Robin.

'That's what she said. And he hit her. A smack loud enough to hear through solid wood, and I heard her shriek. Well, I started hammering and kicking the door. I said, unless he opened it I was going for the police *right now. That* put the fear o' God into him. He opened the door and Margot comes out, hand to her face, it was bright red, you could see his finger marks, and I pulled her behind me and I said to Satchwell, "Don't you *ever* come near her again, and you heard what she said. There'll be trouble if those pictures turn up anywhere."

'And I swear to you, he looked murderous. He stepped right up to me, the way a man will when he wants to remind you what he could do, if he wanted. Almost standing on my toes, he was. I didn't shift,' said Oonagh Kennedy. 'I stood my ground, but I was scared, I won't deny it. And he said to Margot, "Have you told her?" And Margot says, "She doesn't know anything. Yet." And he says, "Well, you know what'll happen if I find out you've talked." And he mimed – well, never mind. It was an – an obscene pose, I suppose you'd say. One of the pictures he'd taken. And he walked back into his flat and slammed the door.'

'Did Margot ever tell you what she meant by the "pillow dream"?' asked Robin.

'She wouldn't. You might t'ink she was scared, but ... you know, I t'ink it's just women,' sighed Oonagh. 'We're socialised that way, but maybe Mother Nature's got a hand in it. How many kids would survive to their first birthday if their mammies couldn't forgive 'em?

'Even that day, with his handprint across her face, she didn't want to tell me, because there was a bit of her that didn't want to hurt him. I saw it all the bloody time with my domestic abuse survivors. Women still protecting them. Still worrying about them! Love dies hard in some women.'

'Did she see Satchwell after that?'

'I wish to *God* I could say she didn't,' said Oonagh, shaking her head, 'but yes, she did. They couldn't stay away from each other.

'She started her degree course, but she was that popular at the club, they let her go part time, so I was still seeing a lot of her. One day, her mammy called the club because her daddy had taken sick, but Margot hadn't come in. I was terrified: where was Margot, what had happened to her, why wasn't she there? I've often t'ought back to that moment, you know, because when it happened for real, I was so sure at first she'd turn up, like she had the first time.

'Anyway, when she saw how upset I'd been, t'inking she'd gone missing, she told me the truth. She and Satchwell had started things up again. She had all the old excuses down: he swore he'd never hit her again, he'd cried his eyes out about it, it was the worst mistake of his life, and anyway, she'd provoked him. I told her, "If you can't see him now for what he is, after what he did to you first time round . . ." Anyway, they split again and, surprise, surprise, he not only knocked her around again, he kept her locked in his flat all day, so she couldn't get to work. That was the first shift she'd ever missed. She nearly lost the job over it, and had to make up some cock-and-bull story.

'So then at last,' said Oonagh, 'she tells me she's learned her lesson, I was right all along, she's never going back to him, that's it, *finito*.'

'Did she get the photographs back?' asked Robin.

'First t'ing I asked, when I found out they were back together. She said he'd told her he'd destroyed them. She believed it, too.'

'You didn't?'

'O' course I didn't,' said Oonagh. 'I'd seen him, when she t'reatened him with his *pillow dream*. That was a frightened man. He'd never have destroyed anyt'ing that gave him bargaining power over her.'

'Would it be all right if I get another cappuccino?' asked Oonagh apologetically. 'My t'roat's dry, all this talking.'

'Of course,' said Strike, hailing a waiter, and ordering fresh coffees all round.

Oonagh pointed at Robin's Fortnum's bag.

'Been stocking up for Christmas, too?'

'Oh, no, I've been buying a present for my new niece. She was born this morning,' said Robin, smiling.

'Congratulations,' said Strike, who was surprised Robin hadn't already told him.

'Oh, how lovely,' said Oonagh. 'My fifth grandchild arrived last month.'

The interval while waiting for the fresh coffees was filled by Oonagh showing Robin pictures of her grandchildren, and Robin showing Oonagh the two pictures she had of Annabel Marie.

'*Gorgeous*, isn't she?' said Oonagh, peering through her purple reading glasses at the picture on Robin's phone. She included Strike in the question, but, seeing only an angry-looking, bald monkey, his acquiescence was half-hearted.

When the coffees had arrived and the waiter moved away again, Robin said,

'While I remember . . . would you happen to know if Margot had family or friends in Leamington Spa?'

'Leamington Spa?' repeated Oonagh, frowning. 'Let's see . . . one of the gorls at the club was from . . . no, that was King's Lynn. They're similar sorts of names, aren't they? I can't remember anyone from there, no . . . Why?'

'We've heard a man claimed to have seen her there, a week after she disappeared.'

'There were a few sightings after, right enough. Nothing in any of them. None of them made sense. Leamington Spa, that's a new one.'

She took a sip of her cappuccino. Robin asked,

'Did you still see a lot of each other, once Margot went off to medical school?'

'Oh yeah, because she was still working at the club part time. How she did it all, studying, working, supporting her family . . . living on nerves and chocolate, skinny as ever. And then, at the start of her second year, she met Roy.'

Oonagh sighed.

'Even the cleverest people can be bloody *stupid* when it comes to their love lives,' she said. 'In fact, I sometimes t'ink, the cleverer they are with books, the stupider they are with sex. Margot t'ought she'd learned her lesson, that she'd grown up. She couldn't see that it was *classic* rebound. He might've *looked* as different from Satchwell as you could get, but really, it was more of the same.

'Roy had the kind of background Margot would've loved. Books, travel, culture, you know. See, there were gaps in what Margot knew. She was insecure about not knowing about the right fork, the right words. "Napkin" instead of "serviette". All that snobby English stuff.

'Roy was mad for her, mind you. It wasn't all one way. I could see what the appeal was: she was like nothing he'd ever known before. She shocked him, but she fascinated him: the Playboy Club and her work ethic, her feminist ideas, supporting her mammy and daddy. They had arguments, intellectual arguments, you know.

'But there was something *bloodless* about the man. Not *wet* exactly, but—' Oonagh gave a sudden laugh. '"Bloodless" – you'll know about his bleeding problem?'

'Yes,' said Robin. 'Von Something Disease?'

'Dat's the one,' said Oonagh. 'He'd been cossetted and wrapped up in cotton wool all his life by his mother, who was a *horror*. I met her a few times. That woman gave me the respect you'd give something you'd got stuck on your shoe.

'And Roy was . . . still waters run deep, I suppose sums it up. He didn't show a lot of emotion. *Their* flirtation wasn't all sex, it really *was* ideas with them. Not that he wasn't good-looking. He was hand-some, in a kind of . . . *limp* way. As different from Satchwell as you could imagine. Pretty boy, all eyes and floppy hair.

'But he was a manipulator. A little bit of disapproval here, a cold look there. He loved how different Margot was, but it still made him uncomfortable. He wanted a woman the exact opposite to his mother, but he wanted Mammy to approve. So the fault lines were dere from the beginning.

'And he could *sulk*,' said Oonagh. 'I *hate* a sulker, now. My mother was the same. T'irty years she wouldn't talk to me, because I moved to London. She finally gave in so she could meet her grandchildren, but then my sister got tipsy at Christmas and let it slip I'd left the church and joined the Anglicans, we were finished for ever. Playboy, she could forgive. Proddy, never.

'Even when they were dating, Roy would stop talking to Margot for days at a time. She told me once he cut her off for a week. She lost patience, she said, "I'm off." That brought him round sharp enough. I said, what was he sulking about? And it was the club. He hated her working there. I said, "Is *he* offering to support your family, while you study?" "Oh, he doesn't like the idea of other men ogling me," she says. Girls like that idea, that little bit of possessiveness. They t'ink it means he only wants her, when o' course, it's the other way round. He only wants her available to *him. He's* still free to look at other girls, and Roy had other people interested in him, girls from his own background. He was a pretty boy with a lot of family money. Well,' said Oonagh, 'look at little cousin Cynthia, lurking in the wings.'

'Did you know Cynthia?' asked Robin.

'Met her once or twice, at their house. Mousy little thing. She never spoke more than two words to me,' said Oonagh. 'But she made Roy feel good about himself. Laughing loike a drain at all his jokes. Such as they were.'

'Margot and Roy must have married right after medical school, did they?'

'Dat's right. I was a bridesmaid. She went into general practice. Roy was a high-flier, he went into one of the big teaching hospitals, I can't remember which.

'Roy's parents had this very nice big house with huge lawns and all the rest of it. After his father died, which was just before they had Anna, the mother made it over to Roy. Margot's name wasn't on the deeds, I remember her telling me dat. But Roy loved the idea of bringing up his family in the same house he'd grown up in, and it was beautiful, right enough, out near Hampton Court. So the mother-in-law moved out and Roy and Margot moved in.

'Except, of course, the mother-in-law felt she had the right to walk back in any time she felt like it, because she'd given it to them and she still looked on it as more hers than Margot's.'

'Did you and Margot still see a lot of each other?' asked Robin.

'We did,' said Oonagh. 'We used to try and meet at least once every couple of weeks. Real best friends, we were. Even after she married Roy, she wanted to hold on to me. They had their middle-class friends, o' course, but I t'ink,' said Oonagh, her voice thickening, 'I t'ink she knew I'd always be on her side, you see. She was moving in circles where she felt alone.'

'At home, or at work, too?' asked Robin.

'At home, she was a fish out of water,' said Oonagh. 'Roy's house, Roy's family, Roy's friends, Roy's everyt'ing. She *saw* her own mammy and daddy plenty, but it was hard, the daddy being in his wheelchair, to get him out to the big house. I t'ink the Bamboroughs felt intimidated by Roy and his mother. So Margot used to go back to Stepney to see them. She was still supporting them financially. Ran herself ragged between all her different commitments.'

'And how were things at work?'

'Uphill, all the way,' said Oonagh. 'There weren't that many women doctors back then, and she was young and working class and that practice she ended up at, the St John's one, she felt alone. It wasn't a happy place,' said Oonagh, echoing Dr Gupta. 'Being Margot, she wanted to try and make it better. That was Margot's whole ethos: make it better. Make it work. Look after everyone. Solve the problem. She tried to bring them together as a team, even though she was the one being bullied.'

'Who was bullying her?'

'The old fella,' said Oonagh. 'I can't remember the names, now. There were two other doctors, isn't that right? The old one and the Indian one. She said *he* was all right, the Indian fella, but she could feel the disapproval off him, too. They had an argument about the pill, she told me. GPs could give it to unmarried women if they wanted – when it was first brought out, it was married women only – but the Indian lad, he still wouldn't hand it out to unmarried women. The first family planning clinics started appearing the same year Margot disappeared. We talked about them. Margot said, t'ank God for it, because she was sure the women coming to their clinic weren't able to get it from either of the other doctors.

'But it wasn't only them. She had trouble with the other staff. I don't t'ink the nurse liked her, either.'

'Janice?' said Robin.

'Was it Janice?' said Oonagh, frowning.

'Irene?' suggested Strike.

'She was blonde,' said Oonagh. 'I remember, at the Christmas party—'

'You were there?' said Robin, surprised.

'Margot *begged* me to go,' said Oonagh. 'She'd set it up and she was afraid it was going to be awful. Roy was working, so *he* couldn't go. This was just a few months after Anna was born. Margot had been on maternity leave and they'd got another doctor in to cover for her, a man. She was convinced the place had worked better without her. She was hormonal and tired and dreading going back. Anna would only have been two or three months old. Margot brought her to the party, because she was breastfeeding. She'd organised the Christmas party to try and make a bit of a fresh start with them all, break the ice before she had to go back in.'

'Go on about Irene,' said Robin, conscious of Strike's pen hovering over his notebook.

'Well, she got drunk, if she's the blonde one. She'd brought some man with her to the party. Anyway, towards the end of the night, Irene accused Margot of *flirting* with the man. Did you ever in your loife hear anything more ridiculous? There's Margot standing there with her new baby in her arms, and the girl having a *proper* go at her. Was she not the nurse? It's so long ago . . . '

'No, Irene was the receptionist,' said Robin.

'I t'ought that was the little Italian girl?'

'Gloria was the other one.'

'Oh, Margot *loved* her,' said Oonagh. 'She said the girl was very clever but in a bad situation. She never gave me details. I t'ink the girl had seen her for medical advice and o' course, Margot wouldn't have shared anything about her health. She took all of dat very seriously. No priest in his confessional treated other people's secrets with more respect.'

'I want to ask you about something sensitive,' said Robin tentatively. 'There was a book about Margot, written in 1985, and you—'

'Joined with Roy to stop it,' said Oonagh at once. 'I did. It was a pack o' lies from start to finish. You know what he wrote, obviously. About—'

Oonagh might have left the Catholic Church, but she baulked at the word.

'—the termination. It was a filthy lie. I never had an abortion and nor did Margot. She'd have told me, if she was thinking about it. We were best friends. Somebody used her name to make dat appointment. I don't know who. The clinic didn't recognise her picture. She'd never been there. The very best t'ing in her life was Anna and she'd *never* have got rid of another baby. *Never.* She wasn't religious, but she'd have t'ought that was a sin, all right.'

'She wasn't a churchgoer?' Robin asked.

'At'eist t'rough and t'rough,' said Oonagh. 'She t'ought it was all superstition. Her mammy was chapel, and Margot reacted against it. The church kept women down, was the way Margot looked at it, and she said to me, "If there's a God, why'd my daddy, who's a good man, have to fall off that step-ladder? Why's my family have to live the life we've had?" Well, Margot couldn't tell me anything about hypocrisy and religion I didn't already know. I'd left the Catholics by then. Doctrine of papal infallibility. No contraception, no matter if women died having their eleventh.

'My own mammy t'ought she was God's deputy on this earth, so she did, and some of the nuns at my school were pure bitches. Sister Mary Theresa – see there?' said Oonagh, pushing her fringe out of her eyes to reveal a scar the size of a five-pence piece. 'She hit me round the head wit' a metal set square. Blood everywhere. "I expect you deserved it," Mammy said.

'Now, I'll tell you who reminded me of Sister Mary Theresa,' said Oonagh. 'Would *she* have been the nurse, now? The older one at Margot's practice?'

'D'you mean Dorothy?'

'She was a widow, the one I'm t'inking of.'

'Yes, that was Dorothy, the secretary.'

'Spit image of Sister Mary Theresa, the eyes on her,' said Oonagh. 'I got cornered by her at the party. They're drawn to the church, women like dat. Nearly every congregation's got a couple. Outward observance, inward poison. They say the words, you know "Father forgive me, for I have sinned", but the Dorothys of this world, they don't believe they *can* sin, not really.

'One t'ing life's taught me: where there's no capacity for joy, there's no capacity for goodness,' said Oonagh Kennedy. 'She had it in for Margot, that Dorothy. I told her I was Margot's best friend and she started asking nosy questions. How we'd met. Boyfriends. How Margot met Roy. None of her bloody business.

'Then she started talking about the old doctor, whatever his name was. There was a bit of Sister Mary Theresa in her, all right, but dat woman's god was sitting a desk away. I told Margot about the talk I'd had with her afterwards, and Margot said I was right. Dorothy was a mean one.'

'It was Dorothy's son who wrote the book about Margot,' said Robin.

'*Was it her son?*' gasped Oonagh. 'Was it? Well, *there you are.* Nasty pieces of work, the pair of them.'

'When was the last time you saw Margot?' Robin asked.

'Exactly two weeks before the night she disappeared. We met at The T'ree Kings then, too. Six o'clock, I had a night off from the club. There were a couple of bars nearer the practice, but she didn't want to run into anyone she worked with after hours.'

'Can you remember what you talked about that night?'

'I remember everyt'ing,' said Oonagh. 'You'll think that's an exaggeration, but it isn't. I started by giving her a row about going for a drink with Satchwell, which she'd told me about on the phone. They'd bumped into each other in the street.

'She said he seemed different to how he used to be and that worried me, I'm not going to lie. She wasn't built for an affair, but she was unhappy. Once we got to the pub, she told me the whole story. He'd asked to see her again and she'd said no. I believed her, and I'll tell you why: because she looked so damn miserable that she'd said no.

'She seemed worn down, that night. Unhappy like I'd never seen her before. She said Roy hadn't been talking to her for ten days when she ran into Satchwell. They'd had a row about his mother walking in and out of the house like she owned it. Margot wanted to redecorate, but Roy said it'd break his mother's heart if they got rid of any of the things his father loved. So there was Margot, an outsider in her own home, not even allowed to change the ornaments.

'Margot said she'd had a line from *Court and Spark* running through her head, all day long. Joni Mitchell's album, *Court and Spark*,' she said, seeing Robin's puzzlement. '*That* was Margot's religion. Joni Mitchell. She *raved* about that album. It was a line from the song "The Same Situation". "*Caught in my struggle for higher achievements, And my search for love that don't seem to cease.*" I can't listen to that album to this day. It's too painful.

'She told me she went straight home after havin' the drink with Paul and told Roy what had just happened. I think partly she felt guilty about going for the drink, but partly she wanted to jolt him awake. She was tired and miserable and she was saying *someone else wanted me, once.* Human nature, isn't it? "Wake up," she was saying. "You can't just ignore me and cut me off and refuse all compromises. I can't live like this."

'Well, being Roy, he wasn't the type to fire up and start throwing things. I t'ink she'd have found it easier if he had. He was furious, all right, but he showed it by gettin' colder and more silent.

'I don't t'ink he said another word to her until the day she disappeared. She told me on the phone when we arranged the drink for the eleventh, "I'm still living in a silent order." She sounded hopeless. I remember thinking then, "She's going to leave him."

'When we met in the pub that last time, I said to her, "Satchwell's not the answer to whatever's wrong with you and Roy."

'We talked about Anna, too. Margot would've given anything to take a year or two out and concentrate on Anna, and that's exactly what Roy and his mother had wanted her to do, stay home with Anna and forget working.

'But she couldn't. She was still supporting her parents. Her mammy was ill now, and Margot didn't want her out cleaning houses any more. While she was working, she could look Roy in the face and justify all the money she was giving them, but his mother wasn't going to let her precious, delicate son work for the benefit of a pair o' chain-smokin' Eastenders.'

'Can you remember anything else you talked about?'

'We talked about the Playboy Club, because I was leaving. I'd got my flat and I was thinking of going and studying. Margot was all for it. What I didn't tell her was, I was thinking of a t'eology degree, what with her attitude to religion.

'We talked about politics, a bit. We both wanted Wilson to win the election. And I told her I was worried I still hadn't found The One. Over t'irty, I was. That was old, then, for finding a husband.

'Before we said goodbye that night, I said, "Don't forget, there's always a spare room at my place. Room for a bassinet, as well."'

Tears welled again in Oonagh's eyes and trickled down her cheeks. She picked up her napkin and pressed it to her face.

'I'm sorry. Forty years ago, but it feels like yesterday. They don't disappear, the dead. It'd be easier if they did. I can see her so clearly. If she walked up those steps now, part of me wouldn't be surprised. She was such a *vivid* person. For her to disappear like that, just thin air where she was . . . '

Robin said nothing until Oonagh had wiped her face dry, then asked,

'What can you remember about arranging to meet on the eleventh?'

'She called me, asked to meet same place, same time. I said yes, o' course. There was something funny in the way she said it. I said, "Everything all right?" She said, "I need to ask your advice about something. I might be going mad. I shouldn't really talk about it, but I t'ink you're the only one I can trust."'

Strike and Robin looked at each other.

'Was that not written down anywhere?'

'No,' said Strike.

'No,' said Oonagh, and for the first time she looked angry. 'Well, I can't say I'm surprised.'

'Why not?' asked Robin.

'Talbot was away with the fairies,' said Oonagh. 'I could see it in the first five minutes of my interview. I called Roy, I said, "That man isn't right. Complain, tell them you want someone else on the case." He didn't, or if he did, nothing was done.

'And Lawson t'ought I was some silly little Bunny Girl,' said Oonagh. 'Probably t'ought I was tellin' fibs, trying to make myself interesting off the back of my best friend disappearing. Margot Bamborough was more like a sister than a friend to me,' said Oonagh fiercely, 'and the on'y person I've ever really talked to about her is my husband. I cried all over him, two days before we got married, because she should've been there. She should've been my matron of honour.'

'Have you got any idea what she was going to ask your advice about?' asked Robin.

'No,' said Oonagh. 'I've t'ought about it often since, whether it could have had anything to do with what happened. Something about Roy, perhaps, but then why would she say she shouldn't talk about it? We'd already talked about Roy. I'd told her as plain as I could, the last time we met, she could come and live with me if she left, Anna as well.

'Then I t'ought, maybe it's something a patient has told her, because like I said, she was scrupulous about confidentiality.

'Anyway, I walked up that hill in the rain to the pub on the eleventh. I was early, so I went to have a look at that church there, over the road, big—'

'Wait,' said Strike sharply. 'What kind of coat were you wearing?'

Oonagh didn't seem surprised by the question. On the contrary, she smiled.

'You're t'inking of the old gravedigger, or whoever he was? The one who t'ought he saw Margot going in there? I *told* them at the time it was me,' said Oonagh. 'I wasn't wearing a raincoat, but it was beige. My hair was darker than Margot's, but it was the same kind of length. I *told* them, when they asked me, did I think Margot might've gone into the church before meeting me – I said, no, she hated church. *I* went there! That was me!'

'Why?' asked Strike. 'Why did you go in there?'

'I was being called,' said Oonagh simply.

Robin repressed a smile, because Strike looked almost embarrassed at the answer.

'God was calling me back,' said Oonagh. 'I kept going into Anglican churches, t'inking, is this the answer? There was so much about the Catholics I couldn't take, but still, I could feel the pull back towards Him.'

'How long d'you think you were in the church?' asked Robin, to give Strike time to recover himself.

'Five minutes or so. I said a little prayer. I was asking for guidance. Then I walked out again, crossed the road and went into the pub.

'I waited nearly the full hour before I called Roy. At first I t'ought, she's been delayed by a patient. Then I t'ought, no, she must've forgotten. But when I called the house, Roy said she wasn't there. He was quite short with me. I wondered whether somethin' more had happened between them. Maybe Margot had snapped. Maybe I was

· going to get home and find her on the doorstep with Anna. So I went dashin' home, but she wasn't there.

'Roy called at nine to see whether I'd had any contact. That's when I started to get really worried. He said he was going to call the police.

'You'll know the rest,' said Oonagh quietly. 'It was like a nightmare. You put all your hopes on t'ings that are less and less likely. Amnesia. Knocked down by a car and unconscious somewhere. She's run away somewhere to t'ink.

'But I knew, really. She'd never've left her baby girl, and she'd *never* have left without telling me. I knew she was dead. I could tell the police t'ought it was the Essex Butcher, but me . . . '

'But you?' prompted Robin gently.

'Well, I kept t'inking, t'ree weeks after Paul Satchwell comes back into her life, she vanishes for ever. I know he had his little alibi, all his arty friends backing him up. I said to Talbot and Lawson: ask him about the pillow dream. Ask him what that means, the pillow dream he was so frightened Margot would tell people about.

'Is that in the police notes?' she asked Strike, turning to look at him. 'Did either of them ask Satchwell about the pillow dream?'

'No,' said Strike slowly. 'I don't think they did.'

25

All those were idle thoughtes and fantasies,
Deuices, dreames, opinions vnsound,
Shewes, visions, sooth-sayes, and prophesies;
And all that fained is, as leasings, tales, and lies.

Edmund Spenser
The Faerie Queene

Three evenings later, Strike was to be found sitting in his BMW
outside a nondescript terraced house in Stoke Newington. The
Shifty investigation, now in its fifth month, had so far yielded no
results. The restive trustees who suspected that their CEO was being
blackmailed by the ambitious Shifty were making ominous noises
of discontent, and were clearly considering taking their business
elsewhere.

Even after being plied with gin by Hutchins, who'd succeeded in
befriending him at the rifle club, Shifty had remained as close lipped
as ever about the hold he had over his boss, so it was time, Strike had
decided, to start tailing SB himself. It was just possible that the CEO,
a rotund, pinstriped man with a bald patch like a monk's tonsure,
was still indulging in the blackmailable behaviour that Shifty had
uncovered and that had leveraged him into a promotion that neither
Shifty's CV, nor his personality, justified.

Strike was sure Shifty wasn't exploiting a simple case of infidelity.
SB's current wife had the immaculate, plastic sheen of a doll newly
removed from cellophane and Strike suspected it would take more
than her husband having an affair to make her relinquish her taloned

grip on a black American Express card, especially as she'd been married barely two years and had no children to guarantee a generous settlement.

Christmas tree lights twinkled in almost every window surrounding Strike. The roof of the house beside him had been hung with brilliant blue-white icicles that burned the retina if looked at too long. Wreaths on doors, glass panels decorated with fake snow and the sparkle of orange, red and green reflected in the dirty puddles all reminded Strike that he really did need to start buying Christmas gifts to take to Cornwall.

Joan had been released from hospital that morning, her drugs adjusted, and determined to get home and start preparing for the family festivities. Strike would need to buy presents not only for Joan and Ted but for his sister, brother-in-law and nephews. This was an irksome extra chore, given the amount of work the agency currently had on its books. Then he reminded himself that he had to buy something for Robin, too, something better than flowers. Strike, who disliked shopping in general, and buying gifts in particular, reached for his cigarettes to ward off a dim sense of persecution.

Having lit up, Strike took from his pocket the copy of *Whatever Happened to Margot Bamborough?* which Robin had given him, but which he hadn't yet had time to read. Small tags marked the places Robin thought might be of some interest to the investigation.

With a quick glance at the still-closed front door of the house he was watching, Strike opened the book and skim-read a couple of pages, looking up at regular intervals to check that SB hadn't yet emerged.

The first chapter, which Robin hadn't marked, but which Strike flicked through anyway, dealt summarily with Margot's childhood and adolescence. Unable to gain access to anybody with particularly clear memories of his subject, Oakden had to fall back on generalities, supposition and a good deal of padding. Thus Strike learned that Margot Bamborough 'would have dreamed of leaving poverty behind', 'would have been caught up in the giddy atmosphere of the 1960s' and 'would have been aware of the possibilities for consequence-free sex offered by the contraceptive pill'. Word count was boosted by the information that the mini-skirt had been popularised by Mary Quant, that London was the heart of a thriving music scene and that the Beatles had appeared on America's *Ed Sullivan Show* around the time of Margot's nineteenth birthday. 'Margot would have been excited by the possibilities offered to the working classes in this new, egalitarian era,' C. B. Oakden informed his readers.

Chapter two ushered in Margot's arrival at the Playboy Club, and here, the sense of strain that had suffused the previous chapter vanished. C. B. Oakden evidently found Playboy Bunny Margot a far more inspiring subject than child Margot, and he devoted many paragraphs to the sense of freedom and liberation she would have felt on lacing herself tightly into her Bunny costume, putting on false ears and judiciously padding the cups of her costume to ensure that her breasts appeared of sufficient fullness to satisfy her employer's stringent demands. Writing eleven years after her disappearance, Oakden had managed to track down a couple of Bunny Girls who remembered Margot. Bunny Lisa, who was now married with two children, reminisced about having 'a good laugh' with her, and being 'devastated' by her disappearance. Bunny Rita, who ran her own marketing business, said that she was 'really bright, obviously going places', and thought 'it must've been dreadful for her poor family'.

Strike glanced up again at the front of the house into which SB had disappeared. Still no sign of him. Turning back to C. B. Oakden, the bored Strike skipped ahead to the first place Robin had marked as of interest.

After her successful stint at the Playboy Club, the playful and flirtatious Margot found it hard to adapt to the life of a general practitioner. At least one employee at the St John's practice says her manner was out of place in the setting of a consulting room.

"She didn't keep them at a proper distance, that was the trouble. She wasn't from a background that had a lot of professional people. A doctor's got to hold himself above the patients.

"She recommended that book *The Joy of Sex*, to a woman who went to see her. I heard people in the waiting room talking about it, after. Giggling, you know. A doctor shouldn't be telling people to read things like that. It reflects poorly on the whole practice. I was embarrassed for her.

"The one who was keen on her, the young fellow who kept coming back to see her, buying her chocolates and what have you – if she was telling people about different sex positions, you can see how men got the wrong idea, can't you?"

There followed several paragraphs that had clearly been cribbed from the press, covering the suicide of Steve Douthwaite's married ex-girlfriend, his sudden flight from his job and the fact that Lawson had re-interviewed him several times. Making the most of his scant material, Oakden managed to suggest that Douthwaite had been at best disreputable, at worst, dangerous: a feckless drifter and an unprincipled lady's man, in whose vicinity women had a habit of dying or disappearing. It was with a slight snort of sudden amusement, therefore, that Strike read the words,

Now calling himself Stevie Jacks, Douthwaite currently works at Butlin's holiday camp in Clacton-on-Sea—

After glancing up again to check that SB hadn't yet emerged, Strike read on:

where he runs events for the campers by day and performs in the cabaret by night. His "Longfellow Serenade" is a particular hit with the ladies. Dark-haired Douthwaite/Jacks remains a handsome man, and clearly popular with female campers.

"I've always liked singing," he tells me in the bar after the show. 'I was in a band when I was younger but it broke up. I came to Butlin's once when I was a kid, with my foster family. I always thought it looked a laugh, being a Redcoat. Plenty of big-time entertainers got their start here, you know."

When talk turns to Margot Bamborough, however, a very different side to this cheeky cabaret singer appears.

"The press wrote a load of balls. I never bought her chocolates or anything else, that was just made up to make me look like some kind of creep. I had a stomach ulcer and headaches. I'd been through a bad time."

After refusing to explain why he'd changed his name, Douthwaite left the bar.

His colleagues at the holiday camp expressed their shock that "Stevie" had been questioned by the police over the disappearance of the young doctor.

"He never told us anything about it," said Julie Wilkes, 22. "I'm quite shocked, actually. You'd think he'd have told us. He never said 'Jacks' wasn't his real name, either."

Oakden treated his readers to a brief history of Butlin's, and ended the chapter with a paragraph of speculation on the opportunities a predatory man might find at a holiday camp.

Strike lit another cigarette, then flicked ahead to the second of Robin's markers, where a short passage dealt with Jules Bayliss, husband of the office-cleaner-turned-social-worker, Wilma. The only piece of new information here was that convicted rapist Bayliss had been released on bail in January 1975, a full three months after Margot went missing. Nevertheless, Oakden asserted that Bayliss 'would have got wind' of the fact that Margot was trying to persuade his wife to leave him, 'would have been angry that the doctor was pressurising his wife to break up the family' and 'would have had many criminal associations in his own community'. The police, Oakden informed his readers, 'would have looked carefully into the movements of any of Bayliss's friends or relatives on the eleventh of October, so we must conclude,' he finished, anticlimactically, 'that no suspicious activity was uncovered.'

Robin's third tab marked the pages dealing with the abortion at Bride Street Nursing Home. Oakden ushered in this part of his story with considerable fanfare, informing his readers that he was about to reveal facts that had never before been made public.

What followed was interesting to Strike only in as far as it proved that an abortion had definitely taken place on the fourteenth of September 1974, and that the name given by the patient had been Margot Bamborough. As proof, Oakden reprinted photographs of the Bride Street medical records that had been provided by an unidentified employee of the nursing home, which had closed down in 1978. Strike supposed the unnamed employee would no longer have been fearful for their job when Oakden had come offering money for information in the eighties. The unnamed employee also told Oakden that the woman who had had the procedure didn't resemble the picture of Margot that had subsequently appeared in the papers.

Oakden then posed a series of rhetorical questions that he and his foolhardy publishers appeared to think circumvented libel laws. Was it possible that the woman who had the abortion had used Margot's name with her support and consent? In which case, who might Margot have been most eager to assist? Was it not most likely that a Roman Catholic would be particularly worried about anyone finding out she had had an abortion? Was it not also the case that complications could arise from such a procedure? Might Margot have returned to the vicinity of the Bride Street Nursing Home on the eleventh of October to visit somebody who had been readmitted to the clinic? Or to ask advice on behalf of that person? Could Margot possibly have been abducted, not from Clerkenwell, but from a street or two away from Dennis Creed's basement?

To which Strike answered mentally, *no, and you deserved to have your book pulped, pal.* The string of events suggested by Oakden had clearly been put together in a determined attempt to place Margot in the vicinity of Creed's basement on the night she disappeared. 'Complications' were necessary to explain Margot returning to the nursing home a month after the abortion, but they couldn't be Margot's own, given that she was fit, well and working at the St John's practice all the way up to her disappearance. Once attributed to a best friend, however, undefined 'complications' could serve two purposes: to give Margot a reason to head back to the clinic to visit Oonagh, and Oonagh a reason to lie about both women's whereabouts that night. All in all, Strike considered Oakden lucky not to have been sued, and surmised that fear of the resultant publicity was all that had held Roy and Oonagh back.

He flicked forward to Robin's fourth tab and, after checking again that the front door of the house he was watching remained closed, read the next marked passage.

"I saw her as clearly as I can see you now. She was standing at that window, *pounding* on it, as if she wanted to attract attention. I especially remember, because I was reading *The Other Side of Midnight* at the time and just thinking about women and what they go through, you know, and I looked up and I saw her.

"If I close my eyes, she's there, it's like a snapshot in my head and it's haunted me ever since, to be honest. People have said to me since, 'you're making it up' or 'you need to let it go', but I'm not changing my story just because other people don't believe it. What would that make me?"

The small printers who then occupied the top floor of the building was run by husband and wife team Arnold and Rachel Sawyer. Police accepted their assurance that Margot Bamborough had never set foot on the premises, and that the woman seen by Mandy that night was probably Mrs Sawyer herself, who claimed one of the windows needed to be hit to close properly.

However, an odd connection between A&R Printing and Margot Bamborough went unnoticed by police. A&R's first major printing job was for the now-closed nightclub Drudge – the very nightclub for which Paul Satchwell, Margot's lover, had designed a risqué mural. Satchwell's designs subsequently featured on flyers printed by A&R Printing, so it is likely that he and the Sawyers would have been in touch with each other.

Might this suggest . . .

'Fuck's sake,' muttered Strike, turning the page and dropping his eyes to a brief paragraph Robin had marked with a thick black line.

However, ex-neighbour Wayne Truelove thinks that Paul Satchwell subsequently went abroad.

"He talked to me about going travelling. I don't think he was making a lot of money from his art and after the police questioned him, he told me he was thinking of clearing out for a bit. Probably smart, going away."

Robin's fifth and final tab came towards the end of the book, and after again checking that SB's car was parked where he had left it, and that the front door of the house had not opened, Strike read:

A month after Margot's disappearance, her husband Roy visited the St John's practice. Roy, who had been unable to conceal his bad temper at the practice barbecue that summer, was unsurprisingly subdued on this visit.

Dorothy remembers: "He wanted to speak to us all, to thank us for cooperating with the police. He looked ill. Hardly surprising.

"We'd boxed up her personal effects because we had a locum working out of her room. The police had already searched it. We put her personal effects together. There was hand cream and her framed degree certificate and a photo of him, Roy, holding their daughter. He looked through the box and got a bit emotional, but then he picked up this thing that she'd had on her desk. It was one of those little wooden figures, like a Viking. He said 'Where did this come from? Where did she get this?' None of us knew, but I thought he seemed upset by it.

"He probably thought a man had given it her. Of course, the police were looking into her love life by then. Awful thing, not to be able to trust your wife."

Strike glanced up yet again at the house, saw no change, and flicked to the end of the book, which concluded in a final burst of speculation, supposition and half-baked theory. On the one hand, Oakden implied that Margot had brought tragedy on herself, that fate had punished her for being too sexual and too bold, for cramming herself into a corset and bunny ears, for hoisting herself hubristically out of the class into which she had been born. On the other hand, she seemed to have lived her life surrounded by would-be killers. No man associated with Margot escaped Oakden's suspicion, whether it was 'charming but feckless Stevie Douthwaite-turned-Jacks', 'domineering blood specialist Roy Phipps', 'resentful rapist Jules Bayliss', 'hot-tempered womaniser Paul Satchwell' or 'notorious sex monster Dennis Creed'.

Strike was on the point of closing the book when he noticed a line of darker page edges in the middle, suggesting photographs, and opened it again.

Other than the familiar press headshot and the picture of Margot and Oonagh in their Bunny Girl costumes – Oonagh curvaceous and grinning broadly, Margot statuesque, with a cloud of fair hair – there were only three photos. All were of poor quality and featured Margot only incidentally.

The first was captioned: 'The author, his mother and Margot'. Square-jawed, iron-grey-haired, and wearing winged glasses, Dorothy Oakden stood facing the camera with her arm around a skinny freckle-faced boy with a pageboy haircut, who had screwed up his face into a grimace that distorted his features. Strike was reminded of Luke, his eldest nephew. Behind the Oakdens was a long expanse of striped lawn and, in the distance, a sprawling house with many pointed gables. Objects appeared to be protruding out of the lawn close to the house: upon closer examination, Strike concluded that they were the beginnings of walls or columns: it looked as though a summerhouse was under construction.

Walking across the lawn behind Dorothy and Carl, unaware that she was being photographed, was Margot Bamborough, barefooted, wearing denim shorts and a T-shirt, carrying a plate and smiling at somebody out of shot. Strike deduced that this picture had been taken at the staff barbecue Margot had organised. The Phipps house was certainly grander than he'd imagined.

After looking up once more to check that SB's car remained parked where he'd left it, Strike turned to the last two pictures, both of which featured the St John's practice Christmas party.

Tinsel had been draped over the reception desk and the waiting room cleared of chairs, which had been stacked in corners. Strike searched for Margot in both pictures and found her, baby Anna in her arms, talking to a tall black woman he assumed was Wilma Bayliss. In the corner of the picture was a slim, round-eyed woman with feathered brown hair, who Strike thought might be a young Janice.

In the second picture, all heads were turned away from the camera or partially obscured, except one. A gaunt, unsmiling older man in a suit, with his hair slicked back, was the only person who seemed to have been given notice that the picture was about to be taken. The flash had turned his eyes red. The picture was captioned 'Margot and Dr Joseph Brenner', though only the back of Margot's head was visible.

In the corner of this picture were three men who, judging from their coats and jackets, had just arrived at the party. The darkness of their clothing made a solid block of black on the right-hand side of the photo. All had their backs to the camera, but the largest, whose face was slightly turned to the left, displayed one long black sideburn, a large ear, the tip of a fleshy nose and a drooping eye. His left hand was raised in the act of scratching his face. He was wearing a large gold ring featuring a lion's head.

Strike examined this picture until noises out on the street made him look up. SB had just emerged from the house. A plump blonde in carpet slippers was standing on her doormat. She raised a hand and patted SB gently on the top of the head, as you would pet a child or a dog. Smiling, SB bade her farewell, then turned and walked back towards his Mercedes.

Strike threw the copy of *Whatever Happened to Margot Bamborough?* into the passenger seat. Waiting for SB to pull out into the road, he set off in pursuit.

After five minutes or so, it became clear that his quarry was driving back to his home in West Brompton. One hand on the steering wheel, Strike groped for his mobile, then pressed the number of an old friend. The call went straight to voicemail.

'Shanker, it's Bunsen. Need to talk to you about something. Let me know when I can buy you a pint.'

26

All were faire knights, and goodly well beseene,
But to faire Britomart they all but shadowes beene.

Edmund Spenser
The Faerie Queene

With five active cases on the agency's books, and only four days to go until Christmas, two of the agency's subcontractors succumbed to seasonal flu. Morris fell first: he blamed his daughter's nursery, where the virus had swept like wildfire through toddlers and parents alike. He continued to work until a high temperature and joint pain forced him to telephone in his apologies, by which time he'd managed to pass the bug to a furious Barclay, who in turn had transmitted it to his own wife and young daughter.

'Stupid arsehole shoulda stayed at home instead o' breathin' all over me in the car,' Barclay ranted hoarsely over the phone to Strike early on the morning of the twentieth, while Strike was opening up the office. The last full team meeting before Christmas was to have taken place at ten o'clock, but as two of the team were now unable to attend, Strike had decided to cancel. The only person he hadn't been able to reach was Robin, who he assumed was on the Tube. Strike had asked her to come in early so they could catch up with the Bamborough case before everyone else arrived.

'We're supposedtae be flying to Glasgow the morra,' Barclay rasped, while Strike put on the kettle. 'The wean's in that much pain wi' her ears—'

'Yeah,' said Strike, who was feeling sub-standard himself, doubtless due to tiredness, and too much smoking. 'Well, feel better and get back whenever you can.'

'Arsehole,' growled Barclay, and then, 'Morris, I mean. Not you. Merry fuckin' Christmas.'

Trying to convince himself that he was imagining the tickle in his throat, the slight clamminess of his back and the pain behind his eyes, Strike made himself a mug of tea, then moved through to the inner office and pulled up the blinds. Wind and heavy rain were causing the Christmas lights strung across Denmark Street to sway on their cables. Just as they'd done on the five previous mornings, the decorations reminded Strike that he still hadn't started his Christmas shopping. He took a seat on his accustomed side of the partners' desk, knowing that he'd now left the job so late that he would be forced to execute it within a couple of hours, which at least obviated the tedious preliminary of carefully considering what anyone might like. Rain lashed the window behind him. He'd have liked to go back to bed.

He heard the glass door open and close.

'Morning,' Robin called from the outer office. 'It's *vile* out there.'

'Morning,' Strike called back. 'Kettle's just boiled and team meeting's cancelled. That's Barclay down with flu as well.'

'Shit,' said Robin. 'How're *you* feeling?'

'Fine,' said Strike, now sorting out his various Bamborough notes.

But when Robin entered the inner office, carrying tea in one hand and her own notebook in the other, she didn't think Strike looked fine at all. He was paler than usual, his forehead looked shiny and there were grey shadows around his eyes. She closed the office door and sat down opposite him without passing comment.

'Not much point to a team meeting anyway,' muttered Strike. 'Fuck-all progress on any of the cases. Twinkletoes is clean. The worst you can say about him is he's with her for the money, but her dad knew that from the start. Two-Times' girlfriend isn't cheating and Christ only knows what Shifty's got on SB. You saw my email about the blonde in Stoke Newington?'

'Yes,' said Robin, whose face had been whipped into high colour by the squally weather. She was trying to comb her hair back into some semblance of tidiness with her fingers. 'Nothing come up on the address?'

'No. If I had to guess, I'd say she's a relative. She patted him on the head as he left.'

'Dominatrix?' suggested Robin.

There wasn't much she hadn't learned about the kinks of powerful men since joining the agency.

'It occurred to me, but the way he said goodbye . . . they looked . . . cosy. But he hasn't got a sister and she looked younger than him. Would cousins pat each other on the head?'

'Well, Sunday night's all wrong for a normal counsellor or a therapist, but patting's quasi-parental . . . life coach? Psychic?'

'That's a thought,' said Strike, stroking his chin. 'Stockholders wouldn't be impressed if he's making business decisions based on what his fortune teller in Stoke Newington's telling him. I was going to put Morris on to the woman over Christmas, but he's out of action, Hutchins is on Two-Times' girl and I'm supposed to be leaving for Cornwall day after tomorrow. You're off to Masham when – Tuesday?'

'No,' said Robin, looking anxious. 'Tomorrow – Saturday. We did discuss this back in September, remember? I swapped with Morris so I could—'

'Yeah, yeah, I remember,' lied Strike. His head was starting to throb, and the tea wasn't making his throat feel much more comfortable. 'No problem.'

But this, of course, meant that if he was going to give Robin a Christmas present, he'd have to buy it and get it to her by the end of the day.

'I'd try and get a later train,' said Robin, 'but obviously, with it being Christmas—'

'No, you're owed time off,' he said brusquely. 'You shouldn't be working just because those careless bastards got flu.'

Robin, who had a strong suspicion that Barclay and Morris weren't the only people at the agency with flu, said,

'D'you want more tea?'

'What? No,' said Strike, feeling unreasonably resentful at her for, as he saw it, forcing him to go shopping. 'And Postcard's a washout, we've got literally noth—'

'I might – *might* – have something on Postcard.'

'What?' said Strike, surprised.

'Our weatherman got another postcard yesterday, sent to the television studio. It's the fourth one bought in the National Portrait Gallery shop, and it's got an odd message on it.'

She pulled the postcard from her bag and handed it over the desk to Strike. The picture on the front reproduced a self-portrait of Joshua Reynolds, his hand shading his eyes in the stereotypical pose of one staring at something indistinct. On the back was written:

> I hope I'm wrong, but I think you sent someone to my work, holding some of my letters. Have you let someone else see them? I really hope you haven't. Were you trying to scare me? You act like you're so kind and down-to-earth, no airs and graces. I'd have thought you'd have the decency to come yourself if you've got something to say to me. If you don't understand this, ignore.

Strike looked up at Robin.

'Does this mean . . . ?'

Robin explained that she'd bought the same three postcards that Postcard had previously sent from the gallery shop, then roamed the gallery's many rooms, holding the postcards so that they were visible to all the guides she passed, until an owlish woman in thick-lensed glasses had appeared to react at the sight of them, and disappeared through a door marked 'Staff Only'.

'I didn't tell you at the time,' Robin said, 'because I thought I might've imagined it, and she also looked exactly like the kind of person I'd imagined Postcard to be, so I was worried I was doing a Talbot, chasing my own mad hunches.'

'But you're not off your rocker, are you? That was a bloody good idea, going to the shop, and this,' he brandished the postcard of the Reynolds, 'suggests you hit the bullseye first throw.'

'I didn't manage to get a picture of her,' said Robin, trying not to show how much pleasure Strike's praise had given her, 'but she was in Room 8 and I can describe her. Big glasses, shorter than me, thick brown hair, bobbed, probably fortyish.'

Strike made a note of the description.

'Might nip along there myself before I head for Cornwall,' he said. 'Right, let's get on with Bamborough.'

But before either could say another word, the phone rang in the outer office. Glad to have something to complain about, Strike glanced at his watch, heaved himself to his feet and said,

'It's nine o'clock, Pat should—'

But even as he said it, they both heard the glass door open, Pat's unhurried tread and then, in her usual rasping baritone,

'Cormoran Strike Detective Agency.'

Robin tried not to smile as Strike dropped back into his chair. There was a knock on the door, and Pat stuck her head inside,

'Morning. Got a Gregory Talbot on hold for you.'

'Put him through,' said Strike. 'Please,' he added, detecting a martial look in Pat's eye, 'and close the door.'

She did so. A moment later, the phone rang on the partners' desk and Strike switched it to speakerphone.

'Hi, Gregory, Strike here.'

'Yes, hello,' said Gregory, who sounded anxious.

'What can I do for you?'

'Er, well, you know how we were clearing out the loft?'

'Yes,' said Strike.

'Well, yesterday I unpacked an old box,' said Gregory, sounding tense, 'and I found something hidden under Dad's commendations and his uniform—'

'Not *hidden*,' said a querulous female voice in the background.

'I didn't know it was there,' said Gregory. 'And now my mother—'

'Let me talk to him,' said the woman in the background.

'My mother would like to talk to you,' said Gregory, sounding exasperated.

A defiant, elderly female voice replaced Gregory's.

'Is this Mr Strike?'

'It is.'

'Gregory's told you all about how the police treated Bill at the end?'

'Yes,' said Strike.

'He could have kept working once he got treatment for his thyroid, but they didn't let him. He'd given them *everything*, the force was his *life*. Greg says he's given you Bill's notes?'

'That's right,' said Strike.

'Well, after Bill died I found this *can* in a box in the shed and it had the Creed mark on it – you've read the notes, you know Bill used a special symbol for Creed?'

'Yes,' said Strike.

'I couldn't take everything with me into sheltered accommodation, they give you virtually *no* storage space, so I put it into the boxes to go in Greg and Alice's attic. I quite forgot it was there until Greg started looking through his dad's things yesterday. The police have made it *quite* clear they weren't interested in Bill's theories, but Greg says you are, so you should have it.'

Gregory came back on the line. They heard movement that seemed to indicate that Gregory was moving away from his mother. A door closed.

'It's a can containing a reel of old 16mm film,' he told Strike, his mouth close to the receiver. 'Mum doesn't know what's on there. I haven't got a camera to run it, but I've held a bit up to the light and . . . it looks like a dirty movie. I was worried about putting it out for the binmen—'

Given that the Talbots were fostering children, Strike understood his qualms.

'If we give it to you – I wonder—'

'You'd rather we didn't say where we got it?' Strike said, eyes on Robin's. 'I can't see why we'd need to.'

Robin noticed that he hadn't promised, but Gregory seemed happy.

'I'll drop it off, then,' he said. 'I'm coming up West this afternoon. Taking the twins to see Father Christmas.'

When Gregory had rung off, Strike said,

'You notice the Talbots are still convinced, forty years on—'

The phone rang in the outer office again.

'—that Margot was killed by Creed? I think I know what the symbol on this can of film is going to be, because—'

Pat knocked on the door of the inner office.

'Fuck's sake,' muttered Strike, whose throat was starting to burn. '*What?*'

'Charming,' said Pat, coldly. 'There's a Mister Shanker on the line for you. It diverted from your mobile. He says you wanted to—'

'Yeah, I do,' said Strike. 'Transfer it back to my mobile – please,' he added, and turning to Robin, he said, 'sorry, can you give me a moment?'

Robin left the room, closing the door behind her, and Strike pulled out his mobile.

'Shanker, hi, thanks for getting back to me.'

He and Shanker, whose real name he'd have been hard pressed to remember, had known each other since they were teenagers. Their lives had been moving in diametrically different directions even then, Strike heading for university, army and detective work, Shanker pursuing a career of ever-deepening criminality. Nevertheless, a strange sense of kinship had continued to unite them and they were, occasionally, useful to each other, Strike paying Shanker in cash for information or services that he could get no other way.

'What's up, Bunsen?'

'I wanted to buy you a pint and show you a photo,' said Strike.

'Up your way later today, as it goes. Going to Hamleys. Got the wrong fackin' Monster High doll for Zahara.'

Everything except 'Hamleys' had been gibberish to Strike.

'OK, call me when you're ready for a drink.'

'Fair dos.'

The line went dead. Shanker didn't tend to bother with goodbyes.

Robin returned carrying two fresh mugs of tea and closed the door with her foot.

'Sorry about that,' said Strike, absent-mindedly wiping sweat off his top lip. 'What was I saying?'

'That you think you know what symbol's on Talbot's can of old film.'

'Oh, yeah,' said Strike. 'Symbol for Capricorn. I've been having a go at deciphering these notes,' he added, tapping the leather-bound notebook sitting beside him, and he took Robin through the reasons Bill Talbot had come to believe that Margot had been abducted by a man born under the sign of the goat.

'Talbot was ruling out suspects on the basis that they weren't Capricorns?' asked Robin in disbelief.

'Yeah,' said Strike, frowning, his throat burning worse than ever. He took a sip of tea. 'Except that Roy Phipps is a Capricorn, and Talbot ruled him out, too.'

'Why?'

'I'm still trying to decipher it all, but he seems to have been using a weird symbol for Phipps that I haven't been able to identify on any astrological site so far.

'But the notes explain why he kept interviewing Janice. Her star sign's Cancer. Cancer is Capricorn's "opposing" sign and Cancerians are psychic and intuitive, according to Talbot's notes. Talbot concluded that, as a Cancerian, Janice was his natural ally against Baphomet, and that she might have supernatural insights into Baphomet's identity, hence the dream diary.

'Even more significant in his mind was that Saturn, Capricorn's ruler—'

Robin hid a smile behind her mug of tea. Strike's expression, as he outlined these astrological phenomena, would have been appropriate to a man asked to eat weeks'-old seafood.

'—was in Cancer on the day of Margot's disappearance. From this, Talbot deduced that Janice knew or had had contact with Baphomet. Hence the request for a list of her sexual partners.'

'Wow,' said Robin quietly.

'I'm just giving you a hint of the nuttery, but there's plenty more. I'll email you the important points when I've finished deciphering it. But what's interesting is that there are hints of an actual detective trying to fight through his illness.

'He had the same idea that occurred to me: that Margot might've been lured somewhere on the pretext of someone needing medical assistance, although he dresses it all up in mumbo-jumbo – there was a stellium in the sixth house, the House of Health, which he decided meant danger associated with illness.'

'What's a stellium?'

'Group of more than three planets. The police did check out patients she'd seen a lot of in the run-up to the disappearance. There was Douthwaite, obviously, and a demented old woman on Gopsall Street, who kept ringing the surgery for something to do, and a family who lived on Herbal Hill, whose kid had had a reaction to his polio vaccination.'

'Doctors,' said Robin, 'have contact with *so many* people.'

'Yeah,' said Strike, 'and I think that's part of what went wrong in this case. Talbot took in a huge amount of information and couldn't see what to discard. On the other hand, the possibility of her being lured into a house on a medical pretext, or attacked by an angry patient isn't crazy. Medics walk unaccompanied into all kinds of people's houses . . . and look at Douthwaite. Lawson really fancied him as Margot's abductor or killer, and Talbot was very interested in him, too. Even though Douthwaite was a Pisces, Talbot tries to make him a Capricorn. He says "Schmidt" thinks Douthwaite's really a Capricorn—'

'Who's Schmidt?'

'No idea,' said Strike, 'but he or she is all over the notes, correcting signs.'

'All the chances to get actual evidence lost,' said Robin quietly, 'while Talbot was checking everyone's horoscope.'

'Exactly. It'd be funny if it wasn't so serious. But his interest in Douthwaite still smacks of sound copper instinct. Douthwaite seems pretty bloody fishy to me, as well.'

'Ha ha,' said Robin.

Strike looked blank.

'Pisces,' she reminded him.

'Oh. Yeah,' said Strike, unsmiling. The throbbing behind his eyes was worse than ever, his throat complaining every time he swallowed, but he couldn't have flu. It was impossible. 'I read that bit you marked in Oakden's book,' he continued. 'The stuff about Douthwaite changing his name when he went to Clacton to sing at a holiday camp, but I can't find any trace of a Steve, Steven or Stevie Jacks after 1976, either. One name change might be understandable after a lot of police attention. Two starts to look suspicious.'

'You think?' said Robin. 'We know he was the nervous type, judging from his medical records. Maybe he was spooked by Oakden turning up at Butlin's?'

'But Oakden's book was pulped. Nobody beyond a couple of Butlin's Redcoats ever knew Stevie Jacks had been questioned about Margot Bamborough.'

'Maybe he went abroad,' said Robin. 'Died abroad. I'm starting to think that's what happened to Paul Satchwell, as well. Did you see, Satchwell's ex-neighbour said he went off travelling?'

'Yeah,' said Strike. 'Any luck on Gloria Conti yet?'

'Nothing,' sighed Robin. 'But I have got a *couple* of things,' she went on, opening her notebook. 'They don't advance us much, but for what they're worth . . .

'I've now spoken to Charlie Ramage's widow in Spain. The hot-tub millionaire who thought he saw Margot in the Leamington Spa graveyard?'

Strike nodded, glad of a chance to rest his throat.

'I think Mrs Ramage has either had a stroke or likes a lunchtime drink. She sounded slurred, but she confirmed that Charlie thought he'd seen Margot in a graveyard, and that he discussed it afterwards with a policeman friend, whose name she couldn't remember. Then suddenly she said, "No, wait – Mary Flanagan. It was Mary Flanagan he thought he saw." I took her back over the story and she said, yes, that was all correct, except that it was Mary Flanagan, not Margot Bamborough, he thought he'd seen. I've looked up Mary Flanagan,' said Robin, 'and she's been missing since 1959. It's Britain's longest ever missing person case.'

'Which of them would you say seemed more confused?' asked Strike. 'Mrs Ramage, or Janice?'

'Mrs Ramage, definitely,' said Robin. 'Janice definitely wouldn't have confused the two women, would she? Whereas Mrs Ramage might have done. She had no personal interest: to her, they were just two missing people whose names began with "M".'

Strike sat frowning, thinking it over. Finally he said, his tonsils burning,

'If Ramage was a teller of tall tales generally, his policeman mate can't be blamed for not taking him seriously. This is at least confirmation that Ramage believed he'd once met a missing woman.'

He frowned so intensely that Robin said,

'Are you in pain?'

'No. I'm wondering whether it'd be worth trying to see Irene and Janice separately. I'd hoped never to have to talk to Irene Hickson again. At the very least, we should keep looking for a connection between Margot and Leamington Spa. Did you say you had another lead?'

'Not much of one. Amanda Laws – or Amanda White, as she was when she supposedly saw Margot at that window on Clerkenwell Road – answered my email. I'll forward her reply if you want to read it, but basically she's angling for money.'

'Is she, now?'

'She dresses it up a bit. Says she told the police and nobody believed her, told Oakden and he didn't give her a penny, and she's tired of not being taken seriously and if we want her story she'd like to be paid for it this time. She claims she's endured a lot of negative attention, being called a liar and a fantasist, and she's not prepared to go through all of that again unless she gets compensated.'

Strike made a second note.

'Tell her it isn't the agency's practice to pay witnesses for their cooperation,' said Strike. 'Appeal to her better nature. If that doesn't work, she can have a hundred quid.'

'I think she's hoping for thousands.'

'And I'm hoping for Christmas in the Bahamas,' said Strike, as rain dotted the window behind him. 'That all you've got?'

'Yes,' said Robin, closing her notebook.

'Well, I've drawn a blank on the Bennie-abusing patient who claimed to have killed Margot, Applethorpe. I think Irene must've got the name wrong. I've tried all the variants that've occurred to me, but nothing's coming up. I might *have* to call her back. I'll try Janice first, though.'

'You haven't told me what you thought of the Oakden book.'

'Bog-standard opportunist,' said Strike, 'who did well to squeeze ten chapters out of virtually nothing. But I'd like to track him down if we can.'

'I'm trying,' sighed Robin, 'but he's another one who seems to have vanished off the face of the planet. His mother seemed to be his primary source, didn't she? I don't think he persuaded anyone who *really* knew Margot to talk to him.'

'No,' said Strike. 'You'd highlighted nearly all the interesting bits.'

'Nearly?' said Robin sharply.

'All,' Strike corrected himself.

'You spotted something else?'

'No,' said Strike, but seeing that she was unconvinced, he added, 'I've just been wondering whether someone might've put a hit on her.'

'Her husband?' said Robin, startled.

'Maybe,' said Strike.

'Or are you thinking about the cleaner's husband? Jules Bayliss, and his alleged criminal connections?'

'Not really.'

'Then why—'

'I just keep coming back to the fact that if she was killed, it was done very efficiently. Which might suggest—'

'—a contract killer,' said Robin. 'You know, I read a biography of Lord Lucan recently. They think he hired someone to kill his wife—'

'—and the killer got the nanny by mistake,' said Strike, who was familiar with the theory. 'Yeah. Well, if that's what happened to Margot, we're looking at an assassin a damn sight more efficient than Lucan's. Not a trace of her left behind, not so much as a drop of blood.'

There was a momentary silence, while Strike glanced behind him to see the rain and wind still buffeting the Christmas lights outside, and Robin's thoughts flew to Roy Phipps, the man whom Oonagh had called bloodless, conveniently bedridden on the day of Margot's disappearance.

'Well, I need to get going,' said Strike, pushing himself up out of his chair.

'I should, too,' sighed Robin, collecting her things.

'You're coming back into the office later, though?' Strike asked.

He needed to give her the as-yet-unbought Christmas present before she left for Yorkshire.

'I wasn't planning to,' said Robin. 'Why?'

'Come back in,' Strike said, trying to think of a reason. He opened the door into the outer office. 'Pat?'

'Yes?' said Pat, without looking round. She was once more typing fast and accurately, her electronic cigarette waggling between her teeth.

'Robin and I both need to head out now, but a man called Gregory Talbot's about to drop off a can of 16mm film. D'you think you can track down a projector that'll play it? Ideally before five o'clock?'

Pat swung slowly around on her desk chair to look at Strike, her monkey-ish face set, her eyes narrowed.

'You want me to find a vintage film projector by five o'clock?'

'That's what I said.' Strike turned to Robin. 'Then we can have a quick look at whatever Talbot had hiding in the attic before you leave for Masham.'

'OK,' said Robin, 'I'll come back at four.'

27

His name was Talus, made of yron mould,
Immoueable, resistlesse, without end.
Who in his hand an yron flale did hould,
With which he thresht out falshood, and did truth vnfould.

Edmund Spenser
The Faerie Queene

Some two and a half hours later, Strike stood beneath the awning of
Hamleys on Regent Street, shopping bags by his feet, telling himself firmly that he was fine in spite of ample empirical evidence that
he was, in fact, shivering. Cold rain was spattering all around him
onto the dirty pavements, where it was kicked out of puddles by the
marching feet of hundreds of passing pedestrians. It splashed over
kerbs in the wake of passing vehicles and dripped down the back of
Strike's collar, though he stood, theoretically, beneath shelter.

While checking his phone yet again for some sign that Shanker
hadn't forgotten they were supposed to be meeting for a drink, he lit
a cigarette, but his raw throat didn't appreciate the sudden ingestion
of smoke. With a foul taste in his mouth, he ground out the cigarette
after one drag. There was no message from Shanker, so Strike picked
up his bulky shopping bags and set off again, his throat burning every
time he swallowed.

He'd imagined optimistically that he might have finished all his
shopping within two hours, but midday had come and gone and
he still wasn't done. How did people decide what to buy, when the
speakers were all shrieking Christmas tunes at you, and the shops

were full of too much choice, and all of it looked like junk? Endless processions of women kept ranging across his path, choosing items with apparently effortless ease. Were they genetically programmed to seek and find the right gift? Was there nobody he could pay to do this for him?

His eyes felt heavy, his throat ached and his nose had started running. Unsure where he was going, or what he was looking for, he walked blindly onwards. He, who usually had an excellent sense of direction, kept turning the wrong way, becoming disorientated. Several times he knocked into carefully stacked piles of Christmas merchandise, or buffeted smaller people, who scowled and muttered and scurried away.

The bulky bags he was carrying contained three identical Nerf blasters for his nephews; large plastic guns which shot foam bullets, which Strike had decided to buy on the dual grounds that he would have loved one when he was eleven, and the assistant had assured him they were one of the must-have gifts of the year. He'd bought his Uncle Ted a sweater because he couldn't think of anything else, his brother-in-law a box of golf balls and a bottle of gin on the same principle, but he still had the trickiest gifts to buy – the ones for the women: Lucy, Joan and Robin.

His mobile rang.

'Fuck.'

He hobbled sideways out of the crowd and, standing beside a mannequin wearing a reindeer sweater, shook himself free from a few of his bags so that he could pull out his mobile.

'Strike.'

'Bunsen, I'm near Shakespeare's 'Ead on Great Marlborough Street. See you there in twenty?'

'Great,' said Strike, who was becoming hoarse. 'I'm just round the corner.'

Another wave of sweat passed over him, soaking scalp and chest. It was, some part of his brain acknowledged, just possible that he had caught Barclay's flu, and if that was the case, he mustn't give it to his severely immunosuppressed aunt. He picked up his shopping bags again and made his way back to the slippery pavement outside.

The black and white timbered frontage of Liberty rose up to his right as he headed along Great Marlborough Street. Buckets and boxes of flowers lay all around the main entrance, temptingly light and portable, and already wrapped; so easy to carry to the Shakespeare's Head and take on to the office afterwards. But, of course, flowers wouldn't do this time. Sweating worse than ever, Strike turned into the store, dumped his bags once more on the floor beside an array of silk scarves, and called Ilsa.

'Hey, Oggy,' said Ilsa.

'What can I get Robin for Christmas?' he said. It was becoming difficult to talk: his throat felt raw.

'Are you all right?'

'I'm fantastic. Give me an idea. I'm in Liberty.'

'Um . . .' said Ilsa. 'Let's th . . . ooh, I know what you can get her. She wants some new perfume. She didn't like the stuff she—'

'I don't need backstory,' said Strike ungraciously. 'That's great. Perfume. What does she wear?'

'I'm trying to tell you, Oggy,' said Ilsa. 'She wants a change. Choose her something new.'

'I can't smell,' said Strike, impatiently, 'I've got a cold.'

But this basic problem aside, he was afraid that a perfume he'd personally picked out was too intimate a gift, like that green dress of a few years back. He was looking for something like flowers, but not flowers, something that said 'I like you', but not 'this is what I'd like you to smell like'.

'Just go to an assistant and say "I want to buy a perfume for some-one who wears Philosykos but wants a—"'

'She what?' said Strike. 'She wears what?'

'Philosykos. Or she did.'

'Spell it,' said Strike, his head thumping. Ilsa did so.

'So I just ask an assistant, and they'll give me something like it?'

'That's the idea,' said Ilsa patiently.

'Great,' said Strike. 'Appreciate it. Speak soon.'

The assistant thought you'd like it.

Yeah, he'd say that. *The assistant thought you'd like it* would effec-tively de-personalise the gift, turn it into a something almost as mundane as flowers, but it would still show he'd taken some care, given it some thought. Picking up his carrier bags again, he limped towards an area he could see in the distance that looked as though it was lined with bottles.

The perfume department turned out to be small, about the size of Strike's office. He sidled into the crowded space, passing beneath a cupola painted with stars, to find himself surrounded by shelves laden with fragile cargos of glass bottles, some of which wore ruffs, or patterns like lace; others which looked like jewels, or the kind of phial suitable for a love potion. Apologising as he forced people aside with his Nerf guns, his gin and his golf balls, he met a slim, black-clad man who asked, 'Can I help you?' At this moment Strike's eye fell on a range of bottled scents which were identically packed with black labels and tops. They looked functional and discreet, with no overt suggestion of romance.

'I'd like one of those,' he croaked, pointing.

'Right,' said the assistant. 'Er—'

'It's for someone who used to wear Philosykos. Something like that.'

'OK,' said the assistant, leading Strike over to the display. 'Well, what about—'

'No,' said Strike, before the assistant could remove the top of the tester. The perfume was called Carnal Flower. 'She said she didn't like that one,' Strike added, with the conscious aim of appearing less strange. 'Are any of the others like Philo—'

'She might like Dans Tes Bras?' suggested the assistant, spraying a second bottle onto a smelling strip.

'Doesn't that mean—?'

'"In your arms",' said the assistant.

'No,' said Strike, without taking the smelling strip. 'Are any of the others like Phi—?'

'Musc Ravageur?'

'You know what, I'll leave it,' said Strike, sweat prickling anew beneath his shirt. 'Which exit is nearest the Shakespeare's Head?'

The unsmiling assistant pointed Strike towards the left. Muttering apologies, Strike edged back out past women who were studying bottles and spraying on testers, turned a corner and saw, with relief, the pub where he was meeting Shanker, which lay just beyond the glass doors of a room full of chocolates.

Chocolates, he thought, slowing down and incidentally impeding a group of harried women. *Everyone likes chocolates*. Sweat was now coming over him in waves, and he seemed to feel simultaneously hot and cold. He approached a table piled high with chocolate boxes, looking for the most expensive one, one that would show appreciation and friendship. Trying to choose a flavour, he thought he recalled a conversation about salted caramel, so he took the largest box he could find and headed for the till.

Five minutes later, another bag hanging from his hands, Strike emerged at the end of Carnaby Street, where music-themed Christmas decorations hung between the buildings. In Strike's now fevered state, the invisible heads suggested by giant headphones and sunglasses seemed sinister rather than festive. Struggling with his bags, he backed into the Shakespeare's Head, where fairy lights twinkled and chatter and laughter filled the air.

'Bunsen,' said a voice, just inside the door.

Shanker had secured a table. Shaven-headed, gaunt, pale and heavily tattooed, Shanker had an upper lip that was fixed in a permanent Elvis-style sneer, due to the scar that ran up towards his cheekbone. He was absent-mindedly clicking the fingers of the hand not holding his pint, a tic he'd had since his teens. No matter where he was, Shanker managed to emanate an aura of danger, projecting the idea that he might, on the slightest provocation, resort to violence. Crowded as the pub was, nobody had chosen to share his table. Incongruously, or so it seemed to Strike, Shanker, too, had shopping bags at his feet.

'What's wrong wiv ya?' Shanker said, as Strike sank down opposite him and disposed of his own bags beneath the table. 'Ya look like shit.'

'Nothing,' said Strike, whose nose was now running profusely and whose pulse seemed to have become erratic. 'Cold or something.'

'Well, keep it the fuck away from me,' said Shanker. 'Last fing we fuckin' need at home. Zahara's only just got over the fuckin' flu. Wanna pint?'

'Er – no,' said Strike. The thought of beer was currently repellent. 'Couldn't get me some water, could you?'

'Fuck's sake,' muttered Shanker, as he got up.

When Shanker had returned with a glass of water and sat down again, Strike said, without preamble,

'I wanted to ask you about an evening, must've been round about '92, '93. You needed to get into town, you had a car, but you couldn't drive it yourself. You'd done something to your arm. It was strapped up.'

Shanker shrugged impatiently, as much as to say, who could be expected to remember something so trivial? Shanker's life had been an endless series of injuries received and inflicted, and of needing to get places to deliver cash, drugs, threats or beatings. Periods of imprisonment had done nothing but temporarily change the environment in which he conducted business. Half the boys with whom he had associated in his teens were dead, most killed by knives or overdoses. One cousin had died in a police car chase, and another had been shot through the back of the head, his killer never caught.

'You had to make a delivery,' Strike went on, trying to jog Shanker's memory. 'Jiffy bag full of something – drugs, cash, I don't know. You came round the squat looking for someone to drive you, urgently. I said I'd do it. We went to a strip club in Soho. It was called Teezers.'

'Teezers, yeah,' said Bunsen. 'Long gone, Teezers. Closed ten, fifteen year ago.'

'When we got there, there was a group of men standing on the pavement, heading inside. One of them was a bald black guy—'

'Your fucking memory,' said Shanker, amused. 'You could do a stage act. "Bunsen, the Amazing Memory Man"—'

'—and there was a big Latin-looking bloke with dyed black hair and sideburns. We pulled up, you wound down the window and he came over and put his hand on the door to talk to you. He had eyes like a basset hound and he was wearing a massive gold ring with a lion's—'

'Mucky Ricci,' said Shanker.

'You remember him?'

'Just said 'is name, Bunsen, d'in I?'

'Yeah. Sorry. What was his real name, d'you know?'

'Nico, Niccolo Ricci, but everyone called 'im "Mucky". Old-school villain. Pimp. 'E owned a few strip clubs, ran a couple of knocking shops. Real bit of old London, 'e was. Got his start as part of the Sabini gang, when 'e was a kid.'

'How're you spelling Ricci? R – I – C – C – I, right?'

'What's this about?'

Strike tugged the copy of *Whatever Happened to Margot Bamborough?* out of his coat pocket, turned to the photographs of the practice Christmas party and held it out to Shanker, who took it suspiciously. He squinted for a moment at the partial picture of the man with the lion ring, then passed the book back to Strike.

'Well?' said Strike.

'Yeah, looks like 'im. Where's that?'

'Clerkenwell. A doctors' Christmas party.'

Shanker looked mildly surprised.

'Well, Clerkenwell, that was the old Sabini stamping ground, warn't it? And I s'pose even gangsters need doctors sometimes.'

'It was a party,' said Strike. 'Not a surgery. Why would Mucky Ricci be at a doctors' party?'

'Dunno,' said Shanker. 'Anyone need killing?'

'Funny you should ask that,' said Strike. 'I'm investigating the disappearance of a woman who was there that night.'

Shanker looked sideways at him.

'Mucky Ricci's gaga,' he said quietly. 'Old man now, innit.'

'Still alive, though?'

'Yer. 'E's in an 'ome.'

'How d'you know that?'

'Done a bit o' business wiv 'is eldest, Luca.'

'Boys in the same line of work as their old man?'

'Well, there ain't no Little Italy gang any more, is there? But they're villains, yeah,' said Shanker. Then he leaned across the table and said quietly, 'Listen to me, Bunsen. You do not wanna screw wiv Mucky Ricci's boys.'

It was the first time Shanker had ever given Strike such a warning.

'You go fuckin' wiv their old man, you try pinnin' anyfing on 'im, the Ricci boys'll skin ya. Understand? They don't fuckin' care. They'll torch your fuckin' office. They'll cut up your girl.'

'Tell me about Mucky. Anything you know.'

'Did you 'ear what I just said, Bunsen?'

'Just tell me about him, for fuck's sake.'

Shanker scowled.

''Ookers. Porn. Drugs, but girls was 'is main thing. Same era as George Cornell, Jimmy Humphries, all those boys. That gold ring 'e wore, 'e used to say Danny the Lion gave it 'im. Danny Leo, the mob boss in New York. Claimed they were related. Dunno if it's true.'

'Ever run across anyone called Conti?' Strike asked. 'Probably a bit younger than Ricci.'

'Nope. But Luca Ricci's a fuckin' psycho,' said Shanker. 'When did this bint disappear?'

'1974,' said Strike.

He expected Shanker to say 'Nineteen seventy fucking four?', to pour scorn on the likelihood of finding any kind of solution after all this time, but his old friend merely frowned at him, his clicking fingers recalling the relentless progress of the deathwatch beetle, and it occurred to the detective that Shanker knew more about old crimes and the long shadows they cast than many policemen.

'Name of Margot Bamborough,' said Strike. 'She vanished on her way to the pub. Nothing ever found, no handbag, door keys, nothing. Never seen again.'

Shanker sipped his beer.

'Professional job,' he said.

'That occurred to me,' said Strike. 'Hence—'

'Fuck your fucking "hence",' said Shanker fiercely. 'If the bint was taken out by Mucky Ricci or any of his boys, she's past fuckin' savin', in't she? I know you like bein' the boy scout, mate, but the last guy who pissed off Luca Ricci, his wife opened the door few days later and got acid thrown in her face. Blind in one eye, now.

'You wanna drop this, Bunsen. If Mucky Ricci's the answer, you need to stop askin' the question.'

28

Greatly thereat was Britomart dismayd,
Ne in that stownd wist, how her selfe to beare . . .
Edmund Spenser
The Faerie Queene

Somehow, Pat had managed to track down a vintage film projector. It had been promised for delivery at four, but Strike and Robin were still waiting for it at a quarter to six, at which time Robin told Strike she really did need to leave. She hadn't yet packed for her trip home to Yorkshire, she wanted an early night before catching the train and, if she was honest, she was feeling insulted by Strike's gift of unwrapped salted caramel chocolates, which he'd pulled hastily out of a Liberty bag when he saw her, and which she now suspected were the whole lousy reason he had forced her to come back to the office in the first place. As this had necessitated a long trip back to Denmark Street on a packed Tube, it was hard not to feel resentful about the time and trouble she had taken to find and wrap the DVD of two old Tom Waits concerts he'd mentioned wanting to watch, a few weeks previously. Robin had never heard of the singer: it had taken her some trouble to identify the man Strike had been talking about, and the concerts he'd never seen as those on *No Visitors After Midnight*. And in return, she got chocolates she was sure had been grabbed at random.

She left Strike's present behind, untouched, in Max's kitchen, before boarding the crowded train to Harrogate next morning. As she travelled north in her mercifully pre-booked seat, Robin tried to tell herself that her feeling of emptiness was merely tiredness. Christmas at home would be a wonderful break. She'd be meeting her new niece for the first time; there'd be lie-ins and home-cooked food and hours in front of the telly.

A toddler was shouting at the back of the carriage, his mother trying just as loudly to entertain and subdue him. Robin pulled out her iPod and put on headphones. She'd downloaded Joni Mitchell's album, *Court and Spark*, which Oonagh had mentioned as Margot Bamborough's favourite. Robin hadn't yet had time to listen to it, or, indeed, to any other music, for weeks.

But *Court and Spark* didn't soothe or cheer her. She found it unsettling, unlike anything she had ever listened to before. Expecting melodies and hooks, Robin was disappointed: everything felt unfinished, left open, unresolved. A beautiful soprano voice tumbled and swooped over piano or guitar chords that never led to anything as mundane as a chorus that you could settle into, or tap your foot to. You couldn't hum along, you couldn't have joined in unless you, too, could sing like Mitchell, which Robin certainly couldn't. The words were strange, and evoked responses she didn't like: she wasn't sure she'd ever felt the things Mitchell sang about, and this made her feel defensive, confused and sad: *Love came to my door, with a sleeping roll and a madman's soul . . .*

A few seconds into track three, she turned off the iPod and reached instead for the magazine she had brought with her. At the back of the carriage, the toddler was now howling.

Robin's mood of mild despondency persisted until she got off the train, but when she saw her mother standing on the platform, ready to drive her back to Masham, she was overtaken by a wave of genuine warmth. She hugged Linda, and for almost ten minutes afterwards, while they wended their way, chatting, towards the car, passing a café out of which jangling Christmas music was emanating, even the dour grey Yorkshire skies and the car interior, which smelled of Rowntree the Labrador, felt comforting and cheery in their familiarity.

'I've got something to tell you,' Linda said, when she had closed the driver's door. Instead of turning the key in the ignition, Linda turned to Robin, looking almost fearful.

A sickening jolt of panic turned Robin's stomach upside down.
'What's happened?' she said.

'It's all right,' Linda said hastily, 'everyone's well. But I want you to know before we get back to Masham, in case you see them.'

'See who?'

'Matthew,' said Linda, 'has brought . . . he's brought that woman home with him. Sarah Shadlock. They're staying with Geoffrey for Christmas.'

'*Oh*,' said Robin. 'Christ, Mum, I thought someone had died.'

She hated the way Linda was looking at her. Though her insides had just grown cold, and the fragile happiness that had briefly kindled inside her had been snuffed out, she forced a smile and a tone of unconcern.

'It's fine. I knew. Her ex-fiancé called me. I should've guessed,' she said, wondering why she hadn't, 'they might be here for Christmas. Can we get home, please? I'm dying for a cup of tea.'

'You *knew*? Why didn't you tell us?'

But Linda herself supplied the answer to that, as they drove. It neither soothed nor comforted Robin to have Linda storming about how outraged she'd been, when a neighbour told her that Matthew had been strolling hand in hand with Sarah through the middle of town. She didn't feel comforted by strictures against her ex-husband's morals and manners, nor did she appreciate having each family member's reaction detailed to her ('Martin was all for *punching* him again'). Then Linda moved on to the divorce: what was going on? Why wasn't it all settled yet? Did Robin *honestly* think mediation would work? Didn't Matthew's behaviour, *flaunting* this woman in front of the whole of Masham, *show* how utterly lost to shame and reason he was? Why, oh why, hadn't Robin agreed to let Harveys of Harrogate deal with it all, was she *sure* this London woman was up to it, because Corinne Maxwell had told Linda that when *her* daughter divorced without children it was all *completely* straightforward . . .

But at least there was little Annabel Marie, was the conclusion of Linda's monologue, as they turned onto Robin's parents' street.

'*Wait* till you see her, Robin, just *wait* . . . '

The front door opened before the car came to a halt. Jenny and

Stephen were standing on the threshold, looking so excited that an onlooker might have suspected it was they who were about to see their baby daughter for the first time, not Robin. Realising what was expected of her, Robin hitched an eager smile onto her face, and within minutes found herself sitting on the sofa in her parents' living room, a warm little sleeping body in her arms, wrapped up in wool, surprisingly solid and heavy, and smelling of Johnson's baby powder.

'She's gorgeous, Stephen,' Robin said, while Rowntree's tail thumped against the coffee table. He was nosing at her, thrusting his head repeatedly under Robin's hand, confused as to why he wasn't receiving the fuss and love he was used to. 'She's gorgeous, Jenny,' Robin said, as her sister-in-law took photos of 'Auntie Robin' meeting Annabel for the first time. 'She's gorgeous, Mum,' Robin said to Linda, who had come back with a tea tray and a craving to hear what Robin thought of their twenty-inch-long marvel.

'Evens things out, doesn't it, having another girl?' said Linda delightedly. Her anger at Matthew was over now: her granddaughter was everything.

The sitting room was more cramped than usual, not only with Christmas tree and cards, but with baby equipment. A changing mat, a Moses basket, a pile of mysterious muslin cloths, a bag of nappies and an odd contraption that Jenny explained was a breast pump. Robin rhapsodised, smiled, laughed, ate biscuits, heard the story of the birth, admired some more, held her niece until she woke, then, after Jenny had taken back possession of the baby and, with a touch of new self-importance, settled herself down to breastfeed, said that she would nip upstairs and unpack.

Robin carried her bag upstairs, her absence unnoticed and unregretted by those below, who were lost in adoration of the baby. Robin closed the door of her old room behind her, but instead of unpacking, lay down on her old bed. Facial muscles aching from all her forced smiling, she closed her eyes, and allowed herself the luxury of exhausted misery.

29

Thus warred he long time against his will,
Till that through weakness he was forced at last
To yield himself unto the mighty ill,
Which, as a victor proud, 'gan ransack fast
His inward parts and all his entrails waste . . .

Edmund Spenser
The Faerie Queene

With three days to go before Christmas, Strike was forced to abandon the pretence that he didn't have flu. Concluding that the only sensible course was to hole up in his attic flat while the virus passed through his system, he took himself to a packed Sainsbury's where, feverish, sweating, breathing through his mouth and desperate to get away from the crowds and the canned carols, he grabbed enough food for a few days, and bore it back to his two rooms above the office.

Joan took the news that he wouldn't be joining the festivities in Cornwall predictably hard. She went so far as to suggest that it would be fine for him to come, as long as they sat at opposite ends of the dinner table, but to Strike's relief, Ted overruled her. Strike didn't know whether he was being paranoid, but he suspected Lucy didn't believe he was genuinely ill. If she did, her tone suggested that he might have caught flu deliberately. He thought he heard a trace of accusation when she informed him that Joan was now entirely bald.

By five o'clock in the afternoon of Christmas Eve, Strike had developed a cough that made his lungs rattle and his ribs ache. Drowsing on his bed in a T-shirt and boxer shorts, his prosthetic

316

leg propped against a wall, he was woken abruptly by a loud noise. Footsteps seemed to be moving down the stairs, away from his attic door. A paroxysm of coughing seized him before he could call out to the person he thought had woken him. Struggling back into a sitting position to clear his lungs, he didn't hear the second approach of footsteps until somebody knocked on his door. He greatly resented the effort it took to shout, 'What?'

'D'you need anything?' came Pat's deep, gravelly voice.

'No,' Strike shouted. The syllable emerged as a croak.

'Have you got food?'

'Yes.'

'Painkillers?'

'Yes.'

'Well, I'm leaving some things outside the door for you.' He heard her setting objects down. 'There are a couple of presents. Eat the soup while it's still hot. See you on the twenty-eighth.'

Her footsteps were clanging down the metal stairs before he could respond.

He wasn't sure whether he'd imagined the mention of hot soup, but the possibility was enough to make him drag his crutches towards himself and make his way laboriously to the door. The chill of the stairwell added gooseflesh to his fever sweats. Pat had somehow managed to carry the old video projector upstairs for him, and he suspected that it was the sound of her setting this down that had woken him. Beside it lay the can of film from Gregory Talbot's attic, a small pile of wrapped Christmas gifts, a handful of cards and two polystyrene tubs of hot chicken soup that he knew she must have walked to Chinatown to fetch. He felt quite pathetically grateful.

Leaving the heavy projector and the can of film where they were, he pulled and prodded the Christmas gifts and card across the floor into the flat with one of his crutches, then slowly bent down to pick up the tubs of soup.

Before eating, he took his mobile from the bedside table and texted Pat:

Thanks very much. Hope you have a good Christmas.

He then wrapped the duvet around himself and ate the soup straight out of the tubs, tasting nothing. He'd hoped the hot liquid would soothe his raw throat, but the cough persisted, and once or twice he thought he was going to choke everything back up again. His intestines also seemed unsure whether they welcomed food. Having finished the two tubs, he settled back down beneath the duvet, sweating while he looked at the black sky outside, guts churning, and wondering why he wasn't yet on the mend.

After a night of intermittent dozing interrupted by prolonged coughing fits, Strike woke on Christmas morning to find his fever unabated, and sweaty sheets tangled about him. His normally noisy flat was unnaturally quiet. Tottenham Court Road was suddenly, weirdly devoid of traffic. He supposed most of the taxi drivers were at home with their families.

Strike was not a self-pitying man, but lying alone in bed, coughing and sweating, his ribs sore and his fridge now virtually empty, he was unable to prevent his thoughts roaming back over Christmases past, especially those spent at Ted and Joan's in St Mawes, where everything proceeded as it did on the television and in story books, with turkey and crackers and stockings.

Of course, today was far from the first Christmas he'd spent away from family and friends. There'd been a couple such in the army, when he'd eaten foil trays of tasteless turkey in field canteens, among camouflage-wearing colleagues wearing Santa hats. The structure he'd enjoyed in the military had then consoled him in the absence of other pleasures, but there was no camaraderie to sustain him today, only the dismal fact that he was alone, ill and one-legged, stuck up in a draughty attic, forced to endure the consequences of his own firm repudiation of any relationship that might offer support in moments of illness or sadness.

The memory of Pat's kindness became, this Christmas morning, still more touching in retrospect. Turning his head, he saw the few gifts that she'd brought upstairs still lying on the floor just inside the door.

He got up from his bed, still coughing, reached for his crutches and swung himself towards the bathroom. His urine was dark, his unshaven face in the mirror ashen. Though dismayed by his own debility and exhaustion, habits ingrained in him by the military prevented Strike from returning to bed. He knew that lying unwashed with his leg off would merely increase his hovering feeling of depression. He therefore showered, moving more carefully than usual to guard against the risk of falls, dried himself off, put on a clean T-shirt, boxers and dressing gown and, still racked with coughs, prepared himself a tasteless breakfast of porridge made with water, because he preferred to conserve his last pint of milk for his tea. As he'd expected to be well on the mend by now, his stocks of food had dwindled to some limp vegetables, a couple of bits of uncooked chicken two days out of date and a small chunk of hard Cheddar.

After breakfast Strike took painkillers, put on his prosthesis and then, determined to use what small amount of physical strength he could muster before the illness dragged him under again, stripped and remade his bed with clean sheets, removed his Christmas presents from the floor to his kitchen table, and carried the projector and roll of film inside from the landing where he had left them. The can, as he'd expected, bore the mark of Capricorn upon it, drawn in faded but clearly legible marker pen.

His mobile buzzed as he propped the can against the wall beneath his kitchen window. He picked it up, expecting a text from Lucy asking when he was going to call and wish everyone in St Mawes a Merry Christmas.

Merry Christmas, Bluey. Are you happy? Are you with someone you love?

It had been a fortnight since Charlotte had last texted him, almost as though she'd telepathically heard his resolution to contact her husband if her messages became any more self-destructive.

It would be so easy to answer; so easy to tell her he was alone, ill, unsupported. He thought of the naked photo she'd sent on his birthday, which he'd forced himself to delete. But he'd come such a long way, to a place of lonely security against emotional storms. However much he'd loved her, however much she could still disturb his serenity with a few typed words, he forced himself, standing beside his small Formica table, to recall the only occasion on which he'd taken her back to St Mawes for Christmas. He remembered the row heard all through the tiny house, remembered her storming out past the family assembled around the turkey, remembered Ted and Joan's faces, because they'd so looked forward to the visit, having not seen Strike for over a year, because he was at that time stationed in Germany with the Special Investigation Branch of the Royal Military Police.

He set his mobile to mute. Self-respect and self-discipline had always been his bulwarks against lethargy and misery. What was Christmas Day, after all? If you disregarded the fact that other people were enjoying feasts and fun, merely a winter's day like any other. If he was currently bodily weak, why shouldn't he use his mental faculties, at least, to continue work on the Bamborough case?

Thus reasoning, Strike made himself a fresh cup of strong tea, added a very small amount of milk, opened his laptop and, pausing regularly for coughing fits, re-read the document he'd been working on before he'd fallen ill: a summary of the contents of Bill Talbot's symbol-laden, leather-bound notebook, which Strike had now spent three weeks deciphering. His intention was to send the document to Robin for her thoughts.

Talbot's Occult Notes
1. Overview
2. Symbol key
3. Possible leads
4. Probably irrelevant
5. Action points

Overview
Talbot's breakdown manifested itself in a belief that he could solve the Bamborough case by occult means. In addition to astrology, he consulted Aleister Crowley's Thoth tarot, which has an astrological dimension. He immersed himself in several occult writers,

including Crowley, Éliphas Lévi and astrologer Evangeline Adams, and attempted magic rituals.

Talbot was a regular churchgoer before his mental health broke down. While ill, he thought he was hunting a literal embodiment of evil/the devil. Aleister Crowley, who seems to have influenced Talbot more than anyone else, called himself 'Baphomet' and also connected Baphomet both with the devil and the sign of Capricorn. This is probably where Talbot got the idea that Margot's killer was a Capricorn.

Most of what's in the notebook is worthless, but I think Talbot left three

Strike now deleted the number 'three' and substituted 'four'. As ever, when immersed in work, he felt a craving for a cigarette. As though in rebellion against the very idea, his lungs immediately treated him to a violent fit of coughing that necessitated the grabbing of kitchen roll to catch what they were trying to expel. Suitably chastened and shivering slightly, Strike drew his dressing gown more tightly around him, took a sip of tea he couldn't taste and continued to work.

Most of what's in the notebook is worthless, but I think Talbot left four possibly genuine leads out of the official police record, only recording them in 'the true book', ie, his leather notebook.

<u>Symbol key</u>
There are no names in the notebook, only zodiacal signs. I'm not listing unidentified eye witnesses – we've got no chance of tracing them on their star signs and nothing else – but by cross-referencing corroborative details, these are my best guesses at the identity of people Talbot thought were important to the investigation.

♈	Aries	Paul Satchwell (ex-boyfriend)
♉	Taurus	Wilma Bayliss (office cleaner)
♊	Gemini	Oonagh Kennedy
♊2	Gemini 2	Amanda Laws (saw M at window)
♋	Cancer	Janice Beattie (nurse)

♋2	Cancer 2	Cynthia Phipps (Anna's nanny/stepmother)
♌	Leo	Dinesh Gupta (GP)
♌2	Leo 2	Willy Lomax (saw M entering church)
♌3	Leo 3	? (from Talbot's notes, ♌3 seems to have been seen coming out of the practice by a member of the public. Hints that ♌3 is known to police and that ♌3 was there at night)

Strike now deleted the last paragraph and substituted a name and a new note.

♌3	Leo 3	Nico 'Mucky' Ricci (gangster who attended practice Christmas party. Nobody seems to have recognised him except an unnamed passer-by)
♍	Virgo	Dorothy Oakden (practice secretary)
♎	Libra	Joseph Brenner (GP)
♎2	Libra 2	Ruby Elliot (saw 2 struggling women)
♏	Scorpio	? (dead person)*
♏2	Scorpio 2	Mrs Fleury (was leading elderly mother across Clerkenwell Green on evening of Margot's disappearance)
♐	Sagittarius	Gloria Conti (receptionist)
♐2	Sagittarius 2	Jules Bayliss (husband of cleaner)
♒	Aquarius	Margot Bamborough (victim)
♑	Capricorn	The Essex Butcher/Baphomet
♓	Pisces	Steven Douthwaite (patient)
🜨	no idea	Roy Phipps (husband) **
⚸	no idea	Irene Bull/Hickson (receptionist)**

* I suggest an identity for Scorpio below, but could be someone we haven't yet heard of.

** No idea what either of these symbols mean. Can't find them on any astrological website. Talbot seems to have invented them. If he'd stuck to birth signs, Irene would have been one of the Geminis and Roy would have been Capricorn. Talbot writes that Phipps 'can't be true Capricorn' (because he's resourceful, sensitive, musical) then comes up with this new symbol for him, on the advice of Schmidt.

Schmidt

The name 'Schmidt' is all over the notebook. 'Schmidt corrects to (different star sign)', 'Schmidt changes everything', 'Schmidt disagrees'. Schmidt mostly wants to change people's star signs, which you'd think would be one certainty, given that birth dates don't change. I've checked with Gregory Talbot, and he can't remember his father ever knowing anyone of the name. My best guess is that Schmidt might have been a figment of Talbot's increasingly psychotic imagination. Perhaps he couldn't help noticing people weren't matching the star signs' supposed qualities and Schmidt was his rational side trying to reassert itself.

<u>Possible leads</u>

Joseph Brenner

In spite of Talbot's early determination to clear Brenner of suspicion on the basis of his star sign (Libra is 'the most trustworthy of the signs' according to Evangeline Adams), he later records in the notebook that an unidentified patient of the practice told Talbot that he/she saw Joseph Brenner inside a block of flats on Skinner Street on the evening Margot disappeared. This directly contradicts Brenner's own story (he went straight home), his sister's corroboration of that story, and possibly the story of the dog-walking neighbour who claims to have seen Brenner through the window at home at 11 in the evening. No time is given for Brenner's alleged sighting in Michael Cliffe House, which was a 3-minute drive from the St John's practice and consequently far nearer Margot's route than Brenner's own house, which was a 20-minute drive away. <u>None of this is in the police notes and it doesn't seem to have been followed up</u>.

Death of Scorpio

Talbot seems to suggest that somebody died, and that Margot may have found the death suspicious. Scorpio's death is connected to Pisces (Douthwaite) and Cancer (Janice), which makes the most likely candidate for Scorpio Joanna Hammond, the married woman Douthwaite had an affair with, who allegedly committed suicide.

The Hammond/Douthwaite/Janice explanation fits reasonably well: Margot could have voiced suspicions about Hammond's death to Douthwaite the last time she saw him, which gives us the reason he stormed out of her surgery. And as a friend/neighbour of Douthwaite's, Janice might have had her own suspicions about him.

The problem with this theory is that I've looked up Joanna Hammond's birth certificate online and she was born under Sagittarius. Either she isn't the dead person in question, or Talbot mistook her date of birth.

Blood at the Phipps house/Roy walking

When Lawson took over the case, Wilma the cleaner told him she'd seen Roy walking in the garden on the day Margot disappeared, when he was supposed to be bedbound. She also claimed she found blood on the spare bedroom carpet and cleaned it up.

Lawson thought this was the first time Wilma had mentioned either fact to the police and suspected she was trying to make trouble for Roy Phipps.

However, turns out Wilma did tell Talbot the story, but instead of recording it in the official police record, he put it in his astrological notebook.

Even though Wilma had already given him what you'd think is significant information, Talbot's notes indicate that he was sure she was concealing something else. He seems to have developed a fixation with Wilma having occult powers/secret knowledge. He speculates that Taurus might have 'magick' and even suggests the blood on the carpet might have been put there by Wilma herself, for some ritual purpose.

Tarot cards associated with Taurus, Wilma's sign, came up a lot when he was using them and he seems to have interpreted them to mean she knew more than she was letting on. He underlined the phrase 'black phantom' in regard to her, and associated her with 'Black Lilith', which is some astrological fixed point associated with taboos and secrets. In the absence of any other explanation, I suspect a good slug of old-fashioned racism.

Out on Charing Cross Road, a car passed, blaring from its radio 'Do They Know It's Christmas?' Frowning, Strike added another bullet point to 'possibly genuine new information', and began to type.

Nico 'Mucky' Ricci

According to Talbot, Leo 3 was seen leaving the practice one night by an unnamed passer-by, who told Talbot about it afterwards. Nico 'Mucky' Ricci was caught on camera in one of Dorothy Oakden's photos of the practice Christmas party in 1973. The picture's reproduced in her son's book. Ricci was a Leo (confirmed by d.o.b. in press report from 1968).

Ricci was a professional gangster, pornographer and pimp who in 1974 was living in Leather Lane, Clerkenwell, a short walk from the St John's practice, so should have been registered with one of the doctors there. He's now in his 90s and living in a nursing home, according to Shanker.

The fact that Ricci was at the party isn't in the official record. Talbot found the fact Ricci was at the practice significant enough to write down in the astrological notebook, but there's no sign he ever followed it up or told Lawson about it. Possible explanations: 1) as Ricci was Leo, not Capricorn, Talbot concluded he couldn't be Baphomet, 2) Talbot didn't trust the person who said he'd seen Ricci leaving the building, 3) Talbot knew, but didn't record in his book, that Ricci had an alibi for that night Margot disappeared, 4) Talbot knew Ricci had alibis for other Essex Butcher abductions.

Whichever applies, the presence of Ricci at that party needs looking into. He's a man who had the contacts to arrange a permanent disappearance. See action points below.

It cost Strike far more effort than it would usually have done to organise his thoughts on Mucky Ricci and set them down. Tired now, his throat raw and his intercostal muscles aching from coughing, he read through the rest of the document, which in his opinion contained little of real value other than the action points. After correcting a couple of typos, he attached the lot to an email and sent it to Robin.

Only after this had gone did it occur to him that some people might think emailing work colleagues on Christmas Day was unacceptable. However, he shrugged off any momentary qualms by telling himself that Robin was currently enjoying a family Christmas, and would be highly unlikely to check her email until tomorrow at the earliest.

He picked up his mobile and checked it. Charlotte hadn't texted again. Of course, she had twins, aristocratic in-laws and a husband to keep happy. He set the phone down again.

Little energy though he had, Strike found the absence of anything to do still more enervating. Without much curiosity, he examined a couple of the Christmas presents lying beside him, both of which were clearly from grateful clients, as they were addressed to both him and Robin. Shaking the larger one, he deduced that it contained chocolates.

He returned to his bedroom and watched a bit of television, but the relentless emphasis on Christmas depressed him and he switched off midway through a continuity announcer's wish that everyone was having a wonderful—

Strike returned to the kitchen and his gaze fell on the heavy projector and can of film lying just inside the door. After a moment's hesitation, he heaved the heavy machine onto his kitchen table, facing a blank stretch of kitchen wall and plugged it in. It seemed to be in working order. He then prised the lid off the tin to reveal a large roll of 16mm film, which he took out and fitted into the projector.

Doubtless because he wasn't thinking as clearly as usual, and also because of the need to stop regularly to cough up more sputum into kitchen roll, it took Strike nearly an hour to work out how to operate the old projector, by which time he realised that he had regained something of an appetite. It was now nearly two o'clock. Trying not to imagine what was going on in St Mawes, where a large turkey with all the trimmings was doubtless reaching the peak of bronzed perfection, but seeing this flicker of returned appetite as a sign of returning health, he took the pack of out-of-date chicken and the limp vegetables out of the fridge, chopped it all, boiled up some dried noodles and made a stir fry.

He could taste nothing, but this second ingestion of food made him feel slightly more human, and ripping the paper and cellophane off the box of chocolates, he ate several of them, too, before flicking the switch on the projector.

Onto the wall, pale in the sunlight, flickered the naked figure of a woman. Her head was covered in a hood. Her hands were bound behind her. A man's black-trousered leg entered the shot. He kicked her: she stumbled and fell to her knees. He continued to kick until she was prone on the ground of what looked like a warehouse.

She'd have screamed, of course, she couldn't have failed to scream, but there was no soundtrack. A thin scar ran from beneath her left breast down to her ribs, as though this wasn't the first time knives had touched her. All the men involved had covered their faces with scarves or balaclavas. She alone was naked: the men merely pulled down their jeans.

She stopped moving long before they had finished with her. At one point, close to the end, when she was barely moving, when blood still dripped from her many stab wounds, the left hand of a man who seemed to have watched, but not participated, slid in front of the camera. It bore something large and gold.

Strike flicked off the projector. He was suddenly drenched in cold sweat. His stomach was cramping. He barely made it to the bathroom before he vomited, and there he remained, heaving until he was empty, until dusk fell beyond the attic windows.

30

Ah dearest Dame, quoth then the Paynim bold,
Pardon the error of enraged wight,
Whome great griefe made forgett the raines to hold
Of reasons rule . . .

Edmund Spenser
The Faerie Queene

Annabel was wailing in Stephen's old bedroom, which was next door
to Robin's own. Her niece had cried through a substantial portion of
Christmas night and Robin had been awake along with her, listening
to Joni Mitchell on her headphones to block out the noise.

Four days stuck in her parents' house in Masham had driven Robin
back to Mitchell's sprawling, wandering tunes and the lyrics that
had made her feel strangely lost. Margot Bamborough had found
something there she had needed, and hadn't Margot Bamborough's
life been far more complicated than her own? Ailing parents to support, a new daughter to love and to miss, a workplace full of cross
currents and bullying, a husband who wouldn't talk to her, another
man lurking in the background, promising that he'd changed. What
were Robin's troubles, compared to those?

So Robin lay in the dark and listened as she hadn't on the train.
Then, she had heard an alienating sophistication in the words the
beautiful voice had sung. Robin hadn't had glamorous love affairs
she could anatomise or lament: she'd had one proper boyfriend and
one marriage, which had gone horribly wrong, and now she was
home at her parents' house, a childless twenty-nine-year-old who was

'travelling in a different direction to the rest of us': in other words, backwards.

But in the darkness, really listening, she began to hear melodies among the suspended chords, and as she stopped comparing the music to anything she would usually have listened to, she realised that the images she had found alienating in their strangeness were confessions of inadequacy and displacement, of the difficulty of merging two lives, of waiting for the soulmate who never arrived, of craving both freedom and love.

It was with a literal start that she heard the words, at the beginning of track eight, '*I'm always running behind the times, just like this train . . .*'

And when, later in the song, Mitchell asked: 'what are you going to do now? You got no one to give your love to', tears started in Robin's eyes. Not a mile from where she lay, Matthew and Sarah would be lying in bed in her ex-father-in-law's spare room, and here was Robin, alone again in a room that for her would forever have a hint of prison cell about it. This was where she had spent months after leaving university, pinioned within four walls by her own memories of a man in a gorilla mask, and the worst twenty minutes of her life.

Since arriving home, everyone in the house had been keen to accompany her into Masham, 'because you shouldn't have to hide'. The implication, no matter their kind intention, was that it would be a natural response for a woman whose ex-husband had found a new partner to hide. There was shame in being single.

But listening to *Court and Spark*, Robin thought that it was perfectly true that she was travelling in a different direction to anyone she knew. She was fighting her way back to the person she should have been before a man in a mask reached for her from the darkness beneath a stairwell. The reason nobody else understood was that they assumed that her true self was to be the wife Matthew Cunliffe had wanted: a woman who worked quietly in HR and stayed home safely after dark. They didn't realise that that woman had been the result of those twenty minutes, and that the authentic Robin might never have emerged if she hadn't been sent, by mistake, to a shabby office in Denmark Street.

With a strange sense of having spent her sleepless hours fruitfully,

Robin turned off her iPod. Four o'clock on Boxing Day morning and the house was silent at last. Robin took out her earbuds, rolled over and managed to fall asleep.

Two hours later, Annabel woke again, and this time, Robin got up and crept downstairs, bare-footed, to the big wooden table beside the Aga, carrying her notebook, her laptop and her phone.

It was pleasant to have the kitchen to herself. The garden beyond the window, covered in a hard frost, was dark blue and silver in the winter pre-dawn. Setting her laptop and phone on the table, she greeted Rowntree, who was too arthritic these days for early morning frolicking, but wagged his tail lazily from his basket beside the radiator. She made herself a cup of tea, then took a seat at the table and opened her laptop.

She hadn't yet read Strike's document summarising the horoscope notes, which had arrived while she was busy helping her mother cook Christmas lunch. Robin had been adding the Brussels sprouts to the steamer when she saw, out of the corner of her eye, the notification on her phone, which was charging on one of the few power points that wasn't taken up by some piece of baby equipment: bottle steriliser, baby alarm or breast pump. Seeing Strike's name, her heart had momentarily lifted, because she was sure that she was about to read thanks for the gift of the Tom Waits DVD, and the fact that he'd emailed on Christmas Day was an indicator of friendship such as she had perhaps never received from him.

However, when she opened the email she simply read:

FYI: summary of Talbot's horoscope notes and action points.

Robin knew her face must have fallen when she looked up and saw Linda watching her.

'Bad news?'

'No, just Strike.'

'On Christmas Day?' said Linda sharply.

And Robin had realised in that instant that Geoffrey, her ex-father-in-law, must have been spreading it around Masham that if Matthew had been unfaithful, it was only after being heinously

330

betrayed himself. She read the truth in her mother's face, and in Jenny's sudden interest in Annabel, whom she was jiggling in her arms, and in the sharp look flung at her by Jonathan, her youngest brother, who was tipping bottled cranberry sauce into a dish.

'It's work,' Robin had said coldly. Each of her silent accusers had returned hastily to their tasks.

It was, therefore, with very mixed feelings towards the author that Robin now settled down to read Strike's document. Emailing her on Christmas Day had felt reproachful, as though she'd let him down by going back to Masham instead of remaining in London and single-handedly running the agency while he, Barclay and Morris were down with flu. Moreover, if he was going to email at all on Christmas Day, some kind of personal message might be seen as common politeness. Perhaps he'd simply treated her Christmas present with the same indifference she'd treated his.

Robin had just read to the bottom of 'Possible leads' and was digesting the idea that a professional gangster had been, on at least one occasion, in close proximity to Margot Bamborough, when the kitchen door opened, admitting baby Annabel's distant wails. Linda entered the room, wearing a dressing gown and slippers.

'What are you doing down here?' she asked, sounding disapproving, as she crossed to the kettle.

Robin tried not to show how irked she felt. She'd spent the last few days smiling until her face ached, helping as much as was physically possible, admiring baby Annabel until she doubted that a pore had been left unpraised; she'd joined in charades and poured drinks and watched films and unwrapped chocolates or cracked nuts for Jenny, who was constantly pinned to the sofa by the demands of breastfeeding. She'd shown an intelligent and sympathetic interest in Jonathan's university friends' exploits; she'd listened to her father's opinions on David Cameron's agricultural policy and she'd noticed, but shown no resentment about, the fact that not a single member of her family had asked what she was doing at work. Was she not allowed to sit quietly in the kitchen for half an hour, while Annabel rendered sleep impossible?

'Reading an email,' said Robin.

'They think,' said Linda (and Robin knew 'they' must be the new parents, whose thoughts and wishes were of all-consuming importance just now) 'it was the sprouts. She's been colicky all night. Jenny's exhausted.'

'Annabel didn't have sprouts,' said Robin.

'She gets it all through the breast milk,' explained Linda, with what felt to Robin like condescension for being excluded from the mysteries of motherhood.

Bearing two cups of tea for Stephen and Jenny, Linda left the room again. Relieved, Robin opened her notebook and jotted down a couple of thoughts that had occurred to her while reading 'Possible leads,' then returned to Strike's document to read his short list of 'Probably irrelevant' items gleaned from Talbot's notebook.

Paul Satchwell

After a few months, Talbot's mental state clearly deteriorated, judging by his notes, which become progressively more detached from reality.

Towards the end of the notebook he goes back to the other two horned signs of the zodiac, Aries and Taurus, presumably because he's still fixated on the devil. As stated above, Wilma comes in for a lot of unfounded suspicion, but he also goes to the trouble of calculating Satchwell's complete birth horoscope, which means he must have got a birth time from him. Probably means nothing, but strange that he went back to Satchwell and spent this much time on his birth chart, which he didn't do for any other suspect. Talbot highlights aspects of the chart that supposedly indicate aggression, dishonesty and neuroses. Talbot also keeps noting that various parts of Satchwell's chart are 'same as AC' without explanation.

Roy Phipps and Irene Hickson

As mentioned above, the signs Talbot uses for Roy Phipps and Irene Hickson (who was then Irene Bull) haven't ever been used in astrology and seem to be inventions of Talbot's.

Roy's symbol looks like a headless stickman. Exactly what it's

supposed to represent I can't find out – presumably a constellation?
Quotations about snakes recur around Roy's name.

Irene's invented sign looks like a big fish and—

The kitchen door opened again. Robin looked around. It was Linda again.

'You still here?' she said, still with a slight sense of disapproval.

'No,' said Robin, 'I'm upstairs.'

Linda's smile was reluctant. As she took more mugs from the cupboard, she asked,

'D'you want another tea?'

'No thanks,' said Robin, closing her laptop. She'd decided to finish reading Strike's document in her room. Maybe she was imagining it, but Linda seemed to be making more noise than usual.

'He's got you working over Christmas as well, then?' said Linda.

For the past four days, Robin had suspected that her mother wanted to talk to her about Strike. The looks she'd seen on her surprised family's faces yesterday had told her why. However, she felt under no obligation to make it easy for Linda to interrogate her.

'As well as what?' asked Robin.

'You know what I mean,' said Linda. 'Christmas. I'd have thought you were owed time off.'

'I get time off,' said Robin.

She took her empty mug over to the sink. Rowntree now struggled to his feet and Robin let him out of the back door, feeling the icy air on every bit of exposed skin. Over the garden hedge she could see the sun turning the horizon green as it made its way steadily up through the icy heavens.

'Is he seeing anyone?' Linda asked. 'Strike?'

'He sees lots of people,' said Robin, wilfully obtuse. 'It's part of the job.'

'You know what I mean,' said Linda.

'Why the interest?'

She expected her mother to back off, but was surprised.

'I think you know why,' she said, turning to face her daughter.

Robin was furious to find herself blushing. She was a twenty-nine-year-old woman. At that very moment, her mobile emitted a beep on the kitchen table. She was convinced that it would be Strike texting her, and so, apparently, was Linda, who, being nearer, picked up the phone to hand it to Robin, glancing at the sender's name as she did so.

It wasn't Strike. It was Saul Morris. He'd written:

Hope you're not having as shit a Christmas as I am.

Robin wouldn't normally have answered. Resentment at her family, and something else, something she didn't particularly want to admit to, made her text back, while Linda watched:

Depends how shit yours is. Mine's fairly shit.

She sent the message, then looked up at Linda.

'Who's Saul Morris?' her mother asked.

'Subcontractor at the agency. Ex-police,' said Robin.

'Oh,' said Linda.

Robin could tell that had given Linda fresh food for thought. If she was honest with herself, she'd meant to do exactly that. Picking her laptop off the table, she left the kitchen.

The bathroom was, of course, occupied. Robin returned to her room. By the time she lay back down on her bed, laptop open again, Morris had texted her again.

Tell me your troubles and I'll tell you mine. Problem shared and all that.

Slightly regretting that she'd answered him, Robin turned the mobile face down on her bed and continued reading Strike's document.

Irene's invented sign looks like a big fish and Talbot's blunt about what he thinks it represents: 'the monster Cetus, Leviathan, the biblical whale, superficial charm, evil in depths. Headstrong, enjoys spotlight, a performer, a liar.' Talbot seems to have suspected Irene was a liar even before she was proven to have lied about her trip to the dentist, which Talbot never found out about, although there's no indication as to what he thinks she was lying about.

Margot as Babalon
This is only of relevance in as much as it shows just how ill Talbot was.

On the night he was finally sectioned, he attempted some kind of magic ritual. Judging by his notes, he was trying to conjure Baphomet, presumably because he thought Baphomet would take the form of Margot's killer.

According to Talbot, what manifested in the room wasn't Baphomet, but the spirit of Margot 'who blames me, who attacks me'. Talbot believed she'd become Babalon in death, Babalon being Baphomet's second–in–command/consort. The demon he 'saw' was carrying a cup of blood and a sword. There are repeated mentions of lions scribbled round the picture of the demon. Babalon rides a seven-headed lion on the card representing Lust in the Thoth tarot.

At some point after Talbot drew the demon, he went back and drew Latin crosses over some of the notes and on the demon itself, and wrote a biblical quotation warning against witchcraft across the picture. The appearance of the demon seems to have pushed him back towards religion, and that's where his notes end.

Robin heard the bathroom door open and close. Now desperate for a pee, she jumped up and headed out of her room.

Stephen was crossing the landing, holding his washbag, puffy-eyed and yawning.

'Sorry about last night, Rob,' he said. 'Jenny thinks it was the sprouts.'

'Yeah, Mum said,' Robin replied, edging around him. 'No problem. Hope she feels better.'

'We're going to take her out for a walk. I'll see if I can buy you some ear plugs.'

335

Once she'd showered, Robin returned to her room. Her phone beeped twice while she was dressing.

Brushing her hair in the mirror, her eyes fell on the new perfume she'd received as a Christmas present from her mother. Robin had told her she was looking for a new fragrance, because the old one reminded her too much of Matthew. She'd been touched that Linda remembered the conversation when she opened the gift.

The bottle was round; not an orb, but a flattish circle: Chanel Chance Eau Fraîche. The liquid was pale green. An unfortunate association of ideas now made Robin think of sprouts. Nevertheless, she sprayed some on her wrists and behind her ears, filling the air with the scent of sharp lemon and nondescript flowers. What, she wondered, had made her mother choose it? What was it about the perfume that made her think 'Robin'? To Robin's nostrils it smelled like a deodorant, generic, clean and totally without romance. She remembered her unsuccessful purchase of Fracas, and the desire to be sexy and sophisticated that had ended only in headaches. Musing about the disparity between the way people would like to be seen, and the way others prefer to see them, Robin sat back down on her bed beside her laptop and flipped over her phone.

Morris had texted twice more.

Lonely and hungover this end. Not being with the kids at Christmas is shit.

When Robin hadn't answered this, he'd texted again.

Sorry, being a maudlin dickhead. Feel free to ignore.

Calling himself a dickhead was the most likeable thing she'd ever known Morris do. Feeling sorry for him, Robin replied,

It must be tough, I'm sorry.

She then returned to her laptop and the last bit of Strike's document, detailing actions to be taken, and with initials beside each to show which of them should undertake it.

<u>Action points</u>

Talk to Gregory Talbot again – CS
I want to know why, even after he got well, Bill Talbot never told colleagues about the leads in this notebook he'd withheld from colleagues during the investigation, ie, sighting of Brenner in Skinner Street the night Margot disappeared/blood on the Phippses' carpet/a death Margot might have been worried about/ Mucky Ricci leaving the practice one night.

Speak to Dinesh Gupta again – CS
He might know who Brenner was visiting in Skinner Street that night. Could have been a patient. He might also be able to shed light on Mucky Ricci appearing at the party. Will also ask him about 'Scorpio' in case this refers to a patient whose death seemed suspicious to Margot.

Interview Roy Phipps – CS/RE
We've tiptoed around Phipps too long. Time to ring Anna and see whether she can persuade him to give us an interview.

Try and secure interview with one of Wilma Bayliss's children – CS/RE
Especially important if we can't get to Roy. Want to re-examine Wilma's story (Roy walking, blood on the carpet).

Find C. B. Oakden – CS/RE
Judging from his book, he's full of shit, but there's an outside possibility he knows things about Brenner we don't, given that his mother was the closest person to Brenner at the practice.

Find & interview Paul Satchwell – CS/RE

Find & interview Steven Douthwaite – CS/RE

Robin couldn't help but feel subtly criticised. Strike had now added his initials to action points that had previously been Robin's alone, such as finding Satchwell, and persuading Wilma Bayliss's children to give them interviews. She set the laptop down again, picked up her phone and headed back to the kitchen for breakfast.

An abrupt silence fell when she walked into the room. Linda, Stephen and Jenny all wore self-conscious looks of those who fear they might have been overheard. Robin put bread in the toaster, trying to tamp down her rising resentment. She seemed to sense mouthed speech and gesticulations behind her back.

'Robin, we just ran into Matthew,' said Stephen suddenly. 'When we were walking Annabel round the block.'

'Oh,' said Robin, turning to face them, trying to look mildly interested.

It was the first time Matthew had been spotted. Robin had avoided midnight mass out of conviction that he and Sarah would be there, but her mother had reported that none of the Cunliffes had attended. Now Linda, Stephen and Jenny were all looking at her, worried, pitying, waiting for her reaction and her questions.

Her phone beeped.

'Sorry,' she said, picking it up, delighted to have a reason to look away from them all.

Morris had texted:

Why's your Christmas so shit?

While the other three watched, she typed back:

My ex-father-in-law lives locally and my ex has brought his new girlfriend home. We're currently the local scandal.

She didn't like Morris, but at this moment he felt like a welcome ally, a lifeline from the life she had forged, with difficulty, away from Matthew and Masham. Robin was on the point of setting down the phone when it beeped again and, still with the other three watching her, she read:

That stinks.

It does, she texted back.

Then she looked up at her mother, Stephen and Jenny, forcing herself to smile.

'D'you want to tell me about it?' Robin asked Stephen. 'Or do I have to ask?'

'No,' he said hurriedly, 'it wasn't much — we were just pushing Annabel up to the Square and back, and we saw them coming towards us. Him and that—'

'Sarah,' supplied Robin. She could just imagine them hand in hand, enjoying the wintry morning, the picturesque town, sleepy in the frost and early sunshine.

'Yeah,' said Stephen. 'He looked like he wanted to double back when he saw us, but he didn't. Said, "Congratulations in order, I see."'

Robin could hear Matthew saying it.

'And that was it, really,' said Stephen.

'I'd've liked to have kicked him in the balls,' said Jenny suddenly. 'Smug bastard.'

But Linda's eyes were on Robin's phone.

'Who are you texting back and forth on Boxing Day?' she asked.

'I've just told you,' said Robin. 'Morris. He works for the agency.'

She knew exactly what impression she was giving Linda, but she had her pride. Perhaps there was no shame in being single, but the pity of her family, the thought of Matthew and Sarah walking through Masham, everyone's suspicion of her and Strike, and the fact that there was nothing whatsoever to tell about her and Strike, except that he thought he'd better start taking over some of her leads because she'd got no results: all made her want to clutch some kind of fig leaf to her threadbare dignity. Smarmy and overfamiliar as he might be, Morris was today, perhaps, more to be pitied than censured, and was offering himself up to save Robin's face.

She saw her mother and brother exchange looks and had the empty satisfaction of knowing that they were already haring after her false scent. Miserable, she opened the fridge and took out half a bottle of carefully re-corked champagne left over from Christmas Day.

'What are you doing?' asked Linda.

'Making myself a mimosa,' said Robin. 'Still Christmas, isn't it?'

One more night and she'd be back on the train to London. Almost as though she had heard Robin's antisocial thought, a cry of anguish issued through the baby monitor just behind her, making Robin jump, and what she was starting to think of as the baby circus relocated from the kitchen to the sitting room, Linda bringing a glass of water for Jenny to drink while breastfeeding and turning on the TV for her, while Stephen ran upstairs to fetch Annabel.

Drink, Robin decided, was the answer. If you splashed in enough orange juice, nobody had to know you were finishing off a bottle of champagne single-handedly, and those feelings of misery, anger and inadequacy that were writhing in the pit of your stomach could be satisfactorily numbed. Mimosas carried her through to lunchtime, when everyone had a glass of red, although Jenny drank 'just a mouthful' because of Annabel, and ignored Robin's suggestion that alcoholic breast milk might help her sleep. Morris was still texting, mostly stupid Christmas knock-knock jokes and updates on his day, and Robin was replying in the same mindless manner that she sometimes continued eating crisps, with a trace of self-loathing.

My mother's just arrived. Send sherry and excuses not to talk to her WI group about policework.

What's your mother's name? Robin texted back. She was definitely a little bit drunk.

Fanny, said Morris.

Robin was unsure whether to laugh or not, or, indeed, whether it was funny.

'Robs, d'you want to play Pictionary?' asked Jonathan.

'What?' she said.

She was sitting on an uncomfortable hard-backed chair in the corner of the sitting room. The baby circus occupied at least half the room. *The Wizard of Oz* was on the television but nobody was really watching.

'Pictionary,' repeated Jonathan, holding up the box. 'Oh, yeah, and Robs, could I come and stay with you for a weekend in February?'

I'm only kidding, texted Morris. **Frances.**

'What?' Robin said again, under the impression somebody had asked her something.

'Morris is obviously a very interesting man,' said Linda archly, and everyone looked around at Robin, who merely said,

'Pictionary, yes, fine.'

Got to play Pictionary, she texted Morris.

Draw a dick, came back the instant answer.

Robin set down her phone again. The drink was wearing off now, leaving in its wake a headache that throbbed behind her right temple. Luckily, Martin arrived at that moment with a tray full of coffees and a bottle of Baileys.

Jonathan won Pictionary. Baby Annabel screamed some more. A cold supper was laid out on the kitchen table, to which neighbours had been invited to admire Annabel. By eight o'clock in the evening, Robin had taken paracetamol and started to drink black coffee to clear her head. She needed to pack. She also needed, somehow, to shut down her day-long conversation with Morris, who, she could tell, was now very drunk indeed.

Mohter gone home, complaining not seeing grandchioldren enough. What shall we talk about now? What are you wearing?

She ignored the text. Up in her bedroom, she packed her case, because she was catching an early train. *Please, God, let Matthew and Sarah not be on it.* She resprayed herself with her mother's Christmas gift. Smelling it again, she decided that the only message it conveyed to bystanders was 'I have washed'. Perhaps her mother had bought her this boring floral antiseptic out of a subconscious desire to wipe her daughter clean of the suggestion of adultery. There was certainly nothing of the seductress about it, and it would forever remind her of this lousy Christmas. Nevertheless, Robin packed it carefully among her socks, having no wish to hurt her mother's feelings by leaving it behind.

By the time she returned downstairs, Morris had texted another five times.

> I was joking.
> Tell me u know I was joking.
> Fukc have I offended u
> Have I?
> Answer me either way fuck's sake

Slightly riled, and embarrassed now by her stupid, adolescent pretence to her family that she, like Matthew, had found another partner, she paused in the hall to text back,

> I'm not offended. Got to go. Need an early night.

She entered the sitting room, where her family were all sitting, sleepy and overfed, watching the news. Robin moved a muslin cloth, half a pack of nappies and one of the Pictionary boards from the sofa, so she could sit down.

'Sorry, Robin,' said Jenny, yawning as she reached out for the baby things and put them by her feet.

Robin's phone beeped yet again. Linda looked over at her. Robin ignored both her mother and the phone, because she was looking down at the Pictionary board where Martin had tried to draw 'Icarus'. Nobody had guessed it. They'd thought Icarus was a bug hovering over a flower.

But something about the picture held Robin fixated. Again, her phone beeped. She looked at it.

> Are you in bed?

Yes and so should you be, she texted back, her mind still on the Pictionary board. The flower that looked like a sun. The sun that looked like a flower.

Her phone beeped yet again. Exasperated, she looked at it.

Morris had sent her a picture of his erect dick. For a moment, and even while she felt appalled and repulsed, Robin continued to stare at it. Then, with a suddenness that made her father start awake in his chair, she got up and almost ran out of the room.

The kitchen wasn't far enough. Nowhere would be far enough. Shaking with rage and shock, she wrenched open the back door and strode out into the icy garden, with the water in the birdbath she'd unfrozen with boiling water already milky hard in the moonlight. Without stopping to pause for thought, she called Morris's number.

'Hey—'

'How fucking dare you — *how fucking dare you send me that?*'

'Fuck,' he said thickly, 'I di'n — I thought — "wish you were here" or—'

'I said I was going to bloody bed!' Robin shouted. 'I did not ask to see your fucking dick!'

She could see the neighbours' heads bobbing behind their kitchen blinds. The Ellacotts were providing rich entertainment this Christmas, all right: first a new baby, then a shouting match about a penis.

'Oh shit,' gasped Morris. 'Oh fuck ... no ... listen, I di'n mean—'

'Who the fuck does that?' shouted Robin. 'What's wrong with you?'

'No ... shit ... fuck ... I'm s'rry ... I thought ... I'm so f'king sorry ... Robin, don't ... oh Jesus ... '

'*I don't want to see your dick!*'

A storm of dry sobs answered her, then Robin thought she heard him lay down the phone on some hard surface. At a distance from the mouthpiece he emitted moans of anguish interspersed with weeping. Heavy objects seemed to be falling over. Then there was a clatter and he picked up his mobile again.

'Robin, I'm so fuckin' sorry ... what've I done, what've I ... ? I thought ... I should fucking kill myself ... don't ... don't tell Strike, Robin ... I'm fuckin' begging you ... if I lose this job ... don't tell, Robin ... I lose this, I lose fuckin' everything ... I can't lose my little girls, Robin ... '

He reminded her of Matthew, the day that she'd found out he was cheating. She could see her ex-husband as clearly as though he was there on the ice-crusted lawn, face in his hands as he gasped his apologies, then looking up at her in panic. '*Have you spoken to Tom? Does he know?*'

What was it about her that made men demand that she keep their dirty secrets?

'I won't tell Strike,' she said, shaking more with rage than with cold, 'because his aunt's dying and we need an extra man. But you'd better never send me anything other than an update on a case again.'

'Oh God, Robin . . . thank you . . . thank you . . . you are such a decent person . . .'

He'd stopped sobbing. His gushing offended her almost as much as the picture of his dick.

'I'm going.'

She stood in the dark, barely feeling the cold, her mobile hanging at her side. As the light in the neighbour's kitchen went off, her parents' back door opened. Rowntree came lolloping over the frozen lawn, delighted to find her outside.

'You all right, love?' Michael Ellacott asked his daughter.

'Fine,' said Robin, crouching to fuss Rowntree to hide her sudden rush of tears. 'It's all fine.'

PART FOUR

Great enemy . . . is wicked Time . . .

Edmund Spenser
The Faerie Queene

31

Deare knight, as deare, as euer knight was deare,
That all these sorrowes suffer for my sake,
High heuen behold the tedious toyle, ye for me take . . .

Edmund Spenser
The Faerie Queene

Strike's gastric upset added days to his illness, and he spent New Year's Eve in bed, reliant on takeaway pizzas but hardly able to touch them when they arrived. For the first time in his life he didn't fancy chocolate, because the truffles he'd consumed after his out-of-date chicken had been the first things to reappear during his prolonged vomiting. The only enjoyable thing he did was to watch the DVD of Tom Waits's *No Visitors After Midnight*, the taped concerts Robin had bought him for Christmas, which he finally unwrapped on New Year's Day. His text thanking her elicited a short 'you're welcome'.

By the time he felt fit enough to travel down to Cornwall, clutching his belated Christmas gifts, Strike had lost over a stone, and this was the first thing an anxious Joan commented on when he finally appeared at her house in St Mawes, full of apologies for his absence at Christmas.

If he'd waited one more day to come down to Joan and Ted's, he'd have been unable to reach them, because no sooner had he arrived than a vicious weather front crashed over the south of Britain. Storms lashed the Cornish coast, train services were suspended, tons of sand washed off the beaches and flooding turned the roads of coastal towns into freezing canals. The Cornish peninsula was temporarily cut off

347

from the rest of England, and while St Mawes had not fared as badly as Mevagissey and Fowey along the coast, sandbags had appeared at the entrances of buildings on the seafront. Waves smashed against the harbour wall, khaki and gunmetal grey. The tourists had melted out of sight like the seals: locals in sodden oilskins greeted each other with nods as they made their way in and out of local shops. All the gaudy prettiness of summertime St Mawes was wiped away and, like an actress when the stage-paint is removed, the town's true self was revealed, a place of hard stone and stiff backbone.

Though pelted with rain and pummelled by gales, Ted and Joan's house was, mercifully, set on high ground. Trapped there, Strike remembered Lucy telling him he was better suited to a crisis than to keeping a commitment going, and knew that there was truth in the accusation. He was well suited to emergencies, to holding his nerve, to quick thinking and fast reactions, but found the qualities demanded by Joan's slow decline harder to summon.

Strike missed the absence of an overriding objective, in pursuit of which he could shelve his sadness; missed the imperative to dismiss pain and distress in the service of something greater, which had sustained him in the military. None of his old coping strategies were admissible in Joan's kitchen, beside the flowered casserole dishes and her old oven gloves. Dark humour and stoicism would be considered unfeeling by the kindly neighbours who wanted him to share and show his pain. Craving diversionary action, Strike was instead expected to provide small talk and homely acts of consideration.

Joan was quietly delighted: hours and days alone with her nephew were compensation for the Christmas he'd missed. Resigned, Strike gave her what she wanted: as much companionship as possible, sitting with her and talking to her all day long. Chemotherapy had been discontinued, because Joan wasn't strong enough for it: she wore a headscarf over the wispy hair she had left, and her husband and nephew watched anxiously as she picked at food, and held themselves constantly ready to assist her when she moved between rooms. Either of them could have carried her with ease, now.

As the days went by, Strike noticed another change in his aunt that surprised him. Just as her storm-ravaged birthplace had revealed a different aspect in adversity, so an unfamiliar Joan was emerging, a Joan who asked open-ended questions that were not designed to elicit confirmation of her own biases, or thinly veiled requests for comforting lies.

'Why haven't you ever married, Cormoran?' she asked her nephew at midday on Saturday morning, when they sat together in the sitting room, Joan in the comfiest armchair, Strike on the sofa. The lamp beside her, which they'd turned on because of the overcast, rainy day, made her skin look as finely translucent as tissue paper.

Strike was so conditioned to tell Joan what she wanted to hear that he was at a loss for an answer. The honest response he'd given Dave Polworth seemed impossible here. She'd probably take it as her fault if he told her that he wasn't the marrying kind; she must have done something wrong, failed to teach him that love was essential to happiness.

'Dunno,' he said, falling back on cliché. 'Maybe I haven't met the right woman.'

'If you're waiting for perfection,' said the new Joan, 'it doesn't exist.'

'You don't wish I'd married Charlotte, do you?' he asked her. He knew perfectly well that both Joan and Lucy considered Charlotte little short of a she-devil.

'I most certainly don't,' said Joan, with a spark of her old fight, and they smiled at each other.

Ted popped his head around the door.

'That's Kerenza here, love,' he said. 'Her car's just pulled up.'

The Macmillan nurse, whom Strike had met on his first day there, was a blessing such as he could never have imagined. A slender, freckled woman his age, she brought into the house no aura of death, but of life continuing, simply with more comfort and support. Strike's own prolonged exposure to the medical profession had inured him to a certain brand of hearty, impersonal cheerfulness, but Kerenza seemed to see Ted and Joan as individuals, not as simple-minded children, and he heard her talking to Ted, the ex-lifeguard, about people trying to take selfies with their backs to the storm waves while she took off her raincoat in the kitchen.

'Exactly. Don't understand the sea, do they? Respect it, or stay well

away, my dad would've said . . . Morning, Joan,' she said, coming into
the room. 'Hello, Cormoran.'

'Morning, Kerenza,' said Strike, getting to his feet. 'I'll get out
of the way.'

'And how're you feeling today, my love?' the nurse asked Joan.

'Not too bad,' said Joan. 'I'm just a bit . . . '

She paused, to let her nephew pass out of earshot. As Strike closed
the door on the two women, he heard more crunching footsteps on
the gravel path outside. Ted, who was reading the local paper at the
table, looked up.

'Who's that, now?'

A moment later, Dave Polworth appeared at the glass panel in
the back door, a large rucksack on his back. He entered, rainswept
and grinning.

'Morning, Diddy,' he said, and they exchanged the handshake
and hug that had become the standard greeting in their later years.
'Morning, Ted.'

'What're you doing here?' asked Ted.

Polworth swung his rucksack off, undid it and lifted out a couple
of polythene-wrapped, frozen dishes onto the table.

'Penny baked a couple of casseroles. I'm gonna get some provisions
in, wanted to know what you needed.'

The flame of pure, practical kindness that burned in Dave Polworth
had never been more clearly visible to Strike, except perhaps on his
very first day at primary school, when the diminutive Polworth had
taken Strike under his protection.

'You're a good lad,' said Ted, moved. 'Say thanks very much to
Penny, won't you?'

'Yeah, she sent her love and all that,' said Polworth dismissively.

'Wanna keep me company while I have a smoke?' Strike asked him.

'Go on, then,' said Polworth.

'Use the shed,' suggested Ted.

So Strike and Polworth headed together across the waterlogged
garden, heads bowed against the strong wind and rain, and entered
Ted's shed. Strike lit up with relief.

'You been on a diet?' asked Polworth, looking Strike up and down.

'Flu and food poisoning.'

'Oh, yeah, Lucy said you'd been ill.' Polworth jerked his head in the direction of Joan's window. 'How is she?'

'Not great,' said Strike.

'How long you down for?'

'Depends on the weather. Listen, seriously, I really appreciate everything you've been—'

'Shut up, you ponce.'

'Can I ask another favour?'

'Go on.'

'Persuade Ted to get a pint with you this lunchtime. He needs to get out of this house for a bit. He'll do it if he knows I'm with her, but otherwise he won't leave.'

'Consider it done,' said Polworth.

'You're—'

'—a prince among men, yeah, I know I am. Arsenal through to the knockout stages, then?'

'Yeah,' said Strike. 'Bayern Munich next, though.'

He'd missed watching his team qualify before Christmas, because he'd been tailing Shifty through the West End. The Champions League, which should have been a pleasure and a distraction, was failing to grip him as it usually did.

'Robin running things in London while you're down here?'

'Yeah,' said Strike.

She'd texted him earlier, asking for a brief chat about the Bamborough case. He'd replied that he'd call her when he had a moment. He, too, had news on the case, but Margot Bamborough had been missing for nearly forty years and, like Kerenza the nurse, Strike was currently prioritising the living.

When he'd finished his cigarette, they returned to the house to find Ted and Kerenza in conversation in the kitchen.

'She'd rather talk to you than to me today,' said Kerenza, smiling at Strike as she shrugged on her raincoat. 'I'll be back tomorrow morning, Ted.'

As she moved towards the back door, Polworth said,

'Ted, come and have a pint.'

'Oh, no, thanks, lad,' said Ted. 'I'll bide here just now.'

Kerenza stopped with her hand on the door knob.

'That's a very good idea. Get a bit of fresh air, Ted – fresh water, today, I should say,' she added, as the rain clattered on the roof. 'Bye-bye, now.'

She left. Ted required a little more persuasion, but finally agreed that he'd join Polworth for a sandwich at the Victory. Once they'd gone, Strike took the local paper off the table and carried it back into the sitting room.

He and Joan discussed the flooding, but the pictures of waves battering Mevagissey meant far less to her than they would have a couple of months ago. Strike could tell that Joan's mind was on the personal, not the general.

'What does my horoscope say?' she asked, as he turned the page of the paper.

'I didn't know you believed in that stuff, Joan.'

'Don't know whether I do or not,' said Joan. 'I always look, though.'

'You're ...' he said, trying to remember her birthday. He knew it was in the summer.

'Cancer,' she said, and then she gave a little laugh. 'In more ways than one.'

Strike didn't smile.

'"Good time for shaking up your routine,"' he informed her, scanning her horoscope so he could censor out anything depressing, '"so don't dismiss new ideas out of hand. Jupiter retrograde encourages spiritual growth."'

'Huh,' said Joan. After a short pause, she said, 'I don't think I'll be here for my next birthday, Corm.'

The words hit him like a punch in the diaphragm.

'Don't say that.'

'If I can't say it to you, who can I say it to?'

Her eyes, which had always been a pale forget-me-not blue, were faded now. She'd never spoken to him like this before, as an equal. Always, she'd sought to stand slightly above him, so that from her perspective the six-foot-three soldier might still be her little boy.

'I can't say it to Ted or Lucy, can I?' she said. 'You know what they're like.'

'Yeah,' he said, with difficulty.

'Afterwards ... you'll look after Ted, won't you? Make sure you see him. He does love you so much.'

Fuck.

For so long, she'd demanded a kind of falseness from all around her, a rose-tinted view of everything, and now at last she offered simple honesty and plain-speaking and he wished more than anything that he could be simply nodding along to news of some neighbourhood scandal. Why hadn't he visited them more often?

'I will, of course,' he said.

'I want the funeral at St Mawes church,' she said quietly, 'where I was christened. But I don't want to be buried, because it'd have to be in the cemetery all the way up in Truro. Ted'll wear himself out, travelling up and down, taking me flowers. I know him.

'We always said we wanted to be together, afterwards, but we never made a plan and he won't talk to me about it now. So, I've thought about it, Corm, and I want to be cremated. You'll make sure this happens, won't you? Because Ted starts crying every time I try and talk about it and Lucy just won't listen.'

Strike nodded and tried to smile.

'I don't want the family at the cremation. I hate cremations, the curtains and the conveyor belt. You say goodbye to me at the church, then take Ted to the pub and let the undertakers deal with the crematorium bit, all right? Then, after, you can pick up my ashes, take me out on Ted's boat and scatter me in the sea. And when his turn comes, you can do the same for Ted, and we'll be together. You and Lucy won't want to be worrying about looking after graves all the way from London. All right?'

The plan had so much of the Joan he knew in it: it was full of practical kindness and forethought, but he hadn't expected the final touch of the ashes floating away on the tide, no tombstone, no neat dates, instead a melding with the element that had dominated her and Ted's lives, perched on their seaside town, in thrall to the ocean, except during that strange interlude where Ted, in revolt against his own father, had disappeared for several years into the military police.

'All right,' he said, with difficulty.

She sank back a little in her chair with an air of relief at having got this off her chest, and smiled at him.

'It's so lovely, having you here.'

Over the past few days he'd become used to her short reveries and her non-sequiturs, so it was less of a surprise than it might have been to hear her say, a minute later,

'I wish I'd met your Robin.'

Strike, whose mind's eye was still following Joan's ashes into the sunset, pulled himself together.

'I think you'd like her,' he said. 'I'm sure she'd like you.'

'Lucy says she's pretty.'

'Yeah, she is.'

'Poor girl,' murmured Joan. He wondered why. Of course, the knife attack had been reported in the press, when Robin had given evidence against the Shacklewell Ripper.

'Funny, you talking about horoscopes,' Strike said, trying to ease Joan off Robin, and funerals, and death. 'We're investigating an old disappearance just now. The bloke who was in charge of the case . . .'

He'd never before shared details of an investigation with Joan, and he wondered why not, now he saw her rapt attention.

'But I remember that doctor!' she said, more animated than he had seen her in days. 'Margot Bamborough, yes! She had a baby at home . . .'

'Well, that baby's our client,' said Strike. 'Her name's Anna. She and her partner have got a holiday home in Falmouth.'

'That poor family,' said Joan. 'Never knowing . . . and so the officer thought the answer was in the stars?'

'Yep,' said Strike. 'Convinced the killer was a Capricorn.'

'Ted's a Capricorn.'

'Thanks for the tip-off,' said Strike seriously, and she gave a little laugh. 'D'you want more tea?'

While the kettle boiled, Strike checked his texts. Barclay had sent an update on Two-Times' girlfriend, but the most recent message was from an unknown number, and he opened it first.

Hi Cormoran, it's your half-sister, Prudence Donleavy, here. Al gave me your number. I do hope you'll take this in the spirit it's meant. Let me firstly say that I absolutely understand and sympathise with your reasons for not wanting to join us for the Deadbeats anniversary/album party. You may or may not know that my own journey to a relationship with Dad has been in many ways a difficult one, but ultimately I feel that connecting with him – and, yes, forgiving him – has been an enriching experience. We all hope very much that you'll reconsider —

'What's the matter?' said Joan.

She'd followed him into the kitchen, shuffling, slightly stooped.

'What are you doing? I can fetch anything you want—'

'I was going to show you where I hide the chocolate biscuits. If Ted knows, he scoffs the lot, and the doctor's worried about his blood pressure. What were you reading? I know that look. You were angry.'

He didn't know whether her new appreciation for honesty would stretch as far as his father, but somehow, with the wind and rain whipping around them, an air of the confessional had descended upon the house. He told her about the text.

'Oh,' said Joan. She pointed at a Tupperware box on a top shelf. 'The biscuits are in there.'

They returned to the sitting room with the biscuits, which she'd insisted he put on a plate. Some things never changed.

'You've never met Prudence, have you?' asked Joan, when she was resettled in her chair.

'Haven't met Prudence, or the eldest, Maimie, or the youngest, Ed,' said Strike, trying to sound matter of fact.

Joan said nothing for a minute or so, then a great sigh inflated, then collapsed, her thin chest, and she said,

'I think you should go to your father's party, Corm.'

'Why?' said Strike. The monosyllable rang in his ears with an adolescent, self-righteous fury. To his slight surprise, she smiled at him.

'I know what went on,' she said. 'He behaved very badly, but he's still your father.'

'No, he isn't,' said Strike. 'Ted's my dad.'

He'd never said it out loud before. Tears filled Joan's eyes.

'He'd love to hear you say that,' she said softly. 'Funny, isn't it . . . years ago, years and years, I was just a girl, and I went to see a proper gypsy fortune teller. They used to camp up the road. I thought she'd tell me lots of nice things. You expect them to, don't you? You've paid your money. D'you know what she said?'

Strike shook his head.

'"You'll never have children." Just like that. Straight out.'

'Well, she got that wrong, didn't she?' said Strike.

Tears started again in Joan's bleached eyes. Why had he never said these things before, Strike asked himself. It would have been so easy to give her pleasure, and instead he'd held tightly to his divided loyalties, angry that he had to choose, to label, and in doing so, to betray. He reached for her hand and she squeezed it surprisingly tightly.

'You should go to that party, Corm. I think your father's at the heart of . . . of a lot of things. I wish,' she added, after a short pause, 'you had someone to look after you.'

'Doesn't work that way these days, Joan. Men are supposed to be able to look after themselves – in more ways than one,' he added, smiling.

'Pretending you don't need things . . . it's just silly,' she said quietly. 'What does *your* horoscope say?'

He picked up the paper again and cleared his throat.

'"Sagittarius: with your ruler retrograde, you may find you aren't your usual happy-go-lucky self . . ."'

32

It was three o'clock in the afternoon and Robin, who was sitting in her Land Rover close to the nondescript house in Stoke Newington that Strike had watched before Christmas, had seen nothing of inter-est since arriving in the street at nine o'clock that morning. As rain drizzled down her windscreen she half-wished she smoked, just for something to do.

She'd identified the blonde owner-occupier of the house online. Her name was Elinor Dean, and she was a divorcee who lived alone. Elinor was definitely home, because Robin had seen her pass in front of a window two hours previously, but the squally weather seemed to be keeping her inside. Nobody had visited the house all day, least of all Shifty's Boss. Perhaps they were relatives, after all, and his pre-Christmas visit was simply one of those things you did in the festive season: pay social debts, give presents, check in. The patting on the head might have been a private joke. It certainly didn't seem to suggest anything sexual, criminal or deviant, which was what they were looking for.

Robin's mobile rang.

'Hi.'

'Can you talk?' asked Strike.

He was walking down the steeply sloping street where Ted

and Joan's house lay, leaning on the collapsible walking stick he'd brought with him, knowing that the roads would be wet and possibly slippery. Ted was back in the house; they'd just helped Joan upstairs for a nap, and Strike, who wanted to smoke and didn't much fancy the shed again, had decided to go for a short walk in the relentless rain.

'Yes,' said Robin. 'How's Joan?'

'Same,' said Strike. He didn't feel like talking about it. 'You said you wanted a Bamborough chat.'

'Yeah,' said Robin. 'I've got good news, no news and bad news.'

'Bad first,' said Strike.

The sea was still turbulent, spray exploding into the air above the wall of the dock. Turning right, he headed into the town.

'The Ministry of Justice isn't going to let you interview Creed. The letter arrived this morning.'

'Ah,' said Strike. The teeming rain ripped through the blueish haze of his cigarette smoke, destroying it. 'Well, can't say I'm surprised. What's it say?'

'I've left it back at the office,' said Robin, 'but the gist is that his psychiatrists agree non-cooperation isn't going to change at this stage.'

'Right,' said Strike. 'Well, it was always a long shot.'

But Robin could hear his disappointment, and empathised. They were five months into the case, they had no new leads worth the name, and now that the possibility of interviewing Creed had vanished, she somehow felt that she and Strike were pointlessly searching rockpools, while yards away the great white slid away, untouchable, into dark water.

'And I went back to Amanda White, who's now Amanda Laws, who thought she saw Margot at the printers' window. She wanted money to talk, remember? I offered her expenses if she wants to come to the office – she's in London, it wouldn't be much – and she's thinking it over.'

'Big of her,' grunted Strike. 'What's the good news?' he asked.

'Anna's persuaded her stepmother to speak to us. Cynthia.'

'Really?'

'Yes, but alone. Roy still doesn't know anything about us,' said Robin. 'Cynthia's meeting us behind his back.'

'Well, Cynthia's something,' said Strike. 'A lot, actually,' he added, after a moment's reflection.

His feet were taking him automatically towards the pub, his wet trouser leg chilly on his remaining ankle.

'Where are we going to meet her?'

'It can't be at their house, because Roy doesn't know. She's suggesting Hampton Court, because she works part time as a guide there.'

'A guide, eh? Reminds me: any news of Postcard?'

'Barclay's at the gallery today,' said Robin. 'He's going to try and get pictures of her.'

'And what're Morris and Hutchins up to?' Strike asked, now walking carefully up the wide, slippery steps that led to the pub.

'Morris is on Two-Times' girl, who hasn't put a foot wrong – Two-Times really is out of luck this time – and Hutchins is on Twinkletoes. Speaking of which, you're scheduled to submit a final report on Twinkletoes next Friday. I'll see the client for you, shall I?'

'That'd be great, thanks,' said Strike, stepping inside the Victory with a sense of relief. The rain dripped off him as he removed his coat. 'I'm not sure when I'm going to be able to get back. You probably saw, the trains have been suspended.'

'Don't worry about the agency. We've got everything covered. Anyway, I haven't finished giving you the Bamborough – oh, hang on,' said Robin.

'D'you need to go?'

'No, it's fine,' said Robin.

She'd just seen Elinor Dean's front door open. The plump blonde emerged wearing a hooded coat which, conveniently, circumscribed her field of vision. Robin slid out of the Land Rover, closed the door and set off in pursuit, still speaking on her mobile.

'Our blonde friend's on the move,' she said quietly.

'Did you just say you've got more good news on Bamborough?' asked Strike.

He'd reached the bar, and by simply pointing, was able to secure himself a pint, which he paid for, then carried to the corner table at which he'd sat with Polworth in the summer.

'I have,' said Robin, turning the corner at the end of the road, the oblivious blonde walking ahead of her. 'Wish I could say I'd found Douthwaite or Satchwell, but the last person to see Margot alive is something, right?'

'You've found Gloria Conti?' said Strike sharply.

'Don't get too excited,' said Robin, still trudging along in the rain. Elinor seemed to be heading for the shops. Robin could see a Tesco in the distance. 'I haven't managed to speak to her yet, but I'm almost sure it's her. I found the family in the 1961 census: mother, father, one older son and a daughter, Gloria, middle name Mary. By the looks of things, Gloria's now in France, Nîmes, to be precise, and married to a Frenchman. She's dropped the "Gloria", and she's now going by Mary Jaubert. She's got a Facebook page, but it's private. I found her through a genealogical website. One of her English cousins is trying to put together a family tree. Right date of birth and everything.'

'Bloody good work,' said Strike. 'You know, I'm not sure she isn't even more interesting than Satchwell or Douthwaite. Last to see Margot alive. Close to her. The only living person to have seen Theo, as well.'

Strike's enthusiasm did much to allay Robin's suspicion that he'd added himself to her action points because he thought she wasn't up to the job.

'I've tried to "friend" her on Facebook,' Robin continued, 'but had no response yet. If she doesn't answer, I know the company her husband works for, and I thought I might email him to get a message to her. I thought it was more tactful to try the private route first, though.'

'I agree,' said Strike. He took a sip of Doom Bar. It was immensely consoling to be in the warm, dry pub, and to be talking to Robin.

'And there's one more thing,' said Robin. 'I think I might have found out which van was seen speeding away from Clerkenwell Green the evening Margot disappeared.'

'What? How?' said Strike, stunned.

'It occurred to me over Christmas that what people thought

might've been a flower painted on the side could have been a sun,' she said. 'You know. The planet.'

'It's technically a st—'

'Sod off, I know it's a star.'

The hooded blonde, as Robin had suspected, was heading into Tesco. Robin followed, enjoying the warm blast of heat as she entered the shop, though the floor underfoot was slippery and dirty.

'There was a wholefoods shop in Clerkenwell in 1974 whose logo was a sun. I found an ad for it in the British Library newspaper archive, I checked with Companies House and I've managed to talk to the director, who's still alive. *I know I couldn't talk to him if he weren't,*' she added, forestalling any more pedantry.

'Bloody hell, Robin,' said Strike, as the rain battered the window behind him. Good news and Doom Bar were certainly helping his mood. 'This is excellent work.'

'Thank you,' said Robin. 'And get this: he sacked the bloke he had making deliveries, he thinks in mid-1975, because the guy got done for speeding while driving the van. He remembered his name – Dave Underwood – but I haven't had time to—'

Elinor turned abruptly, midway up the aisle of tinned foods, and walked back towards her. Robin pretended to be absorbed in choosing a packet of rice. Letting her quarry pass, she finished her sentence.

'—haven't had time to look for him yet.'

'Well, you're putting me to shame,' admitted Strike, rubbing his tired eyes. Though he now had a spare bedroom to himself rather than the sofa, the old mattress was only a small step up in terms of comfort, its broken springs jabbing him in the back and squealing every time he turned over. 'The best I've done is to find Ruby Elliot's daughter.'

'Ruby-who-saw-the-two-women-struggling-by-the-phone-boxes?' Robin recited, watching her blonde target consulting a shopping list before disappearing down a new aisle.

'That's the one. Her daughter emailed to say she's happy to have a chat, but we haven't fixed up a time yet. And I called Janice,' said Strike, 'mainly because I couldn't face Irene, to see whether she can remember the so-called Applethorpe's real name, but she's in Dubai,

361

visiting her son for six weeks. Her answer machine message literally says "Hi, I'm in Dubai, visiting Kevin for six weeks". Might drop her a line advising her it's not smart to advertise to random callers that you've left your house empty.'

'So did you call Irene?' Robin asked. Elinor, she saw, was now looking at baby food.

'Not yet,' said Strike. 'But I have—'

At that very moment, a bleeping on his phone told him that someone else was trying to reach him.

'Robin, that might be him. I'll call you back.'

Strike switched lines.

'Cormoran Strike.'

'Yes, hello,' said Gregory Talbot. 'It's me – Greg Talbot. You asked me to call.'

Gregory sounded worried. Strike couldn't blame him. He'd hoped to divest himself of a problem by handing the can of old film to Strike.

'Yeah, Gregory, thanks very much for calling me back. I had a couple more questions, hope that's OK.'

'Go on.'

'I've been through your father's notebook and I wanted to ask whether your father happened to know, or mention, a man called Niccolo Ricci? Nicknamed "Mucky"?'

'Mucky Ricci?' said Gregory. 'No, he didn't really *know* him. I remember Dad talking about him, though. Big in the Soho sex shop scene, if that's the one I'm thinking of?'

It sounded as though talking about the gangster gave Gregory a small frisson of pleasure. Strike had met this attitude before, and not just in members of the fascinated public. Even police and lawyers were not immune to the thrill of coming within the orbit of criminals who had money and power to rival their own. He'd known senior officers talk with something close to admiration of the organised crime they were attempting to prevent, and barristers whose delight at drinking with high-profile clients went far beyond the hope of an anecdote to tell at a dinner party. Strike suspected that to Gregory Talbot, Mucky Ricci was a name from a fondly remembered childhood, a romantic figure belonging to a lost era, when his father was a sane copper and a happy family man.

'Yeah, that's the bloke,' said Strike. 'Well, it looks as though Mucky Ricci was hanging around Margot Bamborough's practice, and your father seems to have known about it.'

'Really?'

'Yes,' said Strike, 'and it seems odd that information never made it into the official records.'

'Well, Dad was ill,' said Gregory defensively. 'You've seen the notebook. He didn't know what he was up to, half the time.'

'I appreciate that,' said Strike, 'but once he'd recovered, what was his attitude to the evidence he'd collected while on the case?'

'What d'you mean?'

Gregory sounded suspicious now, as though he feared Strike was leading him somewhere he might not want to go.

'Well, did he think it was all worthless, or—?'

'He'd been ruling out suspects on the basis of their star signs,' said Gregory quietly. 'He thought he saw a demon in the spare room. What d'you *think* he thought? He was . . . he was ashamed. It wasn't his fault, but he never got over it. He wanted to go back and make it right, but they wouldn't let him, they forced him out. The Bamborough case tainted everything for him, all his memories of the force. His mates were all coppers and he wouldn't see them any more.'

'He felt resentful at the way he was treated, did he?'

'I wouldn't say – I mean, he was justified, I'd say, to feel they hadn't treated him right,' said Gregory.

'Did he ever look over his notes, afterwards, to make sure he'd put everything in there in the official record?'

'I don't know,' said Gregory, a little testy now. 'I think his attitude was, they've got rid of me, they think I'm a big problem, so let Lawson deal with it.'

'How did your father get on with Lawson?'

'Look, what's all this about?' Before Strike could answer, Gregory said, 'Lawson made it quite clear to my father that his day was done. He didn't want him hanging around, didn't want him anywhere near the case. Lawson did his best to completely discredit my father,

I don't mean just because of his illness. I mean, as a man, and as the officer he'd been before he got ill. He told everyone on the case they were to stay away from my father, even out of working hours. So if information didn't get passed on, it's down to Lawson as much as him. Dad might've tried and been rebuffed, for all I know.'

'I can certainly see it from your father's point of view,' said Strike. 'Very difficult situation.'

'Well, exactly,' said Gregory, slightly placated, as Strike had intended.

'To go back to Mucky Ricci,' Strike said, 'as far as you know, your father never had direct dealings with him?'

'No,' said Gregory, 'but Dad's best mate on the force did, name of Browning. He was Vice Squad. He raided one of Mucky's clubs, I know that. I remember Dad talking about it.'

'Where's Browning now? Can I talk to him?'

'He's dead,' said Gregory. 'What exactly—?'

'I'd like to know where that film you passed to me came from, Gregory.'

'I've no idea,' said Gregory. 'Dad just came home with it one day, Mum says.'

'Any idea when this was?' asked Strike, hoping not to have to find a polite way of asking whether Talbot had been quite sane at the time.

'It would've been while Dad was working on the Bamborough case. Why?'

Strike braced himself.

'I'm afraid we've had to turn the film over to the police.'

Hutchins had volunteered to take care of this, on the morning that Strike had headed down to Cornwall. As an ex-policeman who still had good contacts on the force, he knew where to take it and how to make sure it got seen by the right people. Strike had asked Hutchins not to talk to Robin about the film, or to tell her what he'd done with it. She was currently in ignorance of the contents.

'What?' said Gregory, horrified. 'Why?'

'It isn't porn,' said Strike, muttering now, in deference to the elderly couple who had just entered the Victory and stood, disorientated by the storm outside, dripping and blinking mere feet from his table. 'It's a snuff movie. Someone filmed a woman being gang-raped and stabbed.'

There was another silence on the end of the phone. Strike watched the elderly couple shuffle to the bar, the woman taking off her plastic rain hat as she went.

'Actually killed?' said Gregory, his voice rising an octave. 'I mean . . . it's definitely real?'

'Yeah,' said Strike.

He wasn't about to give details. He'd seen people dying and dead: the kind of gore you saw on horror movies wasn't the same, and even without a soundtrack, he wouldn't quickly forget the hooded, naked woman twitching on the floor of the warehouse, while her killers watched her die.

'And I suppose you've told them where you got it?' said Gregory, more panicked than angry.

'I'm afraid I had to,' said Strike. 'I'm sorry, but some of the men involved could still be alive, could still be charged. I can't sit on something like that.'

'I wasn't concealing anything, I didn't even know it was—'

'I wasn't meaning to suggest you knew, or you meant to hide it,' said Strike.

'If they think – we *foster kids*, Strike—'

'I've told the police you handed it over to me willingly, without knowing what was on there. I'll stand up in court and testify that I believe you were in total ignorance of what was in your attic. Your family's had forty-odd years to destroy it and you didn't. Nobody's going to blame you,' said Strike, even though he knew perfectly well that the tabloids might not take that view.

'I was afraid something like this was going to happen,' said Gregory, now sounding immensely stressed. 'I've been worried, ever since you came round for coffee. Dragging all this stuff up again . . . '

'You told me your father would want to see the case solved.'

There was another silence, and then Gregory said,

'He would. But not at the cost of my mother's peace of mind, or me and my wife having our foster kids taken off us.'

A number of rejoinders occurred to Strike, some of them unkind. It was far from the first time he'd encountered the tendency to believe the dead would have wanted whatever was most convenient to the living.

'I had a responsibility to hand that film over to the police once I'd seen what was on it. As I say, I'll make it clear to anyone who asks that you weren't trying to hide anything, that you handed it over willingly.'

There was little more to say. Gregory, clearly still unhappy, rang off, and Strike called Robin back.

She was still in Tesco, now buying a packet of nuts and raisins, chewing gum and some shampoo for herself while, two tills away, the object of her surveillance bought baby powder, baby food and dummies along with a range of groceries.

'Hi,' Robin said into her mobile, turning to look out of the shop-front window while the blonde walked past her.

'Hi,' said Strike. 'That was Gregory Talbot.'

'What did he—? Oh yes,' said Robin with sudden interest, turning to follow the blonde out of the store, 'what was on that can of film? I never asked. Did you get the projector working?'

'I did,' said Strike. 'I'll tell you about the film when I see you. Listen, there's something else I wanted to say. Leave Mucky Ricci to me, all right? I've got Shanker putting out a few feelers. I don't want you looking for him, or making enquiries.'

'Couldn't I—?'

'*Did you not hear me?*'

'All right, calm down!' said Robin, surprised. 'Surely Ricci must be ninety-odd by—?'

'He's got sons,' said Strike. 'Sons *Shanker's* scared of.'

'*Oh,*' said Robin, who fully appreciated the implication.

'Exactly. So we're agreed?'

'We are,' Robin assured him.

After Strike had hung up, Robin followed Elinor back out into the rain, and back to her terraced house. When the front door had closed again, Robin got back into her Land Rover and ate her packet of dried fruit and nuts, watching the front door.

It had occurred to her in Tesco that Elinor might be a childminder, given the nature of her purchases, but as the afternoon shaded into evening, no parents came to drop off their charges, and no baby's wail was heard on the silent street.

33

For he the tyrant, which her hath in ward
By strong enchauntments and blacke Magicke leare,
Hath in a dungeon deepe her close embard . . .
There he tormenteth her most terribly,
And day and night afflicts with mortall paine . . .

Edmund Spenser
The Faerie Queene

Now that the blonde in Stoke Newington had also become a person of interest, the Shifty case became a two-to-three-person job. The agency was watching Elinor Dean's house in addition to tracking the movements of Shifty's Boss and Shifty himself, who continued to go about his business, enjoying the fat salary to which nobody felt he was entitled, but remaining tight-lipped about the hold he had over his boss. Meanwhile, Two-Times was continuing to pay for surveillance on his girlfriend more, it seemed, out of desperation than hope, and Postcard had gone suspiciously quiet. Their only suspect, the owlish guide at the National Portrait Gallery, had vanished from her place of work.

'I hope to God it's flu, and she hasn't killed herself,' Robin said to Barclay on Friday afternoon, when their paths crossed at the office. Strike was still stuck in Cornwall and she'd just seen the Twinkletoes client out of the office. He'd paid his sizeable final bill grudgingly, having found out only that the West End dancer with whom his feckless daughter was besotted was a clean-living, monogamous and apparently heterosexual young man.

Barclay, who was submitting his week's receipts to Pat before heading out to take over surveillance of Shifty overnight, looked surprised.

'The fuck would she've killed herself?'

'I don't know,' said Robin. 'That last message she wrote sounded a bit panicky. Maybe she thought I'd come to confront her, holding the postcards she'd sent.'

'You need tae get some sleep,' Barclay advised her.

Robin moved towards the kettle.

'No fer me,' Barclay told her, 'I've gottae take over from Andy in thirty. We're back in Pimlico, watchin' Two-Times' bird never cop off wi' any fucker.'

Pat counted out tenners for Barclay, towards whom her attitude was tolerant rather than warm. Pat's favourite member of the agency, apart from Robin, remained Morris, whom Robin had met only three times since New Year: twice when swapping over at the end of a surveillance shift and once when he'd come into the office to leave his week's report. He'd found it difficult to meet her eye and talked about nothing but work, a change she hoped would be permanent.

'Who's next on the client waiting list, Pat?' she asked, while making coffee.

'We havenae got the manpower for another case the noo,' said Barclay flatly, pocketing his cash. 'Not wi' Strike off.'

'He'll be back on Sunday, as long as the trains are running,' said Robin, putting Pat's coffee down beside her. They'd arranged to meet Cynthia Phipps the following Monday, at Hampton Court Palace.

'I need a weekend back home, end o' the month,' Barclay told Pat, who in Strike's absence was in charge of the rota. As she opened it up on her computer, Barclay added, 'Migh' as well make the most of it, while I dinnae need a passport.'

'What d'you mean?' asked the exhausted Robin, sitting down on the sofa in the outer office with her coffee. She was, technically, off duty at the moment, but couldn't muster the energy to go home.

'Scottish independence, Robin,' said Barclay, looking at her from beneath his heavy eyebrows. 'I ken you English've barely noticed, but the union's about tae break up.'

'It won't really, will it?' said Robin.

'Every fucker I know's gonna vote Yes in September. One o' me mates from school called me an Uncle Tam last time I wus home. Arsehole won't be doin' that again,' growled Barclay.

When Barclay had left, Pat asked Robin,

'How's his aunt?'

Robin knew Pat was referring to Strike, because she never referred to her boss by name if she could help it.

'Very ill,' said Robin. 'Not fit for more chemotherapy.'

Pat jammed her electronic cigarette between her teeth and kept typing. After a while, she said,

'He was on his own at Christmas, upstairs.'

'I know,' said Robin. 'He told me how good you were to him. Buying him soup. He was really grateful.'

Pat sniffed. Robin drank her coffee, hoping for just enough of an energy boost to get her off this sofa and onto the Tube. Then Pat said,

'I'd've thought *he'd*'ve had somewhere to go, other than the attic.'

'Well, he had flu really badly,' said Robin. 'He didn't want to give it to anyone else.'

But as she washed up her mug, put on her coat, bade Pat farewell and set off downstairs, Robin found herself musing on this brief exchange. She'd often pondered the, to her, inexplicable animosity that Pat seemed to feel towards Strike. It had been clear from her tone that Pat had imagined Strike somehow immune to loneliness or vulnerability, and Robin was puzzled as to why, because Strike had never made any secret of where he was living or the fact that he slept there alone.

Robin's mobile rang. Seeing an unknown number, and remembering that Tom Turvey had been on the other end of the line the last time she'd answered one, she paused outside Tottenham Court Road station to answer it, with slight trepidation.

'Is this Robin Ellacott?' said a Mancunian voice.

'It is,' said Robin.

'Hiya,' said the woman, a little nervously. 'You wanted to talk to Dave Underwood. I'm his daughter.'

'Oh, yes,' said Robin. 'Thank you so much for getting back to me.'

Dave Underwood was the man who'd been employed to drive a wholefoods shop van at the time that Margot Bamborough went missing. Robin, who'd found his address online and written him a letter three days previously, hadn't expected such a quick response. She'd become inured to people ignoring her messages about Margot Bamborough.

'It was a bit of a shock, getting your letter,' said the woman on the phone. 'The thing is, Dad can't talk to you himself. He had a tracheotomy three weeks ago.'

'Oh, I'm so sorry to hear that,' said Robin, one finger in the ear not pressed to the phone, to block out the rumbling traffic.

'Yeah,' said the woman. 'He's here with me now, though, and he wants me to say ... look ... he's not going to be in trouble, is he?'

'No, of course not,' said Robin. 'As I said in my letter, it really is just about eliminating the van from enquiries.'

'All right then,' said Dave's daughter. 'Well, it *was* him. Amazing, you working it out, because they all swore it was a flower on the side of the van, didn't they? He was glad at the time, because he thought he'd get in trouble, but he's felt bad about it for years. He went the wrong way on a delivery and he was speeding through Clerkenwell Green to try and put himself right. He didn't want to say, because the boss had had a go at him that morning for not getting deliveries out on time. He saw in the paper they were thinking maybe he'd been Dennis Creed and he just ... well, you know. Nobody likes getting mixed up with stuff like that, do they? And the longer he kept quiet, the worse he thought it would look, him not coming forward straight away.'

'I see,' said Robin. 'Yes, I can understand how he felt. Well, this is very helpful. And after he'd made his delivery, did he—?'

'Yeah, he went back to the shop and he got a right telling-off anyway, because they opened the van and saw he'd delivered the wrong order. He had to go back out again.'

So Margot Bamborough clearly hadn't been in the back of the wholefoods van.

'Well, thanks very much for getting back to me,' said Robin, 'and please thank your father for being honest. That's going to be a great help.'

'You're welcome,' said the woman, and then, quickly, before Robin could hang up. 'Are you the girl the Shacklewell Ripper stabbed?'

For a moment, Robin considered denying it, but she'd signed the letter to Dave Underwood with her real name.

'Yes,' she said, but with less warmth than she'd put into her thank you for the information about the van. She didn't like being called 'the girl the Shacklewell Ripper stabbed'.

'Wow,' said the woman, 'I told Dad I thought it was you. Well, at least Creed can't get you, eh?'

She said it almost jauntily. Robin agreed, thanked her again for her cooperation, hung up the phone and proceeded down the stairs into the Tube.

At least Creed can't get you, eh?

The cheery sign-off stayed with Robin as she descended to the Tube. That flippancy belonged only to those who had never felt blind terror, or come up against brute strength and steel, who'd never heard pig-like breathing close to their ear, or seen defocused eyes through balaclava holes, or felt their own flesh split, yet barely registered pain, because death was so close you could smell its breath.

Robin glanced over her shoulder on the escalator, because the careless commuter behind her kept touching the backs of her upper thighs with his briefcase. Sometimes she found casual physical contact with men almost unbearable. Reaching the bottom of the escalator she moved off fast to remove herself from the commuter's vicinity. *At least Creed can't get you, eh?* As though being 'got' was nothing more than a game of tag.

Or was it being in the newspaper had somehow made Robin seem less human to the woman on the end of the phone? As Robin settled herself into a seat between two women on the Tube, her thoughts returned to Pat, and to the secretary's surprise that Strike had nowhere to go when he was ill, and nobody to look after him. Was that at the root of her antipathy? An assumption that newsworthiness meant invulnerability?

When Robin let herself into the flat forty minutes later, carrying a bag of groceries and looking forward to an early night, she found the place empty except for Wolfgang, who greeted her exuberantly, then whined in a way that indicated a full bladder. With a sigh, Robin found his lead and took him downstairs for a quick walk around the block. After that, too tired to cook a proper meal, she scrambled herself some eggs and ate them with toast while watching the news on TV.

She was running herself a bath when her mobile rang again. Her heart sank a little when she saw that it was her brother Jonathan, who was in his final year of university in Manchester. She thought she knew what he was calling about.

'Hi, Jon,' she said.

'Hey, Robs. You didn't answer my text.'

She knew perfectly well that she hadn't. He'd sent it that morning, while she'd been watching Two-Times' girlfriend having a blameless coffee, alone with a Stieg Larsson novel. Jon wanted to know whether he and a female friend could come and stay at her flat on the weekend of the fourteenth and fifteenth of February.

'Sorry,' said Robin, 'I know I didn't, it's been a busy day. I'm not sure, to be honest, Jon. I don't know what Max's plans—'

'He wouldn't mind us crashing in your room, would he? Courtney's never been to London. There's a comedy show we want to see on Saturday. At the Bloomsbury Theatre.'

'Is Courtney your girlfriend?' asked Robin, smiling now. Jonathan had always been quite cagey with the family about his love life.

'Is she my *girlfriend*,' repeated Jonathan mockingly, but Robin had an idea that he was quite pleased with the question really, and surmised that the answer was 'yes'.

'I'll check with Max, OK? And I'll ring you back tomorrow,' said Robin.

Once she'd disposed of Jonathan, she finished running the bath and headed into her bedroom to fetch pyjamas, dressing gown and something to read. *The Demon of Paradise Park* lay horizontally across the top of her neat shelf of novels. After hesitating for a moment, she picked it up and took it back to the bathroom with her, trying as she did so to imagine getting ready for bed with her brother and an unknown girl in the room, as well. Was she prudish, stuffy and old before her time? She'd never finished her university degree:

'crashing' on floors in the houses of strangers had never been part of her life, and in the wake of the rape that had occurred in her halls of residence, she'd never had any desire to sleep anywhere except in an environment over which she had total control.

Sliding into the hot bubble bath, Robin let out a great sigh of pleasure. It had been a long week, sitting in the car for hours or else trudging through the rainy streets after Shifty or Elinor Dean. Eyes closed, enjoying the heat and the synthetic jasmine of her cheap bubble bath, her thoughts drifted back to Dave Underwood's daughter.

At least Creed can't get you, eh? Setting aside the offensively jocular tone, it struck her as significant that a woman who'd known for years that Creed hadn't been driving the sun-emblazoned van was nevertheless certain that he'd abducted Margot.

Because, of course, Creed hadn't *always* used a van. He'd killed two women before he ever got the job at the dry cleaner's, and managed to persuade women to walk into his basement flat even after he'd acquired the vehicle.

Robin opened her eyes, reached for *The Demon of Paradise Park* and turned to the page where she had last left it. Holding the book clear of the hot, foamy water, she continued to read.

One night in September 1972, Dennis Creed's landlady spotted him bringing a woman back to the basement flat for the first time. She testified at Creed's trial that she heard the front gate 'squeak' at close to midnight, glanced down from her bedroom window at the steps into the basement and saw Creed and a woman who 'seemed a bit drunk but was walking OK', heading into the house.

When she asked Dennis who the woman was, he told her the implausible story that she was a regular client of the dry cleaner's. He claimed he'd met the drunk woman by chance in the street, and that she had begged him to let her come into his flat to phone a taxi.

In reality, the woman Violet had seen Dennis steering into the flat was the unemployed Gail Wrightman, who'd been stood up that evening by a boyfriend. Wrightman left the Grasshopper, a bar in Shoreditch, at half past ten in the evening, after consuming several strong cocktails. A woman matching Wrightman's description was seen getting into a white van at a short distance from the bar. Barring Cooper's glimpse of a brunette in a light-coloured coat entering Creed's flat that night, there were no further sightings of Gail Wrightman after she left the Grasshopper.

By now, Creed had perfected a façade of vulnerability that appealed particularly to older women like his landlady, and a convivial, sexually ambiguous persona that worked well with the drunk and lonely. Creed subsequently admitted to meeting Wrightman in the Grasshopper, adding Nembutal to her drink and lying in wait outside the bar where, confused and unsteady on her feet, she was grateful for his offer of a lift home.

Cooper accepted his explanation of the dry-cleaning client who'd wanted to call a taxi 'because I had no reason to doubt it'.

In reality, Gail Wrightman was now gagged and chained to a radiator in Creed's bedroom, where she would remain until Creed killed her by strangulation in January 1973. This was the longest period he kept a victim alive, and demonstrates the degree of confidence he had that his basement flat was now a place of safety, where he could rape and torture without fear of discovery.

However, shortly before Christmas that year, his landlady visited him on some trivial pretext, and she recalled in the witness box that 'he wanted to get rid of me, I could tell. I thought there was a nasty smell about the place, but we'd had problems with next door's drains before. He told me he couldn't chat because he was waiting for a phone call.

'I know it was Christmastime when I went down there, because I remember asking him why he hadn't put any cards up. I knew he didn't have many friends but I thought someone must have remembered him and I thought it was a shame. The radio was playing 'Long-Haired Lover from Liverpool', and it was loud, I remember that, but that wasn't anything unusual. Dennis liked music.'

Cooper's surprise visit to the basement almost certainly sealed Wrightman's death warrant. Creed later told a psychiatrist that he'd been toying with the idea of simply keeping Wrightman 'as a pet' for the foreseeable future, to spare himself the risks that further abductions would entail, but that he reconsidered and decided to 'put her out of her misery'.

Creed murdered Wrightman on the night of January 9th 1973, a date chosen to coincide with a three-day absence of Vi Cooper to visit a sick relative. Creed cut off Wrightman's head and hands in the bath before driving the rest of the corpse in his van to Epping Forest by night, wrapped in tarpaulin, and burying it in a shallow grave. Back at home, he boiled the flesh off Wrightman's head and hands and smashed up the bones, as he'd done to the corpses of both Vera Kenny and Nora Sturrock, adding the powdered bone to the inlaid ebony box he kept under his bed.

On her return to Liverpool Road, Violet Cooper noted that the 'bad smell' had gone from the basement flat and concluded that the drains had been sorted out.

Landlady and lodger resumed their convivial evenings, drinking and singing along to records. It's likely that Creed experimented with drugging Vi at this time. She later testified that she often slept so soundly on nights that Dennis joined her for a nightcap that she found herself still groggy the next morning.

Wrightman's grave remained undisturbed for nearly four months, until discovered by a dog walker whose terrier dug and retrieved a thigh bone. Decomposition, the absence of head and hands or any clothing rendered identification almost impossible given the difficulties of tissue typing in such circumstances. Only after Creed's arrest, when Wrightman's underwear, pantyhose and an opal ring her family identified as having belonged to her were found under the floorboards of Creed's sitting room, were detectives able to add Wrightman's murder to the list of charges against him.

Gail's younger sister had never lost hope that Gail was still alive. 'I couldn't believe it until I saw the ring with my own eyes. Until that moment, I honestly thought there'd been a mistake. I kept telling Mum and Dad she'd come back. I couldn't believe there was wickedness like that in the world, and that my sister could have met it.

'He isn't human. He played with us, with the families, during the trial. Smiling and waving at us every morning. Looking at the parents or the brother or whoever, whenever their relative was mentioned. Then, afterwards, after he was convicted, he keeps telling a bit more, and a bit more, and we've had to live with that hanging over us for years, what Gail said, or how she begged him. I'd murder him with my own bare hands if I could, but I could never make him suffer the way he made Gail suffer. He isn't capable of human feeling, is he? It makes you—'

There was a loud bang from the hall and Robin jumped so severely that water slopped over the edge of the bath.

'Just me!' called Max, who sounded uncharacteristically cheerful, and she heard him greeting Wolfgang. 'Hello, you. Yes, hello, hello . . .'

'Hi,' called Robin. 'I took him out earlier!'

'Thanks very much,' said Max, 'Come join me, I'm celebrating!'

She heard Max climbing the stairs. Pulling out the plug, she continued to sit in the bath as the water ebbed away, crisp bubbles still clinging to her as she finished the chapter.

It makes you pray there's a hell.'

In 1976, Creed told prison psychiatrist Richard Merridan that he tried to 'lie low' following the discovery of Wrightman's remains. Creed admitted to Merriman that he felt a simultaneous desire for notoriety and a fear of capture.

'I liked reading about the Butcher in the papers. I buried her in Epping Forest like the others because I wanted people to know that the same person had done them all, but I knew I was risking everything, not varying the pattern. After that, after Vi had seen me with her, and come in the flat with her there, I thought I'd better just do whores for a bit, lie low.'

But the choice to 'do whores' would lead, just a few months later, to Creed's closest brush with capture yet.

The chapter ended here. Robin got out of the bath, mopped up the spilled water, dressed in pyjamas and dressing gown, then headed upstairs to the living area where Max sat watching television, looking positively beatific. Wolfgang seemed to have been infected by his owner's good mood: he greeted Robin as though she'd been away on a long journey and set to work licking the bath oil off her ankles until she asked him kindly to desist.

'I've got a job,' Max told Robin, muting the TV. Two champagne glasses and a bottle were sitting on the coffee table in front of him. 'Second lead, new drama, BBC One. Have a drink.'

'Max, that's fantastic!' said Robin, thrilled for him.

'Yeah,' he said, beaming. 'Listen. D'you think your Strike would come over for dinner? I'm playing a veteran. It'd be good to speak to someone who's actually ex-army.'

'I'm sure he would,' said Robin, hoping she was right. Strike and Max had never met. She accepted a glass of champagne, sat down and held up her glass in a toast. 'Congratulations!'

'Thanks,' he said, clinking his glass against hers. 'I'll cook, if Strike comes over. It'll be good, actually. I need to meet more people. I'm turning into one of those "he always kept himself to himself" blokes you see on the news.'

'And I'll be the dumb flatmate,' said Robin, her thoughts still with Vi Cooper, 'who thought you were lovely and never questioned why I kept coming across you hammering the floorboards back down.'

Max laughed.

'And they'll blame you more than me,' said Max, 'because they always do. The women who didn't realise ... mind you, some of them ... who was that guy in America who made his wife call him on an intercom before he'd let her into the garage?'

'Jerry Brudos,' said Robin. Brudos had been mentioned in *The Demon of Paradise Park*. Like Creed, Brudos had been wearing women's clothing when he abducted one of his victims.

'I need to get a bloody social life going again,' said Max, more expansive than Robin had ever known him under the influence of alcohol and good news. 'I've been feeling like hell ever since Matthew left. Kept wondering whether I shouldn't just sell this place and move on.'

Robin thought her slight feeling of panic might have shown in her face, because Max said,

'Don't worry, I'm not going to. But it's half-killed me, keeping it going. I really only bought the place because of him. "Put it all into property, you can't lose with property," he said.'

He looked as though he was going to say something else, but if so, decided against it.

'Max, I wanted to ask you something,' said Robin, 'but it's totally fine if the answer's no. My younger brother and a girlfriend are looking for a place to stay in London for the weekend of the fourteenth and fifteenth of February. But if you don't—'

'Don't be silly,' said Max. 'They can sleep on this,' he said, patting the sofa. 'It folds out.'

'Oh,' said Robin, who hadn't known this. 'Well, great. Thanks, Max.'

The champagne and the hot bath had made Robin feel incredibly sleepy, but they talked on for a while about Max's new drama, until at last Robin apologised and said she really did need to go to bed.

As she pulled the duvet over herself, Robin decided against starting a new chapter on Creed. It was best not to have certain things in your head if you wanted to get to sleep. However, once she'd turned out her bedside lamp she found her mind refusing to shut down, so she reached for her iPod.

She never listened to music on headphones unless she knew Max was in the flat. Some life experiences made a person forever conscious of their ability to react, to have advance warning. Now, though, with the front door safely double-locked (Robin had checked, as she always did), and with her flatmate and a dog mere seconds away, she inserted her earbuds and pressed shuffle on the four albums of Joni Mitchell's she'd now bought, choosing music over another bottle of perfume she didn't like.

Sometimes, when listening to Mitchell, which Robin was doing frequently these days, she could imagine Margot Bamborough smiling at her through the music. Margot was forever frozen at twenty-nine, fighting not to be defeated by a life more complicated than she had ever imagined it would be, when she conceived the ambition of raising herself out of poverty by brains and hard work.

An unfamiliar song began to play. The words told the story of the end of a love affair. It was a simpler, more direct lyric than many of

Mitchell's, with little metaphor or poetry about it. *Last chance lost/The hero cannot make the change/Last chance lost/The shrew will not be tamed.*

Robin thought of Matthew, unable to adapt himself to a wife who wanted more from life than a steady progression up the property ladder, unable to give up the mistress who had always, in truth, been better suited to his ideals and ambitions than Robin. So did that make Robin the shrew, fighting for a career that everyone but she thought was a mistake?

Lying in the dark, listening to Mitchell's voice, which was deeper and huskier on her later albums, an idea that had been hovering on the periphery of Robin's thoughts for a couple of weeks forced its way into the forefront of her mind. It had been lurking ever since she'd read the letter from the Ministry of Justice, refusing Strike permission to see the serial killer.

Strike had accepted the Ministry of Justice's decision, and indeed, so had Robin, who had no desire to increase the suffering of the victims' families. And yet the man who might save Anna from a lifetime of continued pain and uncertainty was still alive. If Irene Hickson had been bursting to talk to Strike, how much more willing might Creed be, after decades of silence?

Last chance lost/the hero cannot make the change.

Robin sat up abruptly, pulled out her earphones, turned the lamp back on, sat up and reached for the notebook and pen she always kept beside her bed these days.

There was no need to tell Strike what she was up to. The possibility that her actions might backfire on the agency must be taken. If she didn't try, she'd forever wonder whether there hadn't been a chance of reaching Creed, after all.

34

. . . no Art, nor any Leach's Might . . .
Can remedy such hurts; such hurts are hellish Pain.

Edmund Spenser
The Faerie Queene

The train service between Cornwall and London resumed at last. Strike packed his bags, but promised his aunt and uncle he'd be back soon. Joan clung to him in silence at parting. Incredibly, Strike would have preferred one of the emotional-blackmail-laden farewells that had previously antagonised him.

Riding the train back to London, Strike found his mood mirrored in the monochrome winter landscape of mud and shivering trees he was watching through the dirt-streaked window. Joan's slow decline was a different experience to the deaths with which Strike was familiar, which had almost all been of the unnatural kind. As a soldier and an investigator, he'd become inured to the need to assimilate, without warning, the sudden, brutal extinction of a human being, to accept the sudden vacuum where once a soul had flickered. Joan's slow capitulation to an enemy inside her own body was something new to him. A small part of Strike, of which he was ashamed, wanted everything to be over, and for the mourning to begin in earnest, and, as the train bore him east, he looked forward to the temporary sanctuary of his empty flat, where he was free to feel miserable without either the need to parade his sadness for the neighbours, or to sport a veneer of fake cheerfulness for his aunt.

He turned down two invitations for dinner on Saturday night, one from Lucy, one from Nick and Ilsa, preferring to deal with the agency's books and review case files submitted by Barclay, Hutchins and Morris. On Sunday he spoke again to Dr Gupta and to a couple of relatives of deceased witnesses in the Bamborough case, preparatory to a catch-up with Robin the following day.

But on Sunday evening, while standing beside the spaghetti boiling on his single hob, he received a second text from his unknown half-sister, Prudence.

> **Hi Cormoran, I don't know whether you received my first text. Hopefully this one will reach you. I just wanted to say (I think) I understand your reasons for not wanting to join us for Dad's group photo, or for the party. There's a little more behind the party than a new album. I'd be happy to talk to you about that in person, but as a family we're keeping it confidential. I hope you won't mind me adding that, like you, I'm the result of one of Dad's briefer liaisons (!) and I've had to deal with my own share of hurt and anger over the years. I wonder whether you'd like to have a coffee to discuss this further? I'm in Putney. Please do get in touch. It would be great to meet. Warmest wishes, Pru**

His spaghetti now boiling noisily, Strike lit a cigarette. Pressure seemed to be building behind his eyeballs. He knew he was smoking too much: his tongue ached, and ever since his Christmas flu, his morning cough had been worse than ever. Barclay had been extolling the virtues of vaping the last time they'd met. Perhaps it was time to try that, or at least to cut down on the cigarettes.

He read Prudence's text a second time. What confidential reason could be behind the party, other than his father's new album? Had Rokeby finally been given his knighthood, or was he making a fuss over the Deadbeats' fiftieth anniversary in an attempt to remind those who gave out honours that he hadn't yet had one? Strike tried to imagine Lucy's reaction, if he told her he was off to meet a host of new half-siblings, when her small stock of relatives was about to be diminished by one. He tried to picture this Prudence, of whom he knew nothing at all, except that her mother had been a well-known actress.

Turning off the hob, he left the spaghetti floating in its water, and began to text a response, cigarette between his teeth.

> **Thanks for the texts. I've got no objection to meeting you, but now's not a good time. Appreciate that you're doing what you think is the right thing but I've never been much for faking feelings or maintaining polite fictions to suit public celebrations. I don't have a relationship with—**

Strike paused for a full minute. He never referred to Jonny Rokeby as 'Dad' and he didn't want to say 'our father', because that seemed to bracket himself and Prudence together in a way that felt uncomfortable, as she was a total stranger.

And yet some part of him didn't feel she was a stranger. Some part of him felt a tug towards her. What was it? Simple curiosity? An echo of the longing he'd felt as a child, for a father who never turned up? Or was it something more primitive: the calling of blood to blood, an animal sense of connection that couldn't quite be eradicated, no matter how much you tried to sever the tie?

> **—Rokeby and I've got no interest in faking one for a few hours just because he's putting out a new album. I hold no ill will towards you and, as I say, I'd be happy to meet when my life is less—**

Strike paused again. Standing in the steam billowing from his saucepan, his mind roved over the dying Joan, over the open cases on the agency's books, and, inexplicably, over Robin.

> **—complicated. Best wishes, Cormoran.**

He ate his spaghetti with a jar of shop-bought sauce, and fell asleep that night to the sound of rain hammering on the roof slates, to dream that he and Rokeby were having a fist fight on the deck of a sailing ship, which pitched and rolled until both of them fell into the sea.

Rain was still falling at ten to eleven the following morning, when Strike emerged from Earl's Court Tube station to wait for Robin, who was going to pick him up before driving to meet Cynthia Phipps at Hampton Court Palace. Standing beneath the brick overhang outside the station exit, yet another cigarette in his mouth, Strike read two recently arrived emails off his phone: an update from Barclay on Two-Times, and one from Morris on Shifty. He'd nearly finished them when the mobile rang. It was Al, and rather than let the call go to voicemail, Strike decided to put an end to this badgering once and for all.

'Hey, bruv,' said Al. 'How're you?'

'Been better,' said Strike.

He deliberately didn't reciprocate the polite enquiry.

'Look,' said Al, 'um … Pru's just rung me. She told me what you sent her. Thing is, we've got a photographer booked for next Saturday, but if you're not going to be in the picture – the whole point is that it's from all of us. First time ever.'

'Al, I'm not interested,' said Strike, tired of being polite.

There was a brief silence. Then Al said,

'You know, Dad keeps trying to reach out—'

'Is that right?' said Strike, anger suddenly piercing the fog of fatigue, of his worry about Joan, and the mass of probable irrelevancies he'd found out on the Bamborough case, which he was trying to hold in his head, so he could impart them to Robin. 'When would this be? When he set his lawyers on me, chasing me for money that was legally mine in the first—?'

'If you're talking about Peter Gillespie, Dad didn't know how heavy he was getting with you, I swear he didn't. Pete's retired now—'

'I'm not interested in celebrating his new fucking album,' said Strike. 'Go ahead and have fun without me.'

'Look,' said Al, 'I can't explain right now – if you can meet me for a drink, I'll tell you – there's a reason we want to do this for him now, the photo and the party—'

'The answer's no, Al.'

'You're just going to keep sticking two fingers up at him for ever, are you?'

'Who's sticking two fingers up? I haven't said a word about him publicly, unlike him, who can't give a fucking interview without mentioning me these days—'

'He's trying to put things right, and you can't give an inch!'

'He's trying to tidy up a messy bit of his public image,' said Strike harshly. 'Tell him to pay his fucking taxes if he wants his knighthood. I'm not his pet fucking black sheep.'

He hung up, angrier than he'd expected, his heart thumping uncomfortably hard beneath his coat. Flicking his cigarette butt into the road, his thoughts travelled inescapably back to Joan, with her headscarf hiding her baldness, and Ted weeping into his tea. Why, he thought, furiously, couldn't it have been Rokeby who lay dying, and his aunt who was well and happy, confident she'd reach her next birthday, striding through St Mawes, chatting to lifelong friends, planning dinners for Ted, nagging Strike over the phone about coming to visit?

When Robin turned the corner in the Land Rover a few minutes later, she was taken aback by Strike's appearance. Even though he'd told her by phone about the flu and the out-of-date chicken, he looked noticeably thinner in the face, and so enraged she automatically checked her watch, wondering whether she was late.

'Everything all right?' she asked, when he opened the passenger seat door.

'Fine,' he said shortly, climbing into the passenger seat and slamming the door.

'Happy New Year.'

'Haven't we already said that?'

'No, actually,' said Robin, somewhat aggravated by his surliness. 'But please don't feel pressured into saying it back. I'd hate you to feel railroaded—'

'Happy New Year, Robin,' muttered Strike.

She pulled out into the road, her windscreen wipers working hard to keep the windscreen clear, with a definite sense of déjà vu. He'd been grumpy when she'd picked him up on his birthday, too, and in spite of everything he was going through, she too was tired, she too had personal worries, and would have appreciated just a little effort.

'What's up?' she asked.

'Nothing.'

They drove for a few minutes in silence, until Robin said,

'Did you see Barclay's email?'

'About Two-Times and his girlfriend? Yeah, just read it,' said Strike. 'Ditched, and she'll never realise it was because she was too faithful.'

'He's such a freak,' said Robin, 'but as long as he pays his bill . . . '

'My thoughts exactly,' said Strike, making a conscious effort to throw off his bad temper. After all, none of it – Joan, Pru, Al, Rokeby – was Robin's fault. She'd been holding the agency together while he dealt with matters in Cornwall. She was owed better.

'We've got room for another waiting list client now,' he said, trying for a more enthusiastic tone. 'I'll call that commodities broker who thinks her husband's shagging the nanny, shall I?'

'Well,' said Robin, 'the Shifty job's taking a lot of manpower at the moment. We're covering him, his boss and the woman in Stoke Newington. The boss went back to Elinor Dean yesterday evening, you know. Same thing all over again, including the pat on the head.'

'Really?' said Strike, frowning.

'Yeah. The clients are getting quite impatient for proper evidence, though. Plus, we haven't got any resolution on Postcard yet and Bamborough's taking up quite a bit of time.'

Robin didn't want to say explicitly that with Strike moving constantly between London and Cornwall, she and the subcontractors were covering the agency's existing cases by forfeiting their days off.

'So you think we should concentrate on Shifty and Postcard, do you?'

'I think we should accept that Shifty's currently a three-person-job and not be in a hurry to take anything else on just now.'

'All right, fair enough,' grunted Strike. 'Any news on the guide at the National Portrait Gallery? Barclay told me you were worried she might've topped herself.'

'What did he tell you that for?' Robin said. She regretted blurting out her anxiety now: it felt soft, unprofessional.

'He didn't mean anything by it. Has she reappeared?'

'No,' said Robin.

'Any more postcards to the weatherman?'

'No.'

'Maybe you've scared her off.'

Strike pulled his notebook out of his pocket and opened it, while the rain continued to drum against the windscreen.

'I've got a few bits and pieces on Bamborough, before we meet Cynthia Phipps. That was great work of yours, eliminating the wholefoods van, by the way.'

'Thanks,' said Robin.

'But there's a whole new van on the scene,' said Strike.

'What?' said Robin sharply.

'I spoke to the daughter of Ruby Elliot yesterday. You remember Ruby—'

'The woman who saw the two women struggling from her car.'

'That's the one. I also spoke to a nephew of Mrs Fleury, who was crossing Clerkenwell Green, trying to get her senile mother home out of the rain.'

Strike cleared his throat, and said, reading from his notes:

'According to Mark Fleury, his aunt was quite upset by the description in the papers of her "struggling" and even "grappling" with her mother, because it suggested she'd been rough with the old dear. She said she was chivvying her mother along, not forcing her, but admitted that otherwise the description fitted them to a tee: right place, right time, rain hat, raincoat, etc.

'But Talbot leapt on the "we weren't grappling" discrepancy and tried to pressure Mrs Fleury into retracting her story and admitting that she and the old lady couldn't have been the people Ruby Elliot saw. Mrs Fleury wasn't having that, though. The description of them was too good: she was sure they were the right people.

'So Talbot went back to Ruby and tried to force her to change *her* story. You'll remember that there was another phone box at the opening of Albemarle Way. Talbot tried to persuade Ruby that she'd seen two people struggling in front of *that* phone box instead.

'Which is where things get mildly interesting,' said Strike, turning a page in his notebook. 'According to Ruby's daughter, Ruby was an absent-minded woman, a nervous driver and a poor map reader, with virtually no sense of direction. On the other hand, her daughter claims she had a very retentive memory for small visual details. She might not remember what street she'd met an acquaintance on, but she could describe down to the colour of a shoelace what they'd been wearing. She'd been a window dresser in her youth.

'Given her general vagueness, Talbot should have found it easy to persuade her she'd mistaken the phone box, but the harder he pushed, the firmer she stood, and the reason she stood firm, and said the two women couldn't have been in front of the Albemarle phone box, was because she'd seen *something else* happen beside that particular phone box, something she'd forgotten all about until Talbot mentioned the wedge-shaped building. Don't forget, she didn't know Clerkenwell at all.

'According to her daughter, Ruby kept driving around in a big circle that night, continually missing Hayward's Place, where her daughter's new house was. When he said, "Are you sure you didn't see these two struggling women beside the *other* phone box, near the wedge-shaped building on the corner of Albemarle Way?" Ruby suddenly remembered that she'd had to brake at that point in the road, because a transit van ahead of her had stopped beside the wedge-shaped building without warning. It was picking up a dark, stocky young woman who was standing in the pouring rain, beside the phone box. The woman—'

'Wait a moment,' said Robin, momentarily taking her eyes off the rainy road to glance at Strike. '"Dark and stocky?" It wasn't *Theo*?'

'Ruby thought it was, once she compared her memory of the girl in the rain with the artist's impressions of Margot's last patient. Dark-skinned, solid build, thick black hair – plastered to her face because it was so wet – and wearing a pair of—'

Strike sounded the unfamiliar name out, reading from his notebook.

'—*Kuchi* earrings.'

'What are Kuchi earrings?'

'Romany-style, according to Ruby's daughter, which might

account for Gloria calling Theo "gypsyish". Ruby knew clothes and jewellery. It was the kind of detail she noticed.

'The transit van braked without warning to pick up the-girl-who-could-have-been-Theo, temporarily holding up traffic. Cars behind Ruby were tooting their horns. The dark girl got into the front passenger seat, the transit van moved off in the direction of St John Street and Ruby lost sight of it.'

'And she didn't tell Talbot?'

'Her daughter says that by the time she remembered the second incident, she was exhausted by the whole business, sick to death of being ranted at by Talbot and told she must have been mistaken in thinking the two struggling women hadn't been Margot and Creed in drag, and regretting she'd ever come forward in the first place.

'After Lawson took over the case, she was afraid of what the police and the press would say to her if she suddenly came up with a story of seeing someone who resembled Theo. Rightly or wrongly, she thought it might look as though, having had her first sighting proven to be worthless, she wanted another shot at being important to the inquiry.'

'But her daughter felt OK about telling you all this?'

'Well, Ruby's dead, isn't she? It can't hurt her now. Her daughter made it clear she doesn't think any of this is going to amount to anything, so she might as well tell me the lot. And when all's said and done,' said Strike, turning a page in his notebook, 'we don't know the girl *was* Theo ... although personally, I think she was. Theo wasn't registered with the practice, so probably wasn't familiar with the area. That corner would make an easily identifiable place to meet the transit van after she'd seen a doctor. Plenty of space for it to pull over.'

'True,' said Robin slowly, 'but if that girl really *was* Theo, this lets her out of any involvement with Margot's disappearance, doesn't it? She clearly left the surgery alone, got a lift and drove—'

'Who was driving the van?'

'I don't know. Anyone. Parent, friend, sibling ...'

'Why didn't Theo come forward after all the police appeals?'

'Maybe she was scared. Maybe she had a medical problem she

didn't want anyone to know about. Plenty of people would rather not get mixed up with the police.'

'Yeah, you're not wrong,' admitted Strike. 'Well, I still think it's worth knowing that one of the last people to see Margot alive might've left the area in a vehicle big enough to hide a woman in.

'And speaking of the last person to see Margot alive,' Strike added, 'any response from Gloria Conti?'

'No,' said Robin. 'If nothing's happened by the end of next week, I'll try and contact her through her husband.'

Strike turned a page in his notebook.

'After I spoke to Ruby's daughter and the Fleury bloke, I called Dr Gupta back. Dunno whether you remember, but in my summary of the horoscope notes I mentioned "Scorpio", whose death, according to Talbot, worried Margot.'

'Yes,' said Robin. 'You speculated Scorpio might be Steve Douthwaite's married friend, who killed herself.'

'Well remembered,' said Strike. 'Well, Gupta can't remember any patient dying in unexplained circumstances, or in a way that troubled Margot, although he emphasised that all this is forty years ago and he can't swear there wasn't such a patient.

'Then I asked him whether he knew who Joseph Brenner might have been visiting in a block of flats on Skinner Street on the evening Margot disappeared. Gupta says they had a number of patients in Skinner Street, but he can't think of any reason why Brenner would have lied about going on a house call there.

'Lastly, and not particularly helpfully, Gupta remembers that a couple of men came to pick Gloria up at the end of the practice Christmas party. He remembers one of the men being a lot older, and says he assumed that was Gloria's father. The name "Mucky Ricci" meant nothing to him.'

Midway across Chiswick Bridge, the sun sliced suddenly through a chink in the rain clouds, dazzling their eyes. The dirty Thames beneath the bridge and the shallow puddles flashed laser bright, but, seconds later, the clouds closed again and they were driving again through rain, in the dull grey January light, along a straight dual carriageway bordered by shrubs slick with rain and naked trees.

'What about that film?' said Robin, glancing sideways at Strike. 'The film that came out of Gregory Talbot's attic? You said you'd tell me in person.'

'Ah,' said Strike. 'Yeah.'

He hesitated, looking past the windscreen wipers at the long straight road ahead, glimmering beneath a diagonal curtain of rain.

'It showed a hooded woman being gang-raped and killed.'

Robin experienced a slight prickling over her neck and scalp.

'And people get off on that,' she muttered, in disgust.

He knew from her tone that she hadn't understood, that she thought he was describing a pornographic fiction.

'No,' he said, 'it wasn't porn. Someone filmed . . . the real thing.'

Robin looked around in shock, before turning quickly back to face the road. Her knuckles whitened on the steering wheel. Repulsive images were suddenly forcing their way into her mind. What had Strike seen, that made him look so closed up, so blank? Had the hooded woman's body resembled Margot's, the body Oonagh Kennedy had said was 'all legs'?

'You all right?' asked Strike.

'Fine,' she almost snapped. 'What – what did you see, how—?'

But Strike chose to answer a question she hadn't asked.

'The woman had a long scar over the ribcage. There was never any mention of Margot having a scarred ribcage in press reports or police notes. I don't think it was her.'

Robin said nothing but continued to look tense.

'There were four men, ah, involved,' Strike continued, 'all Caucasian, and all with their faces hidden. There was also a fifth man looking on. His arm came briefly into shot. It could've been Mucky Ricci. There was an out-of-focus big gold ring.'

He was trying to reduce the account to a series of dry facts. His leg muscles had tensed up quite as much as Robin's hands, and he was primed to grab the wheel. She'd had a panic attack once before while they were driving.

'What are the police saying?' Robin asked. 'Do they know where it came from?'

'Hutchins asked around. An ex-Vice Squad guy thinks it's part of a batch they seized in a raid made on a club in Soho in '75. The club was owned by Ricci. They took a load of hardcore pornography out of the basement.

'One of Talbot's best mates was also Vice Squad. The best guess is that Talbot nicked or copied it, after his mate showed it to him.'

'Why would he do that?' said Robin, a little desperately.

'I don't think we're going to get a better answer than "because he was mentally ill",' said Strike. 'But the starting point must have been his interest in Ricci. He'd found out Ricci was registered with the St John's practice and attended the Christmas party. In the notes, he called Ricci—'

'—Leo three,' said Robin. 'Yes, I know.'

Strike's leg muscles relaxed very slightly. This degree of focus and recall on Robin's part didn't suggest somebody about to have a panic attack.

'Did you learn my email off by heart?' he asked her.

It was Robin's turn to remember Christmas, and the brief solace it had been, to bury herself in work at her parents' kitchen table.

'I pay attention when I'm reading, that's all.'

'Well, I still don't understand why Talbot didn't chase up this Ricci lead, although judging by the horoscope notes, there was a sharp deterioration in his mental state over the six months he was in charge of the case. I'm guessing he stole that can of film not long before he got kicked off the force, hence no mention of it in the police notes.'

'And then hid it so nobody else could investigate the woman's death,' said Robin. Her sympathy for Bill Talbot had just been, if not extinguished, severely dented. 'Why the hell didn't he take the film back to the police when he was back in his right mind?'

'I'd guess because he wanted his job back and, failing that, wanted to make sure he got his pension. Setting aside basic integrity, I can't see that he had a great incentive to admit he'd tampered with evidence on another case. Everyone was already pissed off at him: victims' families, press, the force, all blaming him for having fucked up the investigation. And then Lawson, a bloke he doesn't like, takes over and tells him to stay the fuck out of it. He probably told himself the dead woman was only a prostitute or—'

'Jesus,' said Robin angrily.

'*I'm* not saying "only a prostitute",' Strike said quickly. 'I'm guessing at the mindset of a seventies policeman who'd already been publicly shamed for buggering up a high-profile case.'

Robin said nothing, but remained stony-faced for the rest of the journey, while Strike, the muscles of his one-and-a-half legs so tense they ached, tried not to make it too obvious that he was keeping a covert eye on the hands gripping the steering wheel.

35

. . . fayre Aurora, rysing hastily,
Doth by her blushing tell, that she did lye
All night in old Tithonus frosen bed,
Whereof she seemes ashamed inwardly.

Edmund Spenser
The Faerie Queene

'Ever been here before?' Strike asked Robin, as she parked in the Hampton Court car park. She'd been silent since he'd told her about the film, and he was trying to break the tension.

'No.'

They got out of the Land Rover and set off across the car park in the chilly rain.

'Where exactly are we meeting Cynthia?'

'The Privy Kitchen Café,' said Robin. 'I expect they'll give us a map at the ticket office.'

She knew that the film hidden in Gregory Talbot's attic wasn't Strike's fault. He hadn't put it there, hadn't hidden it for forty years, couldn't have known, when he inserted it in the projector, that he was about to watch a woman's last, terrified, excruciating moments. She wouldn't have wanted him to withhold the truth about what he'd seen. Nevertheless, his dry and unemotional description had grated on Robin. Reasonably or not, she'd wanted some sign that he had been repulsed, or disgusted, or horrified.

But perhaps this was unrealistic. He'd been a military policeman long before Robin had known him, where he'd learned a detachment she sometimes envied. Beneath her determinedly calm exterior, Robin felt shaken and sick, and wanted to know that when Strike had watched the recording of the woman's dying moments, he'd recognised her as a person as real as he was.

Only a prostitute.

Their footsteps rang out on the wet tarmac as the great red-brick palace rose up before them, and Robin, who wanted to drive dreadful images out of her mind, tried to remember everything she knew about Henry VIII, that cruel and corpulent Tudor king who'd beheaded two of his six wives, but somehow found herself thinking about Matthew, instead.

When Robin had been brutally raped by a man in a gorilla mask who'd been lurking beneath the stairs of her hall of residence, Matthew had been kind, patient and understanding. Robin's lawyer might be mystified by the source of Matthew's vindictiveness over what should have been a straightforward divorce, but Robin had come to believe that the end of the marriage had been a profound shock to Matthew, because he thought he was owed infinite credit for having helped her through the worst period of her life. Matthew, Robin felt sure, thought she was forever in his debt.

Tears prickled in Robin's eyes. Angling her umbrella so that Strike couldn't see her face, she blinked hard until her eyes were clear again.

They walked across a cobbled courtyard in silence until Robin came to a sudden halt. Strike, who never enjoyed navigating uneven surfaces with his prosthesis, wasn't sorry to pause, but he was slightly worried that he was about to be on the receiving end of an outburst.

'Look at that,' Robin said, pointing down at a shining cobblestone.

Strike looked closer and saw, to his surprise, a small cross of St John engraved upon a small square brick.

'Coincidence,' he said.

They walked on, Robin looking around, forcing herself to take in her surroundings. They passed into a second courtyard, where a school party in hooded raincoats was being addressed by a guide in a medieval jester's costume.

'Oh wow,' said Robin quietly, looking over her shoulder and then walking backwards for a few paces, the better to see the object set high in the wall above the archway. 'Look at *that!*'

Strike did as he was bidden and saw an enormous, ornate, sixteenth-century astronomical clock of blue and gold. The signs of the zodiac were marked on the perimeter, both with the glyphs with which Strike had become unwillingly familiar, and with pictures representing each sign. Robin smiled at Strike's expression of mingled surprise and annoyance.

'What?' he said, catching her look of amusement.

'You,' she said, turning to walk on. 'Furious at the zodiac.'

'If you'd spent three weeks wading through all Talbot's bollocks, you wouldn't be keen on the zodiac, either,' said Strike.

He stood back to allow Robin to enter the palace first. Following the map Strike had been given, they headed along a flagged, covered walkway towards the Privy Kitchen Café.

'Well, I think there's a kind of poetry to astrology,' said Robin, who was consciously trying to keep her mind off Talbot's old can of film, and her ex-husband. 'I'm not saying it works, but there's a kind of – of symmetry to it, an order . . . '

Through a door to the right, a small Tudor garden came into view. Brightly coloured heraldic beasts stood sentinel over square beds full of sixteenth-century herbs. The sudden appearance of the spotted leopard, the white hart and the red dragon seemed to Robin to cheer her on, asserting the potency and allure of symbol and myth.

'It makes a kind of – not literal sense,' Robin said, as the whimsically strange creatures passed out of sight, 'but it's survived for a reason.'

'Yeah,' said Strike. 'People will believe any old shit.'

Slightly to his relief, Robin smiled. They entered the white-walled café, which had small leaded windows and dark oak furniture,

'Find us a discreet table, I'll get the drinks in. What d'you want, coffee?'

Choosing a deserted side room, Robin sat down at a table beneath one of the leaded windows and glanced through the potted history of the palace they'd received with their tickets. She learned that the Knights of St John had once owned the land on which the palace stood, which explained the cross on the cobblestone, and that Cardinal Wolsey had given Henry VIII the palace in a futile bid to stave off his own decline in influence. However, when she read that the ghost of nineteen-year-old Catherine Howard was supposed to run, screaming, along the Haunted Gallery, eternally begging her fifty-year-old-husband, the King, not to have her beheaded, Robin closed the pamphlet without reading the rest. Strike arrived with the coffees to find her with her arms folded, staring into space.

'Everything all right?'

'Yes,' she said. 'Just thinking about star signs.'

'Still?' said Strike, with a slight eye roll.

'Jung says it was man's first attempt at psychology, did you know that?'

'I didn't,' said Strike, sitting down opposite her. Robin, as he knew, had been studying psychology at university before she dropped out. 'But there's no excuse to keep using it now we've got actual psychology, is there?'

'Folklore and superstition haven't gone away. They'll never go away. People need them,' she said, taking a sip of coffee. 'I think a purely scientific world would be a cold place. Jung also talked about the collective unconscious, you know. The archetypes lurking in all of us.'

But Strike, whose mother had ensured that he'd spent a large portion of his childhood in a fug of incense, dirt and mysticism, said shortly,

'Yeah, well. I'm Team Rational.'

'People like feeling connected to something bigger,' said Robin, looking up at the rainy sky outside. 'I think it makes you feel less lonely. Astrology connects you to the universe, doesn't it? And to ancient myths and ideas—'

'—and incidentally feeds your ego,' said Strike. 'Makes you feel less insignificant. "Look how special the universe is telling me I am." I don't buy the idea that I've got anything more in common with other people born on November the twenty-third than I think being born in Cornwall makes me a person better than someone born in Manchester.'

'I never said—'

'You might not, but my oldest mate does,' said Strike. 'Dave Polworth.'

'The one who gets ratty when Cornish flags aren't on strawberries?'

'That's him. Committed Cornish nationalist. He gets defensive about it if you challenge him – "I'm not saying we're better than anyone else" – but he thinks you shouldn't be able to buy property down there unless you can prove Cornish ethnicity. Don't remind him he was born in Birmingham if you value your teeth.'

Robin smiled.

'Same kind of thing, though, isn't it?' said Strike. '"I'm special and different because I was born on this bit of rock." "I'm special and different because I was born on June the twelfth—"'

'Where you're born *does* influence who you are, though,' said Robin. 'Cultural norms and language have an effect. And there have been studies showing people born at different times of the year are more prone to certain health conditions.'

'So Roy Phipps bleeds a lot because he was born—? Hello there!' said Strike, breaking off suddenly, his eyes on the door.

Robin turned and saw, to her momentary astonishment, a slender woman wearing a long green Tudor gown and headdress.

'I'm *so sorry*!' said the woman, gesturing at her costume and laughing nervously as she advanced on their table. 'I thought I'd have time to change! I've been doing a school group – we finished late—'

Strike stood up and held out a hand to shake hers.

'Cormoran Strike,' he said. Eyes on her reproduction pearl necklace with its suspended initial 'B', he said, 'Anne Boleyn, I presume?'

Cynthia's laughter contained a couple of inadvertent snorts, which increased her odd resemblance, middle-aged though she was, to a gawky schoolgirl. Her movements were unsuited to the sweeping velvet gown, being rather exaggerated and ungainly.

'Hahaha, yes, that's me! Only my second time as Anne. You think you've thought of *all* the questions the kids might ask you, then one of them says "How did it feel to get your head cut off?", hahahaha!'

Cynthia wasn't at all what Robin had expected. She now realised that her imagination had sketched in a young blonde, the stereotypical idea of a Scandinavian au pair . . . or was that because Sarah Shadlock had almost white hair?

'Coffee?' Strike asked Cynthia.

'Oh – coffee, yes please, wonderful, thank you,' said Cynthia, over-enthusiastically. When Strike had left, Cynthia made a small pantomime of dithering over which seat to take until Robin, smiling, pulled out the seat beside her and offered her own hand, too.

'Oh, yes, hello!' said Cynthia, sitting down and shaking hands. She had a thin, sallow face, currently wearing an anxious smile. The irises of her large eyes were heavily mottled, an indeterminate colour between blue, green and grey, and her teeth were rather crooked.

'So you lead the tour in character?' asked Robin.

'Yes, exactly, as poor Anne, hahaha,' said Cynthia, with another nervous, snorting laugh. '"I couldn't give the King a son! They said I was a witch!" Those are the sort of things children like to hear; I have to work quite hard to get the politics in, hahaha. Poor Anne.' Her thin hands fidgeted.

'Oh, I'm still – I can take this off, at least, hahaha!'

Cynthia set to work unpinning her headdress. Even though she could tell that Cynthia was very nervous, and that her constant laughter was more of a tic than genuine amusement, Robin was again reminded of Sarah Shadlock, who tended to laugh a lot, and loudly, especially in the vicinity of Matthew. Wittingly or not, Cynthia's laughter imposed a sort of obligation: smile back or seem hostile. Robin remembered a documentary on monkeys she had watched one night when she was too tired to get up and go to bed: chimps, too, laughed back at each other to signal social cohesion.

When Strike returned to the table with Cynthia's coffee, he found her newly bare-headed. Her dark hair was fifty per cent grey, and smoothed back into a short, thin ponytail.

'It's very good of you to meet us, Mrs Phipps,' he said, sitting back down.

'Oh, no, not at all, not at all,' said Cynthia, waving her thin hands and laughing some more. 'Anything I can do to help Anna with – but Roy hasn't been well, so I don't want to worry him just now.'

'I'm sorry to hear—'

'Yes, thank you, no, it's prostate cancer,' said Cynthia, no longer laughing. 'Radiation therapy. Not feeling too chipper. Anna and Kim came over this morning to sit with him, or I wouldn't have been able – I don't like leaving him at the moment, but the girls are there, so I thought I'd be fine to . . .'

The end of the sentence was lost as she took a sip of coffee. Her hand trembled slightly as she replaced the cup onto the saucer.

'Your stepdaughter's probably told—' Strike began, but Cynthia immediately interrupted him.

'*Daughter.* I don't ever call Anna my stepdaughter. Sorry, but I feel *just* the same about her as I do about Jeremy and Ellie. No difference at all.'

Robin wondered whether that was true. She was uncomfortably aware that part of her was standing aside, watching Cynthia with judgemental eyes. *She isn't Sarah*, Robin reminded herself.

'Well, I'm sure Anna's told you why she hired us, and so on.'

'Oh, yes,' said Cynthia. 'No, I must admit, I've been expecting something like this for a while. I hope it isn't going to make things worse for her.'

'Er – well, we hope that, too, obviously,' said Strike, and Cynthia laughed and said, 'Oh, no, of course, yes.'

Strike took out his notebook, in which a few photocopied sheets were folded, and a pen.

'Could we begin with the statement you gave the police?'

'You've got it?' said Cynthia, looking startled. 'The original?'

'A photocopy,' he said, unfolding it.

'How . . . funny. Seeing it again, after all this time. I was eighteen. Eighteen! It seems a century ago, hahaha!'

The signature at the bottom of the uppermost page, Robin saw, was rounded and rather childish. Strike handed the photocopied pages to Cynthia, who took them looking almost frightened.

'I'm afraid I'm awfully dyslexic,' she said. 'I was forty-two before I was diagnosed. My parents thought I was bone idle, hahaha . . . um, so . . .'

'Would you rather I read it to you?' Strike suggested. Cynthia handed it back to him at once.

'Oh, thank you – this is how I learn all my guiding notes, by lis‑
tening to audio discs, hahaha . . . '

Strike flattened out the photocopied papers on the table.

'Please interrupt if you want to add or change anything,' he told
Cynthia, who nodded and said that she would.

'"Name, Cynthia Jane Phipps . . . date of birth, July the twentieth
1957 . . . address, "The Annexe, Broom House, Church Road" . . .
that would be Margot's—?'

'I had self-contained rooms over the double garage,' said Cynthia.
Robin thought she laid slight emphasis on 'self-contained'.

'"I am employed as nanny to Dr Phipps and Dr Bamborough's
infant daughter, and I live in their house—"'

'Self-contained studio,' said Cynthia. 'It had its own entrance.'

'"My hours . . . " Don't think we need any of that,' muttered
Strike. 'Here we go. "On the morning of the eleventh of October I
began work at 7 a.m. I saw Dr Bamborough before she left for work.
She seemed entirely as usual. She reminded me that she would be late
home because she was meeting her friend Miss Oonagh Kennedy for
drinks near her place of work. As Dr Phipps was bedbound due to
his recent accident—"'

'Anna told you about Roy's von Willebrand Disease?' said Cynthia
anxiously.

'Er – I don't think *she* told us, but it's mentioned in the police report.'

'Oh, didn't she say?' said Cynthia, who seemed unhappy to hear
it. 'Well, he's a Type Three. That's serious, as bad as haemophilia.
His knee swelled up and he was in a lot of pain, could hardly *move*,'
said Cynthia.

'Yes,' said Strike, 'it's all in the police—'

'No, because he'd had an accident on the seventh,' said Cynthia,
who seemed determined to say this. 'It was a wet day, pouring with
rain, you can check that. He was walking around a corner of the
hospital, heading for the car park, and an out-patient rode right into
him on a pushbike. Roy got tangled up in the front wheel, slipped,
hit his knee and had a major bleed. These days he has prophylactic
injections so it doesn't happen the way it used to, but back then, if
he injured himself, it could lay him up for weeks.'

'Right,' said Strike, and judging it to be the most tactful thing to do, he made careful note of all these details, which he'd already read in Roy's own statements and police interviews.

'No, Anna knows her dad was ill that day. She's always known,' Cynthia added.

Strike continued reading the statement aloud. It was a retelling of facts Strike and Robin already knew. Cynthia had been in charge of baby Anna at home. Roy's mother had come over during the day. Wilma Bayliss had cleaned for three hours and left. Cynthia had taken occasional cups of tea to the invalid and his mother. At 6 p.m., Evelyn Phipps had gone home to her bungalow to play bridge with friends, leaving a tray of food for her son.

'"At 8 p.m. in the evening I was watching television in the sitting room downstairs when I heard the phone ring in the hall. I would usually only ever answer the phone if both Dr Phipps and Dr Bamborough were out. As Dr Phipps was in, and could answer the phone from the extension beside his bed, I didn't answer.

'"About five minutes later, I heard the gong that Mrs Evelyn Phipps had placed beside Dr Phipps's bed, in case of emergency. I went upstairs. Dr Phipps was still in bed. He told me that it had been Miss Kennedy on the phone. Dr Bamborough hadn't turned up at the pub. Dr Phipps said he thought she must have been delayed at work or forgotten. He asked me to tell Dr Bamborough to go up to their bedroom as soon as she came in.

'"I went back downstairs. About an hour later, I heard the gong again and went upstairs and found Dr Phipps now quite worried about his wife. He asked me whether she'd come in yet. I said that she hadn't. He asked me to stay in the room while he phoned Miss Kennedy at home. Miss Kennedy still hadn't seen or heard from Dr Bamborough. Dr Phipps hung up and asked me what Dr Bamborough had been carrying when she left the house that morning. I told him just a handbag and her doctor's bag. He asked me whether Dr Bamborough had said anything about visiting her parents. I said she hadn't. He asked me to stay while he called Dr Bamborough's mother.

'"Mrs Bamborough hadn't heard from her daughter or seen her. Dr Phipps was now quite worried and asked me to go downstairs and look in the drawer in the base of the clock on the mantelpiece in the sitting room and see whether there was anything in there. I went and looked. There was nothing there. I went back upstairs and told Dr Phipps that the clock drawer was empty. Dr Phipps explained that this was a place he and his wife sometimes left each other private notes. I hadn't known about this previously.

'"He asked me to stay with him while he called his mother, because he might have something else for me to do. He spoke to his mother and asked her advice. It was a brief conversation. When he hung up, Dr Phipps asked me whether I thought he ought to call the police. I said I thought he should. He said he was going to. He told me to go downstairs and let the police in when they arrived and show them up to his bedroom. The police arrived about half an hour later and I showed them up to Dr Phipps's bedroom.

'"I didn't find Dr Bamborough to be unusual in her manner when she left the house that morning. Relations between Dr Phipps and Dr Bamborough seemed completely happy. I'm very surprised at her disappearance, which is out of character. She is very attached to her daughter and I cannot imagine her ever leaving the baby, or going away without telling her husband or me where she was going.

'"Signed and dated Cynthia Phipps, 12 October 1974."'

'Yes, no, that's ... I haven't got anything to add to that,' said Cynthia. 'Odd to hear it back!' she said, with another little snorting laugh, but Robin thought her eyes were frightened.

'This is obviously, ah, sensitive, but if we could go back to your statement that relations between Roy and Margot—'

'Yes, sorry, no, I'm not going to talk about their marriage,' said Cynthia. Her sallow cheeks became stained with a purplish blush. 'Everyone rows, everyone has ups and downs, but it's not up to me to talk about their marriage.'

'We understand that your husband couldn't have—' began Robin.

'*Margot's* husband,' said Cynthia. 'No, you see, they're two completely different people. Inside my head.'

Convenient, said a voice inside Robin's.

'We're simply exploring the possibility that she went away,' said Strike, 'maybe to think or—'

'No, Margot wouldn't have just walked out without saying anything. That wouldn't have been like her.'

'Anna told us her grandmother—' said Robin.

'Evelyn had early onset Alzheimer's and you couldn't take what she said seriously,' said Cynthia, her tone higher and more brittle. 'I've always told Anna that, I've *always* told her that Margot would never have left her. I've *always* told her that,' she repeated.

Except, continued the voice inside Robin's head, *when you were pretending to be her real mother, and hiding Margot's existence from her.*

'Moving on,' said Strike, 'you received a phone call on Anna's second birthday, from a woman purporting to be Margot?'

'Um, yes, no, that's right,' said Cynthia. She took another shaky sip of coffee. 'I was icing the birthday cake in the kitchen when the phone rang, so not in any danger of forgetting what day it was, hahaha. When I picked up, the woman said, "Is that you, Cynthia?" I said "Yes", and she said "It's Margot here. Wish little Annie a happy birthday from her mummy. And make sure you look after her." And the line went dead.

'I just stood there,' she mimed holding an invisible implement in her hand, and tried to laugh again, but no sound came out, 'holding the spatula. I didn't know what to do. Anna was playing in the sitting room. I was . . . I decided I'd better ring Roy at work. He told me to call the police, so I did.'

'Did you think it was Margot?' asked Strike.

'No. It wasn't – well, it *sounded* like her, but I don't think it *was* her.'

'You think somebody was imitating it?'

'Putting it on, yes. The accent. Cockney, but . . . no, I didn't get that feeling you get when you just *know* who it is . . .'

'You're sure it was a woman?' said Strike. 'It couldn't have been a man imitating a woman?'

'I don't think so,' said Cynthia.

'Did Margot ever call Anna "little Annie"?' asked Robin.

'She called her all kinds of pet names,' said Cynthia, looking glum. 'Annie Fandango, Annabella, Angel Face . . . somebody could have guessed, or maybe they'd just got the name wrong . . . But the timing was . . . they'd just found bits of Creed's last victim. The one he threw off Beachy Head—'

'Andrea Hooton,' said Robin. Cynthia looked slightly startled that she had the name on the tip of her tongue.

'Yes, the hairdresser.'

'No,' said Robin. 'That was Susan Meyer. Andrea was the PhD student.'

'Oh, yes,' said Cynthia. 'Of course . . . I'm so bad with names . . . Well, Roy had just been through the whole identification business with, um, you know, the bits of the body that washed up, so we'd had our hopes – not our hopes!' said Cynthia, looking terrified at the word that had escaped her, 'I don't mean that! No, we were obviously relieved it wasn't Margot, but you think, you know, maybe you're going to get an answer . . . '

Strike thought of his own guilty wish that Joan's slow and protracted dying would be over soon. A corpse, however unwelcome, meant anguish could find both expression and sublimation among flowers, speeches and ritual, consolation drawn from God, alcohol and fellow mourners; an apotheosis reached, a first step taken towards grasping the awful fact that life was extinct, and life must go on.

'We'd already been through it once when they found the other body, the one in Alexandra Lake,' said Cynthia.

'Susan Meyer,' muttered Robin.

'Roy was shown pictures, both times . . . And then this phone call, coming right after he'd had to . . . for the second time . . . it was . . . '

Cynthia was suddenly crying, not like Oonagh Kennedy, with her head up and tears sparkling on her cheeks, but hunched over the table, hiding her face, her shaking hands supporting her forehead.

'I'm so sorry,' she sobbed. 'I knew this would be awful . . . we never talk about her any – any more . . . I'm sorry . . . '

She sobbed for a few more seconds, then forced herself to look up again, her large eyes now pink and wet.

'Roy wanted to believe it had been Margot on the phone. He kept saying "Are you sure, are you *sure*, it didn't sound like her?" He was on tenterhooks while the police traced the call . . .

'You're being very polite,' she said, and her laugh this time was slightly hysterical, 'but I know what you want to know, and what Anna wants to know, too, even though I've *told* her and *told* her . . . There was *nothing* going on between me and Roy before Margot disappeared, and not for *four years* afterwards . . . Did she tell you that Roy and I are related?'

She said it as though forcing herself to say it, although a third cousin was not, after all, a very close relationship. But Robin, thinking of Roy's bleeding disorder, wondered whether the Phippses, like the Romanovs, mightn't be well advised not to marry their cousins.

'Yes, she did,' said Strike.

'I was sick of the sound of his name before I went to work for them, actually. It was all, "Just look at Cousin Roy, with all his health problems, getting into Imperial College and studying medicine. If you'd only *work harder*, Cynthia . . ." I used to hate the very idea of him, hahaha!'

Robin recalled the picture of young Roy in the press: the sensitive face, the floppy hair, the poet's eyes. Many women found injury and illness romantic in a handsome man. Hadn't Matthew, in his worst effusions of jealousy against Strike, invoked his amputated leg, the warrior's wound against which he, whole-bodied and fit, felt unable to compete?

'You might not believe this, but as far as I was concerned at seventeen, the best thing about Roy was Margot! No, I thought she was *marvellous*, so – so fashionable and, you know, lots of opinions and things . . .

'She asked me over for dinner, after she heard I ploughed all my exams. Well, I hero-worshipped her, so I was thrilled. I poured my heart out, told her I couldn't face resits, I just wanted to get out in the real world and earn my own money. And she said, "Look, you're wonderful with children, how about coming and looking after my baby when I go back to work? I'll get Roy to do up the rooms over the garage for you."

'My parents were *livid*,' said Cynthia, with another brave but unsuccessful stab at a laugh. 'They were furious with her, *and* Roy, although actually, he didn't want me there in the first place, because he wanted Margot to stay at home and look after Anna herself. Mummy and Daddy said she was just after cheap labour. These days I do see it more from their point of view. I'm not sure *I'd* have been delighted if a woman had persuaded one of my girls to leave school and move in with them, and look after their baby. But no, I loved Margot. I was excited.'

Cynthia fell silent for a moment, a faraway look in her doleful eyes, and Robin wondered whether she was thinking about the huge and unalterable consequences of accepting the job as nanny, which instead of being a springboard to her own independent life had placed her in a house she would never leave, led to her raising Margot's child as her own, sleeping with Margot's husband, forever stuck in the shadow of the doctor she claimed to have loved. What was it like to live with an absence that huge?

'My parents wanted me to go away after Margot disappeared. They didn't like me being alone at the house with Roy, because people were starting to gossip. There were even hints in the press, but I swear to you on the lives of my children,' said Cynthia, with a kind of dull finality, 'there was *nothing* between Roy and me, ever, before Margot disappeared, and not for a long time afterwards, either. I stayed for Anna, because I couldn't bear to leave her . . . she'd become my daughter!'

She hadn't, said the implacable voice in Robin's head. *And you should have told her so.*

'Roy didn't date anyone for a long time after Margot disappeared. Then there was a colleague at work for a while,' Cynthia's thin face flushed again, 'but it only lasted a few months. Anna didn't like her.

'I had a kind of on-off boyfriend, but he packed me in. He said it was like dating a married woman with a child, because I put Anna and Roy first, always.

'And then I suppose . . . ' said Cynthia shakily, one hand balled in a fist, the other clutching it, ' . . . over time . . . I realised I'd fallen in love with Roy. I never dreamed he'd want to be with me, though. Margot was so clever, such a — such a big personality, and he was so much older than me, so much more intelligent and sophisticated . . .

'One evening, after I'd put Anna to bed, I was about to go back

407

to my rooms and he asked me what had happened with Will, my boyfriend, and I said it was over, and he asked what had happened, and we got talking, and he said . . . he said, "You're a very special person and you deserve far better than him." And then . . . then, we had a drink . . .

'That was *four years* after she'd disappeared,' Cynthia repeated. 'I was eighteen when she vanished and I was twenty-two when Roy and I . . . admitted we had feelings for each other. We kept it secret, obviously. It was another three years before Roy could get a death certificate for Margot.'

'That must have been very hard,' said Strike.

Cynthia looked at him for a moment, unsmiling. She seemed to have aged since arriving at the table.

'I've had nightmares about Margot coming back and throwing me out of the house for nearly forty years,' she said, and she tried to laugh. 'I've never told Roy. I don't want to know whether he dreams about her, too. We don't talk about her. It's the only way to cope. We'd said everything we had to say to the police, to each other, to the rest of the family. We'd raked it all over, hours and hours of talking. "It's time to close the door", that's how Roy put it. He said, "We've left the door open long enough. She's not coming back."

'There were a couple of spiteful things said in the press, you know, when we got married. "Husband of vanished doctor marries young nanny." It's always going to sound sordid, isn't it? Roy said not to mind them. My parents were appalled by the whole thing. It was only when I had Jeremy that they came around.

'We never *meant* to mislead Anna. We were waiting . . . I don't know . . . trying to find the right moment, to explain . . . but how are you supposed to do it? She used to call me "Mummy",' whispered Cynthia, 'she was h- happy, she was a completely happy little girl, but then those children at school told her about Margot and it ruined *every*—'

From somewhere close by came a loud synthesiser version of 'Greensleeves'. All three of them looked startled until Cynthia, laughing her snorting laugh, said, 'It's my phone!' She pulled the mobile from a deep pocket in her dress and answered it.

'Roy?' she said.

Robin could hear Roy talking angrily from where she sat. Cynthia looked suddenly alarmed. She tried to get up, but stepped on the hem of her dress and tripped forwards. Trying to disentangle herself, she said,

'No, I'm – oh, she hasn't. Oh, God – Roy, I didn't want to tell you because – no – yes, I'm still with them!'

Finally managing to free herself from both dress and table, Cynthia staggered away and out of the room. The headdress she'd been wearing slid limply off her seat. Robin stooped to pick it up, put it back on the seat of Cynthia's chair and looked up to see Strike watching her.

'What?' asked Robin.

He was about to answer when Cynthia reappeared. She looked stricken.

'Roy knows – Anna's told him. He wants you to come back to Broom House.'

36

He oft finds med'cine who his grief imparts;
But double griefs afflict concealing hearts,
As raging flames who striveth to suppress.

Edmund Spenser
The Faerie Queene

Cynthia hurried away to change out of her Anne Boleyn costume and reappeared ten minutes later in a pair of poorly fitting jeans, a grey sweater and trainers. She appeared extremely anxious as they walked together back through the palace, setting a fast pace that Strike found challenging on cobblestones still slippery with the rain which had temporarily ceased, but the heavy grey clouds, gilt-edged though they were, promised an imminent return. Glancing upwards as they passed back through the gatehouse of the inner court, Robin's eye was caught by the gleaming gold accents on the astronomical clock, and noticed that the sun was in Margot's sign of Aquarius.

'I'll see you there,' said Cynthia breathlessly, as they approached the car park, and without waiting for an answer she half-ran towards a blue Mazda3 in the distance.

'This is going to be interesting,' said Robin.

'Certainly is,' said Strike.

'Grab the map,' said Robin, once both were back in the car. The old Land Rover didn't have a functioning radio, let alone satnav. 'You'll have to navigate.'

'What d'you think of her?' asked Strike, while he looked up Church Road in Ham.

'She seems all right.'

Robin became aware that Strike was looking at her, as he had in the café, a slightly quizzical expression on his face.

'What?' she said again.

'I had the impression you weren't keen.'

'No,' said Robin, with a trace of defensiveness, 'she's fine.'

She reversed out of the parking space, remembering Cynthia's snorting laughter and her habit of jumbling affirmatives and negatives together.

'Well—'

'Thought so,' said Strike, smugly.

'Given what might've happened to Margot, I wouldn't have kicked off the conversation with cheery decapitation jokes.'

'She's lived with it for forty years,' said Strike. 'People who live with something that massive stop being able to see it. It's the backdrop of their lives. It's only glaringly obvious to everyone else.'

It started to rain again as they left the car park: a fine veil laying itself swiftly over the windscreen.

'OK, I'm prejudiced,' Robin admitted, switching on the wipers. 'Feeling a bit sensitive about second wives right now.'

She drove on for a few moments before becoming aware that Strike was looking at her again.

'What?' she asked, for a third time.

'Why're you sensitive about second wives?'

'Because – oh, I didn't tell you, did I? I told Morris.' She'd tried not to think, since, about her drunken Boxing Day spent texting, of the small amount of comfort she had derived from it, or the immense load of discomfort. 'Matthew and Sarah Shadlock are together officially now. She left her fiancé for him.'

'Shit,' said Strike, still watching her profile. 'No, you didn't tell me.'

But he mentally docketed the fact that she'd told Morris, which didn't fit with the idea that he'd formed of Robin and Morris's relationship. From what Barclay had told him about Morris's challenges to Robin's authority, and from Robin's generally lukewarm comments on his new hire, he'd assumed that Morris's undoubted sexual interest in Robin had fizzled out for lack of a return. And yet she'd told Morris this painful bit of personal information, and not told him.

As they drove in silence towards Church Road, he wondered what had been going on in London while he had been in Cornwall. Morris was a good-looking man and he, like Robin, was divorcing. Strike wondered why he hadn't previously considered the implications of this obvious piece of symmetry. Comparing notes on lawyers, on difficult exes, on the mechanics of splitting two lives: they'd have plenty to talk about, plenty of opportunities for mutual sympathy.

'Straight up here,' he said, and they drove in silence across the Royal Paddocks, between high, straight red walls.

'Nice street,' commented Robin, twenty minutes after they'd left Hampton Court Palace, as she turned the Land Rover into a road that might have been deep in countryside. To their left was dense woodland, to the right, several large, detached houses that stood back from the road behind high hedges.

'It's that one,' said Strike, pointing at a particularly sprawling house with many pointed, half-timbered gables. The double gates stood open, as did the front door. They turned into the drive and parked behind the blue Mazda3.

As soon as Robin switched off the engine, they heard shouting coming from inside the house: a male voice, intemperate and high pitched. Anna Phipps's wife, Kim, tall, blonde and wearing jeans and a shirt as before, came striding out of the house towards them, her expression tense.

'Big scenes,' she said, as Strike and Robin got out of the car into the mist of rain.

'Would you like us to wait—?' Robin began.

'No,' Kim said, 'he's determined to see you. Come in.'

They walked across the gravel and entered Broom House. Somewhere inside, male and female voices continued to shout.

Every house has its own deep ingrained smell, and this one was redolent of sandalwood and a not entirely unpleasant fustiness. Kim led them through a long, large-windowed hall that seemed frozen in the mid-twentieth century. There were brass light fittings, water-colours and an old rug on polished floorboards. With a sudden frisson, Robin thought that Margot Bamborough had once walked this very floor, her metallic rose perfume mingling with the scents of polish and old carpet.

As they approached the door of the drawing room, the argument taking place inside became suddenly comprehensible.

'—and if I'm to be talked about,' a man was shouting, 'I should have right of reply – my family deciding to investigate me behind my back, charming, *charming*, it really is—'

'Nobody's investigating *you*, for God's sake!' they heard Anna say. 'Bill Talbot was incompetent—'

'Oh, was he really? Were you there? Did you know him?'

'I didn't *have* to be there, Dad—'

Kim opened the door. Strike and Robin followed Kim inside.

It was like coming upon a tableau. The three people standing inside froze at their entrance. Cynthia's thin fingers were pressed to her mouth. Anna stood facing her father across a small antique table.

The romantic-looking poet of 1974 was no more. Roy Phipps's remaining hair was short, grey and clung only around his ears and the back of his head. In his knitted sweater vest, with his high, domed, shining pate and his wild eyes, slightly sunken in a blotchy face, he'd now be better suited to the role of mad scientist.

So furious did Roy Phipps look, that Robin quite expected him to start shouting at the newcomers, too. However, the haematologist's demeanour changed when his eyes met Strike's. Whether this was a tribute to the detective's bulk, or to the aura of gravity and calm he managed to project in highly charged situations, Robin couldn't tell, but she thought she saw Roy decide against yelling. After a brief hesitation, the doctor accepted Strike's proffered hand, and as the two men shook, Robin wondered how aware men were of the power dynamics that played out between them, while women stood watching.

'Dr Phipps,' said Strike.

Roy appeared to have found the gear change between intemperate rage and polite greeting a difficult one, and his immediate response was slightly incoherent.

'So you're – you're the detective, are you?' he said. Bluish-red blotches lingered in his pale cheeks.

'Cormoran Strike – and this is my partner, Robin Ellacott.'

Robin stepped forwards.

'How d'you do?' Roy said stiffly, shaking her hand, too. His was hot and dry.

'Shall I make coffee?' said Cynthia, in a half-whisper.

'Yes – no, why not,' said Roy, his ill-temper clearly jockeying with the nervousness that seemed to increase while Strike stood, large and unmoving, watching him. 'Sit, sit,' he said, pointing Strike to a sofa, at right angles to another.

Cynthia hurried out of the room to make coffee, and Strike and Robin sat where they'd been instructed.

'Going to help Cyn,' muttered Anna and she hurried out of the room, and Kim, after a moment's hesitation, followed her, leaving Strike and Robin alone with Roy. The doctor settled himself into a high-backed velvet armchair and glared around him. He didn't look well. The flush of temper receded, leaving him looking wan. His socks had bunched up around his skinny ankles.

There ensued one of the most uncomfortable silences Robin had ever endured. Mainly to avoid looking at Roy, she allowed her eyes to roam around the large room, which was as old fashioned as the hall. A grand piano stood in the corner. More large windows looked out onto an enormous garden, where a long rectangular fish pond lay just beyond a paved area, at the far end of which lay a covered, temple-like stone structure where people could either sit and watch the koi carp, now barely visible beneath the rain-flecked surface of the water, or look out over the sweeping lawn, with its mature trees and well-tended flower-beds.

An abundance of leather-bound books and bronzes of antique subjects filled bookcases and cabinets. A tambour frame stood between the sofas, on which a very beautiful piece of embroidery was being worked in silks. The design was Japanese influenced, of two koi swimming in opposite directions. Robin was debating whether to pass polite comment on it, and to ask whether Cynthia was responsible, when Strike spoke.

'Who was the classicist?'

'What?' said Roy. 'Oh. My father.'

His crazy-looking eyes roamed over the various small bronzes and marbles dotted around the room. 'Took a first in Classics at Cambridge.'

'Ah,' said Strike, and the glacial silence resumed.

A squall of wind threw more rain at the window. Robin was relieved to hear the tinkling of teaspoons and the footsteps of the three returning women.

Cynthia, who re-entered the room first, set a tea tray down on the antique table standing between the sofas. It rocked a little with the weight. Anna added a large cake on a stand.

Anna and Kim sat down side by side on the free sofa, and when Cynthia had drawn up spindly side tables to hold everyone's tea, and cut slices of cake for those who wanted some, she sat herself down beside her stepdaughter–in–law, looking scared.

'Well,' said Roy at last, addressing Strike. 'I'd be interested to hear what you think your chances are of finding out what the Metropolitan Police has been unable to discover in four decades.'

Robin was sure Roy had been planning this aggressive opening during the long and painful silence.

'Fairly small,' said Strike matter-of-factly, once he'd swallowed a large piece of the cake Cynthia had given him, 'though we've got a new alleged sighting of your first wife I wanted to discuss with you.'

Roy looked taken aback.

'*Alleged* sighting,' Strike emphasised, setting down his plate and reaching inside his jacket for his notebook. 'But obviously ... Excellent cake, Mrs Phipps,' he told Cynthia.

'Oh, thank you,' she said in a small voice. 'Coffee and walnut was Anna's favourite when she was little – wasn't it, love?' she said, but Anna's only response was a tense smile.

'We heard about it from one of your wife's ex-colleagues, Janice Beattie.'

Roy shook his head and shrugged impatiently, to convey non-recognition of the names.

'She was the practice nurse at the St John's surgery,' said Strike.

'Oh,' said Roy. 'Yes. I think she came here once, for a barbecue. She seemed quite a decent woman ... Disaster, that afternoon.

Bloody disaster. Those children were atrocious – d'you remember?' he shot at Cynthia.

'Yes,' said Cynthia quickly, 'no, there was one boy who was really—'

'Spiked the punch,' barked Roy. 'Vodka. Someone was sick.'

'Gloria,' said Cynthia.

'I don't remember all their names,' said Roy, with an impatient wave of the hand. 'Sick all over the downstairs bathroom. Disgusting.'

'This boy would've been Carl Oakden?' asked Strike.

'That's him,' said Roy. 'We found the vodka bottle empty, later, hidden in a shed. He'd sneaked into the house and taken it out of the drinks cabinet.'

'Yes,' said Cynthia, 'and then he smashed—'

'Crystal bowl of my mother's and half a dozen glasses. Hit a cricket ball right across the barbecue area. The nurse cleaned it all up for me, because – decent of her. She knew I couldn't – broken glass,' said Roy, with an impatient gesture.

'On the bright side,' said Cynthia, with the ghost of a laugh, 'he'd smashed the punch, so nobody else got sick.'

'That bowl was art deco,' said Roy, unsmiling. 'Bloody disaster, the whole thing. I said to Margot,' and he paused for a second after saying the name, and Robin wondered when he'd last spoken it, '"I don't know what you think this is going to achieve." Because *he* didn't come, the one she was trying to conciliate – the doctor she didn't get on with, what was his—?'

'Joseph Brenner,' said Robin.

'Brenner, exactly. *He'd* refused the invitation, so what was the point? But no, we still had to give up our Saturday to entertain this motley collection of people, and our reward was to have our drink stolen and our possessions smashed.'

Roy's fists lay on the arms of his chair. He uncoiled the long fingers for a moment in a movement like a hermit crab unflexing its legs, then curled them tightly in upon themselves again.

'That same boy, Oakden, wrote a book about Margot later,' he said. 'Used a photograph from that damn barbecue to add credibility to the notion that he and his mother knew all about our private lives. So, yes,' said Roy coldly, '*not* one of Margot's better ideas.'

'Well, she was trying to make the practice work better together, wasn't she?' said Anna. 'You've never really needed to manage different personalities at work—'

'Oh, you know all about my work, too, do you, Anna?'

'Well, it wasn't the same as being a GP, was it?' said Anna. 'You were lecturing, doing research, you didn't have to manage cleaners and receptionists and a whole bunch of non-medics.'

'They *were* quite badly behaved, Anna,' said Cynthia, hurrying loyally to support Roy. 'No, they really were. I never told – I didn't want to cause trouble – but one of the women sneaked upstairs into your mum and dad's bedroom.'

'What?' barked Roy.

'Yes,' said Cynthia, nervously. 'No, I went upstairs to change Anna's nappy and I heard movement in there. I walked in and she was looking at Margot's clothes in the wardrobe.'

'Who was this?' asked Strike.

'The blonde one. The receptionist who wasn't Gloria.'

'Irene,' said Strike. 'Did she know you'd seen her?'

'Oh yes. I walked in, holding Anna.'

'What did she say when she saw you?' asked Robin.

'Well, she was a bit embarrassed,' said Cynthia. 'You would be, wouldn't you? She laughed and said "just being nosy" and walked back out past me.'

'Good God,' said Roy Phipps, shaking his head. 'Who *hired* these people?'

'Was she really just looking?' Robin asked Cynthia. 'Or d'you think she'd gone in there to—'

'Oh, I don't think she'd *taken* anything,' said Cynthia. 'And you never – Margot never missed anything, did she?' she asked Roy.

'No, but you should still have told me this at the time,' said Roy crossly.

'I didn't want to cause trouble. You were already . . . well, it was a stressful day, wasn't it?'

'About this alleged sighting,' said Strike, and he told the family the third-hand tale of Charlie Ramage, who claimed to have seen Margot wandering among graves in a churchyard in Leamington Spa.

417

'. . . and Robin's now spoken to Ramage's widow, who confirmed the basic story, though she couldn't swear to it that it was Margot he thought he'd seen, and not another missing woman. The sighting doesn't seem to have been passed to the police, so I wanted to ask whether Margot had any connection with Leamington Spa that you know of?'

'None,' said Roy, and Cynthia shook her head.

Strike made a note.

'Thank you. While we're on the subject of sightings,' said Strike, 'I wonder whether we could run through the rest of the list?'

Robin thought she knew what Strike was up to. However uncomfortable the idea that Margot was still alive might be for the people in this room, Strike wanted to start the interview from a standpoint that didn't presume murder.

'The woman at the service station in Birmingham, the mother in Brighton, the dog walker down in Eastbourne,' Roy rattled off, before Strike could speak. 'Why would she have been out and about, driving cars and walking dogs? If she'd disappeared voluntarily, she clearly didn't want to be found. The same goes for wandering around graveyards.'

'True,' said Strike. 'But there was one sighting—'

'Warwick,' said Roy. 'Yes.'

A look passed between husband and wife. Strike waited. Roy set down his cup and saucer on the table in front of him and looked up at his daughter.

'You're quite sure you want to do this, Anna, are you?' he asked, looking at his silent daughter. 'Quite, *quite* sure?'

'What d'you mean?' she snapped back. 'What d'you think I hired detectives for? Fun?'

'All right, then,' said Roy, 'all right. That sighting caught . . . caught my attention, because my wife's ex-boyfriend, a man called Paul Satchwell, hailed originally from Warwick. This was a man she'd . . . reconnected with, before she disappeared.'

'Oh for God's sake,' said Anna, with a tight little laugh, 'did you *honestly* think I don't know about Paul Satchwell? Of course I do!' Kim reached out and put a hand on her wife's leg, whether in comfort or warning, it was hard to tell. 'Have you never heard of the internet, Dad, or press archives? I've seen Satchwell's ridiculous photograph, with all his chest hair and his medallions, and I know my mother went for a drink with him three weeks before she vanished! But it was only one drink—'

'Oh, was it?' said Roy nastily. 'Thanks for your reassurance, Anna. Thanks for your expert knowledge. How marvellous to be all-knowing—'

'Roy,' whispered Cynthia.

'What are you saying, that it was more than a drink?' said Anna, looking shaken. 'No, it wasn't, that's a horrible thing to say! Oonagh says—'

'Oh, right, yes, I see!' said Roy loudly, his sunken cheeks turning purple as his hands gripped the arms of his chair, '*Oonagh* says, does she? Everything is explained!'

'What's explained?' demanded Anna.

'This!' he shouted, pointing a trembling, rope-veined, swollen-knuckled hand at Strike and Robin. 'Oonagh Kennedy's behind it all, is she? I should have *known* I hadn't heard the last of her!'

'For God's sake, Roy,' said Kim loudly, 'that's a preposterous—'

'*Oonagh Kennedy wanted me arrested!*'

'Dad, that's simply not true!' said Anna, forcibly removing Kim's restraining hand from her leg. 'You've got a morbid fixation about Oonagh—'

'Badgering me to complain about Talbot—'

'Well, why the bloody hell *didn't* you?' said Anna loudly. 'The man was in the middle of a fully fledged breakdown!'

'Roy!' whimpered Cynthia again, as Roy leaned forwards to face his daughter across the too-small circular table, with its precariously balanced cake. Gesticulating wildly, his face purple, he shouted,

'Police swarming all over the house going through your mother's things – sniffer dogs out in the garden – they were looking for any reason to arrest me, and I should lodge a formal complaint against the man in charge? *How would that have looked?*'

'He was incompetent!'

'Were you there, Miss Omniscient? Did you know him?'

'Why did they replace him? Why does everything written about the case say he was incompetent? The truth is,' said Anna, stabbing the air between her and her father with a forefinger, 'you and Cyn loved Bill Talbot because he thought you were innocent from the off and—'

'*Thought* I was innocent?' bellowed Roy. 'Well, thank you, it's good to know that nothing's changed since you were thirteen years old—'

'Roy!' said Cynthia and Kim together.

'—and accused me of building the koi pond over the place I'd buried her!'

Anna burst into tears and fled the room, almost tripping over Strike's legs as she went. Suspecting there was about to be a mass exodus, he retracted his feet.

'When,' Kim said coldly to her father-in-law, 'is Anna going to be forgiven for things she said when she was a confused child, going through a dreadful time?'

'And *my* dreadful time is nothing, of course? Nothing!' shouted Roy, and as Strike expected, he, too, left the room at the fastest pace he could manage, which was a speedy hobble.

'Christ's sake,' muttered Kim, striding after Roy and Anna and almost colliding at the door with Cynthia, who'd jumped up to follow Roy.

The door swung shut. The rain pattered on the pond outside. Strike blew out his cheeks, exchanged looks with Robin, then picked up his plate and continued eating his cake.

'Starving,' he said thickly, in response to Robin's look. 'No lunch. And it's good cake.'

Distantly they heard shouting, and the slamming of another door.

'D'you think the interview's over?' muttered Robin.

'No,' said Strike, still eating. 'They'll be back.'

'Remind me about the sighting in Warwick,' said Robin.

She'd merely skimmed the list of sightings that Strike had emailed her. There hadn't seemed anything very interesting there.

'A woman asked for change in a pub, and the landlady thought she was Margot. A mature student came forward two days later to identify herself, but the landlady wasn't convinced that was who she'd seen. The police were, though.'

Strike took another large mouthful of cake before saying,

'I don't think there's anything in it. Well ...' he swallowed and shot a meaningful look at the sitting room door, 'there's a bit more *now*.'

Strike continued to eat cake, while Robin's eyes roamed the room and landed on an ormolu mantel clock of exceptional ugliness. With a glance at the door, she got up to examine it. A gilded classical goddess wearing a helmet sat on top of the ornate, heavy case.

'Pallas Athena,' said Strike, watching her, pointing his fork at the figure.

In the base of the clock was a drawer with a small brass handle. Remembering Cynthia's statement about Roy and Margot leaving notes for each other here, she pulled the drawer open. It was lined in red felt and empty.

'D'you think it's valuable?' she asked Strike, sliding the drawer shut.

'Dunno. Why?'

'Because why else would you keep it? It's horrible.'

There were two distinct kinds of taste on view in this room and they didn't harmonise, Robin thought, as she looked around, all the time out for the return of the family. The leather-bound copies of Ovid and Pliny, and the Victorian reproductions of classical statues, among them a pair of miniature Medici lions, a reproduction Vestal virgin and a Hermes poised on tiptoe on his heavy bronze base, presumably represented Roy's father's taste, whereas she suspected that his mother had chosen the insipid watercolour landscapes and botanical subjects, the dainty antique furniture and the chintz curtains.

Why had Roy never made a clean sweep and redecorated, Robin wondered. Reverence for his parents? Lack of imagination? Or had the sickly little boy, housebound no doubt for much of his childhood, developed an attachment to these objects that he couldn't put aside? He and Cynthia seemed to have made little impression on the room other than in adding a few family pictures to faded black and white photos featuring Roy's parents and Roy as a child. The only one to hold Robin's interest was a family group that looked as though it had been taken in the early nineties, when Roy had still had all his hair, and Cynthia's had been thick and wavy. Their two biological children, a boy and a girl, looked like Anna. Nobody would have guessed that she'd had a different mother.

Robin moved to the window. The surface of the long, formal koi pond outside, with its stone pavilion at the end, was now so densely rain-pocked that the vivid red, white and black shapes moving beneath the surface were barely discernible as fish. There was one particularly big creature, pearl white and black, that looked as though it might be over two feet long. The miniature pavilion would normally be reflected in the pond's smooth surface, but today it merely added an extra layer of diffuse grey to the far end of the pond. It had a strangely familiar design on the floor.

'Cormoran,' Robin said, at the exact moment Strike said,

'Look at this.'

Both turned. Strike, who'd finished his cake, was now standing beside one of Roy's father's statuettes, which Robin had overlooked. It was a foot-high bronze of a naked man with a cloth around his shoulders, holding a snake. Momentarily puzzled, Robin realised after a second or two why Strike was pointing at it.

'Oh ... the snaky invented sign Talbot gave Roy?'

'Precisely. This is Asclepius,' said Strike. 'Greek god of medicine. What've you found?'

'Look on the floor of the gazebo thing. Inlaid in the stone.'

He joined her at the window.

'Ah,' he said. 'You can see the beginnings of that in one of the photographs of Margot's barbecue. It was under construction.'

A cross of St John lay on the floor of the gazebo, inlaid in darker granite. 'Interesting choice of design,' said Strike.

'You know,' said Robin, turning to look at the room, 'people who're manic often think they're receiving supernatural messages. Things the sane would call coincidences.'

'I was thinking exactly that,' said Strike, turning to look at the figure of Pallas Athena, on top of the ugly mantel clock. 'To a man in Talbot's state of mental confusion, I'm guessing this room would've seemed crammed with astrological—'

Roy's voice sounded in the hall outside.

'—then don't blame me—'

The door opened and the family filed back inside.

'—if she hears things she doesn't like!' Roy finished, addressing Cynthia, who was immediately behind him, and looked scared. Roy's face was an unhealthy purple again, though the skin around his eyes remained a jaundiced yellow.

He seemed startled to see Strike and Robin standing at the window.

'Admiring your garden,' said Strike, as he and Robin returned to their sofa.

Roy grunted and took his seat again. He was breathing heavily.

'Apologies,' he said, after a moment or two. 'You aren't seeing the family at its best.'

'Very stressful for everyone,' said Strike, as Anna and Kim re-entered the room and resumed their seats on the sofa, where they sat holding hands. Cynthia perched herself beside them, watching Roy anxiously.

'I want to say something,' Roy told Strike. 'I want to make perfectly clear—'

'Oh for God's sake, I've had *one* phone call with her!' said Anna.

'I'd appreciate it, Anna,' said Roy, his chest labouring, 'if I could finish.'

Addressing Strike, he said,

'Oonagh Kennedy disliked me from the moment Margot and I first met. She was possessive towards Margot, and she also happened to have left the church, and she was one of those who had to make an enemy of everyone still in it. Moreover—'

'Dr Phipps,' interrupted Strike, who could foresee the afternoon degenerating into a long row about Oonagh Kennedy. 'I think you should know that when we interviewed Oonagh, she made it quite clear that the person she thought we should be concentrating our energies on is Paul Satchwell.'

For a second or two, Roy appeared unable to fully grasp what had just been said to him.

'*See?*' said Anna furiously. 'You just implied that there was more between my mother and Satchwell than one drink. What did you

423

mean? Or were you,' she said, and Robin heard the underlying hope, 'just angry and lashing out?'

'People who insist on opening cans of worms, Anna,' said Roy, 'shouldn't complain when they get covered in slime.'

'Well, go on then,' said Anna, 'spill your slime.'

'Anna,' whispered Cynthia, and was ignored.

'All right,' said Roy. 'All right, then.' He turned back to Strike and Robin. 'Early in our relationship, I saw a note of Satchwell's Margot had kept. "Dear Brunhilda" it said – it was his pet name for her. The Valkyrie, you know. Margot was tall. Fair.'

Roy paused and swallowed.

'Some three weeks before she disappeared, she came home and told me she'd run into Satchwell in the street and that they'd gone for an ... *innocent* drink.'

He cleared his throat. Cynthia poured him more tea.

'After she – after she'd disappeared, I had to go and collect her things from the St John's practice. Among them I found a small—'

He held his fingers some three inches apart.

'—wooden figure, a stylised Viking which she'd been keeping on her desk. Written in ink on this figure's base was "Brunhilda", with a small heart.'

Roy took a sip of coffee.

'I'd never seen it before. Of course, it's *possible* that Satchwell was carrying it around with him for years, on the off chance that he'd one day bump into Margot in the street. However, I concluded that they'd seen each other again and that he'd given her this – this token – on a subsequent occasion. All I know is, I'd never seen it before I collected her things from her surgery.'

Robin could tell that Anna wanted to suggest an alternative explanation, but it was very difficult to find a flaw in Roy's reasoning.

'Did you tell the police what you suspected?' Strike asked.

'Yes,' said Phipps, 'and I believe Satchwell claimed that there'd been no second meeting, that he'd given the figurine to Margot years before, when they were first involved. They couldn't prove it either way, of course. But *I'd* never seen it before.'

Robin wondered which would be more hurtful: finding out that a spouse had hidden a love token from a former partner, and taken to displaying it many years later, or that they'd been given it recently.

'Tell me,' Strike was saying, 'did Margot ever tell you anything about a "pillow dream"?'

'A what?' said Roy.

'Something Satchwell had told her, concerning a pillow?'

'I don't know what you're talking about,' said Roy, suspiciously.

'Did Inspector Talbot ever happen to mention that he believed Satchwell lied about his whereabouts on the eleventh of October?'

'No,' said Roy, now looking very surprised. 'I understood the police were entirely satisfied with his alibi.'

'We've found out,' Strike said, addressing Anna, 'that Talbot kept his own separate case notes – separate from the official police record, I mean. After appearing to rule out Aries, he went back to him and started digging for more information on him.'

'"Aries"?' repeated Anna, confused.

'Sorry,' said Strike, irritated by his own lapse into astrological speak. 'Talbot's breakdown manifested itself as a belief he could solve the case by occult means. He started using tarot cards and looking at horoscopes. He referred to everyone connected with the case by their star signs. Satchwell was born under the sign of Aries, so that's what he's called in Talbot's private notes.'

There was a brief silence, and then Kim said,

'Jesus wept.'

'Astrology?' said Roy, apparently confounded.

'You *see*, Dad?' said Anna, thumping her knee with her fist. 'If Lawson had taken over earlier—'

'Lawson was a fool,' said Roy, who nevertheless looked shaken. 'An idiot! He was more interested in proving that Talbot had been inept than in finding out what happened to Margot. He insisted on going back over *everything*. He wanted to personally interview the doctors who'd treated me for the bleed on my knee, even though they'd given signed statements. He went back to my bank to check my accounts, in case I'd paid someone to kill your mother. He put pressure . . .'

He stopped and coughed, thumping his chest. Cynthia began to rise off the sofa, but Roy indicated with an angry gesture that she should stay put.

'. . . put pressure on Cynthia, trying to get her to admit she'd lied about me being in bed all that day, but he never found out a shred of new information about what had happened to your mother. He was a jobsworth, a bullying, unimaginative jobsworth whose priority wasn't finding *her*, it was proving that Talbot messed up. Bill Talbot may have been . . . he clearly *was*,' Roy added, with a furious glance at Strike, 'unwell, but the simple fact remains: nobody's ever found a better explanation than Creed, have they?'

And with the mention of Creed, the faces of the three women on the sofa fell. His very name seemed to conjure a kind of black hole in the room, into which living women had disappeared, never to be seen again; a manifestation of almost supernatural evil. There was a finality in the very mention of him: the monster, now locked away for life, untouchable, unreachable, like the women locked up and tortured in his basement. And Robin's thoughts darted guiltily to the email she had now written, and sent, without telling Strike what she'd done, because she was afraid he might not approve.

'Do any of you know,' Roy asked abruptly, 'who Kara Wolfson and Louise Tucker were?'

'Yes,' said Robin, before Strike could answer. 'Louise was a teen-age runaway and Kara was a nightclub hostess. Creed was suspected of killing both of them, but there was no proof.'

'Exactly,' said Roy, throwing her the kind of look he might once have given a medical student who had made a correct diagnosis. 'Well, in 1978 I met up with Kara's brother and Louise's father.'

'I never knew you did that!' said Anna, looking shocked.

'Of course not. You were five years old,' snapped Roy. He turned back to Strike and Robin. 'Louise's father had made his own study of Creed's life. He'd gone to every place Creed had ever lived or worked and interviewed as many people who'd admit to knowing him. He was petitioning Merlyn-Rees, the then Home Secretary, to let him go and dig in as many of these places as possible.

'The man was half-insane,' said Roy. 'I saw then what living with something like this could do to you. The obsession had taken over his entire life. He wanted buildings dismantled, walls taken down, foundations exposed. Fields where Creed might once have walked, dug up. Streams dragged, which some schoolboy friend said Creed might have once gone fishing in. Tucker was shaking as he talked, trying to get me and Wolfson, who was a lorry driver, to join him in a TV campaign. We were to chain ourselves to the railings outside Downing Street, get ourselves on the news ... Tucker's marriage had split up. He seemed on bad terms with his living children. Creed had become his whole life.'

'And you didn't want to help?' asked Anna.

'If,' said Roy quietly, 'he'd had actual evidence – any solid clue that linked Margot and Creed—'

'I've read you thought one of the necklaces in the basement might've been—'

'If you will get your information from sensationalist books, Anna—'

'Because you've always made it so *easy* for me to talk to you about my mother,' said Anna. 'Haven't you?'

'Anna,' whispered Cynthia again.

'The locket they found in Creed's basement wasn't Margot's, and I should know, because I gave it to her,' said Roy. His lips trembled, and he pressed them together.

'Just a couple more questions, if you wouldn't mind,' said Strike, before Anna could say anything else. He was determined to avert further conflict if he could. 'Could we talk for a moment about Wilma, the cleaner who worked at the practice and did housework for you here, as well?'

'It was all Margot's idea, hiring her, but she wasn't very good,' said Roy. 'The woman was having some personal difficulties and Margot thought the solution was more money. After Margot disappeared, she walked out. Never turned up again. No loss. I heard afterwards she'd been sacked from the practice. Pilfering, I heard.'

'Wilma told police—'

'That there was blood on the carpet upstairs, the day Margot went missing,' interrupted Roy. From Anna and Kim's startled expressions, Robin deduced that this was entirely new information to them.

'Yes,' said Strike.

'It was menstrual,' said Roy coldly. 'Margot's period had started overnight. There were sanitary wrappers in the bathroom, my mother told me. Wilma sponged the carpet clean. This was in the spare room, at the opposite end of the house to the marital bedroom. Margot and I were sleeping apart at that time, because of,' there was a slight hesitation, 'my injury.'

'Wilma also said that she thought she'd seen you—'

'Walking across the garden,' said Roy. 'It was a lie. If she saw anyone, it would have been one of the stonemasons. We were finishing the gazebo at that time,' he said, pointing towards the stone folly at the end of the fishpond.

Strike made a note and turned over a page in his notebook.

'Can either of you remember Margot talking about a man called Niccolo Ricci? He was a patient at the St John's practice.'

Both Roy and Cynthia shook their heads.

'What about a patient called Steven Douthwaite?'

'No,' said Roy. 'But we heard about him afterwards, from the press.'

'Someone at the barbecue mentioned that Margot had been sent chocolates by a patient,' said Cynthia. 'That was him, wasn't it?'

'We think so. She never talked about Douthwaite, then? Never mentioned him showing an inappropriate interest in her, or told you he was gay?'

'No,' said Roy again. 'There's such a thing as patient confidentiality, you know.'

'This might seem an odd question,' said Strike, 'but did Margot have any scars? Specifically, on her ribcage?'

'No,' said Roy, unsettled. 'Why are you asking that?'

'To exclude one possibility,' said Strike, and before they could ask for further details, he said,

'Did Margot ever tell you she'd received threatening notes?'

'Yes,' said Roy. 'Well, not notes in the plural. She told me she'd got *one.*'

'She did?' said Strike, looking up.

'Yes. It accused her of encouraging young women into promiscuity and sin.'

'Did it threaten her?'

'I don't know,' said Roy. 'I never saw it.'

'She didn't bring it home?'

'No,' said Roy shortly. He hesitated, then said, 'We had a row about it.'

'Really?'

'Yes. There can be serious consequences,' said Roy, turning redder, '*societal* consequences, when you start enabling things that don't take place in nature—'

'Are you worried she told some girl it was OK to be gay?' asked Anna, and yet again Cynthia whispered, '*Anna!*'

'I'm talking,' said Roy, his face congested, 'about giving reckless advice that might lead to marital breakdown. I'm talking about facilitating promiscuity, behind the backs of parents. Some very angry man had sent her that note, and she never seemed to have considered – considered—'

Roy's face worked. For a moment, it looked as though he was going to shout, but then, most unexpectedly, he burst into noisy tears.

His wife, daughter and daughter-in-law sat, stunned, in a row on the sofa; nobody, even Cynthia, went to him. Roy was suddenly crying in great heaving gulps, tears streaming down over his sunken cheeks, trying and failing to master himself, and finally speaking through the sobs.

'She – never seemed – to remember – that I couldn't – protect her – couldn't – do anything – if somebody tried – to hurt – because I'm a useless – bleeder . . . *useless* . . . *bloody* . . . *bleeder* . . .'

'Oh *Dad*,' whispered Anna, horrified, and she slid off the sofa and walked to her father on her knees. She tried to place her hands on his leg, but he batted her consoling hands away, shaking his head, still crying.

'No – no – I don't deserve it – you don't know everything – you don't know—'

'What don't I know?' she said, looking scared. 'Dad, I know more than you think. I know about the abortion—'

'There was never – never – *never* an abortion!' said Roy, gulping and sobbing. 'That was the one – one thing Oonagh Kennedy and

I – we both knew – she'd *never* – *never* – not after you! She told me – Margot told me – after she had you – changed her views completely. *Completely!*'

'Then what don't I know?' whispered Anna.

'I was – I was c- cruel to her!' wailed Roy. 'I was! I made things difficult! Showed no interest in her work. I drove her away! She was going to l- leave me . . . I know what happened. I know. I've always known. The day before – before she went – she left a message – in the clock – silly – thing we used to – and the note said – *Please t- talk to me* . . .'

Roy's sobs overtook him. As Cynthia got up and went to kneel on Roy's other side, Anna reached for her father's hand, and this time, he let her hold it. Clinging to his daughter, he said,

'I was waiting – for an apology. For going to drink – with Satchwell. And because she hadn't – written an apology – I didn't t- talk to her. And the next day—'

'I know what happened. She liked to walk. If she was upset – long walks. She forgot about Oonagh – went for a walk – trying to decide what to do – leave me – because I'd made her – so – so sad. She wasn't – paying attention – and Creed – and Creed – must have . . .'

Still holding his hand, Anna slid her other arm around her father's shaking shoulders and drew her to him. He cried inconsolably, clinging to her. Strike and Robin both pretended an interest in the flowered rug.

'Roy,' said Kim gently, at last. 'Nobody in this room hasn't said or done things they don't bitterly regret. Not one of us.'

Strike, who'd got far more out of Roy Phipps than he'd expected, thought it was time to draw the interview to a close. Phipps was in such a state of distress that it felt inhumane to press him further. When Roy's sobs had subsided a little, Strike said formally,

'I want to thank you very much for talking to us, and for the tea. We'll get out of your hair.'

He and Robin got to their feet. Roy remained entangled with his wife and daughter. Kim stood up to show them out.

'*Well,*' Kim said quietly, as they approached the front door, 'I have to tell you, that was . . . well, close to a miracle. He's never talked about Margot like that, *ever*. Even if you don't find out anything else ... thank you. That was ... healing.'

The rain had ceased and the sun had come out. A double rainbow lay over the woods opposite the house. Strike and Robin stepped outside, into clean fresh air.

'Could I ask you one last thing?' said Strike, turning back to Kim who stood in the doorway.

'Yes, of course.'

'It's about that summer house thing in the garden, beside the koi pond. I wondered why it's got a cross of St John on the floor,' said Strike.

'*Oh*,' said Kim. 'Margot chose the design. Yes, Cynthia told me, ages ago. Margot had just got the job at St John's — and funnily enough, this area's got a connection to the Knights Hospitaller, too—'

'Yes,' said Robin. 'I read about that, at Hampton Court.'

'So, she thought it would be a nice allusion to the two things ... You know, now you mention it, I'm surprised nobody ever changed it. Every other trace of Margot's gone from the house.'

'Expensive, though,' said Strike, 'to remove slabs of granite.'

'Yes,' said Kim, her smile fading a little. 'I suppose it would be.'

37

Spring-headed Hydres, and sea-shouldring Whales,
Great whirlpooles, which all fishes make to flee,
Bright Scolopendraes, arm'd with siluer scales
Mighty Monoceros, with immeasured tayles . . .
The dreadfull Fish, that hath deseru'd the name
Of Death . . .

Edmund Spenser
The Faerie Queene

Rain fell almost ceaselessly into February. On the fifth, the most savage storm yet hit the south. Thousands of homes lost power, part of the sea wall supporting the London-South West railway line collapsed, swathes of farmland disappeared under flood water, roads became rivers and the nightly news featured fields turned to seas of grey water and houses waist-deep in mud. The Prime Minister promised financial assistance, the emergency services scrambled to help the stranded, and high on her hill above the flooded St Mawes, Joan was deprived of a promised visit from Strike and Lucy, because they were unable to reach her either by road or train.

Strike sublimated the guilt he felt for not heading to Cornwall before the weather rendered the journey impossible by working long hours and skimping on sleep. Masochistically, he chose to work back-to-back shifts, so that Barclay and Hutchins could take some of the leave due to them because of his previous trips to see Joan. In consequence, it was Strike, not Hutchins, who was sitting in his BMW in the everlasting rain outside Elinor Dean's house in Stoke

432

Newington on Wednesday evening the following week, and Strike who saw a man in a tracksuit knock on her door and be admitted.

Strike waited all night for the man to reappear. Finally, at six in the morning, he emerged onto the still dark street with his hand clamped over his lower face. Strike, who was watching him through night vision glasses, caught a glimpse of Elinor Dean in a cosy quilted dressing gown, waving him off. The tracksuited man hurried back to his Citroën with his right hand still concealing his mouth and set off in a southerly direction.

Strike tailed the Citroën until they reached Risinghill Street in Pentonville, where Strike's target parked and entered a modern, red-brick block of flats, both hands now in his pockets and nothing unusual about his mouth as far as the detective could see. Strike waited until the man was safely inside, took a note of which window showed a light five minutes later, then drove away, parking shortly afterwards in White Lion Street.

Early as it was, people were already heading off to work, umbrellas angled against the continuing downpour. Strike wound down the car window, because even he, inveterate smoker though he was, wasn't enjoying the smell of his car after a night's surveillance. Then, though his tongue ached from too much smoking, he lit up again and phoned Saul Morris.

'All right, boss?'

Strike, who didn't particularly like Morris calling him 'boss', but couldn't think of any way to ask him to stop without sounding like a dickhead, said,

'I want you to switch targets. Forget Shifty today; I've just followed a new guy who spent the night at Elinor Dean's.' He gave Morris the address. 'He's second floor, flat on the far left as you're looking at the building. Fortyish, greying hair, bit of a paunch. See what you can find out about him – chat up the neighbours, find out where he works and have a dig around online, see if you can find out what his interests are. I've got a hunch he and SB are visiting that woman for the same reason.'

'See, this is why you're the head honcho. You take over for one night and crack the case.'

Strike wished Morris would stop brown-nosing him, too. When he'd hung up, he sat smoking for a while, while the wind nipped at his exposed flesh, and rain hit his face in what felt like icy needle pricks. Then, after checking the time to make sure his early-rising uncle would be awake, he phoned Ted.

'All right, boy?' said his uncle, over the crackling phone line.

'Fine. How are you?'

'Oh, I'm fine,' said Ted. 'Just having some breakfast. Joanie's still asleep.'

'How is she?'

'No change. Bearing up.'

'What about food, have you got enough?'

'We're fine for food, don't you worry about that,' said Ted. 'Little Dave Polworth come over yesterday with enough to feed us for a week.'

'How the hell did he get to you?' asked Strike, who knew that a large chunk of the land between his aunt and uncle and Polworth's house was under several feet of water.

'Rowed part of the way,' said Ted, sounding amused. 'He made it sound like one of his Ironman competitions. All covered in oilskins he was when he got here. Big backpack full of shopping. He's all right, that Polworth.'

'Yeah, he is,' said Strike, momentarily closing his eyes. It oughtn't to be Polworth looking after his aunt and uncle. It should be him. He ought to have left earlier, knowing the weather was looking bad, but for months now he'd been juggling guilt about his aunt and uncle with the guilt he felt about the load he was putting on his subcontractors, and Robin especially. 'Ted, I'll be there as soon as they put the trains back on.'

'Aye, I know you will, lad,' said Ted. 'Don't worry about us. I won't take you to her, because she needs her rest, but I'll tell her you called. She'll be chuffed.'

Tired, hungry and wondering where he might get some breakfast, Strike typed out a text to Dave Polworth, his cigarette jammed between his teeth, using the nickname he'd had for Polworth ever since the latter had got himself bitten by a shark at the age of eighteen.

Ted's just told me what you did yesterday. I'll never be able to repay all this, Chum. Thank you.

He flicked his cigarette end out of the car, wound up the window and had just turned on the engine when his mobile buzzed. Expecting to see a response from Polworth, doubtless asking him when he'd turned into such a poof or a big girl (Polworth's language being always as far from politically correct as you could get), he looked down at the screen, already smiling in anticipation, and read:

Dad wants to call you. When would be a good time?

Strike read the text twice before understanding that it was from Al. At first, he felt only blank surprise. Then anger and profound resentment rose like vomit.

'Fuck off,' he told his phone loudly.

He turned out of the side street and drove away, jaw clenched, wondering why he should be hounded by Rokeby now, of all times in his life, when he was so worried about relatives who'd cared about him when there'd been no kudos to be gained from the association. The time for amends had passed; the damage was irreparable; blood wasn't thicker than fucking water. Consumed by thoughts of frail Joan, with whom he shared no shred of DNA, marooned in her house on the hill amid floods, anger and guilt writhed inside him.

A matter of minutes later, he realised he was driving through Clerkenwell. Spotting an open café on St John Street he parked, then headed through the rain into warmth and light, where he ordered himself an egg and tomato sandwich. Choosing a table by the window, he sat down facing the street, eye to eye with his own unshaven and stony-faced reflection in the rain-studded window.

Hangovers apart, Strike rarely got headaches, but something resembling one was starting to build on the left side of his skull. He ate his sandwich, telling himself firmly that food was making him feel better. Then, after ordering a second mug of tea, he pulled out his mobile again and typed out a response to Al, with the dual objective

435

of shutting down Rokeby once and for all, and of concealing from both his half-brother and his father how much their persistence was disturbing his peace.

I'm not interested. It's too late. I don't want to fall out with you, but take this 'no' as final.

He sent the text and then cast around immediately for something else to occupy his tired mind. The shops opposite were ablaze with red and pink: February the fourteenth was almost here. It now occurred to him that he hadn't heard from Charlotte since he'd ignored her text at Christmas. Would she send him a message on Valentine's Day? Her desire for contact seemed to be triggered by special occasions and anniversaries.

Automatically, without considering what he was doing, but with the same desire for comfort that had pushed him into this café, Strike pulled his phone out of his pocket again and called Robin, but the number was engaged. Shoving the mobile back in his pocket, stressed, anxious and craving action, he told himself he should make use of being in Clerkenwell, now he was here.

This café was only a short walk from the old St John's surgery. How many of these passers-by, he wondered, had lived in the area forty years previously? The hunched old woman in her raincoat with her tartan shopping trolley? The grey-whiskered man trying to flag down a cab? Perhaps the ageing Sikh man in his turban, texting as he walked? Had any of them consulted Margot Bamborough? Could any of them remember a dirty, bearded man called something like Applethorpe, who'd roamed these very streets, insisting to strangers that he'd killed the doctor?

Strike's absent gaze fell on a man walking with a strange, rolling gait on the opposite side of the road. His fine, mousy hair was rain-soaked and plastered to his head. He had neither coat nor umbrella, but wore a sweatshirt with a picture of Sonic the Hedgehog on the front. The lack of coat, the slightly lumbering walk, the wide, childlike stare, the slightly gaping mouth, the stoic acceptance of becoming slowly drenched to the skin: all suggested some kind of cognitive impairment. The man passed out of Strike's line of vision as the detective's mobile rang.

'Hi. Did you just call me?' said Robin, and Strike felt a certain release of tension, and decided the tea was definitely soothing his head.

'I did, yeah. Just for an update.'

He told her the story of the tracksuited man who'd visited Elinor Dean overnight.

'And he was covering up his mouth when he left? That's weird.'

'I know. There's definitely something odd going on in that house. I've asked Morris to dig a bit on the new bloke.'

'Pentonville's right beside Clerkenwell,' said Robin.

'Which is where I am right now. Café on St John Street. I th – think,' a yawn overtook Strike, 'sorry – I think, seeing as I'm in the area, I might have another dig around on the late Applethorpe. Try and find someone who remembers the family, or knows what might've happened to them.'

'How're you going to do that?'

'Walk the area,' said Strike, and he became conscious of his aching knee even as he said it, 'have an ask around in any businesses that look long-established. I kn – know,' he yawned again, 'it's a long shot, but we haven't got anyone else claiming to have killed Margot.'

'Aren't you knackered?'

'Been worse. Where are you right now?'

'Office,' said Robin, 'and I've got a bit of Bamborough news, if you've got time.'

'Go on,' said Strike, happy to postpone the moment when he had to go back out into the rain.

'Well, firstly, I've had an email from Gloria Conti's husband. You know, the receptionist who was the last to see Margot? It's short. *"Dear Mr Ellacott—"'*

'Mister?'

'"Robin" often confuses people. *"I write for my wife, who is been very afflicted by your communications. She has not proofs or information that concern Margot Bamborough and it is not convenient that you contact her at my offices. Our family is private and desires to remain like that. I would*

*like your assurances that you will not contact my wife another time. Yours
sincerely, Hugo Jaubert."'*

'Interesting,' agreed Strike, scratching his unshaven chin. 'Why
isn't Gloria emailing back herself? Too afflicted?'

'I wonder why she's so affli – upset, I mean? Maybe,' Robin said,
answering her own question, 'because I contacted her through
her husband's office? But I tried through Facebook and she
wouldn't answer.'

'You know, I think it might be worth getting Anna to contact
Gloria. Margot's daughter might tug at her heartstrings better than we
can. Why don't you draft another request and send it over to Anna,
see whether she'd be comfortable letting you put her name to it?'

'Good thinking,' said Robin, and he heard her scribbling a note.
'Anyway, in better news, when you called me just now, I was talking
to Wilma Bayliss's second-oldest daughter, Maya. She's the deputy
headmistress. I think I'm close to persuading her to talk to us. She's
worried about her older sister's reaction, but I'm hopeful.'

'Great,' said Strike, 'I'd like to hear more about Wilma.'

'And there's one other thing,' said Robin. 'Only, you might think
this is a bit of a long shot.'

'I've just told you I'm about to go door to door asking about a
dead nutter who definitely wasn't called Applethorpe,' said Strike,
and Robin laughed.

'OK, well, I was back online last night, having another look
for Steve Douthwaite, and I found this old "Memories of Butlin's"
website, where ex-Redcoats chat to each other and reminisce and
organise reunions and stuff – you know the kind of thing. Anyway,
I couldn't find any mention of Douthwaite, or Jacks, as he was calling himself in Clacton-on-Sea, but I did find – I know it's probably
totally irrelevant,' she said, 'and I don't know whether you remember,
but a girl called Julie Wilkes was quoted in *Whatever Happened to
Margot Bamborough?* She said she was shocked that Stevie Jacks hadn't
told his friends that he'd been caught up in a missing woman case.'

'Yeah, I remember,' said Strike.

'Well . . . that girl drowned,' said Robin. 'Drowned at the holiday
camp at the end of the 1985 holiday season. Her body was found one

morning in the camp swimming pool. A group of them were discussing her death on the message boards on the website. They think she got drunk, slipped, hit her head and slid into the pool.

'Maybe it's horrible luck,' said Robin, 'but women do have a habit of dying in Douthwaite's vicinity, didn't they? His married girlfriend kills herself, his doctor goes missing, and then there's this co-worker who drowns ... Everywhere he goes, unnatural death follows ... it's just odd.'

'Yeah, it is,' said Strike, frowning out at the rain. He was about to wonder aloud where Douthwaite had hidden himself, when Robin said in a slight rush,

'Listen, there's something else I wanted to ask you, but it's absolutely fine if the answer's no. My flatmate Max – you know he's an actor? Well, he's just been cast in a TV thing as an ex-soldier and he doesn't know anyone else to ask. He wondered whether you'd come over to dinner so he can ask you some questions.'

'Oh,' said Strike, surprised but not displeased. '... yeah, OK. When?'

'I know it's short notice, but would tomorrow suit you? He really needs it soon.'

'Yeah, that should be all right,' said Strike. He was holding himself ready to travel down to St Mawes as soon as it became practicable, but the sea wall looked unlikely to be repaired by the following day.

When Robin had hung up, Strike ordered a third mug of tea. He was procrastinating, and he knew why. If he was genuinely going to have a poke around Clerkenwell for anyone who remembered the dead man who claimed to have killed Margot Bamborough, it would help if he knew the man's real name, and as Janice Beattie was still in Dubai, his only recourse was Irene Hickson.

The rain was as heavy as ever. Minute to minute, he postponed the call to Irene, watching traffic moving through the rippling sheets of rain, pedestrians navigating the puddle-pocked street, and thinking about the long-ago death of a young Redcoat, who'd slipped, knocked her head and drowned in a swimming pool.

Water everywhere, Bill Talbot had written in his astrological notebook. It had taken Strike some effort to decipher that particular passage. He'd concluded that Talbot was referring to a cluster of water signs apparently connected with the death of the unknown Scorpio. Why, Strike asked himself now, sipping his tea, was Scorpio a water sign? Scorpions lived on land, in heat; could they even swim? He remembered the large fish sign Talbot had used in the notebook for Irene, which at one point he'd described as 'Cetus'. Picking up his mobile, Strike Googled the word.

The constellation Cetus, he read, known also as the whale, was named for a sea monster slain by Perseus when saving Andromeda from the sea god Poseidon. It resided in a region of the sky known as 'The Sea', due to the presence there of many other water-associated constellations, including Pisces, Aquarius the water bearer, and Capricorn, the fish-tailed goat.

Water everywhere.

The astrological notes were starting to tangle themselves around his thought processes, like an old net snagged in a propeller. A pernicious mixture of sense and nonsense, they mirrored, in Strike's opinion, the appeal of astrology itself, with its flattering, comforting promise that your petty concerns were of interest to the wide universe, and that the stars or the spirit world would guide you where your own hard work and reason couldn't.

Enough, he told himself sternly. Pressing Irene's number on his mobile, he waited, listening to her phone ringing and visualising it beside the bowl of pot-pourri, in the over-decorated hall, with the pink flowered wallpaper and the thick pink carpet. At exactly the point where he'd decided, with a mixture of relief and regret, that she wasn't in, she answered.

'Double four five nine,' she trilled, making it into a kind of jingle. Joan, too, always answered her landline by telling the caller the number they'd just dialled.

'Is that Mrs Hickson?'

'Speaking.'

'It's Cormoran Strike here, the—'

'Oh, hello!' she yelped, sounding startled.

'I wondered whether you might be able to help me,' said Strike, taking out his notebook and opening it. 'When we last met, you mentioned a patient of the St John's practice who you thought might've been call Apton or Applethorpe—'

'Oh, yes?'

'—who claimed to have—'

'—killed Margot, yes,' she interrupted him. 'He stopped Dorothy in broad daylight—'

'Yes—'

'—but she thought it was a load of rubbish. I said to her, "What if he really did, Dorothy—?"'

'I haven't been able to find anyone of that name who lived in the area in 1974,' said Strike loudly, 'so I wondered whether you might've misremembered his na—'

'Possibly, yes, I might have done,' said Irene. 'Well, it's been a long time, hasn't it? Have you tried directory enquiries? Not directory enquiries,' she corrected herself immediately. 'Online records and things.'

'It's difficult to do a search with the wrong name,' said Strike, just managing to keep his tone free of exasperation or sarcasm. 'I'm right by Clerkenwell Road at the moment. I think you said he lived there?'

'Well, he was always hanging around there, so I assumed so.'

'He was registered with your practice, wasn't he? D'you remember his first—?'

'Um, let me think . . . It was something like . . . Gilbert, or – no, I can't remember, I'm afraid. Applethorpe? Appleton? Apton? *Everyone* knew him locally by sight because he looked so peculiar: long beard, filthy, blah blah blah. And sometimes he had his kid with him,' said Irene, warming up, 'really *funny*-looking kid—'

'Yes, you said—'

'—with *massive* ears. *He* might still be alive, the son, but he's probably – *you* know . . . '

Strike waited, but apparently he was supposed to infer the end of the sentence by Irene's silence.

'Probably—?' he prompted.

'Oh, *you* know. In a place.'

'In—?'

'A home or something!' she said, a little impatiently, as though

Strike were being obtuse. 'He was never going to be *right*, was he? – with a druggie father and a retarded mother, I don't care what Jan says. Jan hasn't got the same – well, it's not her fault – her family was – different standards. And she likes to look – in front of strangers – well, we all do – but after all, you're after the truth, aren't you?'

Strike noted the fine needle of malice directed at her friend, glinting among the disconnected phrases.

'Have you found Duckworth?' Irene asked, jumping subject.

'Douthwaite?'

'Oh, what am I like, I keep doing that, hahaha.' However little pleased she'd been to hear from him, he was at least someone to talk to. 'I'd *love* to know what happened to him, I really would, *he* was a fishy character if ever there was one. Jan played it down with you, but she was a bit disappointed when he turned out to be gay, you know. She had a soft spot for him. Well, she was very lonely when I first knew her. We used to try and set her up, Eddie and I—'

'Yes, you said—'

'—but men didn't want to take on a kid and Jan was a bit *you* know, when a woman's been alone, I don't mean *desperate*, but clingy – Larry didn't mind, but Larry wasn't exactly—'

'I had one other thing I wanted to ask—'

'—only *he* wouldn't marry her, either. He'd been through a bad divorce—'

'It's about Leamington Spa—'

'You'll have checked Bognor Regis?'

'Excuse me?' said Strike.

'For Douthwaite? Because he went to Bognor Regis, didn't he? To a holiday camp?'

'Clacton-on-Sea,' said Strike. 'Unless he went to Bognor Regis as well?'

'As well as what?'

Jesus fucking Christ.

'What makes you think Douthwaite was ever in Bognor Regis?' Strike asked, slowly and clearly, rubbing his forehead.

'I thought – wasn't he there, at some point?'

'Not as far as I'm aware, but we know he worked in Clacton-on-Sea in the mid-eighties.'

'Oh, it must've been that – yes, someone must've told me that, they're all – old-fashioned seaside – *you* know.'

Strike seemed to remember he'd asked both Irene and Janice whether they had any idea where Douthwaite had gone after he left Clerkenwell, and that both had said they didn't know.

'How did you know he went to work in Clacton-on-Sea?' he asked.

'Jan told me,' said Irene, after a tiny pause. 'Yes, Jan would've told me. *She* was his neighbour, you know, *she* was the one who knew him. Yes, I think she tried to find out where he'd gone after he left Percival Road, because she was worried about him.'

'But this was eleven years later,' said Strike.

'What was?'

'He didn't go to Clacton-on-Sea until eleven years after he left Percival Road,' said Strike. 'When I asked you both if you knew where he'd gone—'

'Well, you meant *now*, didn't you?' said Irene, 'where he is *now*? I've no idea. Have you looked into that Leamington Spa business, by the way?' Then she laughed, and said, 'All these seaside places! No, wait – it isn't seaside, is it, not Leamington Spa? But you know what I mean – *water* – I do *love* water, it's – Greenwich, Eddie knew I'd love this house when he spotted it for sale – *was* there anything in that Leamington Spa thing, or was Jan making it up?'

'Mrs Beattie wasn't making it up,' said Strike. 'Mr Ramage definitely saw a missing—'

'Oh, I didn't mean Jan would make it up, no, I don't mean that,' said Irene, instantly contradicting herself. 'I just mean, you know, odd place for Margot to turn up, Leamington – have you found any connection,' she asked airily, 'or—?'

'Not yet,' said Strike. '*You* haven't remembered anything about Margot and Leamington Spa, have you?'

'Me? Goodness, no, how should I know why she'd go there?'

'Well, sometimes people do remember things after we've talked to—'

'Have you spoken to Jan since?'

'No,' said Strike. 'D'you know when she's back from Dubai?'

'No,' said Irene. 'All right for some, isn't it? I wouldn't mind some sunshine, the winter we're – but it's wasted on Jan, she doesn't sunbathe, and I wouldn't fancy the flight all that way in Economy, which is how she has to – I wonder how she's getting on, six weeks with her daughter-in-law! Doesn't matter how well you get on, that's a long—'

'Well, I'd better let you get on, Mrs Hickson.'

'Oh, all right,' she said. 'Yes, well. Best of luck with everything.'

'Thank you,' he said, and hung up.

The rain pattered on the window. With a sigh, Strike retired to the café bathroom for a long overdue pee.

He was just paying his bill when he spotted the man in the Sonic the Hedgehog sweatshirt walking past the window, now on the same side of the street as the café. He was heading back the way he'd come, two bulging bags of Tesco shopping hanging from his hands, moving with that same odd, rocking, side-to-side gait, his soaking hair flat to his skull, his mouth slightly open. Strike's eyes followed him as he passed, watching the rain drip off the bottom of his shopping bags and from the lobes of his particularly large ears.

38

So long in secret cabin there he held
Her captive to his sensual desire;
Till that with timely fruit her belly swell'd,
And bore a boy unto that salvage sire . . .

Edmund Spenser
The Faerie Queene

Asking himself whether he could possibly have got as lucky as he hoped, Strike threw a tip on the table and hurried outside into the driving rain, pulling on his coat as he went.

If the mentally impaired adult in the sopping Sonic sweatshirt was indeed the big-eared child once marched around these streets by his eccentric parent, he'd have been living in this corner of Clerkenwell for forty years. Well, people did that, of course, Strike reflected, particularly if they had support there and if their whole world was a few familiar streets. The man was still within sight, heading stolidly towards Clerkenwell Road in the pelting rain, neither speeding up, nor making any attempt to prevent himself becoming progressively more sodden. Strike turned up his coat collar and followed.

A short distance down St John Street, Strike's target turned right past a small ironmonger's on the corner, and headed into Albemarle Way, the short street with an old red telephone box at the other end, and tall, unbroken buildings on either side. Strike's interest quickened.

Just past the ironmonger's, the man set down both of his shopping bags on the wet pavement and took out a door key. Strike kept walking, because there was nowhere to hide, but made a note of the door number as he passed. Was it possible that the late Applethorpe had lived in this very flat? Hadn't Strike thought that Albemarle Way presented a promising place to lie in wait for a victim? Not, perhaps, as good as Passing Alley, nor as convenient as the flats along Jerusalem Passage, but better by far than busy Clerkenwell Green, where Talbot had been convinced that Margot had struggled with a disguised Dennis Creed.

Strike heard the front door close behind the large-eared man and doubled back. The dark blue door needed painting. A small push-button bell was beside it, beneath which was stuck the printed name 'Athorn'. Could this be the name Irene had misremembered as Applethorpe, Appleton or Apton? Then Strike noticed that the man had left the key in the lock.

With a feeling that he might have been far too dismissive of the mysterious ways of the universe, Strike pulled out the key and pressed the doorbell, which rang loudly inside. For a moment or two, nothing happened, then the door opened again and there stood the man in the wet Sonic sweatshirt.

'You left this in the lock,' said Strike, holding out the key.

The man addressed the third button of Strike's overcoat rather than look him in eye.

'I did that before and Clare said not to again,' he mumbled, holding out his hand for the key, which Strike gave him. The man began to close the door.

'My name's Cormoran Strike. I wonder whether I could come in and talk to you about your father?' Strike said, not quite putting his foot in the door, but preparing to do so should it be required.

The other's big-eared face stood out, pale, against the dark hall.

'My-Dad-Gwilherm's dead.'

'Yes,' said Strike, 'I know.'

'He carried me on his shoulders.'

'Did he?'

'Yeah. Mum told me.'

'D'you live alone?'

'I live with Mum.'

'Is her name Clare?'

'No. Deborah.'

'I'm a detective,' said Strike, pulling a card out of his pocket. 'My name's Cormoran Strike and I'd really like to talk to your mum, if that's OK.'

The man didn't take the card, but looked at it out of the corner of his eye. Strike suspected that he couldn't read.

'Would that be all right?' Strike asked, as the cold rain continued to fall.

'Yer, OK. You can come in,' said the other, still addressing Strike's coat button, and he opened the door fully to admit the detective. Without waiting to see whether Strike was following, he headed up the dark staircase inside.

Strike felt some qualms about capitalising on the vulnerabilities of a man like Athorn, but the prospect of looking around what he now strongly suspected was the flat in which the self-proclaimed killer of Margot Bamborough had been living in 1974 was irresistible. After wiping his feet carefully on the doormat, Strike closed the door behind him, spotting as he did so a couple of letters lying on the floor, which the son of the house had simply walked over; one of them carried a wet footprint. Strike picked up the letters, then climbed the bare wooden stairs, over which hung a naked, non-functioning light bulb.

As he climbed, Strike indulged himself with the fantasy of a flat which nobody other than the inhabitants had entered for forty years, with locked cupboards and rooms, or even – it had been known to happen – a skeleton lying in open view. For a split-second, as he stepped out onto the landing, his hopes surged: the oven in the tiny kitchen straight ahead looked as though it dated from the seventies, as did the brown wall tiles, but unfortunately, from a detective point of view, the flat looked neat and smelled fresh and clean. There were even recent Hoover marks on the old carpet, which was patterned in orange and brown swirls. The Tesco bags sat waiting to be unpacked on lino that was scuffed, but that had been recently washed.

To Strike's right stood an open door onto a small sitting room. The man he'd followed was standing there, facing a much older woman, who was sitting crocheting in an armchair beside the window. She looked, as well she might, shocked to see a large stranger standing in her hall.

'He wants to talk to you,' announced the man.

'Only if you're comfortable with that, Mrs Athorn,' Strike called from the landing. He wished Robin was with him. She was particularly good at putting nervous women at their ease. He remembered that Janice had said that this woman was agoraphobic. 'My name's Cormoran Strike and I wanted to ask a few questions about your husband. But if you're not happy, of course, I'll leave immediately.'

'I'm cold,' said the man loudly.

'Change your clothes,' his mother advised him. 'You've got wet. Why don't you wear your coat?'

'Too tight,' he said, 'you silly woman.'

He turned and walked out of the room past Strike, who stood back to let him pass. Gwilherm's son disappeared into a room opposite, on the door of which the name 'Samhain' appeared in painted wooden letters.

Samhain's mother didn't appear to enjoy eye contact any more than her son did. At last, addressing Strike's knees, she said,

'All right. Come in, then.'

'Thanks very much.'

Two budgerigars, one blue, one green, chirruped in a cage in the corner of the sitting room. Samhain's mother had been crocheting a patchwork blanket. A number of completed woollen squares were piled on the wide windowsill beside her and a basket of wools sat at her feet. A huge jigsaw mat was spread out on a large ottoman in front of the sofa. It bore a two-thirds completed puzzle of unicorns. As far as tidiness went, the sitting room compared very favourably with Gregory Talbot's.

'You've got some letters,' Strike said, and he held up the damp envelopes to show her.

'You open them,' she said.

'I don't think—'

'You open them,' she repeated.

She had the same big ears as Samhain and the same slight under-bite. These imperfections notwithstanding, there was a prettiness in her soft face and in her dark eyes. Her long, neatly plaited hair was white. She had to be at least sixty, but her smooth skin was that of a much younger woman. There was a strangely otherworldly air about her as she sat, plying her crochet hook beside the rainy window, shut away from the world. Strike wondered whether she could read. He felt safe to open the envelopes that were clearly junk mail, and did so.

'You've been sent a seed catalogue,' he said, showing her, 'and a letter from a furniture shop.'

'I don't want them,' said the woman beside the window, still talking to Strike's legs. 'You can sit down,' she added.

He sidled carefully between the sofa and the ottoman which, like Strike himself, was far too big for this small room. Having successfully avoided nudging the enormous jigsaw, he took a seat at a respectful distance from the crocheting woman.

'This one,' said Strike, referring to the last letter, 'is for Clare Spencer. Do you know her?'

The letter didn't have a stamp. Judging by the address on the back, the letter was from the ironmonger downstairs.

'Clare's our social worker,' she said. 'You can open it.'

'I don't think I should do that,' said Strike. 'I'll leave it for Clare. You're Deborah, is that right?'

'Yes,' she murmured.

Samhain reappeared in the door. He was now barefoot but wearing dry jeans and a fresh sweatshirt with Spider-Man on the front.

'I'm going to put things in the fridge,' he announced, and disappeared again.

'Samhain does the shopping now,' Deborah said, with a glance at Strike's shoes. Though timid, she didn't seem averse to talking to him.

'Deborah, I'm here to ask you about Gwilherm,' Strike said.

'He's not here.'

'No, I—'

'He died.'

'Yes,' said Strike. 'I'm sorry. I'm really here because of a doctor who used to work—'

'Dr Brenner,' she said at once.

'You remember Dr Brenner?' said Strike, surprised.

'I didn't like him,' she said.

'Well, I wanted to ask you about a *different* doc—'

Samhain reappeared at the sitting room door and said loudly to his mother,

'D'you want a hot chocolate, or not?'

'Yes,' she said.

'Do *you* want a hot chocolate, or not?' Samhain demanded of Strike.

'Yes please,' Strike said, on the principle that all friendly gestures should be accepted in such situations.

Samhain lumbered out of sight. Pausing in her crocheting, Deborah pointed at something straight ahead of her and said,

'That's Gwilherm, there.'

Strike looked around. An Egyptian ankh, the symbol of eternal life, had been drawn on the wall behind the old TV. The walls were pale yellow everywhere except behind the ankh, where a patch of dirty green survived. In front of the ankh, on top of the flat-topped television set, was a black object which Strike at first glance took for a vase. Then he spotted the stylised dove on it, realised that it was an urn and understood, finally, what he was being told.

'Ah,' said Strike. 'Those are Gwilherm's ashes, are they?'

'I told Tudor to get the one with the bird, because I like birds.'

One of the budgerigars fluttered suddenly across the cage in a blur of bright green and yellow.

'Who painted that?' asked Strike, pointing at the ankh.

'Gwilherm,' said Deborah, continuing to dextrously ply her crochet hook.

Samhain re-entered the room, holding a tin tray.

'Not on my jigsaw,' his mother warned him, but there was no other free surface.

'Should I—?' offered Strike, gesturing towards the puzzle, but there was no space anywhere on the floor to accommodate it.

'You close it,' Deborah told him, with a hint of reproach, and Strike saw that the jigsaw mat had wings, which could be fastened to protect the puzzle. He did so, and Samhain laid the tray on top. Deborah stuck her crochet hook carefully in the ball of wool and accepted a mug of instant hot chocolate and a Penguin biscuit from her son. Samhain kept the Batman mug for himself. Strike sipped his drink and said, 'Very nice,' not entirely dishonestly.

'I make good hot chocolate, don't I, Deborah?' said Samhain, unwrapping a biscuit.

'Yes,' said Deborah, blowing on the surface of the hot liquid.

'I know this was a long time ago,' Strike began again, 'but there was another doctor, who worked with Dr Brenner—'

'Old Joe Brenner was a dirty old man,' said Samhain Athorn, with a cackle.

Strike looked at him in surprise. Samhain directed his smirk at the closed jigsaw.

'Why was he a dirty old man?' asked the detective.

'My Uncle Tudor told me,' said Samhain. '*Dirty* old man. Hahahaha. Is this mine?' he asked, picking up the envelope addressed to Clare Spencer.

'No,' said his mother. 'That's Clare's.'

'Why is it?'

'I think,' said Strike, 'it's from your downstairs neighbour.'

'He's a bastard,' said Samhain, putting the letter back down. 'He made us throw everything away, didn't he, Deborah?'

'I like it better now,' said Deborah mildly. 'It's good now.'

Strike allowed a moment or two to pass, in case Samhain had more to add, then asked,

'Why did Uncle Tudor say Joseph Brenner was a dirty old man?'

'Tudor knew everything about everyone,' said Deborah placidly.

'Who was Tudor?' Strike asked her.

'Gwilherm's brother,' said Deborah. 'He always knew about people round here.'

'Does he still visit you?' asked Strike, suspecting the answer.

'Passed-away-to-the-other side,' said Deborah, as though it was

451

one long word. 'He used to buy our shopping. He took Sammy to play football and to the swimming.'

'I do all the shopping now,' piped up Samhain. 'Sometimes I don't want to do the shopping but if I don't, I get hungry, and Deborah says, "It's your fault there's nothing to eat." So then I go shopping.'

'Good move,' said Strike.

The three of them drank their hot chocolate.

'Dirty old man, Joe Brenner,' repeated Samhain, more loudly. 'Uncle Tudor used to tell me some stories. Old Betty and the one who wouldn't pay, hahahaha. Dirty old Joe Brenner.'

'I didn't like him,' said Deborah quietly. 'He wanted me to take my pants off.'

'Really?' said Strike.

While this had surely been a question of a medical examination, he felt uncomfortable.

'Yes, to look at me,' said Deborah. 'I didn't want it. Gwilherm wanted it, but I don't like men I don't know looking at me.'

'No, well, I can understand that,' said Strike. 'You were ill, were you?'

'Gwilherm said I had to,' was her only response.

If he'd still been in the Special Investigation Branch, there would have been a female officer with him for this interview. Strike wondered what her IQ was.

'Did you ever meet Dr Bamborough?' he asked. 'She was,' he hesitated, 'a lady doctor.'

'I've never seen a lady doctor,' said Deborah, with what sounded like regret.

'D'you know whether Gwilherm ever met Dr Bamborough?'

'She died,' said Deborah.

'Yes,' said Strike, surprised. 'People think she died, but no one knows for s—'

One of the budgerigars made the little bell hanging from the top of its cage tinkle. Both Deborah and Samhain looked around, smiling.

'Which one was it?' Deborah asked Samhain.

'Bluey,' he said. 'Bluey's cleverer'n Billy Bob.'

Strike waited for them to lose interest in the budgerigars, which took a couple of minutes. When both Athorns' attention had returned to their hot chocolates, he said,

'Dr Bamborough disappeared and I'm trying to find out what happened to her. I've been told that Gwilherm talked about Dr Bamborough, after she went missing.'

Deborah didn't respond. It was hard to know whether she was listening, or deliberately ignoring him.

'I heard,' said Strike – there was no point not saying it; this was the whole reason he was here, after all – 'that Gwilherm told people he killed her.'

Deborah glanced at Strike's left ear, then back at her hot chocolate.

'You're like Tudor,' she said. 'You know what's what. He probably did,' she added placidly.

'You mean,' said Strike carefully, 'he told people about it?'

She didn't answer.

'. . . or you think he killed the doctor?'

'Was My-Dad-Gwilherm doing magic on her?' Samhain enquired of his mother. 'My-Dad-Gwilherm didn't kill that lady. My uncle Tudor told me what really happened.'

'What did your uncle tell you?' asked Strike, turning from mother to son, but Samhain had just crammed his mouth full of chocolate biscuit, so Deborah continued the story.

'He woke me up one time when I was asleep,' said Deborah, 'and it was dark. He said, "I killed a lady by mistake." I said, "You've had a bad dream." He said, "No, no, I've killed her, but I didn't mean it."'

'Woke you up to tell you, did he?'

'Woke me up, all upset.'

'But you think it was just a bad dream?'

'Yes,' said Deborah, but then, after a moment or two, she said, 'but maybe he did kill her, because he could do magic.'

'I see,' said Strike untruthfully, turning back to Samhain.

'What did your Uncle Tudor say happened to the lady doctor?'

'I can't tell you that,' said Samhain, suddenly grinning. 'Uncle Tudor said not to tell. Never.' But he grinned with a Puckish delight

at having a secret. 'My-Dad-Gwilherm did that,' he went on, pointing at the ankh on the wall.

'Yes,' said Strike, 'your mum told me.'

'I don't like it,' said Deborah placidly, looking at the ankh. 'I'd like
it if the walls were all the same.'

'I like it,' said Samhain, 'because it's different from the other
walls ... you silly woman,' he added abstractedly.

'Did Uncle Tudor—' began Strike, but Samhain, who'd finished
his biscuit, now got to his feet and left the room, pausing in the
doorway to say loudly,

'Clare says it's nice I still got things of Gwilherm's!'

He disappeared into his bedroom and closed the door firmly
behind him. With the feeling he'd just seen a gold sovereign bounce
down a grate, Strike turned back to Deborah.

'Do *you* know what Tudor said happened to the doctor?'

She shook her head, uninterested. Strike looked hopefully back
towards Samhain's bedroom door. It remained closed.

'Can you remember *how* Gwilherm thought he'd killed the
doctor?' he asked Deborah.

'He said his magic killed her, then took her away.'

'Took her away, did it?'

Samhain's bedroom door suddenly opened again and he trudged
back into the room, holding a coverless book in his hand.

'Deborah, is this My-Dad-Gwilherm's magic book, is it?'

'That's it,' said Deborah.

She'd finished her hot chocolate, now. Setting down the empty
mug, she picked up her crochet again.

Samhain held the book wordlessly out to Strike. Though the cover
had come off, the title page was intact: *The Magus* by Francis Barrett.
Strike had the impression that being shown this book was a mark
of esteem, and he therefore flicked through it with an expression of
deep interest, his main objective to keep Samhain happy and close
at hand for further questioning.

A few pages inside was a brown smear. Strike halted the cascade of
pages to examine it more closely. It was, he suspected, dried blood,
and had been wiped across a few lines of writing.

This I will say more, to wit, that those who walk in their sleep, do, by no other guide than the spirit of the blood, that is, of the outward man, walk up and down, perform business, climb walls and manage things that are otherwise impossible to those that are awake.

'You can do magic, with that book,' said Samhain. 'But it's my book, because it was My-Dad-Gwilherm's, so it's mine now,' and he held out his hand before Strike could examine it any further, suddenly jealous of his possession. When Strike handed it back, Samhain clutched the book to his chest with one hand and bent to take a third chocolate biscuit.

'No more, Sammy,' said Deborah.

'I went in the rain and got them,' said Samhain loudly. 'I can have what I want. Silly woman. *Stupid* woman.'

He kicked the ottoman, but it hurt his bare foot, and this increased his sudden, childish anger. Pink-faced and truculent, he looked around the room: Strike suspected he was looking for something to disarrange, or perhaps break. His choice landed on the budgies.

'I'll open the cage,' he threatened his mother, pointing at it. He let *The Magus* fall onto the sofa as he clambered onto the seat, looming over Strike.

'No, don't,' said Deborah, immediately distressed. 'Don't do that, Sammy!'

'And I'll open the window,' said Samhain, now trying to walk his way along the sofa seats, but blocked by Strike. 'Hahaha. You stupid woman.'

'No – Samhain, don't!' said Deborah, frightened.

'You don't want to open the cage,' said Strike, standing up and moving in front of it. 'You wouldn't want your budgies to fly away. They won't come back.'

'I know they won't,' said Samhain. 'The last ones didn't.'

His anger seemed to subside as fast as it had come, in the face of rational opposition. Still standing on the sofa, he said grumpily, 'I went out in the rain. I got them.'

'Have you got Clare's phone number?' Strike asked Deborah.

'In the kitchen,' she said, without asking why he wanted it.

'Can you show me where that is?' Strike asked Samhain, although he knew perfectly well. The whole flat was as big as Irene Hickson's sitting room. Samhain frowned at Strike's midriff for a few moments, then said,

'All right, then.'

He walked the length of the sofa, jumped off the end with a crash that made the bookcase shake, and then lunged for the biscuits.

'Hahaha,' he taunted his mother, both hands full of Penguins. 'I got them. Silly woman. *Stupid* woman.'

He walked out of the room.

As Strike inched back out of the space between ottoman and sofa, he stooped to pick up *The Magus*, which Samhain had dropped, and slid it under his coat. Crocheting peacefully by the window, Deborah Athorn noticed nothing.

A short list of names and numbers was attached to the kitchen wall with a drawing pin. Strike was pleased to see that several people seemed interested in Deborah and Samhain's welfare.

'Who're these people?' he asked, but Samhain shrugged and Strike was confirmed in his suspicion that Samhain couldn't read, no matter how proud he was of *The Magus*. He took a photo of the list with his phone, then turned to Samhain.

'It would really help me if you could remember what your Uncle Tudor said happened to the lady doctor.'

'Hahaha,' said Samhain, who was unwrapping another Penguin. 'I'm not telling.'

'Your Uncle Tudor must have really trusted you, to tell you.'

Samhain chewed in silence for a while, then swallowed and said, with a proud little upwards jerk of the chin, 'Yer.'

'It's good to have people you can trust with important information.'

Samhain seemed pleased with this statement. He ate his biscuit and, for the first time, glanced at Strike's face. The detective had the impression that Samhain was enjoying another man's presence in the flat.

'I did that,' he said suddenly and, walking to the sink, he picked up a small clay pot, which was holding a washing-up brush and a sponge. 'I go to class on Tuesdays and we make stuff. Ranjit teaches us.'

'That's excellent,' said Strike, taking it from him and examining it. 'Where were you, when your uncle told you what happened to Dr Bamborough?'

'At the football,' said Samhain. 'And I made this,' he told Strike, prising a wooden photo frame off the fridge, where it had been attached with a magnet. The framed picture was a recent one of Deborah and Samhain, both of whom had a budgerigar perched on their finger.

'That's very good,' said Strike, admiring it.

'Yer,' said Samhain, taking it back from him and slapping it on the fridge. 'Ranjit said it was the best one. We were at the football and I heard Uncle Tudor telling his friend.'

'Ah,' said Strike.

'And then he said to me, "Don't you tell no one."'

'Right,' said Strike. 'But if you tell me, I can maybe help the doctor's family. They're really sad. They miss her.'

Samhain cast another fleeting look at Strike's face.

'She can't come back now. People can't be alive again when they're dead.'

'No,' said Strike. 'But it's nice when their families know what happened and where they went.'

'My-Dad-Gwilherm died under the bridge.'

'Yes.'

'My Uncle Tudor died in the hospital.'

'You see?' said Strike. 'It's good you know, isn't it?'

'Yer,' said Samhain. 'I know what happened.'

'Exactly.'

'Uncle Tudor told me it was Nico and his boys done it.'

It came out almost indifferently.

'You can tell her family,' said Samhain, 'but nobody else.'

'Right,' said Strike, whose mind was working very fast. 'Did Tudor know how Nico and the boys did it?'

'No. He just knew they did.'

457

Samhain picked up another biscuit. He appeared to have no more to say.

'Er – can I use your bathroom?'

'The bog?' said Samhain, with his mouth full of chocolate.

'Yes. The bog,' said Strike.

Like the rest of the flat, the bathroom was old but perfectly clean. It was papered in green, with a pattern of pink flamingos on it, which doubtless dated from the seventies and now, forty years later, was fashionably kitsch. Strike opened the bathroom cabinet, found a pack of razor blades, extracted one and cut the blood-stained page of *The Magus* out with one smooth stroke, then folded it and slipped it in his pocket.

Out on the landing, he handed Samhain the book back.

'You left it on the floor.'

'Oh,' said Samhain. 'Ta.'

'You won't do anything to the budgies if I leave, will you?'

Samhain looked up at the ceiling, grinning slightly.

'*Will* you?' asked Strike.

'No,' sighed Samhain at last.

Strike returned to the doorway of the sitting room.

'I'll be off now, Mrs Athorn,' he said. 'Thanks very much for talking to me.'

'Goodbye,' said Deborah, without looking at him.

Strike headed downstairs, and let himself back onto the street. Once outside, he stood for a moment in the rain, thinking hard. So unusually still was he, that a passing woman turned to stare back at him.

Reaching a decision, Strike turned left, and entered the ironmonger's which lay directly below the Athorns' flat.

A sullen, grizzled and aproned man behind the counter looked up at Strike's entrance. One of his eyes was larger than the other, which gave him an oddly malevolent appearance.

'Morning,' said Strike briskly. 'I've just come from the Athorns, upstairs. I gather you want to talk to Clare Spencer?'

'Who're you?' asked the ironmonger, with a mixture of surprise and aggression.

'Friend of the family,' said Strike. 'Can I ask why you're putting letters to their social worker through their front door?'

'Because they don't pick up their phones at the bloody social work department,' snarled the ironmonger. 'And there's no point talking to *them*, is there?' he added, pointing his finger at the ceiling.

'Is there a problem I can help with?'

'I doubt it,' said the ironmonger shortly. 'You're probably feeling pretty bloody pleased with the situation, are you, if you're a friend of the family? Nobody has to put their hand in their pocket except me, eh? Quick bit of a cover-up and let someone else foot the bill, eh?'

'What cover-up would this be?' asked Strike.

The ironmonger was only too willing to explain. The flat upstairs, he told Strike, had long been a health risk, crammed with the hoarded belongings of many years and a magnet for vermin, and in a just world, it ought not to be *he* who was bearing the costs of living beneath a pair of actual morons—

'You're talking about friends of mine,' said Strike.

'*You* do it, then,' snarled the ironmonger. '*You* pay a bleeding fortune to keep the rats down. My ceiling's sagging under the weight of their filth—'

'I've just been upstairs and it's perfectly—'

'Because they mucked it out last month, when I said I was going to bloody court!' snarled the ironmonger. 'Cousins come down from Leeds when I threaten legal action – nobody give a shit until then – and I come back Monday morning and they've cleaned it all up. Sneaky bastards!'

'Didn't you want the flat cleaned?'

'I want compensation for the money I've had to spend! Structural damage, bills to Rentokil – that pair shouldn't be living together without supervision, they're not fit, they should be in a home! If I have to take it to court, I will!'

'Bit of friendly advice,' said Strike, smiling. 'If you behave in any way that could be considered threatening towards the Athorns, their friends will make sure it's *you* who ends up in court. Have a nice day,' he added, heading for the door.

The fact that the Athorns' flat had recently been mucked out by helpful relatives tended to suggest that Margot Bamborough's remains weren't hidden on the premises. On the other hand, Strike had gained a bloodstain and a rumour, which was considerably more than he'd had an hour ago. While still disinclined to credit supernatural intervention, he had to admit that deciding to eat breakfast on St John Street that morning had been, at the very least, a most fortuitous choice.

39

. . . they thus beguile the way,
Vntill the blustring storme is ouerblowne . . .
They cannot finde that path, which first was showne,
But wander too and fro in waies vnknowne . . .

Edmund Spenser
The Faerie Queene

Robin's alarm went off at half past six on Friday morning, in the middle of a dream about Matthew: he'd come to her in the Earl's Court flat, and begged her to return to him, saying that he'd been a fool, promising he'd never again complain about her job, imploring her to admit that she missed what they'd once had. He'd asked her whether she honestly liked living in a rented flat, without the security and companionship of marriage, and in the dream Robin felt a pull back towards her old relationship, before it had become complicated by her job with Strike. He was a younger Matthew in the dream, a far kinder Matthew, and Sarah Shadlock was dismissed as a mistake, a blip, a meaningless error. In the background hovered Robin's flatmate, no longer the disengaged and courteous Max, but a pale, simpering girl who echoed Matthew's persuasions, who giggled when he looked at her and urged Robin to give him what he wanted. Only when she'd managed to silence her alarm, and dispel the fog of sleep, did Robin, who was lying face down on her pillow, realise how closely the dream-flatmate had resembled Cynthia Phipps.

Struggling to understand why she'd set her alarm so early, she sat up in bed, the cream walls of her bedroom a blueish mauve in the dawn light, then remembered that Strike had planned a full team meeting, the first in two months, and that he'd asked her to come in an hour earlier than the others again, so that they could discuss the Bamborough case before everyone else got there.

Extremely tired, as she always seemed to be these days, Robin showered and dressed, fumbling over buttons, forgetting where she'd put her phone, realising there was a stain on her sweater only when halfway upstairs to the kitchen and generally feeling disgruntled at life and early starts. When she reached the upper floor, she found Max sitting at the dining table in his dressing gown, poring over a cookbook. The TV was on: the breakfast television presenter was asking whether Valentine's Day was an exercise in commercial cynicism or an opportunity to inject some much-needed romance into a couple's life.

'Has Cormoran got any special dietary requirements?' Max asked her, and when Robin looked blank, he said, 'For tonight. Dinner.'

'Oh,' said Robin, 'no. He'll eat anything.'

She checked her emails on her phone as she drank a mug of black coffee. With a small stab of dread, she saw one from her lawyer titled 'Mediation'. Opening it, she saw that an actual date was being proposed: Wednesday March the nineteenth, over a month away. She pictured Matthew talking to his own lawyer, consulting his diary, asserting his power, as ever. *I'm tied up for the whole of next month.* Then she imagined facing him across a boardroom table, their lawyers beside them, and felt panic mixed with rage.

'You should eat breakfast,' said Max, still reading cookbooks.

'I'll get something later,' said Robin, closing her email.

She picked up the coat she'd left draped over the arm of the sofa and said,

'Max, you haven't forgotten my brother and his friend are spending the weekend, have you? I doubt they'll be around much. It's just a base.'

'No, no, all good,' said Max vaguely, lost in recipes.

Robin headed out into the cool, damp early morning, getting all the way to the Tube before she realised that she didn't have her purse on her.

'*Shit!*'

Robin was usually tidy, efficient and organised; she rarely made this kind of mistake. Hair flying, she ran back to the flat, asking herself what the hell she could have done with it, and wondering, now panicking, whether she'd dropped it in the street or had it stolen out of her bag.

Meanwhile, in Denmark Street, the groggy Strike was hopping on his one foot out of the shower, eyes puffy, and similarly exhausted. The after-effects of a week spent covering Barclay's and Hutchins's shifts were now catching up with him, and he slightly regretted having asked Robin to come into work so early.

However, just after pulling on his trousers, his mobile rang and with a stab of fear, he saw Ted and Joan's number.

'Ted?'

'Hi, Corm. There's no need to panic, now,' said Ted. 'I just wanted to give you an update.'

'Go on,' said Strike, standing bare-chested and frozen in the cold grey light filtered by the too-thin curtains of his attic flat.

'She's not looking too clever. Kerenza was talking about trying to get her to hospital, but Joanie doesn't want to go. She's still in bed, she – didn't get up, yesterday,' said Ted, his voice cracking. 'Couldn't manage it.'

'Shit,' muttered Strike, sinking down onto his bed. 'Right, Ted, I'm coming.'

'You can't,' said his uncle. 'We're surrounded by flood water. It's dangerous. Police are telling everyone to stay put, not to travel. Kerenza can ... she says she can manage her pain at home. She's got drugs they can inject ... because she's not eating a lot now. Kerenza doesn't think it's ... you know ... she thinks it'll be ...'

He began to cry in earnest.

'... not immediate, but ... she says ... not long.'

'I'm coming,' said Strike firmly. 'Does Lucy know how bad Joan is?'

'I called you first,' said Ted.

'I'll tell her, don't worry about that. I'll ring you when we've put a plan together, all right?'

Strike hung up and called Lucy.

'Oh God, no,' his sister gasped, when he'd given her an unemotional summary of what Ted had said. 'Stick, I can't leave right now — Greg's stuck in Wales!'

'The hell's Greg doing in Wales?'

'It's for work — oh God, what are we going to do?'

'When's Greg back?'

'Tomorrow night.'

'Then we'll go down Sunday morning.'

'How? The trains are all off, the roads are flooded—'

'I'll hire a jeep or something. Polworth'll meet us the other end with a boat if we have to. I'll ring you back when I've got things sorted.'

Strike dressed, made himself tea and toast, carried them downstairs to the partners' desk in the inner office and called Ted back, overriding his objections, telling him that, like it or not, he and Lucy were coming on Sunday. He could hear his uncle's yearning for them, his desperate need for company to share the burden of dread and grief. Strike then called Dave Polworth, who thoroughly approved of the plan and promised to be ready with boat, tow ropes and scuba equipment if necessary.

'I've got fuck all else to do. My place of work's underwater.'

Strike called a few car hire companies, finally finding one that had a jeep available. He was giving his credit card details when a text arrived from Robin.

Really sorry, I lost my purse, just found it, on my way now.

Strike had entirely forgotten that they were supposed to be catching up on the Bamborough case before the team meeting. Having finished hiring the jeep, he began to assemble the items he'd intended to discuss with Robin: the blood-smeared page he'd cut out of *The Magus*, which he'd now put into a plastic pouch, and the discovery he'd made the previous evening on his computer, which he brought up on his monitor, ready to show her.

He then opened up the rota, to check what shifts he'd have to reallocate now that he was heading back to Cornwall, and saw 'Dinner with Max' written in for that evening.

'*Bollocks*,' he said. He didn't suppose he could get out of it now, having agreed to it the previous day, but this was the last thing he needed.

At that very moment, Robin, who was climbing the escalator at Tottenham Court Road two steps at a time, heard her mobile ringing in her bag.

'Yes?' she gasped into the phone, as she emerged into the station, one among many bustling commuters.

'Hey, Robs,' said her younger brother.

'Hi,' she said, using her Oyster card at the barrier. 'Everything OK?'

'Yeah, fine,' said Jonathan, though he didn't sound quite as cheerful as the last time they'd spoken. 'Listen, is it all right if I bring another guy with me to crash at yours?'

'What?' said Robin, as she emerged into the blustery rain and controlled chaos of the intersection of Tottenham Court Road and Charing Cross Road, at which there had now been building works for three and a half years. She hoped she'd misheard what Jonathan had said.

'Another guy,' he repeated. 'Is that OK? He'll sleep anywhere.'

'Oh Jon,' Robin moaned, half-jogging along Charing Cross Road now, 'we've only got one sofa bed.'

'Kyle'll sleep on the floor, he doesn't care,' said Jonathan. 'It's not that big a deal is it? One more person?'

'OK, fine,' sighed Robin. 'You're still planning on getting here at ten, though?'

'I'm not sure. We might get an earlier train, we're thinking of skipping lectures.'

'Yeah, but the thing is,' said Robin, 'Cormoran's coming over to dinner to talk to Max—'

'Oh great!' said Jonathan, sounding slightly more enthusiastic. 'Courtney'd love to meet him, she's obsessed with crime!'

'No – Jon, I'm trying to tell you, Max needs to interview

Cormoran about a part he's playing. I don't think there'll be enough food for another three—'

'Don't worry about that, if we get there earlier, we'll just order ourselves a takeaway.'

How was she supposed to say, 'Please don't come during dinner'? After he'd hung up, Robin broke into a jog, hoping that Jonathan's time management, which she knew from experience could use improvement, might see him miss enough trains south to delay his arrival.

Taking the corner into Denmark Street at a run, she saw, with a sinking feeling, Saul Morris ahead of her, walking towards the office and carrying a small, wrapped bunch of pink gerberas.

They'd better not be for me.

'Hey, Robs,' he said, turning as she ran up behind him. 'Oh dear,' he added, grinning, 'someone overslept. Pillow face,' he said, pointing at the spot on his cheek where, Robin surmised, her own still bore a faint crease from the way she'd slept, face down and unmoving, because she was so tired. 'For Pat,' he added, displaying his straight white teeth along with the gerberas. 'Says her husband never gets her anything on Valentine's.'

God, you're smarmy, Robin thought, as she unlocked the door. She noticed that he was calling her 'Robs' again, yet another sign that his discomfort in her presence post-Christmas had evaporated over the succeeding seven weeks. She wished she could as easily shrug off the lingering, unreasonable but no less potent sense of shame she felt, forever having seen his erection on her phone.

Upstairs, the harassed Strike was checking his watch when his mobile rang. It was unusually early for his old friend Nick Herbert to be calling him, and Strike, now sensitised to expect bad news, picked up with a sense of foreboding.

'All right, Oggy?'

Nick sounded hoarse, as though he'd been shouting.

'I'm fine,' said Strike, who thought he could hear footsteps and voices on the metal stairs outside. 'What's up?'

'Nothing much,' said Nick. 'Wondered whether you fancied a pint tonight. Just you and me.'

'Can't,' said Strike, very much regretting that this was so. 'Sorry, I've got something on.'

'Ah,' said Nick. 'OK. What about lunchtime, you free then?'

'Yeah, why not?' said Strike, after a slight hesitation. God knew he could use a pint away from work, from family, from his hundred other problems.

Through the open door he saw Robin enter the outer office, followed by Saul Morris, who was holding a bunch of flowers. He closed the dividing door on them, then his tired brain processed the flowers and the date.

'Hang on. Aren't you busy with Valentine's shit?' he asked Nick.

'Not this year,' said Nick.

There was a short silence. Strike had always considered Nick and Ilsa, a gastroenterologist and a lawyer respectively, the happiest couple he knew. Their house on Octavia Street had often been a place of refuge to him.

'I'll explain over a pint,' said Nick. 'I need one. I'll come to you.'

They agreed a pub and a time and rang off. Strike checked his watch again: he and Robin had fifteen minutes left of what he'd hoped would be an hour on Bamborough. Opening the door, he said,

'Ready? We haven't got long.'

'Sorry,' said Robin, hurrying inside. 'You got my text, didn't you? About the purse?'

'Yeah,' said Strike, closing the door on Morris and pointing at the page from *The Magus*, which he'd laid in front of Robin's seat. 'That's the page from the book in the Athorns' house.'

He'd called Robin about finding the Athorns straight after leaving the ironmonger, and she'd responded with excitement and congratulations. His present grumpiness aggravated her. Presumably it was due to her lateness, but was she not allowed a little human fallibility, after all the extra hours she'd put in lately, covering her own work and Strike's, managing the subcontractors, trying as hard as she could not to put extra stress on him when his aunt was dying? However, outside she could hear Barclay and Hutchins entering the outer office, which reminded her that not so very long ago, she'd been the temp, that Strike had laid down his expectations of a partner in uncompromising terms at the start of their professional relationship. There were three men outside who undoubtedly considered themselves better qualified for her position than she was. So, Robin simply sat down, picked up the page and read the passage beneath the smear.

'The writing mentions blood.'

'I know.'

'How fresh does blood have to be, to analyse?'

'The oldest sample I've heard of that was successfully analysed was twenty-something years old,' said Strike. 'If this is blood, and it dates from when Gwilherm Athorn was alive, it's a good decade older. On the other hand, it's been kept away from light and damp, inside that book, which might help. Anyway, I'm going to call Roy Phipps and ask him what Margot's blood group was and then I'll try and find someone to analyse it for us. Might try that bloke your friend Vanessa used to date in forensics, what was his name?'

'Oliver,' said Robin, 'and he's now her fiancé.'

'Well, him, yeah. One other interesting thing came out of my conversation with Samhain . . .'

He told her about Uncle Tudor's belief that 'Nico and his boys' had killed Margot Bamborough.

'"Nico" – d'you think—?'

'Niccolo "Mucky" Ricci? Odds on,' said Strike. 'He wasn't living far away and he must've been a local personality, although no one from the practice seems to have realised who'd walked into their Christmas party.

'I've left a message with the Athorns' social worker, because I want to know how much store we can put in Deborah and Samhain's memories. Shanker's supposed to be digging around on Ricci for me, but I've heard sod all from him. Might give him a prod.'

He held out his hand and Robin passed the blood-smeared page back.

'Anyway, the only other development is that I've found C. B. Oakden,' said Strike.

'What? How?'

468

'Last night,' said Strike. 'I was thinking about names. Irene getting them wrong – Douthwaite and Duckworth, Athorn and Applethorpe. Then I started thinking about how people often don't stray too far from their original name if they change it.'

He swung his computer monitor around to face her, and Robin saw a picture of a man in early middle age. He was slightly freckled, his eyes fractionally too close together and his hair thinning, though he still had enough to sweep across his narrow forehead. He was still just recognisable as the boy screwing up his face at the camera, at Margot Bamborough's barbecue.

The story below read:

SERIAL SWINDLER GETS JAIL SENTENCE

'Despicable Betrayal of Trust'

A serial fraudster who conned over £75,000 from elderly widows over a two-year period has been jailed for four years, nine months.

Brice Noakes, 49, of Fortune Street, Clerkenwell, who was born Carl Oaken, persuaded a total of nine 'vulnerable and trusting women' to part with jewellery and cash, which in one case amounted to £30,000 of life savings.

Noakes was described by Lord Justice McCrieff as 'a cunning and unscrupulous man who capitalised shamelessly on his victims' vulnerability.'

Smartly dressed and well-spoken Noakes targeted widows living alone, usually offering valuations on jewellery. Noakes persuaded his victims to allow him to remove valuable items from their houses, promising to return with an expert assessment.

On other occasions he posed as a representative from the council, who claimed that the householder was in arrears with council tax and about to be prosecuted.

'Using plausible but entirely fraudulent paperwork, you pressured and bullied vulnerable women into transferring money into an account set up for your own benefit,' said Lord Justice McCrieff, while sentencing.

'Some of the women concerned were initially too embarrassed to tell their families that they'd let this individual into their homes,' said Chief Inspector Grant. 'We believe there may be many more victims who are too ashamed to admit that they've been defrauded, and we would urge them, if they recognise Noakes' picture, to contact us.'

'The paper's misspelled his real name,' said Robin. 'They've printed "Oaken", not Oakden.'

'Which is why he wouldn't have shown up on a basic Google search,' said Strike.

Feeling subtly criticised, because she was the one who was supposed to be looking for Oakden, Robin glanced at the date on the news story, which was five years old.

'He'll be out of jail by now.'

'He is,' said Strike, turning the monitor back towards himself, typing another couple of words and turning it to face Robin again. 'I did a bit more searching on variations of his name, and . . .'

She saw an author page of the Amazon website, listing the books written by an author called Carl O. Brice. The photograph showed the same man from the newspaper, a little older, a little balder, a little more creased around the eyes. His thumbs hooked in his jeans pockets, he wore a black T-shirt with a white logo on it: a clenched fist inside the Mars symbol.

Carl O. Brice

Carl O. Brice is a life coach, entrepreneur and award-winning writer on men's issues including masculism, fathers' rights, gynocentrism, men's mental health, female privilege and toxic feminism. Carl's personal experience of the gynocentric family court system, cultural misandry and male exploitation give him the tools and skills to guide men from all walks of life to healthier, happier lives. In his award-winning book series, Carl examines the catastrophic impact that modern feminism has had on freedom of speech, the workplace, men's rights and the nuclear family.

Robin glanced down the list of books beneath the author biography. The covers were cheap and amateurish. All featured pictures of women in various slightly pornified costumes and poses. A scantily dressed blonde wearing a crown was sitting in a throne for *From Courtly Love to Family Courts, A History of Gynocentrism*, whereas a brunette dressed in a rubber stormtrooper outfit pointed at the camera for *Shamed: The Modern War on Masculinity*.

'He's got his own website,' said Strike, turning the monitor back to himself. 'He self-publishes books, offers to coach men on how to get access to their kids, and flogs protein shakes and vitamins. I don't think he'll pass up the chance to talk to us. He seems the type to come running at the sniff of notoriety or money.

'Speaking of which,' said Strike, 'how're you getting on with that woman who thinks she saw Margot at the window on—?'

'Amanda Laws,' said Robin. 'Well, I went back to her offering her expenses if she'll come into the office, and she hasn't answered yet.'

'Well, chase her,' said Strike. 'You realise we're now six months in—?'

'Yes, I do realise that,' said Robin, unable to help herself. 'I learned counting at school.'

Strike raised his eyebrows.

'Sorry,' she muttered. 'I'm just tired.'

'Well, so am I, but I'm also mindful of the fact we still haven't traced some fairly important people yet. Satchwell, for instance.'

'I'm working on him,' said Robin, glancing at her watch and getting to her feet. 'I think they're all out there, waiting for us.'

'Why's Morris brought flowers?' said Strike.

'They're for Pat. For Valentine's Day.'

'Why the hell?'

Robin paused at the door, looking back at Strike.

'Isn't it obvious?'

She let herself out of the room, leaving Strike to frown after her, wondering what was obvious. He could imagine only two reasons to buy a woman flowers: because you were hoping to sleep with her, or to avoid being criticised for not buying flowers on a day when flowers might be expected. Neither seemed to apply in this case.

The team was sitting in a cramped circle outside, Hutchins and Barclay on the fake leather sofa, Morris on one of the fold-up plastic chairs that had been bought when the team outgrew the existing seats, and Pat on her own wheeled desk chair, which left another two uncomfortable plastic chairs for the partners. Robin noticed how all three men stopped talking when Strike emerged from the inner office: when she'd led the meeting alone, she'd had to wait until Hutchins and Morris finished discussing a mutual police acquaintance who'd been caught taking bribes.

The bright pink daisy-like gerberas sat in a small vase on Pat's desk now. Strike glanced at them before saying,

'All right, let's start with Shifty. Morris, did you get anywhere with that bloke in the tracksuit?'

'Yeah, I did,' said Morris, consulting his notes. 'His name's Barry Fisher. He's divorced with one kid and he's a manager at Shifty's gym.'

Appreciative, low-toned growls of approval and interest issued from Strike, Barclay and Hutchins. Robin contented herself with a slight eyebrow raise. It was her experience that the slightest hint of warmth or approval from her was interpreted by Morris as an invitation to flirtation.

'So, I've booked myself in for a trial session with one of their trainers,' said Morris.

Bet it's with a woman, thought Robin.

'While I was talking to her, I saw him wandering about talking to some of the other girls. He's definitely hetero, judging by how he was looking at one of the women on the cross-trainer. I'm going back Monday for a workout, if that's all right with you, boss. Try and find out more about him.'

'Fine,' said Strike. 'Well, this looks like our first solid lead: a link between Shifty and whatever's going on inside Elinor Dean's house.'

Robin, who'd spent the night before last sitting in her Land Rover outside Elinor's house, said,

'It might not be relevant, but Elinor took an Amazon delivery yesterday morning. Two massive boxes. They looked quite light, but—'

'We should open a book,' Morris told Strike, talking over Robin. 'Twenty on dominatrix.'

'Never seen the appeal in bein' whipped,' said Barclay thoughtfully. 'If I want pain, I jus' forget to put the bins oot.'

'Bit mumsy-looking, though, isn't she?' said Hutchins. 'If I had SB's money, I'd go for something a bit more—'

He sketched a slimmer figure in mid-air. Morris laughed.

'Ach, there's no accountin' for taste,' said Barclay. 'Army mate o' mine wouldnae look at anythin' under thirteen stone. We usedtae call him the Pork Whisperer.'

The men laughed. Robin smiled, mainly because Barclay was looking at her, and she liked Barclay, but she felt too tired and demoralised to be truly amused. Pat was wearing a 'boys will be boys' expression of bored tolerance.

'Unfortunately, I've got to go back to Cornwall on Sunday,' said Strike, 'which I appreciate—'

'The fuck are ye gonna get tae Cornwall?' asked Barclay, as the office windows shook with the wind.

'Jeep,' said Strike. 'My aunt's dying. Looks like she's got days.'

Robin looked at Strike, startled.

'I appreciate that leaves us stretched,' Strike continued matter-of-factly, 'but it can't be helped. I think it's worth continuing to keep an eye on SB himself. Morris'll do some digging with this bloke at the gym and the rest of you can divvy up shifts on Elinor Dean. Unless anyone's got anything to add,' said Strike, pausing for comments. The men all shook their heads and Robin, too tired to mention the Amazon boxes again, remained silent. 'Let's have a look at Postcard.'

'I've got news,' said Barclay laconically. 'She's back at work. I've talked tae her. Yer woman,' he added, to Robin, 'short. Big round glasses. Ambled over and started askin' questions.'

'What about?' asked Morris, a smirk playing around his lips.

'Light effects in the landscapes o' James Duffield Harding,' said Barclay. 'What d'ye think I asked, who she fancied for the Champions League?'

Strike laughed, and so did Robin, this time, glad to see Morris looking foolish.

'Yeah, I read the notice by his portrait an' looked him up on my phone round the corner,' said Barclay. 'Wanted a way o' gettin' ontae the subject o' weather wi' her. Anyway,' said the Glaswegian, 'coupla minutes intae the conversation, talkin' light effects an' broodin' skies an' that, she brought up oor weatherman friend. Turned pink when she mentioned him. Said he'd described a viewer's picture as "Turneresque" last week.

'It's her,' said Barclay, addressing Robin. 'She wanted tae mention him for the pleasure of sayin' his name. She's Postcard.'

'Bloody well done,' Strike told Barclay.

'It's Robin's win,' said Barclay. 'She made the pass. I jus' tapped it in.'

'Thanks, Sam,' said Robin, pointedly, not looking at Strike, who registered both the tone and her expression.

'Fair point,' said Strike, 'well done, both of you.'

Aware that he'd been short with Robin during their meeting about the Bamborough case, Strike sought to make amends by asking her opinion on which of the waiting list clients they ought to contact, now that the Postcard case was as good as wrapped up, and she said she thought the commodities broker who thought her husband was sleeping with their nanny.

'Great,' said Strike. 'Pat, can you get in touch and tell her we're ready to roll if she still wants him under surveillance? If nobody's got anything else—'

'I have,' said Hutchins, generally the quietest person in the agency. 'It's about that roll of film you wanted passed to the Met.'

'Oh yeah?' said Strike. 'Is there news?'

'My mate rang last night. There's nothing to be done with it. You won't get any prosecutions now.'

'Why not?' said Robin.

She sounded angrier than she'd meant to. The men all looked at her.

'Perpetrators' faces all hidden,' said Hutchins. 'That arm that appears for a moment: you can't build a prosecution case on an out-of-focus ring.'

'I thought your contact said the roll had come out of a raid on one of Mucky Ricci's brothels?' said Robin.

'He *thinks* it did,' Hutchins corrected her. 'You won't get DNA evidence off a can that old, that's been kept in a shed and an attic and handled by a hundred people. It's a no-go. Shame,' he said indifferently, 'but there you are.'

Strike now heard his mobile ringing back on the partners' desk, where he'd left it. Worried it might be Ted, he excused himself from the meeting and retreated into the inner office, closing the door behind him.

There was no caller ID on the number ringing his mobile.

'Cormoran Strike.'

'Hello, Cormoran,' said an unfamiliar, husky voice. 'It's Jonny.'

There was a brief silence.

'Your father,' Rokeby added.

Strike, whose tired mind was full of Joan, of the agency's three open cases, of guilt about being grumpy with his partner, and the logistical demands he was placing on his employees by disappearing to Cornwall again, said nothing at all. Through the dividing door, he could hear the team still discussing the roll of film.

'Wanted a chat,' said Rokeby. 'Is that all right?'

Strike felt suddenly disembodied; completely detached from everything, from the office, from his fatigue, from the concerns that had seemed all-important just seconds ago. It was as though he and his father's voice existed alone and nothing else was fully real, except Strike's adrenalin, and a primal desire to leave a mark that Rokeby wouldn't quickly forget.

'I'm listening,' he said.

Another silence.

'Look,' said Rokeby, sounding slightly uneasy, 'I don't wanna do this by phone. Let's meet. It's been too fucking long. Water under the bridge. Let's meet, let's . . . I wanna – this can't go on. This fucking – feud, or whatever it is.'

Strike said nothing.

'Come to the house,' said Rokeby. 'Come over. Let's talk, and . . . you're not a kid any more. There are two sides to every story. Nothing's black and white.'

He paused. Strike still said nothing.

'I'm proud of you, d'you know that?' said Rokeby. 'I'm really fucking proud of you. What you've done and . . . '

The sentence petered out. Strike stared, motionless, at the blank wall in front of him. Beyond the partition wall, Pat was laughing at something Morris had said.

'Look,' repeated Rokeby, with just a tiny hint of temper now, because he was a man used to getting his own way. 'I get it, I do, but what the fuck can I do? I can't time travel. Al's told me what you've been saying, and there's a bunch of stuff you don't know, about your mother and all her fucking men. If you just come over, we can have a drink, we can have it all out. And,' said Rokeby, quietly insinuating, 'maybe I can help you out a bit, maybe there's something you want I can help out with, peace offering, I'm open to suggestions . . . '

In the outer office, Hutchins and Barclay were taking their leave, ready to get back to their separate jobs. Robin was thinking only about how much she wanted to go home. She was supposed to have the rest of the day off, but Morris was hanging around, and she was sure he was waiting because he wanted to walk with her to the Tube. Pretending to have paperwork to look at, she was rifling through a filing cabinet while Morris and Pat chatted, hoping he'd leave. She'd just opened an old file on a prolific adulterer, when Strike's voice filled the room from the inner office. She, Pat and Morris turned their heads. Several pages of the file Robin was balancing on top of the drawer slid to the floor.

' . . . so GO FUCK YOURSELF!'

Before Robin could exchange looks with Morris or Pat, the dividing door between inner and outer offices opened. Strike looked alarming: white, livid, his breath coming fast. He stormed through the outer office, grabbed his coat and could be heard heading down the metal staircase outside.

Robin picked up the fallen pages.

'Shit,' said Morris, grinning. 'Wouldn't have wanted to be on the end of *that* call.'

'Nasty temper,' said Pat, who looked weirdly satisfied. 'Knew it, the moment I laid eyes on him.'

40

Thus as they words amongst them multiply,
They fall to strokes, the frute of too much talke . . .

Edmund Spenser
The Faerie Queene

Robin found no polite way of avoiding walking to the Tube with Morris and in consequence was obliged to listen to two off-colour jokes, and to lie about her Valentine's plans, because she could just imagine Morris's response if she told him Strike was coming over. Pretending that she hadn't heard or registered Morris's suggestion that they should get together one night to compare notes on lawyers, she parted from him at the bottom of the escalator with relief.

Tired and mildly depressed, Robin's thoughts lingered on Morris as the Tube sped her back towards Earl's Court. Was he so used to women responding readily to his undeniable handsomeness that he took it for granted he was eliciting a positive response? Or did the fault lie in Robin herself, who, for the sake of politeness, for the cohesion of the team, because she didn't want to make trouble when the agency was so busy, continued to smile at his stupid jokes and chose not to say, loudly and clearly, 'I don't like you. We're never going to date.'

She arrived home to find the flat full of the cheering and delicious smell of simmering beef and red wine. Max appeared to have gone out, but a casserole was sitting in the oven and Wolfgang was lying as close to the hot door as he could manage without burning himself, reminding Robin of fans who camped out overnight in hope of catching a glimpse of pop stars.

Instead of lying down on her bed and trying to get a few hours' sleep before dinner, Robin, who'd been stung by Strike's reminders that she hadn't chased up Amanda Laws or found Paul Satchwell, made herself more coffee, opened her laptop and sat down at the small dining table. After sending Amanda Laws another email, she opened Google. When she did so, each letter of the logo turned one by one into a pastel-coloured, heart-shaped candy with a slogan on it: MR RIGHT, PUPPY LUV and BLIND DATE, and for some reason, her thoughts moved to Charlotte Campbell. It would, of course, be very difficult for a married woman to meet her lover tonight. And who, she wondered, had Strike been telling to fuck off over the phone?

Robin set to work on Satchwell, trying to emulate Strike's success in finding C. B. Oakden. She played around with Satchwell's three names, reversing Paul and Leonard, trying initials and deliberate misspellings, but the men who appeared in answer to her searches didn't look promising.

Was it possible that Margot's tight-jeaned, hairy-chested artist had turned, over the space of four decades, into classic car collector Leo Satchwell, a rotund man with a goatee who wore tinted glasses? Unlikely, Robin decided, after wasting ten minutes on Leo: judging by the photographs on his Facebook page, in which he stood alongside other enthusiasts, he was barely five feet tall. There was a Brian Satchwell in Newport, but he had a lazy eye and was five years too young, and a Colin Satchwell in Eastbourne who ran an antiques business. She was still trying to find an image of Colin when she heard the front door open. A few minutes later, Max walked into the kitchen, with a bag of shopping in his hand.

'How's the casserole doing?' he asked.

'Great,' said Robin, who hadn't checked it.

'Get out of the way, Wolfgang, unless you want to be burned,' said Max, as he opened the oven door. To Robin's relief, the casserole appeared to be doing well, and Max shut the door again.

Robin closed her laptop. A feeling that it was rude to sit typing while someone else was cooking in her vicinity persisted from the days when she'd lived with a husband who'd always resented her bringing work home.

'Max, I'm really sorry about this, but my brother's bringing another friend with him tonight.'

'That's fine,' said Max, unpacking his shopping.

'And they might be arriving early. They aren't expecting to eat with us—'

'They're welcome. This casserole serves eight. I was going to freeze the rest, but we can eat the lot tonight, I don't mind.'

'That's really nice of you,' said Robin, 'but I know you want to talk to Cormoran alone, so I could take them—'

'No, the more the merrier,' said Max, who seemed mildly cheerful at the prospect of company. 'I told you, I've decided to give up the recluse life.'

'Oh,' said Robin. 'OK, then.'

She had some misgivings about what she feared might be quite an ill-assorted group, but telling herself her tiredness was making her pessimistic, she retired to her bedroom, where she spent the rest of the afternoon trying to find a photograph of Colin Satchwell. Finally, at six o'clock, after a great deal of cross-referencing, she located a picture on the website of a local church, where he appeared to be an alderman. Portly, with a low hairline, he in no way resembled the artist she sought.

Aware that she really ought to change and go upstairs to help Max, she was on the point of closing her laptop when a new email arrived. The subject line was one word: 'Creed', and with a spurt of nervous excitement, Robin opened it.

Hi Robin,

Quick update: I've passed the Creed request to the two people I mentioned. My Ministry of Justice contact was a bit more hopeful than I thought he'd be. This is confidential, but another family's been lobbying for Creed to be interviewed again. Their daughter was never found, but they've always believed a pendant in Creed's house belonged to her. My contact thinks something might be achievable if the Bamborough family joined forces with the Tuckers. I don't know whether Cormoran would be allowed to conduct the interview, though. That decision would be taken by

the Broadmoor authorities, the Ministry of Justice and the Home
Office and my MoJ contact thinks it more likely to be police. I'll
let you know what's going on as soon as I hear anything else.

Best, Izzy

Robin read this email through and allowed herself a flicker of
optimism, though she didn't intend to tell Strike what she was up to
just yet. With luck, they'd be allowed to talk to the police interviewer
before he or she went into Broadmoor. She typed an email of thanks,
then began to get ready for dinner.

Her slightly improved mood survived looking in the mirror and
seeing how tired she looked, with grey shadows under her slightly
bloodshot eyes, and hair that definitely needed washing. Making
do with dry shampoo, Robin tied back her hair, changed into clean
jeans and her favourite top, applied undereye concealer and was on
the point of leaving her room when her mobile rang.

Afraid that it would be Strike cancelling, she was positively
relieved to see Ilsa's name.

'Hi, Ilsa!'

'Hi, Robin. Are you with Corm?'

'No,' said Robin. Instead of leaving her bedroom, she sat back
down on the bed. 'Are you OK?'

Ilsa sounded odd: weak and numb.

'D'you know where Corm is?'

'No, but he should be here in ten minutes. D'you want me to give
him a message?'

'No. I – d'you know whether he's been with Nick today?'

'No,' said Robin, now worried. 'What's going on, Ilsa? You sound
terrible.'

Then she remembered that it was Valentine's Day and registered
the fact that Ilsa didn't know where her husband was. Something
more than worry overtook Robin: it was fear. Nick and Ilsa were
the happiest couple she knew. The five weeks she'd lived with them
after leaving Matthew had restored some of Robin's battered faith in
marriage. They couldn't split up: not Nick and Ilsa.

'It's nothing,' said Ilsa.

'Tell me,' Robin insisted. 'What—?'

Wrenching sobs issued through the phone.

'Ilsa, what's happened?'

'I . . . I miscarried.'

'Oh God,' gasped Robin. 'Oh no. Ilsa, I'm so sorry.'

She knew that Nick and Ilsa had been trying for some years to have a child. Nick never talked about it and Ilsa, only rarely. Robin had had no idea she was pregnant. She suddenly remembered Ilsa not drinking, on the night of her birthday.

'It happened – in the – in the supermarket.'

'Oh no,' whispered Robin. 'Oh God.'

'I started bleeding . . . at court . . . we're in the middle of a . . . massive case . . . couldn't leave . . .' said Ilsa. 'And then . . . and then . . . heading home . . .'

She became incoherent. Tears started in Robin's eyes as she sat with the phone clamped to her ear.

' . . . knew . . . something bad . . . so I got out of the cab . . . and I went . . . into the supermarket . . . and I was in . . . the loo . . . and I felt . . . felt . . . and then . . . a little . . . blob . . . a tiny bod – bod – body . . .'

Robin put her face in her hands.

'And . . . I didn't know . . . what to do . . . but . . . there was a woman . . . in the loo with . . . and she . . . it had happened . . . to her . . . so kind . . .'

She dissolved again into incoherence. Snorts, gulps and hiccups filled Robin's ear before words became intelligible again.

'And Nick said . . . it was my fault. Said . . . all my fault . . . working . . . too hard . . . I didn't take . . . enough care . . . didn't put . . . the baby first.'

'He didn't,' said Robin. She liked Nick. She couldn't believe he'd have said such a thing to his wife.

'He did, he said I should've . . . come home . . . that I . . . put w – work . . . before the b – baby—'

'Ilsa, listen to me,' said Robin. 'If you got pregnant once, you can get pregnant again.'

'No, no, no, I can't,' said Ilsa, dissolving again into tears, 'it was our third go at IVF. We agreed ... agreed ... no more after this. No more.'

The doorbell rang.

'Ilsa, I've got to get the door, it might be Cormoran—'

'Yes, yes, go ... it's fine ... it's all fine.'

Before Robin could stop her, Ilsa had hung up. Hardly knowing what she was doing, Robin ran downstairs and flung open the door.

But naturally, it wasn't Strike. He'd never arrived on time for any out-of-work event to which she'd invited him, whether drinks, house-warming party or even her wedding. Instead she found herself facing Jonathan, the brother who most resembled her: tall and slender, with the same strawberry blond hair and blue eyes. The resemblance was even closer this evening, because both siblings looked peaky. Jonathan, too, had shadows under his eyes, not to mention a slightly grey cast to his skin.

'Hey, Robs.'

'Hi,' said Robin, accepting Jonathan's hug and trying to act pleased to see him, 'come in.'

'This is Courtney,' said Jonathan, 'and that's Kyle.'

'Hiya,' giggled Courtney, who was holding a can. She was an exquisitely pretty girl, with large dark eyes and long black hair, and she seemed slightly tipsy. Kyle, who accidentally bashed Robin with his large rucksack on entering, was a couple of inches taller than she was, skinny, with a high-fade haircut, large, bloodshot eyes and a neatly groomed beard.

'Hi there,' he said, holding out his hand and smiling down at Robin. A stranger might have thought he was welcoming her to his flat, rather than the other way around. 'Robin, yeah?'

'Yes,' said Robin, forcing a smile. 'Lovely to meet you. Come upstairs; we're eating on the top floor.'

Lost in thoughts of Ilsa, she followed the three students. Courtney and Kyle were giggling and whispering together, Courtney a little clumsy on her feet. On reaching the living area, Robin introduced all three guests to Max, while Kyle dumped his none-too-clean rucksack on their host's cream sofa.

'Thanks very much for letting us stay,' said Jonathan to Max, who'd laid the table for six. 'Something smells really good.'

'I'm vegan,' piped up Courtney. 'But I can just eat, like, pasta, or whatever.'

'I'll do some pasta, don't you worry about that,' Robin told Max hastily, as she surreptitiously lifted Kyle's dirty rucksack off the sofa, trying not to make a big deal of what she was doing. Courtney promptly knelt on the sofa with her damp trainers still on, and said to Robin,

'Is this the sofa bed?'

Robin nodded.

'We'll have to sort out who sleeps where,' said Courtney, with a glance at Kyle. Robin thought she saw her brother's smile falter.

'Actually, why don't we put all the bags in my bedroom for now?' Robin suggested, as Jonathan swung his holdall onto the sofa, too. 'And keep this area clear for after dinner?'

Neither Courtney nor Kyle showed any inclination to move, so Robin and Jonathan took the bags downstairs together. Once they were in Robin's room, Jonathan took a box of chocolates out of his holdall and gave them to his sister.

'Thanks, Jon, that's lovely. D'you feel OK? You look a bit pale.'

'I was blunted last night. Listen, Robs ... don't say anything to Courtney about her being, like, my girlfriend or whatever.'

'I wasn't going to.'

'Good, because ...'

'You've split up?' Robin suggested sympathetically.

'We weren't ever — we hooked up a couple of times,' muttered Jonathan, 'but — I dunno, I think she might be into Kyle now.'

Courtney's laugh rang out from the upper floor. With a perfunctory smile at his sister, Jonathan returned to his friends.

Robin tried to call Ilsa back, but her number was engaged. Hoping this meant that she'd located Nick, Robin texted:

Just tried to call you. Please let me know what's going on. I'm worried about you. Robin xxx

She went back upstairs and started cooking pumpkin ravioli for Courtney. Apparently sensing that the casserole would soon be leaving the oven, Wolfgang slunk around Max's and Robin's ankles. Checking her watch, Robin noted that Strike was already fifteen minutes late. His record was an hour and a half. She tried, without much success, not to feel angry. After the way he'd treated her for being late this morning . . .

Robin was just draining the ravioli when the doorbell finally rang.

'D'you want me—?' said Max, who was pouring drinks for Jonathan, Courtney and Kyle.

'No, I'll do it,' said Robin shortly.

When she opened the door, she knew immediately that Strike, who was peering down at her with unfocused eyes, was drunk.

'Sorry I'm late,' he said thickly. 'Can I have a pee?'

She stood back to let him pass. He reeked of Doom Bar and cigarettes. Tense as she was, Robin noted that he hadn't thought to bring Max a bottle of anything, in spite of the fact he'd apparently spent all afternoon in the pub.

'The bathroom's there,' she said, pointing. He disappeared inside. Robin waited on the landing. He seemed to take a very long time.

'We're eating up here,' she said, when at last he emerged.

'More stairs?' mumbled Strike.

When they reached the open-plan living area, he seemed to pull himself together. He shook hands with Max and Jonathan in turn and said quite coherently that he was pleased to meet them. Courtney temporarily abandoned Kyle and bounced over to say hello to the famous detective, and Strike looked positively enthusiastic as he took in her looks. Suddenly very conscious of her own washed-out and puffy-eyed appearance, Robin turned back to the kitchen area to put Courtney's ravioli in a bowl for her. Behind her, she heard Courtney saying,

'And this is Kyle.'

'Oh, yeah, you're the detective?' Kyle said, determinedly unimpressed.

Jonathan, Courtney, Kyle and Max already had drinks, so Robin poured herself a large gin and tonic. While she was adding ice, a cheerful Max came back into the kitchen to fetch Strike a beer, then got the casserole out of the oven and on to the table. Wolfgang whined as the object of his devotion was lifted out of his reach.

While Max served everyone at the table, Robin set Courtney's ravioli down in front of her.

'Oh God, no, wait,' said Courtney. 'Is this vegan? Where's the packet?'

'In the bin,' said Robin.

'Tuh,' said Courtney, and she got up and walked into the kitchen. Max and Robin were the only two people at the table whose eyes didn't automatically follow Courtney. Robin downed half her gin before picking up her knife and fork.

'No, it's OK,' called Courtney, from beside the bin. 'It's vegan.'

'Oh good,' said Robin.

To Robin's left, Max began asking Strike's opinion on various aspects of his character's personality and past. Courtney returned to the table and began to wolf down her pasta, drinking and topping up her wine regularly as she went while telling Jonathan and Kyle her plans about a protest march at university. Robin joined in neither conversation, but ate and drank in silence, one eye on the mobile beside her plate in case Ilsa texted or rang back.

'. . . couldn't happen,' Strike was saying. 'He wouldn't've been allowed to join up in the first place, conviction for possession with intent to supply. Total bollocks.'

'Really? The writers did quite a lot of research—'

'Should've known that, then.'

'. . . *so* yeah, basically, you dress up in your underwear and short skirts and stuff,' Courtney was saying, and when Kyle and Jon laughed she said, '*Don't*, it's serious—'

'. . . no, this is useful,' said Max, scribbling in a notebook. 'So if he'd been in jail before the army—'

'If he'd done more than thirty months, the army wouldn't've taken him . . .'

'I'm not wearing *suspenders*, Kyle – anyway, Miranda doesn't want—'

'I don't know how long he's supposed to have done,' said Max. 'I'll check. Tell me about drugs in the army, how common—?'

'—so she says, "D'you not understand how problematic the word 'slut' is, Courtney?" And I'm like, "Er, what d'you think—"'

'"What d'you think a fucking SlutWalk's *for?*"' said Kyle, talking over Courtney. He had a deep voice and the air of a young man who was used to being listened to.

The screen of Robin's mobile lit up. Ilsa had texted back.

'Excuse me,' she muttered, though nobody was paying her any attention, and she headed into the kitchen area to read what Ilsa had said.

Didn't mean to worry you. Nick home, shitfaced. He's been in the pub with Corm. We're talking. He says he didn't mean it the way I took it. What other way was there? X

Robin, who felt entirely on Ilsa's side, nevertheless texted back:

He's a dickhead but I know he really loves you. Xxx

As she poured herself another double gin and tonic, Max called to her, asking her to bring Strike another beer from the fridge. When Robin set the open bottle down in front of Strike he didn't thank her, but merely took a long pull on it and raised his voice, because he was having difficulty trying to make himself heard over Kyle and Courtney, whose conversation had now migrated to the unknown Miranda's views on pornography.

'. . . so I'm, like, you *do* understand that women can actually *choose* what to do with their own bodies, Miran – Oh shit, sorry—'

Courtney's expansive gesture had knocked over her wine glass. Robin jumped up to get the kitchen roll. By the time she got back, Courtney's glass had been refilled by Kyle. Robin mopped up the wine while the two separate conversations grew steadily louder on either side of her, binned the sodden kitchen roll, then sat back down, wishing she could just go to bed.

'. . . troubled background, that's fucking original, guess what, plenty of people join the army because they want to serve, not to escape . . .'

'Pure whorephobia,' boomed Kyle. 'I s'pose she thinks waitresses love every fucking minute of their jobs, does she?'

'. . . and he can't have been in 1 Rifles if he's your age. The battalion was only formed . . .'

'. . . labour for hire, where's the fucking difference?'

'. . . think it was end 2007 . . .'

'. . . and some women enjoy *watching* porn, too!'

Courtney's words fell loudly into a temporary lull. Everyone looked round at Courtney, who'd blushed and was giggling with her hand over her mouth.

'It's all right, we're talking feminism,' said Kyle, with a smirk. 'Courtney isn't suggesting, y'know – after-dinner entertainment.'

'*Kyle!*' gasped Courtney, slapping his upper arm and dissolving into further giggles.

'Who wants pudding?' Robin asked, standing up to collect the empty plates. Max, too, got to his feet.

'I'm sorry Strike's so pissed,' Robin murmured to Max, as she tipped a few uneaten pieces of ravioli into the bin.

'Are you kidding?' said Max, with a slight smile. 'This is pure gold. My character's an alcoholic.'

He'd gone, bearing a homemade cheesecake to the table, before Robin could tell him that Strike didn't usually drink this much; indeed, this was only the second time she'd ever known him drunk. The first time he'd been sad and quite endearing, but tonight there was a definite undercurrent of aggression. She remembered the shouted 'Go fuck yourself' she'd heard through the office door that afternoon and again wondered to whom Strike had been talking.

Robin followed Max back to the table, carrying a lemon tart and a third large gin and tonic. Kyle was now treating the entire table to his views on pornography. Robin didn't much like the expression on Strike's face. He'd often displayed an instinctive antipathy towards the kind of young man you could least imagine in the army; she trusted he was going to keep his feelings to himself tonight.

'. . . form of entertainment, just like any other,' Kyle was saying, with an expansive gesture. Fearful of more accidents, Robin discreetly moved the almost empty wine bottle out of hitting range.

'When you look at it objectively, strip it from all the puritanical bullshit—'

'Yeah, exactly,' said Courtney, 'women have got agency over their own—'

'—movies, gaming, it all stimulates the pleasure centres in your brain,' said Kyle, now pointing at his own immaculately groomed head. 'You could make an argument that movies are emotional pornography. All this moralistic, manufactured outrage about porn—'

'I can't eat either of those if they've got dairy in them,' Courtney whispered to Robin, who pretended she hadn't heard.

'—women want to make a living out of their own bodies, that's the literal definition of female empowerment and you could argue it has more societal benefit than—'

'When I was in Kosovo,' said Strike unexpectedly and all three students turned to look at him, with startled expressions. Strike paused, fumbling to get his cigarettes out of his pocket.

'Cormoran,' said Robin, 'you can't smo—'

'No problem,' said Max, getting up, 'I'll bring an ashtray.'

It took Strike three attempts to make his lighter work and in the meantime everybody watched him in silence. Without raising his voice, he'd dominated the room.

'Who'd like cheesecake?' Robin said into the silence, her voice artificially cheery.

'I can't,' said Courtney, with a slight pout. 'But I might be able to have the lemon tart, if it's—?'

'When I was in Kosovo,' Strike repeated, exhaling as Max returned, placed an ashtray in front of him and sat back down again, ' – cheers – I investigated a porn case – well, human trafficking. Coupla soldiers had paid for sex with underage girls. They were filmed without their knowledge an' the videos ended up on PornHub. Case ended up part of an international civilian investigation. Whole load of pre-pubescent boys and girls had been trafficked into porn. The youngest was seven.'

Strike took a large drag of his cigarette, squinting through the smoke at Kyle.

'What societal benefit would you say that had?' he asked.

There was a short, nasty silence in which the three students stared at the detective.

'Well, obviously,' said Kyle, with a small half-laugh, 'that's – that's a completely different thing. Nobody's talking about kids – that's not – that's illegal, isn't it? I'm talking about—'

'Porn industry's full of trafficking,' said Strike, still watching Kyle through his smoke. 'Women and kids from poor countries. One of the little girls in my case was filmed with a plastic bag over her head, while a bloke anally raped her.'

Out of the corner of her eye, Robin saw Kyle and Courtney throw her darting looks and knew, with an elevator drop in the area of her solar plexus, that her brother must have shared her history with his friends. Max was the only person at the table who seemed entirely relaxed. He was watching Strike with the dispassionate attention of a chemist checking an ongoing experiment.

'The video of that kid was viewed over a hundred thousand times online,' said Strike. Cigarette jammed in his mouth, he now helped himself to a large piece of cheesecake, effectively demolishing it to get a third of it onto his plate. 'Plenty of pleasure centres stimulated there, eh?' he went on, looking up at Kyle.

'No, but that's completely different, though,' said Courtney, rallying to Kyle's defence. 'We were talking about women who – it's up to women, grown women, to decide what they want to do with their own bod—'

'Did you cook all this?' Strike asked Max through a mouthful of cheesecake. He still had a lit cigarette in his left hand.

'Yes,' said Max.

'Bloody good,' said Strike. He turned back to Kyle. 'How many waitresses d'you know who got trafficked into it?'

'Well, obviously none but – I mean, you're bound to've seen that bad stuff, aren't you, being police—'

'As long as you don't have to see it, all good, eh?'

'Well, if you feel like that . . .' said Kyle, red in the face now, 'if you're so against it, you must never've – you've never used porn, then, you don't—?'

'If nobody else wants pudding,' said Robin loudly, standing

up and pointing towards the sofa area, 'shall we have coffee over there?'

Without waiting for an answer, she headed for the kitchen area. Behind her, she heard the scraping of a couple of chairs. After switching on the kettle, she headed downstairs to the bathroom, where, after she'd peed, she sat for five minutes on the toilet with her face in her hands.

Why had Strike turned up drunk? Why did they have to talk about rape and porn? Her attacker had been a voracious consumer of violent pornography, with a particular emphasis on choking, but his internet search history had been deemed inadmissible evidence by the judge. Robin didn't want to know whether Strike used porn; she didn't want to think about trafficked children being filmed, just as she didn't want to remember Morris's dick pic on her phone, or the snuff movie Bill Talbot had stolen. Tired and low, she asked herself why Strike couldn't leave the students alone, if not out of consideration for his host, then for her, his partner.

She headed back upstairs. Halfway to the living area she heard Kyle's heated voice and knew the argument had escalated. Arriving on the top floor, Robin saw the other five sitting around the coffee table, on which stood a cafetière, a bottle and the chocolates Jonathan had brought. Strike and Max were both holding glasses of brandy while Courtney, who was now very obviously drunk, though nowhere near as much as Strike, was nodding along with Kyle's argument, a cup of coffee balanced precariously in her hands. Robin sat back down at the abandoned dining table, away from the rest of the group, took a piece of beef out of the casserole and fed it to a pathetically grateful Wolfgang.

'The *point* is to destigmatise and reclaim derogatory language about women,' Kyle was saying to Strike. 'That's the *point*.'

'And that'll be 'chieved by a bunch'f nice middle-class girls going f'ra walk in their underwear, will it?' said Strike, his voice thick with alcohol.

'Well, not necessar'ly *under*—' began Courtney.

'It's about ending victim-blaming,' said Kyle loudly. 'Surely you can—?'

'An' how's it end victim-blaming?'

'Well, *obv'sly*,' said Courtney loudly, 'by changing the adertu – the underlying attitudes—'

'You think rapists'll see you all marching 'long and think "better jack in the raping", do you?'

Courtney and Kyle both began shouting at Strike. Jonathan glanced anxiously at his sister, who felt another of those sickening drops in her stomach.

'It's about destigmatising—'

'Oh, don't get me wrong, plen'y of men will enjoy watching you all strut past in your bras,' said Strike, taking a sloppy gulp of brandy, ''n 'I'm sure you'll look great on Instagram—'

'It's not about Instagram!' said Courtney, who sounded almost tearful now. 'We're making a serious point about—'

'Men who call women sluts, yeah, you said,' said Strike, talking over her again. 'I'm sure they'll feel properly rebuked, watching you prounce – prance by in your mini-skirt.'

'It's not about *rebuking*,' said Kyle, 'you're missing the—'

'I'm not missing your super-subtle fucking point,' snapped Strike. 'I'm telling you that in the *real* world, this f'cking Whore Walk—'

'SlutWalk,' said Kyle and Courtney loudly.

'—'ll make fuck-all difference. The kind of man who calls women sluts'll look at your fucking sideshow and think "there go a load of sluts, look". Reclaim fucking language all you fucking like. You don't change real altit – att – real-world attitudes by deciding slurs aren't derug – derogat'ry.'

Wolfgang, who was still quivering at Robin's ankle in the hope of getting more beef, emitted a loud whimper, which made Strike glance around. He saw Robin sitting there, pale and impassive.

'What *d'you* think 'bout all this?' Strike asked her loudly, waving his glass in the direction of the students, so that brandy slopped over the rim onto the carpet.

'I think it would be a good idea to change the subject,' said Robin, whose heart was beating so fast it hurt.

'Would *you* go on a fucking Whore—?'

'I don't know, maybe,' said Robin, blood thumping in her ears, wanting only for the conversation to end. Her rapist had grunted 'whore' over and over again during the attack. If her would-be killer had squeezed her neck for another thirty seconds, it would have been the last word she heard on earth.

'She's b'ng polite,' said Strike, turning back to the students.

'Talking for women now, are you?' sneered Kyle.

'For an *actual* rape victim!' said Courtney.

The room seemed to warp. A clammy silence descended. On the edge of Robin's field of vision she saw Max turn to look at her.

Strike got to his feet at the second attempt. Robin knew he was saying something to her, but it was all noise: her ears felt full of cotton wool. Strike lurched off towards the door: he was leaving. He bounced off the doorframe and disappeared from sight.

Everyone continued to stare at Robin.

'Oh God, I'm really sorry if I shouldn't have said that,' whispered Courtney through the fingers she'd pressed to her mouth. Her eyes were brimming with tears. From downstairs came the sound of the door slamming.

'It's fine,' said a distant voice that sounded quite like Robin's own. 'Excuse me a moment.'

She got to her feet, and followed Strike.

41

With that they gan their shiuering speares to shake,
And deadly points at eithers breast to bend,
Forgetfull each to haue bene euer others frend.

Edmund Spenser
The Faerie Queene

The dark, unfamiliar road took the exceptionally drunk Strike by surprise. Rain and high winds battered him as he stood, swaying, wondering which direction the Tube was. His usually reliable sense of direction was telling him to turn right, so he lurched off that way, searching his pockets for cigarettes as he went, savouring the delicious release of tension and temper he'd just enjoyed. The memory of what had just happened presented itself in a few scattered fragments: Kyle's angry red face. *Tosser. Fucking students.* Max laughing at something Strike had said. Lots of food. Even more drink.

Rain sparkled in the street lights and blurred Strike's vision. Objects seemed to shrink and enlarge around him, particularly the parked car that suddenly put itself in his path as he attempted to walk in a straight line down the street. His thick fingers fumbled fruitlessly in his pockets. He couldn't find his cigarettes.

That last brandy might have been a mistake. He could still taste it. He didn't like brandy, and he'd had a hell of a lot of Doom Bar with Nick in the pub.

It was a mighty effort to walk in these high winds. His glow of well-being was wearing off, but he definitely didn't feel sick, even after all that beef casserole and a sizeable bit of cheesecake, though he didn't really want to think about them, nor about the forty or so cigarettes he'd consumed in the past twenty-four hours, nor about the brandy he could still taste.

Without warning, his stomach contracted. Strike staggered to a gap between two cars, bent double and vomited as copiously as he'd done at Christmas, over and over, for several minutes, until he was standing with his hands on his knees, still heaving, but bringing nothing else up.

Sweaty-faced, he stood up, wiping his mouth on the back of his hand, pistons banging in his head. It was several seconds before he became aware of the pale figure standing watching him, its fair hair blowing wildly in the wind.

'Wh—? Oh,' he said, as Robin came into focus. 'It's you.'

It occurred to him that she might have followed him to bring his forgotten cigarettes and looked hopefully at her hands, but they were empty. Strike moved away from the puddle of vomit in the gutter and leaned up against another parked car.

'I was in the pub with Nick all afternoon,' he said thickly, under the impression that Robin might be concerned about him.

Something hard was pressing into his buttock. Now he realised that he did have his cigarettes on him, after all, and he was glad of this, because he'd rather taste tobacco than vomit. He tugged the pack out of his back pocket and, after a few false starts, managed to light up.

At last, it penetrated his consciousness that Robin's demeanour was unusual. Focusing on her face, he registered it as white and oddly pinched.

'What?'

'"What?"' she repeated. 'Fucking "*what?*"'

Robin swore far less often than Strike did. The damp night air, which felt icy on Strike's sweaty face, was rapidly sobering him up. Robin appeared to be angry: angrier, in fact, than he'd ever seen her. But drink was still slowing his reactions, and nothing better occurred to him than to repeat,

'What?'

'You arrive late,' she said, 'because of *course* you do, because when have you ever shown me the common *fucking* courtesy of turning up on time—'

'Wha—?' said Strike again, this time less because he was looking for information than in disbelief. She was the unique woman in his life who'd never tried to change him. This wasn't the Robin he knew.

'You arrive *rat-arsed*, because of *course* you do, because what do I matter? It's only *Robin* who'll be embarrassed, and *my* flatmate, and *my* fam—'

'He wasn't bothered,' Strike managed to say. His memories of the evening weren't particularly distinct, but he was sure of that, at least: Max hadn't minded him being drunk. Max had given him more booze. Max had laughed at a joke he'd made, which he couldn't now remember. He liked Max.

'And then you launch an attack on my guests. And then,' said Robin, 'you lay me open to having something I wanted to keep priv – to keep—'

Her eyes were suddenly wet, her fists clenched, her body rigid.

'—to keep private bandied about in a fucking argument, in front of strangers. Did it *once* occur—'

'Hang on,' said Strike, 'I never—'

'—*once* occur to you that I might not want *rape* discussed, in front of people I barely know?'

'*I* never—'

'Why were you asking me whether I think SlutWalks are a good idea?'

'Well, obv'sly b'cause—'

'Did we need to talk about child rape over dinner?'

'I was making a p—'

'And then you *walk out*, and leave me to—'

'Well,' said Strike, 'by the sounds of it, the sooner I left, the bett—'

'Better for *you*,' she said, advancing on him, her teeth bared: he'd never seen her like this before, 'because you got to dump all your aggression at my house, then walk out and let me clean up your fucking mess, as per usual!'

'"As per fucking usual?"' said Strike, eyebrows raised. 'Wait a—'

'Now I've got to go back in there, and make it all right, soothe everyone's feelings—'

'No, you haven't,' Strike contradicted her. 'Go to fucking bed if you—'

'It's. What. I. DO!' shouted Robin, thumping herself hard on the sternum with each word. Shocked into silence, Strike stared at her. 'Like I remember to say *please* and *thank you* to the secretary, when you don't give a toss! Like I excuse your bad moods to other people when they get offended! Like I suck up a ton of shit on your behalf—'

'Whoa,' said Strike, pushing himself off the stationary car, and looking down at her from his full height. 'Where's all this—?'

'—and you can't be *fucking* bothered, with all I do for you, to arrive sober for *one dinner*—'

'If you must know,' said Strike, temper rising anew from the ashes of his previous euphoria, 'I was in the pub with Nick, who—'

'—whose wife just lost their baby! I know – and what the *fuck* was he doing in the pub with you, leaving her to—'

'She threw him out!' barked Strike. 'Did she tell you that, during the Great Sisterhood Grievance Meeting? And I'm not going to apologise for wanting some fucking R&R after the week I've just had—'

'—whereas *I* don't need R&R, do I? *I* haven't forfeited half my annual leave—'

'How many times have I thanked you for covering for me when I'm in Corn—?'

'So what was with you being an arsehole to me this morning, when I was late for the *first fucking time ever*—'

'I'd had three and a half hours' sleep—'

'You live over the bloody office!'

'Fuck this,' said Strike, throwing his cigarette down. He began to walk away from her, certain now of the direction to the Tube, thinking of the things he could have said: that it was guilt about the pressure he was putting on Robin that had kept him in London, when he should be in St Mawes with his dying aunt; Jonny Rokeby on the phone that morning; and Nick's tears in the pub, and the relief it had been to sit with an old mate and drink, and listen to someone else's troubles instead of fret about his own.

'And *don't*,' bellowed Robin from behind him, 'buy me any more *fucking flowers*!'

'No danger of that!' yelled Strike over his shoulder, as he strode away into the darkness.

42

. . . his late fight
With Britomart, so sore did him offend,
That ryde he could not, till his hurts he did amend.

Edmund Spenser
The Faerie Queene

When Strike woke on Saturday morning, with a thumping headache and a foul-tasting mouth, it took him a while to piece together
exactly what had happened the previous evening. Aside from the
memory of vomiting, which he felt he'd done far too much of lately,
all he could at first recall were Kyle's bright red face and Robin's
pinched white one.

But then, slowly, he reconstructed Robin's complaints: arriving
late and drunk, being rude to her brother and upsetting a dinner
party by telling a couple of students what he considered home truths
about the real world. He also thought there'd been mention of him
being insufficiently touchy-feely with staff.

Gingerly, he got out of bed and, with the aid of the furniture,
hopped his way to the bathroom and then into the shower.

As Strike washed, two separate impulses did battle within him.
One was the urge to self-justify, which patted him on the back and
awarded him a win for what he could remember of his argument with
the students. The other was an innate honesty about his motives that
forced him to recognise that his instant antagonism to Robin's guests
had been rooted in their resemblance to the kinds of people towards
whom his mother would have instantly gravitated.

Leda Strike's whole life had been a battle against constraint of any kind: going for a march in her underwear would have seemed to her just one more fabulous blow against limitations. Strike, who never forgot Leda's generous heart or her ineradicable love of the underdog, was nevertheless clear-eyed about the fact her activism had mostly taken the form of enthusiastic exhibitionism. Not for Leda the tedious toil of door-to-door canvassing, the difficult business of compromise, or the painstaking work structural change entailed. Never a deep or critical thinker, she'd been a sucker for what Strike thought of as intellectual charlatans. The basis for her life's philosophy, if such a word could be used for the loose collection of whims and kneejerk reactions she called beliefs, was that everything of which the bourgeoisie disapproved must be good and right. Naturally, she'd have sided with Kyle and Courtney in championing pornography and SlutWalks, and she'd have seen her son's quibbles as something he must have picked up from her killjoy sister-in-law.

While Strike dried himself and put on his prosthesis, moving cautiously in deference to his throbbing head, the idea of phoning Robin occurred, only to be dismissed. His long-established habit, in the aftermath of a row with a woman, was to wait for her to make the next move, which he considered mere common sense. If she apologised, all well and good; if she wanted further discussion, there was a chance she'd be calmer after a spell of reflection; if she was still angry, it was simply masochistic to volunteer for further grief until she came looking for it. While Strike wasn't in principle opposed to offering an unsolicited apology in the event that he felt himself to have been in the wrong, in practice his apologies tended to be delivered late, and only when it became clear that resolution would come no other way.

This modus operandi owed much to his experiences with Charlotte. Attempting to make up with Charlotte before every last ounce of her fury had been spent had been like trying to rebuild a house during an earthquake. Sometimes, after he refused to accede to some new demand – usually leaving the army, but sometimes giving up contact with another female friend or refusing to spend money he didn't have, all of which were seen by Charlotte as proof he didn't love her – Charlotte would walk out, and only after she came back, by which time Strike might well have met or slept with someone else, would the row be discussed. Their arguments had often lasted a week or more. A couple of times, Strike had returned to postings abroad before anything was resolved.

Yet, as he ate a much-needed bacon roll, drank coffee and downed a couple of Nurofen; after he'd called Ted, heard that Joan was still holding out, and assured him that he and Lucy would be there the following day; while opening a couple of bits of post, and ripping up a large gilt-edged invitation to the Deadbeats' fiftieth anniversary party in May; while food shopping in the everlasting wind and rain, stocking up for what might be a journey of many hours; while he packed clothes for the trip, spoke to Lucy and checked the weather forecast, his thoughts kept returning to Robin.

Gradually he realised that what was bothering him most was the fact that he'd got used to Robin being on his side, which was one of the main reasons he tended to seek reasons to call her if he was at a loose end or feeling low. Over time, they'd developed a most soothing and satisfying camaraderie, and Strike hadn't imagined it could be disrupted by what he categorised as a dinner party row.

When his phone rang at four o'clock in the afternoon, he surprised himself by snatching it up in the hope that it was his partner, only to see yet another unknown number. Wondering whether he was about to hear Rokeby again, or some other unknown blood relative, he answered.

'Strike.'

'What?' said a sharp, middle-class female voice.

'Cormoran Strike here. Who's this?'

'Clare Spencer, the Athorns' social worker. You left a message for me.'

'Oh, yes,' said Strike, pulling out a kitchen chair and sitting down. 'Thanks for getting back to me, Mrs – er – Ms Spencer.'

'Mrs,' she said, sounding very slightly amused. 'Can I just ask – are you *the* Cormoran Strike?'

'I doubt there are many others,' said Strike.

He reached for his cigarettes, then pushed them away again. He really did need to cut down.

'I see,' said Clare Spencer. 'Well, it was a bit of a shock to get a message from you. How d'you know the Athorns?'

'Their name came up,' said Strike, thinking how very inaccurate a statement that was, 'in the course of a case I'm investigating.'

'Was it *you* who went into their downstairs neighbour's shop, and threatened him?'

'I didn't threaten him,' said Strike. 'But his attitude seemed aggressive, so I pointed out that they had friends who might take it amiss if he bullied them.'

'Ha,' said Clare, sounding warmer. 'He's a horror, that man. He's been trying to get them out of that flat for ages. Wants to buy the whole building. He removed a supporting wall, then tried to blame Deborah and Samhain for his ceiling sagging. He's caused them a lot of stress.'

'The flat was –' Strike almost said 'mucked out', but tried to find a politer way of saying it, '– thoroughly cleaned recently, he said?'

'Yes. I'm not denying it was pretty messy, but we've sorted that out now, and as for saying they've caused structural damage, we got a surveyor in who went through the whole place and agreed there's nothing wrong with it. *What* a chancer the man is. Anyway, you did a good thing, there, warning him off. He thinks because they haven't got many close relatives, he can get away with browbeating them. So, what's this case you're investigating?'

Briefly, Strike told her about Margot Bamborough, her disappearance in 1974, and the information that had led him to the Athorns' door.

'. . . and so,' he concluded, 'I wanted to talk to someone who could tell me how much reliance I can put on what they've told me.'

There was a brief silence.

'I see,' said Clare, who sounded a little more guarded now. 'Well, I'm afraid I've got a duty of confidentiality as their social worker, so—'

'Could I ask you some questions? And if you can't answer, obviously I'll accept that.'

'All right,' she said. He had the impression that his actions with regard to the bullying ironmonger had put her on his side.

'They're clearly competent to live alone,' said Strike.

'With support, yes,' said Clare. 'They've done very well, actually. They've got a strong mutual bond. It's probably kept both of them out of institutionalised care.'

'And what exactly—?' Strike wondered how to word the question sensitively. Clare came to his aid.

'Fragile X syndrome,' she said. 'Deborah's relatively high-functioning, although she's got some social difficulties, but she can read and so forth. Samhain copes better socially, but his cognitive impairment's greater than his mother's.'

'And the father, Gwilherm—?'

Clare laughed.

'I've only been their social worker for a couple of years. I never knew Gwilherm.'

'You can't tell me how sane he was?'

There was a longer pause.

'Well,' she said, 'I suppose . . . it seems to be common knowledge that he was very odd. Various family members have spoken to me about him. Apparently he thought he could hex people. With black magic, you know.'

'Deborah told me something I found . . . slightly concerning. It involved a doctor called Dr Brenner, who was a partner of Dr Bamborough's at the St John's practice. She might've been referring to a medical examination, but—'

He thought Clare had said something.

'Sorry?'

'No, nothing. What exactly did she tell you?'

'Well,' said Strike, 'she mentioned having to take her pants off, and not wanting to, but she said Gwilherm told her she had to. I assumed—'

'This was a doctor?'

'Yes,' said Strike.

There was another, longer pause.

'I don't really know what to tell you,' said Clare finally. 'It's possible that was a medical examination, but . . . well, a lot of men used to visit that flat.'

Strike said nothing, wondering whether he was being told what he thought he was being told.

'Gwilherm had to get drink and drugs money somewhere,' said Clare. 'From what Deborah's disclosed to social workers over the years, we think he was – well, not to put too fine a point on it, we think he was pimping her out.'

'Christ,' muttered Strike, in disgust.

'I know,' said Clare. 'From bits and piece she's told caregivers, we think Gwilherm used to take Samhain out whenever she was with a client. It *is* dreadful. She's so vulnerable. On balance, I can't be sorry Gwilherm died young. But please – don't mention any of this to Deborah's family, if you speak to them. I've no idea how much they know, and she's happy and settled these days. There's no need to upset anyone.'

'No, of course not,' said Strike, and he remembered Samhain's words: *old Joe Brenner was a dirty old man.*

'How reliable would you say Samhain's memory is?'

'Why? What's he told you?'

'A couple of things his Uncle Tudor said.'

'Well, people with Fragile X usually have quite good long-term memories,' said Clare cautiously. 'I'd say he'd be more reliable about things his Uncle Tudor told him than on many subjects.'

'Apparently Uncle Tudor had a theory about what happened to Margot Bamborough. It involved some people called "Nico and his boys".'

'Ah,' said Clare, 'yes. D'you know who that is?'

'Go on.'

'There was an old gangster who used to live in Clerkenwell,' said Clare, 'called Niccolo Ricci. Samhain likes talking about "Nico and his boys". Like they're folk heroes, or something.'

They talked for a couple more minutes, but Clare had nothing more of interest to tell.

'Well, thanks very much for getting back to me,' said Strike. 'Social workers work Saturdays as well as detectives, I see.'

'People don't stop needing help at weekends,' she said drily. 'Good luck. I hope you find out what happened to that poor doctor.'

But he could tell by her tone, however friendly, that she thought it highly unlikely.

Strike's headache had now settled into a dull throb that increased if he bent over or stood up too suddenly. He returned to his methodical arrangements for next day's departure to Cornwall, emptying his fridge of perishables, making sandwiches for the trip; listening to the news, which told him that three people had died that day as a result of the adverse weather conditions; packing his kit bag; ensuring his emails were up to date, setting up an out-of-office message redirecting potential clients to Pat, and checking the rota, to make sure it had been altered to accommodate his absence. Through all these tasks he kept an ear out for his mobile, in case a text from Robin arrived, but nothing came.

Finally, at eight o'clock, while he was finishing cooking the fry-up he felt he was owed given his hangover and how hard he'd worked all day, his mobile buzzed at last. From across the table, he saw that three long consecutive texts had arrived. Knowing that he was leaving the following morning without any clear idea of when he'd be back, Robin appeared to have begun the reconciliation process as women were wont to do, with an essay on her various grievances. He opened the first message, magnanimously prepared to accept almost any terms for a negotiated peace, and only then realised that it was from an unknown number.

I thought today was Valentine's day but I've just realised it's the 15th. They've got me on so many drugs in here I can hardly remember my name. I'm in a place again. This isn't my phone. There's another woman here who's allowed one & she lent it to me. Yours is the only mobile number I know by heart. Why didn't you ever change it? Was it because of me or is that my vanity. I'm so full of drugs I cant feel anything but I know I love you. I wonder how much they'd have to give me before that went too. Engouh to kill me I suppose.

The next message, from the same number, read:

How did you spent valentines day. Did you have sex. I'm here partly because I don't want sex. I cant stand him touching me and I know he wants more kids. Id rather die than have more. Actually I'd rather die than most things. But you know that about me. Will I ever see you again? You could come and see me here. Today I imagined you walking in, like I did when your leg. I imagined you telling them to let me go because you loved me and you'd look after me. I cried and

The third message continued:

the psychiatrist was pleased to see me crying because they like emotion. I don't know what the whole address is but it's called Symonds House. I love you don't forget me whatever hpapens to me. I love you.

A fourth and final message read:

It's Charlotte in case that isn't obvious.

Strike read the entire thread through twice. Then he closed his eyes, and like millions of his fellow humans, wondered why troubles could never come singly, but in avalanches, so that you became increasingly destabilised with every blow that hit you.

43

And you faire Ladie knight, my dearest Dame,
Relent the rigour of your wrathfull will,
Whose fire were better turn'd to other flame;
And wiping out remembrance of all ill,
Graunt him your grace . . .

Edmund Spenser
The Faerie Queene

To Robin's relief, her three guests got up early the next morning, because they wanted to spend a full day in London. All were subdued after what Robin thought of as the Nightmare Dinner. She dreaded a tearful plea for forgiveness from Courtney, who seemed especially low, so Robin faked a cheery briskness she certainly didn't feel, making recommendations for cheap places to eat and good things to see before waving the students off. As Robin was due to run surveillance on Elinor Dean overnight, she'd given Jonathan a spare key, and wasn't sorry that she'd probably still be in Stoke Newington when the students returned to Manchester, because they intended to catch a mid-morning Sunday train.

Not wanting to be alone with Max, in case he wanted a post-mortem on the previous evening, Robin made herself a voluntary prisoner in her own bedroom all day, where she continued to work on her laptop, attempting to block out waves of anger towards Strike, and a tearfulness that kept threatening to overcome her. Hard as she tried to concentrate on finding out who'd been living in Jerusalem Passage when Margot had disappeared, however, her thoughts kept returning to her partner.

Robin wasn't in the least surprised not to have heard from him, but was damned if she'd initiate contact. She couldn't in good conscience retract a word of what she'd said after watching him vomit in the gutter, because she was tired of being taken for granted in ways Strike didn't recognise.

But as the afternoon wore on, and the rain continued to fall outside her window, and while she hadn't been nearly as drunk as Strike, she developed a dull headache. Equal parts of misery and rage dragged at her every time she remembered last night's dinner, and all the things she'd shouted at Strike in the street. She wished she could cry, but the tightness in her chest prevented her doing so. Her anger boiled anew every time she remembered the drunk Strike attacking her guests, but then she found herself re-running Courtney and Kyle's arguments in her head. She was sure none of the students had ever brushed up against the ugliness Robin had encountered, not merely under that dark stair in her hall of residence, but during her work with Strike: battered women, raped girls, death. They didn't want to hear Strike's stories, because it was so much more comforting to believe that language alone could remake the world. But none of that made her feel more kindly to her partner: on the contrary, she resented agreeing with him. He'd been looking for someone or something to attack, and it was she who'd paid the price.

Robin forced herself to keep working, because work was her one constant, her salvation. By eight in the evening, Robin was as sure as a thorough perusal of online records could make her that nobody living in Jerusalem Passage had been there for forty years. By this time, she was so hungry that she really did need to eat something, which she feared meant facing Max, and discussing Strike.

Sure enough, when she reached the living area, she found Max sitting watching TV with Wolfgang on his lap. He muted the news the moment he saw her, and Robin's heart sank.

'Evening.'

'Hi,' said Robin. 'I'm going to make myself something to eat. D'you want anything?'

'There's still a bit of casserole, if you want it.'

'Strike didn't finish it all, then?'

508

She mentioned him first in the spirit of getting it over with. She could tell that Max had things to say.

'No,' said Max. He lifted the sleepy Wolfgang onto the sofa beside him, stood up and moved to the kitchen. 'I'll heat it up for you.'

'There's no need, I can—'

But Max did so, and when Robin was settled at the table with her food and a drink, he sat down at the table with her with a beer. This was highly unusual and Robin felt suddenly nervous. Was she being softened up for some kind of unwelcome announcement? Had Max decided, after all, to sell up?

'Never told you how I ended up in such a nice flat, did I?' he said.

'No,' said Robin cautiously.

'I had a big payout, five years ago. Medical negligence.'

'Oh,' said Robin.

There was a pause. Max smiled.

'People usually say, "Shit, what went wrong?" But you never probe, do you? I've noticed that. You don't ask a lot of questions.'

'Well, I have to do a lot of that at work,' said Robin.

But that wasn't why she hadn't asked Max about his finances, and it wasn't why she didn't ask now what had gone wrong with his body or his treatment, either. Robin had too many things in her own past that she didn't want endlessly probed to want to cause other people discomfort.

'I was having palpitations seven years ago,' Max said, examining the label on his beer. 'Arrhythmia. I got referred to a heart specialist and he operated: opened me up and ablated my sinus node. You probably don't know what that is,' he said, glancing up at Robin, and she shook her head. 'I didn't either, until they ballsed mine up. Basically, they knackered my heart's ability to beat for itself. I ended up having to be fitted with a pacemaker.'

'Oh no,' said Robin, a bit of beef suspended in mid-air on her fork.

'And the best bit was,' said Max, 'none of it was necessary. There wasn't anything wrong with my sinus node in the first place. Turned out I hadn't been suffering from atrial tachycardia at all. It was stage fright.'

'I – Max, I'm so sorry.'

'Yeah, it wasn't good,' said Max, taking a sip of his beer. 'Two unnecessary open-heart surgeries, endless complications. I lost jobs, I was unemployed for four years and I'm still on anti-depressants. Matthew said I *had* to pursue a claim against the doctors. I probably wouldn't have done, if he hadn't nagged me. Lawyers' fees. Ton of stress. But I won in the end, got a big payout, and he persuaded me to sink it all into a decent property. He's a barrister, he earns great money. Anyway, we bought this place.'

Max pushed his thick blond hair out of his face and glanced down at Wolfgang, who'd trotted to the table to savour the smell of casserole once more.

'A week after we moved in, he sat me down and told me he was leaving. The ink was barely dry on the mortgage. He said he'd struggled against it, because he felt a loyalty to me, because of what I'd been through, but he couldn't fight his feelings any longer. He told me,' said Max, with a hollow smile, 'he'd realised pity wasn't love. He wanted me to keep the flat, didn't want me to buy him out – as if I could have done – so he signed over his half. That was to make him feel less guilty, obviously. And off he went with Tiago. He's Brazilian, the new guy. Owns a restaurant.'

'That,' said Robin quietly, 'sounds like hell.'

'Yeah, it was ... I really need to stop looking at their bloody Instagram accounts.' Max heaved a deep sigh and absent-mindedly rubbed the shirt over the scars on his chest. 'Obviously I thought of just selling up, but we barely lived here together, so it's not as though it's got a ton of memories. I didn't have the energy to go through more house-hunting and moving, so here I've stayed, struggling to make the mortgage every month.'

Robin thought she knew why Max was telling her all this, and her hunch was confirmed when he looked directly at her and said,

'Anyway, I just wanted to say, I'm sorry about what happened to you. I had no idea. Ilsa only told me you were held at gunpoint—'

'Oh, I didn't get raped *then*,' said Robin, and to Max's evident surprise, she started to laugh. Doubtless it was her tiredness, but it was a relief to find dark comedy in this litany of terrible things humans did to each other, though none of it was really funny at all: his mutilated

510

heart, the gorilla mask in her nightmares. 'No, the rape happened ten years ago. That's why I dropped out of university.'

'Shit,' said Max.

'Yeah,' said Robin, and echoing Max, she said, 'it wasn't good.'

'So when did the knife thing happen?' asked Max, eyes on Robin's forearm, and she laughed again. Really, what else was there to do?

'That was a couple of years ago.'

'Working for Strike?'

'Yes,' said Robin, and she stopped laughing now. 'Listen, about last night—'

'I enjoyed last night,' said Max.

'You can't be serious,' said Robin.

'I'm completely serious. It was really useful for building my character. He's got some proper big man, take-no-bullshit energy about him, hasn't he?'

'You mean he acts like a dick?'

Max laughed and shrugged.

'Is he very different sober?'

'Yes,' said Robin, 'well – I don't know. Less of a dick.' And before Max could ask anything else about her partner, she said quickly, 'He's right about your cooking, anyway. That was fantastic. Thanks so much, I really needed that.'

Having cleared up, Robin returned downstairs, where she showered before changing for the night's surveillance. With an hour to go before she needed to take over from Hutchins, she sat back down on her bed and idly typed variations on the name Paul Satchwell into Google. *Paul L Satchwell. LP Satchwell. Paul Leonard Satchwell. Leo Paul Satchwell.*

Her mobile rang. She glanced down. It was Strike. After a moment or two, she picked it up, but said nothing.

'Robin?'

'Yes.'

'Are you OK to talk?'

'Yes,' she said again, her heart beating faster than usual as she frowned up at the ceiling.

'Calling to apologise.'

Robin was so astonished, she said nothing for several seconds. Then she cleared her throat and said,

'Can you even remember what you're apologising for?'

'Er . . . yeah, I think so,' said Strike. 'I . . . didn't mean *that* to get dragged up. Should've realised it wasn't a subject you'd want discussed over dinner. Didn't think.'

Tears started in Robin's eyes at last.

'OK,' she said, trying to sound casual.

'And I'm sorry for being rude to your brother and his friends.'

'Thank you,' said Robin.

There was a silence. The rain still fell outside. Then Strike said,

'Have you heard from Ilsa?'

'No,' said Robin. 'Have you heard from Nick?'

'No,' said Strike.

There was another silence.

'So, we're OK, yeah?' said Strike.

'Yes,' said Robin, wondering whether it was true.

'If I've taken you for granted,' said Strike, 'I'm sorry. You're the best I've got.'

'Oh, for *fuck's* sake, Strike,' said Robin, abandoning the pretence that she wasn't crying as she snorted back tears.

'What?'

'You just . . . you're bloody infuriating.'

'Why?'

'Saying that. Now.'

'That's not the first time I've said it.'

'It is, actually.'

'I've told other people.'

'Yeah, well,' said Robin, now laughing and crying simultaneously as she reached for tissues, 'you see how that isn't the same thing as telling *me*?'

'Yeah, I s'pose,' said Strike. 'Now you mention it.'

He was smoking at his small Formica kitchen table while the eternal rain fell outside his attic window. Somehow, the texts from Charlotte had made him realise he had to call Robin, had to make things right with her before he set off for Cornwall and Joan. Now the sound of her voice, and her laughter, acted on him as it usually did, by making everything seem fractionally less awful.

'When are you leaving?' Robin asked, drying her eyes.

'Tomorrow at eight. Lucy's meeting me at the car hire. We've got a jeep.'

'Well, be careful,' said Robin. She'd heard on the news that day about the three people who'd died, trying to travel through the wind and the floods.

'Yeah. Can't pretend I don't wish you were driving. Lucy's bloody terrible behind the wheel.'

'You can stop flattering me now. I've forgiven you.'

'I'm serious,' said Strike, his eyes on the relentless rain. 'You and your advanced driving course. You're the only person who doesn't scare the shit out of me behind the wheel.'

'D'you think you'll make it?'

'Possibly not all the way in the jeep. But Polworth's standing by to rescue us. He's got access to dinghies. We've got to do it. Joan might only have days.'

'Well, I'll be thinking about you,' said Robin. 'Keeping everything crossed.'

'Cheers, Robin. Keep in touch.'

After Strike had hung up, Robin sat for a while, savouring the sudden feeling of lightness that had filled her. Then she pulled her laptop towards her, ready to shut it down before she left for her night's surveillance in the Land Rover. Casually, as she might have thrown the dice one last time before turning away from the craps table, she typed 'Paul Satchwell artist' into Google.

... **artist Paul Satchwell** has spent most of his career on the Greek island of ...

'What?' said Robin aloud, as though the laptop had spoken to her. She clicked on the result, and the website of the Leamington Spa Museum and Art Gallery filled the screen. She hadn't once seen it, in all her hours of searching for Satchwell. This page had either just been created or amended.

Temporary Exhibition March 3rd – 7th 2014

Local Artists

The Leamington Spa Museum and Art Gallery will be hosting
a temporary exhibition of artists from the Warwickshire area.
Entrance free.

Robin scrolled down the page past sundry artists' photos until she saw him.

It was, without a doubt, the same man. His face might be leathery and cracked, his teeth might have yellowed, his thick, curly hair turned whiter and thinner, but it still hung to his shoulders, while his open shirt showed thick white chest hair.

Born in Leamington Spa and raised in Warwick, artist Paul
Satchwell has spent most of his career on the Greek island
of Kos. Working mainly in oils, Paul's Hellenic-influenced
exploration of myths challenge the viewer to face primal fears
and examine preconceptions through sensual use of line and
colour . . .

44

Huge sea of sorrow, and tempestuous griefe,
Wherein my feeble barke is tossed long,
Far from the hoped hauen of reliefe,
Why doe thy cruel billowes beat so strong,
And thy moyst mountaines each on others throng,
Threatning to swallow vp my fearefull lyfe?

Edmund Spenser
The Faerie Queene

The storm water, rain and gales they faced were real enough, yet Strike and Lucy's battle to reach St Mawes had a strange, dream-like quality. Both knew death lay at the end; both were resolved that if they managed to reach Joan alive, they would stay with her until she died.

Trees swayed and creaked as they sped along the motorway. They had to divert around great wide lakes where lately there had been fields, forcing them miles out of their way. Twice they were halted at roadblocks and told, by irate police, to turn back. They pressed on, at one point driving fifty miles to progress fifteen, listening to every weather update on the radio and becoming progressively more certain that there would come a point where they had to abandon the jeep. Rain lashed the car, high winds lifted the windscreen wipers from the glass, and brother and sister took it in turns to drive, bound by a single objective, and temporarily freed from all other concerns.

To Strike's grateful surprise, the crisis had revealed a different Lucy, just as illness had uncovered a different Joan. His sister was focused entirely on what needed to be done. Even her driving was different, without three noisy sons in the back seat, squabbling and thumping each other if the journey lasted longer than twenty minutes. He'd forgotten how efficient and practical Lucy could be, how patient, how resolute. Her calm determination only broke when they reached an impasse thirty miles from St Mawes, where flooding and fallen trees had rendered the road impassable.

While Lucy sat slumped at the steering wheel, sobbing with her face in her arms, Strike left the jeep to stand outside under a tree, where, sheltering from the perennial rain and taking the opportunity to smoke, he called Dave Polworth, who was holding himself ready to assist them.

'Yeah, we thought that's where you'd have to stop,' said Polworth, when Strike had given him their position.

'Who's "we"?'

'Well, I can't fucking do this alone, can I, Diddy? Should be with you in an hour. Stay in the car.'

And an hour later, true to his word, Dave Polworth and five other men, two of them members of the local lifeguard, three old schoolfriends of Strike's, emerged out of the gathering gloom. Dressed in waterproofs, and carrying waders ready for the worst passages, the men took charge of Strike and Lucy's bags. Leaving the jeep parked up a side street, the party set off on foot.

The end of Strike's stump began to chafe long before they had walked for two hours solid over boggy ground and slippery tarmac. Soon, he had to abandon pride and allow two of his old schoolfriends to support him on either side. Darkness fell before they reached a couple of dinghies that Polworth had arranged to carry them over flooded fields. Using oars to alternately row and punt themselves along, they navigated with the aid of torches and compasses.

Polworth had called on every friend and acquaintance he knew to arrange Strike and Lucy's passage across the storm-ravaged peninsula. They covered several miles by tractor pulling a trailer, but at some passages were forced to wade through feet of icy flood water, the diminutive Lucy accepting a piggyback from the largest lifeboat man.

Four hours after they'd abandoned the jeep, they reached St

Mawes. At the gate of Ted and Joan's house, brother and sister hugged each of their escorts goodbye.

'Don't start,' said Polworth, as the weary and sore Strike tried to put into words what he felt to be incommunicable. 'Get inside, or what the fuck was it all for?'

Ted, whom they'd updated regularly through their journey, greeted them in pyjamas at the back door, tears running down the deep folds in his craggy face.

'I never thought you'd get here,' he kept saying, as he made them tea. '*Never* thought you'd make it.'

'How is she?' asked the shivering Lucy, as the three of them sat in the kitchen, their hands around mugs of tea, eating toast.

'She managed a bit of soup today,' said Ted. 'She's still . . . she sleeps a lot. But when she's awake, she likes to talk. Oh, she'll be over the moon to have you two here . . .'

And so began days that had the same strange, outside-time quality of their journey. Initially Strike, the end of whose stump was rubbed raw after the painful exigencies of their journey, abandoned his prosthesis and navigated the small house by hopping and holding onto chair backs and walls. He read and responded to Robin's emails about the agency's work, but her news seemed to come from a place far more remote than London.

Joan was now bird-like in her frailty, her bones visible through the translucent skin. She'd made it clear that she wished to die at home, not in the hospital in Truro, so she lay, tiny and shrunken, in the large double bed that dominated the bedroom, a bed that had been purchased to accommodate Ted's bulk back when he'd been a tall, fit and muscular man, late of the Royal Military Police and subsequently a stalwart member of the local lifeguard.

By day, Strike, Ted and Lucy took it in turns to sit beside Joan's bed, because awake or asleep, she liked to know that one of them was nearby. Kerenza came morning and afternoon, and these were the only times when her family left the room. Joan was no longer able to swallow medication, so Kerenza began injecting the morphine through a syringe driver. Strike knew that she washed his aunt, and helped her perform still more private functions: the long convalescence after his amputation had left him under no illusion about what nurses dealt with. Kind, efficient and humane, Kerenza was one of the few people Strike welcomed gladly into the draughty kitchen.

And still Joan clung on. Three days after their arrival, four: she slept almost constantly, but still she clung to life.

'It's you two,' said Ted. 'She doesn't want to go while you two are here.'

Strike was coming to dread silences too large for human voices to fill. His nerves were stretched by the constant clinking of teaspoons in hot drinks made for something to do, by the tears shed by Uncle Ted when he thought nobody was looking, by the hushed enquiries of well-meaning neighbours.

On the fifth day, Lucy's husband Greg arrived with their three boys. Husband and wife had debated how sensible it was to take the boys out of school, and risk a journey that remained tricky, though the storms had at last subsided, but Lucy could bear their absence no longer. When Greg arrived, the boys came running out of the car towards their mother and the whole family clung to each other, while Strike and Ted looked on, united in their aloneness, unmarried man and soon-to-be widower. The boys were led up to Joan's bedroom to see her, and she managed smiles for all of them. Even Luke was subdued afterwards, and Jack cried.

Both spare rooms were now needed to accommodate the new arrivals, so Strike returned, uncomplaining, to sleep on the sofa.

'You look like shit,' Polworth informed him bluntly on day six, and indeed Strike, who'd woken every hour on the horsehair sofa, felt it. 'Let's get a pint.'

'Can I come?' asked Jack hopefully. He was showing a tendency to hang around Strike rather than his father, while Lucy sat upstairs with Joan.

'You can if your dad says it's OK,' said Strike.

Greg, who was currently walking around the garden with his phone clamped to his ear, trying to contribute to a conference call with his London office while Luke and Adam played football around him, agreed with a thumbs up.

So Strike, Polworth and Jack walked down into St Mawes together. Though the sky was dark and the roads still wet, the winds had at last dropped. As they reached the seafront, Strike's mobile rang. He answered it, still walking.

'Strike.'

'It's Shanker. Got your message.'

'I left that ten days ago,' said Strike.

'I've been busy, you ungrateful piece of shit.'

'Sorry,' said Strike.

He waved the other two on and paused again at the harbour wall, looking out at the green-grey sea and the hazy horizon.

'I've nosed around a bit,' said Shanker, 'and you're not gonna find out 'oo that bint was, Bunsen. The one on the film. Nobody knows. She'll 'ave done somethin' fucking serious to get that, though.'

'Deserved it, you reckon,' said Strike, as he surveyed the flat sea. It didn't look capable, now, of the violence it had inflicted upon the town.

'I'm not saying she *deserved* – I'm sayin' even Mucky Ricci didn't make 'an 'abit of *that*,' said Shanker impatiently. 'Are you in solitary?'

'What?'

'Where the fuck are you? There's no noise.'

'In Cornwall.'

For a moment, Strike expected Shanker to ask where that was. Shanker was almost impressively ignorant of the country that lay beyond London.

'The fuck are you doin' in Cornwall?'

'My aunt's dying.'

'Oh shit,' said Shanker. 'Sorry.'

'Where is he now?'

''Oo?'

'Ricci.'

''E's in an 'ome. I told you.'

'All right. Thanks for trying, Shanker. Appreciate it.'

For perhaps the first time ever, it was Shanker who shouted at Strike to stop him hanging up.

'Oi – oi!'

'What?' said Strike, raising the mobile to his ear again.

'Why d'you wanna know where 'e is? You ain't gonna go talkin' to Ricci. You're done.'

'I'm not done,' said Strike, eyes screwed up against the sea breeze. 'I haven't found out what happened to the doctor, yet.'

'*Fuck's* sake. D'you wanna get shot through the fuckin' 'ead?'

'See you, Shanker,' said Strike, and before his old friend could say anything else, he cut the call and muted his phone.

Polworth was already at a table with Jack when Strike reached the Victory, two pints and a Coke on the table.

'Just been telling Jack,' Polworth told Strike, as the detective sat down. 'Haven't I, eh?' he asked Jack, who nodded, beaming. 'For when he's older. *This* is his local.'

'A pub three hundred miles from where he lives?'

'He was born in Cornwall. He was just telling me.'

'Oh yeah,' said Strike. 'I forgot about that.'

The family had been staying with Ted and Joan when Lucy went into labour a month early. Jack had been born in the same Truro hospital as Strike himself.

'And you're a Nancarrow on your mum's side,' Polworth told Jack, who was greatly enjoying Polworth's approval. 'So that makes you a Cornishman, born and bred.'

Polworth turned to Strike.

'Who was the pearly king on the phone there? We could hear his cockney a mile off.'

'Guy called Shanker,' said Strike. 'I've told you about him. My mum scraped him off the street one night when he'd been stabbed. He adopted us.'

Strike sipped his pint, wondering how Polworth and Shanker would get on, in the unlikely event of them ever meeting. He fancied they might end up punching each other. They seemed to Strike like pieces from entirely different jigsaw puzzles: no point of connection. At the mention of stabbing, Polworth had glanced at Jack, but lowering his pint Strike said,

'Don't worry about him. He wants to be a Red Cap, like me and Ted.'

Jack beamed some more. He was having a great time.

'Can I try some of that beer?' he asked his uncle.

'Don't push it,' said Strike.

'Look at this,' said Polworth, pointing at a page in the newspaper he'd picked up. 'Westminster trying to bully the Scots, the bast—'

Strike cleared his throat. Jack giggled.

'Sorry,' said Polworth. 'But come on. Telling them they can't keep the pound if they vote for independence? 'Course they'll keep the pound. It's in everyone's interests . . . '

He talked on for the next ten minutes about small nationalism, the obvious arguments for both Scottish and Cornish independence and the idiocy of those who opposed them, until Jack looked glazed and Strike, as a last resort, dragged the conversation back to football. Arsenal, as he'd foreseen, had lost to defending champions Bayern Munich, and he didn't doubt the second leg would see them knocked out. He and Ted had watched the game together and done a good job of pretending they cared about the result. Strike permitted Polworth to pass censorious comment on the foul that had seen Szczęsny sent off, and politics was mercifully dropped.

Strike thought about Polworth later that night, as he lay in the dark on the horsehair sofa again, unable to sleep. His tiredness now had a feverishness about it, exacerbated by the aching of his body, the perpetual strain of being here, in this overcrowded house, waiting for the tiny body upstairs to give up.

In this near fever state, a jumble of ideas circulated in Strike's mind. He thought of categories and boundaries, of those we want to create and enforce, and those we seek to escape or destroy. He remembered the fanatic glint in Polworth's eye as he argued for a harder boundary between his county and the rest of England. He fell asleep thinking about the spurious groupings of astrology, and dreamed of Leda, laying out her tarot cards in the Norfolk commune of long ago.

Strike was woken at five by his own aching body. Knowing that Ted would be awake soon, he got up and dressed, ready to take over the bedside vigil while his uncle ate breakfast.

Sure enough, hearing Strike's footstep on the upstairs landing, Ted emerged from the bedroom in his dressing gown.

'Just made you tea,' whispered Strike. 'It's in the pot in the kitchen. I'll sit with her for a bit.'

'You're a good lad,' whispered Ted, clapping Strike on the arm. 'She's asleep now, but I had a little chat with her at four. Most she's said for days.'

The talk with his wife seemed to have cheered him. He set off downstairs for his tea and Strike let himself quietly into the familiar room, taking up his position on the hard-backed chair beside Joan.

The wallpaper hadn't been changed, so far as Strike knew, since Ted and Joan had moved into the house, their only home since he'd left the army, in the town where both had grown up. Ted and Joan seemed not to notice that the house had grown shabby over the decades: for all that Joan was meticulous about cleanliness, she'd equipped and decorated the house once and seemed never to have seen any need to do so again. The paper was decorated with small bunches of purple flowers, and Strike could remember tracing geometric shapes between them with his forefinger as a small child, when he climbed into bed with Ted and Joan early in the morning, when both were still sleepy and he wanted breakfast and a trip to the beach.

Twenty minutes after he'd sat down, Joan opened her eyes and looked at Strike so blankly that he thought she didn't know him.

'It's me, Joan,' he said quietly, moving his chair a little closer to her bed and switching on the lamp, with its fringed shade. 'Corm. Ted's having breakfast.'

Joan smiled. Her hand was a tiny claw, now. The fingers twitched. Strike took it into his own. She said something he couldn't hear, and he lowered his large head to her face.

'What did you say?'

'. . . you're . . . good man.'

'Oh, I don't know about that,' muttered Strike.

He held her hand in a light clasp, scared of putting pressure on it. The *arcus senilis* outlining the irises of her pale eyes made the blue seem more faded than ever. He thought of all the times he could have visited, and hadn't. All those missed opportunities to call. All those times he'd forgotten her birthday.

'. . . helping people . . . '

She peered up at him and then, making a supreme effort, she whispered,

'I'm proud of you.'

He wanted to speak, but something was blocking his throat. After a few seconds, he saw her eyelids drooping.

'I love you, Joan.'

The words came out so hoarsely they were almost inaudible, but he thought she smiled as she sank back into a sleep from which she was never to wake.

45

Of auncient time there was a springing well,
From which fast trickled forth a siluer flood,
Full of great vertues, and for med'cine good.

Edmund Spenser
The Faerie Queene

Robin was still at the office when Strike called that evening with the news that Joan had died.

'I'm sorry about this, but I think I'm going to have to stay down here until we get this funeral sorted,' said Strike. 'There's a lot to do and Ted's in pieces.'

He'd just shared Joan's plan for her funeral with Ted and Lucy, thereby reducing both of them to sobs at the kitchen table. Ted's tears were for the poignancy of his wife making arrangements for his own comfort and relief, as she'd done for the fifty years of their marriage, and for the news that she'd wanted, at the end, to enter the sea and wait for him there. In Lucy's case, the sobs were for the lost possibility of a grave she'd hoped to visit and tend. Lucy filled her days with voluntary obligations: they gave purpose and form to a life she was determined would never be like her flighty biological mother's.

'No problem,' Robin reassured him. 'We're coping fine.'

'You're sure?'

'Completely sure.'

'There's a backlog at the crematorium, because of the floods,' said Strike. 'Funeral's pencilled in for March the third.'

This was the day Robin was planning to spend in Leamington

Spa, so she could attend the opening of Paul Satchwell's exhibition. She didn't tell Strike this: she could tell that he had limited mental capacity right now for anything other than Joan, and his life in Cornwall.

'Don't worry,' she repeated. 'I'm so sorry, Cormoran,' she added.

'Thanks,' said Strike. 'I'd forgotten what it's like. Planning a funeral. I've already had to referee one argument.'

After he'd shared Joan's plans for her send-off, and Lucy and Ted had mopped up their tears, Ted had suggested they ask mourners for donations to the Macmillan Cancer Support in lieu of flowers.

'... but Lucy says Joan would've wanted flowers,' Strike told Robin. 'I've suggested we say either. Ted says that'll mean people do both and they can't afford it, but fuck it. Lucy's right. Joan *would* want flowers, and as many as possible. That's how she always judged other people's funerals.'

After they'd bidden each other goodbye, Robin sat for a while at the partners' desk, wondering whether it would be appropriate for the agency to send flowers to Strike's aunt's funeral. She'd never met Joan: she worried that it would seem odd, or intrusive, to send condolences. She remembered how, when she'd offered to pick Strike up from Joan's house in St Mawes the previous summer, he'd quickly cut her off, erecting, as ever, a firm boundary between Robin and his personal life.

Yawning, Robin shut down the computer, closed the completed file on Postcard, which she'd been updating, got to her feet and went to get her coat. At the outer door she stopped, her reflection blank-faced in the dark glass. Then, as though responding to an unheard command, she returned to the inner office, switched the computer back on and, before she could second-guess herself, ordered a sheaf of dark pink roses to be delivered to St Mawes church on March the third, with the message 'With deepest sympathy from Robin, Sam, Andy, Saul and Pat'.

Robin spent the rest of the month working without respite. She conducted a final meeting with the persecuted weatherman and his wife, in which she revealed Postcard's identity, gave them Postcard's real name and address, and took their final payment. She then had

Pat contact their waiting list client, the commodities broker who suspected her husband of sleeping with their nanny and, next day, welcomed the woman to the office to take down her details and receive a down payment.

The commodities broker didn't bother to hide her disappointment that she was meeting Robin instead of Strike. She was a thin, colourless blonde of forty-two, whose over-highlighted hair had the texture, close up, of fine wire. Robin found her unlikeable until the end of the interview, when she talked about her husband, whose business had gone bankrupt and who now worked from home, giving him many long hours alone with the nanny.

'Fourteen years,' said the broker. 'Fourteen years, three kids and now ...'

She hid her eyes behind her shaking hands and Robin, who'd been with Matthew since she was at school, felt, in spite of the woman's brittle façade, an unexpected glow of sympathy.

After the new client had left, Robin called Morris into the office and gave him the job of the first day's surveillance of the nanny.

'Okey-doke,' he said. 'Hey, what d'you say we call the client "RB"?'

'What does that stand for?' Robin asked.

'Rich Bitch,' said Morris, grinning. 'She's loaded.'

'No,' said Robin, unsmiling.

'Whoops,' said Morris, eyebrows raised. 'Feminist alert?'

'Something like that.'

'OK, how about—?'

'We'll call her Mrs Smith, after the street they live on,' said Robin coldly.

Over the next few days, Robin took her turn tailing the nanny, a glossy-haired brunette who somewhat reminded her of Strike's ex-girlfriend Lorelei. The commodities broker's children certainly seemed to adore their nanny, and so, Robin feared, did their father. While he didn't once touch the nanny in any amorous way, he showed every sign of a man completely smitten: mirroring her body language, laughing excessively at her jokes, and hurrying to open doors and gates for her.

A couple of nights later, Robin dozed off at the wheel for a few seconds while driving towards Elinor Dean's house in Stoke Newington. Jerking awake, she immediately turned on the radio and opened the window, so that her eyes streamed with the cold, sooty night air, but the incident scared her. Over the next few days, she increased her caffeine consumption in an effort to keep awake. This made her slightly jittery, and she found it hard to sleep even on the rare occasions the chance presented itself.

Robin had always been as careful with the firm's money as Strike himself, treating every penny spent as though it were to be deducted from her own take-home pay. The habit of parsimony had stayed with her, even though the agency's survival no longer depended on extracting money from clients before the final demands came in. Robin was well aware that Strike took very little money out of the business for his own needs, preferring to plough profits back into the agency. He continued to live a Spartan existence in the two and a half rooms over the office, and there were months when she, the salaried partner, took home more pay than the senior partner and founder of the firm.

All of this added to her feeling of guilt at booking herself into a Premier Inn in Leamington Spa on the Sunday night before Satchwell's art exhibition. The town was only a two-hour drive away; Robin knew she could have got up early on Monday morning instead of sleeping over in the town. However, she was so exhausted, she feared dozing off at the wheel again.

She justified the hotel room to herself by leaving twenty-four hours ahead of the exhibition's opening, thus giving herself time to take a look at the church where Margot had allegedly been sighted a week after her disappearance. She also packed photocopies of all the pages of Talbot's horoscope notes that mentioned Paul Satchwell, with the intention of studying them in the quiet of her hotel room. To these, she added a second-hand copy of Evangeline Adams's *Your Place in the Sun*, a pack of unopened tarot cards and a copy of *The Book of Thoth*. She hadn't told Strike she'd bought any of these items and didn't intend claiming expenses for them.

Much as she loved London, Yorkshire-born Robin sometimes pined for trees, moors and hills. Her drive up the nondescript M40, past hamlets and villages with archaic names like Middleton Cheney, Temple Herdewyke and Bishop's Itchington, gave her glimpses of flat green fields. The cool, damp day bore a welcome whiff of spring on the air, and in the breaks between scudding white clouds, hard, bright sunshine filled the old Land Rover with a light that made a pale grey ghost of Robin's reflection in the dusty window beside her. She really needed to clean the car: in fact, there were sundry small, personal chores piling up while she worked non-stop for the agency, such as ringing her mother, whose calls she'd been avoiding, and her lawyer, who'd left a message about the upcoming mediation, not to mention plucking her eyebrows, buying herself a new pair of flat shoes and sorting out a bank transfer to Max, covering her half of the council tax.

As the hedgerows flashed by, Robin consciously turned her thoughts away from these depressing mundanities to Paul Satchwell. She doubted she'd find him in Leamington Spa, being unable to imagine why the seventy-five-year-old would want to leave his home on Kos merely to visit the provincial art gallery. Satchwell had probably sent his paintings over from Greece, or else given permission for them to be exhibited. Why would he leave what Robin imagined as a dazzling white-walled villa, an artist's studio set among olive groves? Her plan was to pretend an interest in buying or commissioning one of his paintings, so as to get his home address. For a moment or two, she indulged herself in a little fantasy of flying out to Greece with Strike, to interrogate the old artist. She imagined the oven-blast of heat that would hit them on leaving the plane in Athens, and saw herself in a dress and sandals, heading up a dusty track to Satchwell's front door. But when her imagination showed her Strike in shorts, with the metal rod of his prosthetic leg on display, she felt suddenly embarrassed by her own imaginings, and closed the little fantasy down before it took her to the beach, or the hotel.

On the outskirts of Leamington Spa, Robin followed the sign to All Saints church, which she knew from her research was the only possible candidate for the place where Charlie Ramage had seen Margot. Janice had mentioned a 'big church'; All Saints was a tourist attraction due to its size. None of the other churches in Leamington

Spa had graveyards attached to them. Moreover, All Saints was situated directly on the route of anyone travelling north from London. Although Robin found it hard to understand why Margot would have been browsing headstones in Leamington Spa, while her husband begged for information of her whereabouts in the national press and her Leamington-born lover remained in London, she had a strange feeling that seeing the church for herself would give her a better idea as to whether Margot had ever been there. The missing doctor was becoming very real to Robin.

She managed to secure a parking space in Priory Terrace, right beside the church, and set off on foot around the perimeter, marvelling at the sheer scale of the place. It was a staggering size for a relatively small town; in fact, it looked more like a cathedral, with its long, arched windows. Turning right into Church Street, she noted the further coincidence of the street name being so similar to Margot's home address. On the right, a low wall topped with railings provided an ideal spot for a motorbike rider to park, and enjoy a cup of tea from his Thermos, looking at the graveyard.

Except that there was no graveyard. Robin came to an abrupt standstill. She could only see two tombs, raised stone caskets whose inscriptions had been eroded. Otherwise, there was simply a wide stretch of grass intersected with two footpaths.

'Bomb fell on it.'

A cheery-looking mother was walking towards Robin, pushing a double pushchair containing sleeping boy twins. She'd correctly interpreted Robin's sudden halt.

'Really?' said Robin.

'Yeah, in 1940,' said the woman, slowing down. 'Luftwaffe.'

'Wow. Awful,' said Robin, imagining the smashed earth, the broken tombstones and, perhaps, fragments of coffin and bone.

'Yeah – but they missed them two,' said the woman, pointing at the aged tombs standing in the shadow of a yew tree. One of the twin toddlers gave a little stretch in his sleep and his eyelids flickered. With a comical grimace at Robin, the mother took off again at a brisk walk.

Robin walked into the enclosed area that had once been a

graveyard, looking around and wondering what to make of Ramage's story, now. There hadn't been a graveyard here in 1974, when he claimed to have seen Margot browsing among tombstones. Or had an intact cemetery been assumed by Janice Beattie, when she heard that Margot was looking at graves? Robin turned to look at the two surviving tombs. Certainly, if Margot had been examining these, she'd have been brought within feet of a motorcyclist parked beside the church.

Robin placed her hands on the cold black bars that kept the curious from actually touching the old tombs, and examined them. What could have drawn Margot to them? The inscriptions etched on the mossy stone were almost illegible. Robin tilted her head, trying to make them out.

Was she seeing things? Did one of the words say 'Virgo', or had she spent too much time dwelling on Talbot's horoscope notes? Yet the more she studied it, the more like 'Virgo' the name looked.

Robin associated that star sign with two people, these days: her estranged husband, Matthew, and Dorothy Oakden, the widowed practice secretary at Margot's old place of work. Robin had become so adept at reading Talbot's horoscope notes, that she routinely heard 'Dorothy' in her head when looking at the glyph for Virgo. Now she took out her phone, looked up the tomb and felt mildly reassured to discover that she wasn't seeing things: this was the last resting place of one James Virgo Dunn.

But why should it have been of interest to Margot? Robin scrolled down a genealogy page for the Virgos and the Dunns and learned that the man whose bones now lay in dust a few feet from her had been born in Jamaica, where he'd been the owner of forty-six slaves.

'No need to feel sorry for *you*, then,' Robin muttered, returning her phone to her pocket, and she walked on around the perimeter to the front of the church, until she reached the great oak and iron double front doors. As she headed up the stone steps towards them, she heard the low hum of a hymn. Of course: it was Sunday morning.

After a moment's hesitation, Robin opened the door as quietly as possible and peered inside. An immense, sombre space was revealed:

chilly parabolas of grey stone, a hundred feet of cold air between congregation and ceiling. Doubtless a church of this gigantic size had been deemed necessary back in Regency times, when people had flocked to the spa town to drink its waters, but the modern congregation didn't come close to filling it. A black-robed verger looked around at her; Robin smiled apologetically, quietly closed the door and returned to the pavement, where a large modern steel sculpture, part squiggle, part coil, was evidently supposed to represent the medicinal spring around which the town had been built.

A pub nearby was just opening its doors and Robin fancied a coffee, so she crossed the road and entered the Old Library.

The interior was large but hardly less gloomy than the church, the décor mostly shades of brown. Robin bought herself a coffee, settled herself in a tucked-away corner where she couldn't be observed, and sank into abstraction. Her glimpse of the church's interior had told her nothing. Margot had been an atheist, but churches were some of the few places a person could sit and think, undisturbed. Might Margot have been drawn to All Saints out of that unfocused, inchoate need that had once driven Robin herself into an unknown graveyard, there to sit on a wooden bench and contemplate the parlous state of her marriage?

Robin set down her coffee cup, opened the messenger bag she'd brought with her and took out the wad of photocopies of those pages of Talbot's notebook that mentioned Paul Satchwell. Smoothing them flat, she glanced up casually at the two men who'd just sat down at a nearby table. The one with his back to her was tall and broad, with dark, curly hair, and before she could remind herself that he couldn't be Strike, because her partner was in St Mawes, a thrill of excitement and happiness passed through her.

The stranger seemed to have felt Robin looking at him, because he turned before she could avert her eyes. She caught a glimpse of eyes as blue as Morris's, a weak chin and a short neck before she bowed her head to examine the horoscope notes, feeling herself turning red and suddenly unable to take in the mass of drawings and symbols in front of her.

Waves of shame were crashing over her, entirely disproportionate to catching a stranger's eye. In the pit of her stomach, the last sparks of the excitement she'd felt on thinking that she was looking at Strike glimmered and died.

It was a momentary error of perception, she told herself. *There's absolutely nothing to worry about. Calm down.*

But instead of reading the notes, Robin put her face in her hands. In this strange bar, her resistance lowered by exhaustion, Robin knew she'd been avoiding the question of what she really felt about Strike for the past year. Busy trying to disentangle herself from Matthew, familiarising herself with a new flat and a new flatmate, managing and deflecting her parents' anxiety and judgement, fending off Morris's constant badgering, dodging Ilsa's infuriating determination to matchmake and working twice as hard as ever before, it had been easy not to think about anything else, even a question as fraught as what she really felt for Cormoran Strike.

Now, in the corner of this dingy brown pub, with nothing else to distract her, Robin found herself thinking back to those honeymoon nights spent pacing the fine white sand after Matthew had gone to bed, when Robin had interrogated herself about whether she was in love with the man who'd then been her boss, not her partner. She'd worn a deep channel on the beach as she walked up and down in the dark, finally deciding that the answer was 'no', that what she felt was a mixture of friendship, admiration and gratitude for the opportunity he'd given her to embark on a once-dreamed-of career, which she'd thought was closed to her forever. She liked her partner; she admired him; she was grateful to him. That was it. That was all.

Except . . . she remembered how much pleasure it had given her to see him sitting in Notes Café, after a week's absence, and how happy she was, no matter the circumstances, to see Strike's name light up her phone.

Almost scared now, she forced herself to think about how bloody aggravating Strike could be: grumpy, taciturn and ungrateful, and nowhere near as handsome, with his broken nose and hair he himself described as 'pube-like', as Matthew, or even Morris . . .

But he was her best friend. This admission, held at bay for so long, caused an almost painful twist in Robin's heart, not least because she knew it would be impossible ever to tell Strike so. She could just imagine him lumbering away from her like a startled bison at such a naked statement of affection, redoubling the barriers he liked to erect if ever they got too close to each other. Nevertheless, there was a kind of relief in admitting the painful truth: she cared deeply for her partner. She trusted him on the big things: to do the right thing for the right reasons. She admired his brains and appreciated his doggedness, not to mention the self-discipline all the more admirable because many whole-bodied men had never mastered it. She was often astonished by his almost total lack of self-pity. She loved the drive for justice that she shared, that unbreakable determination to settle and to solve.

And there was something more, something highly unusual. Strike had never once made her feel physically uncomfortable. Two of them in the office, for a long time the only workers at the agency, and while Robin was a tall woman, he was far bigger, and he'd never made her feel it, as so many men did, not even in an attempt to intimidate, but because they enjoy the Parade, as a peacock spreads its tail. Matthew hadn't been able to get past the idea of them together all the time, in a small office space, hadn't been able to believe that Strike wasn't capitalising on the situation to make advances, however subtle.

But Robin, who'd forever be hypersensitive to the uninvited touch, the sidelong, lecherous glance, the invasion of personal space, the testing of conventional limits, had never once experienced, with Strike, that shrinking sensation within her own skin evoked by attempts to push a relationship into a different space. A deep reserve lay over Strike's private life, and while that sometimes frustrated her (had he, or had he not, called Charlotte Campbell back?), his love of privacy extended to a respect for other people's boundaries. Never had there been an ostensibly helpful but unnecessary touch, no hand on the small of the back, no grasping of the arm, no look that made her skin prickle, or made her want to cover herself: the legacy of those violent encounters with men that had left her scarred in more ways than the visible.

In truth (why not admit everything to herself now, when she was so tired, her defences lowered?) she was aware of only two moments in four years where she'd been sure that Strike had seen her as a desirable woman, not as a friend, or an apprentice, or a younger sister.

The first had been when she'd modelled that green Cavalli dress for him, in the course of their first investigation together, when he'd looked away from her as a man would if shunning too-bright light. She'd been embarrassed by her own behaviour, afterwards: she hadn't meant to make him think she was trying to be seductive or provocative; all she'd been trying to do was get information out of the sales assistant. But when he'd subsequently given her the green dress, thinking he'd never see her again, she'd wondered whether part of the message Strike had been trying to convey was that he didn't disavow that look, that she had, indeed, looked wonderful in the dress, and this suspicion hadn't made her feel uncomfortable, but happy and flattered.

The second moment, far more painful to remember, had been when she'd stood at the top of the stairs at her wedding venue, Strike below her, and he'd turned when she called his name, and looked up at her, the new bride. He'd been injured and exhausted, and again, she'd seen a flicker of something in his face that wasn't mere friendship, and they'd hugged, and she'd felt . . .

Best not to think about it. Best not to dwell on that hug, on how like home it had felt, on how a kind of insanity had gripped her at that moment, and she'd imagined him saying 'come with me' and known she'd have gone if he had.

Robin swept the horoscope papers off the pub table, stuffed them back into her messenger bag and went outside, leaving half her coffee undrunk.

Trying to walk off her memories, she crossed a small stone bridge spanning the slow-flowing River Leam, which was spotted with clumps of duckweed, and passed the colonnade of the Royal Pump Rooms, where Satchwell's exhibition would open the following day. Striding briskly, her hands in her pockets, Robin tried to focus on the Parade, where shopfronts disfigured what had once been a sweeping white Regency terrace.

But Leamington Spa did nothing to raise her spirits. On the contrary, it reminded her too much of another spa town: Bath, where

Matthew had gone to university. For Robin, long, symmetrical curves of Regency buildings, with their plain, classical façades, would forever conjure once-fond memories disfigured by later discoveries: visions of herself and Matthew strolling hand in hand, overlain by the knowledge that, even then, he'd been sleeping with Sarah.

'Oh, bugger everything,' Robin muttered, blinking tears out of her eyes. She turned abruptly and headed all the way back to the Land Rover.

Having parked the car closer to the hotel, she made a detour into the nearby Co-op to buy a small stash of food, then checked in at a self-service machine in her Premier Inn and headed upstairs to her single room. It was small, bare but perfectly clean and comfortable, and overlooked a spectacularly ugly town hall of red and white brick, which was over-embellished with scrolls, pediments and lions.

A couple of sandwiches, a chocolate éclair, a can of Diet Coke and an apple made Robin feel better. As the sun sank slowly behind the buildings on the Parade, she slipped off her shoes and reached into her bag for the photocopied pages of Talbot's notebook and her pack of Thoth tarot cards, which Aleister Crowley had devised, and in which Bill Talbot had sought the solution to Margot's disappearance. Sliding the pack out of the box into her hand, she shuffled through the cards, examining the images. Just as she'd suspected, Talbot had copied many motifs into his notebook, presumably from those cards which had come up during his frequent attempts to solve the case by consulting the tarot.

Robin now flattened a photocopy of what she thought of as the 'horns page', on which Talbot had dwelled on the three horned signs of the zodiac: Capricorn, Aries and Taurus. This page came in the last quarter of the notebook, in which quotations from Aleister Crowley, astrological symbols and strange drawings appeared far more often than concrete facts.

Here on the horns page was evidence of Talbot's renewed interest in Satchwell, whom he'd first ruled out on the basis that he was an Aries rather than a Capricorn. Talbot had evidently calculated Satchwell's whole birth horoscope and taken the trouble to note various aspects, which he noticed were *same as AC. Same as AC. AND DON'T FORGET LS connection.*

To add to the confusion, the mysterious Schmidt kept correcting signs, although he'd allowed Satchwell to keep his original sign of Aries.

And then an odd idea came to Robin: the notion of a fourteen-sign zodiac was clearly ludicrous (but why was it more ludicrous than a twelve-sign zodiac? asked a voice in her head, which sounded remarkably like Strike's), but certainly if you were going to squeeze in an extra two signs, dates would have to shift, wouldn't they?

She picked up her mobile and Googled 'fourteen-sign zodiac Schmidt'.

'Oh my God,' said Robin aloud, into her still hotel room.

Before she could fully process what she'd read, the mobile in her hand rang. It was Strike.

'Hi,' said Robin, hastily turning him to speakerphone so she could continue reading what she'd just found. 'How are you?'

'Knackered,' said Strike, who sounded it. 'What's happened?'

'What d'you mean?' asked Robin, her eyes rapidly scanning lines of text.

'You sound like you do when you've found something out.'

Robin laughed.

'OK, you won't believe this, but I've just found Schmidt.'

'You've what?'

'Schmidt, first name, Steven. He's a real person! He wrote a book in 1970 called *Astrology 14*, proposing the inclusion of two extra signs in the zodiac, Ophiuchus the Serpent-Bearer, and Cetus the Whale!'

There was a brief silence, then Strike muttered,

'How the hell did I miss that?'

'Remember that statue of the man holding the serpent, at Margot's old house?' said Robin, falling back on her pillows among the scattered tarot cards.

'Asclepius,' said Strike. 'Ophiuchus was the Roman form. God of healing.'

'Well, this explains all the changing dates, doesn't it?' said Robin,

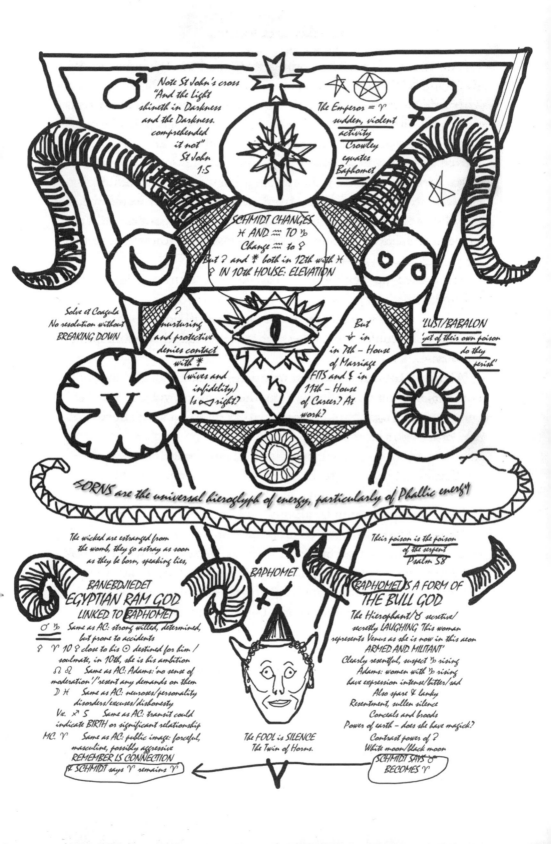

Note St John's cross
"And the Light
shineth in Darkness
and the Darkness
comprehended
it not"
St John
1:5

The Emperor = ♈
sudden, violent
activity
Crowley
equates
Baphomet

SCHMIDT CHANGES
♓ AND ♒ TO ♑
Change ♒ to ♀
But ♀ and ⚹ both in 12th with ♓
♀ IN 10th HOUSE: ELEVATION

Solve et Coagula
No resolution without
BREAKING DOWN

♀?
nurturing
and protective
denies contact
with ⚹
(wives and
infidelity)
Is ☿ right?

But
☿ in
in 7th – House
of Marriage
FITS and ♀ in
11th – House
of Career? At
work?

'LUST/BABALON
'yet of their own poison
do they
perish'

V

SORNS are the universal hieroglyph of energy, particularly of Phallic energy

The wicked are estranged from
the womb, they go astray as soon
as they be born, speaking lies,

BAPHOMET

This poison is the poison
of the serpent
Psalm 58

BANEBDJIEDET
EGYPTIAN RAM GOD
LINKED TO BAPHOMET

♂ ♑   Same as AC: strong willed, determined,
        but prone to accidents
♀ ♈ 10 ♉ close to his ☉ destined for him /
        soulmate, in 10th, she is his ambition
☊ ♌   Same as AC: Adams:'no sense of
        moderation'/resent any demands on them
☽ ♓   Same as AC: neuroses/personality
        disorders/excuses/dishonesty
Vx. ☊ ♐ ♐   Same as AC: transit could
        indicate BIRTH or significant relationship
MC. ♈   Same as AC: public image: forceful,
        masculine, possibly aggressive
REMEMBER LS CONNECTION
♀ SCHMIDT says ♈ remains ♈

The FOOL is SILENCE
The Twin of Horns.

RAPHOMET IS A FORM OF
THE BULL GOD
The Hierophant/♉ secretive/
secretly LAUGHING This woman
represents Venus as she is now in this aeon
ARMED AND MILITANT'
Clearly resentful, suspect ♑ rising
Adams: women with ♑ rising
have expression intense/bitter/sad
Also spare & lanky
Resentment, sullen silence
Conceals and broods
Power of earth – does she have magick?
Contrast power of ♀
White moon/black moon
SCHMIDT SAYS ♀
BECOMES ♈

'and why poor Talbot got so confused! He was trying to put everyone into Schmidt's adjusted dates, but they didn't seem to fit. And all the other astrologers he was consulting were still using the twelve-sign system, so—'

'Yeah,' said Strike, talking over her, 'that'd make a crazy man crazier, all right.'

His tone said, 'This is interesting, but not important.' Robin removed the Three of Disks from beneath her and examined it absent-mindedly. Robin was now so well-versed in astrological symbols that she didn't need to look up the glyphs to know that it also represented Mars in Capricorn.

'How are things with you?' she asked.

'Well, the church isn't going to hold everyone who's coming tomorrow, which Joan would've been thrilled about. I just wanted to let you know I'll be heading back up the road again on Tuesday.'

'Are you sure you don't need to stay longer?'

'The neighbours are all promising they're going to look after Ted. Lucy's trying to get him to come up to London for a bit afterwards. Any other news your end?'

'Er ... let's see ... I wrapped up Postcard,' said Robin. 'I think our weatherman was quite disappointed when he saw who his stalker was. His wife cheered up no end, though.'

Strike gave a grunt of laughter.

'So, we've taken on the commodities broker,' Robin continued. 'We haven't got pictures of anything incriminating between the husband and nanny yet, but I don't think it's going to be long.'

'You're owed a long stretch off for all this, Robin,' said Strike gruffly. 'I can't thank you enough.'

'Don't be silly,' she said.

They hung up shortly afterwards.

Robin's room seemed to have become suddenly much darker. The sun had gone down; in silhouette, the town hall resembled a monstrous Gothic palace. She turned on her bedside lamp and looked around at the bed strewn with astrological notes and tarot cards. Seen in the light of Strike's lack of enthusiasm, Talbot's doodles looked like the determinedly weird drawings in the back of a teenager's jotter, leading nowhere, done purely for the love of strangeness.

Yawning, she refolded the photocopied notes and put them back in her bag, went for a shower, returned in her pyjamas to the bed and gathered up the tarot cards, putting them in order as she did so, to make sure none of them were missing. She didn't particularly want the cleaner to think of her as the kind of person who left tarot cards strewn in her wake.

On the point of replacing the deck in its box, Robin suddenly sat down on the bed and began to shuffle it instead. She was too tired to attempt the fifteen-card layout advocated in the little booklet that accompanied the tarot, but she knew from her exhaustive examination of his notes that Talbot had sometimes tried to see his way through the investigation by laying out just three cards: the first representing 'the nature of the problem', the second, 'the cause', and the third, 'the solution'.

After a minute's shuffling, Robin turned over the top card and laid it down in the pool of light cast by her bedside lamp: the Prince of Cups. A naked blueish-green man rode an eagle, which was diving towards water. He held a goblet containing a snake in one hand and a lotus flower in the other. Robin pulled *The Book of Thoth* out of her bag and looked up the meaning.

> The moral characteristics of the person pictured in this card are sub-tlety, secret violence, and craft. He is intensely secret, an artist in all his ways.

She thought immediately of Dennis Creed. A master of murder, in his way.

She turned over the next card: the Four of Cups, or Luxury. Another lotus was pouring water over four more goblets, golden this time. Robin turned to the book.

> The card refers to the Moon in Cancer, which is her own house; but Cancer itself is so placed that this implies a certain weakness, an abandonment to desire.

Was the tarot criticising her for soft living? Robin glanced around her little box of a room, then turned over the last card.

More cups and yet more lotuses, and two entwined fish, pouring out water into two more golden chalices which stood on a green lake.

Love ... The card also refers to Venus in Cancer. It shows the harmony of the male and the female: interpreted in the largest sense. It is perfect and placid harmony ...

Robin inspected the card for a few more seconds, before laying it down beside the other two. They were all cups. As she knew from her study of the Thoth tarot, cups meant water. Well, here she was in a spa town ...

Robin shook her head, though nobody was there to see her do it, returned the tarot cards to their box, climbed into bed, set her alarm and turned out the light.

46

Whereas that Pagan proud him selfe did rest,
In secret shadow by a fountaine side:
Euen he it was, that earst would haue supprest
Faire Vna . . .

Edmund Spenser
The Faerie Queene

Robin's night was punctuated with sudden wakings from a succession of anxious dreams: that she'd fallen asleep at the wheel again, or had overslept and arrived at the gallery to find Satchwell's exhibition gone. When the alarm on her mobile rang at 7 a.m., she forced herself immediately out of bed, showered, dressed and, glad to leave the impersonal bedroom, headed downstairs with her packed holdall to eat muesli and drink coffee in the dining room, which was painted an oppressive sludge green.

The day outside was fresh but overcast, a cold silver sun trying to penetrate the cloud. Having returned her holdall to the parked Land Rover, she headed on foot towards the Royal Pump Rooms, which housed the gallery where Satchwell's exhibition was about to open. To her left lay the ornamental Jephson Gardens, and a fountain of pinkish stone that might have been the model for one of Crowley's tarot cards. Four scallop-patterned basins sat at the top.

. . . a certain weakness, an abandonment to desire . . .

You're getting like Talbot, Robin told herself crossly. Speeding up, she arrived at the Pump Rooms with time to spare.

The building had just been opened; a young woman in black was walking away from the glass doors, holding a bunch of keys. Robin entered, to find little trace of the Regency pump rooms left inside: the floor was covered in modern grey tiles, the ceiling supported by metal columns. A café took up one wing of the open-plan space, a shop another. The gallery, Robin saw, lay across opposite, through more glass doors.

It comprised one long room, brick-walled and wooden-floored, which had been temporarily given over to an exhibition of local artists. There were only three people inside: a stocky, grey-bobbed woman in an Alice band, a small man with a hang-dog air whom Robin suspected was her husband, and another young woman in black, who she assumed worked there. The grey-haired woman's voice was echoing around the room as though it was a gymnasium.

'I *told* Shona that Long Itchington needs an accent light! You can barely *see* it, this corner's so dark!'

Robin walked slowly around, looking at canvases and sketches. Five local artists had been given space for the temporary exhibition, but she identified Paul Satchwell's work without difficulty: it had been given a prominent position and stood out boldly among the studies of local landmarks, portraits of pallid Britons standing at bus stops, and still lifes.

Naked figures twisted and cavorted in scenes from Greek mythology. Persephone struggled in the arms of Hades as he carried her down into the underworld; Andromeda strained against chains binding her to rock as a dragonish creature rose from the waves to devour her; Leda lay supine in bulrushes as Zeus, in the form of a swan, impregnated her.

Two lines of Joni Mitchell floated back to Robin as she looked at the paintings: '*When I first saw your gallery, I liked the ones of ladies . . .*'

Except that Robin wasn't sure she liked the paintings. The female figures were all black-haired, olive-skinned, heavy-breasted and partially or entirely naked. The paintings were accomplished, but Robin found them slightly lascivious. Each of the women wore a similar expression of vacant abandon, and Satchwell seemed to have a definite preference for those myths that featured bondage, rape or abduction.

'Striking, aren't they?' said the meek-faced husband of the angry painter of Long Itchington, appearing at Robin's side to contemplate a picture of a totally naked Io, whose hair streamed behind her and whose breasts gleamed with sweat as she fled a bull with a gargantuan erection.

'Mm,' said Robin. 'I was wondering whether he was going to come to the exhibition. Paul Satchwell, I mean.'

'I think he said he's going to pop back in,' said the man.

'Back—? You mean he's here? In England?'

'Well, yes,' said the man, looking somewhat surprised. 'He was here yesterday, anyway. Came to see them hung.'

'Visiting family, I think he said,' said the young woman in black, who seemed glad of a reason to talk to somebody other than the fuming artist in the hairband.

'You haven't got contact details for him, have you?' asked Robin. 'Maybe the address of where he's staying?'

'No,' said the young woman, now looking intrigued. Evidently local artists didn't usually engender this much excitement. 'You can leave your name and address, though, if you like, and I'll tell him you want to speak to him if he drops by?'

So Robin accompanied the young woman back to the reception area, where she scribbled her name and phone number onto a piece of paper and then, her heart still beating fast in excitement, went to the café, bought herself a cappuccino and positioned herself beside a long window looking out onto the Pump Room Gardens, where she had a good view of people entering the building.

Should she book back into the Premier Inn and wait here in Leamington Spa until Satchwell showed himself? Would Strike think it worth neglecting their other cases to remain here in the hope of Satchwell turning up? It was Joan's funeral today: she couldn't burden him with the question.

She wondered what her partner was doing now. Perhaps already dressing for the service. Robin had only ever attended two funerals. Her maternal grandfather had died just before she dropped out of university: she'd gone home for the funeral and never gone back. She remembered very little of the occasion: it had taken everything she'd had to preserve a fragile façade of well-being, and she remembered the strange sense of disembodiment that underlay the eggshell brittleness with which she'd met the half-scared enquiries of family members who knew what had happened to her. She remembered, too, Matthew's hand around hers. He hadn't once dropped it, skipping lectures and an important rugby game to come and be with her.

The only other funeral she'd attended had been four years previously, when she and Strike had attended the cremation of a murdered girl in the course of their first murder investigation, standing together at the back of the sparsely populated, impersonal crematorium. That had been before Strike had agreed to take her on permanently, when she'd been nothing but a temp whom Strike had allowed to inveigle her way into his investigation. Thinking back to Rochelle Onifade's funeral, Robin realised that even then, the ties binding her to Matthew had been loosening. Robin hadn't yet realised it, but she'd found something she wanted more than she'd wanted to be Matthew's wife.

Her coffee finished, Robin made a quick trip to the bathroom, then returned to the gallery in the hope that Satchwell might have entered it while she wasn't watching, but there was no sign of him. A few people had drifted in to wander around the temporary exhibition. Satchwell's paintings were attracting the most interest. Having walked the room once more, Robin pretended an interest in an old water fountain in the corner. Covered in swags and lion's heads with gaping mouths, it had once dispensed the health-giving spa waters.

Beyond the font lay another a room, which presented a total contrast to the clean, modern space behind her. It was octagonal and made of brick, with a very high ceiling and windows of Bristol blue glass. Robin stepped inside: it was, or had once been, a Turkish *hammam* or steam room, and had the appearance of a small temple. At the highest point of the vaulted ceiling was a cupola decorated with an eight-pointed star in glass, with a lantern hanging from it.

'Nice to see a bit of *pagan* influence, innit?'

The voice was a combination of self-conscious cockney, overlain with the merest whiff of a Greek accent. Robin spun around and there, planted firmly in the middle of the *hammam*, in jeans and an old denim shirt, was an elderly man with his left eye covered in a surgical dressing, which stood out, stark white against skin as brown as old terracotta. His straggly white hair fell to his stooping shoulders; white chest hair grew in the space left by his undone buttons, a silver chain hung around his crêpe-skinned throat, and silver and turquoise rings decorated his fingers.

'You the young lady 'oo wanted to talk to me?' asked Paul Satchwell, revealing yellow-brown teeth as he smiled.

'Yes,' said Robin, 'I am. Robin Ellacott,' she added, holding out her hand.

His uncovered eye swept Robin's face and figure with unconcealed appreciation. He held her hand a little too long after shaking it but Robin continued to smile as she withdrew it, and delved in her handbag for a card, which she gave him.

'Private detective?' said Satchwell, his smile fading a little as he read the card, one-eyed. 'The 'ell's all this?'

Robin explained.

'Margot?' said Satchwell, looking shocked. 'Christ almighty, that's, what ... forty years ago?'

'Nearly,' said Robin, moving aside to let some tourists claim her spot in the middle of the *hammam*, and read its history off the sign on the wall. 'I've come up from London in hopes of talking to you about her. It'd mean a lot to the family if you could tell me whatever you remember.'

'*Éla ré*, what d'you expect me to remember after all this time?' said Satchwell.

But Robin was confident he was going to accept. She'd discovered that people generally wanted to know what you already knew, why you'd come to find them, whether they had any reason to worry. And sometimes they wanted to talk, because they were lonely or felt neglected, and it was flattering to have somebody hang on your words, and sometimes, as now (elderly as he was, the single eye, which was a cold, pale blue, swept her body and back to her face) they wanted to spend more time with a young woman they found attractive.

'All right, then,' said Satchwell slowly, 'I don't know what I can tell you, but I'm hungry. Let me take you to lunch.'

'That'd be great, but I'll be taking you,' said Robin, smiling. 'You're doing *me* the favour.'

47

. . . the sacred Oxe, that carelesse stands,
With gilden hornes, and flowry girlonds crownd . . .
All suddeinly with mortall stroke astownd,
Doth groueling fall . . .
The martiall Mayd stayd not him to lament,
But forward rode, and kept her ready way . . .

Edmund Spenser
The Faerie Queene

Satchwell bade the attendant in the art gallery farewell by clasping her hands in a double handshake and assuring her he'd look in later in the week. He even took fulsome leave of the disgruntled painter of Long Itchington, who scowled after him as he left.

'Provincial galleries,' he said, chuckling, as he and Robin headed out of the Pump Rooms. 'Funny, seeing my stuff next to that old bat's postcard pictures, though, wasn't it? And a bit of a kick to be exhibited where you were born. I haven't been back here in, Christ, must be fifty-odd years. You got a car? Good. We'll get out of here, go froo to Warwick. It's just up the road.'

Satchwell kept up a steady stream of talk as they walked towards the Land Rover.

'Never liked Leamington.' With only one eye at his service, he had to turn his head in exaggerated fashion to look around. 'Too *genteel* for the likes of me . . .'

Robin learned that he'd lived in the spa town only until he was six, at which point he and his single mother had moved to Warwick. He had a younger half-sister, the result of his mother's second marriage, with whom he was currently staying, and had decided to have his cataract removed while in England.

'Still a British citizen, I'm entitled. So when they asked me,' he said, with a grand wave backwards at the Royal Pump Rooms, 'if I'd contribute some paintings, I thought, why not? Brought them over with me.'

'They're wonderful,' said Robin insincerely. 'Have you got just the one sister?' She had no aim other than making polite conversation, but out of the corner of her eye, she saw Satchwell's head turn so that his unbandaged eye could look at her.

'No,' he said, after a moment or two. 'It was . . . I 'ad an older sister, too, but she died when we were kids.'

'Oh, I'm sorry,' said Robin.

'One of those things,' said Satchwell. 'Severely disabled. Had fits and stuff. She was older than me. I can't remember much about it. Hit my mum hard, obviously.'

'I can imagine,' said Robin.

They had reached the Land Rover. Robin, who'd already mentally calculated the risk to herself, should Satchwell prove to be danger-ous, was confident that she'd be safe by daylight, and given that she had control of the car. She unlocked the doors and climbed into the driver's seat, and Satchwell succeeded in hoisting himself into the passenger seat on his second attempt.

'Yeah, we moved froo to Warwick from 'ere after Blanche died,' he said, buckling up his seatbelt. 'Just me and my mum. Not that Warwick's much better, but it's *aufentic*. Aufentic medieval buildings, you know?'

Given that he was Midlands born and raised, Robin thought his cockney accent must be a longstanding affectation. It came and went, mingled with an intonation that was slightly foreign after so many years in Greece.

'Whereas this place . . . the Victorians 'ad their wicked way with it,' he said, and as Robin reversed out her parking space he said, looking up at the moss-covered face of a stone Queen Victoria, 'there she is, look, miserable old cow,' and laughed. 'State of that building,' he added, as they passed the town hall. 'That's somefing me and Crowley had in common, for sure. Born 'ere, hated it 'ere.'

Robin thought she must have misheard.

'You and . . . ?'

'Aleister Crowley.'

'Crowley?' she repeated, as they drove up the Parade. 'The occult writer?'

'Yeah. 'E was born here,' said Satchwell. 'You don't see that in many of the guidebooks, because they don't like it. 'Ere, turn left. Go on, it's on our way.'

Minutes later, he directed her into Clarendon Square, where tall white terraced houses, though now subdivided into flats, retained a vestige of their old grandeur.

'That's it, where he was born,' said Satchwell with satisfaction, pointing up at number 30. 'No plaque or nothing. They don't like talking about him, the good people of Leamington Spa. I had a bit of a Crowley phase in my youth,' said Satchwell, as Robin looked up at the large, square windows. 'You know he tortured a cat to death when he was a boy, just to see whether it had nine lives?'

'I didn't,' said Robin, putting the car into reverse.

'Probably 'appened in there,' said Satchwell with morbid satisfaction.

Same as AC. Same as AC. Another moment of enlightenment had hit Robin. Talbot had gone looking for identical components between Satchwell's horoscope and Crowley's, the self-proclaimed Beast, Baphomet, the wickedest man in the West. *LS connection.* Of course: Leamington Spa.

Why had Talbot decided, months into the investigation, that Satchwell deserved a full horoscope, the only one of the suspects to be so honoured? His alibi appeared watertight, after all. Had the return of suspicion been a symptom of Talbot's illness, triggered by the coincidence of Satchwell and Crowley's place of birth, or had he uncovered some unrecorded weakness in Satchwell's alibi? Satchwell continued to talk about his life in Greece, his painting and about his disappointment in how old England was faring, and Robin made appropriate noises at regular intervals while mentally reviewing those features of Satchwell's horoscope that Talbot had found so intriguing.

Mars in Capricorn: strong-willed, determined, but prone to accidents.
Moon in Pisces: neuroses/personality disorders/dishonesty
Leo rising: no sense of moderation. Resents demands on them.

They reached Warwick within half an hour and, as Satchwell had promised, found themselves in a town that could hardly have presented a greater contrast to the wide, sweeping white-faced crescents of Leamington. An ancient stone arch reminded Robin of Clerkenwell. They passed timber and beam houses, cobbles, steep sloping streets and narrow alleyways.

'We'll go to the Roebuck,' said Satchwell, when Robin had parked in the market square. 'It's been there for ever. Oldest pub in town.'

'Wherever you like,' said Robin, smiling as she checked that she had her notebook in her handbag.

They walked together through the heart of Warwick, Satchwell pointing out such landmarks as he deemed worth looking at. He was one of those men who felt a need to touch, tapping Robin unnecessarily upon the arm to draw her attention, grasping her elbow as they crossed a street, and generally assuming a proprietorial air over her as they wove their way towards Smith Street.

'D'you mind?' asked Satchwell, as they drew level with Picturesque Art Supplies, and without waiting for an answer he led her into the shop where, as he selected brushes and oils, he talked with airy self-importance of modern trends in art and the stupidity of critics. *Oh, Margot*, Robin thought, but then she imagined the Margot Bamborough she carried with her in her head judging her, in turn, by Matthew, with his endless store of anecdotes of his own sporting achievements, and his increasingly pompous talk of pay rises and bonuses, and felt humbled and apologetic.

At last, they made it into the Roebuck Inn, a low-beamed pub with a sign of a deer's head hanging outside, and secured a table for two towards the rear of the pub. Robin couldn't help but notice the coincidence: the wall behind Satchwell was dotted with horned animal heads, including a stuffed deer and bronze-coloured models of an antelope and a ram. Even the menus had silhouettes of antlered stag heads upon them. Robin asked the waitress for a Diet Coke, all the while trying to repress thoughts of the horned signs of the zodiac.

'Would it be all right,' she asked, smiling, when the waitress had departed for the bar, 'if I ask a few questions about Margot now?'

'Yeah, of course,' said Satchwell, with a smile that revealed his stained teeth again, but he immediately picked up the menu card and studied it.

'And d'you mind if I take notes?' Robin asked, pulling out her notebook.

'Go ahead,' he said, still smiling, watching her over the top of his menu with his uncovered eye, which followed her movements as she opened the book and clicked out the nib of her pen.

'So, I apologise if any of these questions—'

'Are you sure you don't want a proper drink?' asked Satchwell, who had ordered a beer. 'I 'ate drinking on me own.'

'Well, I'm driving, you see,' said Robin.

'You could stay over. Not with me, don't worry,' he said quickly, with a grin that on a man so elderly, resembled a satyr's leer, 'I mean, go to an 'otel, file expenses. I s'pect you're taking a good chunk of money from Margot's family for this, are you?'

Robin merely smiled, and said,

'I need to get back to London. We're quite busy. It would be really useful to get some background on Margot,' she continued. 'How did you meet?'

He told her the story she already knew, about how he'd been taken to the Playboy Club by a client and seen there the leggy nineteen-year-old in her bunny ears and tail.

'And you struck up a friendship?'

'Well,' said Satchwell, 'I don't know that I'd call it *that*.'

With his cold eye upon Robin he said,

'We 'ad a very strong *sexual* connection. She was a virgin when we met, y'know.'

Robin kept smiling formally. He wasn't going to embarrass her.

'She was nineteen. I was twen'y-five. Beau'iful girl,' he sighed. 'Wish I'd kept the pictures I took of her, but after she disappeared I felt wrong about 'aving them.'

Robin heard Oonagh again. 'He took pictures of her. *You* know. *Pictures.*' It must be those revealing or obscene photos Satchwell was talking about, because after all, he'd hardly have felt guilty about having a snapshot.

The waitress came back with Satchwell's beer and Robin's Diet Coke. They ordered food; after swiftly scanning the menu, Robin asked for a chicken and bacon salad; Satchwell ordered steak and chips. When the waitress had gone Robin asked, though she knew the answer,

'How long were you together?'

'Coupla years, all told. We broke up, then got back togevver. She didn't like me using other models. Jealous. Not cut out for an artist's muse, Margot. Didn't like sitting still and not talking, haha ... no, I fell hard for Margot Bamborough. Yeah, there was a damn sight more to her than being a Bunny Girl.'

Of course there was, thought Robin, though still smiling politely. *She became a bloody doctor.*

'Did you ever paint her?'

'Yeah,' said Satchwell. 'Few times. Some sketches and one full-size picture. I sold them. Needed the cash. Wish I 'adn't.'

He fell into a momentary abstraction, his uncovered eye surveying the pub, and Robin wondered whether old memories were genuinely resurfacing behind the heavily tanned face, which was so deeply lined and dark it might have been carved from teak, or whether he was playing the part that was expected of him when he said quietly,

'Hell of a girl, Margot Bamborough.'

He took a sip of his beer, then said,

'It's her 'usband who's hired you, is it?'

'No,' said Robin. 'Her daughter.'

'Oh,' said Satchwell, nodding. 'Yeah, of course: there was a kid. She didn't look as though she'd 'ad a baby, when I met her after they got married. Slim as ever. Both my wives put on about a stone with each of our kids.'

'How many children have you got?' asked Robin, politely.

She wanted the food to hurry up. It was harder to walk out

once food was in front of you, and some instinct told her that Paul Satchwell's whimsical mood might not last.

'Five,' said Satchwell. 'Two with me first wife, and three with me second. Didn't mean to: we got twins on the last throw. All pretty much grown up now, thank Christ. Kids and art don't mix. I love 'em,' he said roughly, 'but Cyril Connolly had it right. The enemy of promise is the pram in the bloody 'all.'

He threw her a brief glance out of his one visible eye and said abruptly,

'So 'er 'usband still thinks I had something to do with Margot disappearing, does 'e?'

'What d'you mean by "still"?' enquired Robin.

''E gave my name to the police,' said Satchwell. 'The night she disappeared. Thought she might've run off with me. Did you know Margot and I bumped into each other a coupla weeks before she disappeared?'

'I did, yes,' said Robin.

'It put ideas into what's-'is-name's head,' he said. 'I can't blame him, I s'pose it did look fishy. I'd've probably thought the same, if my bird had met up with an old flame right before they buggered off – disappeared, I mean.'

The food arrived: Satchwell's steak and chips looked appetising, but Robin, who'd been too busy concentrating on her questions, hadn't read the small print on the menu. Expecting a plate of salad, she received a wooden platter bearing various ramekins containing hot sausage slices, hummous and a sticky mess of mayonnaise-coated leaves, a challenging assortment to eat while taking notes.

'Want some chips?' offered Satchwell, pushing the small metal bucket that contained them towards her.

'No thanks,' said Robin, smiling. She took a bite of a breadstick and continued, her pen in her right hand,

'Did Margot talk about Roy, when you bumped into her?'

'A bit,' said Satchwell, his mouth full of steak. 'She put up a good front. What you do, when you meet the ex, isn't it? Pretend you think you did the right thing. No regrets.'

'Did you think she had regrets?' asked Robin.

'She wasn't 'appy, I could tell. I thought, nobody's paying you attention. She tried to put a brave face on it, but she struck me as miserable. Knackered.'

'Did you only see each other the once?'

Satchwell chewed his steak, looking at Robin thoughtfully. At last he swallowed, then said,

'Have you read my police statement?'

'Yes,' said Robin.

'Then you know perfectly well,' said Satchwell, waggling his fork at her, 'that it was just the once. *Don't* you?'

He was smiling, trying to pass off the implied admonition as waggish, but Robin felt the spindle-thin spike of aggression.

'So you went for a drink, and talked?' said Robin, smiling, as though she hadn't noticed the undertone, daring him to become defensive, and he continued, in a milder tone,

'Yeah, we went to some bar in Camden, not far from my flat. She'd been on an 'ouse call to some patient.'

Robin made a note.

'And can you remember what you talked about?'

'She told me she'd met 'er husband at medical school, 'e was an 'igh-flier and all that. What was 'e?' said Satchwell, with what seemed to Robin a forced unconcern. 'A cardiologist or something?'

'Haematologist,' said Robin.

'What's that, blood? Yeah, she was always impressed by clever people, Margot. Didn't occur to 'er that they can be shits like anyone else.'

'Did you get the impression Dr Phipps was a shit?' asked Robin lightly.

'Not really,' said Satchwell. 'But I was told 'e had a stick up his arse and was a bit of a mummy's boy.'

'Who told you that?' asked Robin, pausing with her pen suspended over her notebook.

'Someone 'oo'd met him,' he replied with a slight shrug. 'You not married?' he went on, his eyes on Robin's bare left hand.

'Living with someone,' said Robin, with a brief smile. It was the answer she'd learned to give, to shut down flirtation from witnesses and clients, to erect barriers. Satchwell said, 'Ah. I always know, if a bird's living with a bloke without marriage, she must be really keen on him. Nothing but 'er feelings holding her, is there?'

'I suppose not,' said Robin, with a brief smile. She knew he was trying to disconcert her. 'Did Margot mention anything that might be worrying her, or causing her problems? At home or at work?'

'Told you, it was all window dressing,' said Satchwell, munching on fries. 'Great job, great 'usband, nice kid, nice 'ouse: she'd made it.' He swallowed. 'I did the same thing back: told her I was having an exhibition, won an award for one of me paintings, in a band, serious girlfriend . . . which was a lie,' he added, with a slight snort. 'I only remember that bird because we split up later that evening. Don't ask me her name now. We 'adn't been together long. She had long black hair and a massive tattoo of a spider's web round her navel, that's what I mainly remember – yeah, anyway, I ended it. Seeing Margot again—'

He hesitated. His uncovered eye unfocused, he said,

'I was thirty-five. It's a funny age. It starts dawning on you forty's really gonna happen to you, not just to other people. What are you, twenty-five?'

'Twenty-nine,' said Robin.

'Happens earlier for women, that worrying about getting old thing,' said Talbot. 'Got kids yet?'

'No,' said Robin, and then, 'so Margot didn't say anything to you that might suggest a reason for disappearing voluntarily?'

'Margot wouldn't have gone away and left everyone in the lurch,' said Satchwell, as positive on the point as Oonagh. 'Not Margot. Responsible was her middle name. She was a good girl, you know? School prefect sort.'

'So you didn't make any plans to meet again?'

'No plans,' said Satchwell, munching on chips. 'I mentioned to 'er my band was playing at the Dublin Castle the following week. Said, "drop in if you're passing", but she said she wouldn't be able to. Dublin Castle was a pub in Camden,' Satchwell added. 'Might still be there.'

'Yes,' said Robin, 'it is.'

'I told the investigating officer I'd mentioned the gig to her. Told 'im I'd've been up for seeing her again, if she'd wanted it. I 'ad nothing to hide.'

Robin remembered Strike's opinion that Satchwell volunteering this information seemed almost too helpful, and, trying to dissemble her sudden suspicion, asked:

'Did anyone spot Margot at the pub, the night you were playing?'

Satchwell took his time before swallowing, then said,

'Not as far as I know.'

'The little wooden Viking you gave her,' said Robin, watching him carefully, 'the one with "Brunhilda" written on the foot—'

'The one she had on her desk at work?' he said, with what Robin thought might have been a whiff of gratified vanity. 'Yeah, I gave her that in the old days, when we were dating.'

Could it be true, Robin wondered. After the acrimonious way Margot and Satchwell had broken up, after he'd locked her in his flat so she couldn't get out to work, after he'd hit her, after she'd married another man, would Margot really have kept Satchwell's silly little gift? Didn't private jokes and nicknames become dead and rotten things after a painful break-up, when the thought of them became almost worse than memories of rows and insults? Robin had given most of Matthew's gifts to charity after she'd found out about his infidelity, including the plush elephant that had been his first Valentine's present and the jewellery box he'd given her for her twenty-first. However, Robin could tell Satchwell was going to stick to his story, so she moved to the next question in her notebook.

'There was a printers on Clerkenwell Road I think you had an association with.'

'Come again?' said Satchwell, frowning. 'A printers?'

'A schoolgirl called Amanda White claims she saw Margot in an upper window belonging to this printers on the night—'

'Really?' said Satchwell. 'I never 'ad no association with no printers. 'Oo says I did?'

'There was a book written in the eighties about Margot's disappearance—'

'Yeah? I missed that.'

'—it said the printers produced flyers for a nightclub you'd painted a mural for.'

'For crying out loud,' said Satchwell, half-amused, half-exasperated. 'That's not an association. It'd be a stretch to call it a coincidence. I've never heard of the bloody place.'

Robin made a note and moved to her next question.

'What did you think of Bill Talbot?'

'Who?'

'The investigating officer. The first one,' said Robin.

'Oh yeah,' said Satchwell, nodding. 'Very odd bloke. When I 'eard afterwards he'd had a breakdown or whatever, I wasn't surprised. Kept asking me what I was doing on random dates. Afterwards, I worked out 'e was trying to decide wevver I was the Essex Butcher. He wanted to know my time of birth, as well, and what the hell that had to do with anything . . . '

'He was trying to draw up your horoscope,' said Robin, and she explained Talbot's preoccupation with astrology.

'*Dén tó pistévo!*' said Satchwell, looking annoyed. 'Astrology? That's not funny. He was in charge of the case – how long?'

'Six months,' said Robin.

'Jesus,' said Satchwell, scowling so that the clear tape holding the dressing over his eye crinkled.

'I don't think the people around him realised how ill he was until it got too obvious to ignore,' said Robin, now pulling a few tagged sheets of paper out of her bag: photocopies of Satchwell's statements to both Talbot and Lawson.

'What's all that?' he said sharply.

'Your statements to the police,' said Robin.

'Why are there – what are they, stars? – all over—'

'They're pentagrams,' said Robin. 'This is the statement Talbot took from you. It's just routine,' she added, because Satchwell was now looking wary. 'We've done it with everyone the police interviewed. I know your statements were double-checked at the time, but I wondered if I could run over them again, in case you remember anything useful?'

Taking his silence for consent, she continued:

'You were alone in your studio on the afternoon of the eleventh of October, but you took a call there at five from a Mr ... Hendricks?'

'Hendricks, yeah,' said Satchwell. 'He was my agent at the time.'

'You went out to eat at a local café around half past six, where you had a conversation with the woman behind the till, which she remembered. Then you went back home to change, and out again to meet a few friends in a bar called Joe Bloggs around eight o'clock. All three friends you were drinking with confirmed your story ... nothing to add to any of that?'

'No,' said Satchwell, and Robin thought she detected a slight sense of relief. 'That all sounds right.'

'Was it one of those friends who'd met Roy Phipps?' Robin asked casually.

'No,' said Satchwell, unsmiling, and then, changing the subject, he said, 'Margot's daughter must be knocking on forty now, is she?'

'Forty last year,' said Robin.

'*Éla*,' said Satchwell, shaking his head. 'Time just—'

One of the mahogany brown hands, wrinkled and embellished with heavy silver and turquoise rings, made a smooth motion, as of a paper aeroplane in flight.

'—and then one day you're old and you never saw it sneaking up on you.'

'When did you move abroad?'

'I didn't mean to move, not at first. Went travelling, late '75,' said Satchwell. He'd nearly finished his steak, now.

'What made you—?'

'I'd been thinking of travelling for a bit,' said Satchwell. 'But after Creed killed Margot – it was such a bloody 'orrible thing – such a shock – I dunno, I wanted a change of scene.'

'That's what you think happened to her, do you? Creed killed her?'

He put the last bit of steak into his mouth, chewed it and swallowed before answering.

'Well, yeah. Obviously at first I 'oped she'd just walked out on 'er husband and was 'oled up somewhere. But then it went on and on and ... yeah, everyone thought it was the Essex Butcher, including the police. Not just the nutty one, the second one, the one who took over.'

'Lawson,' said Robin.

Satchwell shrugged, as much to say as the officer's name didn't matter, and asked,

'Are you going to interview Creed?'

'Hopefully.'

'Why would he tell the truth, now?'

'He likes publicity,' said Robin. 'He might like the idea of making a splash in the newspapers. So Margot disappearing was a shock to you?'

'Well, obviously it was,' said Satchwell, now probing his teeth with his tongue. 'I'd just seen her again and ... I'm not going to pretend I was still *in love* with her, or anything like that, but ... have *you* ever been caught up in a police investigation?' he asked her, with a trace of aggression.

'Yes,' said Robin. 'Several. It was stressful and intimidating, every time.'

'Well, there you are,' said Satchwell, mollified.

'What made you choose Greece?'

'I didn't, really. I 'ad an inheritance off my grandmother and I thought, I'll take some time off, do Europe, paint ... went through France and Italy, and in '76 I arrived in Kos. Worked in a bar. Painted in my free hours. Sold quite a few pictures to tourists. Met my first wife ... never left,' said Satchwell, with a shrug.

'Something else I wanted to ask you,' said Robin, moving the police statements to the bottom of her small stack. 'We've found out about a possible sighting of Margot, a week after she disappeared. A sighting that wasn't ever reported to the police.'

'Yeah?' said Satchwell, looking interested. 'Where?'

'In Leamington Spa,' said Robin, 'in the graveyard of All Saints church.'

Satchwell's thick white eyebrows rose, putting strain on the clear tape that was holding the dressing to his eye.

'In All Saints?' he repeated, apparently astonished.

'Looking at graves. Allegedly, she had her hair dyed black.'

''Oo saw this?'

'A man visiting the area on a motorbike. Two years later, he told the St John's practice nurse about it.'

'He told the *nurse*?'

Satchwell's jaw hardened.

'And what else has the *nurse* told you?' he said, searching Robin's face. He seemed suddenly and unexpectedly angry.

'Do you know Janice?' asked Robin, wondering why he looked so angry.

'That's her name, is it?' said Satchwell. 'I couldn't remember.'

'You *do* know her?'

Satchwell put more chips in his mouth. Robin could see that he was trying to decide what to tell her, and she felt that jolt of excitement that made all the long, tedious hours of the job, the sitting around, the sleeplessness, worthwhile.

'She's shit-stirring,' said Satchwell abruptly. 'She's a shit-stirrer, that one, that nurse. She and Margot didn't like each other. Margot told me she didn't like her.'

'When was this?'

'When we ran into each other, like I told you, in the street—'

'I thought you said she didn't talk about work?'

'Well, she told me that. They'd had a row or something. I don't know. It was just something she said in passing. She told me she didn't like the nurse,' repeated Satchwell.

It was as though a hard mask had surfaced under the leather dark skin: the slightly comical, crêpey-faced charmer had been replaced by a mean old one-eyed man. Robin remembered how Matthew's lower face had tautened when angry, giving him the look of a muzzled dog, but she wasn't intimidated. She sensed in Satchwell the same wily instinct for self-preservation as in her ex-husband. Whatever Satchwell might have meted out to Margot, or to the wives who'd left him, he'd think better of slapping Robin in a crowded pub, in the town where his sister still lived.

'You seem angry,' Robin said.

'*Gia chári tou*, of course I am – that nurse, what's her name? Trying to implicate me, isn't she? Making up a story to make it look like Margot ran away to be with me—'

'Janice didn't invent the story. We checked with Mr Ramage's widow and she confirmed that her late husband told other people he'd met a missing woman—'

'What else has *Janice* told you?' he said again.

'She never mentioned you,' said Robin, now immensely curious. 'We had no idea you knew each other.'

'But she claims Margot was seen in Leamington Spa after she disappeared? No, she knows exactly what she's bloody doing.'

Satchwell took another chip, ate it, then suddenly got to his feet and walked past Robin, who looked over her shoulder to see him striding into the gents. His back view was older than his front: she could see the pink scalp through the thin white hair and there was no backside filling out his jeans.

Robin guessed he considered the interview finished. However, she had something else up her sleeve: a dangerous something, perhaps, but she'd use it rather than let the interview end here, with more questions raised than answered.

It was fully five minutes before he reappeared and she could tell that he'd worked himself up in his absence. Rather than sitting back down, he stood over her as he said,

'I don't think you're a fucking detective. I think you're press.'

Seen from below, the tortoise's neck was particularly striking. The chain, the turquoise and silver rings and the long hair now seemed like fancy dress.

'You can call Anna Phipps and check if you like,' said Robin. 'I've got her number here. Why d'you think the press would be interested in you?'

'I had enough of them last time. I'm off. I don't need this. I'm supposed to be recuperating.'

'One last thing,' said Robin, 'and you're going to want to hear it.'

She'd learned the trick from Strike. Stay calm, but assertive. Make them worry what else you've got.

Satchwell turned back, his one uncovered eye hard as flint. No trace of flirtation remained, no attempt to patronise her. She was an equal now; an adversary.

'Why don't you sit down?' said Robin. 'This won't take long.'

After a slight hesitation, Satchwell eased himself back into his seat. His hoary head now blocked the stuffed deer head that hung on the brick wall behind him. From Robin's point of view, the horns appeared to rise directly out of the white hair that fell in limp curls to his shoulders.

'Margot Bamborough knew something about you that you didn't want to get out,' said Robin. 'Didn't she?'

He glared at her.

'The pillow dream?' said Robin.

Every line of his face hardened, turning him vulpine. The sunburned chest, wrinkled beneath its white hair, caved as he exhaled.

'Told someone, did she? Who?' Before Robin could answer, he said, ''Er husband, I suppose? Or that fucking Irish girl, was it?'

His jaws worked, chewing nothing.

'I should never 'ave told her,' he said. 'That's what you do when you're drunk and you're in love, or whatever the fuck we were. Then I 'ad it playing on my mind for years that she was gonna . . .'

The sentence ended in silence.

'Did she mention it, when you met again?' asked Robin, feeling her way, pretending she knew more than she did.

'She asked after my poor mother,' said Satchwell. 'I fort at the time, are you 'aving a go? But I don't think she was. Maybe she'd learned better, being a doctor, maybe she'd changed her views. She'll have seen people like Blanche. A life not worth living.

'Anyway,' he said, leaning forwards slightly, 'I still think it was a dream. All right? I was six years old. I dreamed it. And even if it wasn't a dream, they're both dead and gone now and nobody can say no different. My old mum died in '89. You can't get 'er for anything now, poor cow. Single mother, trying to cope with us all on 'er own. It's merciful,' said Satchwell, 'putting someone out of their misery. A mercy.'

He got up, drained beneath his tan, his face sagging, turned and walked away, but at the moment he was about to disappear he suddenly turned and tottered back to her, his jaw working.

'I think,' he said, with as much malevolence as he could muster, 'you're a nasty little bitch.'

He left for good this time.

Robin's heart rate was barely raised. Her dominant emotion was elation. Pushing her unappetising ramekins aside, she pulled the little metal bucket he'd left behind towards her, and finished the artist's chips.

48

Sir Artegall, long hauing since,
Taken in hand th'exploit . . .
To him assynd, her high beheast to doo,
To the sea shore he gan his way apply . . .

Edmund Spenser
The Faerie Queene

Joan's funeral service finished with the hymn most beloved of sail-ors, 'Eternal Father, Strong to Save'. While the congregation sang the familiar words, Ted, Strike, Dave Polworth and three of Ted's comrades in the lifeboat service shouldered the coffin back down the aisle of the simple cream-walled church, with its wooden beams and its stained-glass windows depicting purple-robed St Maudez, for whom both village and church were named. Flanked by an island tower and a seal on a rock, the saint watched the coffin-bearers pass out of the church.

O Saviour, whose almighty word
The winds and waves submissive heard,
Who walked upon the foaming deep,
And calm amidst the rage did sleep . . .

Polworth, by far the shortest of the six men, walked directly behind Strike, doing his best to bear a fair share of the load.

The mourners, many of whom had had to stand at the back of the packed church, or else listen as best they could from outside, formed a respectful circle around the hearse outside as the shining oak box was loaded onto it. Barely a murmur was heard as the rear doors slammed shut on Joan's earthly remains. As the straight-backed undertaker in his thick black overcoat climbed back into the driver's seat, Strike put an arm around Ted's shoulders. Together, they watched the hearse drive out of sight. Strike could feel Ted trembling.

'Look at all these flowers, Ted,' said Lucy, whose eyes were swollen shut, and the three of them turned back to the church to examine the dense bank of sprays, wreaths and bunches that created a jubilant blaze against the exterior wall of the tiny church.

'Beautiful lilies, Ted, look . . . from Marion and Gary, all the way from Canada . . .'

The congregation was still spilling out of the church to join those outside. All kept a distance from the family while they moved crab-wise along the wall of the church. Joan would surely have delighted in the mass of floral tributes and Strike drew unexpected consolation from messages that Lucy was reading aloud to Ted, whose eyes, like hers, were puffy and red.

'Ian and Judy,' she told her uncle. 'Terry and Olive . . .'

'Loads, aren't there?' said Ted, marvelling.

The now-whispering, milling crowd of mourners were doubtless wondering whether it would be heartless to set out immediately for the Ship and Castle, where the wake was to be held, Strike thought. He couldn't blame them; he too was craving a pint and perhaps a chaser too.

'"With deepest sympathy, from Robin, Sam, Andy, Saul and Pat",' Lucy read aloud. She turned to look at Strike, smiling. 'How lovely. Did you tell Robin pink roses were Joan's favourite?'

'Don't think so,' said Strike, who hadn't known himself.

The fact that his agency was represented here among the tributes to Joan meant a great deal to him. Unlike Lucy, he'd be travelling back to London alone, by train. Even though he'd been craving solitude for the past ten days, the prospect of his silent attic room was cheerless, after these long days of dread and loss. The roses, which were for Joan, were also for him: they said, you won't be alone, you have something you've built, and all right, it might not be a family, but there are still people who care about you waiting in London. Strike told himself 'people', because there were five names on the card, but he turned away thinking only of Robin.

Lucy drove Ted and Strike to the Ship and Castle in Ted's car, leaving Greg to follow with the boys. None of them talked in the car; a kind of emotional exhaustion had set in.

Joan had known what she was doing, Strike thought, as he watched the familiar streets slide past. He was grateful they weren't following to the crematorium, that they would reclaim the body in a form that could be clutched to the chest and borne on a boat, in the quiet of a sunny afternoon to come, just the family, to say their last, private farewell.

The Ship and Castle's dining-room windows looked out over St Mawes Bay, which was overcast but tranquil. Strike bought Ted and himself pints, saw his uncle safely into a chair among a knot of solicitous friends, returned to the bar for a double Famous Grouse, which he downed in one, then carried his pint to the window.

The sea was Quaker grey, sparkling occasionally where the silvered fringes of the clouds caught it. Viewed from the hotel window, St Mawes was a study in mouse and slate, but the little rowing boats perched on the mudflats below provided welcome dabs of cheerful colour.

'Y'all right, Diddy?'

He turned: Ilsa was with Polworth, and she reached up and hugged Strike. All three of them had been at St Mawes Primary School together. In those days, as Strike remembered it, Ilsa hadn't liked Polworth much. He'd always been unpopular with female classmates. Over Dave's shoulder, Strike could see Polworth's wife, Penny, chatting with a group of female friends.

'Nick really wanted to be here, Corm, but he had to work,' said Ilsa.

'Of course,' said Strike. 'It was really good of you to come, Ilsa.'

'I loved Joan,' she said simply. 'Mum and Dad are going to have Ted over on Friday night. Dad's taking him for a round of golf on Tuesday.'

The Polworths' two daughters, who weren't renowned for their good behaviour, were playing tag among the mourners. The smaller of the two – Strike could never remember which was Roz and which Mel – dashed around them and clung, momentarily, to the back of Strike's legs, as though he were a piece of furniture, looking out at her sister, before sprinting off again, giggling.

'And we're having Ted over Saturday,' said Polworth, as though nothing had happened. Neither Polworth ever corrected their children unless they were directly inconveniencing their parents. 'So don't worry, Diddy, we'll make sure the old fella's all right.'

'Cheers, mate,' said Strike, with difficulty. He hadn't cried in church, hadn't cried all these last horrible days, because there'd been so much to organise, and he found relief in activity. However, the kindness shown by his old friends was seeping through his defences: he wanted to express his gratitude properly, because Polworth hadn't yet permitted him to say all he wanted about the way he'd enabled Strike and Lucy to reach the dying Joan. Before Strike could make a start, however, Penny Polworth joined their group, followed by two women Strike didn't recognise, but who were both beaming at him.

'Hi, Corm,' said Penny, who was dark-eyed and blunt-nosed, and who'd worn her hair pulled back into a practical ponytail since she was five. 'Abigail and Lindy really want to meet you.'

'Hello,' said Strike, unsmiling. He held out his hand and shook both of theirs, sure that they were about to talk about his detective triumphs and already annoyed. Today, of all days, he wanted to be nothing but Joan's nephew. He assumed that Abigail was Lindy's daughter, because if you removed the younger woman's carefully pencilled, geometrically precise eyebrows and fake tan, they had the same round, flat faces.

'She was ever so proud of you,' said Lindy.

'We follow everything about you in the papers,' said plump Abigail, who seemed to be on the verge of giggling.

'What are you working on now? I don't suppose you can say, can you?' said Lindy, devouring him with her eyes.

'D'you ever get involved with the royals, at all?' asked Abigail.

Fuck's sake.

'No,' said Strike. 'Excuse me, need a smoke.'

He knew he'd offended them, but didn't care, though he could imagine Joan's disapproval as he walked away from the group by the window. What would it have hurt him, she'd have said, to entertain her friends by talking about his job? Joan had liked to show him off, the nephew who was the closest thing she'd ever have to a son, and it suddenly came back to him, after these long days of guilt, why he'd avoided coming back to the little town for so long: because he'd found himself slowly stifling under the weight of teacups and doilies and carefully curated conversations, and Joan's suffocating pride, and the neighbours' curiosity, and the sidelong glances at his false leg when nobody thought he could see them looking.

As he stumped down the hall, he pulled out his mobile and pressed Robin's number without conscious thought.

'Hi,' she said, sounding mildly surprised to hear from him.

'Hi,' said Strike, pausing on the doorstep of the hotel to pull a cigarette out of the packet with his teeth. He crossed the road and lit it, looking out over the mudflats at the sea. 'Just wanted to check in, and to thank you.'

'What for?'

'The flowers from the agency. They meant a lot to the family.'

'Oh,' said Robin, 'I'm glad . . . How was the funeral?'

'It was, you know . . . a funeral,' said Strike, watching a seagull bobbing on the tranquil sea. 'Anything new your end?'

'Well, yes, actually,' said Robin, after a fractional hesitation, 'but now's probably not the moment. I'll tell you when you're—'

'Now's a great moment,' said Strike, who was yearning for normality, for something to think about that wasn't connected to Joan, or loss, or St Mawes.

So Robin related the story of her interview with Paul Satchwell, and Strike listened in silence.

'. . . and then he called me a nasty little bitch,' Robin concluded, 'and left.'

'Christ almighty,' said Strike, genuinely amazed, not only that Robin had managed to draw so much information from Satchwell, but at what she'd found out.

'I've just been sitting here looking up records on my phone – I'm back in the Land Rover, going to head home in a bit. Blanche Doris

Satchwell, died 1945, aged ten. She's buried in a cemetery outside Leamington Spa. Satchwell called it a mercy killing. Well,' Robin corrected herself, 'he called it a dream, which was his way of telling Margot, while retaining some plausible deniability, wasn't it? It's a traumatic memory to carry around with you from age six, though, isn't it?'

'Certainly is,' said Strike, 'and it gives him a motive of sorts, if he thought Margot might tell the authorities . . . '

'Exactly. And what d'you think about the Janice bit? Why didn't she tell us she knew Satchwell?'

'Very good question,' said Strike. 'Go over it again, what he said about Janice?'

'When I told him Janice was the one who said Margot was spotted in Leamington Spa, he said she was a shit-stirrer and that she was trying to implicate him somehow in Margot's disappearance.'

'Very interesting indeed,' said Strike, frowning at the bobbing seagull, which was staring at the horizon with concentrated intent, its cruel, hooked beak pointing towards the horizon. 'And what was that thing about Roy?'

'He said somebody had told him Roy was a "mummy's boy" who "had a stick up his arse",' said Robin. 'But he wouldn't tell me who'd said it.'

'Doesn't sound much like Janice, but you never know,' said Strike. 'Well, you've done bloody well, Robin.'

'Thanks.'

'We'll have a proper catch-up on Bamborough when I get back,' said Strike. 'Well, we'll need a catch-up on everything.'

'Great. I hope the rest of your stay's OK,' said Robin, with that note of finality that indicated the call was about to end. Strike wanted to keep her on the line, but she evidently thought she oughtn't monopolise his time in his last afternoon with the grieving family, and he could think of no pretext to keep her talking. They bade each other goodbye, and Strike returned his mobile to his pocket.

'Here you go, Diddy.'

Polworth had emerged from the hotel carrying a couple of fresh pints. Strike accepted his with thanks, and both turned to face the bay as they drank.

'You back up to London tomorrow, are you?' said Polworth.

'Yeah,' said Strike. 'But not for long. Joan wanted us to take her ashes out on Ted's boat and scatter them at sea.'

'Nice idea,' said Polworth.

'Listen, mate – thanks for everything.'

'Shut up,' said Polworth. 'You'd do it for me.'

'You're right,' said Strike. 'I would.'

'Easy to say, you cunt,' said Polworth, without skipping a beat, 'seeing as my mum's dead and I don't know where the fuck my dad is.'

Strike laughed.

'Well, I'm a private detective. Want me to find him for you?'

'Fuck, no,' said Polworth. 'Good riddance.'

They drank their pints. There was a brief break in the cloud and the sea was suddenly a carpet of diamonds and the bobbing seagull, a paper-white piece of origami. Strike was wondering idly whether Polworth's passionate devotion to Cornwall was a reaction against his absent Birmingham-born father when Polworth spoke up again:

'Speaking of fathers ... Joan told me yours was looking for a reunion.'

'She did, did she?'

'Don't be narked,' said Polworth. 'You know what she was like. Wanted me to know you were going through a tough time. Nothing doing, I take it?'

'No,' said Strike. 'Nothing doing.'

The brief silence was broken by the shrieks and yells of Polworth's two daughters sprinting out of the hotel. Ignoring their father and Strike, they wriggled under the chain separating road from damp shingle and ran out to the water's edge, pursued a moment later by Strike's nephew Luke, who was holding a couple of cream buns in his hand and clearly intent on throwing them at the girls.

'OI,' bellowed Strike. 'NO!'

Luke's face fell.

'They started it,' he said, turning to show Strike a white smear down the back of his black suit jacket, newly purchased for his great-aunt's funeral.

'And I'm finishing it,' said Strike, while the Polworth girls giggled, peeking out over the rim of the rowing boat behind which they had taken refuge. 'Put those back where you got them.'

Glaring at his uncle, Luke took a defiant bite out of one of the buns, then turned and headed back into the hotel.

'Little shit,' muttered Strike.

Polworth watched in a detached way as his girls began to kick cold seawater and sand at each other. Only when the younger girl over-balanced and fell backwards into a foot of icy sea, eliciting a scream of shock, did he react.

'Fuck's sake ... get inside. Come on – don't bloody whine, it's your own fault – come on, inside, now!'

The three Polworths headed back into the Ship and Castle, leaving Strike alone again.

The bobbing seagull, which was doubtless used to a tide of tourists, to the chugging and grinding of the Falmouth ferry and the fishing boats passing in and out of the bay every day, had been unfazed by the shrieks and yells of the Polworth girls. Its sharp eyes were fixed upon something Strike couldn't see, far out at sea. Only when the clouds closed again and the sea darkened to iron, did the bird take off at last. Strike's eyes followed it as it soared on wide, curved wings into the distance, away from the shelter of the bay for open sea, ready to resume the hard but necessary business of survival.

PART FIVE

... lusty Spring, all dight in leaues of flowres ...

Edmund Spenser
The Faerie Queene

49

After long storms and tempests overblown,
The sun at length his joyous face doth clear;
So whenas fortune all her spite hath shown,
Some blissful hours at last must needs appear;
Else would afflicted wights oft-times despair . . .

Edmund Spenser
The Faerie Queene

At 8 a.m. on the morning she should have been meeting her estranged husband for mediation, Robin emerged from Tottenham Court Road station beneath a cerulean sky. The sunshine felt like a minor miracle after the long months of rain and storms and Robin, who had no surveillance to do today, had put on a dress, glad to be out of her everlasting jeans and sweatshirts.

Angry as she felt at Matthew for calling off the session with only twenty-four hours' notice ('My client regrets that an urgent matter of a personal nature has arisen. Given my own unavailability for the latter part of March, I suggest we find a mutually convenient date in April'), suspicious as she was that Matthew was dragging out the process merely to demonstrate his power and add pressure to give up her claim on their joint account, her spirits were raised by the dusty glow of the early morning sunshine illuminating the eternal road-works at the top of Charing Cross Road. The truth, which had been borne forcibly upon Robin during the five days off that Strike had insisted she take, was that she was happier at work. With no desire to go home to Yorkshire and face the usual barrage of questions from her mother about the divorce and her job, and insufficient funds to get out of London to take a solitary mini-break, she'd spent most of her time taking care of her backlog of chores, or working on the Bamborough case.

She had, if not precisely leads, then ideas, and was now heading into the office early in the hope of catching Strike before the business of the day took over. The pneumatic drills drowned out the shouts of workmen in the road as Robin passed, until she reached the shadowy calm of Denmark Street, where the shops hadn't yet opened.

Almost at the top of the metal staircase, Robin heard voices emanating from behind the glass office door. In spite of the fact that it was not quite eight-fifteen, the light was already on.

'Morning,' said Strike, when she opened the door. He was standing beside the kettle and looked mildly surprised to see her so early. 'I thought you weren't going to be in until lunchtime?'

'Cancelled,' said Robin.

She wondered whether Strike had forgotten what she'd had on that morning, or whether he was being discreet because Morris was sitting on the fake leather sofa. Though as handsome as ever, Morris's bright blue eyes were bloodshot and his jaw dark with stubble.

'Hello, stranger,' he said. 'Look at you. Proper advert for taking it easy.'

Robin ignored this comment, but as she hung up her jacket, she found herself wishing she hadn't worn the dress. She greatly resented Morris making her feel self-conscious, but it would have been easier just to have worn jeans as usual.

'Morris has caught Mr Smith at it, with the nanny,' said Strike.

'That was quick!' said Robin, trying to be generous, wishing Morris hadn't been the one to do it.

'Red-handed, ten past one this morning,' said Morris, passing Robin a night vision digital camera. 'Hubby was pretending to be out with the boys. Nanny always has a night off on Tuesdays. Silly fuckers said goodbye on the doorstep. Rookie error.'

Robin scrolled slowly through the pictures. The voluptuous nanny who so resembled Strike's ex Lorelei was standing in the doorway of a terraced house, locked in the arms of Mrs Smith's husband.

Morris had captured not only the clinch, but the street name and door number.

'Where's this place?' Robin asked, flicking past pictures of the clinch.

'Shoreditch. Nanny's best mate rents it,' said Morris. 'Always useful to have a friend who'll let you use their place for a sneaky shag, eh? I've got her name and details, too, so she's about to get dragged into it all, as well.'

Morris stretched luxuriously on the sofa, arms over his head, and said through a yawn,

'Not often you get the chance to make three women miserable at once, is it?'

'Not to mention the husband,' said Robin, looking at the handsome profile of the commodity broker's husband, silhouetted against a streetlamp as he made his way back to the family car.

'Well, yeah,' said Morris, holding his stretch, 'him too.'

His T-shirt had ridden up, exposing an expanse of toned abdomen, a fact of which Robin thought he was probably well aware.

'Don't fancy a breakfast meeting, do you?' Strike asked Robin. He'd just opened the biscuit tin and found it empty. 'We're overdue a Bamborough catch-up. And I haven't had breakfast.'

'Great,' said Robin, immediately taking down her jacket again.

'You never take *me* out for breakfast,' Morris told Strike, getting up off the sofa. Ignoring this comment, Strike said,

'Good going on Smith, Morris. I'll let the wife know later. See you tomorrow.'

'Terrible, isn't it,' said Robin, as she and Strike walked back out of the black street door onto the cool of Denmark Street, where sunlight still hadn't penetrated, 'this missing plane?'

Eleven days previously, Malaysia Airlines flight 370 had taken off from Kuala Lumpur and disappeared without trace. More than two hundred people were missing. Competing theories about what had happened to the plane had dominated the news for the last week: hijack, crew sabotage and mechanical failure among them. Robin had been reading about it on the way into work. All those relatives, waiting for news. It must, surely, come soon? An aircraft holding nearly two hundred and fifty people wasn't as easily lost as a single woman, melting away into the Clerkenwell rain.

'Nightmare for the families,' agreed Strike, as they headed out into the sun on Charing Cross Road. He paused, looking up and down the road. 'I don't want to go to Starbucks.'

So they walked to Bar Italia in Frith Street, which lay opposite Ronnie Scott's jazz club, five minutes from the office. The small metal tables and chairs outside on the pavement were all unoccupied. In spite of its sunny promise, the March morning air still carried a chill. Every high stool at the counter inside the café bore a customer gulping down coffee before starting their working day, while reading news off their phones or else examining the shelves of produce reflected in the mirror that faced them.

'You going to be warm enough if we sit out here?' asked Strike doubtfully, looking from Robin's dress to the counter inside. She was starting to really wish she'd worn her jeans.

'I'll be fine,' said Robin. 'And I only want a cappuccino, I already ate.'

While Strike was buying food and drink, Robin sat down on the cold metal chair, drew her jacket more tightly around her and opened her bag, with the intention of taking out Talbot's leather notebook, but after a moment's hesitation, she changed her mind and left it where it was. She didn't want Strike to think that she'd been concentrating on Talbot's astrological musings over the last few days, even though she had, in fact, spent many hours poring over the book.

'Cappuccino,' said Strike, returning to her and setting the coffee in front of her. He'd bought himself a double espresso and a mozzarella and salami roll. Sitting down next to her, he said,

'How come mediation was cancelled?'

Pleased he'd remembered, Robin said:

'Matthew claims something urgent came up.'

'Believe him?'

'No. I think it's more mind games. I wasn't looking forward to it, but at least it would've been over. So,' she said, not wanting to talk about Matthew, 'have you got anything new on Bamborough?'

'Not much,' said Strike, who'd been working flat out on other cases since his return from Cornwall. 'We've got forensics back on that blood smear I found in the book in the Athorns' flat.'

'And?'

'Type O positive.'

'And did you call Roy to find out . . . ?'

'Yeah. Margot was A positive.'

'Oh,' said Robin.

'My hopes weren't high,' said Strike, with a shrug. 'It looked like a smear from a paper cut, if anything.

'I've found Mucky Ricci, though. He's in a private nursing home called St Peter's, in Islington. I had to do a fair bit of impersonation on the phone to get confirmation.'

'Great. D'you want me to—?'

'No. I told you, Shanker issued stern warnings about upsetting the old bastard, in case his sons got wind of it.'

'And you feel, of the two of us, I'm the one who upsets people, do you?'

Strike smirked slightly while chewing his roll.

'There's no point rattling Luca Ricci's cage unless we have to. Shanker told me Mucky was gaga, which I hoped meant he was a bit less sharp than he used to be. Might even have worked in our favour. Unfortunately, from what I managed to wheedle out of the nurse, he doesn't talk any more.'

'Not at all?'

'Apparently not. She mentioned it in passing. I tried to find out whether that's because he's depressed, or had a stroke, or whether he's demented, in which case questioning him is obviously pointless, but she didn't say.

'I went to check out the home. I was hoping for some big institutional place where you might slip in and out unnoticed, but it's more like a B&B. They've only got eighteen residents. I'd say the chances of getting in there undetected or passing yourself off as a distant cousin are close to zero.'

Irrationally, now that Ricci seemed unreachable, Robin, who hadn't been more interested in him than in any of the other suspects, immediately felt as though something crucial to the investigation had been lost.

'I'm not saying I won't take a bash at him, eventually,' said Strike. 'But right now, the possible gains don't justify making a bunch of professional gangsters angry at us. On the other hand, if we've got nothing else come August, I might have to see whether I can get a word or two out of Ricci.'

From his tone, Robin guessed that Strike, too, was well aware that more than half their allotted year on the Bamborough case had already elapsed.

'I've also,' he continued, 'made contact with Margot's biographer, C. B. Oakden, who's playing hard to get. He seems to think he's far more important to the investigation than I do.'

'Is he after money?'

'I'd say he's after anything he can get,' said Strike. 'He seemed as interested in interviewing me as letting me interview him.'

'Maybe,' suggested Robin, 'he's thinking of writing a book about you, like the one he did on Margot?'

Strike didn't smile.

'He comes across as equal parts wily and stupid. It doesn't seem to have occurred to him that I must know a lot about his dodgy past, given that I managed to track him down after multiple name changes. But I can see how he conned all those old women. He puts up a good show over the phone of knowing and remembering everyone around Margot. There was a real fluency to it: "Yes, Dr Gupta, lovely man", "Oh yes, Irene, bit of a handful". It's convincing until you remember he was fourteen when Margot disappeared, and probably met them all a couple of times, tops.

'But he wouldn't tell me anything about Brenner, which is who I'm really interested in. "I'll need to think about that," he said. "I'm not sure I want to go into that." I've called him twice so far. Both times he tried to divert the conversation back onto me, I dragged it back to Brenner, and he cut the call short, pretending he had something urgent to take care of. Both times, he promised to phone me back but didn't.'

'You don't think he's recording the calls, do you?' asked Robin. 'Trying to get stuff about you he can sell to the papers?'

'It occurred to me,' Strike admitted, tipping sugar into his coffee. 'Maybe I should talk to him next time?'

'Might not be a bad idea,' said Strike. 'Anyway,' he took a gulp of coffee, 'that's all I've done on Bamborough since I got back. But I'm planning to drop in on Nurse Janice the moment I've got a couple of clear hours. She'll be back from Dubai by now, and I want to know why she never mentioned she knew Paul Satchwell. Don't think I'll warn her I'm coming, this time. There's something to be said for catching people unawares. So, what's new your end?'

'Well,' said Robin, 'Gloria Conti, or Jaubert, as she is these days, hasn't answered Anna's email.'

'Pity,' said Strike, frowning. 'I thought she'd be more likely to talk to us if Anna asked.'

'So did I. I think it's worth giving it another week, then getting Anna to prod her. The worst that can happen is another definite "no". In slightly better news, I'm supposed to be speaking to Amanda White, who's now Amanda Laws, later today.'

'How much is that costing us?'

'Nothing. I appealed to her better nature,' said Robin, 'and she pretended to be persuaded, but I can tell she's quite enamoured of the idea of publicity, and she likes the idea of you, and of getting her name in the papers again as the plucky schoolgirl who stuck to her woman-in-the-window story even when the police didn't believe her. That's in spite of the fact that her whole shtick, when I first contacted her, was that she didn't want to go through all the stress of press interest again unless she got money out of it.'

'She still married?' asked Strike, taking his cigarettes out of his pocket. 'Because she and Oakden sound like a good match. Mightn't be a bad sideline for us, setting grifters up with each other.'

Robin laughed.

'So they can have dodgy children together, thus keeping us in business for ever?'

Strike lit his cigarette, exhaled and then said,

'Not a perfect business plan. There's no guarantee breeding two shits together will produce a third shit. I've known decent people who were raised by complete bastards, and vice versa.'

'You're nature over nurture, are you?' asked Robin.

'Maybe,' said Strike. 'My three nephews were all raised the same, weren't they? And—'

'—one's lovely, one's a prick and one's an arsehole,' said Robin.

Strike's loud burst of laughter seemed to offend the harried-looking suited man who was hurrying past with a mobile pressed to his ear.

'Well remembered,' Strike said, still grinning as he watched the scowling man march out of sight. Lately he, too, had had moods where the sound of other people's cheerfulness grated, but at this moment, with the sunshine, the good coffee and Robin beside him, he suddenly realised he was happier than he'd been in months.

'People are never raised the same way, though,' said Robin, 'not even in the same house, with the same parents. Birth order matters, and all kinds of other things. Speaking of which, Wilma Bayliss's daughter Maya has definitely agreed to talk to us. We're trying to find a convenient date. I think I told you, the youngest sister is recovering from breast cancer, so I don't want to hassle them.

'And there's something else,' said Robin, feeling self-conscious.

Strike, who'd returned to his sandwich, saw, to his surprise, Robin drawing from her bag Talbot's leather-bound notebook, which Strike had assumed was still in the locked filing cabinet in the office.

'I've been looking back through this.'

'Think I missed something, do you?' said Strike, through a mouthful of bread.

'No, I—'

'It's fine,' he said. 'Perfectly possible. Nobody's infallible.'

Sunshine was slowly making its way into Frith Street now, and the pages of the old notebook glowed yellow as Robin opened it.

'Well, it's about Scorpio. You remember Scorpio?'

'The person whose death Margot might have been worried about?'

'Exactly. You thought Scorpio might be Steve Douthwaite's married girlfriend, who killed herself.'

'I'm open to other theories,' said Strike. His sandwich finished, he brushed off his hands and took out his cigarettes. 'The notes ask whether Aquarius confronted Pisces, don't they? Which I assumed meant Margot confronted Douthwaite.'

In spite of his neutral tone, Strike resented remembering these star signs. The laborious and ultimately unrewarding task of working out which suspects and witnesses were represented by each astrological glyph had been far from his favourite bit of research.

'Well,' said Robin, taking out two folded photocopies, which she'd been keeping in the notebook, 'I've been wondering . . . look at these.'

She passed the two documents to Strike, who opened them and saw copies of two birth certificates, one for Olive Satchwell, the other for Blanche Satchwell.

'Olive was Satchwell's mother,' said Robin, as Strike, smoking, examined the documents. 'And Blanche was his sister, who died aged ten – possibly with a pillow over her face.'

'If you're expecting me to deduce their star signs from these birthdays,' said Strike, 'I haven't memorised the whole zodiac.'

'Blanche was born on the twenty-fifth of October, which makes her a Scorpio,' said Robin. 'Olive was born on the twenty-ninth of March. Under the traditional system, she'd be Aries, like Satchwell . . . '

To Strike's surprise, Robin now took out a copy of *Astrology 14* by Steven Schmidt.

'It was quite hard to track this down. It's been out of print for ages.'

'A masterwork like that? You amaze me,' said Strike, watching Robin turn to a page listing the dates of revised signs according to Schmidt. Robin smiled, but refusing to be deflected said,

'Look here. By Schmidt's system, Satchwell's mother was a Pisces.'

'We're mixing up the two systems now, are we?' asked Strike.

'Well, Talbot did,' Robin pointed out. 'He decided Irene and Roy should be given their Schmidt signs, but other people were allowed to keep the traditional ones.'

'But,' said Strike, well aware that he was trying to impose logic on what was essentially illogical, 'Talbot made massive, sweeping assumptions on the basis of people's original signs. Brenner was ruled out as a suspect solely because he was—'

'—Libra, yes,' said Robin.

'Well, what happens to Janice being psychic and the Essex Butcher being a Capricorn if all the dates start sliding around?'

'Wherever there was a discrepancy between the traditional sign and Schmidt sign, he seems to have gone with the sign he thought suited the person best.'

'Which makes a mockery of the whole business. And also,' said Strike, 'calls all my identifications of signs and suspects into question.'

'I know,' said Robin. 'Even Talbot seems to have got very stressed trying to work across both systems, which is when he began concentrating mainly on asteroids and the tarot.'

'OK,' said Strike, blowing smoke away from her, 'go on with what you were saying – if Satchwell's sister was a Scorpio, and her mother was Pisces ... remind me,' said Strike, 'exactly what that passage about Scorpio says?'

Robin flicked backwards through Talbot's notebook until she found the passage decorated with doodles of the crab, the fish, the scorpion, the fish-tailed goat and the water-bearer's urn.

'"Aquarius worried about how Scorpio died, question mark",' she read aloud. 'And – written in capitals – "SCHMIDT AGREES WITH ADAMS". Then, "Did Aquarius challenge Pisces about Scorpio? Was Cancer there, did Cancer witness? Cancer is kind, instinct is to protect," then, in capitals, "INTERVIEW AGAIN. Scorpio and Aquarius connected, water, water, also Cancer, and Capricorn," in capitals, "HAS A FISH'S TAIL".'

Brow furrowed, Strike said:

'We're assuming Cancer still means Janice, right?'

'Well, Janice and Cynthia are the only two Cancerians connected with the case, and Janice seems to fit this better,' said Robin. 'Let's say Margot decided she was going to act on her suspicion that Satchwell's mother killed his sister. If she phoned Olive from the surgery, Janice might have overheard a phone call, mightn't she? And if Janice knew the Satchwell family, or was involved with them in some way we don't know about, she mightn't have wanted to tell the police what she'd overheard, for fear of incriminating Olive.'

'Why would Margot have waited years to check out her suspicions about the pillow dream?' asked Strike, but before Robin could supply an answer, he did it himself. 'Of course, people do sometimes take years to decide what action to take on something like that. Or to muster up the courage to do it.'

He handed Robin back the two photocopies.

'Well, if that's the story behind the Scorpio business, Satchwell's still a prime suspect.'

'I never got his address in Greece,' said Robin guiltily.

'We'll get at him through his surviving sister if we have to.'

Strike took a swig of coffee then, slightly against his better judgement, asked,

'What did you say about asteroids?'

Robin flicked further on through the notebook, to show Strike the page she'd pored over in Leamington Spa, which she thought of as the 'horns page'.

'As the case went on, he seemed to give up on normal astrology. I think Schmidt had confused him so much he couldn't work it any more, so he starts inventing his own system. He's calculated the asteroids' positions for the evening Margot disappeared. See here—'

Robin was pointing to the symbol ⚲ . . .

'That symbol stands for the asteroid Pallas Athena – remember that ugly clock at the Phippses' house? – and he's using it to mean Margot. The asteroid Pallas Athena was in the tenth house of the zodiac on the night Margot disappeared, and the tenth house is ruled by Capricorn. It's also supposed to govern businesses, upper classes and upper floors.'

'You think Margot's still in someone's attic?'

Robin smiled, but refused to be deflected.

'And see here . . .' She angled the notebook towards him, 'assuming the other asteroids also refer to living people, we've got Ceres, Juno and Vesta.

'I think he's using Vesta, "keeper of the hearth", to represent Cynthia. Vesta was in the seventh house, which is the house of marriage. Talbot's written "FITS" – so I think he's saying Cynthia was in Margot's marital home, Broom House.

'I think "nurturing, protective Ceres" sounds like Janice again. She's in the twelfth house, and so's Juno, who's associated with "wives and infidelity", which might take us back to Joanna Hammond, Douthwaite's married girlfriend . . . '

'What's the twelfth house represent?'

'Enemies, secrets, sorrows and undoing.'

Strike looked at her, eyebrows raised. He'd indulged Robin because it was sunny, and he was enjoying her company, but his tolerance for astrology was now wearing very thin.

'It's also Pisces' house,' said Robin, 'which is Douthwaite's sign, so maybe—'

'You think Janice and Joanna Hammond were both in Douthwaite's flat when Margot was abducted, do you?'

'No, but—'

'Because that'd be tricky, given that Joanna Hammond died weeks before Margot disappeared. Or are you suggesting her ghost was haunting Douthwaite?'

'All right, I know it might mean nothing,' said Robin, half-laughing as she ploughed on, 'but Talbot's written something else here: "Ceres denies contact with Juno. Could Cetus be right?"'

She was pointing at the whale symbol representing Irene.

'I find it hard to imagine Irene Hickson being right about very much,' said Strike. He pulled the leather notebook towards him to look more closely at Talbot's small, obsessive writing, then pushed the notes away again with a slightly impatient shrug. 'Look, it's easy to get sucked into this stuff. When I was going through the notes I started making connections while I was trying to follow his train of thought, but he was ill, wasn't he? Nothing leads anywhere concrete.'

'I was just intrigued by that "Could Cetus be right?" because Talbot mistrusted Irene from the start, didn't he? Then he starts wondering whether she could have been right about . . . about something connected to enemies, secrets and undoing . . . '

'If we ever find out what happened to Margot Bamborough,' said Strike, 'I'll bet you a hundred quid you'll be able to make equally strong cases for Talbot's occult stuff being bang on the money, and completely off beam. You can always stretch this symbolic stuff to fit the facts. One of my mother's friends used to guess everyone's star signs and she was right *every single time*.'

'She was?'

'Oh yeah,' said Strike. 'Because even when she was wrong, she was right. Turned out they had a load of planets in that sign or, I dunno, the midwife who delivered them was that sign. Or their dog.'

'All right,' said Robin, equably. She'd expected Strike's scepticism, after all, and now put both the leather-bound notebook and *Astrology 14* back into her bag. 'I know it might mean nothing at all, I'm only—'

'If you want to go and see Irene Hickson again, be my guest. Tell her Talbot thought she might've had profound insight into something connected to asteroids and – I dunno – cheese—'

'The twelfth house doesn't govern *cheese*,' said Robin, trying to look severe.

'What number's the house of dairy?'

'Oh, bugger off,' she said, laughing against her will.

Robin's mobile vibrated in her pocket, and she pulled it out. A text had just arrived.

Hi Robin, if you want I can talk now? I've just agreed to work a later shift, so I'm not needed at work for a few hours. Otherwise it'll have to be after 8 tonight – Amanda

'Amanda White,' she told Strike. 'She wants to talk now.'

'Works for me,' said Strike, relieved to be back on firm investigative ground. Liar or not, Amanda White would at least be talking about an actual woman at a real window.

Robin pressed Amanda's number, switched the mobile to speakerphone and laid it on the table between her and Strike.

'Hi,' said a confident female voice, with a hint of North London. 'Is that Robin?'

'Yes,' said Robin, 'and I'm with Cormoran.'

'Morning,' said Strike.

'Oh, it's *you*, is it?' said Amanda, sounding delighted. 'I *am* honoured. I've been dealing with your assistant.'

'She's actually my partner,' said Strike.

'Really? Business, or the other?' said Amanda.

'Business,' said Strike, not looking at Robin. 'I understand Robin's been talking to you about what you saw on the night Margot Bamborough disappeared?'

'That's right,' said Amanda.

'Would you mind if we take a recording of this interview?'

'No, I s'pose not,' said Amanda. 'I mean, I want to do the right thing, although I won't pretend it hasn't been a bit of a dilemma, because it was really stressful, last time. Journalists, two police interviews, and I was only fourteen. But I've always been a stubborn girl, haha, and I stuck to my guns . . . '

So Amanda told the story with which Strike and Robin were already familiar: of the rain, and the angry schoolfriend, and the upper window, and the retrospective recognition of Margot, when Amanda saw her picture in the paper. Strike asked a couple of questions, but he could tell that nothing would ever change Amanda's story. Whether she truly believed she'd seen Margot Bamborough at the window that night or not, she was evidently determined never to relinquish her association with the forty-year-old mystery.

' . . . and I suppose I've been haunted ever since by the idea that I didn't do anything, but I was fourteen and it only hit me later, I could've been the one to save her,' she ended the story.

'Well,' said Robin, as Strike nodded at her, signalling he had everything he wanted, 'thank you so much for talking to us, Amanda. I really—'

'There's something else, before you go,' said Amanda. 'Wait until you hear this. It's just an amazing coincidence, and I don't think even the police know about this, because they're both dead.'

'Who're dead?' asked Robin, while Strike lit himself another cigarette.

'Well,' said Amanda, 'how's this for strange? My last job, this young girl at the office's great-aunt—'

Strike rolled his eyes.

'—was in a hospice with, guess who?'

'I don't know,' said Robin politely.

'Violet Cooper,' said Amanda. 'You probably don't—'

'Dennis Creed's landlady,' said Robin.

'*Exactly!*' said Amanda, sounding pleased that Robin appreciated the significance of her story. 'So, anyway, isn't that just *weird*, that I saw Margot at that window, and then, all those years later, I work with someone whose relative met Vi Cooper? Only she was calling herself something different by then, because people hated her.'

'That *is* a coincidence,' said Robin, making sure not to look at Strike. 'Well, thank—'

'That's not all!' said Amanda, laughing. 'No, there's more to it than that! So, this girl's great-aunt said Vi told her she wrote to Creed, once, asking if he'd killed Margot Bamborough.'

Amanda paused, clearly wanting a response, so Robin, who'd already read about this in *The Demon of Paradise Park*, said,

'Wow.'

'*I know*,' said Amanda. 'And apparently, Vi said – this is on her deathbed, so you know, she was telling the truth, because you would, wouldn't you? – Vi said the letter she got back, said he *had* killed her.'

'Really?' said Robin. 'I thought the letter—'

'No, but this is direct from Violet,' Amanda said, while Strike rolled his eyes again, 'and she said, he definitely did, he as good as told her so. He said it in a way only she'd understand, but she knew *exactly* what he meant.

'*Crazy*, though, isn't it? I see Margot at the window, and then, years later—'

'Amazing,' said Robin. 'Well, thanks very much for your time, Amanda, this has been really ... er ...'

It took Robin another couple of minutes, and much more insincere gratitude, to get Amanda off the line.

'What d'you think?' Robin asked Strike, when at last she'd succeeded in getting rid of Amanda.

He pointed a finger at the sky.

'What?' said Robin, looking up into the blue haze.

'If you look carefully,' said Strike, 'you might just see an asteroid passing through the house of bollocks.'

50

Aye me (said she) where am I, or with whom?
Emong the liuing, or emong the dead?

Edmund Spenser
The Faerie Queene

Agency work unconnected with the Bamborough case consumed Strike for the next few days. His first attempt to surprise Nurse Janice Beattie at home was fruitless. He left Nightingale Grove, a nondescript street that lay hard against the Southeastern railway line, without receiving any answer to his knock.

His second attempt, on the following Wednesday, was made on a breezy afternoon that kept threatening showers. Strike approached Janice's house from Hither Green station, along a pavement bordered to the right with railings and hedge, separating the road from the rail tracks. He was thinking about Robin as he trudged along, smoking, because she'd just turned down the opportunity of joining him to interview Janice, saying that there was 'something else' she needed to do, but not specifying what that something was. Strike thought he'd detected a trace of caginess, almost amounting to defensiveness, in Robin's response to the suggestion of a joint interview, where usually there'd have been only disappointment.

Since she'd left Matthew, Strike had become used to more ease and openness between him and Robin, so this refusal, coupled with her tone and lack of an explanation, made him curious. While there were naturally matters he might not have expected her to tell him about – trips to the gynaecologist sprang to mind – he would have expected her to say 'I've got a doctor's appointment', at least.

The sky darkened as Strike approached Janice's house, which was considerably smaller than Irene Hickson's. It stood in a terrace. Net curtains hung at all the windows, and the front door was dark red. Strike didn't immediately register the fact that a light was shining from behind the net curtains at the sitting-room window until he was halfway across the road. When he realised that his quarry must be in, however, he successfully pushed all thoughts about his business partner out of his mind, crossed the road at a quicker pace and knocked firmly on the front door. As he stood waiting, he heard the muffled sounds of a TV on high volume through the glass of the downstairs window. He was just considering knocking again, in case Janice hadn't heard the first time, when the door opened.

In contrast to the last time they'd met, the nurse, who was wearing steel-rimmed spectacles, looked shocked and none too pleased to see Strike. From behind her, two female American voices rang out from the out-of-sight TV: '*So you love the bling?*' '*I love the bling!*'

''Er – 'ave I missed a message, or—?'

'Sorry for the lack of warning,' said Strike insincerely, 'but as I was in the area, I wondered whether you could give me a couple of minutes?'

Janice glanced back over her shoulder. A camp male voice was now saying, '*The dress that Kelly is in love with is a one-of-a-kind runway sample . . .*'

Clearly disgruntled, Janice turned back to Strike.

'Well . . . all right,' she said, 'but the place is in a mess – and can you please wipe your feet properly, because the last bloke who turned up 'ere unannounced brought dog shit in wiv 'im. You can close the door be'ind you.'

Strike stepped over the threshold, while Janice strode out of sight into the sitting room. Strike expected her to turn off the TV but she didn't. While Strike wiped his feet on the coconut mat inside the door, a male voice said: '*This one-of-a-kind runway gown might be impossible to find, so Randy's on the search . . .*' After hesitating for a moment on the doormat, Strike decided that Janice expected him to follow her, and entered the small sitting room.

Having spent a significant part of his youth in squats with his mother, Strike had a very different idea of 'mess' to Janice's. Although cluttered, with something on almost every surface, the only signs of actual disorder in the room were a copy of the *Daily Mirror* lying in one armchair, some crumpled packaging lying beside an open packet of dates on the low coffee table and a hairdryer, which was lying incongruously on the floor beside the sofa, and which Janice was currently unplugging.

'... *Antonella's pulling the closest gown to Kelly's pick, a blinged-out $15,000 dress ...*'

'The mirror down 'ere's better for drying my 'air,' Janice explained, straightening up, pink in the face, hairdryer in her hand and looking slightly cross, as though Strike was forcing her to justify herself. 'I would've appreciated some warning, you know,' she added, looking as stern as such a naturally smiley-looking woman could. 'You've caught me on the 'op.'

Strike was unexpectedly and poignantly reminded of Joan, who'd always been flustered if guests dropped in while the Hoover or the ironing board were still out.

'Sorry. As I say, I happened to be in the area ...'

'*Even as Kelly steps into dress number one, she still can't get her dream dress off her mind,*' said the narrator loudly, and both Strike and Janice glanced towards the TV, where a young woman was wriggling into a clinging, semi-transparent white dress covered in silver rhinestones.

'*Say Yes to the Dress,*' said Janice, who was wearing the same navy jumper and slacks as the last time Strike had seen her. 'My guilty pleasure ... D'you want a cup of tea?'

'Only if it's no trouble,' said Strike.

'Well, it's always *some* trouble, innit?' Janice said, with her first glimmer of a smile. 'But I was going to make myself some at the first advert break, so you might as well 'ave some.'

'In that case, thanks very much,' said Strike.

'*If I don't find this dress,*' said the camp male wedding consultant on-screen, rifling urgently through racks of white dresses, his eyebrows so sharply plucked they looked drawn on, '*it's not gonna be*—'

The screen went blank. Janice had turned it off with her remote control.

'Wanna date?' she asked Strike, holding out the box.

'No thanks,' said Strike.

'Got boxes of 'em in Dubai,' she said. 'I was gonna give 'em as presents, but I just can't stop eating 'em. 'Ave a seat. I won't be two ticks.'

Strike thought he caught another downward glance towards his lower legs as she marched out of the room, hairdryer in one hand, dates in the other, leaving Strike to take an armchair, which creaked beneath his weight.

Strike found the small sitting room oppressive. Predominantly red, the carpet was decorated in a scarlet, swirling pattern, on top of which lay a cheap crimson Turkish rug. Dried flower pictures hung on the red walls, between old photographs, some black and white, and the coloured ones faded, displayed in wooden frames. A china cabinet was full of cheap spun-glass ornaments. The largest, a Cinderella carriage pulled by six glass horses, stood in pride of place on the mantelpiece over the electric fire. Evidently, beneath Janice's no-nonsense clothing, there beat a romantic heart.

She returned a few minutes later, holding a wicker-handled tray bearing two mugs of tea with the milk already added, and a plate of chocolate Hobnobs. The act of making tea seemed to have put her into slightly better humour with her guest.

'That's my Larry,' she said, catching Strike looking towards a double frame on the small side table beside him. On one side was a sleepy-eyed, overweight man with a smoker's teeth. On the other was a blonde woman, heavy but pretty.

'Ah. And is this—?'

'My little sister, Clare. She died '97. Pancreatic cancer. They got it late.'

'Oh, I'm sorry to hear that,' said Strike.

'Yeah,' said Janice, with a deep sigh. 'Lost 'em both around the same time. To tell you the truth,' she said, as she sat down on the sofa and her knees gave audible clicks, 'I walked back in 'ere after

Dubai and I fort, I really need to get some new pictures up. It was depressing, coming back in 'ere, the number of dead people . . .

'I got some gorgeous ones of Kev and the grandkids on 'oliday, but I 'aven't got 'em printed out yet. The lad next door's going to do it for me. All my old ones of Kev and the kids are two years out of date. I gave the boy the memory . . . *board*, is it?'

'Card?' suggested Strike.

'That's the one. The kids next door just laugh at me. Mind you, Irene's worse'n I am. She can 'ardly change a battery. So,' she said, 'why d'you want to see me again?'

Strike, who had no intention of risking an immediate rebuff, was planning to ask his questions about Satchwell last. Drawing out his notebook and opening it, he said,

'A couple of things that have come up since I last saw you. I asked Dr Gupta about this first one, but he couldn't help, so I hoped you might be able to. Would you happen to know anything about a man called Niccolo Ricci, sometimes nicknamed "Mucky"?'

'Old gangster, weren't 'e?' said Janice. 'I knew 'e lived local, in Clerkenwell, but I never met 'im. Why d'you want – oh, 'as Irene been telling you about the foundations thing?'

'The what?' asked Strike.

'Oh, it's nuffing, really. There was this rumour, back when they were doing a load of redevelopment round Clerkenwell in the early seventies, that some builders 'ad found a body buried in concrete under one of the demolished buildings. The story was that Little Italy gangsters 'ad hidden it there, back in the forties. But Eddie – this is Irene's Eddie, the builder she ended up marrying – that's 'ow they met, local pub, when 'is firm was doing a lot of the redevelopment – Eddie told us it was all cobblers. *I* 'adn't ever believed it. I fink Irene 'ad, a bit,' Janice added, dunking a biscuit in her tea.

'How does this tie in with Margot?' Strike asked.

'Well, after Margot disappeared, there was a theory 'er body 'ad been put into one o' the open foundations and covered in concrete. They was still doing a bit of building round there in '74, see.'

'Were people suggesting Ricci had killed her?' asked Strike.

'Gawd, no!' said Janice, with a shocked little laugh. 'What would

Mucky Ricci 'ave to do with Margot? It was only because of that old rumour. It put the idea in people's minds, you know, burying bodies in concrete. People can be bloody silly. My Larry said to me – 'e was a builder, you know – it's not like workmen wouldn't've noticed a load of fresh concrete when they turned up for work.'

'Were you aware that Ricci attended the St John's practice Christmas party?'

''E what?' said Janice, with her mouth full.

'He and another couple of men arrived towards the end of the party, possibly to escort Gloria home.'

'They – *what?*' Janice said, looking unaffectedly astonished. 'Mucky Ricci and *Gloria*? Come off it. Is this because – no, look, you don't wanna pay no attention to Irene, not about Gloria. Irene ... she gets carried away. She never much liked Gloria. And she gets the wrong end of the stick sometimes. *I* never 'eard Gloria's family 'ad any criminal connections. Irene watched way too many *Godfather* movies,' said Janice. 'We saw the first one togevver, at the cinema, and I went back and saw it again twice more on me own. James Caan, you know,' she sighed. 'My dream man.'

'Ricci was definitely at the practice party,' said Strike. 'From what I can tell, he turned up right at the end.'

'Well then, I'd already left. I needed to get 'ome to Kev. Is 'e still alive, Ricci?'

'Yes,' said Strike.

'Must be really getting on, is 'e?'

'He is,' said Strike.

'That's odd, though. What on earth would Ricci be doing at St John's?'

'I'm hoping to find out,' said Strike, flipping over a page of his notebook. 'The next thing I wanted to ask you was about Joseph Brenner. You remember the family you thought might be called Applethorpe? Well, I found—'

'You never tracked 'em down!' said Janice, looking impressed. 'What *was* their name?'

'Athorn.'

'*Athorn!*' said Janice, with an air of relief. 'I *knew* it wasn't

Applethorpe. That bugged me for days, after . . . 'Ow are they? It's Fragile X they've got, isn't it? They're not in an 'ome, or—?'

'Still living together in the old flat,' said Strike, 'and getting on reasonably well, I think.'

'I 'ope they're being well supported, are they?'

'There's a social worker involved, who seems very much on their side, which brings me to what I was going to ask you.

'The social worker says that since Gwilherm's death, Deborah's disclosed . . . ' Strike hesitated, ' . . . well, the way the social worker put it, was that Gwilherm was, er, pimping Deborah out.'

''E was what?' said Janice, the smile sliding off her face.

'It's an unpleasant idea, I know,' said Strike unemotionally. 'When I was talking to her, Deborah told me about Dr Brenner visiting her at home. She said he'd – er – asked her to take off her pants—'

'No!' said Janice, in what seemed instinctive revulsion. 'No, I'm sure – no, that's not right. That's not 'ow it would've 'appened, if she'd needed an intimate examination. It would have 'appened at the surgery.'

'You said she was agoraphobic?'

'Well – yeah, but . . . '

'Samhain, the son, said something about Dr Brenner being a "dirty old man".'

''E . . . but . . . no, it . . . it *must've* been an examination . . . maybe after the baby was born? But that should've been me, the nurse . . . that's upset me, now,' said Janice, looking distressed. 'You think you've 'eard everything, but . . . no, that's really upset me. I mean, I was in the 'ouse that one time to see the kid and she never said a word to me . . . but of course, 'e was there, the father, telling me all about 'is bloody magic powers. She was probably too scared to . . . no, that's really upset me, that 'as.'

'I'm sorry,' said Strike, 'but I have to ask: did you ever hear that Brenner used prostitutes? Ever hear any rumours about him, locally?'

'Not a word,' said Janice. 'I'd've told someone, if I'd 'eard that. It wouldn't be ethical, not in our catchment area. All the women there were registered to our practice. She'd've been a patient.'

'According to Talbot's notes,' said Strike, 'somebody claimed they saw Brenner in Michael Cliffe House on the evening Margot disappeared. The story Brenner gave the police was that he went straight home.'

'Michael Cliffe 'Ouse . . . that's the tower block on Skinner Street, innit?' said Janice. 'We 'ad patients in there, but otherwise . . . ' Janice appeared sickened. 'You've upset me,' she said again. ''Im and that poor Athorn woman . . . and there's me defending 'im to all and sundry, because of 'is experiences in the war. Not two weeks back, I 'ad Dorothy's son sitting exactly where you are now—'

'Carl Oakden was here?' said Strike sharply.

'Yeah,' said Janice, 'and 'e didn't wipe 'is feet, neither. Dog shit all up my 'all carpet.'

'What did he want?' asked Strike.

'Well, 'e *pretended* it was a nice catch-up,' said Janice. 'You'd think I might not recognise 'im after all this time, but actually, 'e don't look that much diff'rent, not really. Anyway, 'e sat in that chair where you are, spouting all sorts of rubbish about old times and 'is mum remembering me fondly – ha! Dorothy Oakden, remember me fondly? Dorothy thought Irene and me were a pair of hussies, skirts above our knees, going out to the pub togevver . . .

''E mentioned *you*,' said Janice, with a beady look. 'Wanted to know if I'd met you, yet. 'E wrote a book about Margot, you know, but it never made it into the shops, which 'e's angry about. 'E told me all about it when 'e was 'ere. 'E's finking of writing another one and it's *you* what's got 'im interested in it. The famous detective solving the case – or the famous detective *not* solving the case. Either one'll do for Carl.'

'What was he saying about Brenner?' asked Strike. There would be time enough later to consider the implications of an amateur biographer tramping all over the case.

'Said Dr Brenner was a sadistic old man, and there I was, sort of sticking up for Dr Brenner . . . but now you're telling me this about Deborah Athorn . . . '

'Oakden said Brenner was sadistic, did he? That's a strong word.'

'I fort so, too. Carl said 'e'd never liked 'im, said Dr Brenner used to go round Dorothy's 'ouse a lot, which I never realised, for Sunday lunch and that. I always fort they were just workmates. You know, Dr Brenner probably told Carl off, that's all. 'E was an 'oly terror when 'e was a kid, Carl, and 'e comes across as the kind of man 'oo 'olds a grudge.'

'If Oakden comes round here again,' said Strike, 'I'd advise you not to let him in. He's done time, you know. For conning . . . ' He just stopped himself saying 'old' ' . . . single women out of their money.'

'*Oh*,' said Janice, taken aback. 'Blimey. I'd better warn Irene. 'E said 'e was going to try 'er next.'

'And he seemed primarily interested in Brenner, did he, when he came round here?'

'Well, no,' said Janice. ''E seemed mostly interested in *you*, but yeah, we talked about Brenner more'n anyone else at the practice.'

'Mrs Beattie, you wouldn't happen to still have that newspaper obituary of Brenner you mentioned? I think you said you kept it?'

'Oh,' said Janice, glancing towards the drawer at the base of her china cabinet, 'yeah . . . Carl wanted to see that, too, when 'e 'eard I 'ad it . . . '

She pushed herself out of the sofa and crossed to the china cabinet. Gripping the mantelpiece to steady herself, she knelt down, opened the drawer and began rummaging.

'They're all in a bit of a state, my clippings. Irene finks I'm bonkers, me and my newspapers,' she added, wrist-deep in the contents of the drawer. 'She's never been much for the news or politics or any of that, but I've always saved interesting bits and pieces, you know: medical fings, and I won't lie, I do like a story on the royals and . . . '

She began tugging on what looked like the corner of a cardboard folder.

' . . . and Irene can fink it's strange all she likes, but I don't see what's wrong – with saving – the story of . . . '

The folder came free.

' . . . a life,' said Janice, walking on her knees to the coffee table. 'Why's that morbid? No worse'n keeping a photo.'

She flipped open the folder and began looking through the clippings, some of them yellow with age.

'See? I saved that for 'er, for Irene,' said Janice, holding up an article about holy basil. 'Supposed to 'elp with digestive problems, I fort Eddie could plant some in the garden for 'er. She takes too many pills for 'er bowels, they do as much 'arm as good, but Irene's one of those 'oo, if it doesn't come in a tablet, she don't wanna know ...'

'Princess Diana,' said Janice with a sigh, flashing a commemorative front page at Strike. 'I was a fan ...'

'May I?' asked Strike, reaching for a couple of pieces of newsprint.

''Elp yourself,' said Janice, looking over her spectacles at the pieces of paper in Strike's hand. 'That article on diabetes is very interesting. Care's changed so much since I retired. My godson's Type One. I like to keep up with it all ... and that'll be the fing about the kid 'oo died of peritonitis, in your other 'and, is it?'

'Yes,' said Strike, looking at the clipping, which was brown with age.

'Yeah,' said Janice darkly, still turning over bits of newspaper, ''e's the reason I'm a nurse. That's what put the idea in me 'ead. 'E lived two doors down from me when I was a kid. I cut that out an' kept it, only photo I was ever gonna 'ave ... bawled my bloody eyes out. The doctor,' said Janice, with a hint of steel, 'was called out and 'e never bloody turned up. 'E would've come out for a middle-class kid, we all knew that, but little Johnny Marks from Bethnal Green, 'oo cared ... and the doctor was criticised, but never struck off ... If there's one thing I '*ate*, it's treating people diff'rent because of where they were born.'

With no apparent sense of irony, she shifted more pictures of the royals out of the way, looking puzzled.

'Where's Dr Brenner's thing?' she muttered.

Still clutching several clippings, she walked on her knees back towards the open drawer and rummaged in there again.

'No, it *really* isn't 'ere,' said Janice, returning to the coffee table. 'That's very odd ...'

'You don't think Oakden took it, do you?' Strike suggested.

Janice looked up.

'That cheeky sod,' she said slowly. ''E could of bloody asked.'

She swept her clippings back into their folder, returned it to her drawer, used the mantelpiece to pull herself back up, knees clicking loudly again, then sat back down on the sofa with a sigh of relief and said,

'You know, 'e was always light-fingered, that boy.'

'What makes you say that?'

'Money went missing, back at the practice.'

'Really?' said Strike.

'Yeah. It all come to 'an 'ead after Margot disappeared. Little bits of money kept going missing and they fort it was Wilma, the cleaner – ev'ryone except me. *I* always fort it was Carl. 'E used to drop in after school, and in the school 'olidays. I dropped a word in Dr Gupta's ear, but I dunno, probably 'e didn't want to upset Dorothy, and it was easier to push Wilma out. True, there were ovver issues wiv Wilma ... she drank,' said Janice, 'and 'er cleaning wasn't the best. She couldn't prove she never nicked it, and after there was a staff meeting about it, she resigned. She could see the way it was going.'

'And did the thefts stop?'

'Yeah,' said Janice, 'but so what? Carl might've thought 'e'd better give it rest, after nearly being found out.'

Strike, who tended to agree, said,

'Just a couple more questions. The first's about a woman called Joanna Hammond.'

'I should know 'oo that is, should I?'

'She was Steve Douthwaite's—'

'—girlfriend, 'oo killed 'erself,' said Janice. 'Oh yeah.'

'Can you remember whether she was registered with the St John's practice?'

'No, she weren't. I fink they lived over in Hoxton.'

'So Margot wouldn't have been involved with the coroner, or had any other professional connection with her death?'

'No, she'll 'ave been same as me: never knew the woman existed till she was already dead and Steve come looking for 'elp. I bet I know why you're asking, though,' said Janice. 'Talbot was dead set on Steve being the Essex Butcher, wasn't 'e? On and on about Steve, in all those interviews I 'ad with 'im. But honestly, Steve Douthwaite was a gentle soul. I grew up wiv a couple of proper violent men. Me father was one. I know the type, and Steve definitely weren't it.'

Remembering how endearing some women had found the apparent vulnerability of Dennis Creed, Strike merely nodded.

'Talbot asked wevver I'd ever visited that Joanna, as a nurse. I told 'im she wasn't a St John's patient, but that didn't put 'im off. Did I think there was anything fishy about 'er death, even so? I kept saying, "I never met the woman. 'Ow do I know?" I was getting worn down wiv it all by then, honestly, being treated like I was Gypsy bloody Rose Lee. I told Talbot, go see what the coroner said!'

'And you don't know whether there *was* a death Margot was worried about?' Strike asked. 'A death that was maybe categorised as natural, or accidental, but where she thought there might have been foul play?'

'What makes you ask that?' said Janice.

'Just trying to clear up something Talbot left in his notes. He seemed to think Margot might've had suspicions about the way somebody died. You were mentioned in connection with the death.'

Janice's round blue eyes widened behind her glasses.

'Mentioned as having witnessed something, or perhaps been present,' Strike elaborated. 'There was no hint of accusation.'

'I should bloody well 'ope not!' said Janice. 'No, I never *witnessed* nothing. I'd've said if I 'ad, wouldn't I?'

There was a short pause, which Strike judged it prudent not to break, and sure enough, Janice piped up again.

'Look, I can't speak for Margot forty years on. She's gone, i'n't she? It isn't fair on either of us. I don't wanna be casting suspicion round, all these years later.'

'I'm just trying to eliminate possible lines of inquiry,' said Strike.

There was a longer pause. Janice's eyes drifted over the tea tray and on to the picture of her late partner, with his stained teeth and his kind, sleepy eyes. Finally, she sighed and said,

'All right, but I want you to write down that this was *Margot's* idea, not mine, all right? I'm not accusing no one.'

'Fair enough,' said Strike, pen poised over his notebook.

'All right then, well – it was very sensitive, because of us working wiv 'er – Dorothy, I mean.

'Dorothy and Carl lived wiv Dorothy's mother. 'Er name was Maud, though I wouldn't remember that if Carl 'adn't been 'ere the ovver day. We were talking and I mentioned 'is gran, and 'e called 'er "bloody Maud", not "Grandma" or nothing.

'Anyway, Maud 'ad an infection on 'er leg, a sore what was taking its time 'ealing. It needed dressing and looking after, so I was visiting the 'ouse a lot. Ev'ry time I was in there, she told me *she* owned the 'ouse, not Dorothy. She was letting 'er daughter and grandson live wiv 'er. She liked saying it, you know. Feeling the power.

'I wouldn't say she'd be much fun to live with. Sour old lady. Nothing ever right for 'er. She moaned a lot about 'er grandson being spoiled – but like I said, 'e was an 'oly terror when 'e was younger, so I can't blame 'er there.

'Anyway,' said Janice, 'before the sore on 'er leg was 'ealed, she died, after falling downstairs. Now, 'er walking wasn't great, because she'd been laid up for a bit with this sore leg, and she needed a stick. People *do* fall downstairs, and if you're elderly, obviously that can 'ave serious consequences, but . . .

'Well, a week afterwards, Margot asked me into 'er consulting room for a word, and . . . well, yeah, I got the impression Margot was maybe a bit uneasy about it. She never said anyfing outright, just asked me what I fort. I knew what she was saying . . . but what could we do? We weren't there when she fell and the family said they was downstairs and just 'eard 'er take the tumble, and there she was at the bottom of the stairs, knocked out cold, and she died two nights later in 'ospital.

'Dorothy never showed no emotion about it, but Dorothy never *did* show much emotion about anything. What could we do?' Janice repeated, her palms turned upwards. 'Obviously I could see the way Margot's mind was working, because she knew Maud owned the 'ouse, and now Dorothy and Carl were sitting pretty, and . . . well, it's the kind of thing doctors consider, of course they do. It'll come back on them, if they've missed anything. But in the end, Margot never done nothing about it and as far as I know there was never any bother.

'There,' Janice concluded, with a slight air of relief at having got this off her chest. 'Now you know.'

'Thank you,' said Strike, making a note. 'That's very helpful. Tell me: did you ever mention this to Talbot?'

'No,' said Janice, 'but someone else mighta done. Ev'ryone knew Maud 'ad died, and 'ow she died, because Dorothy took a day off for the funeral. I'll be honest, by the end of all my interviews wiv Talbot, I just wanted to get out of there. Mostly 'e wanted me to talk about me dreams. It was creepy, honestly. Weird, the 'ole thing.'

'I'm sure it was,' said Strike. 'Well, there's just one more thing I wanted to ask, and then I'm done. My partner managed to track down Paul Satchwell.'

'Oh,' said Janice, with no sign of embarrassment or discomfort. 'Right. That was Margot's old boyfriend, wasn't it?'

'Yes. Well, we were surprised to find out you know each other.'

Janice looked at him blankly.

'What?'

'That you know each other,' Strike repeated.

'Me and Paul Satchwell?' said Janice with a little laugh. 'I've never even met the man!'

'Really?' said Strike, watching her closely. 'When he heard you'd told us about the sighting of Margot in Leamington Spa, he got quite angry. He said words to the effect,' Strike read off his notebook, 'that you were trying to cause trouble for him.'

There was a long silence. A frown line appeared between Janice's round blue eyes. At last she said,

'Did 'e mention me by name?'

'No,' said Strike. 'As a matter of fact, he seemed to have forgotten it. He just remembered you as "the nurse". He also told Robin that you and Margot didn't like each other.'

''E said Margot didn't like *me*?' said Janice, with the emphasis on the last word.

'I'm afraid so,' said Strike, watching her.

'But ... no, sorry, that's not right,' said Janice. 'We used to get on great! Ovver than that one time wiv Kev and 'is tummy ... all right, I *did* get shirty wiv 'er then, but I knew she *meant* it kindly. She fort she was doing me a favour, examining 'im ... I took offence because ... well, you do get a bit defensive, as a mother, if you fink another woman's judging you for not taking care of your kids properly. I was on me own with Kev and . . . you just feel it more, when you're on your own.'

'So why,' Strike asked, 'would Satchwell say he knew you, and that you wanted to get him into trouble?'

The silence that followed was broken by the sound of a train passing beyond the hedge: a great rushing rumble built and subsided, and the quiet of the sitting room closed like a bubble in its wake, holding the detective and the nurse in suspension as they looked at each other.

'I fink you already know,' said Janice at last.

'Know what?'

'Don't give me that. All them fings you've solved – you're not a stupid man. I fink you already know, and all this is to try and scare me into telling you.'

'I'm certainly not trying to *scare*—'

'I know you didn't like 'er,' said Janice abruptly. 'Irene. Don't bovver pretending, I know she annoyed you. If I couldn't read people I wouldn't 'ave been any good at my job, going in and out of strangers' 'ouses all the time, would I? And I was *very* good at my job,' said Janice, and somehow the remark didn't seem arrogant. 'Listen: you saw Irene in one of 'er show-off moods. She was so excited to meet you, she put on a big act.

'It's not easy for women, living alone when they're used to company, you know. Even me, coming back from Dubai, it's been a readjustment. You get used to 'aving family around you and then you're back in the empty 'ouse again, alone . . . Me, I don't mind me own company, but Irene 'ates it.

'She's been a very good friend to me, Irene,' said Janice, with a kind of quiet ferocity. 'Very kind. She 'elped me out financially, after Larry died, back when I 'ad nothing. I've always been welcome in 'er 'ouse. We're company for each other, we go back a long way. So she might 'ave a few airs and graces, so what? So 'ave plenty of people . . .'

There was another brief pause.

'Wait there,' said Janice firmly. 'I need to make a phone call.'

She got up and left the room. Strike waited. Beyond the net curtains, the sun suddenly slid out from behind a bullet-coloured cloud, and turned the glass Cinderella coach on the mantelpiece neon bright.

Janice reappeared with a mobile in her hand.

'She's not picking up,' she said, looking perturbed.

She sat back down on the sofa. There was another pause.

'*Fine*,' said Janice at last, as though Strike had harangued her into speech, 'it wasn't me 'oo knew Satchwell — it was Irene. But don't you go thinking she's done anyfing she shouldn't've! I mean, not in a *criminal* sense. It worried 'er like 'ell, after. I was worried *for* 'er . . . Oh Gawd,' said Janice.

She took a deep breath then said,

'All right, well . . . she was engaged to Eddie at the time. Eddie was a lot older'n Irene. 'E worshipped the ground she walked on, an' she loved 'im, too. She *did*,' said Janice, though Strike hadn't contradicted her. 'And she was *really* jealous if Eddie so much as looked at anyone else . . .

'But she always liked a drink and a flirt, Irene. It was 'armless. *Mostly* 'armless . . . that bloke Satchwell 'ad a band, didn't 'e?'

'That's right,' said Strike.

'Yeah, well, Irene saw 'em play at some pub. I wasn't wiv 'er the night she met Satchwell. I never knew a fing about it till after Margot 'ad gone missing.

'So she watched Satchwell and — well, she fancied 'im. And after the band 'ad finished, she sees Satchwell come into the bar, and 'e goes right to the back of the room to Margot, 'oo's standing there in a corner, in 'er raincoat. Irene fort Satchwell must've seen 'er from the stage. Irene 'adn't spotted Margot before, because she was up the front, wiv 'er friends. Anyway, she watched 'em, and Satchwell and Margot 'ad a short chat — really short, Irene said — and it looked like it turned into an argument. And then Irene reckoned Margot spotted 'er, and that's when Margot walked out.

'So then, Irene goes up to that Satchwell and tells 'im she loved the band and everything and, well, one thing led to another, and . . . yeah.'

'Why would Satchwell think she was a nurse?' asked Strike.

Janice grimaced.

'Well, to tell you the truth, that's what the silly girl used to tell blokes she was, when they were chatting 'er up. She used to pretend to be a nurse because the fellas liked it. As long as they knew naff all about medical stuff she managed to fool 'em, because she'd 'eard the names of drugs and all that at work, though she got most of 'em wrong, God love 'er,' said Janice, with a small eye roll.

'So was this a one-night stand, or . . . ?'

'No. It was a two-, three-week thing. But it didn't last. Margot disappearing . . . well, that put the kibosh on it. You can imagine.

'But for a couple of weeks there, Irene was . . . infatuated, I s'pose you'd say. She *did* love Eddie, you know . . . it was a bit of a feather in 'er cap to 'ave this older man, Eddie, successful business and everything, wanting to marry 'er, but . . . it's funny, isn't it?' said Janice quietly. 'We're all animals, when you take everything else away. She *totally* lost 'er 'ead over Paul Satchwell. Just for a few weeks. Tryin' to see 'im as much as she could, sneaking around . . . I bet she scared the life out of 'im, actually,' said Janice soberly, 'because from what she told me later, I fink 'e only took 'er to bed to spite Margot. Margot was 'oo 'e really wanted . . . and Irene realised that too late. She'd been used.'

'So the story of Irene's sore tooth,' said Strike, 'which then became the story of a shopping trip . . . '

'Yeah,' said Janice quietly. 'She was with Satchwell that afternoon. She took that receipt off 'er sister to use with the police. *I* never knew till afterwards. I 'ad her in floods of tears in my flat, pouring 'er 'eart out. Well, 'oo else could she tell? Not Eddie or 'er parents! She was terrified of it coming out, and losing Eddie. She'd woken up by then. All she wanted was Eddie, and she was scared 'e'd drop 'er if 'e found out about Satchwell.

'See, Satchwell as good as told Irene, the last time they met, 'e was using 'er to get back at Margot. 'E'd been angry at Margot for saying she'd only come to watch the band outta curiosity, and for getting shirty when 'e tried to persuade 'er to go back to 'is flat. 'E gave 'er that little wooden Viking thing, you know. 'E'd 'ad it on 'im, 'oping she'd turn up, and I fink 'e thought she'd just *melt* or somefing when 'e did that, and that'd be the end of Roy . . . like that's all it

takes, to walk out on a kid and a marriage, a little wooden doll . . .
'E said some nasty stuff about Margot to Irene . . . prick tease was the
least of it . . .

'Anyway, after Margot went missing and the police got called in,
Satchwell rings Irene up and says not to mention anyfing 'e'd said
about being angry at Margot, and she begged 'im never to tell anyone
about the both of 'em, and that's 'ow they left it. And I was the only
one 'oo knew, and I kept me mouth shut, too, because . . . well, that's
what you do when it's a friend, isn't it?'

'So when Charlie Ramage said he'd seen Margot in Leamington
Spa,' said Strike, 'were you aware—?'

'—that that's where Satchwell come from? Not then, I wasn't, not
when Charlie first told me. But not long after, there was a news story
about some old geezer in Leamington Spa what 'ad put up a sign in
'is front garden. "Whites united against coloured invasion" or some
such 'orrible thing. Me and Larry was out for dinner with Eddie and
Irene, and Eddie's talking about this old racist in the news, and then,
when Irene and I went to the loo, she says to me, "Leamington Spa,
that's where Paul Satchwell was from." She 'adn't mentioned 'im to
me in ages.

'I won't lie, it give me a proper uncomfortable feeling, 'er telling
me that, because I thought, oh my Gawd, what if Charlie really
did see Margot? What if Margot ran off to be with 'er ex? But then
I fort, 'ang on, though: if Margot only went as far as Leamington
Spa, 'ow come she 'asn't never been seen since? I mean, it's 'ardly
Timbuktu, is it?'

'No,' said Strike. 'It isn't. And is that all Irene's ever told you about
Margot and Satchwell?'

'It's enough, innit?' said Janice. Her pink and white complexion
seemed more faded than when Strike had arrived, the veins beneath
her eyes darker. 'Look, *don't* give Irene an 'ard time. Please. She don't
seem it, but she's soft under all that silly stuff. She worries, you know.'

'I can't see why I'd have to give her a hard time,' said Strike. 'Well,
you've been very helpful, Mrs Beattie. Thank you. That clears up
quite a few points for me.'

Janice slumped backwards on the sofa, frowning at Strike.

'You smoke, don't you?' she said abruptly. 'I can smell it off you. Didn't they stop you smoking after you 'ad that amputation?'

'They tried,' said Strike.

'Very bad for you,' she said. 'Won't 'elp wiv your mobility, either, as you get older. Bad for your circulation *and* your skin. You should quit.'

'I know I should,' said Strike, smiling at her as he returned his notebook to his pocket.

'Hmm,' said Janice, her eyes narrowed. '"'Appened to be in the area", my Aunt Fanny.'

51

. . . neuer thinke that so
That Monster can be maistred or destroyd:
He is not, ah, he is not such a foe,
As steele can wound, or strength can ouerthroe.

Edmund Spenser
The Faerie Queene

The domed turrets of the Tower of London rose behind the wall of dirty yellow brick, but Robin had no attention to spare for ancient landmarks. Not only was the meeting she'd set up without Strike's knowledge supposed to start in thirty minutes' time, she was miles from where she'd expected to be at one o'clock, and completely unfamiliar with this part of London. She ran with her mobile in her hand, glancing intermittently at the map on its screen.

Within a few paces, the phone rang. Seeing that it was Strike, she answered the call.

'Hi. Just seen Janice.'

'Oh good,' said Robin, trying not to pant as she scanned her surroundings for either a Tube sign or a taxi. 'Anything interesting?'

'Plenty,' said Strike, who was strolling back along Nightingale Grove. Notwithstanding his recent exchange with the nurse, he'd just lit a Benson & Hedges. As he walked into the cool breeze, the smoke was snatched from his lips every time he exhaled. 'Where are you at the moment?'

'Tower Bridge Road,' said Robin, still running, still looking around in vain for a Tube sign.

609

'Thought you were on Shifty's Boss this morning?'

'I was,' said Robin. It was probably best that Strike knew immediately what had just happened. 'I've just left him on Tower Bridge with Barclay.'

'When you say "with" Barclay—'

'They might be talking by now, I don't know,' said Robin. Unable to talk normally while jogging, she slowed to a fast walk. 'Cormoran, SB looked as though he was thinking of jumping.'

'Off Tower Bridge?' asked Strike, surprised.

'Why not Tower Bridge?' said Robin, as she rounded a corner onto a busy junction. 'It was the nearest accessible high structure . . .'

'But his office isn't anywhere near—'

'He got off at Monument as usual but he didn't go into work. He looked up at the office for a bit, then walked away. I thought he was just stretching his legs, but then he headed out onto Tower Bridge and stood there, staring down at the water.'

Robin had spent forty anxious minutes watching SB stare down at the cement-coloured river below, his briefcase hanging limply by his side, while traffic rumbled along the bridge behind her. She doubted that Strike could imagine how nerve-racking she'd found the wait for Barclay to come and relieve her.

There was still no sign of a Tube station. Robin broke into a jog again.

'I thought of approaching him,' she said, 'but I was worried I'd startle him into jumping. You know how big he is, I couldn't have held him back.'

'You really think he was—?'

'Yes,' said Robin, trying not to sound triumphant: she'd just caught sight of a circular red Tube sign through a break in the traffic and started running. 'He looked utterly hopeless.'

'Are you running?' asked Strike, who could now hear her feet hitting the ground even over the growl of traffic.

'Yes,' said Robin, and then, 'I'm late for a dental appointment.'

She'd regretted not coming up with a solid reason earlier for not being able to interview Janice Beattie, and had decided on this story, should Strike ask again.

'Ah,' said Strike. 'Right.'

'Anyway,' Robin said, weaving around passers-by, 'Barclay arrived to take over – he agreed SB looked like he was thinking of jumping – and he said—'

She was developing a stitch in her side now.

'—said – he'd go and try – and talk to him – and that's when I left. At least – Barclay's big enough – to hold him back if he tries anything,' she finished breathlessly.

'But it also means SB will recognise Barclay in future,' Strike pointed out.

'Well, yeah, I know that,' said Robin, slowing to a walk again as she was almost at the Underground steps, and massaging the stitch in her side, 'but given that we thought he might be about to kill himself—'

'Understood,' said Strike, who had paused in the shadow of Hither Green station to finish his cigarette. 'Just thinking logistics. 'Course, if we're lucky, he might spill the beans to Barclay about what Shifty's got on him. Desperate men are sometimes willing to—'

'Cormoran, I'm going to have to go,' said Robin, who'd reached the Underground entrance. 'I'll see you back at the office after my appointment and you can fill me in about Janice.'

'Right you are,' said Strike. 'Hope it doesn't hurt.'

'What doesn't hu—? Oh, the dentist, no, it's just a check-up,' said Robin.

Really convincing, Robin, she thought, angry at herself, as she shoved her mobile back into her pocket and ran down the steps into the Underground.

Once on the train, she stripped off her jacket, because she was sweating from running, and neatened her hair with the aid of her reflection in the dirty dark window opposite her. Between SB and his possibly suicidal ideation, lying to Strike, her feeble cover story and the potential risks of the meeting she was about to have, she felt jittery. There'd been another occasion, a couple of years previously, when Robin had chosen to pursue a line of inquiry while keeping it secret from Strike. It had resulted in Strike sacking her.

This is different, she tried to reassure herself, smoothing sweaty strands of hair off her forehead. *He won't mind, as long as it works. It's what he wants, too.*

She emerged at Tottenham Court Road station twenty minutes later and hurried with her jacket over her shoulder into the heart of Soho.

Only when she was approaching the Star café, and saw the sign over the door, did she register the coincidence of the name. Trying not to think about asteroids, horoscopes or omens, Robin entered the café, where round wooden tables stood on a red-brick floor. The walls were decorated with old-fashioned tin signs, one of which was advertising ROBIN CIGARETTES. Directly beneath this, perhaps deliberately, sat an old man wearing a black windcheater, his face ruddy with broken veins and his thick grey hair oiled into a quiff that had the appearance of not having changed since the fifties. A walking stick was propped against the wall beside him. On his other side sat a teenage girl with long neon-yellow hair, who was texting on her phone and didn't look up until Robin had approached their table.

'Mr Tucker?' said Robin.

'Yeah,' said the man hoarsely, revealing crooked brown teeth. 'Miss Ellacott?'

'Robin,' she said, smiling as they shook hands.

'This is my granddaughter, Lauren,' said Tucker.

'Hiya,' said Lauren, glancing up from her phone, then back down again.

'I'll just get myself a coffee,' said Robin. 'Can I buy either of you anything?'

They declined. While Robin bought herself a flat white, she sensed the eyes of the old man on her. During their only previous conversation, which had been by phone, Brian Tucker had talked for a quarter of an hour, without pause, about the disappearance of his eldest daughter, Louise, in 1972, and his lifelong quest to prove that Dennis Creed had murdered her. Roy Phipps had called Tucker 'half-insane'. While Robin wouldn't have gone that far on the evidence to date, there was no doubt that he seemed utterly consumed by Creed, and with his quest for justice.

When Robin returned to the Tuckers' table and sat down with her coffee, Lauren put her phone away. Her long neon extensions, the unicorn tattoo on her forearm, her blatantly false eyelashes and her chipped nail varnish all stood in contrast to the innocent, dimpled face just discernible beneath her aggressively applied contouring.

'I came to help Grandad,' she told Robin. 'He doesn't walk so well these days.'

'She's a good girl,' said Tucker. 'Very good girl.'

'Well, thanks very much for meeting me,' Robin told both of them. 'I really appreciate it.'

Close to, Tucker's swollen nose had a strawberry-like appearance, flecked as it was with blackheads.

'No, I appreciate it, Miss Ellacott,' he said in his low, hoarse voice. 'I think they're really going to let it happen this time, I do. And like I said on the phone, if they don't, I'm ready to break into the television studio—'

'Well,' said Robin, 'hopefully we won't need to do anything that dras—'

'—and I've told them that, and it's shaken them up. Well, that, and your contact nudging the Ministry of Justice,' he conceded, gazing at Robin through small, bloodshot eyes. 'Mind you, I'm starting to think I should've threatened them with the press years ago. You don't get anywhere with these people playing by the rules, they just fob you off with their bureaucracy and their so-called expert opinions.'

'I can only imagine how difficult it's been for you,' said Robin, 'but given that we might be in with a chance to interview him, we don't want to do anything—'

'I'll have justice for Louise if it kills me,' said Tucker. 'Let them arrest me. It'll just mean more publicity.'

'But we wouldn't want—'

'She don't want you to do nothing silly, Grandad,' said Lauren. 'She don't want you to mess things up.'

'No, I won't, I won't,' said Tucker. His eyes were small, flecked and almost colourless, set in pouches of purple. 'But this might be our one and only chance, so it must be done in the right way *and by the right interrogator.*'

'Is he not coming?' said Lauren. 'Cormoran Strike? Grandad said he might be coming.'

'No,' said Robin, and seeing the Tuckers' faces fall, she added quickly, 'He's on another case just now, but anything you'd say to Cormoran, you can say to me, as his part—'

'It's got to be him who interviews Creed,' Tucker said. 'Not you.'

'I under—'

'No, love, you don't,' said Tucker firmly. 'This has been my whole life. I understand Creed better than any of the morons who've written books about him. I've studied him. He's been cut off from any kind of attention for years, now. Your boss is a famous man. Creed'll want to meet him. Creed'll think he's cleverer, of course he will. He'll want to beat your boss, want to come out of it on top, but the temptation of seeing his name in the papers again? He's always thrived on the publicity. I think he'll be ready to talk, as long as your boss can make him believe it's worth his while . . . he's kosher, your boss, is he?'

Under almost any other circumstances, Robin would have said 'he's actually my partner', but today, understanding what she was being asked, she said,

'Yes, he's kosher.'

'Yeah, I thought he seemed it, I thought so,' said Brian Tucker. 'When your contact got in touch, I went online, I looked it all up. Impressive, what he's done. He doesn't give interviews, does he?'

'No,' said Robin.

'I like that,' said Tucker, nodding. 'In it for the right reasons. But the name's known, now, and that'll appeal to Creed, and so will the fact your boss has had contact with famous people. Creed likes all that. I've told the Ministry of Justice and I told your contact, I want this Strike to do it, I don't want the police interviewing him. They've had their go and we all know how well *that* went. And no more bloody *psychiatrists*, thinking they're so smart and they can't even agree on whether the bastard's sane or not.

'I know Creed. I understand Creed. I've made a lifelong study of his psychology. I was there every day in court, during the trial. They didn't ask him about Lou in court, not by name, but he made eye contact with me plenty of times. He'll have recognised me, he'll have known who I was, because Lou was my spitting image.

'When they asked him in court about the jewellery – you know about the pendant, Lou's pendant?'

'Yes,' said Robin.

'She got it a couple of days before she disappeared. Showed it to her sister Liz, Lauren's mother – didn't she?' he asked Lauren, who nodded. 'A butterfly on a chain, nothing expensive, and because it was mass-produced, the police said it could have been anyone's. Liz remembered the pendant differently – that's what threw the police off, she wasn't sure at first that it was Lou's – but she admitted she only saw it briefly. And when they mentioned the jewellery, Creed looked straight at me. He knew who I was. Lou was my spit image,' repeated Tucker. 'You know his explanation for having a stash of jewellery under the floorboards?'

'Yes,' said Robin, 'he said he'd bought it because he liked to cross-dress—'

'That he'd bought it,' said Tucker, talking over Robin, 'to dress up in.'

'Mr Tucker, you said on the phone—'

'Lou nicked it from that shop they all used to go to, what was it—?'

'Biba,' said Lauren.

'Biba,' said Tucker. 'Two days before she disappeared, she played truant and that evening she showed Lauren's mum, Liz, what she'd stolen. She was a handful, Lou. Didn't get on with my second wife. The girls' mum died when Lou was ten. It affected Lou the worst, more than the other two. She never liked my second wife.'

He'd told Robin all of this on the phone, but still, she nodded sympathetically.

'My wife had a row with Lou the morning before she disappeared, and Lou bunked off school again. We didn't realise until she didn't come home that night. Rang round all her friends, none of them had seen her, so we called the cops. We found out later, one of her friends had lied. She'd smuggled Lou upstairs and not told her parents.

'Lou was spotted three times next day, still in her school uniform. Last known sighting was outside a launderette in Kentish Town. She asked some geezer for a light. We knew she'd started smoking. That was partly what she rowed with my wife about.

'Creed picked up Vera Kenny in Kentish Town, too,' said Tucker, hoarsely. 'In 1970, right after he'd moved into the place by Paradise Park. Vera was the first woman he took back to that basement. He chained them up, you know, and kept them alive while he—'

'Grandad,' said Lauren plaintively, 'don't.'

'No,' Tucker muttered, dipping his head, 'sorry, love.'

'Mr Tucker,' said Robin, seizing her chance, 'you said on the phone you had information about Margot Bamborough nobody else knows.'

'Yeah,' said Tucker, groping inside his windcheater for a wad of folded papers, which he unfolded with shaking hands. 'This top one, I got through a warder at Wakefield, back in '79. I used to hang round there every weekend in the late seventies, watch them all coming in and out. Found out where they liked to drink and everything.

'Anyway, this particular warder, I won't say his name, but we got chummy. Creed was on a high-security wing, in a single cell, because all the other cons wanted to take a pop at him. One geezer nearly took out Creed's eye in '82, stole a spoon from the canteen and sharpened the handle to a point in his cell. Tried to stab Creed through the eyeball. Just missed, because Creed dodged. My mate told me he screamed like a little girl,' said Tucker, with relish.

'Anyway, I said to my mate, I said, anything you can find out, anything you can tell me. Things Creed's saying, hints he gives, you know. I paid him for it. He could've lost his job if anyone had found out. And my mate got hold of this and smuggled it out to me. I've never been able to admit to having it, because both of us would be in trouble if it got out, but I called up Margot Bamborough's husband, what was his name—?'

'Roy Phipps.'

'Roy Phipps, yeah. I said, "I've got a bit of Creed's writing here you're going to want to see. It proves he killed your wife."'

A contemptuous smile revealed Tucker's toffee-brown teeth again.

'But he didn't want to know,' said Tucker. 'Phipps thought I was a crank. A year after I called him, I read in the paper he'd married the nanny. Creed did Dr Phipps a good turn, it seems.'

'Grandad!' said Lauren, shocked.

'All right, all right,' muttered Tucker. 'I never liked that doctor. He could've done us a lot of good, if he'd wanted to. Hospital consultant, he was the kind of man the Home Secretary would've listened to. We could've kept up the pressure if he'd helped us, but he wasn't interested, and when I saw he was off with the nanny I thought, ah, right, everything's explained.'

'Could I—?' Robin began, gesturing towards the paper Tucker was still holding flat to the table, but he ignored her.

'So it was just me and Jerry for years,' said Tucker. 'Jerry Wolfson, Kara's brother. You know who that is?' he shot at Robin.

'Yes, the nightclub hostess—'

'Nightclub hostess, hooker on the side, and a drug habit as well. Jerry had no illusions about her, he wasn't naive, but it was still his sister. She raised him, after their mother left. Kara was all the family he had.

'February 1973, three months after my Lou, Kara disappeared as well. Left her club in Soho in the early hours of the morning. Another girl left at exactly the same time. It wasn't far from here, as a matter of fact,' said Tucker, pointing out of the door. 'The two girls go different ways up the street. The friend looks back and sees Kara bending down and talking to a van driver at the end of the road. The friend assumed that Kara knew the driver. She walks off. Kara's never seen again.

'Jerry spoke to all Kara's friends at the club, after, but nobody knew anything. There was a rumour going round, after Kara disappeared, that she'd been a police informer. That club was run by a couple of gangland figures. Suited them, to say she was an informer, see? Scare the other girls into keeping shtum about anything they'd seen or heard in the club.

'But Jerry never believed Kara was a snitch. He thought it was the Essex Butcher from the start – the van was the giveaway. So we joined forces.

'He tried to get permission to visit Creed, same as me, but the authorities wouldn't let us. Jerry gave up, in the end. Drank himself to death. Something like this happens to someone you love, it marks you. You can't get out from under it. The weight of it crushes some people.

'My marriage broke up. My other two daughters didn't speak to me for years. Wanted me to stop going on about Lou, stop talking about Creed, pretend it never—'

'That's not fair, Grandad,' said Lauren, sternly.

'Yeah, all right,' mumbled Tucker. 'All right, I grant you, Lauren's mum, she's come round lately. I said to Liz, "Think of all the time I should've spent with Lou, like I've spent with you and Lisa. Add it all up. Family meals and holidays. Helping her with her homework. Telling her to clean her room. Arguing with her—" My God, she could be bolshie. Watching her graduate, I expect, because she was clever, Lou, even if she did get in trouble at school with all the bunking off. I said to Liz, "I never got to walk her up the aisle, did I? Never got to visit her in hospital when her kids were born. Add up all the time I would've given her if she'd lived—"'

Tucker faltered. Lauren put a plump hand over her grandfather's, which had swollen, purple joints.

'—add all that time together,' Tucker croaked, his eyes filmy with tears, 'and that's what I owe her, to find out what happened to her. That's all I'm doing. Giving her her due.'

Robin felt tears prickle behind her own eyelids.

'I'm so sorry,' she said quietly.

'Yeah, well,' said Tucker, wiping his eyes and nose roughly on the sleeve of his windcheater. He now took the top sheet of writing and thrust it at Robin. 'There you are. That shows you what we're up against.'

Robin took the paper, on which was written two short paragraphs in clear, slanting writing, every letter separate and distinct, and began to read.

She attempts to control through words and sometimes with flattery. Tells me how clever I am, then talks about 'treatment'. The strategy is laughably transparent. Her 'qualifications' and her 'training' are, *compared to my self-knowledge, my self-awareness, the flicker of a damp match beside the light of the sun.*

She promises a diagnosis of madness will mean gentler treatment for me. This she tells me between screams, as I whip her face and breasts. Bleeding, she begs me to see that she could be of use to me. Would testify for me. Her arrogance and her thirst for dominance have been fanned by the societal approval she gained from the position of 'doctor'. Even chained, she believes herself superior. This belief will be corrected.

'You see?' said Tucker in a fierce whisper. 'He had Margot Bamborough chained in his basement. He's enjoying writing about it, reliving it. But the psychiatrists didn't think it was an admission, they reckoned Creed was just churning out these bits of writing to try and draw more attention to himself. They said it was all a game to try and get more interviews, because he liked pitting his wits against the police, and reading about himself in the press, seeing himself on the news. They said that was just a bit of fantasy, and that taking it serious would give Creed what he wanted, because talking about it would turn him on.'

'Gross,' said Lauren, under her breath.

'But my warder mate said – because you know, there was three women they thought Creed had done whose bodies were never found: my Lou, Kara Wolfson and Margot Bamborough – and my warder mate said, it was the doctor he really liked being asked about. Creed likes high-status people, see. He thinks he could've been the boss of some multinational, or some professor or something, if he hadn't of turned to killing. My mate told me all this. He said, Creed sees himself on that sort of level, you know, just in a different field.'

Robin said nothing. The impact of what she'd just read wasn't easily dispelled. Margot Bamborough had become real to Robin, and she'd just been forced to imagine her, brutalised and bleeding, attempting to persuade a psychopath to spare her life.

'Creed got transferred to Belmarsh in '83,' Tucker continued, patting the papers still laid in front of him, and Robin forced herself to concentrate, 'and they started drugging him so he couldn't get a – you know, couldn't maintain . . .

'And that's when I got permission to write to him, and have him write back to me. Ever since he was convicted, I'd been lobbying the authorities to let me question him directly, and let him write back. I wore them down in the end. I had to swear I'd never publicise what he wrote me, or give the letter to the press, but I'm the only member of a victim's family he's ever been allowed direct contact with . . . and there,' he said, turning the next two sheets of paper towards Robin. 'That's what I got back.'

The letter was written on prison writing paper. There was no 'Dear Mr Tucker'.

Your letter reached me three weeks ago, but I was placed in solitary confinement shortly afterwards and deprived of writing materials, so have been unable to answer. Ordinarily I'm not permitted to respond to enquiries like yours, but I gather your persistence has worn the authorities down. Unlikely as it may seem, I admire you for this, Mr Tucker. Resilience in the face of adversity is one of my own defining characteristics.

During my three weeks of enforced solitude, I've wondered how I could possibly explain to you what not one man in ten thousand might hope to understand. Although you think I must be able to recall the names, faces and personalities of my various 'victims', my memory shows me only the many-limbed, many-breasted monster with whom I cavorted, a foul-smelling thing that gave tongue to pain and misery. Ultimately, my monster was never much of a companion, though there was fascination in its contortions. Given sufficient stimulus, it could be raised to an ecstasy of pain, and then it knew it lived, and stood tremulously on the edge of the abyss, begging, screaming, pleading for mercy.

How many times did the monster die, then live again? Too few to satisfy me. Even though its face and voice mutated, its reactions never varied. Richard Merridan, my old psychiatrist, gave what possessed me other names, but the truth is that I was in the grip of a divine frenzy.

Colleagues of Merridan's disputed his conclusion that I'm

sane. Regrettably, their opinions were dismissed by the judge. In conclusion: I might have killed your daughter, or I might not. Either I did so in the grip of some madness which still occludes my memory, and which a more skilful doctor might yet penetrate, or I never met her, and little Louise is out there somewhere, laughing at her daddy's attempts to find her, or perhaps enduring a different hell to the one in which my monster lived.

Doubtless the additional psychiatric support available at Broadmoor would help me recover as much memory as possible. For their own inscrutable reasons, however, the authorities prefer to keep me here at Belmarsh. Only this morning I was threatened under the noses of warders. Regardless of the obvious fact that a cachet attaches to anyone who attacks me, I'm exposed, daily, to intimidation and physical danger. How anyone expects me to regain sufficient mental health to assist police further is a mystery.

Exceptional people ought to be studied only by those who can appreciate them. Rudimentary analysis, such as I've been subjected to thus far, merely entrenches my inability to recollect all that I did. Maybe you, Mr Tucker, can help me. Until I'm in a hospital environment where I can be given the assistance I require, what incentive do I have to dredge my fragmented memory for details that may help you discover what happened to your daughter? My safety is being compromised on a daily basis. My mental faculties are being degraded.

You will naturally be disappointed not to receive confirmation of what happened to Louise. Be assured that, when the frenzy is not upon me, I am not devoid of human sympathy. Even my worst critics concede that I actually understand others much more easily than they understand me! For instance, I can appreciate what it would mean to you to recover Louise's body and give her the funeral you so desire. On the other hand, my small store of human empathy is being rapidly depleted by the conditions in which I am currently living. Recovery from the last attack upon me, which nearly removed my eye, was delayed due to the refusal of the authorities to let me attend a civilian hospital. 'Evil men forfeit the right to fair treatment!' Such seems to be the public's view. However, brutality breeds brutality. Even the most dim-witted psychiatrists agree, there.

Do you have a merciful soul, Mr Tucker? If so, the first letter you'll write upon receiving this will be to the authorities, requesting that the remainder of my sentence will be served in Broadmoor, where the secrets my unruly memory still holds may be coaxed to the surface at last.

Ever yours,
Dennis

Robin finished reading, and looked up.

'You can't see it, can you?' said Tucker, with an oddly hungry expression. 'No, of course you can't. It isn't obvious. I didn't see it myself, at first. Nor did the prison authorities. They were too busy warning me they weren't going to transfer him to Broadmoor, so I needn't ask.'

He jabbed the bottom of the letter with a yellow-nailed finger.

'The clue's there. Last line. *First letter. My sentence.* Put together the first letter of every sentence, and see what you get.'

Robin did as she was bidden.

'Y – O – U – R – D – A – U – G – H – T – E – R ...' Robin read out loud, until, fearing where the message was going to end, she fell silent, until she reached the last sentence, when the taste of milky coffee seemed to turn rancid in her mouth, and she said, 'Oh God.'

'What's it say?' asked Lauren, frowning and straining to see.

'Never you mind,' said Tucker shortly, taking the letter back. 'There you are,' he told Robin, folding up the papers and shoving them back into his inside pocket. 'Now you see what he is. He killed Lou like he killed your doctor and he's gloating about it.'

Before Robin could say anything, Tucker spun his next bit of paper to face her, and she saw a photocopied map of Islington, with a circle inked around what looked like a large house.

'Now,' he said, 'there are two places nobody's ever looked, where I think he might've hid bodies. I've been back over everywhere what had a connection with him, kid or adult. Police checked all the obvious, flats he'd lived and that, but never bothered with these.

'When Lou disappeared in November '72, he wouldn't've been able to bury her in Epping Forest, because—'

'They'd just found Vera Kenny's body there,' said Robin.

Tucker looked grudgingly impressed.

'You do your homework at that agency, don't you? Yeah, exactly. There was still a police presence in the forest at the time.

'But see that, there?' said Tucker, tapping on the marked building. 'That's a private house, now, but in the seventies it was the Archer Hotel, and guess who used to do their laundry? Creed's dry cleaner's. He used to pick up stuff from them once a week in his van, and bring it back again, sheets and bedspreads and what have you ...

'Anyway, after he was arrested, the woman who owned the Archer Hotel gave a quote to the *Mail*, saying he always seemed so nice and polite, always chatty when he saw her ...

'That isn't marked on modern maps,' said Tucker, now moving his finger to a cross marked in the grounds of the property, 'but it's on the old deeds. There's a well out the back of that property. Just a shaft into the ground that collects rainwater. Predated the current building.

'I tracked the owner down in '89, after she'd sold up. She told me the well was boarded up in her time, and she planted bushes round it, because she didn't want no kid going down it accidental. But Creed used to go through that garden to deliver laundry, right past the place where the well was. He'll have known it was there. She couldn't remember telling him,' said Tucker quickly, forestalling Robin's question, 'but that's neither here nor there, is it? She wasn't going to remember every word they said to her, was she, after all that time?

'Dead of night, Creed could've pulled up a van by the rear entrance, gone in through the back gate ... but by the time I realised all this,' said Tucker, gritting his brown teeth in frustration, 'the Archer'd gone back to being a private property, and now there's been a bloody conservatory built over the old well.'

'Don't you think,' said Robin cautiously, 'when they built over it, they might have noticed—'

'Why would they?' said Tucker aggressively. 'I never knew a builder who went looking for work when he could just slap concrete over it. Anyway, Creed's not stupid. He'd've thrown rubbish down there on top of the body, wouldn't he? Cover it up. So *that's* a possibility,' he said firmly. 'And then you've got this.'

Tucker's last piece of paper was a second map.

'That there,' he said, tapping his swollen-knuckled finger on another circled building, 'is Dennis Creed's great-grandmother's house. It's mentioned in *The Demon of Paradise Park*. Creed said, in one of his interviews, the only time he ever saw countryside when he was a kid was when he got taken there.

'And look here,' said Tucker, pointing on a large patch of green. 'The house backs right onto Great Church Wood. Acres of woodland, acres and acres. Creed knew the way there. He had a van. He'd played in those woods as a child.

'We know he chose Epping Forest for most of the bodies, because he had no known connection with the place, but by '75, police were regularly checking Epping Forest by night, weren't they? But here's a different wood he knows, and it's not so far away from London, and Creed's got his van and his spades ready in the back.

'My best guess,' said Tucker, 'is my Lou and your doc are in the well or in the woods. And they've got different technology now to what they had in the seventies. Ground-penetrating radar and what have you. It wouldn't be difficult to see if there was a body in either of those places, not if the will was there.

'But,' said Tucker, sweeping the two maps off the table and folding them up with his shaking hands, 'there's no will, or there hasn't been, not for years. Nobody in authority cares. They think it's all over, they think Creed'll never talk. So that's why it's got to be your boss who interviews him. I wish it could be me,' said Tucker, 'but you've seen what Creed thought I was worth . . .'

As Tucker slid his papers back inside his windcheater, Robin became aware that the café around them had filled up during their conversation. At the nearest table sat three young men, all with amusingly Edwardian beards. So long attuned only to Tucker's low, hoarse voice, Robin's ears seemed suddenly full of noise. She felt as though she'd suddenly been transported from the distant past into a brash and indifferent present. What would Margot Bamborough, Louise Tucker and Kara Wolfson make of the mobile phones in almost every hand, or the sound of Pharrell Williams's 'Happy' now playing somewhere nearby, or the young woman carrying a coffee back from the counter, her hair in high bunches, wearing a T-shirt that read GO F#CK YOUR #SELFIE?

'Don't cry, Grandad,' said yellow-haired Lauren softly, putting her arm around her grandfather as a fat tear rolled down his swollen nose and fell upon the wooden table. Now that he'd stopped talking about Louise and Creed, he seemed to have become smaller.

'It's affected our whole family,' Lauren told Robin. 'Mum and Auntie Lisa are always scared if me and my cousins go out after dark—'

'Quite right!' said Tucker, who was now mopping his eyes on his sleeve again.

'—and all us grew up knowing it's something that can *really happen*, you know?' said the innocent-faced Lauren. 'People *really do* disappear. They *really do* get murdered.'

'Yes,' said Robin. 'I know.'

She reached across the table and briefly gripped the old man's forearm.

'We'll do everything we can, Mr Tucker, I promise. I'll be in touch.'

As she left the café, Robin was aware that she'd just spoken for Strike, who knew absolutely nothing of the plan to interview Creed, let alone to try and find out what had happened to Louise Tucker, but she had no energy left to worry about that just now. Robin drew her jacket more closely around her and walked back to the office, her thoughts consumed by the terrible vacuum left in the wake of the vanished.

52

Oft Fire is without Smoke.

Edmund Spenser
The Faerie Queene

It was one o'clock in the morning, and Strike was driving towards Stoke Newington to relieve Robin, who was currently keeping watch over the terraced house that Shifty's Boss was again visiting, and where he was almost certainly indulging in another bout of the blackmailable behaviour Shifty had somehow found out about. Even though Shifty's hold on his boss had driven the latter onto Tower Bridge, SB didn't appear able or willing to give up whatever it was he was doing inside the house of Elinor Dean.

The night was crisp and clear, although the stars overhead were only dimly visible from brightly lit Essex Road, and Barclay's voice was currently issuing from the speaker of the BMW. A week had passed since the Scot had managed to persuade SB to leave Tower Bridge and get a coffee with him.

'He cannae help himself, the poor bastard.'

'Clearly,' said Strike. 'This is his third visit in ten days.'

'He said to me, "Ah cannae stop." Says it relieves his stress.'

'How does he square that with the fact he's suicidal?'

'It's the blackmail that's makin' him suicidal, Strike, no' whatever he gets up tae in Stoke Newington.'

'And he didn't give *any* indication what he does in there?'

'I told ye, he said he doesnae shag her, but that his wife'll leave him if it gets oot. Could be rubber,' added Barclay, thoughtfully.

626

'What?'

'Rubber,' repeated Barclay. 'Like that guy we had who liked wearin' latex to work under his suit.'

'Oh yeah,' said Strike. 'I forgot about him.'

The various sexual predilections of their clients often blurred in Strike's memory. He could hear the hum of the casino in the background. Shifty had been in there for hours and Barclay had been keeping him company, unnoticed, from across the floor.

'Anyway,' said Barclay, 'ye want me tae stay in here, do ye? Because it's costin' a small fortune and ye said the client's gettin' pissy aboot how much we're chargin'. I could watch when the slimy bastard leaves, from ootside on the street.'

'No, stay on him, keep photographing him, and try and get something incriminating,' said Strike.

'Shifty's coked oot o' his head,' said Barclay.

'Half his colleagues will be cokeheads, as well. We're going to need something worse than that to nail the bastard for blackmailing people onto high bridges ...'

'You're goin' soft, Strike.'

'Just try and get something on the fucker and don't place large bets.'

'It's no' the gamblin' that'll bankrupt us,' said Barclay, 'it's the drinks.'

He hung up, and Strike wound down the window and lit a cigarette, trying to ignore the pain in his stiff neck and shoulders.

Like SB, Strike could have used a respite from life's problems and challenges, but such outlets were currently non-existent. Over the past year, Joan's illness had taken from him that small sliver of time that wasn't given over to work. Since his amputation, he no longer played any kind of sport. He saw friends infrequently due to the demands of the agency, and derived many more headaches than pleasures from his relatives, who were being particularly troublesome just now.

Tomorrow was Easter Sunday, meaning that Joan's family would be gathering together in St Mawes to scatter her ashes at sea. Quite apart from the mournful event itself, Strike wasn't looking forward to yet another long journey to Cornwall, or to further enforced contact with Lucy, who'd made it clear over the course of several phone calls that she was dreading this final farewell. Again and again she returned to her sadness at not having a grave to visit, and Strike detected an undertone of blame, as though she thought Strike ought to have overruled Joan's dying wishes. Lucy had also expressed disappointment that Strike wasn't coming down for the whole weekend, as she and Greg were, and added bluntly that he'd better remember to bring Easter eggs for all three of his nephews, not just Jack. Strike could have done without transporting three fragile chocolate eggs all the way to Truro on the train, with a holdall to manage and his leg sore from days and weeks of non-stop work.

To compound his stress, both his unknown half-sister, Prudence, and his half-brother Al had started texting him again. His half-siblings seemed to imagine that Strike, having enjoyed a moment of necessary catharsis by shouting at Rokeby over the phone, was probably regretting his outburst, and more amenable to attending his father's party to make up. Strike hadn't answered any of their texts, but he'd experienced them as insect bites: determined not to scratch, they were nevertheless the source of a niggling aggravation.

Overhanging every other worry was the Bamborough case which, for all the hours he and Robin were putting into it, was proving as opaque as it had when first they'd agreed to tackle the forty-year-old mystery. The year's deadline was coming ever closer, and nothing resembling a breakthrough had yet occurred. If he was honest, Strike had low hopes of the interview with Wilma Bayliss's daughters, which he and Robin would be conducting later that morning, before Strike boarded the train to Truro.

All in all, as he drove towards the house of the middle-aged woman for whom SB seemed to feel such an attraction, Strike had to admit he felt a glimmer of sympathy for any man in desperate search of what the detective was certain was some form of sexual release. Recently it had been brought home to Strike that the relationships he'd had since leaving Charlotte, casual though they'd been, had been his only unalloyed refuge from the job. His sex life had been moribund since Joan's diagnosis of cancer: all those lengthy trips to Cornwall had eaten up time that might have been given to dates.

Which wasn't to say he hadn't had opportunities. Ever since the agency had become successful, a few of the rich and unhappy women who'd formed a staple of the agency's work had shown a tendency to size up Strike as a potential palliative for their own emotional pain or emptiness. Strike had taken on a new client of exactly this type the previous day, Good Friday. As she'd replaced Mrs Smith, who'd already initiated divorce proceedings against her husband on the basis of Morris's pictures of him with their nanny, they'd nicknamed the thirty-two-year-old brunette Miss Jones.

She was undeniably beautiful, with long legs, full lips and skin of expensive smoothness. She was of interest to the gossip columns partly because she was an heiress, and partly because she was involved in a bitter custody battle with her estranged boyfriend, on whom she was seeking dirt to use in court. Miss Jones had crossed and re-crossed her long legs while she told Strike about her hypocritical ex-partner's drug use, the fact that he was feeding stories about her to the papers, and that he had no interest in his six-month-old daughter other than as a means to make Miss Jones unhappy. While he was seeing her to the door, their interview concluded, she'd repeatedly touched his arm and laughed longer than necessary at his mild pleasantries. Trying to usher her politely out of the door under Pat's censorious eye, Strike had had the sensation of trying to prise chewing gum off his fingers.

Strike could well imagine Dave Polworth's comments had he been privy to the scene, because Polworth had trenchant theories about the sort of women who found his oldest friend attractive, and of whom Charlotte was the purest example of the type. The women most readily drawn to Strike were, in Polworth's view, neurotic, chaotic and occasionally dangerous, and their fondness for the bent-nosed ex-boxer indicated a subconscious desire for something rocklike to which they could attach themselves like limpets.

Driving through the deserted streets of Stoke Newington, Strike's thoughts turned naturally to his ex-fiancée. He hadn't responded to the desperate text messages she'd sent him from what he knew, having Googled the place, to be a private psychiatric clinic. Not only had they arrived on the eve of his departure for Joan's deathbed, he hadn't wanted to fuel her vain hopes that he would appear to rescue her. Was she still there? If so, it would be her longest ever period of hospitalisation. Her one-year-old twins were doubtless in the care of a nanny, or the mother-in-law Charlotte had once assured him was ready and willing to take over maternal duties.

A short distance away from Elinor Dean's street, Strike called Robin.

'Is he still inside?'

'Yes. You'll be able to park right behind me, there's a space. I think number 14 must've gone away for Easter with the kids. Both cars are gone.'

'See you in five.'

When Strike turned into the street, he saw the old Land Rover parked a few houses down from Elinor's front door, and was able to park without difficulty in the space directly behind it. As he turned off his engine, Robin jumped down out of her Land Rover, closed the door quietly, and walked around the BMW to the passenger's side, a messenger bag over her shoulder.

'Morning,' she said, sliding into the seat beside him.

'Morning. Aren't you keen to get away?'

As he said it, the screen of the mobile in her hand lit up: somebody had texted her. Robin didn't even look at the message, but turned the phone over on her knee, to hide its light.

'Got a few things to tell you. I've spoken to C. B. Oakden.'

'Ah,' said Strike.

Given that Oakden seemed primarily interested in Strike, and that Strike suspected Oakden was recording his calls, the two detectives had agreed that it should be Robin who warned him away from the case.

'He didn't like it,' said Robin. 'There was a lot of "it's a free country", and "I'm entitled to talk to anyone I like". I said to him, "Trying to get in ahead of us and talk to witnesses could hamper our investigation." He said, as an experienced biographer—'

'Oh, fuck off,' said Strike under his breath.

'—he knows how to question people to get information out of them, and it might be a good idea for the three of us to pool our resources.'

'Yeah,' said Strike. 'That's exactly what this agency needs, a convicted con man on the payroll. How did you leave it?'

'Well, I can tell he *really* wants to meet you and I think he's determined to withhold everything he knows about Brenner until he comes face to face with you. He wants to keep Brenner as bait.'

Strike reached for another cigarette.

'I'm not sure Brenner's worth C. B. Oakden.'

'Even after what Janice said?'

Strike took a drag on the cigarette, then blew smoke out of the window, away from Robin. 'I grant you, Brenner looks a lot fishier now than he did when we started digging, but what are the odds Oakden's actually got useful information? He was a kid when all this happened and nicking that obituary smacks of a man trying to scrape up things to say, rather than—'

He heard a rustling beside him and turned to see Robin opening her messenger bag. Slightly to his surprise, Robin was pulling out Talbot's notebook again.

'Still carrying that around with you, are you?' said Strike, trying not to sound exasperated.

'Apparently I am,' she said, moving her mobile onto the dashboard so that she could open the book in her lap. Watching the phone, Strike saw a second text arrive, lighting up the screen, and this time, he caught sight of the name: Morris.

'What's Morris texting you about?' Strike said, and even to his ears, the question sounded critical.

'Nothing. He's just bored, sitting outside Miss Jones's boyfriend's house,' said Robin, who was flicking through Talbot's notebook. 'I want to show you something. There, look at that.'

She passed him the book, open to a page Strike remembered from his own perusal of the notes. It was close to the end of the notebook, where the pages were most heavily embellished with strange drawings. In the middle of this page danced a black skeleton holding a scythe.

'Ignore all the weird tarot drawings,' said Robin. 'Look there, though. That sentence between the skeleton's legs. The little symbol, the circle with the cross in it, stands for the Part of Fortune . . .'

☿ holds SECRETS - ☿ primitive instincts, dark side personality, SECRETS ☿ not maternal but SEXUAL, yes, crude sensation, unfaithful, dishonest, was in 11th when ☿ disappeared, house of FRIENDSHIPS yet claims with family?? 11th house also House of ♏, what did she do there? Blood on floor – a ritual? Obeah? THERE THE GOAT DEMONS WILL GREET EACH OTHER AND THERE THE LILIT WILL FIND REST 'Nine drops of impure blood' Question FAMILY of ☿ also neighbours

BAPHOMET HERMAPHRODITE

'She lives in the world of Romance, in the perpetual dream of Rapture' - 'Silently and effortlessly she goes about her work' 'Her image is of extreme purity and beauty, with infinite subtlety; to see the truth of her is hardly possible, for she reflects the nature of the observer in great perfection'

TRUSTED ☿ didn't want to dismiss ☿ IN LOVE WITH ♑?

Contrast ☿ and ♀ black moon/ white moon

⊗ in 2nd MONEY and. POSSESSIONS. Mother's House

ADAMS: ♍ 'outlook is apt to be petty' 'difficult to conceal the fact that she has an axe to grind' TRUE ⊗ says ♀♀♄ 8 are SCARLET WOMEN who RIDE UPON THE BEAST

20° ♋

21° ♍

Lévi: St John agrees sulphur = Ether mercury = Water salt = Dragon's blood or MENSTRUUM OF THE EARTH The things of transcendent symbolism can only be understood rightly by the true children of science.'

♍

'I am the Snake that Knowledge and and bright beasts of men with drunkenness. strange drugs'

giveth Delight glory, and stir the To worship me take wine and A CROWLEY

'What's that?' asked Strike.

'It's a point in the horoscope that's supposed to be about worldly success. "Part of Fortune in Second, MONEY AND POSSESSIONS." And "Mother's House", underlined. The Oakdens lived on Fortune Street, remember? And the Part of Fortune was in the house of money and possessions when Margot disappeared, and he's connecting that with the fact that Dorothy inherited her mother's house, and saying that wasn't a tragedy, but a stroke of luck for Dorothy.'

'You think?' said Strike, rubbing his tired eyes.

'Yes, because look, he then starts rambling about Virgo – which is Dorothy's sign under both systems – being petty and having an axe to grind, which from what we know about her fits. Anyway,' said Robin, 'I've been looking at dates of birth, and guess what? Under both the traditional and Schmidt's systems, Dorothy's mother was a Scorpio.'

'Christ's sake, how many more Scorpios are we going to find?'

'I know what you mean,' said Robin, unfazed, 'but from what I've read, Scorpio's one of the most common birth signs. Anyway, this is the important bit: Carl Oakden was born on the sixth of April. That means he's Aries under the traditional system, but Pisces under Schmidt's.'

A short silence followed.

'How old was Oakden when his grandmother fell downstairs?' asked Strike.

'Fourteen,' said Robin.

Strike turned his face away from Robin to blow smoke out of the window again.

'You think he pushed his grandmother, do you?'

'It might not have been deliberate,' said Robin. 'He could've pushed past her and she lost her balance.'

'"Margot confronted Pisces." It'd be a hell of a thing to accuse a child of—'

'Maybe she never confronted him at all. The confrontation might have been something Talbot suspected, or imagined. Either way—'

'—it's suggestive, yeah. It *is* suggestive . . .' Strike let out a slight groan. 'We're going to *have* to interview bloody Oakden, aren't we? There's a bit of a hotspot developing around that little grouping, isn't there? Brenner and the Oakdens, outward respectability—'

'—inward poison. Remember? That's what Oonagh Kennedy said about Dorothy.'

The detectives sat for a moment or two, watching Elinor Dean's front door, which remained closed, her dark garden silent and still.

'How many murders,' Robin asked, 'd'you think go undetected?'

'Clue's in the question, isn't it? "Undetected" – impossible to know. But yeah, it's those quiet, domestic deaths you wonder about. Vulnerable people picked off by their own families, and everyone thinking it was ill health—'

'—or a mercy that they've gone,' said Robin.

'Some deaths *are* a mercy,' said Strike.

And with these words, in both of their mind's eyes rose an image of horror. Strike was remembering the corpse of Sergeant Gary Topley, lying on the dusty road in Afghanistan, eyes wide open, his body missing from the waist down. The vision had recurred in Strike's nightmares ever since he'd seen it, and occasionally, in these dreams, Gary talked to him, lying in the dust. It was always a comfort to remember, on waking, that Gary's consciousness had been snuffed out instantly, that his wide-open eyes and puzzled expression showed that death had claimed him before his brain could register agony or terror.

But in Robin's mind there was a picture of something she wasn't sure had ever happened. She was imagining Margot Bamborough chained to a radiator (*I whip her face and breasts*), pleading for her life (*the strategy is laughably transparent*), and suffering torments (*it could be raised to an ecstasy of pain, and then it knew it lived, and stood tremulously on the edge of the abyss, begging, screaming, begging for mercy*).

'You know,' said Robin, talking partly to break the silence and dispel that mental image, 'I'd quite like to find a picture of Dorothy's mother, Maud.'

'Why?'

'For confirmation, because – I don't think I told you, look . . .'

She flicked backwards in the notebook to the page littered with water signs. In small writing beneath a picture of a scorpion were the words 'MOLE (Adams).'

'Is that a new sign?' asked Strike. 'The Mole?'

'No,' said Robin, smiling, 'Talbot's alluding to the fact that the astrologer Evangeline Adams said the true Scorpio often has a birth-mark, or a prominent mole. I've read her book, got it second hand.'

There was a pause.

'What?' said Strike, because Robin was looking at him expectantly.

'I was waiting for you to jeer.'

'I lost the will to jeer some way back,' said Strike. 'You realise we're supposed to have solved this case in approximately fourteen weeks' time?'

'I know,' sighed Robin. She picked up her mobile to check the time, and out of the corner of his eye, Strike saw yet another text from Morris. 'Well, we're meeting the Bayliss sisters later. Maybe they'll have something useful to tell us ... are you sure you want to interview them with me? I'd be fine to do it alone. You're going to be really tired after sitting here all night.'

'I'll sleep on the train to Truro afterwards,' said Strike. 'You got any plans for Easter Sunday?'

'No,' said Robin. 'Mum wanted me to go home but ... '

Strike wondered what the silent sequel to the sentence was, and whether she'd made plans with someone else, and didn't want to tell him about it. Morris, for instance.

'OK, I swear this is the last thing I'm going to bring up from Talbot's notebook,' Robin said, 'but I want to flag something up before we meet the Baylisses.'

'Go on.'

'You said yourself, he seemed racist, from his notes.'

'"Black phantom",' Strike quoted, 'yeah.'

'And "Black Moon Lilith—"'

'—and wondering whether she was a witch.'

'Exactly. I think he really harassed her, and probably the family, too,' Robin said. 'The language he uses for Wilma – "crude", "dis-honest" ... ' Robin flicked back to the page featuring the three horned signs, 'and "woman as she is now in this aeon ... armed and militant".'

'A radical feminist witch.'

'Which sounds quite cool when you say it,' said Robin, 'but I don't think Talbot meant it that way.'

'You think this is why the daughters didn't want to talk to us?'

'Maybe,' said Robin. 'So I think we need to be ... you know. Sensitive to what might have gone on. Definitely not go in there looking as though we suspect Wilma of anything.'

'Point well made, and taken,' said Strike.

'Right then,' said Robin with a sigh, as she put the notebook back into her messenger bag. 'I'd better get going ... What *is* he doing in there?' Robin asked quietly, looking at Elinor Dean's front door.

'Barclay thinks it might be a rubber fetish.'

'He'd need a lot of talcum powder to wriggle himself into anything made of rubber, the size of that belly.'

Strike laughed.

'Well, I'll see you in ... ' Robin checked the time on her mobile, 'seven hours, forty-five minutes.'

'Sleep well,' said Strike.

As she walked away from the BMW, Strike saw her looking at her mobile again, doubtless reading Morris's texts. He watched as she got into the ancient Land Rover, then turned the tank-like vehicle in a three-point turn, raising a hand in farewell as she passed him, heading back to Earl's Court.

As Strike reached for the Thermos of tea under his seat, he remembered the supposed dental appointment of the other day, about which Robin had sounded strangely flustered, and which had taken place (though Strike hadn't previously made the connection) on Morris's afternoon off. A most unwelcome possibility crossed his mind: had Robin lied, like Irene Hickson, and for the same reason? His mind darted to what Robin had said a few months previously, when she'd mentioned her ex-husband having a new partner: 'Oh, I didn't tell you, did I? I told Morris.'

As he unscrewed his Thermos, Strike mentally reviewed Robin's behaviour around Morris in the last few months. She'd never seemed to particularly like him, but might that have been an act, designed to deflect attention? Were his partner and his subcontractor actually in a relationship which he, busy with his own troubles, had failed to spot?

Strike poured himself tea, settled back in his seat, and glowered at Elinor Dean's closed door through the steam rising from plastic-tasting tea the colour of mud. He was angry, he told himself, because he should have established a work rule that partners weren't allowed to date subcontractors, and for another reason which he preferred not to examine, because he knew perfectly well what it was, and no good could come of brooding upon it.

53

Seven hours later, in the cool, flat daylight of an overcast morning, Robin, who was back in her Land Rover, took a detour on her way to the café where she and Strike would be meeting the three Bayliss sisters.

When Maya, the middle sister, had suggested meeting in Belgique in Wanstead, Robin had realised how close she'd have to drive to the Flats where Dennis Creed had disposed of his second-to-last known victim, twenty-seven-year-old hairdresser Susan Meyer.

Half an hour ahead of the planned interview, Robin parked the Land Rover beside a stretch of shops on Aldersbrook Road, then crossed the street and headed up a short footpath, which led her to the reedy bank of the man-made Alexandra Lake, a wide stretch of water on which various wildfowl were bobbing. A couple of ducks came paddling hopefully towards Robin, but when she failed to produce bread or other treats, they glided away again, compact, self-sufficient, their onyx eyes scanning both water and bank for other possibilities.

Thirty-nine years ago, Dennis Creed had driven to this lake under cover of night, and rolled the headless, handless corpse of Susan Meyer into it, bound up in black plastic and rope. Susan Meyer's distinctive wedge cut and shy smile had earned her a prominent place on the cover of *The Demon of Paradise Park.*

The milky sky looked as opaque as the shallow lake, which resembled jade silk in which the gliding wildfowl made rippling creases. Hands in her pockets, Robin looked out over the water and the rustling weeds, trying to imagine the scene when a park worker had spotted the black object in the water, which he'd assumed initially was a tarpaulin swollen with air, until he hooked it with a long pole, felt the grisly weight and made an instant connection (or so he told the television crew who arrived shortly after the police and ambulance) with the bodies that kept turning up in Epping Forest, barely ten miles away.

Creed had abducted Susan exactly a month before Margot disappeared. Had they overlapped in Creed's basement? If so, Creed had, for a brief period, held three women there simultaneously. Robin preferred not to think about what Andrea, or Margot, if she'd been there, must have felt on being dragged into Creed's basement, seeing a fellow woman chained there, and knowing that she, too, would be reduced to that emaciated and broken-boned state before she died.

Andrea Hooton was the last woman Creed was known to have killed, and he'd varied the pattern when it came to disposing of her body, driving eighty miles from his house in Liverpool Road to throw the corpse off Beachy Head. Both Epping Forest and Wanstead Flats had become too heavily patrolled by then, and in spite of Creed's evident wish to make sure the Essex Butcher was credited with every kill, as evidenced by the secret store of press clippings he kept beneath the floorboards in his basement flat, he'd never wanted to be caught.

Robin checked her watch: it was time to head to the interview with the Bayliss sisters. Walking back to the Land Rover, she pondered the divide between normalcy and insanity. On the surface, Creed had been far saner than Bill Talbot. Creed had left no half-crazed scribblings behind him to explain his thought processes; he'd never plotted the course of asteroids to guide him: his interviews with psychiatrists and police had been entirely lucid. Not for Creed the belief in signs and symbols, a secret language decipherable only by initiates, a refuge in mystery or magic. Dennis Creed had been a meticulous planner, a genius of misdirection in his neat little white van, dressed in the pink coat he'd stolen from Vi Cooper, and sometimes wearing a wig that, from a distance, to a drunk victim, gave his hazy form a feminine appearance just long enough for his large hands to close over a gasping mouth.

When Robin arrived in the street where the café stood, she spotted Strike getting out of his BMW a short distance away from the entrance. Noticing the Land Rover in turn, Strike raised a hand in greeting and headed up the street towards her, while finishing what looked like a bacon and egg McMuffin, his chin stubbly, the shadows beneath his eyes purple.

'Have I got time for a fag?' were the first words he spoke, checking his watch as Robin got down out of the car and slammed the door. 'No,' he answered himself, with a sigh. 'Ah well . . . '

'You can take the lead on this interview,' he told Robin, as they headed together towards the café. 'You've done all the legwork. I'll take notes. Remind me what their names are?'

'Eden's the eldest. She's a Labour councillor from Lewisham. Maya's the middle one, and she's deputy headmistress of a primary school. The youngest is Porschia Dagley, and she's a social worker—'

'—like her mother—'

'Exactly, and she lives just up the road from here. I think we've come to her neck of the woods because she's been ill, so the others didn't want her to have to travel.'

Robin pushed open the door of the café and led the way inside. The interior was sleekly modern, with a curved counter, a wooden floor and a bright orange feature wall. Close to the door at a table for six sat three black women. Robin found it easy to identify which sister was which, because of the photographs she'd seen on the family's Facebook pages, and on the Lewisham Council website.

Eden, the councillor, sat with her arms folded, a wavy bob casting a shadow over most of her face, so that only a carefully lipsticked, unsmiling plum mouth was clearly visible. She wore a well-tailored black jacket and her demeanour was suggestive of a businesswoman who'd been interrupted during an important meeting.

Maya, the deputy headmistress, wore a cornflower blue sweater and jeans. A small silver cross hung around her neck. She was smaller in build than Eden, the darkest skinned and, in Robin's opinion, the prettiest of the sisters. Her long, braided hair was tied back in a thick ponytail, she wore square-framed glasses over her large, wide-set eyes and her full mouth, with its naturally up-tilted corners, conveyed warmth. A leather handbag sat in Maya's lap, and she was gripping it with both hands as though afraid it might otherwise escape.

Porschia, the youngest sister and the social worker, was also the heaviest. Her hair had been cropped almost to her skull, doubtless because of her recent chemotherapy. She'd pencilled in the eyebrows that were just beginning to grow back; they arched over hazel eyes that shone gold against her skin. Porschia was wearing a purple smock top with jeans and long beaded earrings, which swung like miniature chandeliers as she looked around at Strike and Robin. As they approached the table Robin spotted a small tattoo on the back of Porschia's neck: the trident from the Barbadian flag. Robin knew that Eden and Maya were both well into their fifties, and that Porschia was forty-nine, but all three sisters could have passed for at least ten years younger than their real ages.

Robin introduced herself and Strike. Hands were shaken, Eden unsmiling throughout, and the detectives sat down, Strike at the head of the table, Robin between him and Porschia, facing Maya and Eden. Everyone but Eden made laboured small talk about the local area and the weather, until the waiter came to take their order. Once he'd left, Robin said,

'Thanks very much for meeting us, we really do appreciate it. Would you mind if Cormoran takes notes?'

Maya and Porschia shook their heads. Strike tugged his notebook out of his coat pocket and opened it.

'As I said on the phone,' Robin began, 'we're really after background, building up a complete picture of Margot Bamborough's life in the months—'

'Could *I* ask a couple of questions?' interrupted Eden.

'Of course,' said Robin politely, though expecting trouble.

Eden swept her hair back out of her face, revealing ebony-dark eyes.

'Did you two know there's a guy phoning around everyone who was connected to St John's, saying he's going to write a book about you investigating Bamborough's disappearance?'

Shit, thought Robin.

'Would this be a man called Oakden?' asked Strike.

'No, Carl Brice.'

'It's the same bloke,' said Strike.

'Are you connected to him or—?'

'No,' said Strike, 'and I'd strongly advise you not to talk to him.'

'Yeah, we worked that out for ourselves,' said Eden, coolly. 'But this means there'll be publicity, won't there?'

Robin looked at Strike, who said,

'If we solve the case, there'll be publicity even without Oakden – or Brice, or whatever he's calling himself these days – but that's a big "if". To be frank, the odds are we're not going to solve it, in which case I think Oakden's going to find it very hard to sell any books, and whatever you tell us will never go any further.'

'What if we know something that might help you solve the case, though?' asked Porschia, leaning forwards, so that she could look past Robin at Strike.

There was an infinitesimal pause in which Robin could almost feel Strike's interest sharpening, along with her own.

'Depends what that information is,' Strike answered slowly. 'It *might* be possible not to divulge where we got it, but if the source is important to getting a conviction . . .'

There was a long pause. The air between the sisters seemed charged with silent communications.

'Well?' said Porschia at last, on an interrogative note.

'We *did* decide to,' Maya mumbled to Eden, who continued to sit in silence, arms folded.

'OK, *fine*,' said Eden, with a don't-blame-me-later inflection.

The deputy headmistress reached absently for the little silver cross around her neck, and held it as she began to talk.

'I need to explain a bit of background, first,' she said. 'When we were kids – Eden and I were already teenagers, but Porschia was only nine—'

'Eight,' Porschia corrected her.

'Eight,' Maya said obediently, 'our dad was convicted of – of rape and sent to prison.'

'He didn't do it, though,' said Eden.

Robin reached automatically for her coffee cup and took a sip, so as to hide her face.

'He didn't, OK?' said Eden, watching Robin. 'He had a white girlfriend for a couple of months. The whole of Clerkenwell knew. They'd been seen together in bars all over the place. He tried to end it, and she cried rape.'

Robin's stomach lurched as though the floor had tilted. She very much wanted this story to be untrue. The idea of any woman lying about rape was repugnant to her. She'd had to talk through every moment of her own assault in court. Her soft-spoken fifty-three-year-old rapist and would-be murderer had taken the stand afterwards to explain to the jury how the twenty-year-old Robin had invited him into the stairwell of her hall of residence for sex. In his account, everything had been consensual: she'd whispered that she liked it rough, which had accounted for the heavy bruising around her neck, she'd enjoyed it so much she'd asked him back the following night, and yes (with a little laugh in the dock), of course he'd been surprised, nicely spoken young girl like her, coming on to him like that, out of nowhere . . .

'Easy thing for a white woman to do to a black man,' said Eden, ''specially in 1972. Dad already had a record, because he'd got into a fight a few years before that. He went down for five years.'

'Must've been hard on the family,' said Strike, not looking at Robin.

'It was,' said Maya. 'Very hard. The other kids at school . . . well, you know what kids are like . . . '

'Dad had been bringing in most of the money,' said Porschia. 'There were five of us, and Mum had never had much schooling. Before Dad got arrested, she'd been studying, trying to pass some exams, better herself. We were just about making ends meet while Dad was bringing in a wage, but once he was gone, we struggled.'

'Our mum and her sister married two brothers,' said Maya. 'Nine children between them. The families were really close, right up until

Dad got arrested – but then everything changed. My Uncle Marcus went to court every day while Dad was on trial, but Mum wouldn't go and Uncle Marcus was really angry at her.'

'Well, he knew it would've made a big difference, if the judge had seen Dad had the family united behind him,' snapped Eden. '*I* went. I bunked off school to go. I knew he was innocent.'

'Well, good for you,' said Porschia, though her tone was far from congratulatory, 'but Mum didn't want to sit in open court listening to her husband talk about how often he had sex with his girlfriend—'

'That woman was trash,' said Eden curtly.

'*Dirty water does cool hot iron,*' said Porschia, with a Bajan inflection. 'His choice.'

'So, anyway,' said Maya hastily, 'the judge believed the woman, and Dad got put away. Mum never went to visit him inside, and she wouldn't take me or Porschia or our brothers, either.'

'I went,' piped up Eden again. 'I got Uncle Marcus to take me. He was still our dad. Mum had no right to stop us seeing him.'

'Yeah, so,' continued Maya, before Porschia could say anything, 'Mum wanted a divorce, but she had no money for legal advice. So Dr Bamborough put her in touch with this feminist lawyer, who'd give legal help to women in difficult circumstances, for a reduced fee. When Uncle Marcus told Dad that Mum had managed to get herself a lawyer, Dad wrote to her from prison, begging her to change her mind. He said he'd found God, that he loved her and he'd learned his lesson and all he wanted was his family.'

Maya took a sip of her coffee.

'About a week after Mum got Dad's letter, she was cleaning Dr Bamborough's consulting room one evening after everyone had left, and she noticed something in the bin.'

Maya unfastened the handbag she'd been holding on her lap, and took out a pale blue piece of heavily creased paper, which had clearly been crumpled up into a ball at some point in the past. She held it out to Robin, who laid it flat on the table so that Strike could read it, too.

The faded handwriting was a distinctive mix of capitals and lower-case letters.

LEAVE MY GIRL ALONE YOU CUNT OR I'LL MAKE SURE YOU GO TO HELL SLOW AND PAINFUL.

Robin glanced sideways at Strike and saw her own, barely disguised astonishment mirrored there. Before either of them could say anything, a group of young women passed their table, forcing Strike to push his chair in. Chatting and giggling, the women sat down at the table behind Maya and Eden.

'When Mum read that,' said Maya, speaking more quietly so that the newcomers couldn't hear her, 'she thought Dad had sent it. Not *literally*, because the prison censor would never have let that go out – she thought someone had done it for him.'

'Specifically, Uncle Marcus,' said Eden, arms folded and expression pinched. 'Uncle Marcus, who was a lay preacher and never used the c-word in his life.'

'Mum took the note over to Uncle Marcus and Auntie Carmen's,' said Maya, ignoring this interjection, 'and asked Marcus straight out if he was behind it. He denied it, but Mum didn't believe him. It was the mention of hell: Marcus was a fire-and-brimstone kind of preacher back then—'

'—and he didn't believe Mum really wanted a divorce,' said Porschia. 'He blamed Dr Bamborough for persuading Mum to leave Dad, because, you know, Mum *really* needed a white woman to point out her life was shit. She'd never have noticed otherwise.'

'Going for a cigarette, OK?' said Eden abruptly. She pushed herself up and walked out, her heels rapping on the wooden floorboards.

Both younger sisters seemed to exhale in relief with her departure.

'She was Dad's favourite,' Maya told Strike and Robin quietly, watching through the window as Eden took out a packet of Silk Cut, shook her hair out of her face and lit herself a cigarette. 'She really loved him, even if he was a womaniser.'

'And she never got on with Mum,' said Porschia. 'Their rows would've woken the dead.'

'In fairness,' said Maya, 'them splitting up hit Eden hardest. She left school at sixteen, got herself a job at Marks & Spencer to help support—'

'Mum never wanted her to drop out of school,' said Porschia. 'That was Eden's choice. Eden likes to claim it was a sacrifice she made for the family, but come on. She couldn't *wait* to get out of school, because Mum put so much pressure on her to get good grades. She likes to claim she was a second mother to all of us, but that's not how I remember it. *I* mostly remember her whacking merry hell out of me if I so much as looked at her wrong.'

On the other side of the window, Eden stood smoking with her back to them.

'The whole situation was a nightmare,' said Maya sadly. 'Mum and Uncle Marcus never made it up, and with Mum and Carmen being sisters . . .'

'Let's just tell them now, while she can't stick her oar in,' Porschia urged Maya, and turning to Strike and Robin, she said, 'Auntie Carmen was helping Mum get the divorce, behind Uncle Marcus's back.'

'How?' asked Robin, as a waiter passed their table on the way to the group of women at the next table.

'See, when the lawyer Dr Bamborough had recommended told Mum what she charged, Mum knew she'd never be able to afford her, not even at the reduced rates,' said Porschia.

'Mum came home afterwards and cried,' said Maya, 'because she was desperate to have the divorce done and dusted before Dad got out of jail. She knew otherwise he'd just move right back in and she'd be trapped. Anyway, a few days later, Dr Bamborough asked her how things had gone with the lawyer, and Mum admitted she wasn't going to go through with the divorce, for lack of funds, so,' Maya sighed, 'Dr Bamborough offered to pay the lawyer, in exchange for Mum doing a few hours a week cleaning the house out in Ham.'

The women at the table behind theirs were now flirting with the young waiter, wondering whether it was too early for a cream cake, giggling about breaking their diets.

'Mum didn't feel she could refuse,' said Maya. 'But what with the costs of getting all the way out to Ham, and the time it would take her to get out there, when she already had two other jobs and exams coming up . . .'

'Your Aunt Carmen agreed to do the cleaning for her,' guessed Robin, and out of the corner of her eye she saw Strike glance at her.

'Yeah,' said Maya, eyes widening in surprise. 'Exactly. It seemed like a good solution. Auntie Carmen was a housewife and Uncle Marcus and Dr Bamborough were both out at work all day, so Mum thought neither of them would ever know the wrong woman was turning up.'

'There was one sticky moment,' said Porschia, 'remember, M? When Dr Bamborough asked us all over to a barbecue at her house?' She turned to Robin. 'We couldn't go, because Dr Bamborough's nanny would've realised Mum wasn't the woman turning up once a week to clean. My Auntie Carmen didn't like that nanny,' Porschia added. 'Didn't like her at all.'

'Why was that?' asked Strike.

'She thought the girl was after Dr Bamborough's husband. Went red every time she said his name, apparently.'

The door of the café opened and Eden walked back inside. As she sat down, Robin caught a whiff of smoke mingling with her perfume.

'Where've you got to?' she asked, looking cold.

'Auntie Carmen cleaning instead of Mum,' said Maya.

Eden re-folded her arms, ignoring her coffee.

'So the statement your mother gave the police, about the blood and Dr Phipps walking across the garden—' said Strike.

'—was really her telling him everything Carmen had told *her*, yeah,' said Maya, feeling again for the cross around her neck. 'She couldn't own up that her sister had been going there instead of her, because my Uncle Marcus would've gone *crazy* if he'd found out. Auntie Carmen *begged* Mum not to tell the police and Mum agreed.

'So she had to pretend she was the one who'd seen the blood on the carpet and Dr Phipps walking across the lawn.'

'Only,' interrupted Porschia, with a humourless laugh, 'Carmen changed her mind about Dr Phipps, after. Mum went back to her after her first police interview and said, "They're asking whether I couldn't have got confused and mistaken one of the workmen for Dr Phipps." Carmen said, "Oh. Yeah. I forgot there were workmen round the back. Maybe I did."'

Porschia let out a short laugh, but Robin knew she wasn't truly amused. It was the same kind of laughter Robin had taken refuge in, the night she'd discussed rape with Max over the kitchen table.

'I know it isn't funny,' said Porschia, catching Maya's eye, 'but come on. Carmen was always ditzy as hell, but you'd think she might've made sure of her facts *then*, wouldn't you? Mum was literally sick with stress, like, *retching* if she ate anything. And then that old bitch of a secretary at work found her having a dizzy spell . . .'

'Yeah,' said Eden, suddenly coming to life. 'Next thing was, Mum was accused of being a thief and a drunk and the practice fired her. The old secretary claimed she'd had a secret sniff of Mum's Thermos and smelled booze in it. Total fabrication.'

'That was a few months after Margot Bamborough disappeared, wasn't it?' asked Strike, his pen poised over his notebook.

'Oh, I'm sorry,' Eden said with icy sarcasm, 'did I go off topic? Back to the missing white lady, everyone. Never mind what the black woman went through, who gives a shit?'

'Sorry, I didn't—' began Strike.

'D'you know who Tiana Medaini is?' Eden shot at him.

'No,' he admitted.

'*No*,' said Eden, 'of course you bloody don't. Forty years after Margot Bamborough went missing, here we all are, fussing over her and where she went. Tiana Medaini's a black teenager from Lewisham. She went missing last year. How many front pages has Tiana been on? Why wasn't she top of the news, like Bamborough was? Because we're not worth the same, are we, to the press or to the bloody police?'

Strike appeared unable to find an adequate response; doubtless, Robin thought, because Eden's point was unarguable. The picture of Dennis Creed's only black victim, Jackie Aylett, a secretary and mother of one, was the smallest and the least distinct of the ghostly black and white images of Creed's victims on the cover of *The Demon of Paradise Park*. Jackie's dark skin showed up worst on the gloomy cover. The greatest prominence had been given to sixteen-year-old Geraldine Christie and twenty-seven-year-old Susan Meyer, both of them pale and blonde.

'When Margot Bamborough went missing,' Eden said fiercely, 'the white women at her practice were treated like bone china by the police, OK? Practically mopping their bloody tears for them – but not our mum. They treated her like a hardened con. That policeman in charge, what was his name—?'

'Talbot?' suggested Robin.

'"What are you hiding? Come on, I know you're hiding something."'

The mysterious figure of the Hierophant rose up in Robin's mind. The keeper of secrets and mysteries in the Thoth tarot wore saffron robes and sat upon a bull ('the card is referred to Taurus') and in front of him, half his size, stood a black priestess, her hair braided like Maya's ('Before him is the woman girt with a sword; she represents the Scarlet Woman . . .'). Which had come first, the laying out of tarot cards signifying secrecy and concealment, or the policeman's instinct that the terrified Wilma was lying to him?

'When he interviewed me—' began Eden.

'Talbot interviewed *you*?' asked Strike sharply.

'Yeah, he came to Marks & Spencer unannounced, to my work,' said Eden, and Robin realised that Eden's eyes were suddenly bright with tears. 'Someone else at the practice had seen that anonymous note Bamborough got. Talbot found out Dad was inside and he'd heard Mum was cleaning for the doctor. He went to every man in our family, accusing them of writing the threatening letters, and then he came to me, asking me really strange questions about all my male relatives, wanting to know what they'd been up to on different dates, asking whether Uncle Marcus often stayed out overnight. He even asked me about Dad and Uncle Marcus's—'

'—star signs?' asked Robin.

Eden looked astounded.

'The hell did you know that?'

'Talbot left a notebook. It's full of occult writing. He was trying to solve the case using tarot cards and astrology.'

'Astrology?' repeated Eden. 'Effing *astrology*?'

'Talbot shouldn't have been interviewing you without an adult present,' Strike told Eden. 'What were you, sixteen?'

Eden laughed in the detective's face.

'That might be how it works for white girls, but we're different, aren't you listening? We're hardy. We're *tough*. That occult stuff,' Eden said, turning back to Robin, 'yeah, that makes sense, because he asked me about *obeah*. You know what that is?'

Robin shook her head.

'Kind of magic they used to practise in the Caribbean. Originated in West Africa. We were all born in Southwark, but, you know, we were all black pagans to Inspector Talbot. He had me alone in the back room and he was asking me stuff about rituals using blood, about black magic. I was terrified, I didn't know what he was on about. I thought he meant Mum and the blood on the carpet, hinting she'd done away with Dr Bamborough.'

'He was having a psychotic breakdown,' said Robin. 'That's why they took him off the case. He thought he was hunting a devil. Your mum wasn't the only woman he thought might have supernatural power – but he was definitely racist,' Robin added quietly. 'That's clear from his notes.'

'You never told us about the police coming to Marks & Spencer,' said Porschia. 'Why didn't you tell us?'

'Why would I?' said Eden, angrily blotting her damp eyes. 'Mum was already ill with the stress of it all, I had Uncle Marcus shouting at me that Mum had put the police onto him and his boys, and I was really scared, if Uncle Marcus found out about the officer coming to my work, he'd report him, which was the last thing we needed. God, it was a mess,' said Eden, pressing her hands briefly against her wet eyes, 'such a bloody mess.'

Porschia looked as though she'd like to say something comforting to her elder sister, but Robin had the impression that this would be such a departure from their usual relationship, she didn't know quite how to set about it. After a moment or two, Porschia muttered,

'Need the loo,' pushed her chair away from the table and disappeared into the bathroom.

'I didn't want Porsh to come today,' said Maya, as soon as the bathroom door swung shut behind her younger sister. She was tactfully not looking at her elder sister, who was trying to pretend she wasn't crying, while surreptitiously wiping more tears from her eyes. 'She doesn't need this stress. She's only just finished chemo.'

'How's she doing?' asked Strike.

'She was given the all-clear last week, thank God. She's talking about going back to work on reduced hours. I think it's too early.'

'She's a social worker, isn't she?' asked Robin.

'Yeah,' sighed Maya. 'A backlog of a hundred desperate messages every morning, and you know you're in the firing line if anything goes wrong with a family you haven't been able to reach. I don't know how she does it. But she's like Mum. Two peas in a pod. She was always Mum's baby, and Mum was her hero.'

Eden let out a soft 'huh', which might have been agreement or disparagement. Maya ignored it. There was a short pause, in which Robin reflected on the tangled ties of family. A proxy war between Jules and Wilma Bayliss seemed still to be playing out in the next generation.

The bathroom door swung open again and Porschia reappeared. Instead of taking her seat beside Robin, she swivelled her wide hips around Strike at the end of the table, and edged in behind a startled Maya, who pulled her chair in hastily, until she reached Eden. After thrusting a handful of toilet roll into her elder sister's hand, Porschia slid her plump arms around Eden's neck and dropped a kiss on the top of her head.

'What are you doing?' said Eden huskily, reaching up to clasp her youngest sister's arms, not to remove them, but to hold them there. Strike, Robin saw out of the corner of her eye, was pretending to examine his notebook.

'Thanking you,' said Porschia softly, dropping another kiss on the top of her eldest sister's head before letting her go. 'For agreeing to do this. I know you didn't want to.'

Everyone sat in slightly startled silence while Porschia squeezed her way back around the table and resumed her seat next to Robin.

'Have you told them the last bit?' Porschia asked Maya, while Eden blew her nose. 'About Mum and Betty Fuller?'

'No,' said Maya, who appeared shell-shocked by the act of reconciliation she'd just witnessed. 'You're the one Mum told it to, I thought you should.'

'Right,' said Porschia, turning to look at Strike and Robin. 'This really is the last thing we know, and there might be nothing in it, but you might as well have it, now you know the other stuff.'

Strike waited, pen poised.

'Mum told me this not long after she retired. She shouldn't have, really, because it was about a client, but when you hear what it was, you'll understand.

'Mum kept working in Clerkenwell after she'd qualified as a social worker. It was where all her friends were; she didn't want to move. So she really got to know the local community.

'One of the families she was working with lived in Skinner Street, not that far from the St John's practice—'

'Skinner Street?' repeated Strike. The name rang a bell, but, exhausted as he was, he couldn't immediately remember why that was. Robin, on the other hand, knew immediately why Skinner Street sounded familiar.

'Yeah. The family was called Fuller. They had just about every problem you can think of, Mum said: addiction, domestic abuse, criminality, the lot. The sort of head of the family was a grandmother who was only in her forties, and this woman's main source of income was prostitution. Betty was her name, and Mum said she was like a local news service, if you wanted to know about the underworld, anyway. The family had been in the area for generations.

'Anyway, one day, Betty says to Mum, bit sly, to see her reaction: "Marcus never sent no threatening notes to that doctor, you know."

'Mum was gobsmacked,' said Porschia. 'Her first thought was that Marcus was visiting the woman, you know, as a client – *I know he wasn't*,' said Porschia quickly, holding up a hand to forestall Eden, who'd opened her mouth. 'Mum and Marcus hadn't spoken for years at this point. Anyway, it was all innocent: Betty had met Marcus because the church was doing a bit of outreach in the local area. He'd brought round some Harvest Festival stuff for the family, and tried to persuade Betty to come along to a church service.

'Betty had worked out Marcus's connection with Mum, because Mum was still going by "Bayliss", and Betty claimed she knew who *really* wrote the threatening notes to Margot Bamborough, and that the person who wrote the notes was the same person who killed her. Mum said, "Who was it?" And Betty said if she ever told, Margot's killer would kill her, too.'

There was a short silence. The café clattered around them, and one of the women at the next table, who was eating a cream slice, said loudly, with unctuous pleasure,

'*God* that's good.'

'Did your mother believe Betty?' asked Robin.

'She didn't know what to think,' said Porschia. 'Betty knew some very rough people, so it was possible she'd heard something on the grapevine, but who knows? People talk, don't they, and they like making themselves important,' and Robin remembered Janice Beattie saying exactly this, as she passed on the rumour of Margot Bamborough appearing in a graveyard. 'But if there was anything in it, a woman like Betty, she'd go to the moon before she went to the cops.

'She might well be dead by now,' said Porschia, 'given her life-style, but for what it's worth, there it is. Shouldn't be hard to find out whether she's still alive.'

'Thanks very much for telling us,' said Strike. 'That's definitely worth following up.'

Having told all they knew, the three sisters now lapsed into a pained silence. It wasn't the first time that Robin had had cause to consider how much collateral damage each act of violence left in its wake. The disappearance of Margot Bamborough had evidently wreaked havoc in the lives of the Bayliss girls, and now she knew the full extent of the grief it had brought them, and the painful nature of the memories associated with it, she perfectly understood Eden's initial refusal to talk to detectives. If anything, she had to ask herself why the sisters had changed their minds.

'Thank you so much for this,' she said sincerely. 'I know Margot's daughter will be incredibly grateful that you agreed to talk to us.'

'Oh, it's the daughter who's hired you, is it?' said Maya. 'Well, you can tell her from me, Mum felt guilty all her life that she didn't come clean with the police. She liked Dr Bamborough, you know.

I mean, they weren't close friends or anything, but she thought she was a decent person.'

'It weighed on her,' said Porschia. 'Right up until her death, it weighed on her. That's why she kept that note. She'd have wanted us to do this. There's always handwriting analysis and stuff, isn't there?'

Strike agreed that there was. He went to pay the bill and Robin waited at the table with the sisters, who she could tell wanted the detectives gone, and as quickly as possible. They'd disclosed their personal trauma and their family's secrets, and now a thin layer of polite small talk was too onerous to sustain, and any other form of conversation impossible. Robin was relieved when Strike re-joined her, and after brief farewells, the two of them left the café.

The moment he hit clean air, Strike paused to pull his Benson & Hedges out of his pocket and lit one.

'Needed that,' he muttered, as they walked on. 'So ... Skinner Street ...'

'... is where Joseph Brenner was seen on the night Margot Bamborough disappeared,' said Robin.

'Ah,' muttered Strike, briefly closing his eyes. 'I *knew* there was something.'

'I'll look into Betty Fuller as soon as I get home,' said Robin. 'What did you think of the rest of it?'

'The Bayliss family really went through it, didn't they?' said Strike, pausing beside the Land Rover and glancing back at the café. His BMW lay another fifty yards ahead. He took another drag on his cigarette, frowning. 'Y'know ... it gives us another angle on Talbot's bloody notebook,' he admitted. 'Strip away all the occult shit, and he was right, wasn't he? Wilma *was* hiding stuff from him. A lot of stuff, actually.'

'I thought that, too,' said Robin.

'You realise that threatening note's the first piece of physical evidence we've found?'

'Yes,' said Robin, checking her watch. 'What time are you heading to Truro?'

Strike didn't answer. Looking up, Robin saw that he was staring so fixedly across the open park on the other side of the road that she turned, too, to see what had captured his attention, but saw nothing except a couple of gambolling West Highland terriers and their male owner, who was walking along, swinging a pair of leads.

'Cormoran?'

Strike appeared to recall his attention from a long way away.

'What?' he said, and then, 'Yeah. No, I was just . . . '

He turned to look back at the café, frowning.

'Just thinking. But it's nothing, I think I'm doing a Talbot. Seeing meaning in total coincidence.'

'What coincidence?'

But Strike didn't answer until the café doors opened, and the three Bayliss sisters emerged in their coats.

'We should get going,' he said. 'They must be sick of the sight of us by now. I'll see you Monday. Let me know if you find out anything interesting on Betty Fuller.'

54

But nothing new to him was that same pain;
Nor pain at all; for he so oft had tried
The power thereof, and lov'd so oft in vain.

Edmund Spenser
The Faerie Queene

The train gave a lurch: the sleeping Strike's head rolled sideways and hit the cold window. He woke, feeling drool on his chin. Wiping it on his coat sleeve, he peered around. The elderly couple opposite him were politely immersed in their reading material, but across the aisle, four teenagers were enjoying paroxysms of silent laughter, carefully not looking at him, their shoulders shaking as they feigned interest in the fields out of the window. Apparently he'd been snoring with his mouth wide open, because it was now unpleasantly dry. Checking his watch, he saw that he'd been asleep at least two hours.

Strike reached for the tartan Thermos sitting on the table in front of him, which he'd rinsed out and refilled in McDonald's earlier, and poured himself a black coffee while the teenagers continued to gasp and snort with laughter. Doubtless they thought him comically odd and old, with his snores and his tartan Thermos, but a year of navigating swaying train carriages had taught him that his prosthetic leg appreciated as few trips to the catering car as possible. He drank a cup of plastic-tainted coffee, then re-settled himself comfortably, arms folded, looking out at the fields gliding past, bestridden with power pylons, the flat white cloud given a glaucous glow by the dust on the glass. The landscape registered only incidentally: Strike's attention was focused inwards on the odd idea that had occurred to him after the interview with the Bayliss sisters.

Of course, the idea might be nothing but the product of an overburdened mind making spurious connections between simple coincidences. He mentally turned it this way and that, examining it from different angles, until finally, yawning, he inched sideways over into the empty seat beside him, and laboriously pulled himself up into a standing position in the aisle, so he could access the hold-all in the luggage rack overhead. Beside his holdall sat a Waitrose bag, because he'd made a detour into the supermarket on the way to Paddington station, where he'd grabbed three Easter eggs for his nephews, or rather, three chocolate hedgehogs ('Woodland Friends') because they were relatively compact. Now, groping in his holdall for *The Demon of Paradise Park*, he accidentally knocked over the carrier bag containing the chocolate. The uppermost hedgehog fell out: in his attempt to catch it, he accidentally batted it up into the air; the box bounced off the back of the elderly woman's seat, causing her to squeak in surprise, and the box hit the floor.

The teenagers for whom Strike was unintentionally mounting a one-man comedy show were now openly gasping and crying with laughter. Only when Strike bent down awkwardly to pick up the now cracked chocolate hedgehog, one hand on the teenagers' table to steady himself, did one of the young women spot the metal rod that served as his right ankle. He knew what she'd seen by the abrupt cessation of her laughter, and the frantic, whispered shushing of her friends. Panting, sweating and now aware of half the carriage's eyes on him, he shoved the damaged hedgehog back into its bag, found *The Demon of Paradise Park* in his holdall and then, sweating slightly, but taking malicious pleasure in the po-faced shock of the teenagers beside him, sidled back into his window seat.

After flicking through the book in search of the part he wanted to re-read, Strike finally found the chapter two-thirds of the way through the book, entitled 'Capture'.

Thus far, Creed's relationship with landlady Violet Cooper had been key to his continuing safety. Violet herself admits that for the first five years of his tenancy, she'd never have believed harm of 'Den', who she saw as a lonely and gentle soul, fond of their singalong evenings, and probably gay.

However, the pains he'd once taken to keep Violet happy had begun to irk Creed. Where once he'd drugged her because he was planning to pound bones to dust in the basement, or needed to load a corpse into the van by night, he now began lacing her gin-and-oranges with barbiturates purely to avoid the tedium of her company.

Creed's manner towards Violet also changed. He became 'mean' to her, 'taking the Mickey when there was no need, saying nasty things, laughing at me for using the wrong words and stuff, treating me like I was stupid, which he'd never done before.

'I remember one time, I was telling him about the place my brother bought when he retired, cottage in the country, everything lovely, and I said, "You should've seen the garden, his roses and a gazebo," and he laughed at me, Dennis, well, jeered, really, because I'd said it wrong. *Gazzybo*, I said, and I've never forgotten it, he said, "Don't use words if you can't say 'em, you just look thick."

'It hurt my feelings. I hadn't seen that nasty side of him. I knew he was clever, he used to do the *Times* crossword every day. Knew all the answers on *Mastermind*, when we watched it together, but he'd never put me down before.

'Then, one night, he starts going on about my will. He wants to know who I'm going to leave the house to. He as good as asked me to leave it to him.

'I didn't like that. I wasn't an old woman, I wasn't planning to die any time soon. I changed the subject, but he started on it again a few nights later. I said, "Look, how d'you think that makes me feel, Dennis, you going on like this, like I'm on my last legs? You're making me feel like you're going to do away with me."

'He got uppity and said it was all right for me, but he had

nothing, no security or nothing, and what if he got turfed out on the street by whoever I left the house to? And he flounced out. We made it up, later, but it left a nasty taste.'

It would seem the height of foolhardiness for Creed to persuade Violet into changing her will and then kill her. Quite apart from having an obvious motive, he'd be risking the ingression of police into the basement where he was concealing the remains and belongings of at least five women. However, Creed's arrogance and sense of inviolability seem to have known no bounds by this time. He was also stockpiling pills in larger quantities than ever, which brought him into contact with more than one street dealer. This made him more widely recognisable.

One of his new drugs contacts was Michael Cleat, who sold barbiturates stolen from a contact at a pharmaceutical company. Cleat would later cut a deal with police in exchange for his testimony at the killer's trial. Creed, he testified, had asked Cleat whether he or his contact could procure a doctor's prescription pad. Police suspected that Creed was hoping to fake a prescription for Violet, to explain her possession of the means to overdose . . .

In spite of the coffee, Strike's eyelids began to droop again. After another couple of minutes, his head sank sideways and the book slipped out of his slack grasp.

When he woke up again, the sky outside had turned coral pink, the laughing teenagers were gone, and he found himself ten minutes from Truro station. Stiffer than ever and in no mood for the family reunion, he wished he was heading back to his attic flat for a shower and some peace. Nevertheless, his heart lifted slightly when he saw Dave Polworth waiting for him on the platform. The bag of chocolate hedgehogs rattled slightly as Strike clambered laboriously off the train. He'd have to remember to give the broken one to Luke.

'All right, Diddy?' said Polworth, as they shook hands and patted each other on the back, Strike's Waitrose bag impeding a hug.

'Thanks for picking me up, Chum, really appreciate it.'

They drove to St Mawes in Polworth's Dacia Duster, discussing plans for the following day. Polworth and his family had been invited to the scattering of the ashes, along with Kerenza the Macmillan nurse.

'. . . except it's not going to be a scattering,' said Polworth, driving through country lanes, as the sun turned into a burning coal on the horizon, 'more like a floating.'

'How's that?'

'Lucy's got an urn,' said Polworth. 'Water soluble, cotton and clay. She was showing me last night. It's supposed to look like a flower. You put the ashes inside and the whole thing bobs away and dissolves.'

'Nice idea,' said Strike.

'Prevents stupid accidents,' said Polworth, pragmatically. 'Remember Ian Restarick, from school? His grandad wanted his ashes thrown off Land's End. The dozy fuckers chucked them off in a high wind and ended up with their mouths full of the old boy. Restarick told me he was blowing ash out of his nose for a week after.'

Laughing, Strike felt his phone buzz in his pocket, and pulled it out. He was hoping the text might be Robin, perhaps telling him she'd already located Betty Fuller. Instead, he saw an unknown number.

I hated you as much as I did because I loved you so much. My love never ended but yours did. It wore out. I wore it out

Polworth was still talking, but Strike was no longer listening. He read the text through several times, frowning slightly, then put the phone back in his pocket and tried to concentrate on his old friend's anecdotes.

At Ted's house there were cries of welcome, and hugs from his uncle, Lucy and Jack. Strike tried to look delighted to be there, in spite of his fatigue, and knowing he'd have to wait to sleep until everyone else had gone to bed. Lucy had made pasta for everyone, and when she wasn't tending to everybody else's needs, telling Luke off for kicking Adam or picking at her own plate, she teetered on the verge of tears.

'It's so strange, isn't it?' she whispered to her brother after dinner, while Greg and the boys, at Greg's insistence, were clearing the table, 'Being here without her?' And without a pause she hurried on, 'We've decided we're going to do the ashes in the morning, because the weather looks good, and then come back here for Easter lunch.'

'Sounds great,' said Strike.

He knew how much importance Lucy placed on arrangements and plans, on having everything done in the right way. She fetched the urn and admired the stylised white lily. Ted had already placed Joan's ashes inside.

'That's great. Joan would have loved it,' he said, with no idea whether that was true or not.

'And I've bought pink roses for all of us to throw into the water with it,' said Lucy, tears welling again.

'Nice touch,' said Strike, suppressing a yawn. He really did just want to shower, then lie down and sleep. 'Thanks for sorting all this out, Luce. Oh, and I brought Easter eggs for the boys, where do you want them?'

'We can put them in the kitchen. Did you remember to get some for Roz and Mel, too?'

'Who?'

'Dave and Penny's girls, they'll be coming tomorrow, too.'

Fuck's sake.

'I didn't think—'

'Oh, Stick,' said Lucy, 'aren't you their godfather?'

'No, I'm not,' said Strike, doing his very best not to sound short tempered, 'but fine, yeah, I'll nip down the shops tomorrow morning and buy some more.'

Later, when he was at last alone in the dark sitting room, lying on the sofa with which he'd become so unwillingly familiar over the past year, his prosthetic leg propped against the coffee table, he checked his phone again. There were, he was pleased to see, no more messages from the unknown number, and, exhausted as he was, he managed to fall asleep quickly.

However, at shortly before four in the morning, the phone rang. Jerked out of a profound sleep, Strike groped for it, registered the time then raised it to his ear.

'Hello?'

There was a long silence, although he could hear breathing on the end of the line.

'Who is this?' he said, suspecting the answer.

'Bluey,' came a tiny whisper. 'It's me.'

'It's four in the morning, Charlotte.'

'I know,' she whispered, and gave what might have been a giggle or a sob. She sounded strange; possibly manic. Strike stared up at the dark ceiling, his aunt's ashes a mere twelve feet away.

'Where are you?'

'In hell.'

'Charlotte—'

She hung up.

Strike could hear his own heart beating with ominous force, like a kettle drum deep inside a cave. Red-hot threads of panic and dread darted through him.

How many more burdens was he supposed to bear? Had he not paid enough, given enough, sacrificed enough – loved enough? Joan seemed very close just now, in the darkness of her own sitting room, with her ornamental plates and her dried flowers, closer even than her dusty remains, in that vaguely ludicrous white lily, which would look so puny and insignificant bobbing away on the wide sea, like a discarded paper plate. He seemed to hear her last words as he lay there: 'You're a good man ... helping people ... I'm proud of you ... '

Charlotte had called him from the same unknown number she'd texted from earlier. Strike's exhausted mind now eddied around the known facts, which were that Charlotte had suicide attempts in her past, that she was married with children, and that she'd recently been committed to a mental facility. He remembered his resolution of weeks ago, to phone her husband if she sent him any more self-destructive messages, but Jago Ross wouldn't be at his merchant bank at 4 a.m. on an Easter weekend. He wondered whether it would be cruelty or kindness to ignore the call, and how he'd bear the knowledge that she'd overdosed, if he didn't respond. After a very long ten minutes, during which he half expected her to call him back, Strike sat up to compose a text.

I'm in Cornwall. My aunt's just died. I think you need help, but I'm the wrong person to give it to you. If you're alone, you need to get hold of someone and tell them how you're feeling.

The terrible thing was how well he and Charlotte knew each other. Strike knew just how pusillanimous, how disingenuous, Charlotte would find this bland response. She'd know that some small part of him (shrunken by determined abstinence, though never eradicated) felt a pull back towards her, especially in this extremity, not only because he'd assumed responsibility for her happiness for years, but because he could never forget that she'd come to him when he was at his lowest ebb, lying in a hospital bed with a freshly amputated leg, wondering what possible life there was for him now. He could still remember her appearing in the doorway, the most beautiful woman he'd ever seen, and how she'd walked down the ward towards him and kissed him wordlessly on the mouth, and that moment, more than any other, had told him that life would continue, would contain glorious moments of beauty and pleasure, that he wasn't alone any more, and that his missing leg didn't matter to the woman he couldn't forget.

Sitting in the darkness, atypically cold because of his exhaustion, Strike typed four more words –

It will get better

– and sent the message. Then he lay back down and waited for the phone to vibrate again, but it remained silent, and eventually he fell asleep.

He was woken, inevitably, by Luke bursting into the sitting

room. While he listened to Luke clattering around the kitchen, Strike reached for his phone and looked at it. Charlotte had sent two more texts, one an hour previously, the next half an hour later.

Bluey I'm sorry about your aunt. is it the one I met?

And then, when Strike hadn't answered:

Am I evil? Jago says I am. I used to think I couldn't be, because you loved me

At least she wasn't dead. With a vice-like sensation in his belly, Strike sat up, put on his prosthesis and attempted to shut Charlotte out of his mind.

Breakfast wasn't a particularly relaxing affair. The table was so crowded with Easter eggs, it was like being in some cartoonish nest. Strike ate off a plate on his lap. Lucy had bought Strike and Ted an egg each, and the detective now gathered that he should have bought his sister one, as well. All three boys had tottering piles.

'What's a hedgehog got to do with Easter?' Adam asked Strike, holding up his uncle's offering.

'Eastertime's spring, isn't it?' said Ted, from the end of the table. 'It's when hibernating animals wake up.'

'Mine's all broken,' said Luke, shaking the box.

'That's a shame,' said Strike, and Lucy shot him a sharp look.

She was tense, telling off her sons for looking at their phones during the meal, glaring at Strike when he checked his own, constantly glancing out of the window, to check the state of the weather. The detective was glad of an excuse to get out of the house to buy Polworth's daughters Easter eggs, but he'd walked barely ten yards down the sloping road, cigarette in hand, when the family pulled up in their Dacia. When Strike confided his errand in an undertone, Polworth said,

'Fuck that, they've got enough chocolate for a year at home. Leave it.'

At eleven o'clock, with a leg of lamb left in the oven and the timer set, after Luke had been told that no, he couldn't take his iPad on the boat, and one false start, due to the need to return to the house for the Polworths' younger daughter to have the pee she'd insisted she didn't need before they left, the party made its way successfully down to the harbour, where they met Kerenza the nurse, and boarded Ted's old sailing boat, *Jowanet.*

Strike, who'd once been his uncle's proud helpmeet, no longer had the balance to work either sails or rudder. He sat with the women and children, spared the necessity of making conversation by the noise of wind against canvas. Ted shouted commands to Polworth and Jack. Luke was eating chocolate, his eyes screwed up against the cold breeze; Polworth's daughters were huddled, shivering, beside their mother, who had her arms around them. Tears were already trickling down Lucy's cheeks as she cradled the flat white urn in her lap. Beside her, Kerenza held a bunch of dark pink roses loosely wrapped in cellophane, and it was left to Greg and Polworth to shout at the children to watch out for the boom as they tacked around the peninsula where St Mawes Castle stood sentinel.

The surface of the sea changed from second to second, from rippling plain of sage and grey, to mesh of diamond-bright sparkles. The smell of ozone was as familiar and comforting to Strike as that of beer. He was just thinking how glad he was that Joan had chosen this, and not a grave, when he felt his phone vibrate against his chest. Unable to resist the temptation to read what he knew would be a text from Charlotte, he pulled it out and read it.

I thought you'd come back I thought you'd stop me marrying him I didn't think you'd let me do it

He put the phone back into his pocket. Luke was watching him and Strike thought he saw the idea occur of asking why Uncle Cormoran could look at his phone, whereas he was banned from bringing his iPad, but the look his uncle gave him seemed to make him think better of the idea, and he merely stuffed more chocolate in his mouth.

A feeling of constraint seemed to fall over everyone, even Luke, as Ted turned the boat into the wind and brought the boat slowly to a halt, the sail flapping loudly in the wind, St Mawes Castle now the size of a sandcastle in the distance. Kerenza handed around the roses, one for everyone except Ted, who took the remainder of the bouquet between the hands that were forever sunburned. Nobody spoke, and yet the moment didn't feel anticlimactic. While the sails flapped angrily overhead, Ted bent low over the side of the boat and dropped the urn gently into the sea, murmuring his farewell, and the object Strike had imagined would look inadequate and tawdry became, precisely because of its smallness as it bobbed gallantly on the ocean, affecting, and strangely noble. Soon, the last earthly remains of Joan Nancarrow would dissolve into the sea, and only the pink roses, tossed one by one into the sea by each of them, would remain to show the place where she'd disappeared.

Strike put his arm around Lucy, who rested her head on his shoulder, as they sailed back to shore. Rozwyn, the elder of Polworth's daughters, broke into sobs initially provoked by the sight of the urn vanishing in the distance, but sustained by her enjoyment of her own grief and the sympathy of her mother. Strike watched until he could no longer see the white dot, then turned his eyes towards shore, thinking of the leg of lamb waiting for them back at the house.

His phone vibrated yet again, minutes after he'd regained firm ground. While Polworth helped Ted tie up the boat, Strike lit a cigarette and turned away from the group to read the new text.

I want to die speaking the truth people are such liars everyone I know lies in such if them swant to stop pretending

'I'll walk back,' he told Lucy.

'You can't,' she said at once, 'lunch'll be ready for us—'

'I'm going to want another one of these,' Strike said firmly, holding up his cigarette in her disapproving face. 'I'll meet you up there.'

'Want company, Diddy?' asked Polworth. 'Penny can take the girls back up to the house.'

'No, you're all right, mate,' said Strike. 'Need to make a work call,' he added quietly, so that Lucy couldn't hear. As he said it, he felt his mobile vibrate again.

'Goodbye, Corm,' said Kerenza, her freckled face kindly as ever. 'I'm not coming for lunch.'

'Great,' said Strike, 'no, sorry, I mean – thanks for coming, Kerenza, Joan was so fond of you.'

When Kerenza had finally got into her Mini, and the family's cars were driving away, Strike pulled out his phone again.

Never forget that I loved you goodbye blues x

Strike called the number. After a few rings, it went to voicemail.

'Charlotte, it's me,' said Strike. 'I'm going to keep ringing till you pick up.'

He hung up and dialled again. The number went to voicemail for a second time.

Strike began to walk, because his anxiety required action. The streets around the harbour weren't busy. Most people would be sitting down to Easter lunch. Over and again he dialled Charlotte's number, but she didn't answer.

It was as though a wire was tightening around his skull. His neck was rigid with tension. From second to second his feelings fluctuated between rage, resentment, frustration and fear. She'd always been an expert manipulator. She'd also narrowly escaped death by her own hand, twice.

The phone might be going unanswered because she was already dead. There could be sporting guns at the Castle of Croy, where her husband's family had lived for generations. There'd be heavy-duty medications at the clinic: she might have stockpiled them. She might even have taken a razor blade to herself, as she'd once tried to do during one of her and Strike's more vicious rows.

After calling the number for the tenth time, Strike came to a halt, looking out over the railings at the pitiless sea, which breathed no consolation as it rushed to and then retreated from the shore. Memories of Joan, and the way she'd clung so fiercely to life, flooded his mind: his anxiety about Charlotte was laced with fury, for throwing life away.

And then his phone rang.

'Where are you?' he almost shouted.

'Bluey?'

She sounded drunk, or very stoned.

'*Where are you?*'

' . . . told you,' she mumbled. 'Bluey, d'you 'member . . . '

'Charlotte, WHERE ARE YOU?'

'Told you, S'monds . . . '

He turned and began to half-run, half-hobble back the way he'd come: there was an old-fashioned red telephone box twenty yards back, and with his free hand he was already pulling coins from his trouser pocket.

'Are you in your room? *Where are you?*'

The telephone box smelled urinous, of cigarette butts and dirt from a thousand silt-clogged soles.

'C'n see sky . . . Bluey, I'm so . . . '

She was still mumbling, her breathing slow.

'One one eight, one one eight?' said a cheery voice through the receiver in his left hand.

'Symonds House, it's a residential psychiatric clinic in Kent.'

'Shall I connect—?'

'Yes, connect me . . . Charlotte, are you still there? Talk to me. Where are you?'

But she didn't answer. Her breathing was loud and becoming guttural.

'Symonds House,' said a bright female voice in his other ear.

'Have you got an in-patient there called Charlotte Ross?'

'I'm sorry, sir,' said the receptionist, 'we don't disclose—'

'She's overdosed. She's just called me from your facility, and she's overdosed. You need to find her – she might be outside, have you got grounds there?'

'Sir, can I ask you—?'

'*Check Charlotte Ross's whereabouts, now, I've got her on another line and she's overdosed.*'

He heard the woman speaking to someone away from the phone.

'... Mrs Ross ... first floor, just to make ...'

The voice spoke in his ear again, still professionally bright, but anxious now.

'Sir, what number is Mrs Ross calling from? She – in-patients don't have their own mobiles.'

'She's got one from somewhere,' said Strike, 'as well as a shitload of drugs.'

Somewhere in the background of the call he heard shouting, then loud footsteps. He tried to insert another coin into the slot, but it fell straight through and came out at the bottom.

'Fuck—'

'Sir, I'm going to ask you not to talk to me like that—'

'No, I just—'

The line went dead. Charlotte's breath was now barely audible.

Strike slammed as much change as he had in his pockets into the slot, then redialled telephone enquiries. Within a minute, he was again connected to the female voice at Symonds House.

'Symonds House—'

'Have you found her? I got cut off. Have you found her?'

'I'm afraid I can't disclose—' said the harassed-sounding woman.

'She got hold of a mobile and the means to kill herself on your watch,' said Strike, 'so you can bloody well disclose whether she's dead—'

'Sir, I'd appreciate you not shouting at me—'

But then Strike heard distant male voices through the mobile clamped to his other ear. There was no point hanging up and ringing: Charlotte hadn't heard his ten previous calls. She must have the mobile on silent.

'SHE'S HERE!' he bellowed, and the woman on the payphone line shrieked in shock. 'FOLLOW MY VOICE, SHE'S HERE!'

Strike was bellowing into the phone, well aware of the almost impossible odds of searchers hearing him: he could hear swishing and cracking, and knew that Charlotte was outside, probably in undergrowth.

Then, through the mobile, he heard a man shout.

'Shit, she's here – SHE'S HERE! Fuck . . . get an ambulance!'

'Sir,' said the shell-shocked woman, now that Strike had stopped yelling, 'could I have your name?'

But Strike hung up. Over the sound of his change clattering into the returned coin box, he continued to listen to the two men who'd found Charlotte, one of them shouting details of her overdose to the emergency services, the other repeatedly calling Charlotte's name, until somebody noticed that the mobile beside her was active, and turned it off.

55

Of louers sad calamities of old,
Full many piteous stories doe remaine . . .

Edmund Spenser
The Faerie Queene

As a noted beauty and socialite with a tantalising number of celebrity connections and a rebellious, self-destructive past, Charlotte was an old staple of the gossip columns. Naturally, her emergency hospitalisation out of a private psychiatric clinic made news.

The tabloids ran photo-heavy stories, showing Charlotte at the ages of fourteen (when she'd first run away from her private school and sparked a police hunt), eighteen (arm in arm with her well-known broadcaster father, a thrice-married heavy drinker), twenty-one (with her model-turned-socialite mother, at a cocktail party) and thirty-eight, where, as beautiful as ever, she smiled blankly alongside her white-blond husband, twin babies in her arms, an exquisite drawing room in the background. Nobody had been able to find a picture of her with Cormoran Strike, but the fact that they'd once dated, which Charlotte herself had been careful to mention to the press when she got engaged to Jago, ensured that his name appeared in print alongside hers. 'Emergency hospitalisation', 'history of addiction issues', 'troubled past': though the tabloids didn't say so explicitly, only the most naive reader could be left in doubt that Charlotte had attempted to take her own life. The story gained a second wind when an unnamed 'inside source' at Symonds House confided that the future Viscountess Ross had

671

'allegedly' been found face down in a shrubbery, right behind an old summer house.

The broadsheets' stories led with the questionable practices of the exorbitantly priced Symonds House, 'which' (said the *Telegraph*) 'has a reputation for being the last resort of the wealthy and well-connected. Controversial treatments include transcranial magnetic stimulation and the hallucinogen psilocybin (more commonly known as magic mushrooms).' They, too, used large photographs of Charlotte to embellish their stories, so Robin, who furtively read all of them and felt guilty afterwards, was reminded constantly how very beautiful Strike's ex had always been.

Strike hadn't mentioned a word of the business to Robin, and she hadn't asked. A moratorium had lain over Charlotte's name ever since that night, four years previously, when Robin had still been the temp, and an extremely drunk Strike confided in her that Charlotte had lied about being pregnant with his child. All Robin knew right now was that Strike had returned from Cornwall in a particularly buttoned-up mood, and while she knew that the disposal of his aunt's ashes must have been a sad occasion, she couldn't help suspecting this other source for his moodiness.

Out of loyalty to Strike, she refused to gossip about his ex, even though everyone around her seemed to want to talk about it. A week after Strike returned from Cornwall, Robin entered the office, already in a bad mood because Matthew had again postponed mediation. On seeing the door open, Pat the secretary hastily tried to hide a copy of the *Daily Mail* she'd been poring over with Morris. On realising that the new arrival was Robin rather than Strike, Pat had given her raven's caw of laughter and slapped the paper back onto her desk.

'Caught red-handed,' said Morris with a wink at Robin. 'Seen all this about the boss's ex?'

He's not my boss, he's my partner, thought Robin, but she merely said, 'Yes.'

'Talk about punching above his bloody weight,' said Morris, examining a picture of Charlotte at twenty-one in a beaded mini-dress. 'The fuck did a bloke who looks like him end up with that?'

Robin wasn't even safe from it at home. Max, whose floppy hair had been cropped short to play the ex-army officer, had begun shooting his TV series, and was more cheerful than she'd ever known him. Max was also thoroughly intrigued to know that Strike had been involved with Charlotte for sixteen years.

'I met her once,' he told Robin, who'd come upstairs after several hours in her room, combing online records for Betty Fuller. The one-time prostitute was proving harder to find than she'd anticipated.

'Really?' said Robin, who both wanted and didn't want to hear the story.

'Yeah, I was in a play years ago with her half-brother. Simon Legard? He starred in that mini-series about the financial crash, what was it called? She came to watch our play and took us all out for dinner afterwards. I liked her, actually, she was a real laugh. Some of those posh girls are a lot funnier than you'd think.'

'Mm,' said Robin noncommittally, and she returned immediately to her room with her cup of tea.

'I bet she tried to call Corm before she did it,' was Ilsa's cool comment on the phone, two weeks after Easter, by which time Robin had succeeded, through patient cross-referencing, in identifying the woman she thought was most likely to be the Betty Fuller who'd lived in Skinner Street at the time of Margot Bamborough's disappearance. Betty was now living in sheltered housing in Sans Walk, not far from her original flat, and Robin planned to pay her a visit the following afternoon, after the mediation with Matthew which seemed at last to be going ahead.

Ilsa had rung to wish Robin good luck. Robin had been trying not to think about having to see Matthew, telling herself that the ordeal would be over in a couple of hours, but it had become progressively harder to focus on her list of questions for Betty Fuller as the evening progressed, and she'd been glad, initially, to be interrupted by Ilsa.

'What's Corm saying about the whole Charlotte thing?' Ilsa asked.

'Nothing,' said Robin truthfully.

'No, he never talks about her any more,' said Ilsa. 'I wonder how much longer her marriage is going to last. Must be hanging by a thread. I'm quite surprised it's limped on this long, actually. She only did it to get back at Corm.'

'Well, she's had children with Jago,' Robin pointed out, then instantly regretted it. Ilsa had already told her that she and Nick had decided not to try a fourth round of IVF.

'She never wanted kids,' said Ilsa. 'That was something she and Corm had in common. That, and having really similar mothers. Drink, drugs and a million men each, except Charlotte's is still alive. So, you haven't spoken to him about it all?'

'No,' said Robin, who was feeling marginally worse for this conversation, in spite of Ilsa's kind intentions. 'Ilsa, sorry, but I'd better go. I've got work to do for tomorrow.'

'Can't you take the afternoon off? We could meet for a coffee, you'll probably need some R&R afterwards. Corm wouldn't mind, would he?'

'I'm sure he wouldn't,' said Robin, 'but we're so busy, and I'm following up a lead. Anyway, work gives me something to think about other than Matthew. Let's catch up at the weekend, if you're free.'

Robin slept badly that night. It wasn't Charlotte who wove her way in and out of her dreams, but Miss Jones, the agency's client who, as everyone had now noticed, had taken such a shine to Strike that he'd had to ask Pat to stop putting her calls through. Robin woke before her alarm went off, glad to escape a complicated dream in which it was revealed that Miss Jones had been Matthew's wife all along, and that Robin was defending herself against a charge of fraud at the end of a long, polished table in a dark boardroom.

Wanting to look professional and confident, she dressed in black trousers and jacket, even though Matthew knew perfectly well that she spent most of her investigative life in jeans. Casting one last look in her mirror before leaving her room, she thought she looked washed-out. Trying not to think about all those pictures of Charlotte Ross, who rarely dressed in anything but black, but whose porcelain beauty merely shone brighter in contrast, Robin grabbed her handbag and left her room.

While waiting for the Tube, Robin tried to distract herself from the squirming feeling of nerves in her stomach by checking her emails.

Dear Miss Ellacott,

As previously stated I'm not prepared to talk to anyone except Mr Strike. This is not intended as any slight on you but I would feel more comfortable speaking man to man. Unfortunately, I will be unavailable from the end of next week due to work commitments which will be taking me out of the country. However I can make space on the evening of the 24th. If this is agreeable to Mr Strike, I suggest the American Bar in the Stafford hotel as a discreet meeting place. Kindly let me know if this is acceptable.

Sincerely,

CB Oakden

Twenty minutes later, when she'd emerged from Holborn Tube station and had reception again, Robin forwarded this message to Strike. She had a comfortable quarter of an hour to spare before her appointment and there were plenty of places to grab a coffee in her vicinity, but before she could do so, her mobile rang: it was Pat, at the office.

'Robin?' said the familiar croaking voice. 'D'you know where Cormoran is? I've tried his phone but he's not picking up. I've got his brother Al here in the office, wanting to see him.'

'Really?' said Robin, startled. She'd met Al a couple of years previously, but knew that he and Strike weren't close. 'No, I don't know where he is, Pat. Have you left a message? He's probably somewhere he can't pick up.'

'Yeah, I've left a voicemail,' said Pat. 'All right, I'll keep trying him. Bye.'

Robin walked on, her desire for a coffee forgotten in her curiosity about Al turning up at the office. She'd quite liked Al when she'd met him; he seemed in slight awe of his older half-brother, which Robin had found endearing. Al didn't look much like Strike, being shorter, with straight hair, a narrow jaw and the slight divergent squint he'd inherited from their famous father.

Thinking about Strike's family, she turned the corner and saw, with a thrill of dread that brought her to a halt, Matthew climbing out of a taxi, wearing an unfamiliar dark overcoat over his suit. His head turned, and for a moment they were looking at each other, fifty yards apart like gunslingers ready to fire. Then Robin's mobile rang; she reached for it automatically, and when she'd put it to her ear and looked up, Matthew had disappeared into the building.

'Hello?'

'Hi,' said Strike, 'just got the email from Oakden. "Out of the country", my arse.'

Robin glanced at her watch. She still had five minutes, and her lawyer, Judith, was nowhere in sight. She drew back against the cold stone wall and said,

'Yeah, I thought that, too. Have you rung Pat back?'

'No, why?'

'Al's at the office.'

'Al who?'

'Your brother, Al,' said Robin.

There was a brief pause.

'Fuck's sake,' said Strike under his breath.

'Where are you?' asked Robin.

'At a B&Q in Chingford. Our blonde friend in Stoke Newington's shopping.'

'What for?'

'Rubber foam and MDF, for starters,' said Strike. 'That bloke from Shifty's gym's helping her. Where are you?'

'Waiting outside Matthew's lawyers. It's mediation morning,' said Robin.

'Shit,' said Strike, 'I forgot. Best of luck. Listen – take the rest of the day off, if you'd—'

'I don't want time off,' said Robin. She'd just spotted Judith in the distance, walking briskly towards her in a red coat. 'I'm planning to go and see Betty Fuller afterwards. I'd better go, Cormoran. Speak later.'

She hung up and walked forwards to meet Judith, who smiled broadly.

'All right?' she asked, patting Robin on the arm with the hand not holding her briefcase. 'Should be fine. You let me do the talking.'

'Right,' said Robin, smiling back with as much warmth as she could muster.

They walked up the steps together into a small lobby area, where a stocky, suited man with a haircut like Caesar's came forward with a perfunctory smile, his hand outstretched to Judith.

'Ms Cobbs? Andrew Shenstone. Ms Ellacott? How d'you do?'

His handshake left Robin's hand throbbing. He and Judith walked ahead of Robin through double doors, chatting about London traffic, and Robin followed, dry-mouthed and feeling like a child trailing its parents. After a short walk up a dark corridor, they turned left into a small meeting room with an oval table and a shabby blue carpet. Matthew was sitting there alone, still wearing his overcoat. He readjusted himself in his chair when they entered. Robin looked directly into his face as she sat down, diagonally opposite him. To her surprise, Matthew looked instantly away. She'd imagined him glaring across the table, with that strange muzzle-like whitening around his mouth he'd worn during arguments towards the end of their marriage.

'Right then,' said Andrew Shenstone, with another smile, as Judith Cobbs opened the file she'd brought with her. He had a leather document holder sitting, closed, in front of him. 'Your client's position remains as stated in your letter of the fourteenth, Judith, is that correct?'

'That's right,' said Judith, her thick black glasses perched on the end of her nose as she scanned a copy of said letter. 'Ms Ellacott's perfectly happy to forgo any claim on your client, except in respect of the proceeds from the sale of the flat in – um—'

Hastings Road, thought Robin. She remembered moving into the cramped conversion with Matthew, excitedly carrying boxes of pot plants and books up the short path, Matthew plugging in the coffee machine that had been one of their first joint purchases, the fluffy elephant he'd given her so long ago, sitting on the bed.

'—Hastings Road, yes,' said Judith, scanning her letter, 'from which she'd like the ten thousand pounds her parents contributed to the deposit, upon purchase.'

'Ten thousand,' repeated Andrew Shenstone. He and Matthew looked at each other. 'In that case, we're agreeable.'

'You're ... agreeable?' said Judith Cobbs, as surprised as Robin herself.

'My client's circumstances have changed,' said Shenstone. 'His priority now is securing the divorce as speedily as possible, which I think your client has indicated is also preferable to her, excepting the ten thousand pounds? Of course,' added Shenstone, 'we're almost at the requisite two years, so ... '

Judith looked at Robin, who nodded, her mouth still dry.

'Then I think we can conclude things today. Very good indeed,' said Andrew Shenstone complacently, and it was impossible to escape the suspicion that he was addressing himself. 'I've taken the liberty of drawing up ... '

He opened his document holder, spun it around on the polished table top and pushed it towards Judith, who read the document inside carefully.

'Yes,' she said finally, sliding the document sideways to Robin, who learned that Matthew was promising to transfer the money to Robin's account within seven days of signature. 'Happy?' Judith added in an undertone to Robin.

'Yes,' said Robin, slightly dazed.

What, she wondered, had been the point of dragging her here? Had it been one last demonstration of power, or had Matthew only decided that morning to give in? She reached into her handbag, but Judith was already holding out her own fountain pen, so Robin took it and signed. Judith passed the document back to Andrew Shenstone, who slid it over to Matthew, who scrawled a hasty signature. He glanced up at Robin when he'd done so, then looked quickly away again, and in that moment, Robin knew what had happened, and why he'd given her what she wanted.

'Very good,' said Andrew Shenstone again, and he slapped the table with his thick hand and laughed. 'Well, short and sweet, eh? I think we're . . . ?'

'Yes,' said Judith, with a little laugh, 'I think we are!'

Matthew and Robin rose and watched their lawyers gathering up their things and, in Judith's case, pulling her coat back on. Disorientated by what had just happened, Robin again had the sensation of being a child with its parents, unsure how to quit the situation, waiting for the lawyers to release her.

Andrew Shenstone held the door open for Robin and she passed back into the corridor, heading towards the lobby. Behind her, the lawyers were talking about traffic again. When they paused in the lobby to take leave of each other, Matthew, after a brief word of thanks to Shenstone, walked straight out past Robin, into the street.

Robin waited for Andrew Shenstone to disappear inside the building again before addressing Judith.

'Thanks so much,' she said.

'Well, I didn't really do much, did I?' said Judith, laughing. 'But mediation often brings people to their senses, I've seen it happen before. Much harder to justify yourself in a room with objective observers.'

They shook hands, and Robin headed out into a spring breeze that blew her hair into her mouth. She felt slightly unsettled. Ten thousand pounds. She'd offered to give it back to her parents, knowing that they'd struggled to match Matthew's parents' contribution, but they'd told her to keep it. She'd have to settle her bill with Judith, of course, but the remainder would give her a buffer, maybe even help her back towards her own place.

She turned a corner and there, right in front of her, standing at the kerb, his arm raised in his attempt to hail a taxi, was Matthew.

Catching sight of her, he stood frozen for a moment, his hand still raised, and the taxi he'd been trying to hail slowed ten yards away, and picked up a couple instead.

'Sarah's pregnant, isn't she?' said Robin.

He looked down at her, not quite as tall as Strike, but as good-looking as he'd been at seventeen, on the day he'd asked her out.

'Yeah.' He hesitated. 'It was an accident.'

Was it hell, thought Robin. Sarah had always known how to get what she wanted. Robin realised at last how long a game Sarah had played: always present, giggling, flirting, prepared to settle for Matthew's best friend to keep him close. Then, as her clutch tightened, but Matthew threatened to slip through it, there'd been the diamond earring she'd left in Robin's bed and now, still more valuable, a pregnancy to make sure of him, before he could enter a dangerous state of singledom. Robin had a strong suspicion that this was what had lain behind the two postponements of mediation. Had a newly hormonal and insecure Sarah made scenes, frightened of Matthew coming face to face with Robin while he hadn't yet decided whether he wanted either the baby or its mother?

'And she wants to be married before she has it?'

'Yeah,' said Matthew. 'Well, so do I.'

Did the image of their own wedding flash across his mind, as it flashed across Robin's? The church in Masham that both of them had attended since primary school, the reception in that beautiful hotel, with the swans in the lake that refused to swim together, and the disastrous reception, during which Robin had known, for a few terrifying seconds, that if Strike had asked her to leave with him, she'd have gone.

'How're things with you?'

'Great,' said Robin.

She put up a good front. What you do, when you meet the ex, isn't it? Pretend you think you did the right thing. No regrets.

'Well,' he said, as the traffic rolled past, 'I need to . . .'

He began to walk away.

'Matt.'

He turned back.

'What?'

'I'll never forget . . . how you were, when I really needed you. Whatever else . . . I'll never forget that part.'

For a fraction of a second, his face worked slightly, like a small boy's. Then he walked back to her, bent down, and before she knew what was happening, he'd hugged her quickly, then let go as though she was red hot.

'G'luck, Robs,' he said thickly, and walked away for good.

56

Whereas this Lady, like a sheepe astray,
Now drowned in the depth of sleepe all fearlesse lay.

Edmund Spenser
The Faerie Queene

At the precise moment Matthew turned to walk away from Robin in Holborn, Strike, who was sitting in his parked car three miles away, outside the familiar terraced house in Stoke Newington, decided to call his brother, lest Al sit in wait for him at the office all day. The detective's anger was shot through with other, less easily identifiable feelings, of which the least painful to acknowledge was grudging admiration for Al's persistence. Strike didn't doubt that Al had come to the office for a last-ditch attempt to persuade Strike into some form of reconciliation with his father, preferably before or during the party to celebrate his father's new album. Having always considered Al a fairly weak and sybaritic character, Strike had to admit he was showing guts, risking his older brother's fury.

Strike waited until Elinor Dean had unloaded the foam and the cheap wood from her car and carried it all inside with the aid of her friend from Shifty's gym, watched the front door close, then called Al's number.

'Hi,' said Al, picking up after a single ring.

'Why are you in my office?' asked Strike.

'Wanted to see you, bruv. Talk face to face.'

'Well, I won't be back there today,' lied Strike. 'So I suggest you say whatever it is you've got to say now.'

'Bruv—'

'Who's there with you?'

'Er – your secretary – Pat, is it?' Strike heard Al turn away from his mobile to check, and heard Pat's caw of agreement, 'and a bloke called—'

'Barclay,' said the Scot loudly, in the background.

'Right, well, go into my office for some privacy,' said Strike. He listened while Al told Pat what Strike had asked him to do, heard the familiar sound of his own office door closing, then said,

'If this is about what I think it's about—'

'Cormoran, we didn't want to tell you this, but Dad's got cancer.'

Oh, for fuck's sake.

Strike leaned forwards momentarily and rested his forehead on the steering wheel of his car, before he sat up again.

'Prostate,' Al continued. 'They reckon they've caught it early. But we thought you should know, because this party isn't just about celebrating the band's anniversary, and the new album. It's about giving him something to look forward to.'

There was a silence.

'We thought you should know,' Al repeated.

Why should I fucking know? thought Strike, eyes on the closed door of Elinor Dean's house. He had no relationship with Rokeby. Did Al expect him to weep, to rush to Rokeby's side, to express compassion or pity? Rokeby was a multimillionaire. Doubtless he'd enjoy the very best treatment. The memory of Joan's lily urn bobbing away on the sea recurred as Strike said,

'OK, well, I don't really know how to respond to that. I'm sure it's a bugger for everyone who cares about him.'

Another long silence followed.

'We thought this might make a difference,' said Al quietly.

'To what?'

'To your attitude.'

'As long as they've caught it early, he'll be fine,' said Strike bracingly. 'Probably live to father another couple of kids he never sees.'

'Jesus Christ!' said Al, really angry now. 'You might not give a shit, but he happens to be my dad—'

'I give a shit about people who've ever given a shit about me,' said Strike, 'and keep your fucking voice down, those are my employees you're airing my private business in front of.'

'*That's* your priority?'

Strike thought of Charlotte who, according to the papers, remained in hospital, and of Lucy, who was agitating to know whether Strike would be able to take the weekend off, to join Ted at her house in Bromley for the weekend. He thought of the clients in the Shifty case, who were hinting they'd terminate payment in a week's time unless the agency found out what hold Shifty had on his boss. He thought of Margot Bamborough, and the rapidly vanishing year they'd been allotted to find out what had happened to her. Inexplicably, he thought of Robin, and the fact that he'd forgotten that today was her mediation session with Matthew.

'I've got a life,' said Strike, keeping a curb on his temper only by exercising maximum self-control, 'which is hard and complicated, just like everyone else's. Rokeby's got a wife and half a dozen kids and I'm at maximum capacity for people who need me. I'm not coming to his fucking party, I'm not interested in hearing from him, I don't want a relationship with him. I don't know how much clearer I can make this, Al, but I'm—'

The line went dead. Without regretting anything he'd said, but nevertheless breathing heavily, Strike threw his mobile onto the passenger seat, lit a cigarette and watched Elinor Dean's front door for another fifteen minutes until, on a sudden whim, he snatched up the phone from beside him again, and called Barclay.

'What are you doing right now?'

'Filin' my expenses,' said the Scot laconically. 'That casino cost ye a fortune.'

'Is my brother still there?'

'No, he left.'

'Good. I need you to come and take over in Stoke Newington.'

'I havenae got my car wi' me.'

'OK, well, fuck it, then,' said Strike angrily.

'I'm sorry, Strike,' said Barclay, 'but I'm s'posed tae have this afternoon off—'

'No, *I'm* sorry,' said Strike, closing his eyes. He had the same sensation of a wire tightening around his forehead that he'd experienced in St Mawes. 'Getting frustrated. Enjoy your afternoon off. Seriously,' he added, in case Barclay thought he was being sarcastic.

Having hung up on Barclay, Strike rang Robin.

'How did mediation go?'

'Fine,' said Robin, though she sounded strangely flat. 'We've settled.'

'Great!'

'Yeah. It's a relief.'

'Did you say you're going to Betty Fuller's?'

'Yes, I was just about to head into the Tube.'

'Remind me where she lives?'

'Sheltered housing on Sans Walk in Clerkenwell.'

'OK, I'll meet you there,' said Strike.

'Really? I'm fine to—'

'I know, but I want to be there,' Strike cut across her.

He pulled away from Elinor Dean's house knowing that he'd just been abrasive towards his two favourite colleagues. If he was going to vent his temper, it could at least have been at Pat and Morris's expense.

Twenty minutes later, Strike entered Clerkenwell via Percival Street. To his right were the nondescript red-brick flats where Janice Beattie and Steve Douthwaite had once lived, and he wondered yet again what had become of Margot's one-time patient, whose whereabouts, in spite of his and Robin's best efforts, remained unknown.

Sans Walk was a narrow pedestrianised one-way street. Strike parked his BMW as close to it as possible. The day was surprisingly warm, in spite of a good amount of cloud. As he approached Sans Walk, he saw Robin waiting for him at the entrance.

'Hi,' she said. 'It's up the other end, that red-brick modern building with the circular tower thing on top.'

'Great,' said Strike, as they set off together. 'Sorry for earlier, I—'

'No, it's fine,' said Robin, 'I know we really need results soon.'

But Strike thought he detected a slight coolness.

'Al pissed me off,' he explained. 'So I might've been a bit—'

'Cormoran, it's fine,' repeated Robin, but with a smile that reassured Strike.

'Great news about the mediation,' he said.

'Yes,' said Robin, though she didn't look particularly pleased. 'So, what d'you think's the best tack to take with Betty Fuller?'

'Be honest and direct about who we are and what we're investigating,' said Strike, 'and then play it by ear, I think. And hope to Christ she's not demented . . .'

Priory House was a modern, multi-level building with a shared garden at the back. As they approached the front doors, a middle-aged couple came out; they had the relieved look of people who'd just done their duty, and, smiling at Strike and Robin, they held open the door to let them walk inside.

'Thanks very much,' said Robin, smiling at them, and as the couple walked on, she heard the woman say,

'At least she remembered who we are, this time . . .'

Had it not been for the mobility scooters, the place would have resembled a hall of residence, with its hardy dark grey carpet underfoot, its bulletin board bristling with pamphlets and a depressing smell of communal cooking hanging in the air.

'She's on the ground floor,' said Robin, pointing towards a corridor. 'I checked the names on the buzzer.'

They passed a number of identical pine doors until they reached the one with 'Elizabeth Fuller' printed on a card in a metal holder. Through the wood came the muffled sounds of voices. Just as it had been when he'd visited Janice Beattie, the TV was turned up very high inside. Strike rapped hard on the door.

After a lengthy wait, the door opened very slowly to reveal a panting old lady wearing a nasal cannula, who'd pulled her oxygen tank to the door with her. Over her shoulder, Strike saw a TV blaring the reality show *The Only Way is Essex*.

'*I'm fine. You just upset me, Arg,*' a heavily made-up girl in bright blue was saying onscreen.

Betty Fuller looked as though she'd been subject to heavier gravity than the rest of humankind. Everything about her had sagged and drooped: the corners of her lipless mouth, her papery eyelids, her loose jowls, the tip of her thin nose. It appeared that the flesh had been sucked down out of her upper body into her lower: Betty had almost no bust, but her hips were broad and her poor bare legs were immensely swollen, both ankles thicker than her neck. She wore what looked like a pair of men's slippers and a dark green knitted dress on which there were several stains. A yellowish scalp was clearly visible through the sparse grey hair slicked back off her face and a hearing aid was prominent in her left ear.

'Who're you?' she wheezed, looking from Robin to Strike.

'Afternoon, Mrs Fuller,' said Strike loudly and clearly, 'my name's Cormoran Strike and this is Robin Ellacott.'

He pulled his driver's licence out of his pocket and showed it to her, with his card. She made an impatient gesture, to show she couldn't read them; her eyes were milky with glaucoma.

'We're private detectives,' said Strike, voice still raised over the arguing pair on-screen (*'At the end of the day, Lucy, she slept, on a one-night stand, wiv a boy—' 'Arg – Arg – Arg – this is irrelevant—'*).

'We've been hired to try and find out what happened to Margot Bamborough. She was a doctor who—'

''Oo?'

'Dr Margot Bamborough,' Strike repeated, still more loudly. 'She went missing from Clerkenwell in 1974. We heard you—'

'Oh yeah . . .' said Betty Fuller, who appeared to need to draw breath every few words. 'Dr Bamborough . . . yeah.'

'Well, we wondered whether we could talk to you about her?'

Betty Fuller stood there for what seemed a very long twenty seconds, thinking this over, while onscreen a young man in a maroon suit said to the over-made-up girl, *'I didn't wanna bring it up but you come over to me—'*

Betty Fuller made an impatient gesture, turned and shuffled back inside. Strike and Robin glanced at each other.

'Is it all right to come in, Mrs Fuller?' asked Strike loudly.

She nodded. Having carefully positioned her oxygen tank, she fell back into her armchair, then tugged the knitted dress in an effort to make it cover her knees. Strike and Robin entered the room and Strike closed the door. Watching the old lady struggle to pull her dress down, Robin had an urge to take a blanket off the unmade bed, and place it decorously over her lap.

Robin had discovered during her research that Betty was eighty-four. The old lady's physical state shocked her. The small room smelled of BO and urine. A door showed a small toilet leading off the single bedroom. Through the open wardrobe door, Robin saw crumpled clothes which had been thrown there, and two empty wine bottles, half hidden in underwear. There was nothing on the walls except a cat calendar: the month of May showed a pair of ginger kittens peeking out from between pink geranium blossoms.

'Would it be all right to turn this down?' Strike shouted over the TV, where the couple onscreen continued to argue, the woman's eyelashes as thick as woolly bear caterpillars.

'Turn it . . . off,' said Betty Fuller. ''S a recording.'

The Essex voices were suddenly extinguished. The two detectives looked around. There were only two choices for seats: the unmade bed and a hard, upright chair, so Robin took the former, Strike the latter. Removing his notebook from his pocket, Strike said,

'We've been hired by Dr Bamborough's daughter, Mrs Fuller, to try and find out what happened to her.'

Betty Fuller made a noise like 'hurhm', which sounded disparaging, although Strike thought it might also have been an attempt to clear phlegm out of her throat. She rocked slightly to one side in her chair and pulled ineffectually at the back of her dress. Her swollen lower legs were knotted with varicose veins.

'So, you remember Dr Bamborough disappearing, do you, Mrs Fuller?'

'. . . 'es,' she grunted, still breathing heavily. In spite of her incapacity and unpromising manner, Strike had the impression of somebody both more alert than they might appear at first glance, and happier to have company and attention than the unprepossessing exterior might suggest.

'You were living in Skinner Street then, weren't you?'

She coughed, which seemed to clear her lungs, and in a slightly steadier voice, she said,

'Was there till . . . last year. Michael Cliffe . . . 'Ouse. Top floor. Couldn't manage, no more.'

Strike glanced at Robin; he'd expected her to lead the interrogation, assumed Betty would respond better to a woman, but Robin seemed oddly passive, sitting on the bed, her gaze wandering over the small room.

'Were you one of Dr Bamborough's patients?' Strike asked Betty.

'Yeah,' wheezed Betty. 'I was.'

Robin was thinking, is this where single people end up, people without children to look out for them, without double incomes? In small boxes, living vicariously through reality stars?

Next Christmas, no doubt, she'd run into Matthew, Sarah and their new baby in Masham. She could just imagine Sarah's proud strut through the streets, pushing a top-of-the-range pushchair, Matthew beside her, and a baby with Sarah's white-blonde hair peeking over the top of the blankets. Now, when Jenny and Stephen ran into them, there'd be common ground, the shared language of parenthood. Robin decided there and then, sitting on Betty Fuller's bed, to make sure she didn't go home next Christmas. She'd offer to work through it, if necessary.

'Did you like Dr Bamborough?' Strike was asking Betty.

'She were . . . all right,' said Betty.

'Did you ever meet any of the other doctors at the practice?' asked Strike.

Betty Fuller's chest rose and fell with her laboured breathing. Though it was hard to tell with the nasal cannula in the way, Strike thought he saw a thin smile.

'Yeah,' she said.

'Which ones?'

'Brenner,' she said hoarsely, and coughed again. 'Needed an 'ouse call . . . 'mergency . . . she weren't available.'

'So Dr Brenner came out to see you?'

'Hurhm,' said Betty Fuller. 'Yeah.'

There were a few small, cheaply framed photographs on the windowsill, Robin noticed. Two of them showed a fat tabby cat, presumably a lamented pet, but there were also a couple showing toddlers, and one of two big-haired teenaged girls, wearing puff-sleeved dresses from the eighties. So you could end up alone, in near squalor, even if you had children? Was it solely money, then, that made the difference? She thought of the ten thousand pounds she'd be receiving into her bank account later that week, which would be reduced immediately by legal bills and council tax. She'd need to be careful not to fritter it away. She really needed to start saving, to start paying into a pension.

'You must have been seriously unwell, were you?' Strike was asking Betty. 'To need a house call?'

He had no particular reason for asking, except to establish a friendly conversational atmosphere. In his experience of old ladies, there was little they enjoyed more than discussing their health.

Betty Fuller suddenly grinned at him, showing chipped yellow teeth.

'You ever taken it ... up the shitter ... with a nine-inch cock?'

Only by exercising the utmost restraint did Robin prevent herself letting out a shocked laugh. She had to hand it to Strike: he didn't so much as grin as he said,

'Can't say I have.'

'Well,' wheezed Betty Fuller, 'you can ... take it from me ... fuckin' ... agony ... geezer went at me ... like a fucking power drill ... split my arsehole open.'

She gasped for air, half-laughing.

'My Cindy 'ears me moanin' ... blood ... says "Mum, you gotta ... get that seen to ..." called ... doctor.'

'Cindy's your—?'

'Daughter,' said Betty Fuller. 'Yeah ... got two. Cindy and Cathy ...'

'And Dr Brenner came out to see you, did he?' asked Strike, trying not to dwell on the mental image Betty had conjured.

'Yeah ... takes a look ... sends me to A&E, yeah ... nineteen stitches,' said Betty Fuller. 'And I sat on ... an ice pack ... for a week ... and no fuckin' money ... comin' in ... After that,' she panted, 'no anal ... unless they was ... payin' double and nuthin' over ... six inches ... neither.'

She let out a cackle of laughter, which ended in coughs. Strike and Robin were carefully avoiding looking at each other.

'Was that the only time you met Dr Brenner?' asked Strike, when the coughing had subsided.

'No,' croaked Betty Fuller, thumping her chest. 'I seen 'im regular . . . ev'ry Friday night . . . for monfs . . . after.'

She didn't seem to feel any qualms about telling Strike this. On the contrary, Strike thought she seemed to be enjoying herself.

'When did that arrangement start?' asked Strike.

'Couple o' weeks . . . after 'e seen me . . . for me arse,' said Betty Fuller. 'Knocked on me door . . . wiv 'is doctor's bag . . . pretendin' 'e'd . . . come to check . . . then 'e says . . . wants a regular 'pointment. Friday night . . . 'alf past six . . . tell the neighbours . . . medical . . . if they ask . . . '

Betty paused to cough noisily. When she'd quelled her rattling chest, she went on,

' . . . and if I told anyone . . . 'e'd go to the cops . . . say I was . . . extorting 'im . . . '

'Threatened you, did he?'

'Yeah,' panted Betty Fuller, though without rancour, 'but 'e wasn't . . . try'na get it . . . free . . . so I kep' . . . me mouf shut.'

'You never told Dr Bamborough what was going on?' asked Robin.

Betty looked sideways at Robin who, in Strike's view, had rarely looked as out of place as she did sitting on Betty's bed: young, clean and healthy, and perhaps Betty's drooping, occluded eyes saw his partner the same way, because she seemed to resent both question and questioner.

''Course I fuckin' . . . didn't. She tried ta get me to . . . stop working . . . Brenner . . . easiest job of the week.'

'Why was that?' asked Strike.

Betty laughed wheezily again.

''E liked me . . . lyin' still, like I was . . . coma . . . playin' dead. 'E fucked me . . . sayin' 'is dirty words . . . I pretended . . . couldn't 'ear . . . except once,' said Betty, with a half-chuckle, half-cough, 'the bleedin' fire alarm . . . went off 'alfway . . . I said . . . in 'is ear . . .

"I'm not stayin' dead . . . if we're on fuckin' fire . . . I've got kids . . . next room . . . " 'E was livid . . . turned out it was . . . false alarm . . . '

She cackled, then coughed again.

'D'you think Dr Bamborough suspected Dr Brenner of visiting you?' asked Robin.

'No,' said Betty, testily, with another sideways glance. ''Course she fuckin' didn't . . . was eivver of us gonna tell 'er?'

'Was Brenner with you,' asked Strike, 'the night she went missing?'

'Yeah,' said Betty Fuller indifferently.

'He arrived and left at the usual times?'

'Yeah,' said Betty again.

'Did he keep visiting you, after Dr Bamborough disappeared?'

'No,' said Betty. 'Police . . . all over the surgery . . . no, 'e stopped comin' . . . I 'eard . . . 'e retired, not long after . . . Dead now, I s'pose?'

'Yes,' said Strike, 'he is.'

The ruined face bore witness to past violence. Strike, whose own nose had been broken, was sure Betty's hadn't originally been the shape it was now, with its crooked tip.

'Was Brenner ever violent to you?'

'Never.'

'While your – arrangement was going on,' said Strike, 'did you ever mention it to anyone?'

'Nope,' said Betty.

'What about after Brenner retired?' asked Strike. 'Did you happen to tell a man called Tudor Athorn?'

'Clever, aincha?' said Betty, with a cackle of mild surprise. 'Yeah, I told Tudor . . . 'e's long gawn, 's well . . . used to drink . . . wiv Tudor. 'Is nephew's . . . still round 'ere . . . grown up . . . I seen 'im . . . about. Retarded,' said Betty Fuller.

'In your opinion,' said Strike, 'given what you know about Brenner, d'you think he'd have taken advantage of a patient?'

There was a pause. Betty's milky eyes surveyed Strike.

'On'y . . . if she was out cold.'

'Not otherwise?' said Strike.

Taking a deep breath of oxygen through her crooked nose, Betty said,

'Man like that . . . when there's one fing . . . what really . . . gets 'im off . . . that's all 'e wants . . . '

'Did he ever want to drug you?' asked Strike.

'No,' said Betty, 'didn't need to . . . '

'D'you remember,' asked Strike, turning a page in his notebook, 'a social worker called Wilma Bayliss?'

'Coloured girl?' said Betty. 'Yeah . . . you smoke, dontcha?' she added. 'Can smell it . . . give us one,' she said, and out of the wrecked old body came a whiff of flirtatiousness.

'I don't think that's a good idea,' said Strike, smiling. 'Seeing as you're on oxygen.'

'Oh fuck off, then,' said Betty.

'Did you like Wilma?'

''Oo?'

'Wilma Bayliss, your social worker.'

'She were . . . like they all are,' said Betty, with a shrug.

'We spoke to Mrs Bayliss's daughters recently,' said Strike. 'They were telling us about the threatening notes that were sent to Dr Bamborough, before she disappeared.'

Betty breathed in and out, her collapsed chest doing its valiant best for her, and a small squeak issued from her ruined lungs.

'Do you know anything about those notes?'

'No,' said Betty. 'I 'eard . . . they'd bin sent. Everyone 'eard, round 'ere.'

'Who did they hear it from?'

'Probably that Irene Bull . . . '

'You remember Irene, do you?'

With many more pauses to catch her breath, Betty Fuller explained that her youngest sister had been in the same year as Irene at school. Irene's family had lived in a road off Skinner Street: Corporation Row.

'Thought . . . 'er shit . . . smelled of roses . . . that one,' said Betty. She laughed, but then broke yet again into a volley of hoarse coughs. When she'd recovered, she said, 'The police . . . asked 'em all ... not to talk ... but the mouth on ... that girl ... everyone knew ... there'd been threats made.'

'According to Wilma's daughters,' said Strike, watching for Betty's reaction, 'you knew who sent those notes.'

'No, I never,' said Betty Fuller, no longer smiling.

'You were sure Marcus Bayliss hadn't sent them, though?'

'Marcus never ... 'e was a lovely ... y'know, I always liked ... a darkie, me,' said Betty Fuller, and Robin, hoping Betty hadn't seen her wince, looked down at her hands. 'Very 'andsome ... I'd've given it ... 'im for free ... hahaha ... big, tall man,' said Betty wistfully, '... kind man ... no, 'e never freatened no doctor.'

'So who d'you think—?'

'My second girl ... my Cathy ...' continued Betty, determinedly deaf, 'er dad was a darkie ... dunno 'oo 'e was ... condom split ... I kept 'er 'cause ... I like kids, but ... she don't give a shit ... about me. Smackhead!' said Betty fiercely. '*I* never touched it ... seen too many ... go that way ... stole from me ... I told 'er ... keep the fuck ... my 'ouse ...

'Cindy's good,' gasped Betty. She was fighting her breathlessness now, though still relishing Strike's captive attention. 'Cindy ... drops by. Earning ... decent money ...'

'Really?' said Strike, playing along, waiting for his opportunity. 'What does Cindy do?'

'Escort,' wheezed Betty. 'Lovely figure ... up West ... makin' more'n I ever ... Arabs an' whatnot ... but she says ... "Ma, you wouldn't ... like it these days ... all they want ... is anal."' Betty cackled, coughed and then, without warning, turned her head to look at Robin perched on the bed and said with vitriol: '*She* don't find it ... funny, this one ... do you?' she demanded of Robin, who was taken aback. ''S'pect ... you give it away ... for meals an' jewellery ... an' fink it's ... fink it's free ... look at 'er face,' wheezed Betty, eyeing Robin with dislike, 'you're the same as ... the sniffy fuckin' ... social worker ... we 'ad round ... when I ... minding Cathy's kids ... gorn now,' said Betty, angrily. 'Took into care ...

'"*New*, Mrs Fuller",' said Betty, adopting a grotesquely genteel accent, '"*new*, it meks . . . *new* diff'rence to *me* . . . 'ow yew ladies mek . . . ends meet . . . *sex work is work*" . . . they'll tell yer that . . . patronisin' . . . fuckin' . . . but would they . . . want *their* daughters . . . doin' it? *Would they fuck*,' said Betty Fuller, and she paid for her longest speech yet with her most severe spate of coughing.

'Cindy does . . . too much coke,' Betty wheezed, her eyes watering, when she could talk again. ' . . . keeps the weight off . . . Cathy, it was smack . . . boyfriend . . . workin' for 'im . . . beat 'er blue . . . pregnant and lost it . . . '

'I'm sorry to hear that,' said Strike.

'It's all kids . . . on the street . . . these days,' said Betty, and a glimmer of what Strike thought was real distress showed through the determinedly tough exterior. 'Firteen, fourteen . . . children . . . my day . . . we'd've marched 'em . . . right back 'ome . . . it's all right, grown women, but kids – whatchew fucking starin' at?' she barked to Robin.

'Cormoran, I might—' said Robin, standing up and gesturing towards the door.

'Yeah, off you fuck,' said Betty Fuller, watching with satisfaction as Robin left her room. 'You doin' 'er, are you?' she wheezed at Strike, once the door had clicked shut behind Robin.

'No,' he said.

'What the fuck's . . . point, then?'

'She's very good at the job,' said Strike. 'When she's not up against someone like you, that is,' and Betty Fuller grinned, displaying her Cheddar-yellow teeth.

'Hahaha . . . I know . . . 'er type . . . knows fuckin' nothing . . . 'bout real life . . . '

'There was a man living in Leather Lane, back in Margot Bamborough's day,' said Strike. 'Name of Niccolo Ricci? "Mucky", they used to call him.'

Betty Fuller said nothing, but the milky eyes narrowed.

'What d'you know about Ricci?' asked Strike.

'Same as . . . ev'ryone,' said Betty.

Out of the corner of his eye, Strike saw Robin emerge into the daylight. She lifted her hair briefly off her neck, as though needing to remove weight from herself, then walked out of sight with her hands in her jacket pockets.

'It warn't Mucky ... what freatened 'er,' said Betty. ''E wouldn't ... write notes. Not 'is ... style.'

'Ricci turned up at the St John's practice Christmas party,' said Strike. 'Which seemed odd.'

'Don't know ... nuffin' 'bout that ... '

'Some of the people at the party assumed he was Gloria Conti's father.'

'Never 'eard of 'er,' wheezed Betty.

'According to Wilma Bayliss's daughters,' said Strike, 'you told their mother you were scared of the person who wrote the notes. You said the writer of the notes killed Margot Bamborough. You told Wilma he'd kill you, too, if you said who he was.'

Betty's milky eyes were expressionless. Her thin chest laboured to get enough oxygen into her lungs. Strike had just concluded that she definitely wasn't going to talk, when she opened her mouth.

'Local girl I knew,' she said, 'friend o' mine ... *she* met Mucky ... 'e come cruisin' ... our corner ... 'e says to Jen ... "You're bet-ter'n this ... workin' the street ... body like yours ... I could get you ... five times what ... you're earnin' 'ere ... " so off Jen goes,' said Betty, 'up West ... Soho ... strippin' for punters ... sex wiv 'is mates ... '

'I met 'er ... coupla years later ... visitin' 'er mum ... and she tole me a story.

'Girl at their club ... gorgeous girl, Jen said ... got raped ... knifepoint. Cut ... ' said Betty Fuller, indicating her own sagging torso, 'right down the ribs ... by a mate ... of Ricci's ...

'Some people,' said the old woman, 'fink a hooker ... being raped ... it just means she never ... got paid ... 'spect your Miss Stick-Up-'Er-Arse,' said Betty, glancing at the window, 'finks that ... but it ain't that ...

'This girl ... angry ... wants revenge ... get back ... at Ricci ... so the silly bitch ... turns police informer ...

'And Mucky found out,' wheezed Betty Fuller, 'and 'e filmed it ... as they killed 'er. My mate Jen was told ... by someone ... what 'ad seen ... the film ... Ricci kept it ... in the safe ... show people ... if they needed ... scaring ...

'Jen's dead now,' said Betty Fuller. 'Overdosed ... firty-odd years ago ... fort she'd be better ... up West ... and 'ere's me ... workin' the streets ... still alive.

'I ain't got nuffing ... to say ... about no notes ... it warn't Marcus ... that's all ... That's my meals on wheels,' said Betty, her head turning, and Strike saw a man heading towards the outside door, with a pile of foil trays in his arms.

'I'm done,' Betty said, who seemed suddenly tired and cross. 'You can turn ... telly back on ... and move ... that table over ... pass me that knife and fork ... in the loo ... '

She'd rinsed them off in the bathroom sink, but they were still dirty. Strike washed them again before taking them to her. After arranging the table in front of her armchair, and turning *The Only Way is Essex* back on, he opened the door to the meals-on-wheels man, who was grey-haired and cheery.

'Oh hello,' said the newcomer in a loud voice. 'This your son, Betty?'

'Is he fuck,' wheezed Betty Fuller. 'Whatchew got?'

'Chicken casserole and jelly and custard, love ... '

'Thanks very much for talking to me, Mrs Fuller,' said Strike, but Betty's stock of goodwill had plainly been exhausted, and she was now far more interested in her food.

Robin was leaning against a nearby wall, reading something off her phone, when Strike emerged from the building.

'I thought it was best to clear out,' she said, in a flat voice. 'How did it go?'

'She won't talk about the notes,' said Strike, as the pair of them headed back down Sans Walk, 'and if you ask me why, I'd say it's because she thinks Mucky Ricci wrote them. I've found out a bit more about that girl in the snuff movie.'

'You're joking?' said Robin, looking worried.

'Apparently she was a police informer in one of Ricci's—'

Robin gasped.

'Kara Wolfson!'

'What?'

'Kara Wolfson. One of the women they thought Creed might have killed. Kara worked at a nightclub in Soho – the owners put it about after she disappeared that she'd been a police informer!'

'How did you know that?' asked Strike, taken aback. He couldn't remember this information from *The Demon of Paradise Park*.

Robin suddenly remembered that she'd heard this from Brian Tucker, back at the Star Café. She hadn't yet heard back from the Ministry of Justice about the possibility of interviewing Creed, and as Strike still had no inkling what she was up to, she said,

'Think I read it online . . . '

But with a new heaviness pressing on her heart, Robin remembered that Kara's only remaining close relative, the brother she'd raised, had drunk himself to death. Hutchins had said the police weren't able to do anything about that film. Kara Wolfson's body might be anywhere. Some stories didn't have neat endings: there was nowhere to lay flowers for Kara Wolfson, unless it was on the corner near the strip joint where she'd last been seen.

Fighting the depression now threatening to overwhelm her, Robin raised her phone to show Strike what she'd been looking up, and said in a determinedly matter-of-fact voice,

'I was just reading about somnophilia, otherwise known as sleeping princess syndrome.'

'Which, I take it—?'

'Was Brenner's kink,' said Robin, and reading off her phone, she said, '"Somnophilia is a paraphilia in which the individual is sexually aroused by someone non-responsive . . . some psychologists have linked somnophilia with necrophilia." Cormoran . . . you know how he had barbiturates stocked up in his office?'

'Yeah,' said Strike slowly, as they walked back towards his car. 'Well, this is going to give us something to talk to Dorothy's son about, isn't it? I wonder whether she was game for playing dead? Or whether she found herself sleeping a long time, after Brenner had been round for lunch?'

Robin gave a small shudder.

'I know,' Strike continued, as he lit up, 'I said he'd be a last resort, but we've only got three months left. I'm starting to think I'm going to have to pay Mucky Ricci a visit.'

57

But all his mind is set on mucky pelfe,
To hoord vp heapes of euill gotten masse,
For which he others wrongs, and wreckes himself.

Edmund Spenser
The Faerie Queene

Adding daytime surveillance of St Peter's Roman Catholic Nursing Home to the rota meant that as May progressed, the agency was again struggling to cover all open cases. Strike wanted to know how many visitors were going in and out, and at what times, so that he might ascertain when he'd have the best chance of entering the building without running into one of the old gangster's relatives.

The nursing home lay in a quiet Georgian street on the very edge of Clerkenwell, in a quiet, leafy enclave where dun-coloured brick houses sported neo-classical pediments and glossy black front doors. A dark wood plaque on the exterior wall of the nursing home was embellished with a cross, and a biblical quotation, in gold:

For you know that it was not with perishable things such as silver or gold that you were redeemed from the empty way of life handed down to you from your ancestors, but with the precious blood of Christ, a lamb without blemish or defect.

Peter 1:18–19

'Nice sentiment,' as Strike commented to Robin, on one of their handovers, 'but nobody's getting in there without a good bit of cash.'

700

The private nursing home was small and clearly expensive. The staff, all of whom the agency quickly grew to know by sight, wore dark blue scrubs and hailed mostly from abroad. There was a black male nurse who sounded as though he'd come from Trinidad, and two blondes who talked Polish to each other every morning as they passed whichever agency member happened to be loitering in the area at the time, feigning a call on their mobile, reading a newspaper or appearing to wait, slightly impatiently, for a friend who never showed up.

A podiatrist and a hairdresser went regularly in and out of the home, but after two weeks' daytime surveillance, the agency tentatively concluded that Ricci only received visits on Sundays, when his two sons appeared, wearing the resigned looks of people for whom this was an unwelcome chore. It was easy to identify which brother was which from pictures that had appeared in the press. Luca looked, in Barclay's phrase, 'like a piano fell oan his heid', having a bald, flat, noticeably scarred skull. Marco was smaller, slighter and hairier, but gave off an air of barely contained violence, slamming his hand repeatedly on the nursing home's doorbell if the door wasn't opened immediately, and slapping a grandson around the back of the head for dropping a chocolate bar on the pavement. Both the brothers' wives had a hard-boiled look about them, and none of the family had the good looks Robin associated with Italians. The great-grandfather sitting mutely behind the doors of the nursing home might have been a true Latin, but his descendants were disappointingly pallid and Saxon in appearance, right down to the little ginger-haired boy who dropped his chocolate.

It was Robin who first laid eyes on Ricci himself, on the third Saturday the agency was watching the home. Beneath her raincoat, Robin was wearing a dress, because she was meeting Strike later at the Stafford hotel in Mayfair, to interview C. B. Oakden. Robin, who'd never been to the hotel, had looked it up and learned that the five-star establishment, with its bowler-hatted doormen, was one of the oldest and smartest hotels in London, hence her atypical choice of surveillance wear. As she'd previously disguised herself while lurking outside St Peter's (alternately beanie hat, hair up, dark contact lenses and sunglasses), she felt safe to look like herself for once as she strolled up and down the street, pretending to talk on the phone, although she'd added clear-lensed glasses she'd remove for the Stafford.

The elderly residents of St Peter's were occasionally escorted or wheeled down the street in the afternoon to the nearby square, which had a central private garden enclosed by railings, open only to keyholders, there to doze or enjoy the lilac and pansies while well wrapped up against the cold. Hitherto, the agency had seen only elderly women taken on the outings, but today, for the first time, an old man was among the group coming down a ramp at the side of the building.

Robin recognised Ricci instantly, not by his lion ring, which, if he was wearing it, was well hidden beneath a tartan rug, but by the profile that time might have exaggerated, but could not disguise. His thick black hair was now dark grey and his nose and earlobes enormous. The large eyes that reminded Strike of a Basset hound had an even more pronounced droop these days. Ricci's mouth hung slightly open as one of the Polish nurses pushed him towards the square, talking to him brightly, but receiving no response.

'You all right, Enid, love?' the black male nurse called ahead to a frail-looking old lady wearing a sheepskin hat, and she laughed and nodded.

Robin gave the group a head start, then followed, watching as one of the nurses unlocked the gate to the garden, and the party disappeared inside. Walking around the square with her phone clamped to her ear, pretending to be in conversation, Robin thought how typical it was that today, of all days, she'd worn heels, never imagining that there might have been a possibility of approaching Ricci and chatting to him.

The group from the nursing home had come to a halt beside flower-beds of purple and yellow, Ricci parked in his wheelchair beside an empty park bench. The nurses chatted amongst themselves, and to those old ladies capable of doing so, while the old man stared vacantly across the lawns.

If she'd been wearing her usual trainers, Robin thought, she might possibly have been able to scale the railings and get into the garden unseen: there was a clump of trees that would provide cover from the nurses, and she could have sidled over to Ricci and found out, at the very least, whether he had dementia. Unfortunately, she had absolutely no chance of managing that feat in her dress and high heels.

As she completed her walk around the square, Robin spotted Saul Morris walking towards her. Morris was early, as he always tended to be, whenever it was Robin from whom he was taking over.

He's going to mention either the glasses or the heels first, Robin thought.

'High heels,' said Morris, as soon as he was within earshot, his bright blue eyes sweeping over her. 'Don't think I've ever seen you in heels before. Funny, I never think of you as tall, but you are, aren't you? Sexy specs, too.'

Before Robin could stop him, he'd stooped and kissed her on the cheek.

'I'm the guy you're meeting on a blind date,' he told her, straightening up again and winking.

'How do we account for the fact that I'm about to leave you standing here?' Robin asked, unsmiling, and Morris laughed too hard, just as he did at Strike's mildest jokes.

'Dunno – what would it take to make you walk out on a blind date?' asked Morris.

You turning up, thought Robin, but ignoring the question she checked her watch and said,

'If you're OK to take over now, I'll head—'

'Here they come,' said Morris quietly. 'Oh, the old fella's outside this time, is he? I wondered why you'd abandoned the front door.'

The comment aggravated Robin almost as much as his flirtatious manner. Why did he think she'd leave the front door, unless the target had moved? Nevertheless, she waited beside him while the small group of nurses and residents, having decided that twenty minutes was enough fresh air, passed them on the other side of the street, heading back to the home.

'My kids were taken out like that at nursery,' said Morris quietly, watching the group pass. 'All bundled up in pushchairs, the helpers wheeling them out. Some of that lot are probably wearing nappies, too,' he said, his bright blue eyes following the St Peter's party.

'Christ, I hope I never end up like that. Ricci's the only man, too, poor sod.'

'I think they're very well looked after,' Robin said, as the Trinidadian nurse shouted,

'Up we go, Enid!'

'Like being a kid again, though, isn't it?' said Morris, as they watched the wheelchairs rolling along in procession. 'But with none of the perks.'

'S'pose so,' said Robin. 'I'll head off, then, if you're ready to take over.'

'Yeah, no problem,' said Morris, but he immediately added, 'where're you going, all dressed up like that?'

'I'm meeting Strike.'

'*Oh,*' said Morris, eyebrows raised, 'I see—'

'No,' said Robin, 'you don't. We're interviewing someone at a really smart hotel.'

'Ah,' said Morris. 'Sorry.'

But there was a strange complacency, bordering on complicity, about the way Morris bade her goodbye, and it wasn't until Robin had reached the end of the street that the unwelcome thought occurred to her that Morris had entirely misread the sharpness of her denial that she was going on a date with Strike; that he might, in fact, have interpreted it as Robin wanting to make it quite clear that her affections weren't engaged elsewhere.

Was Morris – *could* he be – so deluded as to think that Robin was secretly hoping that his unsubtle flirtation might lead to something happening between them? Even after what had happened on Boxing Day, when she'd shouted at him for sending her that dick pic? Little though she wanted to believe it, she was afraid that the answer was 'yes'. Morris had been extremely drunk when she'd shouted at him, and possibly incapable of judging just how truly angry and disgusted she'd been. He'd seemed sincerely ashamed of himself in the imme-diate aftermath, so she'd forced herself to be friendlier than she wanted to be, purely out of a desire to foster team cohesion. The result had been that Morris had returned to his pre-dick pic ways. She only answered his late-night texts, mostly containing jokes and attempts at banter, to stop him pestering her with 'have I offended you?' follow-ups. Now it occurred to her that what she considered professionalism Morris took as encouragement. Everything he said to her about work suggested that he saw her as less able and less experienced than the rest of the agency: perhaps he also thought her naive enough to be flattered by the attentions of a man she actually found condescending and slimy.

Morris, Robin thought, as she headed towards the Tube, didn't actually like women. He desired them, but that, of course, was an entirely different matter: Robin, who was forever marked by the ineradicable memory of the man in the gorilla mask, knew better than most that desire and liking were different, and sometimes mutually exclusive, things. Morris gave himself away constantly, not only in the way he spoke to Robin, but in his desire to call Mrs Smith 'Rich Bitch', his attribution of venal or provocative motives to every woman under surveillance, in the barely disguised disgust with which he noted that Mucky Ricci was now forced to live in a houseful of females. *Christ, I hope I never end up like that.*

Robin walked another few steps, and suddenly stopped dead, earning herself a curious glance from a passing traffic warden. She'd had an idea, triggered by what Morris had just said to her: or rather, the idea had slammed its way into the forefront of her mind and she knew that it had been there in her subconscious all along, waiting for her to admit it.

Moving aside so as not to get in the way of passers-by, Robin pulled out her phone and checked the list of paraphilias she'd last consulted when looking up sleeping princess syndrome.

Autonepiophilia.

'Oh God,' Robin muttered. 'That's it. That's got to be it.'

Robin called Strike, but his number went to voicemail; he was doubtless already on the Tube, heading for the Stafford. After a moment or two's thought, she called Barclay.

'Hiya,' said the Scot.

'Are you still outside Elinor Dean's?'

'Yeah.'

'Is there anyone in there with her?'

'No.'

'Sam, I think I know what she's doing for those men.'

'Whut?'

Robin told him. The only answer was a long silence. Finally, Barclay said,

'You're aff yer heid, Robin.'

'Maybe,' said Robin, 'but the only way to know for sure is to knock on her door and ask if she'll do it for you. Say you were recommended to her by SB.'

'Will I fuck,' said Barclay. 'Does Strike know ye're asking me tae do this?'

'Sam, we've got a week left before the client pulls the plug. The worst that can happen is that she denies it. We're not going to have many more chances.'

She heard Barclay exhale, hard.

'All right, but it's on ye if ye're wrong.'

Robin hurried onwards towards the Tube station, second-guessing herself as she went. Would Strike think she was wrong to tell Barclay to go in, on her hunch? But they had a week left before the client withdrew funding: what was there, now, to lose?

It was Saturday evening, and Robin arrived on the crowded Tube platform to find she'd just missed a train. By the time she exited at Green Park station, she'd lost the chance of arriving at the American Bar early, which she'd hoped to do, so that she and Strike could have a few words together before Oakden arrived. Worse still, when she hurried down St James's Street, she saw, with a sense of déjà vu, a large crowd blocking the bottom of the road, being marshalled by police. As Robin slowed down, wondering whether she'd be able to get through the dense mass of people to the Stafford, a couple of sprinting paparazzi overtook her, in pursuit of a series of black Mercedeses. As Robin watched them pressing their lenses against windows, she became aware that the crowd in the distance was chanting *'Jonn-ny! Jonn-ny!'* Through the windows of one of the cars heading towards the event, Robin glimpsed a woman in a Marie Antoinette wig. Only when she was nearly knocked sideways by a sprinting pair of autograph hunters, both of them holding Deadbeats posters, did Robin realise with a thrill of shock that Strike's father was the Jonny whose name was being chanted.

'Shit,' she said aloud, wheeling around and hurrying back up the road, pulling out her mobile as she went. She knew there was another entrance to the Stafford via Green Park. Not only was she going to be late, but a horrible suspicion had just hit her. Why had Oakden been so determined to meet on this specific evening? And why had it had to be this bar, so close to what she was afraid was an event involving Strike's father? Did Strike know, had he realised, what was happening close by?

She called him, but he didn't pick up. Still walking, she typed out a text:

Cormoran I don't know whether you know this, but Jonny Rokeby's having an event around the corner. I think it's possible Oakden's trying to set you up.

Breaking into a jog, because she was already five minutes late, she knew she'd just told Strike, for the very first time, that she knew who his father was.

On her arrival in Green Park, she saw from a distance a policeman at the rear entrance, who, with one of the hotel's bowler-hatted attendants, was politely but firmly turning away two men with long-lensed cameras.

'Not this way, sorry,' said the policeman. 'Only for tonight. If it's the hotel you want, you'll have to go round the front.'

'What's going on?' demanded a suited man hand in hand with a beautiful Asian woman in a cheongsam. 'We've got a dinner booking! Why can't we go through?'

'Very sorry, sir, but there's an event on at Spencer House,' explained the doorman, 'and police want us to stop people using this as a short cut.'

The two men with cameras swore and turned away, jogging back the way Robin had come. She lowered her head as they passed her, glad that she was still wearing her unneeded glasses, because her picture had appeared in the press during a court case a couple of years back. Maybe she was being paranoid, but Robin was worried the pressmen had been trying to use the Stafford not as a short cut to Rokeby and his guests, but as a means of getting to his estranged son.

Now that the photographers had gone, the bowler-hatted attendant permitted the woman in the cheongsam and her companion to enter, and after giving Robin a shrewd up-and-down glance, evidently decided she wasn't a photographer and allowed her to proceed through the gate into a courtyard, where well-dressed drinkers were smoking beneath exterior heaters. After checking her mobile and seeing that Strike hadn't answered her text, she hurried up the steps into the American Bar.

It was a comfortable, elegant space of dark wood and leather, with pennants and baseball caps from many American states and universities hanging from the ceiling. Robin immediately spotted Strike standing in a suit at the bar, his surly expression lit by the rows of illuminated bottles on the wall.

'Cormoran, I just—'

'If you're about to tell me my father's just round the corner,' said Strike tersely, 'I know. This arsehole doesn't realise I'm wise to his attempted set-up, yet.'

Robin glanced into the far corner. Carl Oakden was sitting there, legs spread wide, an arm along the back of the leather bench. He was wearing a suit, but no tie, and his attitude was clearly meant to suggest a man at ease in these cosmopolitan surroundings. With his slightly too-close-together eyes and his narrow forehead, he still resembled the boy who'd smashed Roy's mother's crystal bowl all those years ago.

'Go and talk to him. He wants some food, I'm getting menus,' muttered Strike. 'We'd just got started on Steve Douthwaite. Apparently, Dorothy always thought the bloke was suspicious.'

Heading towards Oakden, Robin prayed that Strike was going to keep his temper. She'd only once seen him lose his cool with a witness, and had no desire to see it happen again.

'Mr Oakden?' she said, smiling as she reached him and extending her hand. 'I'm Robin Ellacott, we've emailed—'

'I know,' said Oakden, turning his head slowly to look her up and down with a smirk. He ignored her outstretched hand and Robin could tell he did so deliberately. Refusing to show that she realised that he was trying to be offensive, she shrugged off her raincoat.

'Nice bar,' she said pleasantly, sitting down opposite him. 'I've never been here before.'

'Normally takes you cheaper places, does he?' asked Oakden.

'Cormoran was just telling me you remember your mother talking about Steve Douth—'

'Love,' said Oakden, legs still wide apart, arm along the back of the leather bench, 'I told you all along, I'm not interested in being palmed off with assistants or secretaries. I'll talk to him, or nobody.'

'I'm actually Cormoran's—'

'I'll bet you are,' said Oakden, with a snigger. 'Don't suppose he can get rid of you now, can he?'

'Sorry?'

'Not now you've been knifed, trying to do a man's job,' said Oakden, with a glance towards her forearm as he raised his cocktail to his lips. 'You'd probably sue the shit out of him, if he tried.'

Oakden, who'd evidently done his homework on the detectives, was clearly revelling in his rudeness. Robin could only suppose that the con man assumed she was too desperate for his information to take offence at his manner. He seemed determined to derive maximum pleasure from this encounter: to enjoy free alcohol and food, and bait a woman who was unlikely to walk away. Robin wondered which paper or picture agency he'd contacted, to propose luring Strike within a few hundred yards of his father's party, and how much Oakden stood to gain, if they could get a picture of Strike apparently publicly snubbing his father, or catch the detective on record saying something angry and quotable.

'There you go,' said Strike, throwing a couple of leather-bound menus onto the table and sitting down. He hadn't thought to bring Robin anything to drink. Oakden picked up a menu and perused it slowly, and he seemed to enjoy keeping them waiting.

'I'll have the club sandwich,' he said at last, and Strike hailed a waiter. The order given, Strike turned back to Oakden and said,

'Yeah, so you were saying, your mother found Douthwaite—'

'Oh, she definitely thought he was a charmer,' said Oakden. His eyes, Robin noted, kept moving to the entrance of the bar, and she was sure Oakden was waiting for photographers to burst in. 'Wide boy, you know the type. Chatting up the slags on reception. The old woman said he tried it on with everyone. The nurse got all giggly when he was around and all.'

Robin remembered the gambolling black skeleton of Talbot's notebook, and the words written beside Crowley's figure of death: *Fortuna says Pallas Athena, Ceres, Vesta and Cetus are SCARLET WOMEN who RIDE UPON THE BEAST* . . .

'And did your mother think he fancied Dr Bamborough?'

Oakden took a sip of his cocktail and smacked his lips.

'Well, I mean, Margot,' he said, with a small snort of laughter, and Robin found herself irrationally resentful of Oakden using the missing doctor's first name, 'you know, she was the classic wanted-it-all-ways, wasn't she?'

'What ways were those?' said Strike.

'Bunny Girl,' said Oakden, taking another sip of his drink, 'legs out, tits out. Then, quick, get the white coat on—'

'Don't think GPs wear white coats,' said Strike.

'I'm talking metaphorically,' said Oakden airily. 'Child of her time, wasn't she?'

'How's that?'

'The rise of gynocentric society,' said Oakden, with a slight bow towards Robin, who suddenly thought his narrow head resembled a stoat's. 'Late sixties, early seventies, it's when it all started changing, isn't it? You've got the pill: consequence-free fucking. Looks like it benefits the male, but by enabling women to avoid or subvert the reproductive function, you're repressing natural and healthy patterns of sex behaviour. You've got a gynocentric court system, which favours the female even if she didn't want the kids in the first place. You've got misandrist authoritarianism masquerading as a campaign for equal rights, policing men's thoughts and speech and natural behaviour. And you've got widespread sexual exploitation of men. Playboy Club, that's all bullshit. Look, but don't touch. It's the old courtly love lie. The woman's there to be worshipped, the man's there to spew cash, but never get satisfaction. Suckers, the men who hang round those places.

'Bamborough didn't look after her own kid,' said Oakden, his eyes again darting to the entrance and back to Strike, 'didn't fuck her own husband, from what I heard, he was nearly always too ill to perform. He had plenty of cash though, so she gets a nanny and goes lording it over men at work.'

'Who, specifically, did she lord it over?' asked Strike.

'Well, Douthwaite ran out of there practically crying last time he saw her, my old woman said. But that's been our culture since the sixties, hasn't it? Male suffering, nobody gives a shit. People whine when men break, when they can't handle it any more, when they lash out. If Douthwaite did her in – I don't *personally* think he did,' said Oakden with an expansive gesture, and Robin reminded herself that Carl Oakden had almost certainly never laid eyes on Steven Douthwaite, and that he'd been fourteen years old when Margot disappeared, 'but *if* he did, I'd lay odds it's because she kicked his pain back in his teeth. Only women bleed,' said Oakden, with a contemptuous little laugh, 'isn't that right?' he shot at Robin. 'Ah, there's my sandwich.'

While the waiter served him, Robin got up and headed to the bar, where the beautiful woman in the cheongsam, whose hair hung like black silk in the light of the banked bottles of spirits, was standing with her partner. Both were ordering cocktails and looked delighted to be in each other's company. For a few seconds Robin suddenly wondered whether she'd ever again feel as they did. Her job reminded her almost daily of the many ways in which men and women could hurt each other.

As she ordered herself a tonic water, Robin's phone rang. Hoping it was Barclay, she instead saw her mother's name. Perhaps Linda had got wind of Sarah's pregnancy. Matthew might have taken his wife-to-be back to Masham by now, to share the good news. Robin muted the phone, paid for her drink, wishing it was alcoholic, and carried it back to the table in time to hear Oakden say to Strike,

'No, that didn't happen.'

'You didn't add vodka to the punch at Dr Bamborough's barbecue?'

Oakden took a large bite of his free sandwich, and chewed it insolently. In spite of his thin hair and the many wrinkles around his eyes, Robin could clearly see the spoiled teenager inside the fifty-four-year-old.

'Nicked some,' said Oakden thickly, 'then drank it in the shed. Surprised they missed it, but the rich are tight. How they stay minted, isn't it?'

'We heard the punch made someone sick.'

'Not my fault,' said Oakden.

'Dr Phipps was pretty annoyed, I hear.'

'Him,' said Oakden, with a smirk. 'Things worked out all right for old Phipps, didn't they?'

'In what way?' asked Strike.

'Wife out the way, marrying the nanny. All very convenient.'

'Didn't like Phipps, did you?' said Strike. 'That came across in your book.'

'You've read it?' said Oakden, momentarily startled. 'How come?'

'Managed to track down an advance copy,' said Strike. 'It should've come out in '85, right?'

'Yeah,' said Oakden.

'D'you remember the gazebo that was under construction in the garden when the barbecue happened?'

One of Oakden's eyelids flickered. He raised a hand quickly to his face and made a sweep of his forehead, as though he felt a hair tickling him.

'No,' he said.

'It's in the background of one of your photos. They'd just started building the columns. I expect they'd already put down the floor.'

'I can't remember that,' said Oakden.

'The shed where you took the vodka wasn't near there, then?'

'Can't've been,' said Oakden.

'While we're on the subject of nicking things,' said Strike, 'would you happen to have the obituary of Dr Brenner you took from Janice Beattie's house?'

'I never stole no obituary from her house,' said Oakden, with a display of disdain. 'What would I want that for?'

'To get some information you could try and pass off as your own?'

'I don't need to look up old Joe Brenner, I know plenty about him. He came round our house for his dinner every other Sunday. My old woman used to cook better than his sister, apparently.'

'Go on, then,' said Strike, his tone becoming combative, 'amaze us.'

Oakden raised his sparse eyebrows. He chewed another bite of sandwich and swallowed it, before saying,

'Hey, this was all your idea. You don't want the information, I'm happy to go.'

'Unless you've got more than you put in your book—'

'Brenner wanted Margot Bamborough struck off the bloody medical register. Come round our house one Sunday full of it. Couple of weeks before she disappeared. There,' said Oakden pugnaciously, 'I kept that out of the book, because my mother didn't want it in there.'

'Why was that?'

'Still loyal to him,' said Oakden, with a little snort of laughter. 'And I wanted to keep the old dear happy at the time, because noises had been made about writing me out of the will. Old women,' said the convicted con man, 'are a bit too persuadable if you don't keep an eye on them. She'd got chummy with the local vicar by the eighties. I was worried it was all going to go to rebuild the bloody church steeple unless I kept an eye on her.'

'Why did Brenner want Bamborough struck off?'

'She examined some kid without parental permission.'

'Was this Janice's son?' asked Robin.

'Was I talking to you?' Oakden shot at her.

'You,' growled Strike, 'want to keep a civil tongue in your bloody head. Was it Janice's son, yes or no?'

'Maybe,' said Oakden, and Robin concluded that he couldn't remember. 'Point is, that's unethical behaviour, looking at a kid without a parent there, and old Joe was all worked up about it. "I'll have her struck off for this," he kept saying. There. Didn't get *that* from no obituary, did I?'

Oakden drank the rest of his cocktail straight off, then said,

'I'll have another one of those.'

Strike ignored this, saying,

'And this was two weeks before Bamborough disappeared?'

'About that, yeah. Never seen the old bastard so excited. He loved disciplining people, old Joe. Vicious old bastard, actually.'

'In what way?'

'Told my old woman in front of me she wasn't hitting me enough,' said Oakden. 'She bloody listened, too. Tried to lay about me with a slipper a couple of days later, silly cow. She learned not to do that again.'

'Yeah? Hit her back, did you?'

Oakden's too-close-together eyes raked Strike, as though trying to ascertain whether he was worth educating.

'If my father had lived, he'd've had the right to punish me, but her trying to humiliate me because Brenner told her to? I wasn't taking that.'

'Exactly how close were your mother and Brenner?'

Oakden's thin brows contracted.

'Doctor and secretary, that's all. There wasn't anything else between them, if that's what you're implying.'

'They didn't have a little lie down after lunch, then?' said Strike. 'She didn't come over sleepy, after Brenner had come over?'

'You don't want to judge everyone's mother by yours,' said Oakden.

Strike acknowledged the jibe with a dark smile and said,

'Did your mother ask Brenner to sign the death certificate for your grandmother?'

'The hell's that got to do with anything?'

'Did she?'

'I dunno,' said Oakden, his eyes darting once again towards the bar's entrance. 'Where did you get that idea? What're you even asking that for?'

'Your grandmother's doctor was Margot Bamborough, right?'

'I dunno,' said Oakden.

'You can remember every word your mother told you about Steve Douthwaite, right down to him flirting with receptionists and looking tearful the last time he left the surgery, but you can't remember details of your own grandmother falling downstairs and killing herself?'

'I wasn't there,' said Oakden. 'I was out at a mate's house when it happened. Come home and seen the ambulance.'

'Just your mother at home, then?'

'The hell's this relevant to—?'

'What's the name of the mate whose house you were at?' asked Strike, for the first time taking out his notebook.

'What're you doing?' said Oakden, with an attempt at a laugh, dropping the last portion of his sandwich on his plate. 'What are you fucking implying?'

'You don't want to give us his name?'

'Why the fuck should – he was a schoolmate—'

'Convenient for you and your mother, old Maud falling down-stairs,' said Strike. 'My information is she shouldn't have been trying to navigate stairs alone, in her condition. Inherited the house, didn't you?'

Oakden began to shake his head very slowly, as though marvelling at the unexpected stupidity of Cormoran Strike.

'Seriously? You're trying to ... wow. *Wow.*'

'Not going to tell me the name of your schoolfriend, then?'

'*Wow,*' said Oakden, attempting a laugh. 'You think you can—'

'—drop a word in a friendly journalist's ear, to the effect that your long career of screwing over old ladies started with a good hard push in the small of your grandmother's back? Oh yeah, I definitely can.'

'Now you wait a fucking—'

'I know you think it's me being set up tonight,' said Strike, leaning in. His body language was unmistakeably menacing, and out of the corner of her eye, Robin saw the black-haired woman in the cheong-sam and her partner watching warily, both with their drinks at their lips. 'But the police have still got a note written to them in 1985, telling them to dig beneath the cross of St John. DNA techniques have moved on a lot since then. I expect they'll be able to get a good match from the saliva under the envelope flap.'

Oakden's eyelid twitched again.

'You thought you were going to stir up a bit of press interest in the Bamborough case, to get people interested in your shitty book, didn't you?'

'I never—'

'I'm warning you. You go talking to the papers about me and my father, or about me working the Bamborough case, and I'll make sure you get nailed for that note. And if by chance that doesn't work, I'll put my whole agency onto turning over every part of your miserable fucking life, until I've got something else on you to take to the police. Understand?'

Oakden, who looked momentarily unnerved, recovered himself quickly. He even managed another little laugh.

'You can't stop me writing about whatever I want. That's freedom of—'

'I'm warning you,' repeated Strike, a little more loudly, 'what'll happen if you get in the way of this case. And you can pay for your own fucking sandwich.'

Strike stood up and Robin, caught off guard, hastened to grab her raincoat and get up, too.

'Cormoran, let's go out the back,' she said, thinking of the two photographers lurking at the front of the building, but they hadn't gone more than two steps when they heard Oakden call after them.

'You think I'm scared of your fucking agency? Some fucking detective you are!' he said, and now most of the heads in their vicinity turned. Glancing back, Robin saw that Oakden had got up, too: he'd come out from behind the table and was planted in the middle of the bar, clearly set on making a scene.

'Strike, please, let's just go,' said Robin, who now had a presentiment of real trouble. Oakden was clearly determined to come out of the encounter with something sellable, or at the very least, a narrative in which he'd come out on top. But Strike had already turned back towards their interviewee.

'You didn't even know your own fucking father's having a party round the corner,' said Oakden loudly, pointing in the direction of Spencer House. 'Not going to pop in, thank him for fucking your mother on a pile of beanbags while fifty people watched?'

Robin watched what she had dreaded unfold in apparent slow motion: Strike lunged for Oakden. She made a grab for the arm Strike had drawn back for a punch, but too late: his elbow slammed into Robin's forehead, breaking her glasses in two. Dark spots popped in front of Robin's eyes and the next thing she knew, she'd fallen backwards onto the floor.

Robin's attempted intervention had given the con man a few seconds in which to dodge, and instead of receiving what might have been a knockout punch, he suffered no worse than a glancing blow to the ear. Meanwhile the enraged Strike, who'd barely registered his arm being impeded, realised what he'd done only when he saw drinkers all over the bar jumping to their feet, their eyes on the floor behind him. Turning, he saw Robin lying there, her hands over her face, a trickle of blood issuing from her nose.

'Shit!' Strike bellowed.

The young barman had run out from behind the bar. Oakden was shouting something about assault. Still slightly dizzy, tears of pain streaming from her eyes, the humiliated Robin was assisted back onto her feet by a couple of affluent-looking grey-haired Americans, who were fussing about getting her a doctor.

'I'm absolutely fine,' she heard herself saying. She'd taken the full force of Strike's elbow between her eyebrows, and she realised her nose was bleeding only when she accidentally sprayed blood onto the kind American's white shirt front.

'Robin, shit—' Strike was saying.

'Sir, I'm going to have to—'

'Yes, we're *absolutely* going to leave,' Robin told the waiter, absurdly polite, while her eyes watered and she tried to stem the bleeding from her nostrils. 'I just need – oh, thank you so much,' she said to the American woman, who'd handed Robin her raincoat.

'Call the police!' Oakden was shouting. Thanks to Robin's intervention, he was entirely unmarked. 'Someone call the bloody police!'

'I won't be pressing charges,' Robin said to nobody in particular.

'Robin – I'm so—'

Grabbing a handful of Strike's sleeve, warm blood still trickling down onto her chin, Robin muttered,

'Let's just go.'

She trod on the cracked lens of her glasses as they headed out of the silent bar, the drinkers staring after them.

58

His louely words her seemd due recompence
Of all her passed paines: one louing howre
For many yeares of sorrow can dispence:
A dram of sweete is worth a pound of sowre:
Shee has forgott, how many, a woeful stowre
For him she late endurd; she speakes no more
Of past . . .
Before her stands her knight, for whom she toyld so sore.

Edmund Spenser
The Faerie Queene

'Robin—'

'*Don't* tell me I shouldn't have tried to stop you,' she said through gritted teeth, as they hurried through the outside courtyard. Her vision was blurred with tears of pain. Smokers turned to gape as she passed, trying to staunch her bleeding nose. 'If that punch had connected, we'd be back there waiting for the police.'

To Robin's relief, there were no paparazzi waiting for them as they headed into Green Park, but she was scared that it wouldn't take long, after the scene Strike had just made, for them to come hunting again.

'We'll get a cab,' said Strike, who was currently consumed with a mixture of total mortification and rage against Oakden, his father, the press and himself. 'Listen, you're right—'

'I know I'm right, thanks!' she said, a little wildly.

Not only was her face throbbing, she was now wondering why Strike hadn't warned her about Rokeby's party; why, in fact, he'd let himself get lured there by a second-rate chancer like Oakden, careless of consequences for their case and for the agency.

'TAXI!' bellowed Strike, so loudly that Robin jumped. Somewhere nearby, she heard running footsteps.

A black cab pulled up and Strike pushed Robin inside.

'Denmark Street,' he yelled at the cabbie, and Robin heard the shouts of photographers as the taxi sped up again.

'It's all right,' said Strike, twisting to look out of the back window, 'they're on foot. Robin ... I'm so fucking sorry.'

She'd pulled a mirror out of her bag to try and clean up her smarting face, wiping blood from her upper lip and chin. It looked as though she was going to have two black eyes: both were rapidly swelling.

'D'you want me to take you home?' said Strike.

Furious at him, fighting the urge to cry out of pain, Robin imagined Max's surprise and curiosity at seeing her in this state; imagined having to make light, again, of the injuries she'd sustained while working for the agency. She also remembered that she hadn't gone food shopping in days.

'No, I want you to give me something to eat and a strong drink.'

'You've got it,' said Strike, glad to have a chance to make reparations. 'Will a takeaway do?'

'No,' said Robin sarcastically, pointing at her rapidly blackening eyes, 'I'd like to go to the Ritz, please.'

Strike started to laugh but cut himself off, appalled at the state of her face.

'Maybe we should go to casualty.'

'Don't be ridiculous.'

'Robin—'

'You're sorry. I know. You said.'

Strike's phone rang. He glanced down: Barclay could wait, he decided, and muted it.

Three-quarters of an hour later, the taxi dropped them at the end of Denmark Street, with a takeaway curry and a couple of clinking bottles. Once upstairs, Robin repaired to the toilet on the landing, where she washed dried blood from her nostrils and chin with a wad of wet toilet paper. Two increasingly swollen, red-purplish mounds containing her eyes looked back at her out of the cracked mirror. A blue bruise was spreading over her forehead.

Inside the office, Strike, who'd normally have eaten the curry straight out of the foil tray it had come in, had brought out mismatched plates, knives and forks, then, because Robin wanted a strong drink, went upstairs to his flat where he had a bottle of his favourite whisky. There was a small freezer compartment in his fridge, where he kept ice packs for his stump in addition to an ice tray. The cubes within this had been there for over a year, because although Strike enjoyed the odd drink of spirits, he generally preferred beer. About to leave the flat with the ice tray, he had second thoughts, and doubled back for one of the ice packs, as well.

'Thank you,' muttered Robin, when Strike reappeared, accepting the proffered ice pack. She was sitting in Pat's seat, behind the desk where she'd once answered the phone, where Strike had laid out the curry and plates. 'And you'd better re-do next week's rota,' she added, applying the ice pack gingerly to her left eye first, 'because there isn't a concealer in the world that's going to cover up this mess. I'm not going to have much chance of going unnoticed on surveillance with two black eyes.'

'Robin,' said Strike yet again, 'I'm so fucking sorry. I was a tit, I just . . . What d'you want, vodka, whisky—?'

'Whisky,' she said. 'On the rocks.'

Strike poured both of them a triple measure.

'I'm sorry,' he said, yet again, while Robin took a welcome gulp of Scotch, then began helping herself to curry. Strike sat down on the fake leather sofa opposite the desk. 'Hurting you's the last thing – there's no excuse for – I saw red, I lost it. My father's other kids have been pestering me for months to go to that fucking party,' said Strike, running his hand through the thick, curly hair that never looked disarranged. He felt she was owed the whole story now: the reason, if not the excuse, that he'd fucked up so badly. 'They wanted us to get a group photo taken together for a present. Then Al tells me Rokeby's got prostate cancer – which doesn't seem to have prevented him having four hundred mates over for a good old knees-up . . . I ripped up the invitation without registering where the thing was being held. I should've realised Oakden was up to something, I took my eye off the ball, and—'

He downed half his drink in one.

'There's no excuse for trying to punch him, but everything – these last few months – Rokeby rang me in February. First time ever. Tried to bribe me into meeting him.'

'He tried to *bribe* you?' said Robin, pressing the ice pack to her other eye, remembering the shouted 'go fuck yourself' from the inner office, on Valentine's Day.

'As good as,' said Strike. 'He said he was open to suggestions for helping me out . . . well, it's forty years too fucking late for that.'

Strike downed the rest of his whisky, reached for the bottle and poured the same again into his glass.

'When did you last see him?' Robin asked.

'When I was eighteen. I've met him twice,' Strike said. 'First time was when I was a kid. My mother tried to ambush him with me, outside a recording studio.'

He'd only ever told Charlotte this. Her family was at least as dysfunctional and peculiar as his own, riven with scenes that to other people might've been epoch defining – 'it was a month before Daddy torched Mummy's portrait in the hall, and the panelling caught fire, and the fire brigade came, and we all had to be evacuated via the upstairs windows' – but to the Campbells were so normalised they seemed routine.

'I thought he wanted to see me,' said Strike. The shock of what he'd done to Robin, and the whisky scorching his throat, had liberated memories he usually kept locked up tight inside him. 'I was seven. I was so fucking excited. I wanted to look smart, so he'd be – so he'd be proud of me. Told my mum to put me in my best trousers. We got outside this studio – my mother had music industry contacts, someone had tipped her off he was going to be there – and they wouldn't let us in. I thought there'd been some mistake. The bloke on the door obviously didn't realise my dad wanted to see me.'

Strike drank again. The curry lay cooling between them.

'My mother kicked off. They were threatening her when the

band's manager got out of his car behind us. He knew who my mother was and he didn't want a public scene. He took us inside, into a room away from the studio.

'The manager tried to tell her it was a dumb move, turning up. If she wanted more money, she should go through lawyers. That's when I realised my father hadn't invited us at all. She was just trying to force her way in. I started crying,' said Strike roughly. 'Just wanted to go . . .

'And then, while my mother and Rokeby's manager are going at it hammer and tongs, Rokeby walks in. He heard shouting on the way back from the bathroom. Probably just done a line; I realised that later. He was already wound up when he came in the room.

'And I tried to smile,' said Strike. 'Snot all over my face. I didn't want him to think I was a whiner. I'd been imagining a hug. "There you are, at last." But he looked at me like I was nothing. Some fan's kid, in too-short trousers. My trousers were always too fucking short . . . I grew too fast . . .

'Then he clocked my mother, and he twigged. They started rowing. I can't remember everything they said. I was a kid. The gist was how dare she butt in, she had his lawyer's contact details, he was paying enough, it was her problem if she pissed it all away, and then he said, "This was a fucking accident." I thought he meant, he'd come to the studio accidentally or something. But then he looked at me, and I realised, he meant me. *I* was the accident.'

'Oh God, Cormoran,' said Robin quietly.

'Well,' said Strike, 'you've got to give him points for honesty. He walked out. We went home.

'For a while afterwards, I held out a bit of hope he'd regretted what he'd said. It was hard to let go of the idea he wanted to see me, deep down. But nothing.'

While the sun was far from setting, the room was becoming steadily darker. The high buildings of Denmark Street cast the outer office into shadow at this time of the evening, and neither detective had turned on the interior lights.

'Second time we met,' said Strike, 'I made an appointment with his management. I was eighteen. Just got into Oxford. We hadn't touched any of Rokeby's money for years. They'd been back to court to put restrictions on what my mother could do with it, because she was a nightmare with cash, just threw it away. Anyway, unbeknownst to me, my aunt and uncle had informed Rokeby I'd got into Oxford. My mother got a letter saying he had no obligations to me now I'd turned eighteen, but reminding her I could use the money that had been accumulating in the bank account.

'I arranged to see him at his manager's office. He was there with his long-time lawyer, Peter Gillespie. Got a smile off Rokeby this time. Well, I was off his hands financially now, but old enough to talk to the press. Oxford had clearly been a bit of a shock to him. He'd probably hoped, with a background like mine, I'd slide quietly out of sight for ever.

'He congratulated me on getting into Oxford and said I had a nice little nest egg all built up now, because my mother hadn't spent any of it for six, seven years.

'I told him,' said Strike, 'to stick his fucking money up his arse and set fire to it. Then I walked out.

'Self-righteous little prick, I was. Didn't occur to me that Ted and Joan were going to have to stump up if Rokeby didn't, which is what they did . . . I only realised that later. But I didn't take their money long. After my mother died, midway through my second year, I left Oxford and enlisted.'

'Didn't he contact you after your mum died?' asked Robin quietly.

'No,' said Strike, 'or if he did, I never got it. He sent me a note when my leg got blown off. I'll bet that put the fear of God into him, hearing I'd been blown up. Probably worried sick about what the press might make of it all.

'Once I was out of Selly Oak, he tried to give me the money again. He'd found out I was trying to start the agency. Charlotte's friends knew a couple of his kids, which is how he got wind of it.'

Robin felt something flip in her stomach at the sound of Charlotte's name. Strike so rarely acknowledged her existence.

'I said no, at first. I didn't want to take the money, but no other fucker wanted to lend a one-legged ex-soldier without a house or any savings enough money to set up a detective agency. I told his prick of a lawyer I'd take just enough money to start the agency and pay it back in instalments. Which I did.'

'That money was yours all along?' said Robin, who could remember Gillespie pressing Strike for repayment every few weeks, when she'd first joined the agency.

'Yeah, but I didn't want it. Resented even having to borrow a bit of it.'

'Gillespie acted as though—'

'You get people like Gillespie round the rich and famous,' said Strike. 'His whole ego was invested in being my father's enforcer. The bastard was half in love with my old man, or with his fame, I dunno. I was pretty blunt on the phone about what I thought about Rokeby, and Gillespie couldn't forgive it. I'd insisted on a loan agreement between us, and Gillespie was going to hold me to it, to punish me for telling him exactly what I thought of the pair of them.'

Strike pushed himself off the sofa, which made its usual farting noises as he did so, and began helping himself to curry. When they both had full plates, he went to fetch two glasses of water. He'd already got through a third of the whisky.

'Cormoran,' said Robin, once he was settled back on the sofa and had started eating. 'You do realise, I'm never going to gossip about your father to other people? I'm not going to talk to *you* about him if you don't want to, but . . . we're partners. You could have told me he was hassling you, and let off steam that way, instead of punching a witness.'

Strike chewed some of his chicken jalfrezi, swallowed, then said quietly,

'Yeah, I know.'

Robin ate a bit of naan. Her bruised face was aching less now: the ice pack and the whisky had both numbed her, in different ways. Nevertheless, it took a minute to marshal the courage to say,

'I saw Charlotte's been hospitalised.'

Strike looked up at her. He knew, of course, that Robin was well aware who Charlotte was. Four years previously, he'd got almost too drunk to walk, and told her a lot more than he'd ever meant to, about the alleged pregnancy Charlotte had insisted was his, which had broken them apart for ever.

'Yeah,' said Strike.

And he told Robin the story of the farewell text messages, and his dash to the public payphone, and how he'd listened until they'd found Charlotte lying in undergrowth in the grounds of her expensive clinic.

'Oh my Christ,' said Robin, setting down her fork. 'When did you know she was alive?'

'Knew for sure two days later, when the press reported it,' said Strike. He heaved himself back out of his chair, topped up Robin's whisky, then poured himself more before sitting back down again. 'But I'd concluded she must be alive before that. Bad news travels faster than good.'

There was a long silence, in which Robin hoped to hear more about how being drawn into Charlotte's suicide attempt, and by the sounds of it, saving her life, had made him feel, but Strike said nothing, merely eating his curry.

'Well,' said Robin at last, 'again, in future, maybe we could try that talking thing, before you die of a stress-induced heart attack or, you know, end up killing someone we need to question?'

Strike grinned ruefully.

'Yeah. We could try that, I s'pose . . . '

Silence closed around them again, a silence that seemed to the slightly drunk Strike to thicken like honey, comforting and sweet, but slightly dangerous if you sank too far into it. Full of whisky, contrition and a powerful feeling he preferred at all times not to dwell upon, he wanted to make some kind of statement about Robin's kindness and her tact, but all the words that occurred to him seemed clumsy and unserviceable: he wanted to express something of the truth, but the truth was dangerous.

How could he say, look, I've tried not to fancy you since you first took off your coat in this office. I try not to give names to what I feel for you, because I already know it's too much, and I want peace from the shit that love brings in its wake. I want to be alone, and unburdened, and free.

725

But I don't want you to be with anyone else. I don't want some other bastard to persuade you into a second marriage. I like knowing the possibility's there, for us to, maybe . . .

Except it'll go wrong, of course, because it always goes wrong, because if I were the type for permanence, I'd already be married. And when it goes wrong, I'll lose you for good, and this thing we've built together, which is literally the only good part of my life, my vocation, my pride, my greatest achievement, will be forever fucked, because I won't find anyone I enjoy running things with, the way I enjoy running them with you, and everything afterwards will be tainted by the memory of you.

If only she could come inside his head and see what was there, Strike thought, she'd understand that she occupied a unique place in his thoughts and in his affections. He felt he owed her that information, but was afraid that saying it might move this conversation into territory from which it would be difficult to retreat.

But, from second to second, sitting here, now with more than half a bottle of neat whisky inside him, a different spirit seemed to move inside him, asking himself for the first time whether determined solitude was what he really wanted, for evermore.

Joanie reckons you're gonna end up with your business partner. That Robin girl.

All or nothing. See what happens. Except that the stakes involved in making any kind of move would be the highest of his life; higher by far than when he'd staggered across a student party to chat up Charlotte Campbell, when, however much agony he'd endured for her later, he'd risked nothing more than minor humiliation, and a good story to tell.

Robin, who'd eaten as much curry as she could handle, had now resigned herself to not hearing what Strike felt for Charlotte. She supposed it had been a forlorn hope, but it was something she was very keen to know. The neat whisky she'd drunk had given the night a slight fuzziness, like a rain haze, and she felt slightly wistful. She knew that if it hadn't been for the alcohol, she might feel simply unhappy.

'I suppose,' said Strike, with the fatalistic daring of a trapeze artist, swinging out into the spotlight, only black air beneath him, 'Ilsa's been trying to matchmake, your end, as well?'

Across the room, sitting in shadow, Robin experienced something like an electric shock through her body. That Strike would even allude to a third party's idea of them being romantically involved was unprecedented. Didn't they always act as though nothing of the sort could be further from anyone's mind? Hadn't they always pretended certain dangerous moments had never happened, such as when she'd modelled that green dress for him, and hugged him while wearing her wedding dress, and felt the idea of running away together pass through his mind, as well as hers?

'Yes,' she said, at last. 'I've been worried . . . well, embarrassed about it, because I haven't . . . '

'No,' said Strike quickly, 'I never thought *you* were . . . '

She waited for him to say something else, suddenly acutely aware, as she'd never been before, that a bed lay directly above them, barely two minutes from where they sat. And, like Strike, she thought, everything I've worked and sacrificed for is in jeopardy if I take this conversation to the wrong place. Our relationship will be forever marred by awkwardness and embarrassment.

But worse than that, by far: she was scared of giving herself away. The feelings she'd been denying to Matthew, to her mother, to Ilsa and to herself must remain hidden.

'Well, sorry,' said Strike.

What did that mean, Robin wondered, her heart thumping very hard: she took another large gulp of whisky before she said,

'Why are you apologising? You're not—'

'She's *my* friend.'

'She's mine, too, now,' said Robin. 'I . . . don't think she can help herself. She sees two friends of the opposite sex getting on . . . '

'Yeah,' said Strike, all antennae now: was that all they were? Friends of the opposite sex? Not wanting to leave the subject of men and women, he said,

'You never told me how mediation went. How come he settled, after dragging it out all this time?'

'Sarah's pregnant. They want to get married before she has it . . .

or before she gets too big for a designer dress, knowing Sarah.'

'Shit,' said Strike quietly, wondering how upset she was. He couldn't read her tone or see her clearly: the office was now full of shadow, but he didn't want to turn on the lights. 'Is he – did you expect that?'

'S'pose I should have,' said Robin, with a smile Strike couldn't see, but which hurt her bruised face. 'She was probably getting annoyed with the way he was dragging out our divorce. When he was about to end their affair, she left an earring in our bed for me to find. Probably getting worried he wasn't going to propose, so she forgot to take her pill. It's the one way women can control men, isn't it?' she said, momentarily forgetting Charlotte, and the baby she claimed to have lost. 'I've got a feeling she'd just told him she was pregnant when he cancelled mediation the first time. Matthew said it was an accident . . . maybe he didn't want to have it, when she first told him . . . '

'Do you want kids?' Strike asked Robin.

'I used to think so,' said Robin slowly. 'Back when I thought Matthew and I were . . . you know. For ever.'

As she said it, memories of old imaginings came to her: of a family group that had never existed, but which had once seemed quite vivid to her. The night that Matthew had proposed, she'd formed a clear mental picture of the pair of them with three children (a compromise between his family, where there had been two children, and her own, which had had four). She'd seen it all quite clearly: Matthew cheering on a young son who was learning to play rugby, as he'd done himself; Matthew watching his own little girl onstage, playing Mary in the school nativity play. It struck her now how very conventional her imaginings had been, and how much Matthew's expectations had become her own.

Sitting here in the darkness with Strike, Robin thought that Matthew would, in fact, be a very good father to the kind of child he'd be expecting: in other words, a little boy who wanted to play rugby, or a little girl who wanted to dance in a tutu. He'd carry their pictures around in his wallet, he'd get involved at their schools, he'd hug them when they needed it, he'd care about their homework. He wasn't devoid of kindness: he felt guilty when he did wrong. It was simply that what Matthew considered right was so heavily coloured by what other people did, what other people considered acceptable and desirable.

'But I don't know, any more,' said Robin, after a short pause. 'I can't see myself having kids while doing this job. I think I'd be torn ... and I don't ever want to be torn again. Matthew was always trying to guilt me out of this career: I didn't earn enough, I worked too many hours, I took too many risks ... but I love it,' said Robin, with a trace of fierceness, 'and I don't want to apologise for that any more ...

'What about you?' she asked Strike. 'Do *you* want children?'

'No,' said Strike.

Robin laughed.

'What's funny?'

'I give a whole soul-searching speech on the subject and you're just: *no*.'

'I shouldn't be here, should I?' said Strike, out of the darkness. 'I'm an accident. I'm not inclined to perpetuate the mistake.'

There was a pause, then Robin said, with asperity,

'Strike, that's just bloody self-indulgent.'

'Why?' said Strike, startled into a laugh. When he'd said the same to Charlotte, she'd both understood and agreed with him. Early in her teens, her drunken mother had told Charlotte she'd considered aborting her.

'Because ... for God's sake, you can't let your whole life be coloured by the circumstances of your conception! If everyone who was conceived accidentally stopped having kids—'

'We'd all be better off, wouldn't we?' said Strike robustly. 'The world's overpopulated as it is. Anyway, none of the kids I know make me particularly keen to have my own.'

'You like Jack.'

'I do, but that's one kid out of God knows how many. Dave Polworth's kids – you know who Polworth is?'

'Your best mate,' said Robin.

'He's my oldest mate,' Strike corrected her. 'My best mate ...'

For a split-second he wondered whether he was going to say it, but the whisky had lifted the guard he usually kept upon himself: why not say it, why not let go?

'. . . is you.'

Robin was so amazed, she couldn't speak. Never, in four years, had Strike come close to telling her what she was to him. Fondness had had to be deduced from offhand comments, small kindnesses, awkward silences or gestures forced from him under stress. She'd only once before felt as she did now, and the unexpected gift that had engendered the feeling had been a sapphire and diamond ring, which she'd left behind when she walked out on the man who'd given it to her.

She wanted to make some kind of return, but for a moment or two, her throat felt too constricted.

'I . . . well, the feeling's mutual,' she said, trying not to sound too happy.

Over on the sofa, Strike dimly registered that somebody was on the metal staircase below their floor. Sometimes the graphic designer in the office beneath worked late. Mostly Strike was savouring the pleasure it had given him to hear Robin return his declaration of affection.

And now, full of whisky, he remembered holding her on the stairs at her wedding. This was the closest they'd come to that moment in nearly two years, and the air seemed thick with unspoken things, and again, he felt as though he stood on a small platform, ready to swing out into the unknown. *Leave it there*, said the surly self that coveted a solitary attic space, and freedom, and peace. *Now*, breathed the flickering demon the whisky had unleashed, and like Robin a few minutes previously, Strike was conscious that they were sitting mere feet from a double bed.

Footsteps reached the landing outside the glass outer door. Before either Strike or Robin could react, it had opened.

'Is the power oot?' said Barclay, and he flicked on the light. After a moment in which the three blinked at each other in surprise, Barclay said,

'You're a friggin' genius, R – the fuck happened tae yer face?'

59

Blinking in the bright light, Robin reached again for the ice pack.

'Strike hit me. Accidentally.'

'Jesus,' said Barclay. 'Wouldnae wanna see what he can do deliberately. How'd that happen?'

'My face got in the way of his elbow,' said Robin.

'Huh,' said Barclay, hungrily eyeing the almost empty curry cartons, 'what wus that? Compensation?'

'Exactly,' said Robin.

'Tha' why neither of yiz have been answerin' yer phones fer the last three hours?'

'Shit, sorry, Sam,' said Robin, pulling out her mobile and looking at it. She'd had fifteen missed calls from Barclay since muting her mother in the American Bar. She was also pleased to see that she'd missed a couple of texts from Morris, one of which seemed to have a picture attached.

'Beyond the call of duty to come in person,' said the slightly drunk Strike. He wasn't sure whether he was more glad or annoyed that Barclay had interrupted, but on balance, he thought annoyance was uppermost.

'The wife's at her mother's wi' the bairn overnight,' said Barclay. 'So I thought I'd come deliver the good news in person.'

He helped himself to a poppadum and sat down on the arm of the sofa at the other end to Strike.

'I've found oot what SB gets up tae in Stoke Newington. All down tae Robin. You ready for this?'

'What?' said Strike, looking between Barclay and Robin. 'When—?'

'Earlier,' said Robin, 'before I met you.'

'Rang the doorbell,' said Barclay, 'said I'd bin recommended by SB, wondered whether she could help me oot. She didnae believe me. I had to get a foot in the door to stop her slammin' it on me. Then she says SB told her a Scottish guy talked him doon off Tower Bridge the other day.

'So I decide it's cut our losses time,' said Barclay. 'I said, yeah, that wuz me. I'm a friend. We know what ye're up to in here. You're gonnae wanna talk to me, if ye care aboot your client.

'So she let me in.'

Barclay ate a bit of poppadum.

'Sorry, starvin'. Anyway, she takes me in the back room, and there it all is.'

'There what all is?'

'Giant playpen she's knocked up, out o' some foam an' MDF,' said Barclay, grinning. 'Big old changin' mat. Stack of adult nappies. Johnson's baby powder.'

Strike appeared to have been struck momentarily speechless. Robin began to laugh, but stopped quickly, because it made her face hurt.

'Poor old SB gets aff on bein' a baby. She's only got one other client, that guy at the gym. Doesnae need any more, because SB pays her so much. She dresses 'em up. Changes 'em. Powders their fucking arses—'

'You're having a laugh,' said Strike. 'This can't be real.'

'It is real,' said Robin, with the ice pack pressed to her face. 'It's called . . . hang on . . . '

She brought up the list of paraphilias on her phone again.

'Autonepiophilia. "Being aroused by the thought of oneself as an infant."'

'How the hell did you—?'

'I was watching the old people being wheeled out of the nursing home,' said Robin. 'Morris said they were like kids, that some of them were probably wearing nappies and it just . . . *clicked*. I saw her buying a ton of baby powder and dummies in the supermarket, but we've never once seen a child go in or out of that house. Then there was that patting on the head business, like the men were little kids . . . '

Strike remembered following the gym manager home, the man's hand over his lower face as he left Elinor Dean's house, as though he'd had something protruding from his mouth that he wanted to conceal.

' . . . and big boxes being delivered, of something really light,' Robin was saying.

'That'll be the adult nappies,' said Barclay. 'Anyway . . . she's no' a bad woman. Made me a cup of tea. She kens aboot the blackmail, but here's something interestin': she and SB don't think Shifty knows what's really goin' on inside that hoose.'

'How come?'

'The gym manager let it slip tae Shifty he knew a big man at Shifty's company. SB and the gym guy sometimes go in the playpen together, see. Like it's a nurs – like it's a nurser—'

Barclay suddenly broke into peals of laughter and Strike followed suit. Robin pressed the ice pack to her face and joined in. For a minute, all three of them roared with laughter at the mental image of the two men in nappies, sitting in their MDF playpen.

'—like it's a nursery,' said Barclay in a falsetto, wiping tears out of his eyes. 'Fuck me, it takes all sorts, eh? Anyway, the tit at the gym lets this slip, an' Shifty, knowin' old SB never went tae a gym in his life, an' that he lives on the other side o' London, probes a wee bit, and notices the other guy gettin' uncomfortable. So Shifty follows

SB. Watches him going in and oot Elinor's place. Draws the obvious conclusion: she's a hooker.

'Shifty then walks intae SB's office, closes the door, gives him Elinor's address, and says he kens what's goin' on in there. SB was shittin' himself, but he's no fool. He reckons Shifty thinks it's just straight sex, but he's worried Shifty might do more diggin'. See, SB found Elinor online, advertisin' her services in some dark corner o' the net. SB's scared Shifty'll go looking for whut she really does if he denies it's sex, an' if anyone finds oot whut really goes on in there, SB's gonna be straight back up Tower Bridge.

'So, that bit's no' so funny,' said Barclay, more soberly. 'The guy at the gym only came clean tae SB and Elinor a coupla months ago, about talking tae Shifty. He's aboot ready tae kill himself, for what he's done. Elinor's taken her ad down, but the internet never forgets, so that's no bloody use . . .

'The worst thing, Elinor says, is Shifty himself is a right cock. SB's told her all aboot him. Apparently Shifty takes his coke habit tae work and he's always feelin' up his PA, but SB cannae do anything about it, for fear of retribution. So,' said Barclay, 'what are we gonnae do, eh? Tell the board SB's suit troosers dinnae fit him properly because he's wearin' a nappy underneath?'

Strike didn't smile. The amount of whisky he'd consumed didn't particularly help his mental processes. It was Robin who spoke first.

'Well, we can tell the board everything, and accept that's going to ruin a few lives . . . or we can let them terminate our contract without telling them what's going on, and accept that Shifty's going to keep blackmailing SB . . . or . . .'

'Yeah,' said Strike heavily, 'that's the question, isn't it? Where's the third option, where Shifty gets his comeuppance and SB doesn't end up in the Thames?'

'It sounds,' said Robin to Barclay, 'as though Elinor would back SB up, if he claimed it was just an affair? Of course, SB's wife mightn't be happy.'

'Aye, Elinor'd back him up,' said Barclay. 'It's in her interests.'

'I'd like to nail Shifty,' said Strike. 'That'd please the client no end, if we helped them get rid of Shifty without the company's name getting splashed all over the papers ... which it definitely will if it gets out their CEO likes having his arse powdered ...

'If that PA's being sexually harassed,' Strike said, 'and watching him do coke at work, why isn't she complaining?'

'Fear of not being believed?' Robin suggested. 'Of losing her job?'

'Could you,' Strike said to Robin, 'ring Morris for me? He'll still have the girl's contact details. And, Barclay,' Strike added, getting up from the sofa on the third attempt, and heading for the inner office, 'come in here, we're going to have to change next week's rota. Robin can't follow people looking like she just did three rounds with Tyson Fury.'

The other two went into Strike's office. Robin stayed sitting at Pat's desk for a moment, thinking not about what Barclay had just told them, but about the moments before he'd arrived, when she and Strike had been sitting in semi-darkness. The memory of Strike telling her she was his best friend made her heart feel immeasurably lightened, as though something she hadn't realised was weighing on it had been removed for ever.

After a moment's pleasurable savouring of this feeling, she pulled out her mobile, and opened the texts Morris had sent her earlier. The first, which had the picture attached, said '**lol**'. The image was of a sign reading: 'Viagra Shipment Stolen. Cops Looking For Gang of Hardened Criminals.' The second text said, '**Not funny?**'

'No,' Robin muttered. 'Not funny.'

Getting to her feet, she pressed Morris's number, and began to clear up the curry one-handed, while she held the phone to her ear.

'Evening,' said Morris, after a couple of rings. 'Calling to tell me you've found a hardened criminal?'

'Are you driving?' asked Robin, ignoring the witticism.

'On foot. Just seen the old folks' home locked up for the night. I'm actually right by the office, I'm on my way to relieve Hutchins. He's outside the Ivy, keeping an eye on Miss Jones's boyfriend.'

'Well, we need the details of Shifty's PA,' said Robin.

'What? Why?'

'We've found out what he's blackmailing SB about, but,' she hesitated, imagining the jokes she'd have to hear at SB's expense, if she told Morris what Elinor Dean was doing for him, 'it's nothing illegal and he's not hurting anyone. We want to talk to Shifty's PA again, so we need her contact details.'

'No, I don't think we should go back to her,' said Morris. 'Bad idea.'

'Why?' Robin asked, as she dropped the foil tins into the pedal bin, suppressing her frown because it made her bruised face ache.

'Because . . . fuck's sake,' said Morris, who usually avoided swearing to Robin. 'You were the one who said we shouldn't use her.'

Behind Robin, in the inner office, Barclay laughed at something Strike had said. For the third time that evening, Robin had a feeling of impending trouble.

'Saul,' she said, 'you aren't still seeing her, are you?'

He didn't answer immediately. Robin picked up the plates from the desk and put them in the sink, waiting for his answer.

'No, of course I'm not,' he said, with an attempt at a laugh. 'I just think this is a bad idea. You were the one who said, before, that she had too much to lose—'

'But we wouldn't be asking her to entrap him or set him up this time—'

'I'll need to think about this,' said Morris.

Robin put the knives and forks into the sink, too.

'Saul, this isn't up for debate. We need her contact details.'

'I don't know whether I kept them,' said Morris, and Robin knew he was lying. 'Where's Strike right now?'

'Denmark Street,' said Robin. Not wanting another sly joke about her and Strike being together after dark, she purposely didn't say she was there, too.

'OK, I'll ring him,' said Morris, and before Robin could say anything else, he'd hung up.

The whisky she'd drunk was still having a slightly anaesthetic effect. Robin knew that if she were entirely sober, she'd be feeling still more incensed at yet another example of Morris treating her not as a partner in the firm, but as Strike's secretary.

Turning on the taps in the cramped kitchen area, she began rinsing off the plates and forks, and as curry sauce dripped down the drain, her thoughts drifted again to those moments before Barclay had

736

arrived, while she and Strike had still been sitting in semi-darkness.

Out on Charing Cross Road, a car passed, blaring Rita Ora's 'I Will Never Let You Down', and softly, under her breath, Robin sang along:

> *'Tell me baby what we gonna do*
> *I'll make it easy, got a lot to lose . . . '*

Putting the plug into the sink, she began to fill it, squirting washing-up liquid on top of the cutlery. Singing, her eyes fell on the unopened vodka Strike had bought, but which neither of them had touched. She thought of Oakden stealing vodka at Margot's barbecue . . .

> *'You've been tired of watching me*
> *forgot to have a good time . . . '*

. . . and claiming that he hadn't spiked the punch. Yet Gloria had vomited . . . At the very moment Robin drew breath into her lungs to call to Strike, and tell him her new idea, two hands closed on her waist.

Twice in Robin's life, a man had attacked her from behind: without conscious thought, she simultaneously stamped down hard with her high heel on the foot of the man behind her, threw back her head, smashing it into his face, grabbed a knife in the sink and spun around as the grip at her waist disappeared.

'FUCK!' bellowed Morris.

She hadn't heard him coming up the stairs over the noise of water splashing into the sink and her own singing. Morris was now doubled up, hands clamped over his nose.

'FUCK!' he shouted again, taking his hands away from his face, to reveal that his nose was bleeding. He hopped backwards, the imprint of her stiletto imprinted in his shoe, and collapsed onto the sofa.

'What's going on?' said Strike, emerging at speed from the inner office and looking from Morris on the sofa to Robin, who was still holding the knife. She turned off the taps, breathing hard.

'He grabbed me,' she said, as Barclay emerged from the inner room behind Strike. 'I didn't hear him coming.'

'It – was – a – fucking – *joke*,' said Morris, examining the blood smeared on his hands. 'I only meant to make you jump – fuck's *sake*—'

But adrenalin and whisky had suddenly unleashed an anger in Robin such as she hadn't felt since the night she'd left Matthew. Light-headed, she advanced on Morris.

'Would you sneak up on Strike and grab him round the waist? D'you creep up on Barclay and hug him? *D'you send either of them pictures of your dick?*'

There was a silence.

'You bitch,' said Morris, the back of his hand pressed to his nostrils. 'You said you wouldn't—'

'He did what?' said Strike.

'Sent me a dick pic,' snapped the furious Robin, and turning back to Morris, she said, 'I'm not some sixteen-year-old work experience girl who's scared of telling you to stop. I don't want your hands on me, OK? I don't want you kissing me—'

'He sent you—?' began Strike.

'I didn't tell you because you were so stressed,' said Robin. 'Joan was dying, you were up and down to Cornwall, you didn't need the grief, but I'm done. I'm not working with him any more. I want him gone.'

'Christ's sake,' said Morris again, dabbing at his nose, 'it was a *joke*—'

'Ye need tae learn tae read the fuckin' room, mate,' said Barclay, who was standing against the wall, arms folded, and seemed to be enjoying himself.

'You can't fucking fire me over—'

'You're a subcontractor,' said Strike. 'We're not renewing your contract. Your non-disclosure agreement remains in operation. One word of anything you've found out working here, and I'll make sure you never get another detective job. Now get the fuck out of this office.'

Wild-eyed, Morris stood up, still bleeding from his left nostril.

'Fine. You want to keep her on because you've got a hard-on for her, fine.'

Strike took a step forwards; Morris nearly fell over the sofa, backing away.

'Fine,' he said again.

He turned and walked straight out of the office, slamming the glass door behind him. While the door vibrated, and Morris's footsteps clanged away down the metal stairs, Barclay pushed himself off the wall, plucked the knife Robin was still holding out of her hand and went to drop it into the sink with the dirty crockery.

'Never liked that tosser,' he said.

Strike and Robin looked at each other, then at the worn carpet, where a couple of drops of Morris's blood still glistened.

'One all, then,' said Strike, clapping his hands together. 'What say, first to break Barclay's nose wins the night?'

PART SIX

So past the twelue Months forth, and their dew places found.

Edmund Spenser
The Faerie Queene

60

Fortune, the foe of famous cheuisaunce
Seldome (said Guyon) yields to vertue aide,
But in her way throwes mischiefe and mischaunce,
Whereby her course is stopt, and passage staid.

Edmund Spenser
The Faerie Queene

What would have happened had Sam Barclay not opened the door that evening and switched on the light was a question that pre-occupied both detective partners over the weekend, each of them re-running the conversation in their head, wondering what the other was thinking, and whether too much had been said, or given away.

Sober now, Strike had to be glad he hadn't done what whisky had been urging him to do. Had he acted on that alcohol-fuelled impulse, he might now be in a state of bitter remorse, with no way back to the friendship that was unique in his life. Yet in his free moments, he wondered whether Robin had known how dangerously close he'd come to pushing the conversation into territory that had previously been fenced around with barbed wire, or that, seconds before Barclay flicked the light switch, Strike had been trying to remember when he'd last changed his sheets.

Robin, meanwhile, had woken on Sunday morning with her face aching as though it had been trodden on, a slight hangover, and a volatile mixture of pleasure and anxiety. She went back over everything she'd said to Strike, hoping she hadn't betrayed any of those feelings she habitually denied, even to herself. The memory of him telling her she was his best friend caused a little spurt of happiness every time she returned to it, but as the day wore on, and her bruising worsened, she wished she'd been brave enough to ask him directly how he now felt about Charlotte Campbell.

An image of Charlotte hung permanently in Robin's head these days, like a shadowy portrait she'd never wanted hung. The picture had acquired shape and form in the four years since they'd passed on the stairs in the Denmark Street office, because of the many details Ilsa had given her, and the snippets she'd read in the press. Last night, though, that image had become stark and fixed: a darkly romantic vision of a lost and dying love, breathing her final words in Strike's ear as she lay among trees.

And this was, however you looked at it, an extraordinarily powerful image. Strike had once, when extremely drunk, told Robin that Charlotte was the most beautiful woman he'd ever seen, and as she hovered between life and death, that beautiful woman had chosen to contact Strike, to tell him she loved him still. What did prosaic Robin Ellacott have to offer that was in any way equal to such high-stakes drama, such extremity of emotion? An up-to-date rota, nearly docketed invoices and cups of strong tea? Doubtless because of the pain in her face, Robin's mood vacillated between diminishing cheerfulness and a tendency to brood. Finally, she gave herself a stern talking to: Strike had given her an unprecedented assurance of affection, and she'd never have to see Saul Morris again, and she should be delighted about both.

Predictably, it was Pat who took the sudden firing of Saul Morris hardest. Strike delivered the news on Monday morning, as he and the secretary narrowly missed colliding in the doorway onto Denmark Street, Strike on his way out, Pat on her way in. Both of them were preparing for the ingestion of nicotine, Pat having just taken out the electronic cigarette she used during work hours, Strike already holding the Benson & Hedges he rarely smoked in the office.

'Morning,' said Strike. 'I've left a note on your desk, couple of things I'd like you to do while I'm out. Robin'll be in at ten. Oh—'

He'd taken a couple of steps before turning back.

'—and can you calculate Morris's pay up to Friday and transfer it into his account right away? He's not coming back.'

He didn't wait for a reaction, so it was Robin who took the brunt of their secretary's disappointment when she arrived at ten to ten. Pat had Radio Two playing, but turned it off the moment the door handle turned.

'Morning. Why – what 'appened to you?' said Pat.

Robin's face looked worse, two days on, than it had on Saturday. While the swelling had subsided, both eyes were ringed in dark grey tinged with red.

'It was an accident. I bumped into something,' said Robin, stripping off her coat and hanging it on a peg. 'So I won't be on surveillance this week.'

She took a book out of her handbag and crossed to the kettle, holding it. She hadn't particularly enjoyed the covert staring on the Tube that morning, but wasn't going to mention Strike's elbow to Pat, because she tried, wherever possible, not to fuel Pat's antipathy for her partner.

'Why won't Saul be coming back?' Pat demanded.

'He didn't work out,' said Robin, her back to Pat as she took down two mugs.

'What d'you mean?' said Pat indignantly. 'He caught that man who was having it away with the nanny. He always kept his paperwork up to date, which is more'n you can say for that Scottish nutter.'

'I know,' said Robin. 'But he wasn't a great team player, Pat.'

Pat took a deep drag of nicotine vapour, frowning.

'He,' she nodded towards the empty chair where Strike usually sat, 'could take a few lessons from Morris!'

Robin knew perfectly well that it wasn't Pat's decision who the partners hired and fired, but unlike Strike, she also thought that in such a small team, Pat deserved the truth.

'It wasn't Cormoran who wanted him gone,' she said, turning to face the secretary, 'it was me.'

'You!' said Pat, astounded. 'I thought the pair of you were keen on each other!'

'No. I didn't like him. Apart from anything else, he sent me a picture of his erect penis at Christmas.'

Pat's deeply lined face registered an almost comical dismay.

'In . . . in the post?'

Robin laughed.

'What, tucked inside a Christmas card? No. By text.'

'You didn't—?'

'Ask for it? No,' said Robin, no longer smiling. 'He's a creep, Pat.'

She turned back to the kettle. The untouched bottle of vodka was still standing beside the sink. As Robin's eyes fell on it, she remembered the idea that had occurred to her on Saturday night, shortly before Morris's hands closed around her waist. After giving the secretary her coffee, she carried her own into the inner office, along with the book she'd taken from her bag. Pat called after her,

'Shall I update the rota, or will you?'

'I'll do it,' said Robin, closing the door, but instead, she called Strike.

'Morning,' he said, answering on the second ring.

'Hi. I forgot to tell you an idea I had on Saturday night.'

'Go on.'

'It's about Gloria Conti. Why did she vomit in the bathroom at Margot's barbecue, if Oakden didn't spike the punch?'

'Because he's a liar, and he *did* spike the punch?' suggested Strike. He was currently in the same Islington square that Robin had patrolled on Friday, but he paused now and reached for his cigarettes, eyes on the central garden, which today was deserted. Beds densely planted with purple pansies looked like velvet cloaks spread upon the glistening grass.

'Or did she throw up because she was pregnant?' said Robin.

'I thought,' said Strike, after a pause while lighting a cigarette, 'that only happens in the mornings? Isn't that why it's called—'

On the point of saying 'morning sickness', Strike remembered the expectant wife of an old army friend, who'd been hospitalised for persistent, round-the-clock vomiting.

'My cousin threw up any time of the day when she was pregnant,' said Robin. 'She couldn't stand certain food smells. And Gloria was at a barbecue.'

'Right,' said Strike, who was suddenly remembering the odd notion that had occurred to him after talking to the Bayliss sisters.

Robin's theory struck him as stronger than his. In fact, his idea was weakened if Robin's was true.

'So,' he said, 'you're thinking it might've been Gloria who—'

'—had the abortion at the Bride Street clinic? Yes,' said Robin. 'And that Margot helped her arrange it. Irene mentioned Gloria being closeted in Margot's consulting room, remember? While Irene was left on reception?'

The lilac bush in the central garden was casting out such a heavy scent that Strike could smell it even over the smoke of his cigarette.

'I think you could be on to something here,' said Strike slowly.

'I also thought this might explain—'

'Why Gloria doesn't want to talk to us?'

'Well, yes. Apart from it being a traumatic memory, her husband might not know what happened,' said Robin. 'Where are you just now?'

'Islington,' said Strike. 'I'm about to have a crack at Mucky Ricci.'

'What?' said Robin, startled.

'Been thinking about it over the weekend,' said Strike, who, unlike Robin, had had no time off, but had run surveillance on Shifty and Miss Jones's boyfriend. 'We're nearly ten months into our year, and we've got virtually nothing. If he's demented, obviously it'll be no-go, but you never know, I could be able to get something out of him. He might even,' said Strike, 'get a kick out of reliving the good old days . . . '

'And what if his sons find out?'

'He can't talk, or not properly. I'm banking on him being unable to tell them I've been in. Look,' said Strike, in no particular hurry to hang up, because he wanted to finish his cigarette, and would rather do it talking to Robin, 'Betty Fuller thinks Ricci killed her, I could tell. So did Tudor Athorn; he told his nephew so, and they were the kind of people who were plugged into local gossip and knew about local low life.

'I keep going back to the thing Shanker said, when I told him about Margot vanishing without a trace. "Professional job." When you take a step back and look at it,' said Strike, now down to the last centimetre of his cigarette, 'it seems borderline impossible for every trace of her to have disappeared, unless someone with plenty of practice handled it.'

'Creed had practice,' said Robin quietly.

'D'you know what I did last night?' said Strike, ignoring this interjection. 'Looked up Kara Wolfson's birth certificate online.'

'Why? Oh,' said Robin, and Strike could hear her smiling, 'star-sign?'

'Yeah. I know it breaks the means before motive rule,' he added, before Robin could point it out, 'but it struck me that someone might've told Margot about Kara's murder. Doctors know things, don't they? In and out of people's houses, having confidential consultations. They're like priests. They hear secrets.'

'You were checking whether Kara was a Scorpio,' said Robin. It was a statement rather than a question.

'Exactly. And wondering whether Ricci looked into that party to show his goons which woman they were going to pick off.'

'Well?'

'Well what?'

'*Was* Kara a Scorpio?'

'Oh. No. Taurus — seventeenth of May.'

Strike now heard pages turning at Robin's end of the call.

'Which means, according to Schmidt . . .' said Robin, and there was a brief pause, '. . . she was Cetus.'

'Huh,' said Strike, who'd now finished his cigarette. 'Well, wish me luck. I'm going in.'

'Good l—'

'*Cormoran Strike!*' said somebody gleefully, behind him.

As Strike hung up on Robin, a slender black woman in a cream coat came alongside him, beaming.

'You don't remember me, do you?' she said. 'Selly Oak. I'm—'

'Marjorie!' said Strike, the memory coming back to him. 'Marjorie the physiotherapist. How are you? What're you—?'

'I do a few hours in the old folks' home up the road!' said Marjorie. 'And look at *you*, all famous . . .'

Fuck.

It took Strike twenty-five minutes to extricate himself from her.

'. . . so that's bloody that,' he told Robin later at the office. 'I pre-tended I was in the area to visit my accountant, but if she's working at St Peter's, there's no chance of us getting in to see Ricci.'

'No chance of *you* getting in there—'

'I've already told you,' said Strike sharply. The state of Robin's face was a visible warning against recklessness, of the perils of failing to think through consequences. 'You're not going anywhere near him.'

'I've got Miss Jones on the line,' Pat called from the outer office.

'Put her through to me,' said Robin, as Strike mouthed 'thanks'.

Robin talked to Miss Jones while continuing to readjust the rota on her computer, which, given Robin's own temporary unavailability for surveillance, and Morris's permanent absence, was like trying to balance a particularly tricky linear equation. She spent the next forty minutes making vague sounds of agreement whenever Miss Jones paused to draw breath. Their client's objective, Robin could tell, was staying on the line long enough for Strike to come back to the office. Finally, Robin got rid of her by pretending to get a message from Pat saying Strike would be out all day.

It was her only lie of the day, Robin thought, while Strike and Pat discussed Barclay's expenses in the outer office. Given that Strike was adept himself at avoiding pledging his own word when he didn't want to, he really ought to have noticed that Robin had made no promises whatsoever about staying away from Mucky Ricci.

61

Then when the second watch was almost past,
That brasen dore flew open, and in went Bold
Britomart . . .

Edmund Spenser
The Faerie Queene

In the first week of June, a blind item appeared in the *Metro*, concerning Strike's presence in the American Bar on the night of his
father's party.

> Which famous son of a famous father preferred to spend
> the night of his old man's celebrations brawling in a
> bar five hundred yards from the party, rather than hob-
> nobbing with his family? Our spies tell us a punch was
> thrown, and his faithful assistant was unable to *Hold it*
> *Back*. A father-son competition for publicity? Dad defi-
> nitely won this round.

As *Hold it Back* was the name of one of Jonny Rokeby's albums,
nobody could really be in much doubt which father and son were in
question. A couple of journalists called Strike's office, but as neither
he nor Rokeby were disposed to comment, the story fizzled out for
lack of details. 'Could've been worse,' was Strike's only comment.
'No photos, no mention of Bamborough. Looks like Oakden's been
frightened out of the idea of selling stories about us.'

Feeling slightly guilty, Robin had already scrolled through the pictures of Jonny Rokeby's party on her phone, while on surveillance outside Miss Jones's boyfriend's house. Rokeby's guests, who included celebrities from both Hollywood and the world of rock 'n' roll, had all attended in eighteenth-century costumes. Buried in the middle of all the famous people was a single picture of Rokeby surrounded by six of his seven adult children. Robin recognised Al, grinning from beneath a crooked powdered wig. She could no more imagine Strike there, trussed up in brocade, with patches on his face, than she could imagine him pole-vaulting.

Relieved as she was that Oakden appeared to have given up the idea of discussing the agency with the press, Robin's anxiety mounted as June progressed. The Bamborough case, which mattered to her more than almost anything else, had come to a complete standstill. Gloria Conti had met Anna's request for her cooperation with silence, Steve Douthwaite remained as elusive as ever, Robin had heard no news about the possibility of interviewing Dennis Creed, and Mucky Ricci remained cloistered inside his nursing home, which, owing to the agency's reduced manpower, nobody was watching any more.

Even temporary replacements for Morris were proving impossible to find. Strike had contacted everyone he knew in the Special Investigation Branch, Hutchins had asked his Met contacts, and Robin had canvassed Vanessa, but nobody was showing any interest in joining the agency.

'Summer, isn't it?' said Barclay, as he and Robin crossed paths in the office one Saturday afternoon. 'People don't want tae start a new job, they want a holiday. I ken how they feel.'

Both Barclay and Hutchins had booked weeks off with their wives and children months in advance, and neither partner could begrudge their subcontractors a break. The result was that by mid-July, Strike and Robin were the only two left working at the agency.

While Strike devoted himself to following Miss Jones's boyfriend, still trying to find out anything that might prove that he was an unsuitable person to have custody of his daughter, Robin was trying to kindle an acquaintance with Shifty's PA, which wasn't proving easy. So far that month, wearing a different wig and coloured contacts each time, Robin had tried to engage her in conversation in a bar, deliberately tripped over her in a nightclub, and followed her into the ladies in Harvey Nichols. While the PA didn't seem to have the slightest idea that it was the same woman opportuning or inconveniencing her, she showed no inclination to chat, let alone confess that her boss was a lech or a coke user.

Having tried and failed to sit next to the PA in a sandwich bar in Holborn one lunchtime, Robin, who today had dark hair and dark brown eyes courtesy of hair chalk and contact lenses, decided the moment had come to try and wheedle information out of a very old man, instead of a pretty young woman.

She hadn't reached this decision lightly, nor did she approach it in any casual spirit. While Robin was vaguely fond of Strike's old friend Shanker, she was under no illusions about how evil a person would have to be to scare a man who'd been steeped in criminal violence since the age of nine. Accordingly, she'd worked out a plan, of which the first step was to have a full and effective disguise. Today's happened to be particularly good: she'd learned a lot about make-up since starting the job with Strike, and she'd sometimes had the satisfaction of seeing her partner double-take before he realised who she was. After checking her reflection carefully in the mirror of a McDonald's bathroom, and reassuring herself that she not only looked utterly unlike Robin Ellacott, but that nobody would guess she'd recently had two black eyes, she set off for the Tube, and just under twenty minutes later, arrived at Angel station.

The garden where the old residents of St Peter's sometimes sat was empty as she passed it, in spite of the warm weather. The pansies were gone, replaced by pink asters and the broad, sunny street where the nursing home lay was almost deserted.

The quotation from St Peter gleamed gold in the sunshine as Robin approached the front door.

. . . it was not with perishable things such as silver or gold that you were redeemed . . . but with the precious blood of Christ . . .

Robin rang the bell. After a few moments, a chubby black-haired woman in the familiar blue uniform opened it.

'Afternoon,' she said, sounding Spanish.

'Hi,' said Robin, her North London accent copied from her friend Vanessa. 'I'm here to visit Enid? I'm her great-granddaughter.'

She'd stored up the only first name she'd heard for any of the old ladies in the home. Her great fear had been that Enid might have died before she got to use it, or that Enid had no family.

'Oh, that's nice,' said the nurse, smiling and gesturing towards a visitors' book just inside the door. 'Sign in, please, and don't forget to sign out when you leave. She's in her room. Might be asleep!'

Robin stepped into a dark, wood-panelled hall. She deliberately hadn't asked which number Enid's room was, because she intended to get lost finding it.

A number of walking frames and a couple of collapsible wheelchairs were lined up against the wall. The hall was dominated by an enormous crucifix facing the door, on which a pallid plaster Jesus hung, his six-pack rendered with startling precision, scarlet blood dripping from hands, feet and the punctures left by his crown of thorns. The home smelled better than Betty Fuller's sheltered accommodation: though there was a definite undertone of old cooking smells, it mingled with that of furniture wax.

Sunlight poured through the fan window behind Robin as she bent over the visitors' book and wrote in the date, the time she'd entered the building and the fake name she'd decided on: *Vanessa Jones.* Over the table where the visitors' book lay hung a board showing the name of each resident. Beside each was a little sliding door, which could be adjusted to show whether the occupant was 'in' or 'out'. Niccolo Ricci was currently – and, Robin suspected, almost permanently – 'in'.

There was a lift, but she chose to take the red-carpeted and wooden-banistered stairs, passing the Trinidadian nurse she'd often seen while on surveillance, who was descending. He smiled and wished her a good afternoon, his arms laden with packs of incontinence pads.

A doorway led off the first landing, a small sign beside it announcing that this way lay bedrooms 1 to 10. Robin set off along the corridor, reading names off doors. Unfortunately, 'Mrs Enid Billings' lived behind door number 2 and, as Robin swiftly discovered, Ricci wasn't on her floor. Aware that this was going to make any claim of having got lost on the way to Enid's room implausible in the extreme, Robin doubled back, and climbed up to the second floor.

A few steps along an identical corridor to the one below, she heard a woman with a strong Polish accent in the distance, and backed hastily into an alcove where a sink and cupboard had been placed.

'D'you need the bathroom? *Do – you – need – the – bathroom, Mister – Ricci?*'

A low moan answered.

'*Yes?*' said the voice. '*Or no?*'

There was a second, answering moan.

'*No?* All right then . . . '

Footsteps grew louder: the nurse was about to pass the alcove, so Robin stepped boldly out from it, smiling.

'Just washing my hands,' she told the approaching nurse, who was blonde and flat-footed and merely nodded as she passed, apparently preoccupied with other matters.

Once the nurse had disappeared, Robin proceeded down the corridor, until she reached the door of number 15, which bore the name 'Mr Nico Ricci'.

Unconsciously holding her breath, Robin knocked gently, and pushed. There was no lock on the inside of the door; it swung open at once.

The room inside, while small, faced south, getting plenty of sun. A great effort had been made to make the room homely: watercolour pictures hung on the walls, including one of the Bay of Naples. The mantelpiece was covered in family photographs, and a number of children's paintings had been taped up on the wardrobe door, including one captioned 'Grandpa and Me and a Kite'.

The elderly occupant was bent almost double in an armchair beside the window. In the minute that had elapsed since the nurse left him, he'd fallen fast asleep. Robin let the door close quietly behind her, crept across to Ricci and sat down on the end of his single bed, facing the one-time pimp, pornographer and orchestrator of gang-rape and murder.

There was no doubt that the staff looked after their charges well. Ricci's dark grey hair and his fingernails were as clean as his bright white shirt collar. In spite of the warmth of the room, they'd dressed him in a pale blue sweater. On one of the veiny hands lying limp on the chair beside him glistened the gold lion's head ring. The fingers were curled up in a way that made Robin wonder whether he could still use them. Perhaps he'd had a stroke, which would account for his inability to talk.

'Mr Ricci?' said Robin quietly.

He made a little snorting snuffle, and slowly raised his head, his mouth hanging open. His enormous, drooping eyes, though not as filmy as Betty Fuller's, nevertheless looked dull, and like his ears and nose seemed to have grown while the rest of him shrank, leaving loose folds of dark skin.

'I've come to ask you some questions,' said Robin quietly. 'About a woman called Margot Bamborough.'

He gaped at her, open-mouthed. Could he hear her? Could he understand? There was no hearing aid in either of his overlarge ears. The loudest noise in the room was the thumping of Robin's heart.

'Do you remember Margot Bamborough?' she asked.

To her surprise, Ricci made his low moan. Did that mean yes or no?

'You do?' said Robin.

He moaned again.

'She disappeared. D'you know——?'

Footsteps were coming along the corridor outside. Robin got up hastily and smoothed away the impression she'd left on the bedspread.

Please God, don't let them be coming in here.

But God, it seemed, wasn't listening to Robin Ellacott. The footsteps grew louder, and then the door opened to reveal a very tall man whose face was pitted with acne scars and whose knobbly bald head looked, as Barclay had said, as though something heavy had been dropped on it: Luca Ricci.

'Who're you?' he said. His voice, which was far softer and higher than she'd imagined, made the hairs on the back of her neck prickle. For a second or two, Robin's terror threatened to derail her carefully

worked out contingency plan. The very worst she'd expected to have
to deal with was a nurse. None of the Riccis should have been here;
it wasn't Sunday. And of all the Riccis she would have wanted to
meet, Luca was the last.

'You his relative?' Robin asked in her North London accent. 'Oh,
fank Gawd! He was making a weird moaning noise. I've just been
visiting my gran, I fort he was ill or somefing.'

Still standing in the doorway, Luca looked Robin up and down.

'He doesthn't mean anything by it,' said Luca, who had a lisp.
'He moanth a bit, but it don't mean nothing, do it, eh, Dad?' he said
loudly to the old man, who merely blinked at his eldest son.

Luca laughed.

'What'th your name?' he asked Robin.

'Vanessa,' she said promptly. 'Vanessa Jones.'

She took half a step forwards, hoping he'd move aside, but he
remained planted exactly where he was, though smiling a little more
widely. She knew he'd understood that she wanted to leave, but
couldn't tell whether his evident determination to keep her inside was
done for the simple pleasure of keeping her momentarily trapped, or
because he hadn't believed her reason for being in his father's room.
Robin could feel sweat under her armpits and over her scalp, and
hoped to God that her hair chalk wouldn't come off.

'Never theen you around here before,' said Luca.

'No, it's my first time,' said Robin, forcing herself to smile. 'They
look after 'em well, don't they?'

'Yeah,' said Luca, 'not bad. I usually come Thundayth, but we're off
to Florida tomorrow. Gonna mith hith birthday. Not that he knowth
it'th hith birthday – do you, eh?' he said, addressing his father, whose
mouth continued to hang open, his eyes fixed vacantly on his son.

Luca took a small wrapped package from under his jacket, leaned
over to the chest of drawers and laid it on top without moving his
large feet so much as an inch.

'Aw, that's nice,' said Robin.

She could feel the sweat on her breastbone now, where it would be
visible to Luca. The room was as warm as a greenhouse. Even had she
not known who Luca was, she'd have known *what* he was. She could

feel the potential for violence coming off him like radiation. It was in the greedy smile he was giving her, in the way he was now leaning up against the door jamb, revelling in the silent exercise of power.

'It'th only chocolateth,' said Luca. 'Who'th your granny?'

'Great-granny, really, but I call her "Gran",' Robin said, playing for time, trying to remember any of the names she'd passed on the way to Ricci's room. 'Sadie.'

'Where'th she?'

'Couple of rooms that way,' said Robin, pointing left. She hoped he couldn't hear how dry her mouth was. 'Promised my mum I'd pop in and visit her while she's on holiday.'

'Yeah?' said Luca. 'Where'th your Mum gone?'

'Florence,' Robin invented wildly. 'Art galleries.'

'Yeah?' said Luca again. 'Our family'th from Napleth, originally. Innit, Dad?' he called over Robin's head at the gaping old man, before looking Robin up and down again. 'Know what my old man uthed to be?'

'No,' said Robin, trying to maintain her smile.

'He owned thtrip clubth,' said Luca Ricci. 'Back in the old dayth, he'd've had your pantieth right off you.'

She tried to laugh, but couldn't, and saw that Luca was delighted to see her discomfort.

'Oh yeah. Girl like you? He'd've offered you a hothtess job. It wath good money, too, even if you did have to blow thome of Dad'th mateth, hahaha.'

His laugh was as high-pitched as a woman's. Robin couldn't join in. She was remembering Kara Wolfson.

'Well,' she said, feeling the sweat trickling down her neck, 'I really need—'

'Don't worry,' said Luca, smiling, still standing firmly between her and the door, '*I'm* not in that game.'

'What do you do?' asked Robin, who'd been on the verge of asking him to move aside, but lost her nerve.

'I'm in inthuranthe,' said Luca, smiling broadly. 'What about you?'

'Nursery nurse,' said Robin, taking the idea from the children's daubs on the wardrobe door.

'Yeah? Like kidth, do you?'

'I love them,' said Robin.

'Yeah,' said Luca. 'Me too. I got thix.'

'Wow,' said Robin. 'Six!'

'Yeah. And I'm not like him,' said Luca, looking over Robin's head again, at his gaping father. 'He wathn't interethted in uth until we were grown up. I like the littl'unth.'

'Oh, me too,' said Robin fervently.

'You needed to get knocked down by a car to get *hith* attention, when we were kidth,' said Luca. 'Happened to my brother Marco, when he wath twelve.'

'Oh no,' said Robin politely.

He was playing with her, demanding that she give him appropriate responses, while both of them were equally aware that she was too scared to ask him to move aside, afraid of what he might do. Now he smiled at her feigned concern for his brother Marco's long-ago car accident.

'Yeah, Dad thtayed at the hothpital with Marco for three weekth tholid, till Marco wath out of danger,' said Luca. 'At leatht, I think it wath Marco he wath thtaying for. Might've been the nurtheth. In the old dayth,' said Luca, looking Robin up and down again, 'they wore black thtockingth.'

Robin could hear footsteps again, and this time she prayed, *please be coming in here*, and her prayer was answered. The door behind Luca opened, hitting him in the back. The flat-footed blonde nurse was back.

'Oh, sorry, Mr Ricci,' she said, as Luca stepped aside. 'Oh,' she repeated, becoming aware of Robin's presence.

''E was moaning,' Robin said again, pointing at Mucky, in his chair. 'Sorry, I shouldn't've – I fort he might be in pain or something.'

And right on cue, Mucky Ricci moaned, almost certainly to contradict her.

'Yeah, he does a bit of that, if he wants something,' said the nurse. 'Probably ready for the bathroom now, are you, Mr Ricci?'

'I'm not thtaying to watch him crap,' said Luca Ricci, with a little laugh. 'I only came to drop off hith prethent for Thurthday.'

Robin was already halfway out of the door, but to her horror, she'd walked barely three steps when Luca appeared behind her, taking one stride to her every two.

'Not going to thay goodbye to Thadie?' he asked, as they passed the door of Mrs Sadie O'Keefe.

'Oh, she fell asleep while I was in there, bless her,' said Robin. 'Flat out.'

They walked down the stairs, Luca slightly behind her all the way. She could feel his eyes, like lasers, on the nape of her neck, on her legs and her backside.

After what felt like ten minutes, though it was barely three, they reached the ground floor. The almost life-size plaster Jesus looked sadly down upon the killer and the impostor as they headed towards the door. Robin had just placed her hand on the handle when Luca said,

'Hang on a moment, Vanetha.'

Robin turned, a pulse thrumming in her neck.

'You've got to thign out,' said Luca, holding out a pen to her.

'Oh, I forgot,' said Robin, with a breathless giggle. 'I told you – it's my first time here.'

She bent over the visitors' book. Directly below the signature she'd written on entering the building was Luca's.

LUCA RICCI

In the space left for 'Comments' he'd written,

BROUGHT HIM SOME CHOCOLATES FOR HIS BIRTHDAY ON THURSDAY. PLEASE GIVE HIM THEM ON THE MORNING OF THE 25TH JULY.

Robin scrawled the time beside her signature, then turned back to the door. He was holding it open for her.

'Fanks very much,' she said breathlessly, sidling past him into the fresh air.

'Give you a lift anywhere?' Luca asked her, pausing at the top of the steps to the street. 'My car'th round the corner. Athton Martin.'

'Oh, no, fanks very much, though,' said Robin. 'I'm meeting my boyfriend.'

'Be good, then,' said Luca Ricci. 'And if you can't be good, be thafe, hahaha.'

'Yes,' said Robin, a little wildly. 'Oh, and enjoy Florida!'

He raised a hand to her and began to walk away, whistling 'Begin the Beguine'. Light-headed with relief, Robin walked off in the opposite direction. It took the utmost restraint to stop herself breaking into a run.

Once she'd reached the square, she slid behind the lilac bush and watched the front of the nursing home for a full half an hour. Once she was certain that Luca Ricci had genuinely left, she doubled back.

62

Oftimes it haps, that sorrowes of the mynd
Find remedie vnsought, which seeking cannot fynd.

Edmund Spenser
The Faerie Queene

The row, for which Robin was braced, was one of the worst she and Strike had ever had. His fury that she'd approached Mucky Ricci, after his clear warnings and instructions not to, remained unabated even after a solid hour's argument in the office that evening, which culminated in Robin seizing her bag and walking out while Strike was mid-sentence, leaving him facing the vibrating glass door, wishing it had shattered, so he could bill her.

A night's sleep only slightly mitigated Strike's anger. Yes, there were major differences between Robin's actions this time, and those that had seen him sack her three years previously: she hadn't, for instance, spooked a suspect into hiding. Nor was there any indication, at least in the first twenty-four hours following her visit, that either the Ricci family or the nursing home suspected 'Vanessa Jones' of being anyone other than she'd claimed to be. Above all (but this fact rankled, rather than soothed), Robin was now a partner in the firm, rather than a lowly subcontractor. For the first time, Strike was brought up against the hard fact that if they ever parted ways, a legal and financial tangle would engulf him. It would, in fact, be akin to a divorce.

He didn't want to split from Robin, but his newly awakened awareness that he'd made it very difficult to do so increased his ire.

The atmosphere between them remained strained for a fortnight after her visit to St Peter's until, on the first morning in August, Robin received a terse text from Strike asking her to abandon her fresh attempt to befriend Shifty's PA, and come back to the office.

When she entered the inner room, she found Strike sitting at the partners' desk, with bits and pieces of the Bamborough police file laid out in front of him. He glanced up at her, noted that her eye and hair colour were her own, then said brusquely,

'The Shifty clients have just rung up. They've terminated the job, for lack of results.'

'Oh no,' said Robin, sinking into the chair opposite him. 'I'm sorry, I really tried with Shifty's PA—'

'And Anna and Kim want to talk to us. I've set up a conference call at four o'clock.'

'They aren't—?'

'Winding things up?' said Strike unemotionally. 'Probably. Apparently they've had a spur-of-the-moment invitation from a friend to join them on holiday in Tuscany. They want to talk to us before they go, because they'll still be away on the fifteenth.'

There was a long silence. Strike didn't appear to have anything else to say, but resumed his perusal of various bits of the case file.

'Cormoran,' said Robin.

'What?'

'Can we please talk about St Peter's?'

'I've said everything I've got to say,' said Strike, picking up Ruby Elliot's statement about the two women struggling together in the rain, and pretending to read it again.

'I don't mean about me *going* there. I've already said—'

'You said you wouldn't approach Ricci—'

'I "agreed" not to go near Ricci,' said Robin, sketching quotation marks in the air, 'just like you "agreed" with Gregory Talbot not to tell the police where you got that roll of film.' Hyperaware of Pat typing away in the outer office, Robin was speaking quietly. 'I didn't set out to *defy* you; I left him up to you, remember? But it needed doing, and you couldn't. In case you hadn't noticed, I'm a damn sight better than you are at disguising my appearance.'

'That's not in question,' said Strike, throwing aside Ruby Elliot's statement and picking up Gloria's description of Theo, instead. 'What bugs me, as you *bloody well know*, is that you didn't tell me you were going to—'

'D'you ring *me* every three seconds and tell me what you're going to do next? You're happy enough for me to work on my own initiative when it suits—'

'Luca Ricci's done time for putting electrodes on people's genitals, Robin!' said Strike, dropping the pretence that the description of Theo had his attention.

'How many times are we going to go over this? D'you think I was *pleased* when he walked in the room? I'd *never* have gone in there if I'd known he was about to make a surprise appearance! The fact remains—'

'—it's not a fact—'

'—if I hadn't—'

'—this theory—'

'*It isn't a bloody theory, Strike, it's reality, and you're just being pig-headed about it.*' Robin pulled her mobile out of her back pocket and brought up the photo she'd taken on her second visit to the nursing home, which had lasted barely two minutes, and involved her taking a quick, unwitnessed photograph of Luca Ricci's handwriting in the visitors' book.

'Give me the anonymous note,' she ordered Strike, holding out her hand for the piece of crumpled blue paper they'd taken away from their meeting with the Bayliss sisters. '*There.*'

She set them side by side, facing Strike. To Robin, the similarities were undeniable: the same odd mixture of capital and lower-case letters, all distinct and separate, but with odd and unnecessary little flourishes, rather like the incongruous lisp of a tall, dangerous-looking man whose skin was as pitted as a partly peeled orange.

'You can't prove it's the same writing from a photograph,' said Strike. He knew he was being ungracious, but his anger wasn't yet fully spent. 'Expert analysis relies on pen pressure, apart from anything else.'

'OK, fine,' said Robin, who now had a hard, angry lump in her throat. She got up and walked out, leaving the door slightly ajar. Through the gap, Strike heard her talking to Pat, followed by the tinkle of mugs. Annoyed though he was, he still hoped she was going to get him a cup of tea, as well.

Frowning slightly, he pulled Robin's mobile and the anonymous note towards him and looked again from one to the other. She was right, and he'd known, though not acknowledged it, from the moment she'd shown him the picture on her phone, on her return from St Peter's. Though he hadn't told Robin so, Strike had forwarded a picture of both the anonymous note and Luca Ricci's visitors' book message to an expert handwriting analyst he'd reached through his police contacts. The woman had expressed caution about reaching a hard and fast conclusion without having the original samples in front of her, but said that, on the evidence, she was 'seventy to eighty per cent certain' that both had been written by the same person.

'Does handwriting remain that consistent, forty years apart?' Strike asked.

'Not always,' the expert replied. 'You expect changes, typically. Mostly, people's handwriting deteriorates with age because of physical factors. Mood can have an influence, too. My research tends to show that handwriting alters least in people who write infrequently, compared with those who write a lot. Occasional writers seem to stick with the style they adopted early, possibly in school. In the case of these two samples, there are certainly distinctive features that seem to have hung around from youth.'

'I think it's fair to say this guy doesn't write a lot in his line of work,' said Strike.

Luca's last spell in jail, as Shanker had told him, had been for ordering and overseeing a stabbing. The victim had been knifed in the balls. By a miracle, he'd survived, 'but 'e won't be 'avin' any more kids, poor cunt,' Shanker had informed Strike, two nights previously. 'Can't get a fuckin' 'ard-on wivvout agony. Not worf living, is it, after that? The knife sliced straight through the right bollock, I 'eard – course, they 'ad him pinned down—'

'No need for details,' Strike had said. He'd just experienced a nasty sensation radiating out of his own balls up to his chest.

Strike had called Shanker on some slight pretext, purely to see whether any rumour had reached his old friend of Luca Ricci being concerned that a female detective had turned up in his father's nursing home. As Shanker hadn't mentioned anything, Strike had to conclude that no such whispers were abroad.

While this was a relief, it wasn't really a surprise. Once he'd calmed down, Strike had been forced to admit to himself that he was sure Robin had got away with it. Everything Strike knew about Luca Ricci suggested he'd never have let her walk away unscathed if he'd believed she was there to investigate any member of his family. The kinds of people whose darkest impulses were kept in check by their own consciences, the dictates of the law, by social norms and common sense might find it hard to believe anyone would be so foolish or reckless as to hurt Robin inside a nursing home bedroom, or march her out of the building with a knife to her back. *He wouldn't do it in broad daylight*, they'd say. *He wouldn't dare, with witnesses all around!* But Luca's fearsome reputation rested on his propensity for brazen violence, no matter where he was, or who was watching. He operated on an assumption of impunity, for which he had much justification. For every prison term he'd served, there'd been many incidents that should have seen him convicted, but which he'd managed to escape by intimidating witnesses, or terrifying others into taking the rap.

Robin returned to the inner office, stony-faced, but carrying two mugs of tea. She pushed the door closed with her foot, then set down the darker of the two teas in front of Strike.

'Thanks,' muttered Strike.

'You're welcome,' she replied stiffly, checking her watch as she sat down again. They had twenty minutes to go, before the conference call with Anna and Kim.

'We can't,' said Strike, 'tell Anna we think Luca Ricci wrote the anonymous notes.'

Robin simply looked at him.

'We can't have two nice middle-class women walking around telling people Ricci threatened Margot, and maybe killed her,' said Strike. 'We'd be putting them in danger, quite apart from ourselves.'

'Can't we at least show the samples to an expert?'

'I have,' said Strike, and he explained what the woman had said.

'Why didn't you tell—?'

'Because I was still bloody angry,' said Strike, sipping his tea. It was exactly the way he liked it, strong, sweet and the colour of creosote. 'Robin, the reality is, if we take the photo and the note to the police, whether or not anything comes of it, you'll have painted a giant target on your back. Ricci'll start digging around on who could have photographed his handwriting in that visitors' book. It won't take him long to find us.'

'He was twenty-two when Margot went missing,' said Robin quietly. 'Old enough and big enough to abduct a woman. He had contacts to help with the disposal of a body. Betty Fuller thought the person who wrote the notes was the killer, and she's still scared of telling us who it was. That could imply the son, just as well as the father.'

'I grant you all that,' said Strike, 'but it's time for a reality check. We haven't got the resources to go up against organised criminals. You going to St Peter's was reckless enough—'

'Could you explain to me why it was reckless when I did it, but not when you were planning to do it?' said Robin.

Strike was momentarily stymied.

'Because I'm less experienced?' said Robin. 'Because you think I'll mess it up, or panic? Or that I can't think on my feet?'

'None of those,' said Strike, though it cost him some pain to admit it.

'Well then—'

'Because my chances of surviving if Luca Ricci comes at me with a baseball bat are superior to yours, OK?'

'But Luca doesn't come at people with baseball bats,' said Robin reasonably. 'He comes at them with knives, electrodes and acid, and I don't see how you'd withstand any of them better than I would. The truth is, you're happy to take risks you don't want me to take. I don't know whether it's lack of confidence in me, or chivalry, or one dressed up as the other—'

'Look—'

'No, *you* look,' said Robin. 'If you'd been recognised in there, the whole agency would have paid the price. I've read up on Ricci, I'm not stupid. He goes for people's families and associates and even their *pets* as often as he goes for them personally. Like it or not, there are places I can go more easily than you. I'm less distinctive-looking, I'm easier to disguise, and people trust women more than men, especially around kids and old people. We wouldn't know *any* of this if I hadn't gone to St Peter's—'

'We'd be better off not knowing it,' Strike snapped back. 'Shanker said to me months back, "If Mucky's the answer, you need to stop asking the question." Same goes for Luca, in spades.'

'You don't mean that,' said Robin. 'I know you don't. You'd never choose not to know.'

She was right, but Strike didn't want to admit it. Indeed, one of the things that had kept his anger simmering for the past two weeks was that he knew there was a fundamental lack of logic in his own position. If trying to get information on the Ricci family had been worth doing at all, it should have been done, and as Robin had proven, she'd been the best person for the job. While he resented the fact that she hadn't warned him what she was about to do, he knew perfectly well that if she'd done so, he'd have vetoed it, out of a fundamentally indefensible desire to keep her out of harm's way, when the logical conclusion of that line of thinking was that she oughtn't to be doing this job at all. He wanted her to be open and direct with him, but knew that his own incoherent position on her taking physical risks was the reason she hadn't been honest about her intentions. The long scar on her forearm reproached him every time he looked at it, even though the mistake that had led to the attack had been entirely her own. He knew too much about her past; the relationship had become too personal: he didn't want to visit her in hospital again. He felt precisely that irksome sense of responsibility that kept him determinedly single, but without any of the compensatory pleasures. None of this was her fault, but it had taken a fortnight for him to look these facts clearly in the face.

'OK,' he muttered at last. 'I wouldn't choose not to know.' He made a supreme effort. 'You did bloody well.'

'Thank you,' said Robin, as startled as she was gratified.

'Can we agree, though – please? That in future, we talk these things through?'

'If I'd asked you—'

'Yeah, I might've said no, and I'd've been wrong, and I'll bear that in mind next time, OK? But as you keep reminding me, we're partners, so I'd be grateful—'

'All right,' said Robin. 'Yes. We'll discuss it. I'm sorry I didn't.'

At that moment, Pat knocked on the door and opened it a few inches.

'I've got a Ms Phipps and a Ms Sullivan on the line for you.'

'Put them through, please,' said Strike.

Feeling as though she was sitting in on the announcement of bad medical news, Robin let Strike do the talking to Anna and Kim. He took the couple systematically through every interview the agency had conducted over the past eleven and a half months, telling them the secrets he and Robin had unearthed, and the tentative conclusions they'd drawn.

He revealed that Irene Hickson had been briefly involved with Margot's ex-boyfriend, and that both had lied about it, and explained that Satchwell might have been worried that Margot would tell the authorities about the way his sister died; that Wilma the cleaner had never set foot in Broom House, and that the story of Roy walking was almost certainly false; that the threatening notes had been real, but (with a glance at Robin) that they hadn't managed to identify the writer; that Joseph Brenner had been a more unsavoury character than anyone had realised, but that there was nothing to tie him to Margot's disappearance; that Gloria Conti, the last person to see Margot alive, was living in France, and didn't want to talk to them; and that Steve Douthwaite, Margot's suspicious patient, had vanished without trace. Lastly, he told them that they believed they'd identified the van seen speeding away from Clerkenwell Green on the night that Margot disappeared, and were confident that it hadn't been Dennis Creed's.

The only sound to break the silence when Strike first stopped talking was the soft buzzing emitted by the speaker on his desk, which proved the line was still open. Waiting for Anna to speak, Robin suddenly realised that her eyes were full of tears. She'd so very much wanted to find out what had happened to Margot Bamborough.

'Well . . . we knew it would be difficult,' said Anna at last. 'If not impossible.'

Robin could tell that Anna was crying, too. She felt wretched.

'I'm sorry,' said Strike formally. 'Very sorry, not to have better news for you. However, Douthwaite remains of real interest, and—'

'No.'

Robin recognised Kim's firm negative.

'No, I'm sorry,' said the psychologist. 'We agreed a year.'

'We're actually two weeks short,' said Strike, 'and if—'

'Have you got any reason to believe you can find Steve Douthwaite in the next two weeks?'

Strike's slightly bloodshot eyes met Robin's wet ones.

'No,' he admitted.

'As I said in my email, we're about to go on holiday,' said Kim. 'In the absence of actually finding Margot's body, there was always bound to be another angle you could try, one more person who might know something, and as I said at the start of this, we haven't got the money, or, frankly, the emotional stamina, to keep this going for ever. I think it's better – cleaner – if we accept that you've done your best, and thank you for the trouble you've clearly taken. This has been a worthwhile exercise, even if – I mean, Anna and Roy's relationship's better than it's been in years, thanks to your visit. He'll be glad to hear that the cleaner accepted he wasn't able to walk that day.'

'Well, that's good,' said Strike. 'I'm only sorry—'

'I knew,' said Anna, her voice wavering, 'that it was going to be . . . almost impossible. At least I know I tried.'

After Anna had hung up, there was a silence in the room. Finally Strike said 'Need a pee', pulled himself up and left the room.

Robin got up, too, and began to gather together the photocopied pages from the police file. She couldn't believe it was all over. Having put the records into a neat pile, she sat down and began to flick through them one more time, knowing that she was hoping to see something – anything – they'd overlooked.

From Gloria Conti's statement to Lawson:

She was a short, dark, stocky woman who looked like a gypsy. I judged her to be in her teens. She came in alone and said she was in a lot of pain. She said her name was Theo. I didn't catch her surname and I didn't ask her to repeat it because I thought she needed urgent attention. She was clutching her abdomen. I told her to wait and I went to ask Dr Brenner if he'd see her, because Dr Bamborough was still with patients.

From Ruby Elliot's statement to Talbot:

I saw them beside a telephone box, two women sort of struggling together. The tall one in the raincoat was leaning on the short one, who wore a plastic rain hood. They looked like women to me, but I didn't see their faces. It looked to me like one was trying to make the other walk quicker.

From Janice Beattie's statement to Lawson:

I've been on speaking terms with Mr Douthwaite since he was assaulted at the flats, but I wouldn't call him a friend. He did tell me how upset he was his friend had killed herself. He told me he had headaches. I thought it was tension. I know he grew up in foster care, but he never told me the names of any of his foster mothers. He never talked to me about Dr Bamborough except to say he'd gone to her about his headaches. He didn't tell me he was leaving Percival House. I don't know where he's gone.

From Irene Hickson's second statement to Lawson:

The attached receipt proves that I was in Oxford Street on the afternoon in question. I deeply regret not being honest about my whereabouts, but I was ashamed of lying to get the afternoon off.

And beneath the statement was the photocopy of Irene's receipt: Marks & Spencer, three items, which came to a total of £4.73.

From Joseph Brenner's statement to Talbot:

I left the practice at my usual time, having promised my sister that I'd be home in time for dinner. Dr Bamborough kindly agreed to see the emergency patient, as she had a later appointment with a friend in the area. I have no idea whether Dr Bamborough had personal troubles. Our relationship was entirely professional. I have no knowledge of anyone who wanted to do her harm. I remember one of her patients sending her a small box of chocolates, although I can't say for certain that it was from Steven Douthwaite. I don't know Mr Douthwaite. I remember Dr Bamborough seemed displeased when Dorothy handed the chocolates to her, and asked Gloria, the receptionist, to throw them straight in the bin, although she later took them back out of the bin. She had a very sweet tooth.

Strike re-entered the office and dropped a five-pound note onto the table in front of Robin.

'What's that for?'

'We had a bet,' he said, 'about whether they'd extend the year if we had any outstanding leads. I said they would. You said they wouldn't.'

'I'm not taking that,' said Robin, leaving the fiver where it lay. 'There are still two more weeks.'

'They've just—'

'They've paid till the end of the month. I'm not stopping.'

'Did I not make myself clear just now?' said Strike, frowning down at her. 'We're leaving Ricci.'

'I know,' said Robin.

She checked her watch again.

'I'm supposed to be taking over from Andy in an hour. I'd better go.'

After Robin had left, Strike returned the photocopied papers to the boxes of old police records that still lay underneath the desk, then went out into the office where Pat sat, electronic cigarette between her teeth as always.

'We've lost two clients,' he told her. 'Who's next on the waiting list?'

'That footballer,' said Pat, bringing up the encrypted file on her monitor to show Strike a well-known name. 'And if you want to replace both of them, there's that posh woman who's got the chihuahua.'

Strike hesitated.

'We'll just take the footballer for now. Can you ring his assistant and say I'm available to take details any time tomorrow?'

'It's Saturday,' said Pat.

'I know,' said Strike. 'I work weekends and I doubt he'll want anyone to see him coming in here. Say I'm happy to go to his place.'

He returned to the inner office and pushed up the window, allowing the afternoon air, heavy with exhaust fumes and London's particular smell of warm brick, soot and, today, a faint trace of leaves, trees and grass, to permeate the office. Tempted to light up, he restrained himself out of deference to Pat, because he'd asked her not to smoke in the office. Clients these days were nearly all non-smokers and he felt it gave a poor impression to have the place reeking like an ashtray. He leaned on the windowsill and watched the Friday-night drinkers and shoppers walking up and down Denmark Street, half-listening to Pat's conversation with the Premier League footballer's assistant, but mostly thinking about Margot Bamborough.

He'd known all along there was only the remotest chance of find-ing out what had happened to her, but where had fifty weeks gone? He remembered all the time spent with Joan in Cornwall, and the other clients who'd come and gone, and asked himself if they might have found out what had happened to Margot Bamborough if none of these things had got in the way. Tempting though it was to blame distractions, he believed the outcome would have been the same. Perhaps Luca Ricci was the answer they weren't ever going to be able to admit. A plausible answer, in many ways: a professional hit, done for some inscrutable underworld reason, because Margot had got too close to a secret, or interfered in the gangsters' business. *Leave my girl alone* ... she'd been the type to advise a stripper, or a hooker, or a porn actress, or an addict, to choose a different life, to give evidence against men who abused her ...

'Eleven tomorrow,' rasped Pat, from behind Strike. 'At 'is place. I've left his address on the desk for you.'

'Thanks very much,' he said, turning to see her already in her coat. It was five o'clock. She looked vaguely surprised to hear his thanks, but ever since Robin had shouted at him for being rude to Pat, Strike had been consciously trying to be politer to the secretary. For a moment she hesitated, electronic cigarette between her yellow teeth, then removed it to say,

'Robin told me what that Morris did. What he sent her.'

'Yeah,' said Strike. 'Sleazy bastard.'

'Yeah,' said Pat. She was scrutinising him closely, as though seeing things she hadn't ever expected to find. ''Orrible. And 'e always reminded me,' she said surprisingly, 'of a young Mel Gibson.'

'Really?' said Strike.

'Funny fing, looks,' she said. 'You make assumptions.'

'I s'pose,' said Strike.

'You've got a real look of my first 'usband,' Pat told him.

'Is that right?' said Strike, startled.

'Yeah. Well ... I'll be off. 'Ave a good weekend.'

'You too,' said Strike.

He waited until her footsteps had died away on the metal staircase, before pulling out his cigarettes, lighting one and returning to the inner office, where the window was still open. Here, he took an old ashtray out of the desk drawer and Talbot's leather notebook out of the top drawer of the filing cabinet, and settled down in his usual chair to flick through it once more, stopping at the final page.

Strike had never given Talbot's final jottings more than cursory attention, partly because his patience had run out by the time he got there, partly they were among the most shambolic and incoherent parts of the notes. Tonight, though, he had a melancholy reason for examining the last page of Talbot's notebook, because Strike, too, had come to the end of the case. So he examined Talbot's drawing of the demon he believed he'd conjured before the ambulance came

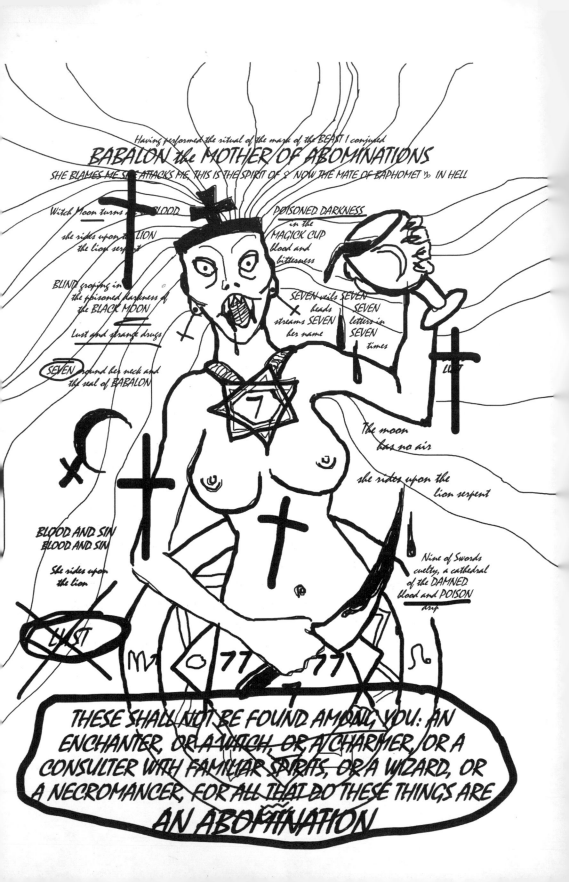

to take him away: the spirit of Margot Bamborough, returned from some astral plane to haunt him in the form of Babalon, the Mother of Abominations.

There was no pressure to understand any more. Strike defocused his mind as he'd have relaxed his eyes, the better to spot one of those apparently three-dimensional images hidden in what appeared to be a flat pattern. His eyes glided over the phrases and fragments Talbot had half-remembered from Crowley's writings, and of consultation of the Thoth tarot. As he scrutinised the picture of the heavy-breasted demon, on whose belly the penitent Talbot had subsequently inscribed a Christian cross, he remembered Robin's words all those months previously in Hampton Court Palace, about the allure of myth and symbol, and the idea of the collective unconscious, where archetypes lurked. This demon, and the disconnected phrases that had seemed pertinent to Talbot in his psychotic state, had sprung from the policeman's own subconscious: it was too easy, too simplistic, to blame Crowley and Lévi for what Talbot's own mind had chosen to retain. This was what it generated, in a last spasm of madness, in a final attempt at resolution. *Seven veils, seven heads, seven streams. Lust and strange drugs. Seven around her neck. The poisoned darkness of the BLACK MOON. Blood and sin. She rides upon the lion serpent.*

Strike bent the lamp closer to the page, so that he could scrutinise the drawing more closely. Was he deluding himself, or did some of these crazy jottings indicate that Talbot had noticed the odd coincidences that Strike had, after talking to the Bayliss sisters? As his gaze moved from one fragment of mystic writing to another, Strike thought he saw, not just a penitent churchgoer trying to make amends for his descent into witchcraft, but the last desperate effort of a good detective, trying to salvage clues from chaos, sense from madness.

63

At last resoluing forward still to fare,
Till that some end they finde or in or out,
That path they take, that beaten seemd most bare,
And like to lead the labyrinth about . . .

Edmund Spenser
The Faerie Queene

Over the next couple of weeks, Robin noticed that *Astrology 14* by Steven Schmidt, the second-hand book she'd left at the office, kept changing position. One morning it was on top of the filing cabinet where she'd left it, a few days later on Strike's half of the desk, and the following evening lying beside the kettle. Similarly, various bits of the Bamborough police records kept appearing, then disappearing again, while Bill Talbot's leather-bound notebook had vanished from the filing cabinet and, she suspected, made its way upstairs to Strike's attic flat.

The agency was once again very busy. The new client, a Premier League footballer, had sunk two million pounds into a proposed nightclub which had failed to materialise. His partner in the venture had now disappeared, along with all the money. The footballer, nick-named Dopey by an unsympathetic Barclay, feared press exposure almost as much as not getting his cash back.

Meanwhile, Miss Jones's boyfriend continued to live a frustrat-ingly law-abiding life, but she appeared happy to keep paying the agency's bills, as long as Strike endured twice-weekly phone calls with her. During these supposed catch-ups, she told Strike all her

problems, and hinted broadly that a dinner invitation would be happily accepted.

In addition to these clients, and leapfrogging those on the waiting
list, was Shifty's Boss, who'd been forced into early retirement by the
board. SB walked in off Denmark Street one morning looking for
Barclay, who'd left his contact details with Elinor Dean. To Strike's
surprise, early retirement seemed not to have spurred SB into despair,
but liberated him.

'If you can believe it, I was genuinely thinking of killing myself,
just a few months back,' he told Strike. 'But I'm out from under that
bastard's thumb now. Now I've told my wife about Elinor—'

'Told her, have you?' said Strike, surprised.

'And she's been very understanding,' said SB. 'In my previous marriage, my – well, my needs – were taken care of by my ex-wife, but
since we split . . . anyway, Portia and I have talked it all through, and
she's perfectly happy for my arrangement with Elinor to continue,
as long as there's no infidelity.'

Strike hid his expression behind his mug. He could well imagine
that Portia, with her inch-long nails and her professional blow-dries,
her thrice-yearly holidays, her black American Express card and her
six-bedroomed house with swimming pool in West Brompton, preferred someone else to change SB's nappy.

'No, all I want *now*,' said SB, his satisfied smile replaced by a hard
glare, 'is to make sure that shifty bastard gets what's coming to him.
And I'm prepared to pay.'

So the agency had resumed surveillance on both Shifty and
his PA.

The upshot of three demanding cases meant that most of the communication between the two partners was done by phone for the rest
of the month. Their paths finally crossed one Thursday afternoon
in late August, when Strike entered the office as Robin was about
to leave it.

Pat, who was listening to the radio while paying a slew of bills,
offered to turn it off on seeing Strike, whose attention had just been
caught by the figure-hugging blue dress Robin was wearing.

'No, it's fine,' he said. 'Nice to hear some music.'

'Cormoran, can I have a quick word before I go?' Robin asked, beckoning him into the inner office.

'... next up, in our hundred hits of the seventies, an oldie but goodie from one-hit-wonder Middle of the Road: "Chirpy Chirpy Cheep Cheep ..."'

'Where're you off to?' said Strike, closing the internal door on Pat. He'd spent most of the previous night on his feet, watching Shifty get drunk and coked up in a nightclub, and today driving between the various addresses Dopey's business partner had used over the previous two years. Unshaven and aching all over, he grunted in relief as he sank into his usual chair.

'The Vintry. Wine bar in the City,' said Robin. 'Gemma's going to be there later, Andy heard her arranging it. I'm hoping she's with girlfriends. I'm going to try and infiltrate the group somehow.'

Gemma was Shifty's PA. Through the closed door they now heard strains of a jaunty song playing on the radio, with its incongruous lyric,

'*Where's your mamma gone?*'

'You're still working on Bamborough, aren't you?' Robin asked.

'Just going back over a few things,' Strike admitted.

'And?'

'And nothing. It's like a maze. Moment I start thinking I'm getting somewhere, I turn a corner and come up against a dead end. Or find myself back where I started. Why are you looking so pleased?'

'I'm just glad you haven't given up,' said Robin.

'You won't say that when they cart me off to the same asylum as Bill Talbot. If I never see another fucking star sign, it'll be too soon ... Where the *hell* is Douthwaite? What happened to him?'

'You think—?'

'I think he's bloody fishy, I always did. His alibi amounts to fuck all. Then he changes his name. Then, as you found out, another young woman dies in his vicinity – that drowned Redcoat. Then he vanishes again.

'If I could just speak to Douthwaite,' said Strike, drumming his fingers on the desk, 'I'd give it up.'

'Really?' said Robin.

He glanced at her, then, frowning, looked away. She was looking particularly sexy in that blue dress, which he'd never seen before.

'Yeah, if I could speak to Douthwaite, that'd do me.'

'Last night I heard my mamma singing a song . . .'

'And maybe Gloria Conti,' said Strike.

'Woke up this morning, and my mamma was gone . . .'

'And Creed,' said Strike. 'I'd like to talk to Dennis Creed.'

Robin felt a little skip of excitement. She'd received an email earlier, telling her to expect a decision by the end of the day on whether or not Creed could be re-interviewed.

'I'd better get going,' she said. 'Gemma's supposed to be there at six. It was nice of you,' she added, as she reached for the door handle, 'to let Pat keep the radio on.'

'Yeah, well,' said Strike, with a shrug. 'Trying to be friendly.'

As Robin was putting on her coat in the outer office, Pat said,

'That's a very good colour on you.'

'Thanks. It's quite old. Miracle it still fits, all the chocolate I've been eating lately.'

'Would he like a cuppa, d'you think?'

'I'm sure he would,' said Robin, surprised. Apparently Strike wasn't the only one who was trying to be friendly.

'Oooh, I used to love this,' said Pat, as the opening bars of 'Play That Funky Music' filled the office, and as Robin walked down the stairs, she heard Pat singing along, in her raspy baritone:

> *Once I was a funky singer,*
> *Playin' in a rock and roll band . . .*

The Vintry, which Robin reached twenty minutes later, lay near Cannon Street Tube station in the heart of the financial district, and was precisely the kind of place her ex-husband had most enjoyed. Undemandingly modern in a conventional, high-spec manner, with its sleek mixture of steel beams, large windows and wooden floors, it had a hint of open-plan office about it, in spite of the long bar with padded stools. There was the odd quirky touch, such as the two stuffed rabbits on a windowsill, which carried model guns and wore shooting caps, but in the main the clientele, which consisted overwhelmingly of men in suits, were cocooned in an atmosphere of tasteful beige blandness. They stood in cliques, fresh from the day's work, drinking, laughing together, reading newspapers or their phones, or eyeing up the few female customers – to Robin they seemed to exude not just confidence, but self-satisfaction. She received a number of appreciative looks as she sidled between stockbrokers, bankers and traders on her way to the bar.

Looking carefully around the large open-plan area, Robin gathered that Gemma hadn't yet arrived, so she took a free bar stool, ordered a tonic water and pretended to be reading the day's news off her phone, purely to avoid the open staring of the two young men to her right, one of whom seemed determined to make Robin look up, if only to ascertain where the annoying, braying laugh was coming from. To her left, a pair of older men were discussing the imminent Scottish independence referendum.

'Polls are looking shaky,' said the first man. 'Hope Cameron knows what he's doing.'

'They'd be bloody mad to do it. Mad.'

'There's opportunity in madness – for a few, anyway,' said the first man. 'I remember, when I was in Hong Kong – oh, I think that's our table free ...'

The two speakers departed for their dinner. Robin glanced around again, carefully avoiding meeting the eyes of the young man with the braying laugh, and a patch of scarlet at the far end of the bar caught her eye. Gemma had arrived, and was standing alone, trying to catch the barman's eye. Robin slid off her bar stool, and carried her drink over to Gemma, whose long dark hair fell in gypsyish curls to the middle of her back.

'Hi – Linda?'

'What?' said Gemma, startled. 'No, sorry.'

'Oh,' said Robin, looking crestfallen. 'Maybe I've got the wrong bar. Has this place got other branches?'

'I've no idea, sorry,' said Gemma, still with her hand raised, trying to attract the barman's attention.

'She said she'd be wearing red,' said Robin, looking around at the sea of suits.

Gemma glanced at Robin, mildly interested.

'Blind date?'

'I wish,' said Robin, rolling her eyes. 'No, it's a friend of a friend who thinks there might be an opening at Winfrey and Hughes. The woman said she'd meet me for a quick drink.'

'Winfrey and Hughes? That's where I work.'

'You're kidding!' said Robin, with a laugh. 'Hey – you're not really Linda, are you? And pretending to be someone different, because you don't like the look of me or something?'

'No,' said the other woman, smiling. 'I'm Gemma.'

'Oh. Are you meeting someone, or—?'

'S'posed to be,' said Gemma, 'yeah.'

'D'you mind me sitting here with you? Just till they arrive? I was getting some properly lechy looks over there.'

'Tell me about it,' said Gemma, as Robin climbed up onto the barstool beside her. The barman now approached a pinstriped, grey-haired man who'd just arrived.

'Oi,' Robin called, and half a dozen businessmen's heads turned, as well as the barman's. 'She was here first,' said Robin, pointing sideways at Gemma, who laughed again.

'Wow. *You* don't mess around, do you?'

'No point, is there?' said Robin, taking a sip of her water. She'd subtly broadened her Yorkshire accent, as she often did when pretending to be a bolder, brasher character than she really felt herself to be. 'Gotta take charge, or they'll walk all bloody over you.'

'You're not wrong there,' sighed Gemma.

'Winfrey and Hughes isn't like that, is it?' said Robin. 'Full of tossers?'

'Well . . . '

The barman arrived at that moment to take Gemma's order. Once the PA had her large glass of red wine, she took a swig and said,

'It's OK, actually. Depends which bit you're working in. I'm PA to one of the high-ups. The work's interesting.'

'Nice guy?' asked Robin casually.

Gemma drank several mouthfuls of wine before saying,

'He's ... all right. Devil you know, isn't it? I like the job and the company. I've got a great salary and a ton of friends there ... oh damn—'

Her handbag had slipped off the barstool. As Gemma bent to retrieve it, Robin, whose eyes had roamed across the vista of cream, grey and beige in front of her, suddenly spotted Saul Morris.

He'd just walked into the bar, wearing a suit, an open-necked shirt and a remarkably smug smile. He glanced around, picked out Gemma and Robin by the bright colours of their dresses, and froze. For a second or two, he and Robin simply stared at each other; then Morris turned abruptly and hurried back out of the bar.

Gemma settled herself back onto her barstool, bag safely on her lap. The mobile phone she'd left lying on the counter now lit up.

'Andy?' said Gemma, answering quickly. 'Yeah ... no, I'm here already ...'

There was a long silence. Robin could hear Morris's voice. He was using the same wheedling tone in which he'd tried to talk her into bed, with all those puerile jokes and have-I-upset-yous.

'Fine,' said Gemma, her expression hardening. 'Fine. I just ... I'm going to take your number off my phone now and I'd like you ... no, actually, I ... oh just *fuck off*!'

She hung up, flushed, her lips trembling.

'Why,' she said, 'do they always want to be told they're still nice guys, after they've been total shits?'

'Often wondered that meself,' said Yorkshire Robin. 'Boyfriend?'

'Yeah,' said the shaken Gemma. 'For six months. Then he just stands me up one night, with no explanation. *Then* he comes back a couple of times – booty calls, basically,' she said, taking another big swig of wine. 'And finally he just ghosts me. I texted him yesterday, I said, look, I just wanna meet, just want an explanation—'

'Sounds like a right twat,' said Robin, whose heart was racing with excitement at this perfect opportunity to have a heart-to-heart. 'Hey,' she called to the barman, 'can we have a couple more wines and a menu, please?'

And after that, Robin found getting confidences out of Gemma as easy as shelling peas. With three large glasses of wine inside her, and her new friend from Yorkshire being so funny, supportive and understanding, a plate of chicken and polenta to eat, and a bottle of wine ('Yeah, why the hell not?'), she moved seamlessly from the misdemeanours of 'Andy' to the inappropriate and unsolicited groping by her boss that had escalated until she was on the verge of quitting.

'Can't you go to HR?' asked Robin.

'He says nobody'll believe me because of what happened when we were on a course last year ... although ... To tell you the truth, I don't really know *what* happened,' said Gemma, and looking away from Robin she mumbled, 'I mean ... we had sex ... but I was so out of it ... so drunk ... I mean, it wasn't, you know ... it wasn't *rape* ... I'm not saying *that* ... '

'Were you in a fit state to give consent?' said Robin, no longer laughing. She'd only drunk half a glass of wine.

'Well, not ... but ... no, I'm not putting myself through *that*,' said Gemma, flushed and tearful. 'Not the police and everything, God no ... he's a big shot, he could afford great lawyers ... an' if I didn't win, how'm I gonna get another job in the City? ... Court, and the papers ... anyway, it's too late now ... people saw me ... coming out of his room. I pretended it was all OK. I had to, I was so embarrassed ... rumour mill's been in overdrive since. We both denied anything happened, so how would it look if I ...

'Andy told me I shouldn't report it,' said Gemma, pouring the last of the bottle into her glass.

'Did he?'

'Yeah ... I told him about it, firs' time we had sex ... see, it was the firs' time I'd slept with anyone since ... and he said, "Yeah, you'll want to keep that quiet ... be loads of grief for you, an' he'll probably get off" ... He was ex-police, Andy, he knew all about that kind of thing.'

You total shit, Morris.

'No, if I was going to tell about *anything*,' said Gemma, hazily, 'it'd be the insider bloody trading ... Oh yeah ... nobody knows 'cept me ... '

One hour later, Robin and Gemma emerged into the darkening

street, Robin almost holding Gemma up, because she showed a tendency to sag if unsupported. After a ten-minute wait, she succeeded in flagging down a taxi, and loaded the very drunk Gemma into it.

'Le's go out Saturday!' Gemma called to Robin, trying to stop her closing the door.

'Fantastic!' said Robin, who'd given the PA a fake number. 'Ring me!'

'Yeah, I will ... thanks so much for dinner!'

'No problem!' said Robin, and she succeeded at last in slamming the door on Gemma, who waved at her until the cab turned the corner.

Robin turned away and walked quickly back past the Vintry. A young man in a suit wolf-whistled as she passed.

'Oh bugger off,' muttered Robin, pulling out her phone to call Strike.

To her surprise, she saw she'd missed seven calls from him. She'd also received an email whose subject line read: Creed.

'Oh my God,' said Robin out loud.

She sped up, wanting to get away from the hordes of suited men still walking the streets, to be alone and able to concentrate. Retreating at last into the dark doorway of a grey stone office block, she opened the email. After reading it through three times, to make absolutely sure her eyes weren't deceiving her, she called Strike back.

'There you are!' he said, answering on the first ring. 'Guess what?'

'What?'

'I've found Douthwaite!'

'You've *what*?' gasped Robin, attracting the startled attention of a sober-looking City gent shuffling past in the dark, holding a tightly furled umbrella. '*How?*'

'Names,' said Strike, who sound elated. 'And Pat listening to hits of the seventies.'

'I don't—'

'He called himself Jacks first time, right? Well, Terry Jacks had a massive hit with a song called "Seasons in the Sun" in '74. They played it this afternoon. We know Douthwaite fancied himself a singer, so I thought, bet that's where he got the idea for "Jacks" ...'

Robin could hear Strike pacing. He was evidently as excited as she felt.

'So then I went back to Oakden's book. He said Douthwaite's "Longfellow Serenade" was a particular hit with the ladies. I looked it up. That was one of Neil Diamond's. So then,' said Strike, 'I start Googling Steve Diamond . . .

'I'm about to text you a picture,' said Strike. 'Stand by.'

Robin took the phone away from her ear and waited. Within a few seconds, the text arrived, and she opened the accompanying picture.

A sweaty, red-faced, balding man in his sixties was singing into a microphone. He wore a turquoise T-shirt stretched over a sizeable belly. A chain still hung around his neck, but the only other resemblance to the picture of the spiky-haired, cheeky chap in his kipper tie were the eyes, which were as dark and bright as ever.

'It's him,' Robin said.

'That picture came off the website of a pub in Skegness,' said Strike. 'He's still a karaoke king and he co-owns and runs a bed and breakfast up there, with his wife Donna. I wonder,' said Strike, 'whether she realises his name hasn't always been Diamond?'

'This is *amazing*!' said Robin, so jubilant that she began to walk down the street again, purely to use the energy now surging through her. 'You're brilliant!'

'I know,' said Strike, with a trace of smugness. 'So, we're going to Skegness. Tomorrow.'

'I'm supposed to be—'

'I've changed the rota,' said Strike. 'Can you pick me up early? Say, eight o'clock? I'll come out to Earl's Court.'

'Definitely,' said Robin.

'Then I'll see you—'

'Wait,' said Robin.

'Oh, shit, yeah,' said Strike politely. 'Should've asked. How'd it go with Gemma?'

'Great,' said Robin. 'Shifty's insider trading, but never mind that now.'

'He's—?'

'Strike, I don't want to upstage you or anything,' she said, failing to suppress the note of triumph in her voice, 'because finding Douthwaite's incredible, but I think you ought to know ... you're going to be allowed to interview Dennis Creed in Broadmoor, on September the nineteenth.'

64

. . . his hand did quake,
And tremble like a leafe of Aspin greene,
And troubled blood through his pale face was seene
To come, and goe with tidings from the heart,
As it a ronning messenger had beene.

Edmund Spenser
The Faerie Queene

'*Well,*' said Strike, getting into the Land Rover next morning.

They beamed at each other: for a moment, Robin thought she saw the idea of hugging her cross Strike's mind, but instead he held out his hand, and shook hers.

'My Christ, you wait a year for a breakthrough . . .'

Robin laughed, put the Land Rover into gear and pulled out onto the road. The day was unusually hot: she was driving in sunglasses, yet Strike noted a scarf protruding from the bag behind her seat.

'Don't think you're going to need that. Proper summer weather,' he said, looking out at the clear sky.

'We'll see,' said Robin sceptically. 'We used to visit Skegness when we were kids. Mum's sister used to live in Boston, up the road. There's usually a bracing breeze off the North Sea.'

'So, I read the email,' said Strike, referring to the message Robin had forwarded him, which laid out both the terms and conditions of him interviewing Dennis Creed, and the reasoning which had led the authorities to permit Strike to do it.

'What did you think?' Robin asked.

'Other than being bloody astounded you pulled this off—'

'It took ages.'

'I'm not surprised. Other than that, I won't lie ... I'm feeling the pressure.'

'You mean, because of the Tuckers?'

'Yeah,' said Strike, opening the window so he could light a cigarette. 'Anna doesn't know I'm getting this shot, so she won't get their hopes up, but that poor bastard Tucker ...'

Absolute secrecy about the interview, including signing a non-disclosure agreement that guaranteed Strike would never talk to the press about it, had been the first precondition set by the authorities.

'He really wants it to be you,' said Robin. 'Tucker. He says Creed's got a big ego and he'll want to meet you. And the psychiatrists must agree, mustn't they, or they wouldn't be allowing it? Brian Tucker says Creed always saw himself as high status, and deserving of associating with famous, successful people.'

'It isn't a psychiatrist's job to decide whether I'll be able to get anything out of him,' said Strike. 'I'd imagine all they'll care about is whether I'm going to rile him up. You don't get put in Broadmoor for being mildly eccentric.'

Strike was silent for a long time, looking out of the window, and Robin too remained quiet, not wanting to interrupt his train of thought. When at last Strike spoke again, he sounded matter of fact, and focused on the plan for Skegness.

'I looked up the B&B on TripAdvisor. It's called the Allardice, which is his wife's maiden name. We won't walk in there cold, because if he isn't there and the wife smells a rat, she can call him and warn him not to come back, so we'll park, get ourselves into a position where we can see the building, and ring him. If he's there, we walk straight in before he's got a chance to run – or catch him as he leaves, as the case might be. And if he isn't in, we wait.'

'For how long?' said Robin.

'I'd like to say "as long as it takes",' said Strike, 'but we're not actually being paid for this, so I've got to be back in town on Monday.'

'I could stay behind,' suggested Robin.

'I don't think so,' said Strike.

788

'Sorry,' said Robin, immediately regretting the suggestion, afraid that Strike might think she was simply after another weekend away in a hotel. 'I know we're short-staffed—'

'It isn't that. You were the one who pointed out women have a habit of dying or disappearing around Steve Douthwaite. Could be a case of bad luck, but on the other hand . . . three different surnames is a lot for a man with nothing to hide. I'm taking the lead on this one.'

They arrived in the small seaside town at eleven, leaving the Land Rover in a car park beside Skegness Bowl, an enormous red-walled seafront bowling alley. Strike could smell and taste the sea as he got out of the car, and turned instinctively towards it, but the ocean was invisible from where he stood. Instead he found himself looking at a manmade waterway of a murky green, along which a laughing young woman and her boyfriend were pedalling a dinghy-sized boat. The driver's door slammed and Strike turned to see Robin, still in sunglasses, wrapping the scarf around her neck.

'Told you,' she said to the mystified Strike, to whom the day felt unequivocally hot. Not for the first time wondering what it was about women and their bizarre ability to feel non-existent chills, Strike lit up, waited beside the Land Rover while Robin bought a parking permit, then walked with her up to Grand Parade, a wide street that ran along the seafront.

'"The Savoy",' said Strike, smirking as he read the names of the larger hotels, whose upper windows could surely see the distant sea. '"The Quorn". "The Chatsworth".'

'Don't jeer,' said Robin. 'I used to love coming to Skegness when I was a kid.'

'The Allardice should be up there,' Strike said, as they crossed the road, pointing up broad Scarbrough Avenue. 'Yeah, that's it, the one with the blue awning.'

They paused on the corner, beside an enormous mock Tudor hotel which boasted the Jubilee Carvery and Café. Early-morning drinkers of both beer and coffee were sitting at outside tables, enjoying the sunshine.

'Perfect place to keep an eye out,' said Strike, pointing at one of these pavement tables. 'I could use a cup of tea.'

'OK, I'll order,' said Robin. 'I need the loo, anyway. Are you going to call him or d'you want me to do it?'

'I will,' said Strike, already sinking onto one of the chairs, and taking out his mobile.

As Robin disappeared into the bar, Strike lit a cigarette, then keyed in the Allardice's number, his eyes on the front of the B&B. It stood in a row of eight tall red buildings, several of which had been converted into small boarding houses and had similar scalloped PVC awnings over the entrances. Spotless white net curtains hung at almost every window.

'Morning, the Allardice,' said a Scottish woman, who sounded on the irritable side of brisk.

'Steve there?' said Strike, faking casualness and confidence.

'That you, Barry love?'

'Yeah,' said Strike.

'He's on his way now,' she said. 'We only had a small, sorry. But do me a favour, Barry, and don't hold him up, because there are four beds to change here and he's supposed to be getting me more milk.'

'Righto,' said Strike, and not wanting to speak another syllable that might reveal him to be anyone other than Barry, he hung up.

'Is he there?' asked Robin anxiously, dropping into the seat opposite Strike. She'd washed her hands in the bathroom, but they were still damp, because she'd been in such a hurry to get back to Strike.

'No,' said Strike, knocking his cigarette ash into the small pink metal bucket placed on the table for that purpose. 'He's delivering something to a bloke up the road and will be back shortly, bringing milk.'

'Oh,' said Robin quietly, turning to look over her shoulder at the Allardice's royal blue awning, on which the name was inscribed in curly white lettering.

The barman brought out two metal pots and china teacups, and the detectives drank their tea in silence, Strike keeping a watchful eye on the Allardice, Robin on Grand Parade. The sea was blocked from her view by the wide, multicoloured frontage of the entrance to Skegness Pier, which advertised, among other attractions, the optimistically named Hollywood Bar and Diner. Elderly people rode mobility scooters up and down Grand Parade. Families strolled past, eating ice cream. Plume-tailed Maltese, fat pugs and panting chihuahuas trotted over the hot pavements alongside their owners.

'Cormoran,' muttered Robin suddenly.

A man had just turned the corner into Scarbrough Avenue, a heavy carrier bag dangling from his hand. His grey hair was close cropped around the ears, but a few strands had been combed over a wide expanse of sweaty forehead. His round shoulders and hangdog look gave him the air of a man whom life had ground down to a sullen obedience. The same turquoise T-shirt he'd worn in the karaoke picture was stretched tightly over his beer belly. Douthwaite crossed the road, climbed the three steps leading to the Allardice's front door and, with a flash of sun on glass, disappeared from view.

'Have you paid for this?' Strike asked, downing the rest of his tea and putting his empty cup back onto the saucer.

'Yes.'

'Then let's go,' said Strike, dropping his cigarette into the metal bucket and pulling himself to his feet, 'before he can disappear upstairs and start changing beds.'

They crossed the road as fast as Strike could walk and headed up the front steps, which had been painted pale blue. Baskets of purple petunias hung beneath the ground-floor windows and an assortment of stickers adorned the glass portion of the front door, one of which announced that this was a three-star residence, another asking guests to wipe their feet.

A tinkling bell announced their arrival. The deserted hall was narrow, its stairs carpeted in dark blue and green tartan. They waited beside a table laden with leaflets about local attractions, breathing in a combination of fried food and a powerful rose-scented air-freshener.

'... and Paula's got new tubes in her sunbeds,' said a Scottish voice, and a woman with short hair dyed canary yellow emerged through a door to the right. A deep vertical line was graven down the middle of her forehead. Barelegged, she wore an apron decorated with a Highland cow over her T-shirt and denim skirt, and a pair of Dr Scholl's sandals.

'We've no vacancies, sorry,' she said.

'Are you Donna?' asked Strike. 'We were hoping for a word with Steve.'

'What about?'

'We're private detectives,' said Strike, pulling out his wallet to hand her a card, 'and we're investigating—'

A hugely obese old lady came into view on the landing above them. She was clad in shocking-pink leggings and a T-shirt bearing the slogan 'The More People I Meet, The More I Like My Dog'. Panting audibly, she began a sideways descent, both hands clutching the banister.

'—a missing person case,' Strike finished quietly, as he handed Donna his card.

At that moment, Steve Douthwaite emerged from behind his wife, a pile of towels in his arms. Close up, his dark eyes were bloodshot and puffy. Every feature had coarsened with age and, possibly, drink. His wife's demeanour, the card in her hand and the presence of the two strangers now looking at him brought him to a halt, the dark eyes frightened above his pile of towels.

'Cormoran Strike?' murmured Donna, reading the card. 'Aren't you the one . . . ?'

The old lady, who was barely halfway down the stairs, was now audibly wheezing.

'Get in here,' muttered Donna, pointing Strike and Robin towards the room from which she'd just emerged. 'And you,' she snapped at her husband.

They entered a small public sitting room, with a wall-mounted TV, a sparsely stocked bookcase and a miserable-looking spider plant sitting in a pedestalled urn. Through an arch was a breakfast room, where five tightly packed dining tables were being wiped down by a discontented-looking young woman in glasses, who sped up appreciably when she realised Donna had returned. Robin guessed that they were mother and daughter. Though the younger woman was dark rather than blonde, life had carved an identical groove of dissatisfaction in her forehead.

'Leave that, Kirsty,' said Donna abruptly. 'Take these towels upstairs, will you? And close the door.'

Kirsty relieved Douthwaite silently of his pile of towels and left the room, her slides slapping the bottoms of her sockless feet. The door clicked shut behind her.

'Sit down,' Donna instructed Strike and Robin, who did so, on a small sofa.

Douthwaite took up a standing position, arms folded, with his back to the TV. Frowning slightly, his eyes flickered over Strike and Robin and back to his wife. The sunlight filtering through the net curtains cast an unforgiving light over his hair, which looked like wispy strands of steel wool.

'He's the one who caught that Shacklewell Ripper,' Donna said to her husband, jerking her head at Strike. 'Why's he after you?' Her voice rose in both pitch and volume. 'Been dicking around with the wrong woman again, have you? *Have you?*'

'What?' said Douthwaite, but it was obvious this was a stalling tactic: he had understood well enough. His right forearm was tattooed with an hourglass, and around it was wrapped a ribbon with the words 'Never Enough'.

'Mr Douthwaite,' Strike began, but Douthwaite said quickly, 'Diamond! It's Diamond!'

'Why're you calling him Douthwaite?' asked Donna.

'I'm sorry,' said Strike insincerely. 'My mistake. Your husband was born Steven Douthwaite, as I'm sure you—'

But Donna clearly hadn't known this. She turned, astonished, from Strike to Douthwaite, who'd frozen, mouth slightly open.

'*Douthwaite?*' repeated Donna. She turned on her husband. 'You told me your name used to be Jacks!'

'I—'

'When were you *Douthwaite?*'

'—ages—'

'Why didn't you tell me?'

'I – what's it matter?'

The bell tinkled again and a group of people was heard out in the hall. Still looking shocked and angry, Donna strode outside to see what was needed, her wooden-soled sandals banging over the tiles. The moment she'd disappeared, Douthwaite addressed Strike.

793

'What d'you want?'

'We've been hired by Dr Margot Bamborough's daughter, to look into her disappearance,' said Strike.

The parts of Douthwaite's face that weren't ruddy with broken veins blanched.

The enormous old lady who'd been descending the stairs now walked into the room, her wide, innocent face demonstrating total immunity to the atmosphere within.

'Which way's the seal sanctuary?'

'End of the road,' said Douthwaite hoarsely. 'Turn left.'

She sidled out of the room again. The bell outside tinkled.

'Listen,' said Douthwaite quickly, as the sound of his wife's footsteps grew louder again. 'You're wasting your time. I don't know anything about Margot Bamborough.'

'Perhaps you could have a look over your old police statement, at least,' asked Strike, taking a copy out of his inside pocket.

'What?' said Donna, now back in the room. 'What police statement? Oh, for *Christ's* sake,' she said, as the bell tinkled again, and she clunked back out of the room and bellowed up the stairs, 'Kirsty! *KIRSTY!*'

'That doctor,' Douthwaite said, looking at Strike through blood-shot eyes, his forehead sweaty, 'it all happened forty-odd years ago, I don't know anything about what happened, I never did.'

The harried Donna reappeared.

'Kirsty'll mind the front door,' she said, glaring at her husband. 'We'll go upstairs. Lochnagar's empty. We can't go in ours,' she added to Strike and Robin, pointing towards the basement, 'me grandkids are down there, playing computer games.'

Douthwaite hitched up his waistband and threw a wild look outside the net curtains, as though contemplating flight.

'Come on,' said Donna fiercely, and with a return to his hangdog look, he followed his wife out of the door.

Kirsty passed them, heading for the ground floor, as they climbed the steep tartan stairs, Strike making liberal use of the banister to haul himself up. He'd hoped Lochnagar might be on the first floor, but he was disappointed. It lay, as the name might have suggested, right at the top of the B&B, and faced out of the rear of the building.

The furniture inside was made of cheap pine. Kirsty had arranged towels in the shape of kissing swans on the maroon bedspread, which matched the patterned wallpaper of maroon and deep purple. Leads dangled from behind the wall-mounted TV. A plastic kettle sat in the corner on a low table, beside the Corby trouser press. Through the window Strike glimpsed the sea at last: a gleaming golden bar lying low between buildings, in the misty haze created by the net curtains.

Donna crossed the room and took the only chair. Her hands were gripping her own upper arms so tightly that the flesh showed white.

'You can sit down,' she told Strike and Robin.

Having nowhere else to do it, both sat down on the end of the double bed, with its slippery maroon cover. Douthwaite remained at the door, back against it, arms folded, displaying the hourglass tattoo.

'Diamond, Jacks, Douthwaite,' Donna recited. 'How many other names have you had?'

'None,' said Douthwaite, trying for a laugh, but failing.

'Why'd you change your name from Douthwaite to Jacks?' she demanded. 'Why were the police after you?'

'They weren't after me,' croaked Douthwaite. 'This was ages ago. I wanted a fresh start, that's all.'

'How many fresh starts does one man need?' said Donna. 'What did you do? Why'd you have to give a police statement?'

'A doctor went missing,' said Douthwaite, with a glance at Strike.

'What doctor? When?'

'Her name was Margot Bamborough.'

'Bamborough?' repeated Donna, her forehead bifurcated by that deep frown line, 'But that ... that was all over the news ...'

'They interviewed all the patients she'd seen before she disappeared,' Douthwaite said quickly. 'It was routine! They didn't have anything on me.'

'You must think I was born bloody yesterday,' said Donna. '*They,*' she pointed at Strike and Robin, 'haven't tracked you down because it was *routine enquiries,* have they? You didn't change your bloody name because it was *routine enquiries*! Screwing her, were you?'

'No, I wasn't bloody screwing her!' said Douthwaite, with his first sign of fight.

'Mr Douthwaite,' began Strike.

'Diamond!' said Douthwaite, more in desperation than in anger.

'I'd be grateful if you'd read through your police statement, see whether you've got anything to add.'

Douthwaite looked as though he'd have liked to refuse, but after a slight hesitation he took the pieces of paper and began to read. The statement was a long one, covering as it did the suicide of Joanna Hammond, his married ex-lover, the beating he'd endured at the hands of her husband, the anxiety and depression which had led to so many visits to the St John's surgery, his assertion that he'd felt nothing more for Margot Bamborough than mild gratitude for her clinical expertise, his denial that he'd ever brought or sent her gifts and his feeble alibi for the time of her disappearance.

'Yeah, I've got nothing to add to that,' Douthwaite said at last, holding the pieces of paper back out to Strike.

'I want to read it,' said Donna at once.

'It's got nothing to do with – it's forty years ago, it's nothing,' said Douthwaite.

'Your real name's Douthwaite and I never knew till five minutes ago! I've got a right to know who you are,' she said fiercely, 'I've got a right to know, so I can decide whether I was a bloody mug to stay with you, after the last—'

'Fine, read it, go on,' said Douthwaite with unconvincing bravado, and Strike handed the statement over to Donna.

She'd read for barely a minute when she burst out,

'You were sleeping with a married – and she *killed* herself?'

'I wasn't – we weren't – once, it happened, once! Nobody kills themselves over that!'

'Why'd she do it, then? Why?'

'Her husband was a bastard.'

'*My* husband's a bastard. I haven't topped myself!'

'Christ's sake, Donna—'

'*What happened?*'

'It was nothing!' said Douthwaite. 'We used to hang out together, few of the lads at work and their wives and whatever, and one night I was out with some other mates and ran into Joanna, who was with some girlfriends and ... some cunt tipped off her husband we'd left the pub together and—'

'And then this doctor disappeared and all, and the police came calling?'

Donna got to her feet, Douthwaite's crumpled statement quivering in her hand. Still sitting on the slippery maroon coverlet, Robin remembered the day she'd found Sarah Shadlock's diamond earring in her bed, and thought she knew a little, a very little, of what Donna was experiencing.

'I knew you were a bloody cheat and a liar, but *three girlfriends dead*? One's a tragedy,' said Donna furiously, and Strike wondered whether they were about to hear a Wildean epigram, 'but *three*? How bloody unlucky can one man get?'

'I never had anything going on with that doctor!'

'You'll try it on with anyone!' shrieked Donna, and addressing Robin, she said, 'Year before last, I catch him in a guest bedroom with one of my best friends—'

'Christ's sake, Donna!' whimpered Douthwaite.

'—and six months ago—'

'*Donna*—'

'—I find out he's been sneaking around with one of our regulars – and now –' said Donna, advancing on Douthwaite, his statements clutched in her fist. 'You creepy bastard, *what happened to all these women?*'

'I had nothing to do with any of them *dying*, fuck's sake!' said Douthwaite, trying for an incredulous laugh and merely looking terrified. 'Donna, come on – you think I'm some kind of *murderer?*'

'You expect me to believe—'

To Strike's surprise, Robin suddenly jumped to her feet. Taking Donna by the shoulders, she guided her back into her chair.

'Put your head down,' Robin was saying, 'head down.'

When Robin moved to untie Donna's apron, which was tight around her waist, and Strike saw that Donna's forehead, which was

797

all he could see now she had sunk her face into her hands, was as white as the net curtain behind her.

'Donna?' said Douthwaite feebly, but his wife whispered,

'You stay away from me, you bastard.'

'Breathe,' Robin was saying, crouching beside Donna's chair. 'Get her some water,' she told Strike, who got up and went into the tiny shower room, where a plastic beaker sat in a holder over the sink.

Almost as pale as his wife, Douthwaite watched as Robin persuaded Donna to drink.

'Stay there, now,' Robin told the landlady, one hand resting on her shoulder. 'Don't get up.'

'Did he have something to do with them dying?' Donna whispered, looking sideways at Robin, her pupils enormous with shock.

'That's what we're here to find out,' Robin murmured back.

She turned and looked meaningfully at Strike, who silently agreed that the best thing he could do for the stricken Donna was to get information out of Douthwaite.

'We've got a number of questions we'd like to ask you,' Strike told him. 'Obviously you're not obliged to answer them, but I'd put it to you that it would be in the best interests of everyone, yourself included, to cooperate.'

'What questions?' said Douthwaite, still flat against the door. Then, in a torrent of words, he said, 'I've never hurt anyone, never, I'm not a violent man. Donna will tell you, I've never laid a finger on her in anger, that's not who I am.'

But when Strike merely continued to look at him, Douthwaite said pleadingly,

'Look, I've told you – with Joanna – it was a one-night stand. I was just a kid,' he said, and in an echo of Irene Hickson, he said, 'You do those kinds of things when you're young, don't you?'

'And when you're old,' whispered Donna. 'And all the bloody years in between ...'

'Where were you,' Strike asked Douthwaite, 'when Joanna killed herself?'

'In Brent,' said Douthwaite. 'Miles away! And I had witnesses to prove it. We used to work in pairs, selling, each do one side of the street, and I was out with a bloke called Tadger,' and he tried to laugh again. Nobody smiled. 'Tadger, you can imagine the grief he . . . well, he was with me all day . . .

'Got back to the office late in the afternoon, and there was a group of lads in there, and they told us Hammond had just got the message his wife had topped herself . . .

'Terrible,' said the pale and sweating Douthwaite, 'but except for that one night together, I had nothing to do with it. But her old man – well, it was easier to blame me,' said Douthwaite, 'wasn't it, than think about his own bloody behaviour?

'I got home a couple of nights later and he was lying in wait. Ambush. He beat the shit out of me.'

'Good!' said Donna, on a half-sob.

'And your neighbour, Janice the nurse, looked after—'

'Straight off with the neighbour, were you, Steve?' said Donna, with a hollow laugh. 'Get the nurse to mop you up?'

'It wasn't like that!' said Douthwaite with surprising vehemence.

'It's his little trick,' the white-faced Donna told Robin, who was still kneeling by her chair. 'Always got a sob story on the go. Fell for it myself. Heartbroken after the love of his life drowned . . . oh my God,' Donna whispered, slowly shaking her head. 'And she was the third.' With a hysterical little laugh, she said, 'As far as we know. Maybe there are others. Who knows?'

'Christ's sake, Donna!' said Douthwaite, yet again. Patches of underarm sweat were visible through his thin turquoise T-shirt: Strike could literally smell his fear. 'Come on, you know me, you know I'd never hurt anyone!'

'Janice says she advised you to see the doctor about your symp—'

'*She* never told me to go to the doctor!' snapped Douthwaite, one eye on his wife. 'I didn't need telling, I went off my own bat because I was just getting worried about the . . . headaches and . . . mostly headaches. I felt really bad.'

'You visited Margot six times in one two-week period,' said Strike.

'I felt ill, stomach pains and what have you . . . I mean, it obviously affected me, Joanna dying, and then people talking about me . . .'

'Oh, poor you, poor you,' murmured Donna. 'Jesus effing Christ. You hate going to the doctor. Six times in two weeks?'

'Donna, come on,' said Douthwaite imploringly, 'I was feeling like shit! And then the bloody police come and make out like I was stalking her or something. It was all my health!'

'Did you buy her—?' began Strike.

'—chocolates? No!' said Douthwaite, who suddenly seemed very agitated. 'If someone sent her chocolates, maybe you should find *them*. But it wasn't me! I told the police I never bought her anything, it weren't like that—'

'Witnesses said you seemed distressed and possibly angry, the last time you left Dr Bamborough's surgery,' said Strike. 'What happened during that last visit?'

Douthwaite's breath was coming fast now. Suddenly, almost aggressively, he looked directly into Strike's eyes.

Experienced in the body language of suspects who yearn for the release and relief of unburdening themselves, no matter the consequences, Strike suddenly knew that Douthwaite was teetering on the brink of a disclosure. He'd have given almost anything to spirit the man away now, to a quiet interrogation room, but exactly as he'd feared, the precious moment was snatched away by Donna.

'Turned you down, did she? What did you think, Steve – a scrubby little failed salesman had a chance with a doctor?'

'*I wasn't bloody looking for a chance!*' said Douthwaite, rounding on his wife, 'I was there for my health, I was in a state!'

'He's like a bloody tomcat,' Donna told Robin, 'slinking around behind everyone's backs. He'll use anything to get his end away, anything. His girlfriend's topped herself and he's using it to chat up nurses and doctors—'

'I wasn't, I was ill!'

'That last meeting—' Strike began again.

'I don't know what you're on about, it was nothing,' Douthwaite said, now avoiding looking Strike in the face. 'The doc was just telling me to take it easy.'

'Like you ever needed telling that, you lazy bastard,' spat Donna.

'Perhaps,' said Strike, 'as you're feeling unwell, Mrs Diamond, I could speak to Steve somewhere sep—'

'Oh no you don't!' said Donna. 'No way! I want—'

She exploded into tears, shoulders sagging, face in her hands.

'I'm going to hear it all now . . . last chance . . .'

'Donna—' said Douthwaite plaintively.

'Don't,' she sobbed into her fingers. 'Don't you dare.'

'Perhaps,' said Strike, hoping to return to the last visit with Margot in due course, 'we could go over your alibi for the time Dr Bamborough disappeared?'

Donna was sobbing, tears and mucus flowing freely now. Robin grabbed a paper napkin off the tray beside the kettle and handed it to her.

Cowed by his wife's distress, Douthwaite allowed Strike to lead him back over his shaky alibi for the evening in question, sticking to the story that he'd been sitting unnoticed in a café, scanning the newspapers for flats to rent.

'I wanted to clear out, get away from all the gossip about Joanna. I just wanted to get away.'

'So the desire to move wasn't triggered by anything that passed between you and Dr Bamborough during your last visit?' Strike asked.

'No,' said Douthwaite, still not looking at Strike. 'How could it be?'

'Given up on her?' Donna asked from behind the wet napkin with which she was blotting her eyes. 'Knew he'd made a fool of himself. Same as with that young lassie from Leeds, eh, Steve?'

'Donna, for *fuck's* sake—'

'He forgets,' Donna said to Robin, 'he's not that cocky little sod in his twenties any more. Deluded, b – baldy bastard,' she sobbed.

'*Donna*—'

'So you moved to Waltham Forest . . .' prompted Strike.

'Yeah. Police. Press. It was a nightmare,' said Douthwaite. 'I thought of ending it, to tell you the—'

'Shame you didn't,' said Donna savagely. 'Save us all a lot of time and trouble.'

As though he hadn't heard this, and ignoring Douthwaite's look of outrage, Strike asked,

'What made you go to Clacton-on-Sea? Did you have family there?'

'I haven't got family, I grew up in care—'

'Oh, someone pass him a bloody violin,' said Donna.

'Well, it's true, isn't it?' said Douthwaite, displaying unvarnished anger for the first time. 'And I'm allowed to tell the truth about my own bloody life, aren't I? I just wanted to be a Redcoat, because I sing a bit and it looked like a fun way to earn a living—'

'Fun,' muttered Donna, 'oh yeah, as long as *you're* having fun, Steve—'

'—get away from people treating me like I'd killed someone—'

'And *whoops*!' said Donna. 'There's another one gone, in the pool—'

'You know *bloody well* I had nothing to do with Julie drowning!'

'How could I know?' said Donna, 'I wasn't there! It was before we even met!'

'I showed you the story in the paper!' said Douthwaite. 'I *showed* you, Donna, come on!' He turned to Strike. 'A bunch of us were drinking in our chalet. Me and some mates were playing poker. Julie was tired. She left before we finished our game, walked back to her chalet. She walked round the pool, slipped in the dark, knocked herself out and—'

For the first time, Douthwaite showed real distress.

'—she drowned. I won't ever forget it. Never. I ran outside in me underpants next morning, when I heard the shouting. I saw her body when they were taking her out of the pool. You don't forget something like that. She was a kid. Twenty-two or something. Her parents came and . . . it was a horrible thing. Horrible. I never . . . that someone can go like that. A slip and a trip . . .

'Yeah, so . . . that's when I applied for a job at the Ingoldmells Butlin's up the road from here. And that's where I met Donna,' he said, with an apprehensive glance at his wife.

'So you leaving Clacton-on-Sea and changing your name again had nothing to do with a man called Oakden coming to question you about Margot Bamborough?' asked Strike.

Donna's head jerked up.

'Oh my God,' she said, 'so even the *Julie* bit's a lie?'

'It's not a lie!' said Douthwaite loudly. 'I *told* you Julie and I had an argument a couple of days before she died, I *told* you that, because I felt so guilty after! This man, this – what did you say his name was? Oakden? – yeah, he turned up, saying he was writing a book about Dr Bamborough disappearing. Went round all the other Redcoats talking to them about me, telling them all I'd been a suspect and how I'd changed my name afterwards, making me sound dodgy as hell. And Julie was really pissed off with me because I hadn't told her—'

'Well, you really learned *that* lesson, didn't you, Steve?' said Donna. 'Run and hide, that's all you know, and when you're found out, you just sneak off and find some other woman to whine to, until she finds you out, and then—'

'Mr Douthwaite,' said Strike, cutting across Donna, 'I want to thank you for your time. I know it's been a shock, having all this raked up again.'

Robin looked up at Strike, astonished. He couldn't be leaving the interview here, surely? The Douthwaites (or Diamonds, as they thought of themselves), looked similarly taken aback. Strike extracted a second card from his pocket and held it out to Douthwaite.

'If you remember anything,' the detective said, 'you know where to find me. It's never too late.'

The hourglass tattoo on Douthwaite's forearm rippled as he held out his hand for the card.

'Who else've you talked to?' Douthwaite asked Strike.

Now that his ordeal was over, he seemed curiously averse to it ending. Perhaps, thought Robin, he feared being alone with his wife.

'Margot's husband and family,' said Strike, watching Douthwaite's reactions. 'The co-workers who're still alive – Dr Gupta. One of the receptionists, Irene Hickson. Janice Beattie, the nur—'

'That's nice,' piped up Donna, 'the nurse is still available, Steve—'

'—an ex-boyfriend of Margot's, her best friend, and a few other people.'

Douthwaite, who'd flushed at his wife's interjection, said, 'Not Dennis Creed?'

'Not yet,' said Strike. 'Well,' he looked from husband to wife, 'thanks for your time. We appreciate it.'

Robin got to her feet.

'I'm sorry,' she said quietly to Donna. 'I hope you feel better.'

'Thanks,' mumbled Donna.

As Strike and Robin reached the top of the stairs, they heard shouting break out again behind the door of Lochnagar.

'Donna, babes—'

'Don't you dare call me babes, you fucking bastard!'

'No point carrying on,' said Strike quietly, setting off down the steep tartaned stairs as slowly as the obese old lady had moved. 'He's not going to say it with her there.'

'Say what?'

'Well, that,' said Strike, as the Douthwaites' shouts echoed down the stairs, 'is the question, isn't it?'

65

'I'm hungry,' Strike announced, once they stepped down onto the sunny pavement outside the Allardice.

'Let's get some fish and chips,' said Robin.

'Now you're talking,' said Strike enthusiastically, as they headed off towards the end of Scarbrough Avenue.

'Cormoran, what makes you think Douthwaite knows something?'

'Didn't you see the way he looked at me, when I asked him about his last appointment with Margot?'

'I must've been looking at Donna. I was seriously worried she was going to pass out.'

'Wish she had,' said Strike.

'Strike!'

'He was definitely thinking about telling me something, then she bloody ruined it.' As they reached the end of the road, he said, 'That was a scared man, and I don't think he's only scared of his wife . . . Do we go left or right?'

'Right,' said Robin, so they headed off along Grand Parade, passing a long open-fronted building called Funland, which was full of beeping and flashing video games, claw machines and coin-operated mechanical horses for children to ride. 'Are you saying Douthwaite's guilty?'

'I think he feels it,' Strike said, as they wove their way in and out of cheerful, T-shirted families and couples. 'He looked at me back there as though he was bursting to tell me something that's weighing on him.'

'If he had actual evidence, why didn't he tell the police? It would've got them off his back.'

'I can think of one reason.'

'He was scared of the person he thought had killed her?'

'Exactly.'

'So . . . Luca Ricci?' said Robin.

At that moment, a male voice from the depths of Funland called, 'White seven and four, *seventy-four.*'

'Possibly,' said Strike, though he didn't sound entirely convinced. 'Douthwaite and Ricci were living in the same area at the time. Maybe going to the same pubs. I suppose he might've heard a rumour about Ricci being out to get her. But that doesn't fit with the eye-witness accounts, does it? If Douthwaite was issuing the warning, you'd think it'd be Margot looking distressed afterwards, whereas we know *he* was the one who came running out of there looking scared and worried . . . but my gut feeling is that Douthwaite thinks whatever happened between them at that last appointment is relevant to her disappearance.'

The entrance to a well-maintained park on their right was ablaze with petunias. Ahead, on an island in the middle of a traffic island, stood a sixty-foot-high clock tower of brick and stone, with a faintly Gothic appearance, and faces like a miniature Big Ben.

'Exactly how many chippies has Skegness got?' Strike asked, as they came to a halt on the busy intersection beside the clock tower. They were standing right beside two establishments which had tables spilling out onto the pavement, and he could see a further two fish and chip shops on the other side of the junction.

'I never counted,' said Robin. 'I was always more interested in the donkeys. Shall we try here?' she asked, pointing at the nearest free table, which was pistachio green and belonged to Tony's Chippy ('We Sell on Quality not Price').

'Donkeys?' repeated Strike, grinning, as he sat down on the bench.

'That's right,' said Robin. 'Cod or haddock?'

'Haddock, please,' said Strike, and Robin headed into the chip shop to order.

After a minute or so, looking forward to his chips and enjoying the feeling of sun on his back, Strike became aware that he was still watching Robin, and fixed his eyes instead on a fluttering mass just above him. Even though the top of the yellow railings separating Tony's from Harry Ramsbottom's had been fitted with fine spikes to stop birds landing on them, a handful of speckled starlings were doing just that, delicately poised between the needles, and balanced in the iron circles just below them, waiting for the chance to swoop on an abandoned chip.

Watching the birds, Strike wondered what the chances were of Douthwaite ringing the number on his card. He was a man with a long track record of hiding from his past, but Strike had definitely read in his face a desperation he'd only ever seen in the faces of men who could no longer bear the pressure of a terrible secret. Idly rubbing his chin, Strike decided to give the man a short period of grace, then either call him again, or even return, unannounced, to Skegness, where he might waylay Douthwaite in the street or a pub, where Donna couldn't interfere.

Strike was still watching the starlings when Robin set down two polystyrene trays, two small wooden forks and two cans of Coke on the table.

'Mushy peas,' said Strike, looking at Robin's tray, where a hefty dollop of what looked like green porridge sat alongside her fish and chips.

'Yorkshire caviar,' said Robin, sitting down. 'I didn't think you'd want any.'

'You were right,' said Strike, picking up a sachet of tomato sauce while watching with something like revulsion as Robin dipped a chip into the green sludge and ate it.

'Soft Southerner, you are,' she said, and Strike laughed.

'Don't ever let Polworth hear you say that,' he said, breaking off a bit of fish with his fingers, dipping it in ketchup and eating it. He then, without warning, broke into song:

> *A good sword and a trusty hand!*
> *A merry heart and true!*
> *King James's men shall understand,*
> *What Cornish lads can do.*

'What on earth's that?' asked Robin, laughing.

'First verse of "The Song of the Western Men",' said Strike. 'The gist is that Cornishmen are the antithesis of soft bastards. Bloody hell, this is good.'

'I know. You don't get fish and chips like this in London,' said Robin.

For a few minutes they ate in silence. The greaseproof paper in which the trays of chips were wrapped was printed with old pages of the *Mirror* newspaper. *Paul Quits the Beatles.* There were cartoons too, of the dirty postcard type: a busty blonde in bed with her elderly boss was saying 'Business must be booming. You've never given me so much overtime.' It reminded her of Gemma the PA, who'd perhaps already called the fake number Robin had given her, and realised that it wasn't only her ex, 'Andy', who wasn't all he appeared to be. But Robin had a recording on her phone of everything Gemma knew about Shifty's insider trading and Pat, at that moment, was transcribing it into a document shorn of anything that might identify the informant. Shifty, Robin hoped, would soon be jobless and, with any luck, in court.

A long stretch of fairground rides on the other side of the road hid the sea from her sight. The seats of the distant Ferris wheel were enclosed in casings shaped like pastel-coloured hot-air balloons. Nearby stood a gigantic climbing frame for adults, with ropes and swinging tyres, a hundred feet up in the air. Watching the harnessed people navigating the obstacles, Robin felt a strange mixture of contentment and melancholy: the possibility of an unknown development in the Bamborough case, the delicious chips and peas, the companionship of Strike and the sunshine were all cheering, but she was also remembering chasing along the out-of-sight beach as a small child, trying to outrun her brother Stephen to reach the donkeys and have first pick. Why did the memory of innocence sting so much, as you got older? Why did the memory of the child who'd thought she was invulnerable, who'd never known cruelty, give her more pain than pleasure?

Her childhood had been happy, unlike Strike's; it ought not to hurt. Over the space of summer weekends spread years apart, Robin and her brothers had competed to ride the black donkey called Noddy, who was doubtless long gone. Was it mortality, then, which turned cheerful memories bittersweet? Maybe, Robin thought, she'd bring Annabel here when she was old enough, and treat her to her first donkey ride. It was a nice idea, but she doubted Stephen and Jenny would see Skegness as a desirable weekend destination. Annabel's great-aunt had moved away from Boston: there was no longer any family connection to the area. Times changed, and so did childhoods.

'You all right?' said Strike, watching Robin's face.

'Fine,' she said. 'Just thinking ... I'm going to be thirty in a few weeks.'

Strike snorted.

'Well, you're getting no sympathy from me,' he said. 'I'll be forty the month after.'

He snapped open his can of Coke and drank. Robin watched a family pass, all four eating ice creams, accompanied by a waddling dachshund that was nosing the Union Jack carrier bag which swung from the father's hand.

'D'you think Scotland's going to leave?'

'Go for independence? Maybe,' said Strike. 'The polls are close. Barclay thinks it could happen. He was telling me about some old mates of his at home. They sound just like Polworth. Same hate figures, same promises everything'll be rainbows and unicorns if only they cut themselves free of London. Anyone pointing out pitfalls or difficulties is scaremongering. Experts don't know anything. Facts lie. "Things can't be any worse than they are."'

Strike put several chips in his mouth, chewed, swallowed, then said,

'But life's taught me things can always get worse than they are. I thought I had it hard, then they wheeled a bloke onto the ward who'd had both his legs and his genitals blown off.'

He'd never before talked to Robin about the aftermath of his life-changing injury. Indeed, he rarely mentioned his missing leg. A barrier had definitely fallen, Robin thought, since their whisky-fuelled talk in the dark office.

'Everyone wants a single, simple solution,' he said, now finishing his last few chips. '*One weird trick to lose belly fat.* I've never clicked on it, but I understand the appeal.'

'Well, reinvention's such an inviting idea, isn't it?' said Robin, her eyes on the fake hot-air balloons, circling on their prescribed course. 'Look at Douthwaite, changing his name and finding a new woman every few years. Reinventing a whole country would feel amazing. Being part of that.'

'Yeah,' said Strike. 'Of course, people think if they subsume themselves in something bigger, and that changes, they'll change too.'

'Well, there's nothing wrong with wanting to be better, or different, is there?' asked Robin. 'Nothing wrong with wanting to improve things?'

'Not at all,' said Strike. 'But *people* who fundamentally change are rare, in my experience, because it's bloody hard work compared to going on a march or waving a flag. Have we met a single person on this case who's radically different to the person they were forty years ago?'

'I don't know . . . I think *I've* changed,' said Robin, then felt embarrassed to have said it out loud.

Strike looked at her without smiling for the space it took him to chew and swallow a chip, then said,

'Yeah. But you're exceptional, aren't you?'

And before Robin had time for anything other than a slight blush, Strike said,

'Are you not finishing those chips?'

'Help yourself,' said Robin, shoving the tray towards him. She pulled her phone out of her pocket. 'I'll look up that one weird tip to lose belly fat.'

Strike smirked. After wiping her hands on her paper napkin, Robin checked her emails.

'Have you seen this from Vanessa Ekwensi? She's copied you in.'

'What?'

'She might know someone who could replace Morris ... woman called Michelle Greenstreet ... she wants to leave the police. She's been in eight years,' said Robin, scrolling slowly down the email, 'not enjoying response policing ... she's in Manchester ... wants to relocate to London, very keen on the detective side ...'

'Sounds promising,' said Strike. 'Let's schedule an interview. She's already cleared the first hurdle with flying colours.'

'What hurdle?' said Robin, looking up.

'Doubt she's ever sent a dick pic.'

He patted his pockets, pulled out his packet of Benson & Hedges but found it empty.

'I need more fags, let's—'

'Wait,' said Robin, who was still staring down at her mobile. 'Oh my God. Cormoran – Gloria Conti's emailed me.'

'You're kidding,' said Strike. Having partly risen, he now let himself fall back onto the bench.

'"Dear Miss Ellacott,"' Robin read aloud, '"I'm sorry I haven't answered your emails. I wasn't aware you were trying to contact me and have only just found out. If convenient, I'd be available to talk to you tomorrow evening at 7pm. Yours sincerely ..." and she's given her phone number,' said Robin, looking up at Strike, astonished. 'How can she only just have found out? It's been *months* of me emailing her without any response ... unless Anna's prompted her?'

'Could be,' said Strike. 'Which doesn't suggest someone who wants the investigation over.'

'Of *course* she doesn't,' said Robin. 'But for sanity's sake, you'd have to draw the line somewhere.'

'So what does that make us?'

Robin smiled and shook her head.

'Dedicated?'

Strike lit himself another cigarette.

'Conti: last person to see Margot alive. Closest person to Margot at the practice ...'

'I'm thanking her,' said Robin, who was typing fast onto her mobile, 'and agreeing to the call tomorrow.'

'We could do it from the office, together,' said Strike. 'Maybe FaceTime her, if she's agreeable?'

'I'll ask,' said Robin, still typing.

They set off a few minutes later in search of cigarettes, Robin reflecting on how casually she'd just agreed to go into work on a Saturday evening, so she could conduct Gloria's interview with Strike. There was no angry Matthew at home any more, furious about her committing herself to long hours, suspicious about what she and Strike were up to, alone in the office in the evening. And she thought back to Matthew's refusal to look her in the eye across the table at the mediation. He'd changed his partner, and his firm; he'd soon be a father. His life had changed, but had he?

They turned the corner to find themselves facing what Strike mentally categorised as 'acres of tat'. As far as the eye could see were racks of merchandise laid out on the pavement: beach balls, keyrings, cheap jewellery, sunglasses, buckets of candyfloss, fudge and plush toys.

'Look at that,' said Robin suddenly, pointing to her right. A bright yellow sign read: *Your Life Within Your Hands.* On the dark glass of the door below was written: *Palm Reader. Clairvoyant*, along with a circular chart, all twelve signs of the zodiac represented by the glyphs around a central sun.

'What?' said Strike.

'Well, you've had your chart done. Maybe I'd like mine.'

'Fuck's sake,' muttered Strike, and they walked on, Robin smiling to herself.

She waited outside, examining postcards, while Strike entered the newsagent's to buy cigarettes.

Waiting to be served, Strike was seized by a sudden, quixotic impulse (stimulated no doubt by the gaudy colour all around him, by the sunshine and sticks of rock, the rattle and clang of amusement arcades and a stomach full of some of the best fish and chips he'd ever eaten) to buy Robin a toy donkey. He came to his senses almost before the idea had formed: what was he, a kid on a daytime date with his first girlfriend? Emerging again into the sunlight as he left the shop, he noted that he couldn't have bought a donkey if he'd wanted to. There wasn't a single one in sight: the bins full of plushes held only unicorns.

'Back to the car, then?' said Robin.

'Yeah,' said Strike, ripping the cellophane off his cigarettes, but then he said, 'we'll go down to the sea before we head off, shall we?'

'OK,' said Robin, surprised. 'Er – why?'

'Just fancy it. It's wrong, being by the sea without actually laying eyes on it.'

'Is this a Cornish thing?' asked Robin, as they headed back to Grand Parade.

'Maybe,' said Strike, lighting the cigarette between his teeth. He took a drag on his cigarette, exhaled then sang,

> *And when we come to London Wall,*
> *A pleasant sight to view,*
> *Come forth! come forth! ye cowards all:*
> *Here's men as good as you.*

'"The Song of the Western Men?"'

'That's the one.'

'Why d'you think they feel the need to tell Londoners they're just as good? Isn't that a given?'

'Just London, isn't it?' said Strike, as they crossed the road. 'Pisses everyone off.'

'I love London.'

'Me too. But I can see why it pisses everyone off.'

They passed a fountain with a statue in the middle of the Jolly Fisherman, that rotund, bearded sailor skipping along in high wind, who'd been used on posters advertising Skegness for nearly a century, and progressed across a smooth paved area towards the beach.

At last they saw what Strike had felt the need to see: a wide expanse of flat ocean, the colour of chalcedony, beneath a periwinkle sky. Far out at sea, spoiling the horizon, were an army of tall white wind turbines, and while Strike personally enjoyed the chill breeze coming off the wide ocean, he understood at last why Robin had brought a scarf.

Strike smoked in silence, the cool wind making no difference whatsoever to his curly hair. He was thinking about Joan. It hadn't occurred to him until this moment that her plan for her final resting place had given them a grave to visit any time they were at the British coast. Cornish-born, Cornish-bred, Joan had known that this need to reconnect with the sea lived in all of them. Now, every time they made their way to the coast they paid her tribute, along with the obeisance due to the waves.

'They were Joan's favourites, pink roses,' he said, after a while. 'What you sent, to the funeral.'

'Oh, really?' said Robin. 'I . . . well, I had a kind of picture in my head of Joan, from things you'd told me, and . . . pink roses seemed to suit her.'

'If the agency ever fails,' said Strike, as they both turned away from the sea, 'you could come back to Skegness and set yourself up as a clairvoyant.'

'Bit niche,' said Robin, as they walked back towards the car park. 'Guessing dead people's favourite flowers.'

'No donkeys,' said Strike, glancing back over his shoulder at the beach.

'Never mind,' said Robin kindly. 'I think you'd have been a bit heavy.'

66

Speak, thou frail woman, speak with confidence.

Edmund Spenser
The Faerie Queene

The following evening, Strike and Robin sat down together on the same side of the partners' desk. They were alone in the office for the first time since the night Strike had given her two black eyes. The lights were on this time, there were no glasses of whisky in their hands, but each of them was very conscious of what had happened on the previous occasion, and both felt a slight self-consciousness, which manifested itself, on Strike's side, in a slightly brisker tone as they set up the computer monitor so that both could see it well, and on Robin's, in focusing herself on all the questions she wanted to ask Gloria.

At six o'clock – which was seven o'clock, Gloria's time – Strike dialled Gloria's number, and after a moment's suspense, they heard ringing, and a woman appeared onscreen, looking slightly nervous, in what looked like a book-lined study. Framed on the wall behind her was a large photograph of a family: Gloria herself, a distinguished-looking husband and three adult children, all wearing white shirts, all of them notably attractive.

Of all the people they'd met and interviewed in connection with Margot Bamborough, Gloria Conti, Robin thought, looked most like her younger self, although she hadn't made any obvious efforts to disguise the ageing process. Her hair, which was pure white, had been cut into a short and flattering bob. Although there were fine lines on her brow and around her eyes, her fair complexion seemed never to have been exposed to much sun. She was slim and high-cheekboned, so that the structure of her face was much as it had been when she was younger, and her high-necked navy shirt, small gold earrings and square-framed glasses were stylish and simple. Robin thought that Gloria looked far more like her idea of a college professor than the scion of a criminal family, but perhaps she was being influenced by the lines of books on the shelves behind her.

'Good evening,' said Gloria nervously.

'Good evening,' said Strike and Robin together.

'It's very good of you to talk to us, Mrs Jaubert,' said Strike. 'We appreciate it.'

'Oh, not at all,' she said, politely.

Robin hadn't imagined received pronunciation from Irene Hickson's descriptions of a girl from a rough background, but of course, as with Paul Satchwell, Gloria had now spent longer outside the country of her birth than in it.

'We've been hoping to talk to you for a long time,' said Robin.

'Yes, I'm very sorry about that,' said Gloria. 'My husband, Hugo, didn't tell me about any of your messages, you see. I found your last email in the trash folder, by accident. That's how I realised you were trying to contact me. Hugo – well, he thought he was doing the right thing.'

Robin was reminded of that occasion when Matthew had deleted a voicemail from Strike on Robin's phone in an attempt to stop Robin going back to work at the agency. She was surprised to see Gloria didn't seem to hold her husband's intervention against him. Perhaps Gloria could read her mind, because she said:

'Hugo assumed I wouldn't want to talk about what happened with strangers. He didn't realise that, actually, you're the only people I'd ever want to talk to, because you're trying to find out what really happened, and if you succeed, it'll be – well, it would lift a huge weight off me.'

'D'you mind if I take notes?' Strike asked her.

'No, not at all,' said Gloria politely.

As Strike clicked out the nib of his pen, Gloria reached out of shot for a large glass of red wine, took a sip, appeared to brace herself and said rather quickly,

'Please – if you don't mind – could I explain some things first? Since yesterday, I've been going over it, in my head, and I think if I tell you my story it will save you a lot of time. It's key to understanding my relationship with Margot and why I behaved . . . as I behaved.'

'That'd be very helpful,' said Strike, pen poised. 'Please, go on.'

Gloria took another sip of wine, put her glass back where they couldn't see it, drew a deep breath and said,

'Both my parents died in a house fire when I was five.'

'How awful,' said Robin, startled. The 1961 census record had shown a complete family of four. 'I'm so sorry.'

Strike gave a kind of commiserative growl.

'Thank you,' said Gloria. 'I'm only telling you that to explain – you see, I survived because my father threw me out of the window into a blanket the neighbours were holding. My mother and father didn't jump, because they were trying to reach my elder brother, who was trapped. All three of them died, so I was raised by my mother's parents. They were adorable people. They'd have sold their own souls for me, which makes everything I'm about to say even worse . . .

'I was quite a shy girl. I really envied the girls at school who had parents who were – you know – *with it*. My poor granny didn't really understand the sixties and seventies,' said Gloria, with a sad smile. 'My clothes were always a bit old-fashioned. No mini-skirts or eye make-up, you know . . .

'I reacted by developing a very elaborate fantasy life. I know most teenagers are fantasists, but I was . . . extreme. Everything sort of spun out of control when I was sixteen, and I went to see the movie *The Godfather* . . .

'It's ridiculous,' said Gloria soberly, 'but it's the truth. I . . . *cleaved* to that movie. I became *obsessed* with it. I don't know how many times I saw it; at least twenty, I expect. I was an English schoolgirl from seventies Islington, but what I *really* wanted was to be Apollonia from forties Sicily, and meet a handsome American Mafioso, and *not* to be blown up by a car bomb, but go and live with Michael Corleone in New York and be beautiful and glamorous while my husband did

817

glamorously violent, criminal things, all underpinned, you know, by a strict moral code.'

Strike and Robin both laughed, but Gloria didn't smile. On the contrary, she looked sad and ashamed.

'I somehow thought all this might be achievable,' she went on, 'because I had an Italian surname. I'd never really cared about that, before *The Godfather*. Now, out of nowhere, I asked my grandparents to take me to the Italian church on Clerkenwell Road for mass, instead of their regular church – and bless them, they did it. I wish they hadn't. I wish they'd told me not to be so selfish, because their regular church gave them a lot of support and it was the centre of their social life.

'I'd always felt entirely English, which I *was* on my mum's side, but now I started trying to find out as much as I could about my dad's family. I hoped to find out I was descended from Mafiosi. Then I could get my grandparents to give me the money to go and meet them all in Sicily and maybe marry a distant cousin. But all I found out was that my Italian grandfather immigrated to London to work in a coffee shop. I already knew my dad had worked for London Transport. Everyone I found out about, no matter how far back I went, was completely respectable and law-abiding. It was a real disappointment,' said Gloria, with a sigh.

'Then one Sunday, at St Peter's, somebody pointed out a man called Niccolo Ricci, sitting at the back of the Italian church. They said he was one of the very last of the Little Italy gangsters.'

Gloria paused to take another mouthful of wine, replaced the glass out of shot again, then said,

'Anyway . . . Ricci had sons.'

Strike now set pen to paper for the first time.

'There wasn't much resemblance, really, between Luca Ricci and Al Pacino,' said Gloria drily, 'but I managed to find one. He was four years older than I was, and everyone I asked about him said he was trouble, which was exactly what I wanted to hear. It started with a few smiles in passing . . .

'We went on our first date a couple of months before I was due to sit my exams. I told Granny and Gramps I was revising at a schoolfriend's house. I'd always been such a good girl; they never dreamed I could be fibbing.

'I *desperately* wanted to like Luca, because this was my way into my fantasy. He had a car, and he was definitely criminal. He didn't tell me anything about summit meetings between heads of crime families, though . . . mostly he talked about his Fiat, and drugs and beating people up.

'After a few dates, it was obvious Luca was quite keen on me, or . . . no,' said Gloria, unsmiling, 'not keen, because that implies genuine affection. He really just wanted to fix me down, to keep me his. I was so stupid and lost to my fantasy, I found that quite exciting, because it seemed – you know – the proper Mafioso attitude. But I liked Luca best when I wasn't actually with him, when I was mixing him up with Michael Corleone in my head, in my bed at night.

'I stopped studying. My fantasy life took me over completely. Gangsters' molls didn't need A-levels. Luca didn't think I needed A-levels, either. I failed all of them.

'My grandparents were really disappointed, although they were so kind about it,' said Gloria. For the first time, her voice quivered slightly. 'Then – I think it was the following week – they found out about me seeing Luca. They were desperately worried and upset, but by this time, I didn't really care. I told them I'd given up on the idea of college. I wanted to go out to work.

'I only applied for the job at the St John's practice because it was in the heart of Little Italy, even though Little Italy didn't really exist any more. Luca's father was one of the very last relics. But it was all part of my fantasy: I was a Conti, I should be there, where my fore-fathers had been. It made it easier to see Luca, too, because he lived there.

'I should never have got that receptionist's job. I was far too young and I had no experience. It was Margot who wanted me to have it.'

Gloria paused, and Robin was sure it was because she'd just had to say Margot's name for the first time. Drawing another deep breath, she said,

'So, there I was, on reception with Irene all day. My grandparents weren't registered at St John's, because they lived in Islington, so I got away with telling Irene a bunch of lies about my background.

'I'd created a whole persona by now. I told her the Contis were an old Sicilian family, how my grandfather and father had been part of a crime family and I don't know what else. Sometimes I used bits and pieces Luca had told me about the Riccis. Some of it was straight out of *The Godfather*. Ironically,' said Gloria, with a slight eye roll, 'the one authentically criminal thing I could have told her, I didn't. I kept my mouth shut about my boyfriend. Luca had told me never to talk about him and his family to other people, so I didn't. I took him seriously.

'I remember, a few months after I got the job, a rumour went round the local area that they'd found a body buried in concrete in one of the builder's sites up the road. I pretended I knew all about that through my underworld contacts. I told Irene I had it on good authority that the corpse had been a member of the Sabini gang. I really was a fool,' said Gloria quietly. 'A little idiot . . .

'But I always had the feeling Margot could see right through me. She told me not long after I started there that she'd "seen something" in me, at the interview. I didn't like that, I felt as though she was patronising me. She never treated me the way I wanted to be treated, as some street-smart Mafia girl with dark secrets, but always as though I was just a sweet young girl. Irene didn't like Margot, either, and we used to moan about her all the time on reception. Margot had a big thing about education and keeping your career, and we used to say what a hypocrite she was, because she'd married this rich consultant. When you're living a lie, nothing's more threatening than people who tell the truth . . .

'I'm sorry,' said Gloria, with an impatient shake of the head, 'this probably doesn't seem relevant at all, but it is, if you just bear with me . . .'

'Take your time,' said Strike.

'Well . . . the day after my eighteenth birthday, Luca and I got into a row. I can't remember what it was about, but he put his hand round my throat and pushed me up against the wall until I couldn't breathe. I was terrified.

'He let go, but there was this horrible look in his eye. He said,

"You've got only yourself to blame." And he said, "You're starting to sound like that doctor."

'I'd talked to him quite a lot about Margot, you see. I'd told him she was a complete killjoy, really bossy and opinionated. I kept repeating things she'd said, to denigrate them, to tell myself there was nothing in them.

'She quoted Simone de Beauvoir once, during a staff meeting. She'd sworn when she dropped her pen, and Dr Brenner said, "People are always asking me what it's like working with a lady doctor, and if I ever meet one, I'll be able to tell them." Dorothy laughed – she hardly ever laughed – and Margot snapped right back at him – I know the quotation off by heart now, in French, too – "Man is defined as a human being and a woman as a female – whenever she behaves as a human being she is said to imitate the male."

'Irene and I talked about it afterwards. We called her a show-off for quoting some French woman, but things like that got in my head and I couldn't get them out again. I thought I wanted to be a fifties Mafia housewife, but sometimes Margot was really funny, and I watched her never backing down to Brenner, and you couldn't help admiring her for it . . . '

Gloria took yet another gulp of wine.

'Anyway, the evening Luca half-throttled me, I went home and lay awake crying half the night. The next morning, I put on a polo-neck for work to hide the bruises, and at five o'clock that afternoon, when I left work, I went straight to a call box near the surgery, rang Luca and finished with him. I told him he'd scared me and that I didn't want to see him any more.

'He took it quite quietly. I was surprised, but so relieved . . . for three or four days I thought it was all over, and I felt amazing. It was like waking up, or coming up for air after being underwater. I still wanted to be a mobster's girlfriend, but the fantasy version was fine. I'd had a little bit too much contact with reality.

'Then, at the end of our practice Christmas party, in walked Luca, with his father and one of his cousins.

'I was absolutely *terrified* to see them there. Luca said to me, "Dad just wanted to meet my girlfriend." And – I don't know why, except

I was petrified of there being a scene – I just said, "Oh, OK." And I grabbed my coat and left with the three of them, before anyone could talk to them.

'They walked me to my bus stop. On the way, Nico said, "You're a nice girl. Luca was very upset by what you said to him on the phone. He's very fond of you, you know. You don't want to make him unhappy, do you?" Then he and Luca's cousin walked away. Luca said, "You didn't mean what you said, did you?" And I . . . I was so scared. Him bringing his father and cousin along . . . I told myself I'd be able to get out of it later. Just keep him happy for now. So I said, "No, I didn't mean it. You won't do anything like that ever again, though, will you?" And he said, "Like what?" As if he'd never pressed on my windpipe till I couldn't breathe. As though I'd imagined it.

'So, we carried on seeing each other,' said Gloria. 'Luca started talking about getting married. I kept saying I felt too young. Every time I came close to ending it, he'd accuse me of cheating on him, which was the worst crime of all, and there was no way of proving I wasn't, except to keep going out with him.'

Now Gloria looked away from them, her eyes on something off screen.

'We were sleeping together by then. I didn't want to. I'm not saying he forced me – not really,' said Gloria, and Robin thought of Shifty's PA, Gemma, 'but keeping him happy was the only way to keep going. Otherwise there'd be a slap or worse. One time, he made some comment about hurting my grandmother if I didn't behave. I went crazy at him, and he laughed, and said it was an obvious joke, but he wanted to plant the idea in my mind, and he succeeded.

'And he didn't believe in contraception. We were supposed to be using the . . . you know, the rhythm method,' said Gloria, reaching again for her wine. 'But he was . . . let's say, he was careless, and I was sure he wanted me pregnant, because then he'd have me cornered, and I'd marry him. My grandparents would probably have backed him up. They were devout people.

'So, without telling Luca, I went to Margot for the pill. She said she was happy to give it to me, but she didn't know I had a boyfriend, even, I'd never said . . .

'And even though I didn't really like her,' said Gloria, 'I told her some of it. It was the only place I could drop the pretence, I suppose. I knew she couldn't tell anyone outside her consulting room. She tried to talk sense into me. Tried to show me there were ways out of the situation, apart from just giving in to Luca all the time. I thought it was all right for her, with all her money and her big safe house . . .

'But she gave me a bit of hope, I suppose. Once, after he'd hit me, and told me I'd asked for it, and told me I should be grateful I had someone offering me a way out of living at home with two old people, I said, "There are other places I could go," and I think he got worried someone had offered to help me get away. I'd stopped making fun of Margot by this time, and Luca wasn't a stupid man . . .

'That's when he wrote her threatening notes. Anonymously, you know – but I knew it was him,' said Gloria. 'I knew his writing. Dorothy was off one day because her son was having his tonsils out, so Irene was opening the post and she unfolded one of the notes, right at the desk beside me. She was gloating about it, and I had to pretend to find it funny, but not to recognise the handwriting.

'I confronted Luca about it. He told me not to be so stupid, of course he hadn't written the notes, but I knew he had . . .

'Anyway – I think it was right after the second note – I found out what I'd been terrified about happening had happened. I was pregnant. I hadn't realised that the pill wouldn't work if you'd had a stomach upset, and I'd had a bug, a month before. I knew I was cornered, and it was too late, I'd have to marry Luca. The Riccis would want it, and my grandparents wouldn't want me to be an unwed mother.

'That's when I admitted it to myself for the first time,' said Gloria, looking directly at Strike and Robin. 'I absolutely hated Luca Ricci.'

'Gloria,' said Robin quietly, 'I'm sorry to interrupt, but could I ask you: when you were sick at Margot's barbecue—?'

'You heard about that, did you? Yes, that was when I had the tummy bug. People said one of the kids had spiked the punch, but I don't think so. Nobody else was as ill as I was.'

Out of the corner of Robin's eye, she saw Strike writing something in his notebook.

'I went back to Margot to find out for sure whether I was pregnant,' said Gloria. 'I knew I could trust her. I broke down again in her surgery, and cried my eyes out, when she confirmed it. And then . . . well, she was just lovely. She held my hand and talked to me for ages.

'I thought abortion was a sin,' said Gloria. 'That's the way I was raised. She didn't think it was a sin, not Margot. She talked to me about the life I was likely to have with Luca, if I had the baby. We discussed me keeping it, alone, but we both knew Luca wouldn't want that, that he'd be in my life for ever if I had his kid. It was hard, then, being on your own with a child. I was watching Janice the nurse doing it. Always juggling her son and the job.

'I didn't tell Luca, obviously,' said Gloria. 'I knew that if I was going to – to *do anything* – I had to do it quickly, before he noticed my body change, but most of all, before the baby could feel it or . . . '

Gloria suddenly bowed her head, and covered her face with her hands.

'I'm so sorry,' said Robin. 'It must have been awful for you . . . '

'No – well –' said Gloria, straightening up and again pushing back her white hair, her eyes wet. 'Never mind that. I'm only telling you, so you understand . . .

'Margot made the appointment for me. She gave the clinic her name and contact details and she bought us both wigs, because if she was recognised, someone might recognise me by association. And she came with me – it was a Saturday – to this place in Bride Street. I've never forgotten the name of the street, because a bride is exactly what I *didn't* want to be, and that's why I was there.

'The clinic had been using Margot's name as the referring doctor, and I think somewhere there were crossed wires, because they thought "Margot Bamborough" was the one having the procedure. Margot said, "It doesn't matter, nobody'll ever know, all these records are confidential." And she said, in a way it was convenient, if there was any follow-up needed, they could contact her and arrange it.

'She held my hand on the way in, and she was there when I woke up,' said Gloria, and now tears leaked from her dark eyes, and she brushed them quickly away. 'When I was ready to go home, she took me to the end of my grandparents' street in a taxi. She told me what to do afterwards, how to take care of myself . . .

'I wasn't like Margot,' said Gloria, her voice breaking. 'I didn't believe it was right, what I did. September the fourteenth: I don't think that date's come by once, since, that I haven't remembered, and thought about that baby.

'When I went back to work after a couple of days off, she took me into her office and asked me how I was feeling, and then she said, "Now, Gloria, you've got to be brave. If you stay with Luca, this will happen again." She said, "We need to find you a job away from London, and make sure he doesn't know where you've gone." And she said something that's stayed with me always, "We aren't our mistakes. It's what we do *about* the mistake that shows who we are."

'But I wasn't like Margot,' said Gloria again. 'I wasn't brave, I couldn't imagine leaving my grandparents. I pretended to agree, but ten days after the abortion I was sleeping with Luca again, not because I wanted to, but because there didn't seem any other choice.

'And then,' said Gloria, 'about a month after we'd been to the clinic, it happened. Margot disappeared.'

A muffled male voice was now heard at Gloria's end of the call. She turned towards the door behind her and said,

'*Non, c'est toujours en cours!*'

Turning back to her computer she said,

'*Pardon.* I mean, sorry.'

'Mrs Jaubert – Gloria,' said Strike, 'could we please take you back through the day Margot disappeared?'

'The whole day?'

Strike nodded. Gloria took a slow inward breath, like somebody about to dive into deep water, then said,

'Well, the morning was all normal. Everyone was there except Wilma the cleaner. She didn't come in on Fridays.

'I remember two things about the morning: meeting Janice by the kettle at the back, and her going on about the sequel to *The Godfather* coming out soon, and me pretending to be excited about it, and actually feeling as though I'd run a mile rather than go and see it . . . and Irene being quite smug and pleased because Janice had just been on a date with some man she'd been trying to set Janice up with for ages.

'Irene was funny about Janice,' said Gloria. 'They were supposed to be such great friends, but she was always going on about Janice being a bit of a man-eater, which was funny if you'd known Irene. She used to say that Janice needed to learn to cut her cloth, that she was deluded, waiting for someone like James Caan to show up and sweep her off her feet, because she was a single mother and not that great a catch. Irene thought the best she could hope for was this man from Eddie's work, who sounded a bit simple. Irene was always laughing about him getting things wrong . . .

'We were quite busy, as I remember it, all three doctors coming in and out of the waiting room to call for their patients. I can't remember anything unusual about the afternoon except that Irene left early. She claimed she had toothache, but I thought it was a fib at the time. She hadn't seemed in pain to me, when she was going on about Janice's love life.

'I knew Margot was meeting her friend later in the pub. She told me, because she had a doughnut in cling film in the fridge, and she asked me to bring it through to her, right before she saw her last patient, to keep her going. She loved sugar. She was always in the biscuit tin at five o'clock. She had one of those metabolisms, never put on weight, full of nervous energy.

'I remember the doughnut, because when I took it in to her, I said, "Why didn't you just eat those chocolates?" She had a box she'd taken out of the bin, I think it was the day before. I mean, they were still in their cellophane when she took them out of the bin, it wasn't unhygienic. Someone had sent them to her—'

'Someone?' repeated Strike.

'Well, we all thought it was that patient the police were so interested in, Steve Douthwaite,' said Gloria. 'Dorothy thought that, anyway.'

'Wasn't there a message attached?'

'There was a card saying "Thank you",' said Gloria, 'and Dorothy might've made the assumption it was Steve Douthwaite, because we all thought he was turning up a lot. I don't think the card was signed, though.'

'So Margot threw the box in the bin, and then took it out again, afterwards?'

'Yes, because I laughed at her about it,' said Gloria. 'I said, "I knew you couldn't resist," and she laughed, too. And next day, when I said, "Why don't you eat them?" she said, "I have, I've finished them."'

'But she still had the box there?'

'Yes, on the shelf with her books. I went back to the front desk. Dr Brenner's patient left, but Brenner didn't, because he was writing up the notes.'

'Could I ask you whether you knew about Dr Brenner's barbiturate addiction?' asked Strike.

'His what?' said Gloria.

'Nobody ever told you about that?'

'No,' she said, looking surprised. 'I had no idea.'

'You never heard that Janice had found an Amytal capsule in the bottom of a cup of tea?'

'No . . . oh. Is that why Margot started making her own tea? She told me Irene made it too milky.'

'Let's go back to the order in which everyone left.'

'OK, so, Dr Gupta's patient was next, and Dr Gupta left immediately afterwards. He had some family dinner he needed to attend, so off he went.

'And then, just when I was thinking we were done for the day, in walked that girl, Theo.'

'Tell us about Theo,' said Strike.

'Long black hair . . . dark-skinned. She looked Romanian or Turkish. Ornate earrings, you know: gypsy-ish. I actually thought she looked like a gypsy. I'd never seen her before, so I knew she wasn't registered with us. She looked as though she was in a lot of pain, with her stomach. She came up to the desk and asked to see a doctor urgently. I asked her name, and she said Theo . . . something or other. I didn't ask her again because she was obviously suffering, so I told her to wait and went to see whether a doctor was free. Margot's door was still closed, so I asked Dr Brenner. He didn't want to see her. He was always like that, always difficult. I never liked him.

'Then Margot's door opened, and the mother and child who'd

been seeing her left, and she said she'd see the girl who was waiting.'

'And Theo was definitely a girl?' asked Strike.

'Without any doubt at all,' said Gloria firmly. 'She was broad-shouldered, I noticed that when she came to the desk, but she was definitely a woman. Maybe it was the shoulders that made Dr Brenner say, afterwards, she looked like a man, but honestly . . .

'I was thinking about him last night, knowing I was going to be talking to you. Brenner was probably the biggest misogynist I ever met. He'd denigrate women for not looking feminine or talking "like a lady", but he also despised Irene, who was giggly and blonde and very feminine, you know. I suppose what he wanted was for us all to be like Dorothy, subordinate and respectful, high collars, low hemlines. Dorothy was like a really humourless nun.'

Robin thought of Betty Fuller, lying on a bed, pretending to be comatose, while Brenner poured filthy words into her ear.

'Women patients really didn't like Brenner. We were always having them asking to switch to Margot, but we had to turn most of them down, because her list was so full. But Brenner was coming up for retirement and we were hoping we'd get someone better when he went.

'So, yes, he left, and Theo went in to see Margot. I kept checking the time, because I was supposed to be meeting Luca, and if I kept him waiting, there was always trouble. But Theo's appointment just went on and on. At a quarter past six, Theo finally came back out of the surgery and left.

'Margot came through just a couple of minutes later. She seemed absolutely exhausted. It had been a full day. She said, "I'm going to write her notes up tomorrow, I've got to go, Oonagh's waiting. Lock up with the spare key." I didn't really answer,' said Gloria, 'because I was so worried about Luca getting angry with me. So, I never said goodbye, or have a good evening, to this woman who saved my life . . .

'Because she did, you know. I never said it to her, but she did . . . '

A tear trickled down her face. Gloria paused to wipe it away, then said,

'I remember, as she put her umbrella up, she slipped. Turned over on her heel. It was raining, the pavement was wet. Then she straightened up and walked out of sight.

'I started dashing round, turning off lights, locking the records up in the filing cabinets. Then I made sure the back door was locked, which it was – the police asked me about that. I closed and locked the front door, and ran straight up Passing Alley, which was right beside the surgery, to meet Luca in St John Street.

'And that was the last time I ever saw Margot.'

Gloria reached again for her almost empty wine glass, and drained it.

'Did you have any idea what might have happened to her?' asked Strike.

'Of course,' said Gloria quietly. 'I was terrified Luca had got someone to hurt her, or kidnap her. She'd become a bugbear to him. Every time I stood up for myself, he'd say horrible things about Margot influencing me. He was convinced she was trying to persuade me to leave him, which, of course, she was. My greatest fear was that he'd somehow find out what she'd helped me do . . . you know. In Bride Street.

'I knew he couldn't have abducted her personally, because I met him on St John Street, not five minutes after she left the surgery, and I know it can't have been his father, because his brother Marco was in hospital at the time, and the parents were with him round the clock. But Luca had friends and cousins.

'I couldn't tell the police. Luca had stopped pretending he was joking, when he threatened my grandparents. I asked him whether he was behind it, though. The anxiety was too much: I had to ask. He got really angry, called me names – dumb bitch, things like that. He said, of course he hadn't. But he'd told me stories about his father "making people disappear", so I just didn't know . . . '

'Did you ever have reason to suppose he knew . . . ' Robin hesitated ' . . . what happened in Bride Street?'

'I'm absolutely positive he never knew,' said Gloria. 'Margot was too good for him. The wigs and using her name and giving me a plausible story for why I couldn't have sex with him for a while . . . She's the reason I got away with it. No, I don't believe he ever knew.

So, in my best moments, I thought, he didn't really have a strong enough reason—'

The door behind Gloria opened, and in walked a handsome aquiline-nosed, grey-haired man in a striped shirt and jeans, carrying a bottle of red wine. A large German Shepherd dog followed him into the room, its tail wagging.

'*Je m'excuse,*' he said, smiling at Strike and Robin onscreen. 'I am sorry for . . . *Comment dit-on "interrompre"?*' he asked his wife.

'Interrupt,' she said.

'*Oui.* I am sorry for interrupt.'

He refilled his wife's glass, handed it back to her, patted her on the shoulder, then walked out again, calling the dog.

'*Viens, Obélix.*'

When both man and dog had disappeared, Gloria said, with a little laugh,

'That was Hugo.'

'How long did you stay at the St John's practice, after Margot disappeared?' asked Strike, although he knew the answer.

'Six, seven months, I think,' said Gloria. 'Long enough to see the new policeman take over. We were all pleased, because the first – Talbot, wasn't it? – was quite strange. He bullied the life out of Wilma and Janice. I think that's what made Wilma ill, actually. She had quite enough on her plate without the police hounding her.'

'You don't think she drank, then?' asked Robin.

'Drank? That was all Dorothy's malice,' said Gloria, shaking her head. 'Dorothy was trying to pin the thefts on Wilma. Have you heard about that?'

Strike and Robin nodded.

'When she couldn't prove that Wilma was taking money out of people's bags, she put it about that she was drinking and the poor woman resigned. She was probably glad to leave, but it was still losing a salary, wasn't it?

'I wanted to leave myself,' said Gloria, 'but I was paralysed. I had this really strange feeling that, if I just stayed there, the world would right itself. Margot would come back. It was only after she disappeared that I realised . . . what she'd been to me . . .

'Anyway,' sighed Gloria, 'one night, months after she'd disappeared, Luca was *really* violent to me. I'd smiled at a man who opened a door for me as I left the pub with Luca, that's what sparked it. He beat me like he'd never beaten me before, at his place – he had this little flat.

'I remember saying "I'm sorry, I'm sorry, I shouldn't have smiled at him". And all the time I was saying it, I could see – in here –' Gloria tapped her head, 'Margot watching me, and even while I was begging Luca to stop, and agreeing I'd behaved like a little slut, and I shouldn't ever smile at strange men, I was thinking, *I'm going, Margot. I'm going where he'll never find me.*

'Because it had clicked in my head at last. She'd told me I needed to be brave. It was no good waiting for anyone else to save me. *I* had to save me.

'After he'd calmed down, he let me go home to my grandparents' house, but he wanted to see me again later. It was always like that after he'd been really violent. He wanted extra contact.

'He hadn't beaten me in the face. He never did, he never lost control like that, so I went back to my grandparents' and acted as though everything was fine. Went out to meet Luca that night, and he took me out for dinner, and that was the night he proposed, with a ring and everything.

'And I said yes,' said Gloria, with a strange smile and a shrug. 'I put that ring on, and I looked down at it, and I didn't even have to act happy, because I genuinely was. I thought *That'll buy some of my plane ticket.* Mind you, I'd never flown before in my life. The idea of it scared me. But all the time, I could see Margot in my head. *You've got to be brave, Gloria.*

'I had to tell my grandparents I was engaged. I couldn't tell them what I was really planning, because I was scared they wouldn't be able to act, or that they'd try and confront Luca or, worse, go to the police. Anyway, Luca came round to the house to meet them properly, pretending to be a nice guy, and it was awful, and I had to act as though I was thrilled about all of it.

'Every single day after that, I bought all the newspapers, and circled all of the jobs abroad that I might have a chance of getting. I had to do all of it in secret. Typed up a CV at work and got a bus to the West End to post all the applications, because I was scared someone who knew Luca would see me putting lots of envelopes in the post.

'After a few weeks, I got an interview with a French woman who was looking for an English home help, to teach her kids English. What really got me the job was being able to type. She ran her own business from home, so I could do a bit of admin for her while the kids were at nursery. The job came with room and board, and my employer would buy my plane ticket, so I didn't have to sell Luca's ring, and pretend I'd lost it . . .

'You know, the day I went into St John's and told them I was resigning, a funny thing happened. Nobody had mentioned Margot for weeks. Immediately after she disappeared, it was all any of us could talk about, but then it became taboo, somehow. We had a new locum doctor in her room. I can't remember his name. A new cleaner, too. But this day, Dorothy arrived, quite flustered, and she never showed any emotion, usually . . .

'This local . . . what's the word?' said Gloria, clicking her fingers, for the first time lost in her native language. 'We'd say *un dingue* . . . oh, you know, a crazy man, a loon . . . harmless, but strange. Big long beard, dirty, you used to see him wandering up and down Clerkenwell Road with his son. Anyway, he'd sort of accosted Dorothy in the middle of the street, and told her he killed Margot Bamborough.

'It had shaken Dorothy up, but in an odd way . . . please don't think this is awful . . . I hoped it was true. Because although I'd have given *anything* to know Margot was alive, I was sure she was dead. She wasn't the type to run away. And my worst nightmare was that Luca was responsible, because that meant it was all my fault.'

Robin shook her head, but Gloria ignored her.

'I only told my grandparents the truth the night before I was due to leave for France. I hadn't let them spend any money on the wedding that wasn't going to happen, but even so, it was a huge shock to them. I sat them down, and told them everything, except for the termination.

'Of course, they were appalled. At first, they didn't want me to leave, they wanted me to go to the police. I had to explain why that was a terrible idea, tell them about the threats Luca had made, and all of that. But they were so glad I wasn't marrying him, they accepted it in the end. I told them it would all die down, and I'd be back soon . . . even though I wasn't sure that was true, or if it would be possible.

'My grandfather took me to the airport, early next day. We'd worked out a story, for when Luca came asking where I was. They were to say I'd been having doubts, because he'd been violent, and that I'd gone over to Italy to stay with some of Dad's relatives, to think things over. We even concocted a fake address to give him. I don't know whether he ever wrote to it.

'And that's everything,' said Gloria, sitting back in the desk chair. 'I stayed with my first employer for seven years, and ended up with a junior position in her firm. I didn't visit London again until I heard Luca was safely married.' She took another sip of wine from the glass her husband had refilled. 'His first wife drank herself to death at the age of thirty-nine. He used to beat her badly. I found all that out later.

'And I've never told another lie about myself,' said Gloria, raising her chin. 'Never exaggerated, never pretended, only ever told the absolute truth, except on one point. Until tonight, the only person who knew about the abortion was Hugo, but now you two know, too.

'Even if you find out Luca was behind what happened to Margot, and I have to have that on my conscience for ever, I owe her the truth. That woman saved me, and I've never, ever forgotten her. She was one of the bravest, kindest people I've ever known.'

67

There by th'vncertaine glims of starry night,
And by the twinkling of their sacred fire,
He mote perceiue a litle dawning sight . . .

Edmund Spenser
The Faerie Queene

They thanked Gloria for her time and her honesty. Having bidden her goodbye, Strike and Robin sat at the partners' desk, each of them sunk in thought, until Strike offered Robin one of the pots of dehydrated noodles he kept for snacks in the office. She declined, instead taking a bag of mixed nuts unenthusiastically out of her bag, and opening it. Once Strike had added boiling water to the plastic pot, he returned to the desk, stirring the noodles with a fork.

'It's the efficiency,' he said, sitting down again. 'That's what's bugging me. Literally no trace of her anywhere. Somebody was either extraordinarily clever, or unprecedentedly lucky. And Creed still fits that picture best, with Luca Ricci a close second.'

'Except it can't have been Luca. He's got an alibi: Gloria.'

'But as she says, he knew people who could take care of making someone disappear – because what are the odds, if Margot was abducted off the street, that this was a *truly* one-person job? Even Creed had his unwitting accomplices. The dozy landlady, giving him that safe basement, and the dry cleaner letting him have the van that day and n—'

'Don't,' said Robin sharply.

'Don't what?'

'Blame them.'

'I'm not blaming them, I'm—'

'Max and I were talking about this,' said Robin. 'About the way people – women, usually – get blamed for not knowing, or seeing – but everyone's guilty of that kind of bias. Everyone does it.'

'You think?' said Strike thickly, through his first mouthful of noodles.

'Yes,' said Robin. 'We've all got a tendency to generalise from our own past experiences. Look at Violet Cooper. She thought she knew who Creed really was, because she'd met a couple of men who behaved like him, in her theatre days.'

'Men who wouldn't let anyone in their basement flats because they were boiling down skulls?'

'You know what I mean, Strike,' said Robin, refusing to be amused. 'Soft-spoken, apparently gentle, slightly feminine. Creed liked putting on her feather boa, and he pretended to like show tunes, so she thought he was a gay man. But if the only gay man she'd met had been Max, my flatmate . . . '

'He's gay, is he?' said Strike, whose memories of Max were indistinct.

'Yes, and he isn't remotely camp, and hates musicals. Come to that, if she'd met a couple of Matt's straight mates down the rugby club, who couldn't wait to shove oranges up their T-shirts and prance around, she might've drawn a different conclusion, mightn't she?'

'S'pose so,' said Strike, chewing noodles and considering this point. 'And in fairness, most people don't know any serial killers.'

'Exactly. So even if somebody's got some unusual habits, our direct experience tends to suggest they're just eccentric. Vi had never met a man who fetishised women's clothing or . . . sorry, I'm boring you,' Robin added, because Strike's eyes seemed to have glazed over.

'No, you aren't,' he muttered. 'You're actually making me think . . . I had an idea, you know. I thought I'd spotted some coincidences, and it got me wondering . . . '

He set down the pot of noodles, reached under the desk and

pulled one of the boxes of police evidence towards him, on top of which lay the pages he'd last been re-examining. He now took these bits of paper out, spread them in front of himself again, and resumed his noodle-eating.

'Are you going to tell me about the coincidences?' said Robin with a trace of impatience.

'Hang on a minute,' said Strike, looking up at her. 'Why was Theo standing *outside* the phone box?'

'What?' said Robin, confused.

'I don't think we can doubt, now, can we, that Ruby Elliot saw Theo by that phone box near Albemarle Way? Her description and Gloria's tally exactly ... so why was Theo standing *outside* the phone box?'

'She was waiting for the van to pick her up.'

'Right. But, not to state the bleeding obvious, the sides of the old red telephone boxes have windows. It was pissing down with rain. Theo didn't have an umbrella, and Ruby said Theo's hair was plastered down — so why didn't she shelter in the telephone box, and keep watch for her lift? Clerkenwell Road's long and straight. She'd've had a perfectly good view from that telephone box, and plenty of time to come out and show herself to the van driver. Why,' said Strike for the third time, 'was she standing *outside* the phone box?'

'Because ... there was someone in it?'

'That would seem the obvious explanation. And that phone box at the end of Albemarle Way would give you a view of the top of St John's Lane.'

'You think someone was lying in wait for Margot? Watching out from that phone box?'

Strike hesitated.

'Do me a favour and look up Fragile X syndrome?'

'OK ... why?' said Robin, setting down her almonds and beginning to type.

'That phone box is at the end of the Athorns' street.'

While Robin brought up the search results, Strike pulled the copy of Irene Hickson's receipt towards him. It had the time 3.10 p.m. on it. Eating noodles, Strike was still looking at the slip of paper when Robin said, reading off her screen,

'"First called Martin–Bell syndrome . . . the FMR1 gene on the X chromosome was sequenced in 1991" . . . Sorry, what exactly do you need?'

'What specific disabilities does it cause?'

'"Social anxiety",' said Robin, reading again, '"lack of eye contact . . . challenges forming relationships . . . anxiety with unfamiliar situations and people . . . poor ability to recognise faces you've seen before", but "good long-term memory, good imitation skills and good visual learning". Men are more severely affected than women . . . good sense of humour, usually . . . "can be creative, especially visually" . . . '

She looked around the computer monitor.

'Why d'you want to know all this?'

'Just thinking.'

'About Gwilherm?'

'Yeah,' said Strike. 'Well, about the whole family.'

'*He* didn't have Fragile X, though, did he?'

'No, I don't know what Gwilherm's problem was. Maybe just the Bennies.'

He didn't smile as he said the name this time.

'Cormoran, what coincidences did you notice?'

Instead of answering, Strike pulled a couple of pages of police notes towards him and read through them again. Out of force of habit, Robin reached out for Talbot's notebook, and turned to the first page. For a couple of minutes, there was silence in the office, and neither partner noticed any of the noises that were as familiar to them as their own breathing: the traffic rolling down Charing Cross Road, occasional shouts and snatches of music from Denmark Street below.

The very first page of Bill Talbot's notebook began with untidy jottings of what Robin knew to be genuine evidence and observations. It was the most coherent part of the notes but the first pentagrams appeared at the very bottom of the page, as did the first astrological observation.

(Theo? MALE?) white van speeding Aylesbury St away from Clerkenwell Green Two women struggling by phone boxes, smaller in rainhat, taller in raincoat, seems unsteady on feet, then VAN speeding away from Clerkenwell Green ♃ is currently retrograde in ♓ meaning planet of OBJECTIVE TRUTH in sign of ILLUSION and FANTASY

Robin re-read this final paragraph twice, frowning slightly. Then she set aside her bag of almonds to delve in the nearest box of police evidence. It took her five minutes to find the original police record of Ruby Elliot's statement, and while she searched, Strike remained deeply immersed in his own portion of the notes.

> I saw them beside a telephone box, two women sort of struggling together. The tall one in the raincoat was leaning on the short one, who was in a plastic rain hood. They both looked like women to me, but I didn't see their faces. It looked to me like one was trying to make the other walk quicker.

Pulse now quickened, Robin set aside this piece of paper, got back onto her knees and began to search for the record of Ruby's statement to Lawson, which took her another five minutes.

> I saw them beside the two telephone boxes in Clerkenwell Green, two women struggling with each together. The tall one in the raincoat was trying to make the little one in the rain hood walk faster.

'Cormoran,' said Robin urgently.
Strike looked up.
'The heights are round the wrong way.'
'What?'
'In Ruby's very first statement to Talbot,' Robin said, 'she said, "I saw them beside a telephone box, two women sort of struggling together. The tall one in the raincoat was leaning on the short one, who was in a plastic rain hood. They both looked like women to me, but I didn't see their faces. It looked to me like one was trying to make the other walk quicker."'

838

'Right,' said Strike, frowning slightly.

'And that's what Talbot wrote in his horoscope notes, too,' said Robin. 'But that's not how it should have been, if those two women were the Fleurys. Where's that picture?'

'Box one,' said Strike, shoving it towards Robin with his real foot.

She crouched down beneath the desk and began searching the photocopied papers until she found the sheaf of newspaper clippings Strike had shown her, months previously, in the Three Kings.

'There,' said Robin. 'Look. *There.*'

And there was the old picture, of the two women who'd come forward to say that they were Ruby's struggling women: the tall, broad, younger woman with her cheery face, and her aged mother, who was tiny and stooped.

'It's the wrong way round,' repeated Robin. 'If Fiona Fleury had leaned on her mother, she'd have flattened her ... ' Robin scanned the few lines beneath the picture. 'Cormoran, *it doesn't fit.* Fiona says *she* was wearing the rain hat, but Ruby says it was the short woman who had the rainhat on.'

'Ruby was vague,' said Strike, but Robin could see his interest sharpening as he reached out for these pieces of paper. 'She could've been confused ... '

'Talbot never thought the Fleurys were the people Ruby saw, and this is why!' said Robin. 'The heights were reversed. It was the taller woman Ruby saw who was unsteady, not the little one ... '

'So how come she didn't tell Lawson the Fleurys couldn't be the people she saw?'

'Same reason she never told anybody she'd seen Theo? Because she'd been flustered by Talbot trying to force her to bend her story to fit his theories? Because she lost confidence in herself, and didn't know what she'd really seen? It was raining, she was lost, she was panicked ... by the time it got to Lawson, maybe she just wanted to agree she'd seen the Fleurys and be left alone?'

'Plausible,' admitted Strike.

'How tall was Margot?'

'Five nine,' said Strike.

'And Creed?' said Robin.

'Five seven.'

'Oh God,' said Robin quietly.

There was another minute's silence, while Strike sat lost in thought and Robin re-read the statements laid out in front of her.

'The phone boxes,' said Strike, at last. 'Those bloody phone boxes . . .'

'What about them?'

'Talbot wanted Ruby to have seen the two struggling women beside the two boxes in Clerkenwell Green, right? So he could tie them to the van that was speeding away up Aylesbury Street, which was supposed to contain Creed.'

'Right,' said Robin.

'But after the Fleurys came forward, Talbot tried to get Ruby to agree she'd seen the two struggling women beside the first phone box, the one at the end of Albemarle Way.'

'But she wouldn't change her story,' said Robin, 'because she'd seen Theo there.'

'Precisely,' said Strike, 'but that doesn't make sense.'

'I don't—'

'She's driving round in an enormous circle in the rain, right, looking for this house she can't find, right?'

'Yes . . .'

'Well, just because Ruby saw Theo get into a van by the phone box on one of her circuits doesn't mean she can't have seen two struggling women on her second or third circuit. We know she was hazy about landmarks, unfamiliar with the area and with no sense of direction, her daughter was very clear about that. But she had this very retentive visual memory, she's somebody who notices clothes and hairstyles . . .'

Strike looked down at the desk again, and for the second time, picked up Irene Hickson's receipt and examined it. Then, so suddenly that Robin jumped, Strike let the receipt fall and stood up, both hands clasped over the back of his head.

'Shit,' he said. '*Shit! Never* trust a phone call whose provenance you haven't checked!'

'What phone call?' said Robin nervously, casting her mind back over any phone calls she'd taken over the course of the case.

'Fuck's sake,' said Strike, walking out of the room into the outer office and then back again, still clasping the back of his head, apparently needing to pace, just as Robin had needed to walk when she'd found out Strike could interview Creed. *'How did I not fucking see it?'*

'Cormoran, what—?'

'Why did Margot keep an empty chocolate box?' said Strike.

'I don't know,' said Robin, confused.

'You know what?' said Strike slowly. 'I think I do.'

68

. . . an Hyena was,
That feeds on wemens flesh, as others feede on gras.

Edmund Spenser
The Faerie Queene

The high-security mental hospital that is Broadmoor lies slightly over an hour outside London, in the county of Berkshire. The word 'Broadmoor' had long since lost all bucolic associations in the collective mind of the British public, and Strike was no exception to this rule. Far from connoting a wide stretch of grassland or heath, the name spoke to Strike only of violence, heinous crimes and two hundred of the most dangerous men in Britain, whom the tabloids called monsters. Accordingly, and in spite of the fact that Strike knew he was visiting a hospital and not a prison, he took all the common sense measures he'd have taken for a high-security jail: he wore no tie, ensured that neither he or his car was carrying anything likely to trigger a burdensome search, brought two kinds of photographic ID and a copy of his letter from the Ministry of Justice, set out early, certain, though he'd never been there before, that getting inside the facility would be time-consuming.

It was a golden September morning. Sunshine pouring down upon the road ahead from between fluffy white clouds, and as Strike drove through Berkshire in his BMW, he listened to the news on the radio, the lead item of which was that Scotland had voted, by 55 per cent to 45 per cent, to remain in the United Kingdom. He was wondering how Dave Polworth and Sam Barclay were taking the news, when his mobile rang.

'It's Brian, Brian Tucker,' said the hoarse voice. 'Not interrupting, am I? Wanna wish you good luck.'

'Thanks, Brian,' said Strike.

They'd finally met three days previously, at Strike's office. Tucker had shown Strike the old letter from Creed, described the butterfly pendant taken from the killer's basement, which he believed was his daughter's, shared his theories and trembled with emotion and nerves at the thought of Strike coming face to face with the man he believed had murdered his eldest daughter.

'I'll let you go, I won't keep you,' said Tucker. 'You'll ring me when it's over, though?'

'I will, of course,' said Strike.

It was hard to concentrate on the news now that he'd heard Tucker's anxiety and excitement. Strike turned off the radio, and turned his thoughts instead to what lay ahead.

Gratifying though it would be to believe that he, Cormoran Strike, might trick or persuade Creed into confessing where all others had failed, Strike wasn't that egotistical. He'd interviewed plenty of suspects in his career; the skill lay in making it easier for a suspect to disclose the truth than to continue lying. Some were worn down by patient questioning, others resistant to all but intense pressure, still others yearned to unburden themselves, and the interrogator's methods had to change accordingly.

However, in talking to Creed, half of Strike's interrogatory arsenal would be out of commission. For one thing, he was there at Creed's pleasure, because the patient had had to give his consent for the interview. For another, it was hard to see how Strike could paint a frightening picture of the consequences of silence, when his interviewee was already serving life in Broadmoor. Creed's secrets were the only power he had left, and Strike was well aware that persuading him to relinquish any of them might prove a task beyond any human investigator. Standard appeals to conscience, or to the desire to figure as a better person to the self or to others, were likewise useless. As Creed's entire life demonstrated, his primary sources of enjoyment were inflicting pain and establishing dominance, and it was doubtful that anything else would persuade him into disclosures.

Strike's first glimpse of the infamous hospital was of a fortress on raised ground. It had been built by the Victorians in the middle of woodland and meadows, a red-brick edifice with a clocktower the highest point in the compound. The surrounding walls were twenty feet high, and as Strike drove up to the front gates, he could see the heads of hundreds of Cyclopean security cameras on poles. As the gates opened, Strike experienced an explosion of adrenalin, and for a moment the ghostly black and white images of seven dead women, and the anxious face of Brian Tucker, seemed to swim before him.

He'd sent his car registration number in advance. Once through the first set of double gates he encountered an inner wire fence, as tall as the wall he'd just passed through. A white-shirted, black-trousered man of military bearing unlocked a second set of gates once the first had closed behind the BMW, and directed Strike to a parking space. Before leaving his car, and wanting to save time going through the security he was about to face, the detective put his phone, keys, belt, cigarettes, lighter and loose change into the glove compartment and locked it.

'Mr Strike, is it?' said the smiling, white-shirted man, whose accent was Welsh and whose profile suggested a boxer. 'Got your ID there?'

Strike showed his driver's licence, and was led inside, where he encountered a scanner of the airport security type. Good-humoured, inevitable amusement ensued when the scanner announced shrill disapproval of Strike's metal lower leg, and his trousers had to be rolled up to prove he wasn't carrying a weapon. Having been patted down, he was free to join Dr Ranbir Bijral, who was waiting for him on the other side of the scanners, a slight, bearded psychiatrist whose open-necked yellow shirt struck a cheerful note against the dull green-grey tiled floors, the white walls and the unfresh air of all medical institutions, part disinfectant, part fried food, with a trace of incarcerated human.

'We've got twenty minutes until Dennis will be ready for you,' said Dr Bijral, leading Strike off along an eerily empty corridor, through

many sets of turquoise swing doors. 'We coordinate patient movements carefully and it's always a bit of a feat moving him around. We
have to make sure he never comes into contact with patients who
have a particular dislike for him, you see. He's not popular. We'll
wait in my office.'

Strike was familiar with hospitals, but had never been inside one
with so little bustle or shuffle of patients in the corridors. The emptiness was slightly unnerving. They passed many locked doors. A
short female nurse in navy scrubs marched past. She smiled at Strike,
who smiled back.

'You've got women working here,' he said, slightly surprised.

'Of course,' said Dr Bijral.

Strike had somehow imagined an all-male staff, even though he
knew that male prisons had female warders. Dr Bijral pushed open a
door to a small office that had the air of a converted treatment room,
with chipped paint on the walls and bars on the windows.

'Have a seat,' said Dr Bijral, waving his hand at the chair opposite
his desk, and with slightly forced politeness, he asked, 'Did you have
a good journey? Come up from London?'

'Yeah, it was a nice drive,' said Strike.

As he sat down behind the desk, Dr Bijral became business-like.

'All right, so: we're going to give you forty-five minutes
with Creed.'

'Forty-five minutes,' repeated Strike.

'If Dennis wants to admit to another killing, that should be ample
time,' said Dr Bijral, 'but . . . may I be honest with you, Mr Strike?'

'Of course.'

'If it had been down to Dennis's treatment team, we prob-
ably wouldn't have permitted this visit. I know the MoJ feel the
Bamboroughs and the Tuckers ought to be given a last chance to ask
Dennis about their relatives, but—'

Dr Bijral leaned back in his seat and sighed.

'—he's a classic sociopath, you see, a pure example of the type. He
scores very highly on the dark triad: narcissism, Machiavellianism
and psychopathy. Devious, sadistic, unrepentant and extremely
egotistical.'

'Not a fan, then?' said Strike, and the doctor permitted himself a perfunctory smile.

'The problem, you see, is if he admitted to another murder under your questioning, you'd get the credit. And Dennis can't have that, he can't allow somebody else to come out on top. He had to give his consent to meeting you, of course, and I think he's agreed because it feeds his ego to be questioned, especially by a man who's been in the papers, and I think he'd like to manipulate you into being an advocate for him in some way. He's been lobbying to get out of Broadmoor and back into prison for a long time now.'

'I thought he was desperate to get in here?'

'He was, once,' said Bijral. 'High-profile sex offenders are usually under risk of attack in the prison system, as you probably know. You might have seen in the papers, one man nearly took his eye out with a sharpened spoon handle. Dennis wanted to come to Broadmoor when he was first convicted, but there were no grounds to admit him to hospital back then. Psychopathy isn't, in itself, treatable.'

'What changed?'

'He was exceptionally difficult to manage in the prison system. He managed to talk a young offender with Asperger's syndrome into killing himself. For that, he was put into solitary confinement. They ended up keeping him there for almost a year. By night, he took to re-enacting what had happened in the basement in Liverpool Road, screaming through the night, doing his voice and the women's. Warders couldn't stand hearing it, let alone prisoners.

'After eleven months in solitary, he became suicidal. First he went on hunger strike. Then he began trying to bite his own wrists open, and smashing his head against the wall. He was assessed, judged psychotic and transferred here.

'Once we'd had him a couple of months, he claimed he'd been faking his mental illness, which is pure Dennis. Nobody else can be cleverer than he is. But actually, his mental health was very poor when he came to us, and it took many months of medication and therapy to stop him self-harming and trying to kill himself.'

'And now he wants to leave?'

'Once he was well enough to fully appreciate the difference

between jail and hospital, I think it's fair to say he was disappointed. He had more freedom in Belmarsh. He did a lot of writing and drawing before he got ill. I read the autobiography he'd been working on, when he was admitted. It was useful in assessing him. He writes very well for a man who had hardly any education, but ... ' Dr Bijral laced his fingers together, and Strike was reminded of another doctor, who'd talked of teamwork while eating fig rolls. 'You see, persuading patients to discuss their crimes is usually an important part of the therapeutic process. You're trying to find a pathway to accountability and remorse, but Dennis feels no remorse. He's still aroused by the thought of what he did to those women, and he enjoys talking and writing about it. He used to draw episodes from the basement, as well; essentially producing his own hardcore pornography. So when he came here, we confiscated all writing and drawing materials.

'Dennis blames us for his deteriorating mental faculties, although in fact, for a seventy-seven-year-old man, he's remarkably sharp. Every patient is different, and we manage Dennis on a strict reward and penalty system. His chosen rewards are unusual. He enjoys chess; he taught himself in Belmarsh, so sometimes I'll give him a game. He likes crosswords and logic puzzles, too. We allow him access to those when he's behaving himself.

'But you mustn't think he's typical of our patients,' added Dr Bijral earnestly. 'The vast majority of mentally ill people pose absolutely no risk of violence, as I'm sure you know. And people do leave Broadmoor, they do get better. People's behaviour can change, if they're motivated, if they're given the right help. Our aim is always recovery. One can hate the crime, but feel compassion for the perpetrator. Many of the men in here had appallingly abusive childhoods. Dennis's childhood was pure hell – though, of course, other people have upbringings as bad and never do what Dennis did. In fact, one of our former patients—'

There was a knock on the door and a cheery blonde poked her head inside.

'That's Dennis ready in the room, Ranbir,' she said, and withdrew.

'Shall we?' said Dr Bijral, getting to his feet. 'I'll be sitting in on the interview, and so will Dennis's primary nurse.'

847

The woman who'd announced Dennis's arrival in the meeting room walked with Strike and the psychiatrist down another couple of corridors. Now there were doors that had to be unlocked and relocked at every passage. Through the third set of locked doors, Strike saw an obese man shuffling along in Nike tracksuit bottoms, flanked by a pair of nurses, each of whom held one of the patient's stiff arms behind his back. The patient gave Strike a glazed look as the trio passed in silence.

Finally, Strike's party reached a deserted open-plan area, with armchairs and a switched-off TV. Strike had assumed the blonde woman was Creed's nurse, but he was wrong: a burly man with tattoos down both arms, and a prominent, square jaw, was introduced as 'Marvin, Dennis's lead nurse', and the blonde woman smiled at Strike, wished him luck and walked away.

'Well, shall we?' said Dr Bijral, and Marvin opened the door onto a Spartan meeting room, with a single window and a whiteboard on the wall.

The only occupant, a small, obese, bespectacled man, wore jeans and a black sweatshirt. He had a triple chin, and his belly kept him a foot and a half away from the white Formica-topped table at which he was sitting. Transplanted to a bus stop, Dennis Creed would have been just another old man, a little unkempt, his light grey hair in need of a trim.

(He'd pressed hot-irons to the bare breasts of secretary Jackie Aylett. He'd pulled out all of hairdresser Susan Meyer's finger and toenails. He'd dug the eyeballs out of estate agent Noreen Sturrock's face while she was still alive and manacled to a radiator.)

'Dennis, this is Cormoran Strike,' said Dr Bijral, as he sat down in a chair against the wall. Marvin stood, tattooed arms folded, beside him.

'Hello, Dennis,' said Strike, sitting down opposite him.

'Hello, Cormoran,' said Creed, in a flat voice which retained its working-class, East London accent.

The sunlight fell like a gleaming pane across the table between them, highlighting the smears on the lenses of Creed's wire-rimmed glasses and the dust motes in the air. Behind the dirt, Strike saw irises of such pale grey that they faded into the sclera, so that the enormous pupils seemed surrounded by whiteness. Close to, Strike could see the jagged scar which ran from temple to nose, dragging at his left lower eyelid, a relic of the attack that had almost taken half Creed's sight. The plump, pale hands on the table were slightly shaking and the slack mouth trembled: side-effects, Strike guessed, of Creed's medication.

'Who're you working for?' Creed asked.

''Spect you'll be able to work that out, from my questions,' said Strike.

'Why not say, then?' asked Creed, and when Strike didn't answer, he said, 'Sign of narcissism, withholding information to make yourself feel powerful, you know.'

Strike smiled.

'It's not a question of trying to feel powerful. I'm simply familiar with the King's Gambit.'

Creed pushed his wire-rimmed glasses back up his nose.

'Told you I play chess, did they?'

'Yeah.'

'D'you play?'

'Badly.'

'So how does the King's Gambit apply to this situation?'

'Your opening move appears to open an easy route to your king. You're offering to jump straight into discussing the missing woman I'm investigating.'

'But you think that's a ploy?'

'Maybe.'

There was a short pause. Then Creed said,

'I'll tell you who I think sent you, then, shall I?'

'Go on.'

'Margot Bamborough's daughter,' said Dennis Creed, watching carefully for Strike's reaction. 'The husband gave up on her long since, but her daughter'll be forty-odd now and she'll be well-heeled. Whoever hired you's got money. You won't come cheap. I've read all about you, in the paper.

'The second possibility,' said Creed, when Strike didn't respond, 'is old Brian Tucker. He pops up every few years, making a spectacle of himself. Brian's skint, though . . . or did he put out the begging bowl on the internet? Get on the computer and whine out some hard-luck story, so mugs send in cash? But I think, if he'd done that, it would've been in the papers.'

'D'you get online much?' asked Strike.

'We're not allowed, in here,' said Creed. 'Why are you wasting time? We've only got forty-five minutes. Ask a question.'

'That was a question, what I just asked you.'

'Why won't you tell me which so-called victim you're interested in?'

'"So-called" victim?'

'Arbitrary labels,' said Creed. '"Victim". "Patient". *This* one deserves pity . . . *this* one gets caged. Maybe those women I killed were the real patients, and I'm the true victim?'

'Novel point of view,' said Strike.

'Yeah, well, does people good to hear novel points of view,' said Creed, pushing his glasses up his nose again. 'Wake them up, if they're capable of it.'

'What would you say you were curing those women of?'

'The infection of life? Diagnosis: life. Terminal. "Pity not the fallen! I never knew them. I am not for them. I console not: I hate the consoled and the consoler . . ."'

(He'd slit open the corners of schoolgirl Geraldine Christie's mouth, and photographed her crying and screaming, before, as he told her parents from the dock, slitting her throat because she was making so much noise.)

'"... I am unique and conqueror. I am not of the slaves that perish." Know who said that?'

'Aleister Crowley,' said Strike.

'Unusual reading matter,' said Creed, 'for a decorated soldier in the British army.'

'Oh, we're all satanists on the sly,' said Strike.

'You think you're joking,' said Creed, whose expression had become intense, 'but you kill and you get given a medal and called a hero. I kill and get called evil and locked up for ever. Arbitrary categories. Know what's just down the road from here?'

'Sandhurst,' said Strike.

'Sandhurst,' repeated Creed, as though Strike hadn't spoken. 'Institutions for killers, side by side, one to make them, one to break them. Explain to me why's it more moral to murder little brown children on Tony Blair's say-so, than to do what I did? I'm made the way I am. Brain scans will show you, they've studied people like me. It's how we're wired. Why's it more evil to kill because you've got to, because it's your nature, than to blow up poor brown people because we want oil? Properly looked at, I'm the innocent, but *I* get fattened up and drugged like a captive pig, and you get a state pension.'

'Interesting argument,' said Strike. 'So you had no control over what you did?'

'Control,' scoffed Creed, shaking his head. 'That shows how far removed — I can't explain it in terms someone like you would understand. "You have your way. I have my ways. As for the right way, the correct way, and the only way, it does not exist." Know who said that?'

'Sounds like Nietzsche,' said Strike.

'Nietzsche,' said Creed, talking over him. 'Obviously, yes. I read a lot in Belmarsh, back before I got stuffed full of so many drugs I couldn't concentrate from one end of the sentence to another.

'I've got diabetes now, did you know that?' Creed continued. 'Yeah. Hospital-acquired diabetes. They took a thin, fit man, and piled the weight on me, with these drugs I don't need and the pig-swill we're forced to eat. Eight hundred so-called healers leeching a living off us. They need us ill, because we're their livelihoods. Morlocks. Understand that word?'

'Fictional underbeings,' said Strike, 'in *The Time*—'

'Obviously, yes,' said Creed again, who seemed irritated that Strike understood his references. 'H. G. Wells. Primitive beings preying on the highly evolved species, who don't realise they're being farmed to eat. Except *I* realise it, *I* know what's going on.'

'See yourself as one of the Eloi, do you?' asked Strike.

'Interesting thing about the Eloi,' said Creed, 'is their total lack of conscience. The higher race is intellectual, refined, with no so-called remorse . . . I was exploring all this in my book, the book I was writing before they took it off me. Wells's thing was only a superficial allegory, but he was groping towards a truth . . . What I was writing, part autobiography, part scientific treatise – but it was taken away from me, they've confiscated my manuscript. It could be an invaluable resource, but no, because it's mine, it's got to be destroyed. I've got an IQ of 140, but they want my brain flabby like my body.'

'You seem pretty alert to me. What drugs have they got you on?'

'I shouldn't be on any drugs at all. I should be in assertive rehab but they won't let me out of high dependency. They let the little schizophrenics loose in the workshops with knives over there, and I can't have a pencil. When I came here, I thought I'd meet intelligent people . . . any child who can memorise a seven times table could be a doctor, it's all rote learning and dogma. The patient's supposed to be a partner in this therapeutic process, and I say I'm well enough to go back to prison.'

'Certainly seem sane to me,' said Strike.

'Thank you,' said Creed, who'd become flushed. 'Thank you. *You're* an intelligent man, it appears. I thought you would be. That's why I agreed to this.'

'But you're still on medication—'

'I know all about their drugs, and they're giving me too much. I could prescribe better for myself than they know how to, here.'

'How d'you know about that stuff?' asked Strike.

'Obvious, easy,' said Creed, with a grandiose gesture. 'I used myself as a guinea pig, developed my own series of standardised tests. How well I could walk and talk on twenty milligrams, thirty milligrams . . . made notes on disorientation, drowsiness, differences in side-effects . . . '

'What kinds of drugs were these?' asked Strike.

'Amobarbital, pentobarbital, phenobarbital,' rattled off Creed: the names of barbiturates of the early seventies, mostly replaced, now, by other drugs.

'Easy to buy on the street?'

'I only bought off the street occasionally, I had other channels, that were never widely known . . . '

And Creed launched into a meandering speech that couldn't properly be called a story, because the narrative was disjointed and full of mysterious hints and oblique allusions, but the gist seemed to be that Creed had been associating with many unnamed but powerful people in the sixties and seventies, and that a steady supply of prescription drugs had been an incidental perk, either of working for gangsters, or spying on them for the authorities. He hinted at having been recruited by the security services, spoke of flights to America there was no evidence he'd ever taken, of barbiturate-addicted politicians and celebrities, and the dangerous desire of humans from all walks of life to dope themselves to cope with the cruel realities of the world, a tendency and temptation which Dennis Creed deplored and had always resisted.

Strike surmised that these fake reminiscences were designed to feed Creed's overweening craving for status. No doubt his decades in high-security prisons and mental hospitals had taught him that rape and torture were considered almost as contemptible there as they'd been on the outside. He might continue to derive sexual pleasure from reliving his crimes, but in others, they elicited only contempt. Without a fantasy career in which he was part-spy, part-gangster, the man with the 140 IQ was merely a dry-cleaning delivery man, a sexual deviant buying handfuls of downers from street dealers who'd exploited, then betrayed him.

'. . . see all that security all round me, at the trial? There were other forces at play, that's all I'll say . . . '

There'd been a solid cordon of police around Creed on his way in and out of court because the crowd had wanted to tear him apart. The details of his torture chamber had leaked: police had found the hot-irons and the pliers, the ball gags and the whips, the photographs Creed had taken of his victims, alive and dead, and the decomposing head and hands of Andrea Hooton, sitting in his bathroom sink. But the image of himself Creed now presented Strike turned murder into something incidental to a much more prestigious criminal life, a hobby that for some reason the public continued to harp on, when there was so much more to tell, and admire.

'. . . because they like salivating over dirty little things that excite them, as an outlet for their own unacceptable urges,' said Creed. 'I could've been a doctor, probably should have been, actually . . . '

(He'd poured cooking oil over dinner lady Vera Kenny's head, then set her hair on fire and photographed her while it burned, a ball gag in her mouth. He'd cut out unemployed Gail Wrightman's tongue. He'd murdered hairdresser Susan Meyer by stamping repeatedly on her head.)

'Never killed anyone by overdose, did you?' said Strike.

'It takes far more skill to disorientate them but keep them on their feet. Any fool can shove an overdose down someone's throat. The other takes knowledge and experience. That's how I know they're using too much on me in here, because I understand side-effects.'

'What were you giving the women in the basement?'

'I never drugged a woman, once I had her at home. Once she was inside, I had other ways of keeping her quiet.'

Andrea Hooton's mouth had been sewn shut by Creed while she was still alive: the traces of thread had still been present on the rotting head.

The psychiatrist glanced at his watch.

'What if a woman was already drunk?' asked Strike. 'Gail Wrightman: you picked her up in a bar, right? Wasn't there a danger of overdose, if you drugged her on top of the drink?'

'Intelligent question,' said Creed, drinking Strike in with his enormous pupils. 'I can usually tell what a woman's had to the exact unit. Gail was on her own, sulking. Some man had stood her up . . . '

Creed was giving nothing away: these weren't secrets. He'd admitted to it all already, in the dock, where he'd enjoyed relaying the facts, watching the reaction of the victims' relatives. The photographs hidden under the floorboards, of Gail and Andrea, Susan and Vera, Noreen, Jackie and Geraldine, bound, burned and stabbed, alive and maimed, their mutilated and sometimes headless corpses posed in pornographic attitudes, had damned him before he opened his mouth, but he'd insisted on a full trial, pleading guilty by reason of insanity.

' . . . in a wig, bit of lipstick . . . they think you're harmless, odd . . .

maybe queer. Talked to her for a minute or two, little dark corner. You act concerned . . .

'Bit of Nembutal in her drink . . . tiny amount, tiny,' said Creed, holding his trembling fingers millimetres apart. 'Nembutal and alcohol, potentially dangerous, if you don't know what you're doing, but I did, obviously . . .

'So I say, "Well, I got to go now, sweetheart, you be careful." "Be careful!" It always worked.' Creed affected squeaky tones to imitate Gail, '"Aw, don't go, have a drink!" "No, darling, I need my beauty sleep." That's when you prove you're not a threat. You make as if you want to leave, or actually walk away. Then, when they call you back, or run into you ten minutes later, when they're starting to feel like shit, they're relieved, because you're the nice man who's safe . . .

'It was all in my book, the different ways I got them. Instructive for women who want to keep out of trouble, you'd think, to read how a highly efficient killer works, but the authorities won't let it be published, which makes you question, are they happy for slags to be picked off on the streets? Maybe they are.

'Why're there people like me at all, Cormoran? Why's evolution let it happen? Because humans are so highly developed, we can only thin ourselves out with intraspecies predators. Pick off the weak, the morally depraved. It's a good thing that degenerate, drunk women don't breed. That's just a fact, it's a fact,' said Dennis Creed.

'I'd wind down my window. "Want a lift, love?" Swaying all over the place. Glad to see me. Got in the van, no trouble, grateful to sit down . . .

'I used to say to Gail, once I had her in the basement: "Should've gone to the bathroom instead, you dirty little bitch, shouldn't you? I bet you're the type to piss in the street. Filthy, that is, filthy" . . . Why're you so interested in drugging?'

The flow of talk had suddenly dried up. Creed's blank grey and black eyes darted left and right between each of Strike's.

'You think Dr Bamborough would be too clever to get herself drugged by the likes of me, do you?'

'Doctors can make mistakes, like anyone else,' said Strike. 'You met Noreen Sturrock on a bus, right?'

Creed considered Strike for several seconds, as though trying to work something out.

'Buses, now, is it? How often did Margot Bamborough take the bus?'

'Frequently, I'd imagine,' said Strike.

'Would she've taken a can of Coke from a stranger?'

'That's what you offered Noreen, right? And the Coke was full of phenobarbital?'

'Yeah. She was almost asleep by the time we came to my stop. I said, "You've missed yours, darling. Come on, I'll take you to a taxi rank." Walked her straight off the bus, arm round her. She wasn't a big girl, Noreen. That was one of the easiest.'

'Did you adjust dosage for weight?'

There was another slight pause.

'Buses and cans of pop, and adjusting drugs for weight? ... You know what, Cormoran? I think my second guess was right. You're here for little Louise Tucker.'

'No,' said Strike with a sigh, settling back in his chair. 'As it happens, you were spot on first time round. I was hired by Margot Bamborough's daughter.'

There was a longer silence now, and the psychiatrist again checked his watch. Strike knew that his time was nearly up, and he thought Creed knew it, too.

'I want to go back to Belmarsh, Cormoran,' said Creed, leaning in now that Strike had leaned back. 'I want to finish my book. I'm sane, you know it, too, you just said it. I'm not ill. It's costing the taxpayer five times as much to keep me in here as it would in jail. Where would the British public say I should be, eh?'

'Oh, they'd want you back in prison,' said Strike.

'Well, I agree with them,' said Creed. 'I agree.'

He looked sideways at Dr Bijral, who had the look of a man about to call a halt.

'I'm sane and if I'm treated like it, I'll act like it,' said Creed.

He leaned further forwards.

'I killed Louise Tucker,' said Creed in a soft voice, and in Strike's peripheral vision the psychiatrist and the nurse both froze, astonished. 'Picked her up off a street corner in my van, November 1972. Freezing cold that night. She wanted to go home and she had no money. I couldn't resist, Cormoran,' said Creed, those big black pupils boring into Strike's. 'Little girl in her school uniform. No man could resist. Did it on impulse ... no planning ... no wig, no drugged Coke, nothing ... '

'Why wasn't there any trace of her in the basement?' said Strike.

'There was. I had her necklace. But I never had *her* in the basement, see? You want proof, I'll give you proof: she called her stepmother "Claws". Tell Tucker she told me that, all right? Yeah, we had a five-minute chat about how pissed off she was at home, before she realised we were going the wrong way. Then she starts screaming and banging on the windows.

'I turned into a dark car park,' said Creed quietly, 'put my hand over her mouth, dragged her into the back of the van, fucked her and throttled her. I'd've liked to keep her longer, but she was loud, too loud.

'Dumb thing to do, but I couldn't resist, Cormoran. No planning – school uniform! But I had work next day, I needed the van empty. I wanted to take the body back to the basement, but old Vi Cooper was wide awake when I drove back up Liverpool Road. She was looking down at me out the top window when I drove past, so I didn't stop. Told her later she'd imagined it was me. The old bitch used to sit up to see what time I came in. I usually drugged her if I was off on the prowl, but this was a spur-of-the-moment treat ... '

'What did you do with the body?' said Strike.

'Ah,' said Creed, sitting back in his seat. The wet lips slid over each other, and the wide pupils gaped. 'I think I'm going to need a transfer back to Belmarsh before I tell anyone that. You go and tell the newspapers I've decided to confess to killing Louise, and that I'm sane, and I should be in Belmarsh, and if I'm transferred, I'll tell old Brian Tucker where I put his little girl. You go tell the authorities, that's my offer ...

'You never know, I might even feel up to talking about Margot Bamborough when I'm out of here. Let's get these drugs out of my system, and maybe I'll remember better.'

ROBERT GALBRAITH

'You're full of shit,' said Strike, getting to his feet, looking angry. 'I'm not passing this on.'

'Don't be like that, because it's not the one you came for,' said Creed, with a slow smile. 'You're coming across like a proper narcissist, Cormoran.'

'I'm ready to go,' Strike told Dr Bijral.

'Don't be like that,' said Creed. 'Oi!'

Strike turned back.

'All right . . . I'll give you a little clue about where I put Louise's body, and we'll see whether you're as clever as you think you are, all right? We'll see whether you or the police work it out first. If they find the body, they'll know I'm sane, and I'm ready to talk about Margot Bamborough, as long as I get moved where I want to go. And if nobody can figure out the clue, someone'll have to come back and talk to me, won't they? Maybe even you. We could play chess for more clues, Cormoran.'

Strike could tell that Creed was imagining weeks of front pages, as he laid a trail for investigators to follow. Psychological torture for the Tuckers, manipulation of public opinion, Strike, perhaps, at his beck and call: it was a sadist's wet dream.

'Go on then,' said Strike, looking down at him. 'What's the clue?'

'You'll find Louise Tucker's body where you find M54,' said Creed, and Strike knew Creed had thought out the clue well ahead of time, and was certain that it would have been a clue about Margot, had Strike said he'd been hired by the Tuckers. Creed needed to believe he hadn't given Strike what he really wanted. He had to come out on top.

'Right,' said Strike. He turned to Dr Bijral. 'Shall we?'

'M54, all right, Cormoran?' called Creed.

'I heard you,' said Strike.

'Sorry not to be able to help with Dr Bamborough!' called Creed, and Strike could hear his pleasure at the idea that he'd thwarted the detective.

Strike turned back one last time, and now he stopped pretending to be angry, and grinned, too.

'I was here for Louise, you silly fucker. I know you never met

858

Margot Bamborough. She was murdered by a far more skilful killer than you ever were. And just so you know,' Strike added, as the nurse's keys jangled, and Creed's slack, fat face registered dismay, 'I think you're a fucking lunatic, and if anyone asks me, I'll say you should be in Broadmoor till you rot.'

69

Beare ye the picture of that Ladies head?
Full liuely is the semblaunt, though the substance dead.

Edmund Spenser
The Faerie Queene

After almost an hour's debrief with Dr Bijral, during which the shaken psychiatrist phoned Scotland Yard, the detective left the hospital feeling as though he'd been there twice as long as he really had. The village of Crowthorne didn't lie on Strike's route back to London, but he was hungry, he wanted to call Robin and he felt a powerful need to place himself among ordinary people going about their lives, to expel the memory of those empty, echoing corridors, the jangle of keys and the widely dilated pupils of Dennis Creed.

He parked outside a pub, lit himself the cigarette he'd been craving for the past two and a half hours, then turned his phone back on. He'd already missed two calls from Brian Tucker, but instead of phoning the old man back, he pressed Robin's number. She answered on the second ring.

'What happened?'

Strike told her. When he'd finished, there was a short silence.

'Say the clue again,' said Robin, who sounded tense.

'"You'll find her where you find M54."'

'Not *the* M54? Not the motorway?'

'He could've meant that, but he left out the definite article.'

'The M54's twenty-odd miles long.'

'I know.'

Reaction was setting in: Strike should have felt triumphant, but in fact he was tired and tense. His phone beeped at him and he glanced at the screen.

'That's Brian Tucker again, trying to ring me,' he told Robin.

'What are you going to tell him?'

'The truth,' said Strike heavily, exhaling smoke out of his open window. 'Dr Bijral's already called Scotland Yard. Trouble is, if that clue's meaningless, or unsolvable, it leaves Tucker knowing Creed killed his daughter, but never getting the body back. This could well be Creed's idea of the ultimate torture.'

'It's something to have a confession, though, isn't it?' said Robin.

'Tucker's been convinced Creed killed her for decades. Confession without a body just keeps the wound open. Creed'll still have the last laugh, knowing where she is and not telling . . . How've you got on in the British Library?'

'Oh. Fine,' said Robin. 'I found Joanna Hammond a couple of hours ago.'

'And?' said Strike, now alert.

'She had a large mole on her face. Left cheek. You can see it in the picture of her wedding in the local paper. I'll text it to you now.'

'And the holy—?'

'It would've been on the back of her obituary. Same local paper.'

'Jesus Christ,' said Strike.

There was a longer silence. Strike's phone beeped again, and he saw that Robin had texted him a picture.

Opening it, he saw a couple on their 1969 wedding day: a blurry black and white picture of a toothy, beaming brunette bride, her hair worn in ringlets, in a high-necked lace dress, a pillbox hat on top of her veil, a large mole on her left cheekbone. The blond husband loomed over her shoulder, unsmiling. Even minutes into married life, he had the air of a man ready to wield a baseball bat.

'She wasn't Sagittarius under Schmidt,' said Robin, and Strike put the phone back up to his ear, 'she was Scorpio—'

'—which Talbot thought fitted her better, because of the mole,' said Strike, with a sigh. 'I should've gone back through all the identifications once you found out about Schmidt. We might've got here sooner.'

'What are we going to do about Douthwaite?'

'I'll ring him,' said Strike, after a moment's pause. 'Now. Then I'll call you back.'

His stomach rumbled as he called the Allardice boarding house in Skegness, and heard the familiar cross Scottish accent of Donna, Douthwaite's wife.

'Oh Christ,' she said, when Strike identified himself. 'What now?'

'Nothing to worry about,' lied Strike, who could hear a radio playing in the background. 'Just wanted to double-check a couple of points.'

'Steve!' he heard her yell, away from the receiver. 'It's *him!* . . . What d'you mean, "Who?", who d'you bloody think?'

Strike heard footsteps and then Douthwaite, who sounded half-angry, half-scared.

'What d'you want?'

'I want to tell you what I think happened during your last appointment with Margot Bamborough,' said Strike.

He spoke for two minutes, and Douthwaite didn't interrupt, though Strike knew he was still there, because of the distant sounds of the boarding house still reaching him over the line. When Strike had finished his reconstruction of Douthwaite's final consultation, there was silence but for the distant radio, which was playing 'Blame' by Calvin Harris.

So blame it on the night . . . don't blame it on me . . .

'Well?' said Strike.

He knew Douthwaite didn't want to confirm it. Douthwaite was a coward, a weak man who ran away from problems. He could have prevented further deaths had he had the courage to tell what he knew, but he'd been scared for his own skin, scared he'd be seen as complicit, stupid and shabby, in the eyes of newspaper readers. And so he'd run, but that had made things worse, and nightmarish consequences had ensued, and he'd run from those, too, barely admitting to himself what he feared, distracting himself with drink, with karaoke, with women. And now Strike was presenting him with a dreadful choice that was really no choice at all. Like Violet Cooper, Steve Douthwaite was facing a lifetime of opprobrium from the censorious public, and how much better would it have been if he'd come clean to Talbot forty years previously, when Margot Bamborough's body could have been found quickly, and a killer could have been brought to justice before others had to die.

'Am I right?' Strike said.

'Yes,' said Douthwaite, at last.

'OK, well, if you'll take my advice, you'll go straight to your wife and tell her, before the press do it. There's going to be no hiding from this one.'

'Shit,' said Douthwaite quietly.

'See you in court, then,' said Strike briskly, and he hung up, and called Robin straight back.

'He's confirmed it.'

'Cormoran,' said Robin.

'I advised him to tell Donna—'

'Cormoran,' said Robin, again.

'What?'

'I think I know what M54 is.'

'Not—'

'—the motorway? No. M54 is a globular cluster—'

'A what?'

'A spherical cluster of stars.'

'Stars?' said Strike, with a sinking sensation. 'Hang on—'

'Listen,' said Robin. 'Creed thought he was being clever, but it only takes a Google search—'

'They haven't got internet in there,' said Strike. 'He was whining about it—'

'Well, M54 is a cluster of stars in the constellation Sagittarius,' said Robin.

'Not astrology again,' said Strike, closing his eyes. 'Robin—'

'*Listen to me.* He said "You'll find her where you find M54", right?'

'Yeah—'

'The constellation Sagittarius is also known as the Archer.'

'So?'

863

'Brian showed us the map, Strike! Dennis Creed was a regular visitor to the Archer Hotel in Islington in the early seventies, when he was delivering their dry cleaning. There was a well on the property, in the back garden. Boarded up, and now covered over with a conservatory.'

A pair of jolly men with matching beer bellies walked into the pub across the road. Strike barely registered them. He'd even forgotten to take drags of the cigarette burning between his fingers.

'Think this through,' said Robin in his ear. 'Creed's got a body he didn't expect in the van, but he can't take it to Epping Forest, because there was still an active crime scene there. They'd just found the remains of Vera Kenny. I don't know why he didn't take the body to the basement—'

'I do,' said Strike. 'He's just told me. He drove past the house and Vi Cooper was awake and at the window.'

'OK – right – so he's got to empty the van before work. He knows his way around the Archer garden, and he knows there's a back gate. He's got tools in the back of the van, he could prise those boards up easily. Cormoran, I'm *sure* she's in the old Archer well.'

There was a brief pause, then hot ash fell into Strike's lap from his neglected cigarette.

'Bollocks—'

He flicked the end out of the window, earning himself a look of disapproval from a passing old woman pulling a tartan shopping trolley.

'All right, here's what we're going to do,' he told Robin. 'I'll phone Tucker and tell him what's just happened, including your deduction. You call George Layborn and tell him about the well at the Archer. The quicker the police search it, the better for the Tuckers, especially if the news leaks that Creed's confessed.'

'OK, I'll get on to that right—'

'Hang on, I haven't finished,' said Strike. He'd closed his eyes now, and he was rubbing his temples as he thought through everything the agency needed to do, and quickly. 'When you've spoken to Layborn, I want you to ring Barclay and tell him he's going on a job with you, tomorrow morning. He can forget Miss Jones's boyfriend

864

for a few hours. Or, most probably, all day, if what I think's going to happen happens.'

'What job are Barclay and I doing?' asked Robin.

'Isn't it obvious?' said Strike, opening his eyes again. 'We're up against the clock if Douthwaite talks to anyone.'

'So Barclay and I are . . . ?'

'Finding Margot's body,' said Strike. 'Yes.'

There was a long silence. Strike's stomach rumbled again. Now a pair of young women entered the pub, giggling at something one had shown the other on her phone.

'You really think she's there?' said Robin, a little shaken.

'I'm sure of it,' said Strike.

'And you're—?'

'I'm going to call Brian Tucker, eat some chips, make that long-distance phone call – I think they're three hours ahead of us, so that should work fine – then drive back to the office. I'll be back late afternoon and we can talk it all over properly.'

'Right,' said Robin, 'good luck.'

She rang off. Strike hesitated for a moment before calling Brian Tucker: he'd have liked to do it with a pint in his hand, but he still needed to drive back to London, and being arrested for drink driving on the eve of catching Margot Bamborough's killer was a complication he really didn't want to risk. Instead, he lit himself a second cigarette, and prepared to tell a grieving father that after a forty-two year wait, he might soon be in a position to bury his daughter.

70

The morning was so mild it might have been summer, but the leaves of the plane trees beside the telephone box at the mouth of Albemarle Way were starting to turn yellow. A patchwork blue and white sky gave and withdrew warmth as the sun slid in and out behind clouds, and Robin felt shivery in spite of the sweater she was wearing beneath her raincoat, as though a cold wind was blowing up Albemarle Way, the short side street whose tall, unbroken buildings kept it forever in shadow.

She was standing beside the telephone box where once, nearly forty years previously, the killer of Margot Bamborough had waited and watched, feeling, Robin imagined, much as she did now. There must have been fear, and nervousness, and doubt that the plan could possibly work, and terror of the consequences of failure. But this sense of kinship didn't make Robin feel any more kindly to the killer. Looking across the road at the ancient arch of St John's Gate, she could imagine Margot Bamborough walking through it on a rainy evening forty years previously, or perhaps weaving, feeling strangely groggy and not knowing why . . . or had she realised? Possibly. Margot was a clever woman, and that was why she'd had to die . . .

Clerkenwell Road was busy with traffic and pedestrians. Robin felt entirely isolated from all of them. Nobody passing Robin could have the slightest idea of what she was about to try and do. How bizarre they'd think her morning's plans, how macabre ... a trickle of panic ran down Robin's spine ...

Think about something else.

There'd been a picture in the *Metro* that morning of Charlotte Ross wearing sunglasses and a long dark coat, walking along a street in Mayfair with her sister, Amelia. There had been no sign of Charlotte's husband or young twins, and the short non-story beneath the picture had told Robin nothing she wanted to know.

Charlotte Campbell was spotted enjoying a morning walk in London with her sister, Amelia Crichton, yesterday. Charlotte, who is married to Jago, heir to the Viscountcy of Croy, was recently released from hospital, following a prolonged stay in Symonds House, an addiction and mental health facility much favoured by the rich and famous.

Charlotte, who once topped *Tatler*'s list of 100 Most Beautiful Londoners, has been a favourite of the gossip columns since she first ran away from school, aged 14. Daughter of ...

Think about something else, Robin told herself, and consciously groped around for another subject.

It was September the twentieth. A person born today would be born under the sign of Virgo. Robin wondered how long it was going to take to rid herself of the mental tic of tying dates to star signs. She thought of Matthew, who was the Virgoan she knew best. The sign was supposed to be clever, and organised, and nervous. He was certainly organised, and bright in a book-smart way ... she remembered Oonagh Kennedy saying, 'I sometimes t'ink, the cleverer they are with books, the stupider they are with sex,' and wondered whether he was now happy about the pregnancy he'd said was accidental ...

Think about something else.

She checked her watch. Where was Barclay? True, Robin had arrived very early, and technically Barclay wasn't late, but she didn't like standing here alone, trying to distract herself from thoughts of what they were about to do.

Theo had once stood almost exactly where Robin now was, watching the traffic roll up and down Clerkenwell Road, dark-haired Theo of the Kuchi earrings and the painful abdomen, waiting for the silver van that would take her away. Why Theo had never come forward afterwards, why she'd never felt enough gratitude to the woman who'd seen her at short notice, at least to rule herself out of suspicion and stop Talbot haring after a delusion, remained a minor mystery. But of course, that assumed that Theo felt grateful. Nobody ever really knew what happened between a doctor and patient: it was the secular equivalent of the confession box. Robin's thoughts had moved to Douthwaite when, at last, she spotted Barclay, who was approaching, carrying a holdall. When he got close enough, Robin heard the tools inside it clinking.

'Havin' a wee bit o' déjà vu, here,' he said, coming to halt beside her. 'Didn't we once go diggin' fer a body before?'

'I don't think this qualifies as digging,' said Robin.

'What's the latest?'

'He's gone out,' said Robin. 'Strike says we've got to wait until he comes back.'

'What's in there?' asked Barclay, nodding at the carrier bag in Robin's hand.

'Chocolate biscuits,' said Robin.

'Bribe?'

'Basically.'

'And has Strike—?'

'Not yet. He's in position. He wants us to . . . '

Robin waited for a group of what looked like students to walk out of earshot.

' . . . do our bit, first. Were you pleased,' Robin continued, still trying not to think about what they were about to do until it was absolutely necessary, 'about the referendum result?'

'Aye, but don't kid yerself oan,' said Barclay darkly, 'this isn't finished. That stupid fucker Cameron's playing right into the nats' hands. "English votes for English laws", the day after Scotland decides to stay? You don't fight fuckin' nationalism with more fuckin' nationalism. He wants tae get his head out of Farage's arse – is this oor wee fella now?'

Robin looked around. Silhouetted against the end of Albemarle Way was a man walking along with a strange, rolling gait, who was carrying two full carrier bags. He stopped at a door, set down his shopping, put his key in the lock, picked up his shopping bags, stepped over the threshold and vanished from sight.

'That's him,' said Robin, as her insides seemed to wobble. 'Let's go.'

They walked side by side down the street to the dark blue front door.

'He's left the key in the lock,' said Barclay, pointing.

Robin was about to the ring the bell when the door opened, and Samhain Athorn reappeared. Pale, big-eared and mousy-haired, he gaped slightly. He was wearing a Batman sweatshirt. Disconcerted to find two people on his doorstep, he blinked, then addressed Robin's left shoulder.

'I left the key.'

He reached around to pull it out of the lock. As he made to close the door, Barclay dextrously inserted a foot.

'You're Samhain, aren't you?' said Robin, smiling at him, while Samhain gaped. 'We're friends of Cormoran Strike's. You were very helpful to him, a few months ago.'

'I need to put the shopping away,' said Samhain. He tried to close the front door, but Barclay's foot was in the way.

'Could we come in?' asked Robin. 'Just for a little while? We'd like to talk to you and your mum. You were so helpful, before, telling Cormoran about your Uncle Tudor—'

'My Uncle Tudor's dead,' said Samhain.

'I know. I'm sorry.'

'He died in the hospital,' said Samhain.

'Really?' said Robin.

'My-Dad-Gwilherm died under the bridge,' said Samhain.

'That's so sad,' said Robin. 'Could we come in, please, just for a moment? Cormoran wanted me to bring you these,' she added, pulling the tin of chocolate biscuits out of her bag. 'As a thank you.'

'What's them?' asked Samhain, looking at the tin out of the corner of his eye.

'Chocolate biscuits.'

He took the tin out of her hand.

'Yeah. You can come in,' he said, and turning his back, he marched up the dark interior stairs.

With a glance at Barclay, Robin led the way inside. She heard her companion close the door behind her, and the clinking of the tools in his holdall. The staircase was steep, narrow and dark after daylight, the light bulb overhead dead. When Robin reached the landing she saw, through the open door, a white-haired woman with big ears like Samhain's, wiping the surfaces of a brown-tiled kitchen while Samhain, who had his back to her, eagerly peeled the plastic wrapper off the tin of chocolate biscuits.

Deborah turned, her neat white plait sliding over her shoulder, to fix her dark eyes on the two strangers.

'Hello, Mrs Athorn,' said Robin, coming to a halt in the hall.

'Are you from the social work department?' asked Deborah slowly. 'I phoned Clare . . . '

'We can help wi' anythin' Clare can,' said Barclay, before Robin could answer. 'What's the problem?'

'Him downstairs is a bastard,' said Samhain, who was now digging busily in the tin of chocolate biscuits, and selecting the one wrapped in gold foil. 'These are the best ones, in the shiny paper, that's how you know.'

'Is the man downstairs complaining again?' asked Robin, with a sudden upswell of excitement that bordered on panic.

'Can we have a look at whut the problem is?' asked Barclay. 'Where's he think his ceilin's crackin'?'

Deborah pointed towards the sitting room.

'I'll have a wee look,' said Barclay confidently, and he set off towards the sitting room.

'Don't eat all of them, Sammy,' said Deborah, who'd returned to the methodical wiping of the kitchen sides.

'They gave them to me, you silly woman,' said Samhain, his mouth full of chocolate.

Robin followed, fighting a sense of utter unreality. Could what Strike suspected really be true?

Two budgerigars were twittering in a cage in the corner of the small sitting room, which, like the hall, was carpeted in swirls of brown and orange. A crocheted blanket had been spread over the back of the sofa. Barclay was looking down at the almost completed jigsaw of unicorns leaping over a rainbow. Robin glanced around. The place was sparsely furnished. Apart from the sofa and the budgies' cage, there was only a small armchair, a television set on top of which stood an urn, and a small shelving unit on which sat a few old paperbacks and some cheap ornaments. Her eyes lingered on the Egyptian symbol of eternal life painted on a patch of dirty green wall.

She lies in a holy place.

'Floorboards?' she murmured to Barclay.

He shook his head, looked meaningfully down at the jigsaw of the unicorns, then pointed with his foot at the overlarge ottoman on which it lay.

'Oh God, no,' whispered Robin, before she could stop herself. 'You think?'

'Otherwise the carpet would've had tae come up,' murmured Barclay. 'Move furniture, take up floorboards ... and would it make the ceilin' crack, down below? An' what aboot the smell?'

Samhain now came ambling into the room, eating his second foil-wrapped biscuit.

'D'you want a hot chocolate, or not?' he asked, looking at Robin's knees.

'Um ... no, thank you,' said Robin, smiling at him.

'Does he want a hot chocolate, or not?'

'No thanks, mate,' said Barclay. 'Can we move this jigsaw? Need tae have a look beneath it.'

'Deborah don't like her jigsaw touched,' said Samhain sternly.

'We need to prove the man downstairs is lying, though,' said Robin. 'About his ceiling cracking.'

'Deborah,' called Samhain. 'They want to move your jigsaw.'

He walked out of the room with his rocking gait, and his mother took his place at the door, eyeing Robin's shoes as she said,

'You can't move my unicorns.'

'We need to have a little look underneath it,' said Robin. 'I promise we'll take very good care of it, and not break it. We could move
it . . .'

She looked around, but there was no stretch of floor big enough
to accommodate it.

'In my bedroom, you can put it,' said Samhain, bobbing back into
sight. 'On my bed, they can put it, Deborah.'

'Excellent idea,' said Barclay heartily, bending to pick it up.

'Close it up first,' said Robin hastily, and she folded the wings of
the jigsaw mat over the puzzle, containing all the pieces.

'Good job,' said Barclay, and he carried the jigsaw mat carefully out
through the sitting-room door, followed by Deborah, who looked
both anxious and alarmed, and by the self-important Samhain,
who seemed proud to have had his plan adopted by this new man
in the flat.

For a few seconds, Robin stood alone in the sitting room, looking down at the ottoman that was far too big for this small room. It
had been covered with a cloth that Robin suspected dated from the
sixties, being of thin, faded purple cotton, and carrying the design
of a mandala. If a tall woman curled herself up, she might fit inside
that ottoman, as long as she was thin, of course.

I don't want to look, Robin thought suddenly, panic rising again. *I
don't want to see . . .*

But she had to look. She had to see. That was what she was
there for.

Barclay returned, followed by both an interested-looking Samhain
and a troubled Deborah.

'That doesn't open,' said Deborah, pointing at the exposed ottoman. 'You can't open that. You leave that alone.'

'I had my toys in there,' said Samhain. 'Didn't I, Deborah?
Once I did. But My-Dad-Gwilherm didn't want me to keep them
there no more.'

'You can't open that,' repeated Deborah, now distressed. 'Leave
it, don't touch that.'

'Deborah,' said Robin quietly, walking towards the older woman, 'we've got to find out why the ceiling downstairs is cracking. You know how the man downstairs is always complaining, and saying he'd like you and Samhain to move out?'

'I don't want to go,' said Deborah at once, and for a split-second her dark eyes almost met Robin's, before darting back to the swirly carpet. 'I don't want to move. I'm going to ring Clare.'

'No,' said Robin, moving quickly around Deborah and blocking her way back to the kitchen, with its old wall-mounted phone beside the fridge. She hoped Deborah hadn't heard her panic. 'We're here instead of Clare, you see? To help you with the man downstairs. But we think – Sam and I—'

'My-Dad-Gwilherm called me Sam,' said Samhain. 'Didn't he, Deborah?'

'That's nice,' said Robin, and she pointed at Barclay. 'This man's called Sam, too.'

'Is his name Sam, is it?' said Samhain gleefully, and boldly he raised his eyes to Barclay's face before looking away again, grinning. 'Two Sams. Deborah! Two Sams!'

Robin addressed the perplexed Deborah, who was now shifting from foot to foot in a manner reminiscent of her son's rolling walk.

'Sam and I want to sort this out, Deborah, so you don't have any more trouble with the man downstairs.'

'Gwilherm didn't want that opened,' said Deborah, reaching nervously for the end of her white plait. 'He didn't want that opened, he wanted that kept shut.'

'Gwilherm would want you and Samhain to be allowed to stay here, though, wouldn't he?'

Deborah put the end of her plait in her mouth and sucked at it, as though it was an ice lolly. Her dark eyes wandered as though in search of help.

'I think,' said Robin gently, 'it would be good if you and Samhain wait in his bedroom while we have a look at the ottoman.'

'Knotty man,' said Samhain, and he cackled again. 'Sam! Hey – Sam! Knotty man!'

'Good one,' said Barclay, grinning.

'Come on,' said Robin, sliding an arm around Deborah. 'You wait in the bedroom with Samhain. You haven't done anything wrong, we know that. Everything's going to be fine.'

As she led Deborah slowly across the landing, she heard Samhain say cheerily,

'I'm staying here, though.'

'No, mate,' Barclay replied, as Robin and Deborah entered Samhain's tiny bedroom. Every inch of wall was covered in pictures of superheroes and gaming characters. Deborah's gigantic jigsaw took up most of the bed. The floor around the PlayStation was littered with chocolate wrappers.

'Look after yer mam and, after, I'll teach ye a magic trick,' Barclay was saying.

'My-Dad-Gwilherm could do magic!'

'Aye, I know, I heard. That make it easy fer you tae do magic, if yer dad could do it, eh?'

'We won't be long,' Robin told Samhain's frightened mother. 'Just stay in here for now, all right? Please, Deborah?'

Deborah simply blinked at her. Robin was particularly afraid of the woman trying to reach the phone on the kitchen wall, because she didn't want to have to physically restrain her. Returning to the sitting room, she found Barclay still bargaining with Samhain.

'Do it now,' Samhain was saying, grinning, looking from Barclay's hands to his chin to his ear. 'Go on, show me now.'

'Sam can only do magic after we've done our job,' said Robin. 'Samhain, will you wait in the bedroom with your mum, please?'

'Go on, mate,' said Barclay. 'Just fer a bit. Then I'll teach ye the trick.'

The smile faded off Samhain's face.

'Silly woman,' he said sulkily to Robin. 'Stupid woman.'

He walked out of the room, but instead of going into his bedroom, he made for the kitchen.

'Shit,' Robin muttered, 'don't do anything yet, Sam—'

Samhain reappeared, holding the tin of chocolate biscuits, walked into his bedroom and slammed the door behind him.

'Now,' said Robin.

'Stay by the door,' said Sam, 'keep an eye on them.'

Robin closed the sitting-room door, leaving a tiny crack through which she could spy on Samhain's bedroom, and gave Barclay the thumbs up.

He pulled the mandala covering off the ottoman, bent down, gripped the edge of the lid and heaved. The lid wouldn't budge. He put all his strength into it, but still it didn't shift. From Samhain's room came the sound of raised voices. Deborah was telling Samhain not to eat any more chocolate biscuits.

'It's like – it's locked – on the inside,' said Barclay, panting and letting go.

He unzipped his holdall and, after some rummaging, pulled out a crowbar, which he wedged the end of into the crack separating the lid from the body of the ottoman. '*Come – oan – you – fucker,*' he gasped, as the end of the crowbar lost its grip and nearly hit Barclay in the face. 'Somethin's stickin' it doon.'

Robin peeked back at Samhain's bedroom door. It remained closed. Mother and son were still arguing about the chocolate biscuits. The budgerigars chirruped. Beyond the window, Robin could see an aeroplane trail, a fuzzy white pipe cleaner stretched across the sky. Everyday things became so strange, when you were waiting for something dreadful to happen. Her heart was pounding fast.

'Help me,' said Barclay through gritted teeth. He'd managed to get the end of the crowbar deeper into the crack in the ottoman. 'It's gonnae take two.'

After another glance at Samhain's closed door, Robin hurried over to Barclay and gripped the crowbar alongside him. Using all their weight and force, both pushed the handle towards the floor.

'Jesus,' panted Robin. 'What's holding it?'

'Where's – Strike – when you need—'

There was a loud crunching, cracking noise. The crowbar suddenly gave way as the lid of the ottoman opened. Robin turned and saw a cloud of dust rising into the air. Barclay pushed the lid up.

The ottoman had been filled with concrete, which had stuck the lid down upon itself. The grey matter was lumpy and looked as though it might have been badly mixed. In two places, something smooth broke through the uneven, ashen surface: one resembling a few inches of walrus tusk, the other, a curved surface that hinted at a dark ivory globe. Then Robin saw, stuck to a bit of the concrete that had adhered to the lid of the ottoman, a few fair hairs.

They heard footsteps on the landing. Barclay slammed the lid of the ottoman down as Samhain opened the door. He was followed by Deborah.

'I'll teach you that magic trick now,' said Barclay, walking towards Samhain. 'Come in the kitchen, we'll do it there.'

The two men left. Deborah shuffled into the room, and picked up the faded purple throw that Robin had cast aside.

'Did you open it?' she mumbled, eyes on the old carpet.

'Yes,' said Robin, far more calmly than she felt. She sat down on the ottoman, even though she felt sacrilegious doing it. *I'm sorry, Margot. I'm so sorry.*

'I need to make a phone call now, Deborah. Then I think we should all have some hot chocolate.'

71

Such is the face of falshood, such the sight
Of fowle Duessa, when her borrowed light
Is laid away, and counterfesaunce knowne.

Edmund Spenser
The Faerie Queene

A train came roaring and rattling along the Southeastern railway line. Strike, who was standing on the opposite side of the road, felt his mobile vibrate in his pocket and pulled it out, but for a few seconds the din was such that he couldn't immediately hear Robin.

'. . . found her.'

'Say that again?' he shouted, as the train rumbled away.

'We've – found – her. Inside the ottoman inside the sitting room. Concrete was poured in all around her, but we can see a bit of her skull and maybe a femur.'

'Shit.'

Strike had expected the presence of the body in the Athorns' flat, but there was nothing routine, ever, about finding a dead human. 'Concrete?' he repeated.

'Yes. It doesn't look that well mixed. Amateurish. But it's done the job. It probably killed most of the smell.'

'Hell of a weight on a supporting beam.'

'Well, exactly. Where are you?'

'Outside, about to go in. Right: call 999, then call Layborn and tell him where I am, and why. That should speed things up.'

'OK. Good luck.'

877

Strike hung up. The nondescript street of terraced houses was quiet now the train had gone, birdsong replacing its thunderous clamour. Strike, who'd been waiting where he couldn't be seen, now walked up the street, passing three small houses, and at the fourth, turned left up a short garden path, then beat a tattoo on the dark red front door.

The net curtains twitched, and Janice Beattie's cross face appeared. Strike raised a hand in greeting. The curtain fell.

After a slightly longer wait than might have been expected, given the short distance from sitting room to hall, Janice opened the door. She was dressed all in black today, with sheepskin carpet slippers on her feet. Her clear china-blue eyes, rimmed in steel, looked as kind and innocent as ever. Silver-haired, apple-cheeked, she frowned up at the detective, but didn't speak.

'Can I come in?' asked Strike.

There was a long pause. The wild birds tweeted, and Strike thought fleetingly of the budgies in the Athorns' flat, where part of his mind was dwelling on the image of a skull and a femur, poking up through concrete.

'If you must,' said Janice slowly.

He followed Janice into the red sitting room, with its cheap crimson Turkish rug, its dried-flower pictures and its faded photographs. The sun was making the spun-glass Cinderella carriage and its six horses twinkle on top of the fire, which Janice had on, in spite of the mildness of the September day.

'Wanna cup of tea?' said Janice.

'That'd be great,' said Strike, fully alive to the unreality of the situation.

He listened to her sheepskin-muffled footsteps receding and the sound of the kitchen door opening. Taking out his mobile phone, he switched it to record and laid it on the arm of the chair in which he'd sat last time. He then pulled on a pair of latex gloves and followed Janice quietly out of the room, the worn carpet muffling his footsteps.

At the door, he paused, listening to the soft bubbling of boiling water against a kettle lid, and the tinkle of teaspoons, and the opening of a cupboard. With one fingertip, he pushed open the kitchen door.

Janice spun round, eyes wide. On seeing him, she grabbed one of the china mugs on the tray and raised it hurriedly to her lips, but Strike had already taken a stride towards her. Gripping the thin wrist with his latex-gloved hand, forcing the mug away from her mouth, he felt bone beneath the soft flesh and the papery skin of the elderly. With his free hand, he pulled the mug out of hers, and examined it. A good inch of viscous white liquid was swimming in the bottom of it. Still holding Janice's wrist, he looked into the teapot, which contained more of the same, then opened the cupboard over the kettle.

It was jammed with bottles of pills, weedkiller, bleach and jam jars full of what looked like home-dried plants, leaves and fungus: a poisoner's storehouse, a testimony to a lifetime's careful study of the means by which death could be delivered in the guise of healing.

'Think I'll skip tea,' said Strike. 'Let's have a chat, shall we?'

She offered no resistance as he led her by the wrist back through to the sitting room and pushed her down onto the sofa.

'A murder-suicide would be a hell of a way to go out,' said Strike, standing over her, 'but I don't much fancy being victim number . . . how many is it?'

Janice said nothing. Her round blue eyes registered only shock.

Strike looked up at the wall of old photographs. One showed a toothy, beaming brunette bride, her hair worn in ringlets, in a high-necked lace dress, a pillbox hat on top of her veil, a large mole on her left cheekbone. Just above it was a picture of a young blonde with her hair worn in a frizzy eighties perm. She was wearing a red coat. He hadn't noticed, hadn't seen, because he'd walked into the room with certain expectations, making assumptions no less sweeping than Talbot had, with his conviction that Cancerians were intuitive, gentle and perceptive. Nurses were angels, ministering to the vulnerable: he'd been as guilty of bias as Vi Cooper, seeing Janice through the prism of his grateful memories of the nurses in Selly Oak who'd helped him manage pain and depression, and of Kerenza down in Cornwall, bringing comfort and kindness every single day. And on top of it all, he'd been fooled by a veritable genius for lies and misdirection.

'I thought,' said Strike, 'I should come and tell the Athorns' social worker in person that a body's been found in their flat. You do a very good middle-class accent, Janice. I s'pose the phone Clare uses is round here somewhere?'

He looked around. Possibly she'd hidden it when she'd seen who was at the door. He suddenly spotted the hairdryer, tucked away behind the sofa, but with its lead protruding. He sidled past the coffee table, bent down and pulled it out, along with a roll of cellophane, a small phial with the label pulled off, a syringe and some chocolates.

'Leave them,' said Janice suddenly and angrily, but he laid the items on the coffee table instead.

'How ill would I have been if I'd eaten one of those dates you were doctoring when I arrived last time?' he asked. 'You use the hairdryer to fix the cellophane back round them, right?' When she didn't answer, he said, 'I haven't thanked you for those chocolates you sent Robin and me at Christmas. I had flu. Only managed to eat a couple before puking my guts up. Chucked the rest away, because they had bad associations. Lucky for me, eh?'

Strike now sat down in the armchair, beside his mobile, which was still recording.

'Did you kill *all* these people?' Strike asked, gesturing up at the wall of photographs, 'Or do some of them just have recurrent bowel problems around you? No,' he said, scrutinising the wall, 'Irene's not up there, is she?'

She blinked at him through the lenses of her round silver glasses, which were far cleaner than Dennis Creed's.

A car came trundling up the road beyond the net curtains. Janice watched it pass, and Strike thought she was half expecting to see a police car. Perhaps she wasn't going to talk at all. Sometimes, people didn't. They preferred to leave it all up to the lawyers.

'I spoke to your son on the phone last night,' said Strike.

'You never!'

The words had burst out of her, in shock.

'I did,' said Strike. 'Kevin was quite surprised to hear you'd been visiting him in Dubai, because he hasn't seen you in nearly seven years. Why d'you pretend you're visiting him? To get a break from Irene?'

She pressed her lips together. One hand was playing with the worn wedding ring on the other.

'Kevin told me he's had barely any contact with you, since leaving home. You weren't ever close, he said. But he paid for you to fly out there seven years ago, because he thought he should give you "another chance", as he put it . . . and his young daughter managed to ingest quite a lot of bleach while you were looking after her. She survived – just – and since then, he's cut you off completely.'

'We ended up talking for nearly two hours,' said Strike, watching Janice's colour fluctuate. 'It was hard for Kevin to say out loud what he's suspected all these years. Who wants to believe their own mum's been poisoning people? He preferred to think he was paranoid about all those "special drinks" you used to give him. And apparently your first husband—'

'He wasn't my 'usband,' muttered Janice. 'We were never married.'

'—left because he thought you were doing things to his meals, too. Kevin used to think his father was making it all up. But after our chat last night, I think he's seeing things very differently. He's ready to come over and testify against you.'

Janice gave a small convulsive jerk. For almost a minute there was silence.

'You're recording this,' she whispered at last, looking at the mobile lying on the arm of Strike's chair.

'I am, yeah,' said Strike.

'If you turn that off, I'll talk to you.'

'I'll still be able to testify to whatever you tell me.'

'I'm sure a lawyer would tell me not to let meself be recorded, though.'

'Yeah,' Strike acknowledged, 'you're probably right.'

He picked up the mobile, turned it to face her so she could watch, switched off the recording, then laid it down on the small coffee table beside the chocolates, the empty phial, the syringe, the cellophane and the hairdryer.

'Why d'you do it, Janice?'

She was still stroking the underside of her wedding ring.

'I don't know why,' she said. 'I just . . . like it.'

881

ROBERT GALBRAITH

Her eyes wandered over the wall of photographs.

'I like seeing what 'appens to them, if they take poison or too many drugs. Sometimes I like 'elping 'em and 'aving them be grateful, and sometimes I like watching 'em suffer, and sometimes I like watching 'em go . . . ' A prickle ran up the back of Strike's neck. 'I don't know why,' she said again. 'I sometimes fink it's because I 'ad a bang on the 'ead, when I was ten. My dad knocked me downstairs. I was out for fifteen minutes. Ever since then, I've 'ad 'eadaches . . . 'Ead trauma can do fings to you, you know. So maybe it's not my fault, but . . . I dunno . . .

'Wiv me granddaughter,' said Janice, frowning slightly, 'I just wanted 'er gone, honestly . . . spoiled and whiny . . . I don't like kids,' she said, looking directly back at Strike. 'I've never liked kids. I never wanted 'em, never wanted Kev, but I fort if I 'ad it, 'is dad might marry me . . . but 'e never, 'e wouldn't . . .

'It was 'aving a baby what killed my mum,' said Janice. 'I was eight. She 'ad it at 'ome. Placenta previa, it was. Blood everywhere, me trying to 'elp, no doctor, my father drunk, screaming at everyone . . .

'I took this,' said Janice quietly, showing Strike the wedding ring on her finger, 'off Mum's dead 'and. I knew my father would sell it for drink. I took it and 'id it so 'e couldn't get it. It's all I got of 'er. I loved my mum,' said Janice Beattie, stroking the wedding ring, and Strike wondered whether it was true, whether head trauma and early abuse had made Janice what she was, and whether Janice had the capacity to love at all.

'Is that really your little sister, Clare?' Strike asked, pointing at the double frame beside Janice, where the sleepy-eyed, overweight man with smoker's teeth faced the heavy but pretty blonde.

'No,' said Janice, looking at the picture. After a short pause, she said, 'She was Larry's mistress. I killed both of 'em. I'm not sorry. They deserved it. 'E was wiv me, 'e wasn't much of a catch, but 'e was wiv me, the pair of 'em carryin' on be'ind my back. Bitch,' said Janice quietly, looking at the picture of the plump blonde.

'I assume you kept the obituaries?'

She got slowly up from the sofa, and Strike heard her knees click as she walked towards the china cabinet in the corner which housed

882

most of her cheap spun-glass ornaments, and knelt down, again steadying herself with one hand on the mantelpiece. But now, instead of one folder, she tugged two out of the drawer in the base of the cabinet, and Strike remembered how she'd shifted things around in the drawer last time, doubtless removing those things she didn't want him to see.

'That one,' she said, showing him the fatter of the two folders, 'is all the stuff about Margot. I cut out everyfing I could find. Needed a second folder for all 'er clippings ... '

She opened the thinner folder, which was the one Strike had seen before, and extracted an old work newsletter headed *Hickson & Co.* The blonde's colour photograph featured prominently at the top.

'Clare Martin,' said Janice. ''Eavy drinker, she was. "Accidental overdose" ... liver failure. I knew she was taking too many paraceta-mol for 'er endometriosis, I watched 'er doing it. Me and Larry 'ad a bunch of people over to the 'ouse. They fort I was stupid. Eye contact between 'em all night long. Thick as mince, the pair of 'em. I was mixing drinks. Every cocktail I gave 'er was 'alf liquid paracetamol. She died eight days later ... '

'And there's Larry's,' she said indifferently, holding up a second newsletter from Hickson & Co.

'I waited six, seven monfs. That was easy. 'E was a walkin' time-bomb, Larry, the doctors 'ad warned 'im, 'is 'eart was wrecked. Pseudoephedrine, that was. They never even checked 'im for drugs in 'is system. They knew what it was: smoking and eating like a pig. Nobody looked further than 'is dodgy ticker ... '

Strike detected not the slightest sign of remorse as she shuffled the obituaries of her victims as though they were so many knitting patterns. Her fingers trembled, but Strike thought that was down to shock, not shame. Mere minutes ago she'd thought of suicide. Perhaps that cool and clever brain was working very hard beneath the apparently frank surface, and Strike suddenly reached out and removed the drugged chocolates from the table beside Janice, and put them down on the floor beside his chair. Her eyes followed them, and he was sure he'd been right to suspect she was thinking of eating them. Now he leaned forwards again and picked up the old yellow clipping he'd examined last time, showing little Johnny Marks from Bethnal Green.

'He was your first, was he?'

Janice took a deep breath and exhaled. A couple of the cuttings fluttered.

'Yeah,' she said heavily. 'Pesticide. You could get all sorts in them days, buy it over the counter. Organophosphates. I fancied 'im something rotten, Johnny Marks, but 'e made fun of me. Yeah, so they fort it was peritonitis and 'e died. It's true the doctor didn't turn up, mind. People didn't care, when it was kids from a slum . . . That was a bad death, 'e 'ad. I was allowed to go in and look at 'im, after 'e died. I give 'im a little kiss on the cheek,' said Janice. ''E couldn't stop me then, could 'e? Shouldn't of made fun of me.'

'Marks,' said Strike, examining the clipping, 'gave you the idea for Spencer, right? It was the name that first connected her with you, but I should've twigged when Clare phoned me back so promptly. Social workers never do that. Too overworked.'

'Huh,' said Janice, and she almost smiled. 'Yeah. That's where I got the name: Clare Martin and Johnny Marks.'

'You didn't keep Brenner's obituary, did you?'

'No,' said Janice.

'Because you didn't kill him?'

'No. 'E died of old age somewhere in Devon. I never even read 'is obituary, but I 'ad to come up wiv somefing, didn't I, when you asked for it? So I said Oakden took it.'

She was probably the most accomplished liar Strike had ever met. Her ability to come up with falsehoods at a moment's notice, and the way she interwove her plausible lies with truth, never attempting too much, and delivering everything with such an air of authenticity and honesty, placed her in a class apart.

'Was Brenner really addicted to barbiturates?'

'No,' said Janice.

She was shuffling the obituaries back into their folder now, and Strike spotted the clipping about holy basil, on the reverse of which was Joanna Hammond's death notice.

'No,' she repeated, as she put the obituaries back into her bottom drawer and closed it, as though it mattered any more whether she tidied these things away, as though they wouldn't soon be used in evidence against her. Knees clicking, she got slowly to her feet again, and returned to the sofa.

'I was getting Brenner to sign for drugs for me,' she said. ''E fort I was selling them on the street, dopey old sod.'

'How did you persuade him to over-order drugs? Blackmail?'

'S'pose you'd call it that, yeah,' she said. 'I found out 'e was going to see a prostitute locally. One of 'er kids told me Brenner was visiting 'er once a week. I fort, right, I'll get you, you dirty old bastard. 'E was coming up for retirement. I knew 'e didn't want to end 'is career in disgrace. I went in to see 'im one day in his consulting room and told 'im I knew. 'E nearly 'ad an 'eart attack,' said Janice, with a malicious smile. 'I told 'im I knew 'ow to keep me mouf shut, and then I asked 'im to get me some drugs. 'E signed like a lamb. I was using stuff Brenner got me for years, after.'

'The prostitute was Betty Fuller, right?'

'Yeah,' said Janice. 'I fort you'd find that out.'

'Did Brenner really assault Deborah Athorn?

'No. 'E checked 'er stitches after she had Samhain, that's all.'

'Why did Clare Spencer tell me that story? Just blowing a bit more smoke around?'

Janice shrugged.

'I dunno. I fort maybe you'd fink Brenner was a sex pest and Margot found out 'e was fiddling with patients.'

'Was there ever really an Amytal capsule in Brenner's mug?'

'No,' said Janice. 'It was in Irene's mug ... that was stupid,' she said, her pink and white brow furrowed. The wide blue eyes drifted over her wall of victims' photographs, to the window and back to Strike. 'I shouldn't of done that. Sometimes I sailed a bit close to the wind. Took silly risks. Irene was pissing me off one day on reception, flirting wiv – just flirting,' said Janice, 'so I took 'er a mug of tea wiv a couple of capsules in it. She talks till you could throttle 'er, I just wanted 'er to shut the hell up for a bit. But she let it go cold ...

'I was sort of glad, after I'd calmed down. I got the mug and took it out the back to wash up, but Margot come creepin' up behind me in 'er flat shoes. I tried to 'ide it, but she saw.

'I fort she'd go tellin' tales, so I 'ad to get in first. I went straight to Dr Gupta and said I'd found a capsule in Dr Brenner's tea, and told 'im I fort 'e was over-ordering drugs and was addicted. What else could I do? Gupta was a nice man but he was a coward. Bit scared of Brenner. I fort 'e probably wouldn't confront 'im, and 'e didn't, but honestly, I knew even if 'e 'ad, Brenner would rather pretend to be an addict than risk me tellin' anyone about a 'is dirty little fing wiv Betty Fuller.'

'And was Margot really worried about how Dorothy Oakden's mother died?'

'No,' said Janice again. 'But I 'ad to tell you somefing, didn't I?'

'You're a genius of misdirection,' said Strike, and Janice turned slightly pink.

'I've always been clever,' she mumbled, 'but that don't 'elp a woman. It's better to be pretty. You 'ave a better life if you're good-looking. Men always went for Irene, not me. She talked shit all night long, but they liked 'er better. I wasn't bad-looking ... I just didn't 'ave what men liked.'

'When we first met the two of you,' said Strike, ignoring this, 'I thought Irene might've wanted you interviewed together to make sure you didn't spill her secrets, but it was the other way round, wasn't it? You wanted to be there to control what *she* said.'

'Yeah, well,' said Janice, with another sigh, 'I didn't do that well, did I? She was blabbing left, right and centre.'

'Tell me, did Charlie Ramage really see a missing woman in Leamington Spa?'

'No. I just needed to give you somefing to fink about instead of Margot prodding Kev in the tummy. Charlie Ramage told me 'e saw Mary Flanagan in a country churchyard in ... Worcestershire somewhere, I fink it was. I knew nobody could say no diff'rent, I knew 'e was dead and I knew 'e talked such bollocks, nobody round 'im would remember one more tall story.'

'Was the mention of Leamington Spa supposed to nudge me towards Irene and Satchwell?'

'Yeah,' said Janice.

'Did you put drugs in Wilma Bayliss's Thermos? Is that why she seemed drunk to people at the surgery?'

'I did, yeah.'

'Why?'

'I already told you,' said Janice restlessly, 'I don't know why I do it, I just do . . . I wanted to see what would 'appen to 'er. I like knowing why fings are 'appening, when nobody else does . . .

''Ow did you work all this out?' she demanded. 'Talbot and Lawson never suspected.'

'Lawson might not have done,' said Strike, 'but I think Talbot did.'

''E never,' said Janice, at once. 'I 'ad 'im eating out me 'and.'

'I'm not so sure,' said Strike. 'He left a strange set of notes, and all through them he kept circling back to the death of Scorpio, or Juno, which are the names he gave Joanna Hammond. Seven interviews, Janice. I think he subconsciously knew there was something off about you. He mentions poison a lot, which I think had stuck in his mind because of the way Joanna died. At one point – I was reading the notes again, last night – he copies out a long description of the tarot card the Queen of Cups. Words to the effect that she reflects the observer back at themselves. "To see the truth of her is almost impossible." And on the night they hauled him off to hospital, he hallucinated a female demon with a cup in her hand and a seven hanging round her neck. He was too ill to string his suspicions together, but his subconscious kept trying to tell him you weren't all you seemed. At one point, he wrote: "Is Cetus right?" – he called Irene Cetus – and eventually I asked myself what she could've been right about. Then I remembered that the first time we met the pair of you, she told us she thought you were "sweet on" Douthwaite.'

At the sound of Douthwaite's name, Janice winced slightly.

'Oakden said you got giggly around Douthwaite, too,' Strike continued, watching her closely. 'And Dorothy bracketed you with Irene and Gloria as some kind of scarlet woman, which implies you'd done some flirting in front of her.'

'Is that all you went on: me flirting once, and being the Queen of

Cups?' said Janice, managing to get a note of scorn into her voice, though he thought she seemed shaken.

'No,' said Strike, 'there were plenty of other things. Strange anomalies and coincidences. People kept telling me Margot didn't like "the nurse", but they got you confused with Irene a lot, so it took me a while to twig that they really did mean you.

'Then there was Fragile X. When I saw you that first time, with Irene, you claimed you'd only been to visit the Athorns once, but the second time I met you, you seemed to know a hell of a lot about them. Fragile X was called Martin-Bell syndrome back in the early seventies. If you'd only seen them that one time, it seemed odd you knew exactly what was wrong with them, and used the modern term . . .

'And then I started noticing how many people were getting stomach upsets or acting drugged. Did you put something in the punch at Margot and Roy's barbecue?'

'I did, yeah,' she said. 'Ipecac syrup, that was. I fort it would be funny if they all thought they'd got food poisoning from the barbecue, but then Carl broke the bowl, and I was glad, really . . . I just wanted to see 'em all ill, and maybe look after 'em all, and ruin 'er party, but it was stupid, wasn't it? . . . That's what I mean, I sailed close to the wind sometimes, they were doctors, what if they'd known? . . . It was only Gloria who 'ad a big glassful and was sick. Margot's 'usband didn't like that . . . ruined their smart house . . .'

And Strike saw the almost indiscriminate desire for disruption that lay behind the meek exterior.

'Gloria throwing up at the barbecue,' said Strike. 'Irene and her irritable bowel syndrome – Kevin and his constant stomach aches – Wilma swaying on her feet and vomiting while she was working at St John's – me, puking up my Christmas chocolates – and, of course, Steve Douthwaite and his vision problems, his headaches and his churning guts . . . I'm assuming it was Douthwaite Irene was flirting with, the day you put Amytal capsules in her tea?'

Janice pressed her lips together, eyes narrowed.

'I suppose you told her he was gay to try and get her to back off?'

'She already 'ad Eddie gagging to marry 'er,' Janice burst out. 'She 'ad all these blokes down the pub flirting with 'er. If I'd told 'er 'ow much I liked Steve, she'd've taken 'im for the fun of it, that's what she was. So yeah, I told 'er 'e was queer.'

'What are you drugging her with, these days?'

'It varies,' said Janice quietly. 'Depends 'ow much she's pissing me off.'

'So tell me about Steve Douthwaite.'

Suddenly, Janice was breathing deeply. Her face was flushed again: she looked emotional.

''E was . . . such a beautiful man.'

The passionate throb in her voice took Strike aback, almost more than the full stock of poisons she was keeping in her kitchen. He thought of the cheeky chap in his kipper tie, who'd become the puffy, bloodshot-eyed proprietor of the Allardice in Skegness, with his strands of greying hair stuck to his sweating forehead, and not for the first time, Strike had reason to reflect on the extraordinarily unpredictable nature of human love.

'I've always been one to fall 'ead over 'eels,' said Janice, and Strike thought of Johnny Marks dying in agony, and Janice kissing him farewell on his cold dead cheek. 'Oh, Steve could make you laugh. I *love* a man what can make you laugh. *Really* 'andsome. I used to walk past 'is flat ten times a day just to get an 'ello . . . we got friendly . . .

''E started dropping in, telling me all 'is problems . . . and 'e tells me 'ow 'e's mad about this married woman. Fallen for 'is mate's wife. On and on and on about 'ow 'ard 'er life is, and there's me sitting there wiv a kid on me own. What about *my* 'ard life? She 'ad an 'usband, didn't she? But no, I could tell I wasn't gonna get nowhere wiv 'im unless she was out the way, so I fort, right, well, she'll 'ave to go . . .

'She was no better lookin' than I was,' muttered Janice, pointing at the picture of Joanna Hammond on the wall. 'State of that fing on 'er face . . .

'So I looked 'er up in the phone book and I just went round 'er 'ouse when I knew 'er 'usband was at work. I used to 'ave this wig I wore to parties. Put that on, and me uniform, and a pair of glasses I used to 'ave, but I didn't need. Rang the doorbell, told 'er I'd 'ad a tip-off about 'er domestic situation.

'People will always let a nurse in,' said Janice. 'She was desperate to talk to someone. I got 'er good and emotional, cryin' and all that. She told me about sleeping with Steve, and 'ow she fort she was in love wiv 'im ...

'I made 'er a drink wiv latex gloves on. ''Alf of it was weedkiller. She knew, the moment she tasted it, but I grabbed 'er 'air from be'ind,' Janice mimed the motion in mid-air, 'pulled 'er 'ead back, forced it down 'er fuckin' throat. Oh yeah. Once she was on the floor, chokin', I poured some more down, neat.

''Ad to stay a while, to make sure she didn't try an' phone anyone. Once I knew she was too far gone to recover, I took off me uniform an' left.

'It takes nerve,' said Janice Beattie, her colour high and her eyes bright, 'but act normal and people don't see nothing strange ... you just got to 'old your nerve. And maybe I wasn't showy-looking when I was young, but that 'elped. I wasn't the kind people remembered ...

'Next day, near enough, I 'ad Steve crying 'is eyes out round my place. It was all going great,' said the woman who'd poured neat weedkiller down her rival's throat, 'I saw 'im loads after that, 'e was round my place all the time. There was somefing there between us, I could feel it.

'I never drugged 'im a lot,' said Janice, as though this was true evidence of affection. 'Only enough to stop 'im going out, make 'im feel 'e needed me. I used to look after 'im really well. Once, 'e slept on my sofa, and I wiped 'is face for 'im, while 'e was asleep,' she said, and again, Strike thought of the kiss she'd given the dead Johnny Marks.

'But sometimes,' said Janice, with bitterness, 'men fort I was the mumsy type and didn't see me as anyfing else. I could tell Steve liked me, but I fort 'e might not be seeing me the right way, you know, wiv bein' a nurse, and Kev always dragging round after me. One evening, Steve come over, and Kev was 'aving a tantrum, and Steve said, he thought 'e'd be off, let me look after Kev ... and I could tell, I fort, you're not gonna want me wiv a kid. So I fort, Kev needs to go.'

She said it as though talking about taking out the bins.

'But you gotta be careful when it's your own kid,' said Janice. 'I needed to get an 'istory going. 'E couldn't just die, not after being perfectly 'ealthy. I started experimenting wiv stuff, I was finking, maybe a salt overdose, claim 'e did it on a dare or somefing. I started putting stuff in 'is food 'ere and there. Get 'im complaining to teachers about stomach aches an' that, and then I'd say, "Oh, I know, I think it's a bit of schoolitis" . . . '

'But then Margot examined him,' said Strike.

'But then,' repeated Janice slowly, nodding, 'that hoity-toity bitch takes 'im into 'er surgery and examines 'im. And I knew she was suspicious. She asked me after, what drinks it was I'd given 'im, because the little bastard 'ad told 'er Mummy was givin' 'im special drinks . . .

'Not a week later,' said Janice, twisting the old wedding ring on her finger, 'I realise Steve's going to see 'er about 'is 'ealf, instead of coming to see me. Next fing I know, Margot's asking me all about Joanna's death, out the back by the kettle, and Dorothy and Gloria were listening in. I said, "'Ow the 'ell should I know what 'appened?" but I was worried. I fort, what's Steve been telling 'er? 'As 'e said 'e finks there was somefing wrong wiv it? 'As someone said they saw a nurse leaving the 'ouse?

'I was getting worried. I sent 'er chocolates full of phenobarbital. Irene 'ad told me Margot 'ad 'ad freatening notes, and I'm not surprised, interfering bitch, she was . . . I fort, they'll fink it's 'ooever sent them notes, sent the chocolates . . .

'But she never ate 'em. She frew 'em in the bin in front of me, but after, I 'eard she'd taken 'em out the bin and kept 'em. And that's when I knew, I really knew. I fort, she's gonna get 'em tested . . . '

'And that's when you finally agreed to go on a date with simple old Larry,' said Strike.

''Oo says 'e was simple?' said Janice, firing up.

'Irene,' said Strike. 'You needed access to concrete, didn't you? Didn't want to be seen buying it, I'd imagine. What did you do, tell Larry to take some and not mention it to anyone?'

She simply looked at him out of those round blue eyes that nobody who hadn't heard this conversation could possibly mistrust.

'What gave you the idea of concrete?' Strike asked. 'That rumour of the body in the foundations?'

'Yeah,' said Janice, finally. 'It seemed like the way to stop the body smelling. I needed 'er to disappear. It was too near 'ome, what wiv 'er examining Kev, and asking me about Joanna, and keeping those chocolates. I wanted people to fink maybe the Essex Butcher got 'er, or the bloke 'oo sent the threatening notes.'

'How many times had you visited the Athorns before you killed Margot?'

'A few.'

'Because they needed a nurse? Or for some other reason?'

The longest pause yet ensued, long enough for the sun to slide out from a cloud, and the glass Cinderella coach to burn briefly like white fire, and then turn back into the tawdry gewgaw it really was.

'I sort of fort of killing them,' said Janice slowly. 'I don't know why, really. Just from the time I met 'em . . . they were odd and nobody ever went there. Those cousins of theirs visited once every ten years. I met 'em back in January, those cousins, when the flat needed cleaning out, to stop that man downstairs going to court . . . they stayed an hour and let "Clare" do all the rest . . .

'Yeah, I just fort I might kill the Athorns one day,' she said, with a shrug. 'That's why I kept visiting. I liked the idea of watching an 'ole family die togevver, and waiting to see when people realised, and then it'd be on the news, probably, and I'd know what 'appened when everyone was gossiping, local . . .

'I did a bit of experimenting on 'em. Vitamin injections, I told them it was. Special treatments. And I used to hold their noses while they were asleep. Used to pull up their eyelids and look at their eyes, while they were unconscious. Nurses don't never give anaesthetics, see, but Dr Brenner was letting me 'ave all sorts, and the Athorns just let me do stuff to 'em, even Gwilherm. 'E loved me coming over. 'E'd spend days on benzedrine and then 'e'd get sedatives off me. Proper junkie.

'I used to say to 'im, now, don't you go telling anyone what we're doing. These are expensive treatments. It's only because I like your family.

'Some days, I used to fink, I'll kill the kid and then give evidence against Gwilherm. That was one idea I 'ad. I fort, I'll get in the papers, all dressed up, give evidence against 'im, you know. My picture on the front page ... and I fort that'd be somefing interesting to talk to Steve about, when 'e seen my picture in the paper. Men love nurses. That was the on'y fing I 'ad going for me when I was out wiv Irene, and then the bitch starts pretending she's a nurse an' all ...

'Only fank Gawd I never did any of that, fank Gawd I saved the Athorns, because what would I 'ave done wiv Margot if I 'adn't 'ad them up the road? I'd nicked their spare key by then. They never noticed.

'I never fort it would work,' said Janice, ''cause I 'ad to frow the plan togevver in about five minutes. I knew she was onto me, when she saved the chocolates, and I was up all night, finking, worrying ... and it was the next day, or maybe the day after, Steve went charging out of her surgery that last time. I was scared she'd warned 'im about me, because when I went round that night, 'e made some excuse not to let me in ... I mean, 'e never went to the police, so now I know I was being paranoid, but at the time—'

'You weren't being paranoid,' said Strike. 'I spoke to him yesterday. Margot told him he ought to stop eating anything you prepared him. Just that. He understood what she was saying, though.'

Janice's face grew redder.

'That bitch,' she said venomously. 'What did she do that for? She 'ad a rich 'usband and a lover wanting her back, why's she got to take Steve off me?'

'Go on,' said Strike, 'about how you did it.'

A subtle change now came over Janice. Previously, she'd seemed diffident, matter-of-fact, or even ashamed of her own impetuousness, but now, for the first time, she seemed to enjoy what she was saying, as though she killed Margot Bamborough all over again, in the telling.

'Went out wiv Larry. Told 'im some bullshit about this poor family what needed to concrete over somefing on their roof terrace. Said they were dirt-poor. 'E was so keen to impress me, silly sod, 'e wanted to go do the building work for 'em.'

She rolled her eyes.

'I 'ad to give 'im all this crap about 'ow that would made the dad feel inadequate . . . I said just nicking a few bags of concrete mix off the building site'd be enough.

'Larry drove it to Albemarle Way for me and carried it up to their landing. I wouldn't let 'im come any further, said it would be uneffical for 'im to see patients. 'E was silly, Larry, you could tell 'im anyfing . . . But he wouldn't marry me,' said Janice suddenly. 'Why is that? Why wouldn't anyone marry me? What 'aven't I got, that ovver women 'ave?' asked the nurse who'd pulled back the eyelids from her drugged victims to stare into their unseeing eyes. 'Nobody ever wanted to marry me . . . never . . . I wanted to be in the paper in a white dress. I wanted my day in church and I never got it. Never . . . '

'You needed an alibi as well as concrete, presumably?' said Strike, ignoring her question. 'I assume you chose the demented old lady in Gopsall Street because she couldn't say one way or another whether you'd been with her when Margot disappeared?'

'Yeah,' said Janice, returning to her story, 'I went to see 'er late morning and I left drugs there and a note, to prove I'd been in. I knew she'd agree I was there early evening. She didn't 'ave no family, she'd agree with anyfing you said to 'er . . .

'I went from 'er place to buy a cinema ticket for the late-night show, and I called up my babysitter and told 'er I'd be later than I fort because we were getting the last viewing. I knew Irene wouldn't wanna go wiv me. She'd been makin' noises about not feelin' up to it all morning. I knew she didn't 'ave no bad toof, but I pretended to go along wiv it. Irene never wanted to go anywhere we weren't gonna meet men.'

'So, you went back to the surgery that afternoon – in through the back door, I suppose?'

'Yeah,' said Janice, her eyes slightly unfocused now. 'Nobody saw me. I knew Margot 'ad a doughnut in the fridge, because I'd been in there that morning and seen it, but there was people around all the time, so I couldn't do nuffing. I injected it wiv Nembutal sodium solution, froo the cellophane.'

'You must've been well practised by now? You knew how much to give her, so she could still walk up the road?'

'Nuffing's certain,' said the nurse. Unlike Creed, she didn't pretend omnipotence, but then, she'd also been, however reluctantly, in the business of healing as well as killing. 'I 'ad a good feeling for dosages, but you can't never be an 'undred per cent sure. I'd 'eard she was going to meet some friend in a pub up the road, and she usually ate somefing before she went, but I couldn't be sure she'd eat it, or still be able to walk up the road after, or when it would really hit 'er . . .

'All the time I was doing it, getting the concrete and drugging the doughnut, I was finking, this won't work, it can't work. You're gonna go to prison, Janice . . . And you know somefing?' said the nurse, now pink cheeked and fierce, 'By then, I didn't even care. Not if she'd told Steve about me. I fort, I'll go on trial and I'll tell 'em 'ow 'e treated me like a mum and a nurse and took advantage, round my flat all hours. 'E'll 'ave to bloody notice me and 'ear me then, won't 'e? I didn't care. I just fort, I want you dead, lady. I want you dead, you wiv your 'usband and your boyfriend on the side, and my man coming to see you three times a week . . .

'Eivver she dies, I fort, and I get away wiv it, or I'll be famous, I'll be in the papers . . . and I liked the idea, then.'

She looked around her small sitting room, and Strike was certain that she wondered what her cell would be like.

'I left the surgery and went round the long way to the Athorns', but when I let myself in, Gwilherm wasn't there. I fort, OK, that's a problem. Where is 'e?

'And then Deborah and Samhain started moaning. They didn't want their vitamin injections. I 'ad to get strict wiv 'em. I said to Deborah, it's these injections what's keeping you well. You don't take 'em, I'll have to ring an ambulance and get 'em to take you into 'ospital for an assessment . . . You could scare 'er into anyfing if you told 'er she'd 'ave to go outside. I give Deborah and Samhain their "vitamin injections", lying side by side in the double bedroom. Rolled 'em onto their sides. They were out for the count.

'So then I goes outside, and I waits in the phone box, pretending to be on the phone, keepin' watch.

'It didn't feel real, none of it. I didn't fink it'd work. Probably I'd go into work next day and 'ear Margot passed out in the street, and then she'd start yelling the place down saying she was drugged, and I knew she'd point the finger at me . . .

'She didn't come for ages. I fort, it's over. She's eaten the doughnut and got ill in the surgery. She's called an ambulance. She's guessed, she's got sick. There was this girl, standing in front of the phone box, and I'm trying to see round 'er, trying to see . . .

'And then I saw Margot coming up the road. I fort, well, this is it. It was raining hard. People weren't watchin'. It was all umbrellas and cars splashing. She crossed the road and I could see she was in a bad way. Wobbling all over the place. She got to my side of the road and leaned up against the wall. 'Er legs were about to go. I come out the phone box and I says, "Come on, love, you need to sit down." Kept my face down. She come wiv me, a few steps, then she realised it was me. We 'ad a bit of a struggle. I got 'er a few more feet, just inside Albemarle Way, but she was a tall girl . . . and I fort, this is where it ends . . .

'And then I seen Gwilherm coming up the other way. It was me only chance. I called 'im to 'elp me. 'E fort 'e was 'elping 'er. 'E 'elped me drag 'er up the stairs. There wasn't much fight in 'er by then. I told Gwilherm some rubbish to stop 'im phoning the ambulance. Said I could treat 'er myself . . . said 'e didn't want no police coming up, looking round the flat . . . 'E was a very paranoid man about the auforities, so that worked . . .

'I says, you go and see if Deborah and Samhain are still asleep. They've both been very worried about where you've been, and I 'ad to give 'em a little sedative.

'I suffocated 'er while 'e was out of the room. It didn't take much. 'Eld 'er nose, kept 'er mouth shut. Did to Margot what I'd been planning to do to the Athorns.

'When I knew she was dead,' said Janice, 'I left 'er sitting on the sofa and I went into the barfroom. I sat on the bog, looking at the flamingos on the wallpaper and I fort, now what? Gwilherm's here. 'E's seen 'er . . . and the on'y fing I could fink of was, let 'im fink 'e's done it. 'E's crazy enough. I fort, I'll probably 'ave to kill 'im, too, in the end, but I'll worry about that later . . .

'So I waited in the bog and let 'im go in the room and find 'er.

'I give 'im five minutes alone wiv the body, then I walk back in, talkin' to Margot, like I left 'er alive. "You feeling all right now, Margot, love?" And then I says, "What've you done, Gwilherm? What've you done?"

'And he says, "Nuffing, nuffing, I ain't done nuffing," and I'm saying, "You told me you can kill people with your powers. P'rhaps we better call the police," and 'e's begging me not to, 'e didn't mean to, it was all a mistake. So in the end I says, all right, I won't give you away. I'll make it disappear. I'll take care of it.

''E was crying like a baby and he asked me for one of my sedatives. 'E *asked* me to put 'im out, can you believe that? I give 'im some downers. Left 'im curled up asleep on Samhain's bed.

'It was really 'ard, putting her in that big box fing all on me own. I 'ad to take out all the crap they kept in there. Folded 'er up. Once I 'ad 'er in there, I checked on all the Athorns. Made sure the airways weren't obstructed. Then I ran back outside to the phone box. I says to Irene, are we still on for the cinema? And she says no, like I fort she would, fank Gawd.

'So I go back inside. I was there till midnight, near enough. I 'ad to mix the concrete bit by bit, by 'and, in a bucket. It took ages. Margot filled up most of that box fing, but it took a long time to get all the concrete round her. Then I closed the lid. It stuck to the concrete. I couldn't get it up again, so that was good.

'When they was all awake, I told Gwilherm I'd taken care of it. I said to 'im quietly, the lid on that box thing 'as jammed. Best find somewhere else to put Samhain's toys.

''E knew, obviously. I fink 'e pretended to 'imself 'e didn't, but 'e did. I was there free times a week, afterwards. I 'ad to be. Keeping 'im happy. One time I went round and 'e'd painted all those symbols on the walls, like it was some sort of pagan temple or something.

'Weeks after, monfs after, I was worried sick. I knew 'e was tellin' people 'e'd killed 'er. Luckily, everyone fort 'e was a nutcase, local. But it got bad, towards the end. 'E 'ad to go. I still can't believe I waited a year to get rid of 'im ... '

'And around the time you killed him, you phoned Cynthia Phipps and pretended to be Margot, didn't you? To give the police another lead to hare after, and distract from Gwilherm, in case anyone had taken him seriously?'

'Yeah. That's right,' mumbled Janice, twisting the old wedding ring.

'And you kept visiting Deborah and Samhain as Clare Spencer?'

'Well, yeah,' said Janice. 'I 'ad to. They needed watching. Last fing I wanted was real social workers fiddling around in there.'

'And Deborah and Samhain never realised Clare was the same as Janice the nurse?'

'People with Fragile X don't recognise faces easy,' said Janice. 'I changed me 'air colour and used me glasses. I done a lot to keep 'em 'ealfy, you know. Vitamin D for Deborah, cause she never goes outside. She's younger'n me . . . I fort, I might well be dead before anyone finds the body. Longer it went on, less likely it was anyone would ever know I 'ad anyfing to do wiv it . . . '

'And what about Douthwaite?'

''E scarpered,' said Janice, her smile fading. 'That near enough broke my 'eart. There was me 'aving to go out on foursomes wiv Irene and Eddie, and act like I was 'appy wiv Larry, and the love of my life's disappeared. I asked ev'ryone where Steve 'ad gone, and no one knew.'

'So why's Julie Wilkes on your wall?' asked Strike.

''Oo?' said Janice, lost in her self-pitying reverie.

'The Redcoat who worked at Clacton-on-Sea,' said Strike, pointing at the young blonde with her frizzy hair, who was framed on Janice's wall.

'Oh . . . 'er,' said Janice, with a sigh. 'Yeah . . . I ran into someone 'oo knew someone 'oo'd met Steve at Butlin's, few years later . . . oh, I was excited. Gawd, I was bored wiv Larry by then. I really wanted to see Steve again. I *love* a man 'oo can make me laugh,' repeated the woman who'd planned the murder of a family, for the pleasure of watching them die. 'I *knew* there'd been somefing there between us, I *knew* we coulda bin a couple. So I booked me and Larry an 'oliday at Butlin's. Kev didn't wanna come – suited me. I got meself a perm and I went on a diet. Couldn't wait. You build things up in your mind, don't you?

'And we went to the club night and there 'e was,' said Janice quietly. 'Oh, 'e looked gorgeous. "Longfellow Serenade". All the girls went crazy for 'im when 'e finished singing. There's Larry boozing . . . After Larry went to bed in the chalet I went back out again. Couldn't find 'im.

'Took me free days to get a word wiv 'im. I said, "Steve, it's me. Janice. Your neighbour. The nurse!"'

She turned slowly redder than she'd been all interview. Her eyes watered with the intensity of her blush.

'He goes "Oh yeah. All right, Janice?" And 'e walks away. And I seen 'im,' said Janice, and her jaw quivered, 'kiss that girl, that Julie, and look back at me, like 'e wanted me to see . . .

'And I fort, *no*. After all what I've done for you, Steve? *No*.

'I did it on the last night but one of our 'oliday. Larry snoring 'is 'ead off as usual. 'E never noticed I wasn't in bed.

'They all used to go to Steve's chalet after work, I found that out, following 'em. She come out on 'er own. Pissed. Two in the morning.

'It wasn't 'ard. There wasn't anyone round. They didn't 'ave cameras around like they do nowadays. I pushed 'er, and I jumped in after 'er, and I 'eld 'er under. It was the surprise what killed 'er. She took in a load of water on the way down. That was the only one I ever did wivvout drugs, but I was angry, see . . .

'Got out, towelled meself off. Mopped up all the footprints, but it was a warm night, you couldn't see nuffing by morning.

'Next day, I seen 'im. I says, "Terrible fing, that girl, Steve. You look awful. Wanna get a drink?"'

'E went white as a sheet, but I fort, well, you used me, Steve, and then you left me high and dry, didn't you?'

A police siren sounded somewhere in the distance, and Strike, glancing at his watch, thought it was likely to be heading here, for Nightingale Grove.

'You took my sympafy and my kindness and you let me cook for you,' said Janice, still addressing an imaginary Steve Douthwaite. 'I was even ready to kill my kid for you! And then you go off messing around wiv ovver women? *No*. Actions 'ave consequences,' said Janice, her cheeks still burning. 'Men need to learn that, and take some responsibility. Women 'ave to,' she said, as the police siren grew ever louder. 'Well, I'll see 'im again in court, won't I? You know, I'm quite looking forward to it, now I'm finking about it,' said Janice. 'It's not fun, living 'ere all on me own. It'll be funny seeing Irene's face. I'll be all over the papers, won't I? And maybe some men will read about why I done it, and realise they want to be careful 'oo they lead on. Useful lesson for men everywhere, if you ask me. Actions,' repeated Janice Beattie, as the police car drew to a halt outside her front door, and she squared her shoulders, ready to accept her fate, ''ave consequences.'

PART SEVEN

Then came October full of merry glee . . .

Edmund Spenser
The Faerie Queene

72

. . . they for nought would from their worke refraine . . .

Edmund Spenser
The Faerie Queene

Success, as Cormoran Strike had long since learned, is a much more complex business than most people suppose.

It wasn't the first time that the press had turned its sights upon the detective agency, and while the acclaim was undoubtedly flattering and a good advert for the business, it was, as ever, severely prejudicial to the partners' ability to keep working. Robin, whose home address was swiftly discovered by the press, took refuge at the house of Vanessa Ekwensi, and with the aid of a number of wigs and some skilful make-up, managed to continue to cover a certain amount of work, so that Barclay and Hutchins didn't have to do everything themselves. Strike, on the other hand, was forced back into Nick and Ilsa's spare room, where he let his beard grow, and lay low, directing the agency's subcontractors by phone. Pat Chauncey alone remained based at the office in Denmark Street, taking care of administrative matters, stolidly opening and closing up each morning and evening.

'I've got no comment. You'd all do better sodding off,' she croaked twice a day at the knot of journalists hanging around Denmark Street.

The eruption of publicity that followed the twin discoveries of a woman's body encased in concrete in a quiet flat in Clerkenwell, and a teenager's skeleton hidden beneath debris in the depths of an underground well in Islington, showed no sign of abating quickly. There were far too many exciting angles to this story: the separate excavations and positive identifications of the bones of Margot Bamborough and Louise Tucker, the comments from two bereaved families, who scarcely knew whether they felt more relief or grief, the profiles of two very different killers and, of course, the private detectives now widely acclaimed as the capital's most talented.

Gratifying though this was, Strike took no satisfaction in the way the press hounded either Gregory Talbot ('What would you say to people who say your father had blood on his hands?') or Dinesh Gupta ('Do you regret giving Janice Beattie that glowing reference, doctor?') nor in seeing the Athorns led out of their flat by genuine social workers, frightened, displaced and uncomprehending. Carl Oakden made a brief appearance in the *Daily Mail*, trying to sell himself as an expert on both Strike and Margot Bamborough, but as the article began with the words 'Convicted con man Carl Brice, son of the old practice secretary, Dorothy ...' it was perhaps unsurprising that Oakden soon slunk back into the shadows. Strike's father, on the other hand, was happy to continue associating his name with Strike's, issuing a fulsome statement of pride in his eldest son through his publicist. Fuming quietly, Strike ignored all requests for comment.

Dennis Creed, who for so long had received top billing in any news story including him, was relegated almost to a footnote in this one. Janice Beattie had outdone him, not only in the number of her suspected victims, but in remaining undetected for decades longer. Photographs of her sitting room in Nightingale Grove were leaked to the press, who highlighted the framed pictures of the dead on the walls, the folder of obituaries kept in her china cabinet, and the syringe, the cellophane and the hairdryer that Strike had found behind the sofa. The store of drugs and poisons retrieved from her kitchen were carried out of her house by forensics experts, and the rosy-cheeked, silver-haired nurse dubbed 'the Poisoner Granny' blinked impassively at news cameras as she was led into court and remanded in custody.

Meanwhile, Strike could barely open a newspaper or switch on the TV without seeing Brian Tucker, who was giving interviews to anybody who'd speak to him. In a cracked voice he wept, exulted, praised Strike and Robin, told the world they deserved knighthoods ('Or the other thing, what is it for women?' 'Damehood,' murmured the sympathetic blonde presenter, who was holding the emotional Tucker's hand), cried as he reminisced about his daughter, described the preparations for her funeral, criticised the police and informed the world that he'd suspected all along that Louise was hidden in the well. Strike, who was happy for the old man, nevertheless wished, both for his own sake and for Tucker's, that he'd go and grieve quietly somewhere, rather than taking up space on an endless succession of daytime television sofas.

A trickle of relatives, suspicious about the way their loved ones had died under Janice's care, soon turned into a tide. Exhumation orders were made, and Irene Hickson, the contents of whose food cupboards had been removed and analysed by the police, was profiled in the *Daily Mail*, sitting in her swagged and flounced sitting room, flanked by two voluptuous daughters who closely resembled her.

'I mean, Jan was always a bit of a man-eater, but I never suspected anything like this, never. I'd've called her my best friend. I don't know how I could've been such a fool! She used to offer to go food shopping for me, before I came back from staying at my daughter's. Then I'd eat some of the stuff she'd put in the fridge, get ill, call her and ask her to come over. I suppose this is a comfier house than hers, and she liked staying here, and I sometimes gave her money, so that's why I'm not dead. I don't know whether I'll ever get over the shock, honestly. I can't sleep, I feel sick all the time, I can't stop thinking about it. I look back now, and ask myself, *how did I never see*? And if it turns out she killed Larry, poor Larry who Eddie and I introduced her to, I don't know how I'm going to live with myself, honestly, it's all just a nightmare. You don't expect this from a nurse, do you?'

And on this count, if no other, Strike was forced to agree with Irene Hickson. He asked himself why it had taken him so long to look closer at an alibi he'd known from the first was barely adequate, and why he'd taken Janice's word at face value, when he'd challenged almost everyone else's. He was forced to conclude that, like the women who'd climbed willingly into Dennis Creed's van, he'd been hoodwinked by a careful performance of femininity. Just as Creed had camouflaged himself behind an apparently fey and gentle façade, so Janice had hidden behind the persona of the nurturer, the selfless giver, the compassionate mother. Strike had preferred her apparent modesty to Irene's garrulity and her sweetness to her friend's spite, yet knew he'd have been far less ready to take those traits at face value, had he met them in a man. *Ceres is nurturing and protective. Cancer is kind, instinct is to protect.* A hefty dose of self-recrimination tempered Strike's celebrations, which puzzled Ilsa and Nick, who were inclined to gloat over the newspaper reports of their friend's latest and most celebrated detective triumph.

Meanwhile, Anna Phipps was longing to thank Strike and Robin in person, but the detective partners postponed a meeting until the first effusion of press attention died down. The hypercautious Strike, whose beard was now coming along nicely, finally agreed to a meeting over two weeks after Margot's body had been found. Though he and Robin had been in daily contact by phone, this would also be the first time they'd met since solving the case.

Rain pattered against the window of Nick and Ilsa's spare bedroom as Strike dressed that morning. He was pulling a sock over his false foot when his mobile beeped from the bedside table. Expecting to see a message from Robin, possibly warning him that press were on the prowl outside Anna and Kim's house, he saw, instead, Charlotte's name.

Hello Bluey. I thought Jago had thrown this phone away, but I've just found it hidden at the back of a cupboard. So, you've done another amazing thing. I've been reading all about you in the press. I wish they had some decent pictures of you, but I suppose you're glad they don't? Congratulations, anyway. It must feel good to prove everyone who didn't believe in the agency wrong. Which includes me, I suppose. I wish I'd been more supportive, but it's too late now. I don't know whether you'll be glad to hear from me or not. Probably not. You never called the hospital, or if you did,

nobody told me. Maybe you'd have been secretly glad if I'd died? A problem solved, and you like solving things ... Don't think I'm not grateful. I suppose I am, or I will be, one day. But I know you'd have done what you did for anyone. That's your code, isn't it? And I always wanted something particular from you, something you wouldn't give anyone else. Funny, I've started to appreciate people who're decent to everyone, but it's too late for that, too, isn't it? Jago and I are separating, only he doesn't want to call it that yet, because leaving your suicidal wife isn't a good look and nobody would believe it's me leaving him. I still mean the thing I said to you at the end. I always will.

Strike sat back down on the spare bed, mobile in his hands, one sock on, one off. The rainy daylight illuminated the phone's screen, reflecting his bearded face back at him as he scowled at a text so Charlottian he could have written it himself: the apparent resignation to her fate, the attempts to provoke him into reassurance, the vulnerability wielded like a weapon. Had she really left Jago? Where were the now two-year-old twins? He thought of all the things he could have told her, which would have given her hope: that he'd wanted to call the hospital, that he'd dreamed about her since the suicide attempt, that she retained a potent hold over his imagination that he'd tried to exorcise but couldn't. He considered ignoring the message, but then, on the point of setting the mobile back down, changed his mind, and, character by careful character, typed out his brief response.

You're right, I'd have done what I did for anyone. That doesn't mean I'm not glad you're alive, because I am. But you need to stay alive for yourself and your kids now. I'm about to change my number. Look after yourself.

He re-read his words before sending. She'd doubtless experience the words as a blow, but he'd done a lot of thinking since her suicide attempt. Having always told himself that he'd never changed his number because too many contacts had it, he'd lately admitted to himself that he'd wanted to keep a channel of communication open between himself and Charlotte, because he wanted to know she couldn't forget him, any more than he could forget her. It was time to cut that last, thin thread. He pressed 'send' on the text, then finished dressing.

Having made sure that both of Nick and Ilsa's cats were shut up in the kitchen, he left the house. Another text from Charlotte arrived as he was walking up the road in the rain.

I don't think I've ever felt so envious in my life as I am of that girl Robin.

And this, Strike decided to ignore.

He'd set off for Clapham South station deliberately early, because he wanted time for a cigarette before Robin picked him up and drove them the short distance to Anna and Kim's flat. Standing beneath the overhang outside the station, he lit up, looking out over a row of bicycles at a muddy corner of Clapham Common, where ochre-leaved trees shivered in the downpour. He'd only taken a couple of drags on his cigarette when his mobile rang in his pocket. Resolving not to answer if it was Charlotte, he pulled it out and saw Polworth's name.

'All right, Chum?'

'Still got time for the little people, then, Sherlock?'

'I can spare you a minute or two,' said Strike, watching the rain. 'Wouldn't want people to think I've lost the common touch. How's things?'

'We're coming up to London for a weekend.'

Polworth sounded about as excited as a man facing a colonoscopy.

'I thought London was the heart of all evil?'

'Not my choice. It's Roz's birthday. She wants to see the fucking *Lion King* and Trafalgar Square and shit.'

'If you're looking for somewhere to stay, I've only got one bedroom.'

'We're booked into an Airbnb. Weekend after next. Just wondered if you were up for a pint. Could bring your Robin along, so Penny's got someone to talk to. Unless, I dunno, the fucking Queen's got a job for you.'

'Well, she has, but I told her the waiting list's full. That'd be great,' said Strike. 'What else is new?'

'Nothing,' said Polworth. 'You saw the Scots bottled it?'

The old Land Rover had appeared in a line of traffic. Having no desire to get onto the subject of Celtic nationalism, Strike said,

'If "bottling"'s what you want to call it, yeah. Listen, I'm gonna have to go, mate, Robin's about to pick me up in the car. I'll ring you later.'

Chucking his cigarette end down a nearby storm drain, he was ready to climb into the Land Rover as soon as Robin pulled up.

'Morning,' she said, as Strike hoisted himself into the passenger seat. 'Am I late?'

'No, I was early.'

'Nice beard,' said Robin, as she pulled away from the kerb in the rain. 'You look like a guerrilla leader who's just pulled off a successful coup.'

'Feel like one,' said Strike, and in fact, right now, reunited with Robin, he felt the straightforward sense of triumph that had eluded him for days.

'Was that Pat you were just talking to?' asked Robin. 'On the phone?'

'No, Polworth. He's coming up to London weekend after next.'

'I thought he hated London?'

'He does. One of his kids wants to visit. He wants to meet you, but I wouldn't advise it.'

'Why not?' asked Robin, who was mildly flattered.

'Women don't usually like Polworth.'

'I thought he was married?'

'He is. His wife doesn't like him.'

Robin laughed.

'Why did you think Pat would be calling me?' asked Strike.

'I've just had her on the phone. Miss Jones is upset at not getting updates from you personally.'

'I'll FaceTime her later,' said Strike, as they drove across the common, windscreen wipers working. 'Hopefully the beard'll put her off.'

'Some women like them,' said Robin, and Strike couldn't help wondering whether Robin was one of them.

'Sounds like Hutchins and Barclay are closing in on Dopey's partner,' he said.

'Yes,' said Robin. 'Barclay's offering to go out to Majorca and have a look around.'

'I'll bet he is. Are you still on for interviewing the new subcontractor together, Monday?'

'Michelle? Yes, definitely,' said Robin

'Hopefully we'll be back in the office by then.'

Robin turned into Kyrle Road. There was no sign of press, so she parked outside a Victorian terraced house divided into two flats.

When Strike rang the bell labelled 'Phipps/Sullivan', they heard footsteps on stairs through the door, which opened to reveal Anna Phipps, who was wearing the same baggy blue cotton jumpsuit and white canvas shoes as the first time they'd met her, in Falmouth.

'Come in,' she said, smiling as she retreated so that they could enter a small square of space at the bottom of the staircase. The walls were painted white: a series of abstract, monochrome prints covered the walls, and the fanned window over the door cast pools of light onto the uncarpeted stairs, reminding Robin of the St Peter's nursing home, and the life-size Jesus watching over the entrance.

'I'm going to try not to cry,' said Anna quietly, as though scared of being overheard, but in spite of her resolution, her eyes were already full of tears. 'I'm sorry, but I – I'd really like to hug you,' she said, and she promptly did so, embracing first Robin, then Strike. Stepping back, she shook her head, half-laughing, and wiped her eyes.

'I can't ever express to you how grateful ... how grateful I am. What you've given me ... ' She made an ineffable gesture and shook her head. 'It's just so ... so strange. I'm incredibly happy and relieved, but at the same time, I'm grieving ... Does that make sense?'

'Totally,' said Robin. Strike grunted.

'Everyone's here,' said Anna, gesturing upstairs. 'Kim, Dad, Cyn, and Oonagh, too. I invited her down for a few days. We're planning the funeral, you see – Dad and Cyn are really leaving it up to me – anyway . . . come up, everyone wants to thank you . . . '

As they followed Anna up the steep stairs, Strike using the banister to heave himself along, he remembered the tangle of emotions that had hit him when he'd received the phone call telling him of his own mother's death. Amid the engulfing wave of grief had been a slight pinprick of relief, which had shocked and shamed him, and which had taken a long time to process. Over time, he'd come to understand that in some dark corner of his mind, he'd been dreading and half-expecting the news. The axe had fallen at last, suspense was forever over: Leda's appalling taste in men had culminated in a sordid death on a dirty mattress, and while he'd missed her ever since, he'd be a liar if he claimed to miss the toxic mixture of anxiety, guilt and dread he'd endured over her last couple of years of life.

He could only imagine the mixture of emotions currently possessing Margot's husband, or the nanny who'd taken Margot's place in the family. As he reached the upper landing, he glimpsed Roy Phipps sitting in an armchair in the sitting room. Their eyes met briefly, before Kim came out of the room, blocking Strike's view of the haematologist. The blonde psychologist was smiling broadly: she, at least, seemed to feel unalloyed pleasure.

'Well,' she said, shaking first Strike's hand, then Robin's, 'what can we say, really? Come through . . . '

Strike and Robin followed Anna and Kim into the sitting room, which was as large and airy as their Falmouth holiday home, with long gauze curtains at the windows, stripped floorboards, a large white rug and pale grey walls. The books had been arranged by colour. Everything was simple and well designed; very different from the house in which Anna had grown up, with its ugly Victorian bronzes and chintz-covered chairs. The only art on the walls was over the fireplace: a black and white photograph of sea and sky.

Rain was beating on the large bay window behind Roy, who was already on his feet. He wiped his hand nervously on his trousers before holding it out to Strike.

'How are you?' he asked jerkily.

'Very well, thanks,' said Strike.

'Miss Ellacott,' said Roy, holding out his hand to Robin in turn. 'I understand *you* actually . . . ?'

The unspoken words *found her* seemed to ring around the room.

'Yes,' said Robin, and Roy nodded and pursed his lips, his large eyes leaving her to focus on one of the ragdoll cats, which had just prowled into the room, its aquamarine eyes shrewd.

'Sit down, Dad,' said Anna gently, and Roy did as he was told.

'I'll just go and see whether Oonagh's found everything; she's making tea,' said Kim cheerfully, and left.

'Please, have a seat,' said Anna to Strike and Robin, who sat down side by side on the sofa. The moment Strike was settled, the ragdoll cat leapt up lightly beside him and stepped into his lap. Robin, meanwhile, had noticed the ottoman that stood in place of a coffee table. It was upholstered in grey and white striped canvas, and far smaller than the one in the Athorns' flat, too small for a woman to curl up in, but even so, it was a piece of furniture Robin doubted she'd ever own, no matter how useful they might be. She'd never forget the dusty mass of hardened concrete, and the skull of Margot Bamborough curving up out of it.

'Where's Cyn?' Anna asked her father.

'Bathroom,' said Roy, a little hoarsely. He threw a nervous glance at the empty landing beyond the door, before addressing the detective:

'I – I have to tell you how ashamed I am that I never hired anybody myself. Believe me, the thought that we could have known all this ten, twenty years ago . . .'

'Well, that's not very good for our egos, Roy,' said Strike, stroking the purring cat. 'Implying that anyone could have done what we did.'

Roy and Anna both laughed harder than the comment deserved, but Strike understood the need for the release of jokes, after a profound shock. Mere days after he'd been airlifted out of the bloody crater where he'd lain after his leg had been blown off, fading in and out of consciousness with Gary Topley's torso beside him, he seemed to remember Richard Anstis, the other survivor, whose face had been mangled in the explosion, making a stupid joke about the savings Gary could have made on trousers, had he lived. Strike could still remember laughing at the idiotic, tasteless joke, and enjoying a few seconds' relief from shock, grief and agony.

Women's voices now came across the landing: Kim had returned with a tea tray, followed by Oonagh Kennedy, who was bearing a large chocolate cake. She was beaming from beneath her purple-streaked fringe, her amethyst cross bouncing on her chest as before, and when she'd put down the cake, she said,

'Here dey are, then, the heroes of the hour! I'm going to hug the pair of you!'

Robin stood to receive her tribute, but Strike, not wanting to disarrange the cat, received his hug awkwardly while sitting.

'And here I go again!' said Oonagh, laughing as she straightened up, and wiping her eyes. 'I swear to God, it's loike being on a roller-coaster. Up one minute, down the next—'

'I did the same, when I saw them,' said Anna, laughing at Oonagh. Roy's smile, Robin noticed, was nervous and a little fixed. What did it feel like, she wondered, to be face to face with his dead wife's best friend, after all these years? Did the physical changes in Oonagh make him wonder what Margot would have looked like, had she lived to the age of seventy? Or was he wondering anew, as he must have done over all the intervening years, whether his marriage would have survived the long stretch of icy silence that had followed her drink with Paul Satchwell, whether the strains and tensions in the relationship could have been overcome, or whether Margot would have taken Oonagh up on her offer of refuge in her flat?

They'd have divorced, Robin thought, with absolute certainty, but then she wondered whether she wasn't tangling up Margot with herself, as she'd tended to do all through the case.

'Oh, hello,' said a breathless voice, from the doorway, and everyone looked around to see Cynthia, on whose thin, sallow face was a smile that didn't quite reach her anxious, mottled eyes. She was wearing a black dress, and Robin wondered whether she'd consciously put it on to suggest mourning. 'Sorry, I was – how are you both?'

'Fine,' said Robin.

'Great,' said Strike.

Cynthia let out one of her nervous, breathless laughs, and said, 'Yes, no – so wonderful—'

Was it wonderful for Cynthia, Robin wondered, as Anna's stepmother pulled up a chair, and she declined a piece of the cake which, it transpired, Oonagh had gone out in the rain to purchase. How did it feel to have Margot Bamborough back, even in the form of a skeleton in a box? Did it hurt to see her husband so shaken and emotional, and to have to receive Oonagh, Margot's best friend, into the heart of the family, like a newly discovered aunt? Robin, who seemed to be on something of a clairvoyant streak, felt sure that if Margot had never been killed, but had simply divorced Roy, Cynthia would never have been the haematologist's choice of second wife. Margot would probably have begged the young Cynthia to accompany her into her new life, and continue looking after Anna. Would Cynthia have agreed, or would her loyalties have lain with Roy? Where would she have gone, and who would she have married, once there was no place for her at Broom House?

The second cat now entered the room, staring at the unusually large group it found inside. She picked her way past the armchairs, the ottoman and the sofa, jumped up onto the windowsill and sat with her back to them, watching the raindrops sliding down the window.

'Now, listen,' said Kim, from the upright chair she'd brought out of a corner of the room, 'we really do want to pay you for the extra month you put in. I know you said no—'

'It was our choice to keep working on the case,' said Strike. 'We're glad to have helped and we definitely don't want more money.'

He and Robin had agreed that, as the Margot Bamborough case looked likely to pay for itself three times over in terms of publicity and extra work, and as Strike felt he really should have solved it sooner, taking more cash from Anna and Kim felt unnecessarily greedy.

'Then we'd like to make a donation to charity,' said Kim. 'Is there one you'd like us to support?'

'Well,' said Strike, clearing his throat, 'if you're serious, Macmillan nurses ...'

He saw a slight look of surprise on the family's faces.

'My aunt died this year,' he explained, 'and the Macmillan nurse gave her a lot of support.'

'Oh, I see,' said Kim, with a slight laugh, and there was a little pause, in which the spectre of Janice Beattie seemed to rise up in the middle of them, like the wisp of steam issuing from the teapot spout.

'A nurse,' said Anna quietly. 'Who'd suspect a nurse?'

'Margot,' said Roy and Oonagh together.

They caught each other's eye, and smiled: a rueful smile, doubtless surprised at finding themselves in agreement at long last, and Robin saw Cynthia look away.

'She didn't like that nurse. She told me so,' said Oonagh, 'but I got the woman confused with that blonde at the Christmas party who made a scene.'

'No, she never took to the nurse,' said Roy. 'She told me, too, when she joined the practice. I didn't take much notice ...'

He seemed determined to be honest, now, however much it hurt.

'... I thought it was a case of two women being too similar: both working class, both strong characters. When I met the woman at the barbecue, I actually thought she seemed quite ... well ... decent. Of course, Margot never told me her suspicions ...'

There was another silence, and everyone in the room, Strike was sure, was remembering that Roy hadn't spoken to his wife at all in those few weeks before her murder, which was precisely the time period during which Margot's suspicions of Janice must have crystallised.

'Janice Beattie's probably the best liar I've ever met,' Strike said, into the tense atmosphere, 'and a hell of an actress.'

'I've had the most extraordinary letter,' said Anna, 'from her son, Kevin. Did you know he's coming over from Dubai to testify against her?'

'We did,' said Strike, who George Layborn was briefing regularly on the progress of the police investigation.

'He wrote that he thinks Mum examining him saved his life,' said Anna.

Robin noticed how Anna was now calling Margot 'Mum', when previously she'd only said 'my mother'.

'It's a remarkable letter,' said Kim, nodding. 'Full of apologies, as though it's somehow his fault.'

'Poor man,' said Oonagh quietly.

'He says he blames himself for not going to the police about her, but what child would believe his mother's a serial killer? I really *can't*,' said Anna again, over the purring of Cagney the cat in Strike's lap, 'explain adequately to you both what you've done for me . . . for all of us. The not knowing's been so terrible, and now I know for sure that Mum didn't leave willingly and that she went . . . well, quite peacefully . . .'

'As deaths go,' said Strike, 'it was almost painless.'

'And I know for sure she loved me,' said Anna.

'We always—' began Cynthia, but her stepdaughter said quickly,

'I know you always told me she did, Cyn, but without knowing what really happened, there was always going to be a doubt, wasn't there? But when I compare my situation with Kevin Beattie's, I actually feel lucky . . . D'you know,' Anna asked Strike and Robin, 'what they found when they – you know – got Mum out of the concrete?'

'No,' said Strike.

Cynthia's thin hands were playing with her wedding ring, twisting it around her finger.

'The locket Dad gave her,' said Anna. 'It's tarnished, but when they opened it up, it had a picture of me in it, which was as good as new,' said Anna, and her eyes suddenly shone with tears again. Oonagh reached out and patted Anna on the knee. 'They say I'll be able to have it back, once they've completed all the forensics.'

'How lovely,' said Robin quietly.

'And did you hear what was in her handbag?' asked Kim.

'No,' said Strike.

'Notes from her consultation on Theo,' said Kim. 'They're completely legible – protected by the leather, you know. Her full name was Theodosia Loveridge and she was from a traveller family.

Margot suspected an ectopic pregnancy and wanted to ring an ambulance, but Theo said her boyfriend would take her. Margot's notes suggest Theo was scared of her family knowing she was pregnant. They don't seem to have approved of the boyfriend.'

'So that's why she never came forward, afterwards?' said Robin.

'I suppose so,' said Kim. 'Poor girl. I hope she was OK.'

'May I ask,' said Roy, looking at Strike, 'how strong you think the case against Janice Beattie is? Because – I don't know what your police contacts have told you – but the latest we've heard is that forensics haven't been able to prove Margot was drugged.'

'Not so far,' said Strike, who'd spoken to George Layborn the previous evening, 'but I've heard they're going to try some new-fangled way of getting traces of drugs and chemicals out of the concrete surrounding the body. No guarantees, but it was used successfully in a case in the States recently.'

'But if they can't prove she was drugged,' said Roy, his expression intense, 'the case against Janice is entirely circumstantial, isn't it?'

'Her lawyer's certainly trying to get her off, judging by his comments to the press,' said Kim.

'He'll have his work cut out for him,' said Strike. 'The defence has got to come up with reasons the police found a phone belonging to a non-existent social worker in her house, and why the Athorns had the number. The Athorns' cousins in Leeds can identify her as the woman who helped them muck out the flat. Gloria Conti's willing to come over to testify about the doughnut in the fridge and the vomiting attacks she and Wilma suffered, and Douthwaite's going to take the stand—'

'He is?' said Oonagh, her expression clearing. 'Oh, that's good, we've been worried about him—'

'I think he finally realises the only way out of this is going through with it,' said Strike. 'He's ready to testify that from the moment he started eating food prepared by Janice, he had symptoms of poisoning, and, most importantly, that during their last consultation, Margot advised him not to eat anything else prepared by Janice.

'Then we've got Kevin Beattie testifying that his daughter drank bleach while Janice was supposedly looking after her, and that his mother used to feed him "special drinks" that made him feel ill . . . What else?' said Strike, inviting Robin to continue, mainly so he could eat some cake.

'Well, there are all the lethal substances they've taken out of Janice's kitchen,' said Robin, 'not to mention the fact that she tried to poison Cormoran's tea when he went round there to confront her. There's also the drugged food the police have found at Irene's, and the framed photographs on her wall, including Joanna Hammond, who she claimed never to have met, and Julie Wilkes, who drowned at the Clacton-on-Sea Butlin's. And the police are confident they're going to be able to get forensic evidence out of other victims' graves, even if Margot's results are inconclusive. Janice had her ex-partner, Larry, cremated, but his lover Clare was buried and she's being exhumed.'

'Personally,' said Strike, who'd managed to eat half his slice of chocolate cake while Robin was talking, 'I think she's going to die in jail.'

'Well, that's good to hear,' said Roy, looking relieved, and Cynthia said breathlessly,

'Yes, no, definitely.'

The cat at the window looked around and then, slowly, turned to face the rain again, while its twin pawed idly at Strike's sweater.

'You two will come to the funeral, won't you?' asked Anna.

'We'd be honoured,' said Robin, because Strike had just taken another big mouthful of cake.

'We're, ah, leaving the arrangements up to Anna,' said Roy. 'She's taking the lead.'

'I'd like Mum to have a proper grave,' said Anna. 'Somewhere to visit, you know . . . all these years, without knowing where she is. I want her where I can find her.'

'I can understand that,' said Strike.

'You really *don't* know what you've given me,' said Anna, for the third time. She'd reached out a hand to Oonagh, but she was looking at Cynthia. 'I've got Oonagh, now, as well as Cyn, who's been the most wonderful mother . . . Mum certainly chose the right person to raise me . . . '

As Cynthia's face crumpled, Strike and Robin both looked tact-fully away, Robin at the cat at the window and Strike at the seascape over the mantelpiece. The rain drummed against the window, the cat in his lap purred, and he remembered the lily urn bobbing away. With a twist in his chest, and in spite of his satisfaction at having done what he'd set out to do, he wished he could have called Joan, and told her the end of Margot Bamborough's story, and heard her say she was proud of him, one last time.

73

For naturall affection soone doth cesse,
And quenched is with Cupids greater flame:
But faithfull friendship doth them both suppresse,
And them with maystring discipline doth tame,
Through thoughts aspyring to eternall fame.
For as the soule doth rule the earthly masse,
And all the seruice of the bodie frame,
So loue of soule doth loue of bodie passe,
No lesse then perfect gold surmounts the meanest brasse.

Edmund Spenser
The Faerie Queene

Robin woke a few days later to autumn sunshine streaming through the gap in her curtains. Glancing at her mobile, she saw to her amazement that it was ten in the morning, which meant she'd just enjoyed the longest sleep she'd had all year. Then she remembered why she was having a lie-in: today was the ninth of October, and it was her birthday.

Ilsa had arranged a dinner in her honour the following evening, which was a Friday. Ilsa had chosen and booked the smart restaurant, to which she and Nick, Vanessa and her fiancé Oliver, Barclay, Hutchins and their wives, Max, his new boyfriend (the lighting director on his TV show) and Strike were all invited. Robin had no plans for today, her actual birthday, which Strike had insisted she take off. She now sat up in bed, yawning, and looked at the packages lying on her chest of drawers opposite, which were all from her family. The small package from her mother had the appearance of a piece of jewellery, doubtless in tribute to this milestone birthday. Just as she was about to get out of bed, her phone beeped and she saw a text from Strike.

> **I know you're supposed to be having a day off but something's come up. Please can you meet me at the Shakespeare's Head, Marlborough St, 5pm. Dress smart, might need to go on somewhere upmarket.**

Robin read this twice, as though she might have missed a 'happy birthday'. Surely — *surely* — he hadn't forgotten again? Or did he think that, by planning to turn up at the dinner Ilsa had planned, he was doing all that was required, and the actual day of her birth required no acknowledgement? True, she felt at a slightly loose end without work and with none of her friends available, but Strike wasn't to know that, so it was with very mixed feelings that she texted back: **OK**.

However, when she arrived upstairs in her dressing gown to fetch a cup of tea, Robin found a large box sitting on the kitchen table, with a card on top of it, her name on the envelope in Strike's unmistakeable cramped, hard-to-read writing. Max, she knew, had left the flat early to film outdoor scenes in Kent, taking Wolfgang with him, who'd sleep in the car and enjoy a lunchtime walk. As she hadn't heard the doorbell, she had to conclude that Strike had somehow transferred both box and card to Max ahead of time, to surprise her with this morning. This argued degrees of planning and effort that seemed highly uncharacteristic. Moreover, she'd never received a proper card from Strike, not even when he'd bought her the green dress after solving their first case.

The front of the birthday card was somewhat generic and featured a large glittery pink number thirty. Inside, Strike had written:

> Happy birthday. This isn't your real present,
> you'll get that later. (Not flowers)
> Love Strike x

Robin looked at this message for far longer than it warranted. Many things about it pleased her, including the kiss and the fact that he'd called himself 'Strike'. She set the card on the table and picked up the large box which, to her surprise, was so light it felt empty. Then she saw the product name on the side: Balloon in a Box.

Opening the lid, she pulled out a balloon in the shape of a donkey's head, tied by a thick ribbon to a weighted base. Grinning, she set it down on the table, made herself tea and breakfast, then texted Strike.

Thanks for the balloon donkey. Perfect timing. My old one's nearly deflated.

She received an answer sixty seconds later.

Great. I was worried it was so obvious, everybody would've got you one. See you at 5.

Light-hearted now, Robin drank tea, ate her toast and returned downstairs to open her family's presents. Everybody had bought her slightly more expensive versions of last year's gifts, except for her parents, who'd sent a beautiful pendant: a single round opal, which was her birthstone, shimmering green and blue, surrounded by tiny diamonds. The accompanying card read: 'Happy thirtieth, Robin. We love you, Mum and Dad x.'

Robin felt her luck, these days, at having two loving parents. Her work had taught her how many people weren't that fortunate, how many people had families that were broken beyond repair, how many adults walked around carrying invisible scars from their earliest childhood, their perceptions and associations forever altered by lack of love, by violence, by cruelty. So she called Linda to thank her, and ended up talking to her mother for over an hour: inconsequential chatter, most of it, but cheering, nevertheless. It was easier to ring home now that her divorce was over. Robin hadn't told her mother that Matthew and Sarah were expecting a baby: she'd let Linda find that out in her own time, and work off her initial outrage out of Robin's earshot.

Towards the end of the call, Linda, who'd disapproved of Robin's dramatic change of career ever since her first injury incurred on the job, mentioned the continuing press coverage concerning Margot Bamborough.

'You really did an incredible thing, there,' said Linda. 'You and, er . . . Cormoran.'

'Thanks, Mum,' said Robin, as surprised as she was touched.

'How's Morris?' her mother asked, in a would-be casual tone.

'Oh, we sacked him,' said Robin cheerfully, forgetting that she hadn't told her mother that, either. 'His replacement's starting next week. Woman called Michelle Greenstreet. She's great.'

After showering, Robin returned to her bedroom to blow dry her hair properly, ate lunch watching TV, then returned downstairs to change into the figure–hugging blue dress that she'd last worn when persuading Shifty's PA to give up her secrets. She added the opal necklace, which, since she'd left her engagement ring behind when leaving Matthew, was now the most valuable piece of jewellery she owned. The beautiful stone, with its iridescent flecks, lifted the appearance of the old dress, and for once pleased with her appearance, Robin picked up the second of her handbags, which was slightly smarter than the one she usually took to the office, and went to pick up her mobile phone from her bedside table.

The drawer of the bedside table was slightly open and, looking down, Robin glimpsed the Thoth tarot pack, sitting inside. For a moment, she hesitated; then, under the smiling eyes of the balloon donkey she'd installed in the corner of her bedroom, she checked the time on her phone. It was still early to leave the house, if she wanted to meet Strike in Marlborough Street at five. Setting down her bag, she took out the tarot pack, sat down on her bed and began shuffling the cards before turning the first card over and laying it down in front of her.

Two swords intersected a blue rose against a green background. She consulted the *Book of Thoth*.

Peace . . . The Two of Swords. It represents a general shaking-up, resulting from the conflict of Fire and Water in their marriage . . .

This comparative calm is emphasized by the celestial attribution: the Moon in Libra ...

Robin now remembered that this first card was supposed to represent 'the nature of the problem'.

'Peace isn't a problem,' she muttered, to the empty room. 'Peace is good.'

But of course, she hadn't actually asked the cards a question; she'd simply wanted them to tell her something today, on the day of her birth. She turned over the second card, the supposed cause of the problem.

A strange green masked female figure stood beneath a pair of scales, holding a green sword.

Adjustment ... This card represents the sign of Libra ... she represents The Woman Satisfied. Equilibrium stands apart from any individual prejudices ... She is therefore to be understood as assessing the virtue of every act and demanding exact and precise satisfaction ...

Robin raised her eyebrows and turned over the third and last card: the solution. Here again were the two entwined fish, which poured out water into two golden chalices floating on a green lake: it was the same card she'd turned over in Leamington Spa, when she still didn't know who'd killed Margot Bamborough.

Love ... The card also refers to Venus in Cancer. It shows the harmony of the male and the female: interpreted in the largest sense. It is perfect and placid harmony ...

Robin took a deep breath, then returned all the cards to their pack and the pack to her bedside drawer. As she stood and picked up her raincoat, the balloon donkey swayed slightly on its ribbon.

Robin could feel the new opal resting in the hollow of the base of her throat as she walked towards the Tube station along the road, and having slept properly for once, and having clean hair, and carrying a feeling of lightness with her that had persisted ever since she took the balloon donkey out of his box, she attracted many pairs of male eyes in the street and on the train. But Robin ignored all of them, heading up the stairs at Oxford Circus, and then proceeded down Regent Street and, finally, to the Shakespeare's Head where she saw Strike standing outside, wearing a suit.

'Happy birthday,' he said, and after a brief hesitation he bent down and kissed her on the cheek. He smelled, Robin noticed, not only of cigarettes, but of a subtle lavender aftershave, which was unusual.

'Thanks ... aren't we going into the pub?'

'Er – no,' said Strike. 'I want to buy you some new perfume.' He pointed towards the rear entrance of Liberty, which lay a mere ten yards away. 'It's your real birthday present – unless you've already bought some?' he added. He really hoped not. He couldn't think of anything else to offer her that didn't take them back into the realm of awkwardness and possible misunderstanding.

'I ... no,' said Robin. 'How did you know I've ...?'

'Because I phoned Ilsa, last Christmas ...'

As he held open the glass door for her, which led to a chocolate department now full of Hallowe'en treats, Strike explained about his failed attempt to buy Robin perfume, the previous December.

' ... so I asked the assistant, but he kept showing me things with names like ... I dunno ... "Shaggable You" ...'

The laugh Robin failed to repress was so loud that people turned to look at her. They moved past tables stacked with expensive truffles.

' ... and I panicked,' Strike admitted, 'which is why you ended up with chocolates. Anyway,' he said, as they came to the threshold of the perfume room, with its cupola painted with moon and stars, 'you choose whatever you want and I'll pay.'

'Strike,' said Robin, 'this is ... this is *thoughtful.*'

'Yeah, well,' said her partner, with a shrug. 'People can change. Or so a psychiatrist in Broadmoor told me. I'm going to stand here,' he said, pointing at a corner where he hoped his bulk wouldn't impede anyone. 'Take your time.'

So Robin spent a pleasurable quarter of an hour browsing among bottles, spraying testers onto strips, enjoying a brief consultation with the helpful assistant, and finally narrowing her choice down to two perfumes. Now she hesitated, wondering whether she dare do what she wanted . . . but surely, if they were best friends, it was all right?

'OK, there are two I really like,' Robin said, reappearing at Strike's side. 'Give me your opinion. You've got to live with it, in the Land Rover.'

'If they're strong enough to cover up the smell of that car, they aren't fit for human inhalation,' he said, but nevertheless, he took the two smelling strips.

The first smelled of vanilla, which reminded him of cake, and he liked it. The second put him in mind of warm, musky skin, with a suggestion of bruised flowers.

'That one. The second one.'

'Huh. I thought you'd prefer the first.'

'Because it smells like food?'

She grinned as she sniffed the smelling strips.

'Yes . . . I think I prefer two, as well. It isn't cheap.'

'I'll cope.'

So he carried a heavy cube of white glass which bore the unexceptional name 'Narciso' to the desk.

'Yeah, it's a gift,' Strike said when asked, and he waited patiently as the price sticker was peeled off and a ribbon and wrapping added. He couldn't personally see the point, but he felt that Robin was owed a little ceremony, and her smile as she took the bag from him told him he'd answered correctly. Now they walked together back through the store and out of the main entrance, where buckets of flowers surrounded them.

'So where—?' asked Robin.

'I'm taking you to the Ritz for champagne,' said Strike.

'Are you serious?'

'Yeah. It's why I'm wearing a suit.'

For a moment Robin simply looked at him, then she reached up and hugged him tightly. Surrounded by banked flowers, both remembered the hug they'd shared at the top of the stairs on her wedding day, but this time, Robin turned her face and kissed Strike deliberately on the cheek, lips to stubble.

'Thanks, Strike. This really means a lot.'

And that, thought her partner, as the two of them headed away towards the Ritz in the golden glow of the early evening, really was well worth sixty quid and a bit of an effort ...

Out of his subconscious rose the names Mazankov and Krupov, and it was a second or two before he remembered where he'd heard them, why they sounded Cornish, and why he thought of them now. The corners of his mouth twitched, but as Robin didn't see him smiling, he felt no compulsion to explain.

ACKNOWLEDGEMENTS

My thanks, as ever, to my superb editor David Shelley, who always makes the job a pleasure; to my wonderful agent Neil Blair; to the management team who keep me sane, Mark Hutchinson, Rebecca Salt and Nicky Stonehill; to my home and office team, without whom this book would never have been finished: Di Brooks, Simon Brown, Danny Cameron, Angela Milne, Ross Milne, Fi Shapcott and Kaisa Tiensuu; to Neil Murray, the world's best reader of works-in-progress; to Kenzie, for spotting that cross of the Knights of St John where I didn't expect to find one; to William Leone and Lynne Corbett, for inspiration and for checking my calculations; to Russell Townsend, for helping me check out all these locations and for saving my dead laptop; and to Tom Burke, for fascinating Crowleyana and the Atlantis bookshop.

CREDITS

Help us make the next generation of readers

We – both author and publisher – hope you enjoyed this book.
We believe that you can become a reader at any time in your life,
but we'd love your help to give the next generation a head start.

Did you know that 9% of children don't have a book of their
own in their home, rising to 12% in disadvantaged families*?
We'd like to try to change that by asking you to consider the role
you could play in helping to build readers of the future.

We'd love you to think of sharing, borrowing, reading, buying or talking
about a book with a child in your life and spreading the love of reading.
We want to make sure the next generation continue to have access
to books, wherever they come from.

And if you would like to consider donating to charities that help
fund literacy projects, find out more at www.literacytrust.org.uk
and www.booktrust.org.uk.

Thank you.

hachette
CHILDREN'S GROUP

little, brown
BOOK GROUP

*As reported by the National Literacy Trust